THE
Revelation
Code

By Andy McDermott

Featuring Nina Wilde and Eddie Chase
The Hunt for Atlantis
The Tomb of Hercules
The Secret of Excalibur
The Covenant of Genesis
The Pyramid of Doom
The Sacred Vault
Empire of Gold
Return to Atlantis
The Valhalla Prophecy
Kingdom of Darkness
The Last Survivor (ebook)
The Revelation Code

Standalone Novel
The Shadow Protocol

THE
Revelation
Code

A NOVEL

Andy McDermott

DELL
NEW YORK

The Revelation Code is a work of fiction. Names, characters, places, and incidents either are the products of the author's imagination or are used fictitiously. Any resemblance to actual persons, living or dead, events, or locales is entirely coincidental.

A Dell Mass Market Original

Copyright © 2015 by Andy McDermott
Excerpt from *The Midas Legacy* by Andy McDermott copyright © 2016 by Andy McDermott

Published in the United States by Dell, an imprint of Random House, a division of Penguin Random House LLC, New York.

DELL and the HOUSE colophon are registered trademarks of Penguin Random House LLC.

Originally published in the United Kingdom by the Headline Publishing Group Ltd., in 2015.

This book contains an excerpt from the forthcoming book *The Midas Legacy* by Andy McDermott. This excerpt has been set for this edition only and may not reflect the final content of the forthcoming edition.

ISBN 978-1-101-96529-0
ebook ISBN 978-1-101-96530-6

Cover art: Mike Bryan
Art direction: Carlos Beltrán

Printed in the United States of America

randomhousebooks.com

9 8 7 6 5 4 3 2

Dell mass market edition: May 2016

For Sebastian
and all the adventures that await

THE
Revelation
Code

Southern Iraq

The half-moon cast a feeble light over the desolate sand-swept plain. The region had been marshland not long ago, but war had changed that. Not directly; the islands spattering the expanse between the great rivers of the Tigris and the Euphrates had not been destroyed by shells and explosives. Instead spite had drained it, the dictator Saddam Hussein taking his revenge upon the Ma'dan people for daring to rise against him following the Gulf War. Dams and spillways had reduced the wetlands to a dust bowl, forcing the inhabitants to leave in order to survive.

That destruction was, ironically, making the mission of the trio of CIA operatives crossing the bleak landscape considerably easier. The no-fly zone established over southern Iraq gave the United States and its allies total freedom to operate, and the agents had parachuted to the Euphrates's northern bank earlier that night, their ultimate objective the toppling of the Iraqi leader. Had the marshes not been drained, they would have been forced to make a circuitous journey by boat, dragging it over reed-covered embankments whenever the water became too shallow to traverse. Instead, they had been able to drive the battered Toyota four-by-four waiting at their insertion point almost in a straight line across the lowlands.

"Not far now," said the team's leader, Michael Rosemont, as he checked a handheld GPS unit. "Two miles."

The driver, Gabe Arnold, peered ahead through his night-vision goggles. He was driving without headlights to keep them hidden from potential observers. "I can see the lake."

"Any sign of Kerim and his people?"

"Not yet."

"Might have known these Arabs would be late," said the third man, from behind them. Ezekiel Cross was using a small flashlight to check a map, focusing it on an almost perfectly circular patch of pale blue marked UMM AL BINNI. "Nobody in this part of the world can even do anything as basic as keep time. Savages."

Rosemont let out a weary huff but let the remark pass. "How close is the nearest Iraqi unit, Easy?" he asked instead.

"Based on today's intel, about six miles to the northeast. Near the Tigris." Cross's pale gray eyes flicked toward his superior. "And I'd prefer not to be called that."

"Okay, *Cross*," Rosemont replied with a small shake of his head. Arnold suppressed a grin. "Any other units nearby?"

"There's another nine miles north of here. Forces have been building up there over the past week."

"They know Uncle Sam's gonna come for 'em sooner or later," said Arnold.

Cross made an impatient sound. "We should have flattened the entire country the day after 9/11."

"Iraq didn't attack us," Rosemont pointed out.

"They're supporting al-Qaeda. And they're building weapons of mass destruction. To me, that justifies any action necessary to stop them."

"Well, that's what we're waiting on the UN to confirm, ain't it?" Arnold said. "Got to give 'em a chance to give up their WMDs before we put the hammer down."

"The United Nations!" Cross spat. "We should kick

them out of our country. As if New York isn't enough of a pit of degeneracy already, we let a gang of foreign socialists and atheists squat there telling us what to do!"

"Uh-huh." Rosemont had only known the Virginian for a few days, but that had been long enough to learn to tune out the agent's frequent rants about anything he considered an ungodly affront to his values—which, it seemed, was everything in the modern world. He turned his attention back to the driver. "Still no sign of Kerim?"

"Nothing—no, wait," replied Arnold, suddenly alert. "I see a light."

Cross immediately flicked off the flashlight, dropping the off-roader's interior into darkness. Rosemont narrowed his eyes and stared ahead. "Where?"

"Twelve o'clock."

"Is it them?" said Cross, wary.

The CIA leader picked out a tiny point of orange against the darkness. "It's them. Right where they're supposed to be."

"On schedule too," added Arnold. "Guess they *can* keep time after all, huh?" Cross glowered at him.

The lake came into clearer view as the Toyota crested a low rise, a black disk against the moonlit wash covering the plain. Arnold surveyed it through his goggles. "Man, that's weird. It looks like a crater or something."

"That's the theory," Rosemont told him. "They think a meteorite made it a few thousand years ago; that's what the background data on the region said, anyhow. The lake used to be a lot bigger, but nobody knew that was at the bottom until Saddam drained the marshes." His tone turned business-like. "Okay, this is it. I'll do the talking, get the intel off Kerim. You two ready the weapons for transfer." He turned to regard the cases stacked in the Toyota's cargo bed.

"And after?" Cross asked.

"Depends on what Kerim tells me. If he's got new information about the Iraqi defenses, then we call it in and maybe go see for ourselves if HQ needs us to. If he doesn't, we give the Marsh Arab rebels their weapons and prep them for our invasion."

"Assuming the UN doesn't try to stop us," said Cross scathingly.

"Hey, hey," Arnold cut in. "There's something by the lake. Looks like a building, some ruins."

Rosemont peered ahead, but there wasn't enough light to reveal any detail on the shore. "There wasn't anything marked on the maps."

"It's in the water. Musta been exposed when the lake dried up."

"Are Kerim and his people by it?"

"No, they're maybe two hundred meters away."

"It's not our problem, then." Rosemont raised the M4 carbine on his lap and clicked off the safety. Cross did the same with his own weapon. They were meeting friendlies, but those at the sharp end of intelligence work in the CIA's Special Activities Division preferred to be ready for any eventuality.

Arnold brought the Toyota in. The point of orange light was revealed as a small campfire, figures standing around the dancing flames. All were armed, the fire's glow also reflecting dully off assorted Kalashnikov rifles. To Rosemont's relief, none were pointed at the approaching vehicle.

Yet.

The four-by-four halted. The men around the fire stood watching, waiting for its occupants to make the first move. "All right," said Rosemont. "I'll go meet them."

The CIA commander opened the door and stepped out. The action brought a response, some of the Ma'dan raising their guns. He took a deep breath. "Kerim! Is Kerim here?"

Mutterings in Arabic, then a man stepped forward. "I am Kerim. You are Michael?"

"Yes."

Kerim waved him closer. The Ma'dan leader was in his early thirties, but a hard life in the marshes had added a decade of wear to his face. "Michael, hello," he said, before embracing the American and kissing him on both cheeks.

"Call me Mike," Rosemont said with a smile.

The Arab returned it. "It is very good to see you . . . Mike. We have waited a long time for this day. When you come to kill Saddam"—a spitting sound, echoed by the others as they heard the hated dictator's name—"we will fight beside you. But his soldiers, they have tanks, helicopters. These are no good." He held up his dented AK-47. "We need more."

"You'll have more." Rosemont signaled to the two men in the Toyota. "Bring 'em their toys!"

"You've got the intel?" asked Cross as he got out.

"Show of good faith. Come on."

Cross was aggrieved by the change of plan, but he went with Arnold to the truck's rear. Each took out a crate and crunched through dead reeds to bring it to the group. "This fire'll be visible for miles," the Virginian complained. "Stupid making it out in the open, real stupid."

Kerim bristled. Rosemont shot Cross an irritated look but knew he was right. "You should put this out now we're here," he told the Ma'dan leader. Kerim gave an order, and one of his men kicked dirt over the little pyre. "Why didn't you set up in those ruins?"

The suggestion seemed to unsettle his contact. "That is . . . not a good place," said Kerim, glancing almost nervously toward the waterlogged structure. "If it had been up to us, we would not have chosen to meet you here."

"Why not?" asked Arnold, setting down his case.

"It is a place of death. Even before the water fell, all the marsh tribes stayed away from it. It is said that . . ." He hesitated. "That the end of the world will begin there. Allah, praise be unto Him, will send out His angels to burn the earth."

"You mean God," snapped Cross.

Kerim was momentarily confused. "Allah *is* God, yes. But it is a place we fear."

With the fire extinguished, the ragged ruins were discernible in the moon's pallid light. They were not large, the outer buildings and walls having crumbled, but it seemed to Rosemont that the squat central structure had remained mostly intact. How long had it been submerged? Centuries, millennia? There was something indefinably ancient about it.

Not that it mattered. His only concerns were of the present. "Well, here's something that'll make Saddam fear *you*," he said, switching on a flashlight and opening one of the crates.

Its contents produced sounds of awe and excitement from the Ma'dan. Rosemont lifted out an olive-drab tube. "This is an M72 LAW rocket—*LAW* stands for 'light anti-tank weapon.' We'll show you how to use them, but if you can fire a rifle, you can fire one of these. We've also brought a couple thousand rounds of AK ammunition."

"That is good. That is very good!" Kerim beamed at the CIA agent, then translated for the other Ma'dan.

"I guess they're happy," said Arnold on seeing the enthusiastic response.

"Guess so," Rosemont replied. "Okay, Kerim, we need your intel on Saddam's local troops before—"

A cry of alarm made everyone whirl. The Marsh Arabs whipped up their rifles, scattering into the patches of dried-up reeds. "What's going on?" Cross demanded, raising his own gun.

"Down, down!" Kerim called. "The light, turn it off!"

Rosemont snapped off the torch and ducked. "What is it?"

"Listen!" He pointed across the lake. "A helicopter!"

The CIA operatives fell silent. Over the faint sigh of the wind, a new sound became audible: a deep percussive rumble. The chop of heavy-duty rotor blades.

Growing louder.

"Dammit, it's a Hind!" said Arnold, recognizing the distinctive thrum of a Soviet-made Mil Mi-24 gunship. "What the hell's it doing here? We're in the no-fly zone—why haven't our guys shot it down?"

"We first saw it two days ago," said Kerim. "It flies low, very low."

"So it gets lost in the ground clutter," said Arnold. "Clever."

"More like lucky," Cross corrected. "Our AWACS should still pick it up."

"We've got some new intel, then," Rosemont said with a wry smile. "They need to point their radar in this direction."

Arnold tried to locate the approaching gunship. "Speaking of direction, is it comin' in ours?"

"Can't tell. Get the NVGs from the truck . . . Shit!" A horrible realization hit Rosemont. "The truck, we've got to move it! If they see it—"

"On it!" cried Arnold, sprinting for the Toyota. "I'll hide it in the ruins."

"They might still see its tracks," warned Cross.

"We'll have to chance it," Rosemont told him. "Kerim! Get your men into cover over there." He pointed toward the remains of the building.

The Ma'dan leader did not take well to being given orders. "No! We will not go into that place!"

"Superstition might get you killed."

"The helicopter will not see us if we hide in the reeds," Kerim insisted.

"Let them stay," said Cross dismissively. "We need to move."

"Agreed," said Rosemont, putting the LAW back into its case. The Toyota's engine started, then sand kicked from its tires as Arnold swung it toward the ruins. "Come on."

Gear jolting on their equipment webbing, they ran after the four-by-four, leaving the Marsh Arabs behind. It took almost half a minute over the uneven ground to reach cover, the outer edge of the ruins marked by the jagged base of a pillar sticking up from the sands like a broken tooth. By now, Arnold had stopped the Toyota beside the main structure, its wheels in the water. He jumped out. "Where's the chopper?"

Rosemont looked over a wall. He couldn't see the helicopter itself, but caught the flash of its navigation lights. A reflection told him that it was less than thirty feet above the water. A couple of seconds later the lights flared again, revealing that while the Hind wasn't heading straight at them, it would make landfall a couple hundred yards beyond Kerim's position.

"If it's got its nav lights on, they don't know we're here," said Cross. "They'd have gone dark if they were on an attack run."

"Yeah, but they gotta be using night vision to fly that low without a spotlight," Arnold warned. "They might still see us."

The helicopter neared the shore, the roar of its engines getting louder. Tension rose among the three men. The Hind was traveling in a straight line; if it suddenly slowed or altered course, they would know they had been spotted.

The gunship's thunder reached a crescendo . . .

And passed. It crossed the shore and continued across the barren plain, a gritty whirlwind rising in its wake.

Arnold blew out a relieved whistle. "Goddamn. That was close."

Rosemont kept watching the retreating strobes. "Let's give it a minute to make sure it's gone—Cross, what the hell? Turn that light out!"

Cross was shining his flashlight over the ruined structure. "I want to see this."

"Yeah, and the guys in that chopper might see *you*!"

"They won't. Look, there's a way in." A dark opening was revealed in the dirty stone: an arched entrance, still intact. Cross waded into the lake, the water rising up his shins as he approached the passage. "There's something written above it." Characters carved into the stonework stood out in the beam from his flashlight.

"What does it say?" asked Arnold, moving to the water's edge.

Rosemont reluctantly joined him. "I don't know what language that is," he said, indicating a line of angular runes running across the top of the opening, "but the letters above it? I think they're Hebrew. No idea what they say, though."

"We should find out." Cross aimed his light into the

entrance, revealing a short tunnel beyond, then stepped deeper into the water.

"Cross, get back—goddammit," Rosemont growled as the other man ducked through the entrance. He traded exasperated looks with Arnold. "Wait here and watch for the chopper. I'll get him."

He splashed into the lake. Cross had by now disappeared inside the ruined structure, spill from his flashlight washing back up the tunnel. "Cross! Get out of there. We've got a job to do."

There was no reply. Annoyed, Rosemont sluiced through the opening and made his way into the building's heart, turning on his own flashlight. The water rose to his knees. "Hey! When I tell you to—"

He stopped in amazement.

The room was not large, only a few yards along each wall. But it had clearly been a place of great importance to its builders. Stone columns coated in flaked gilding supported each corner of the ceiling, bands of pure gold and silver around them inset with numerous gemstones. Not even the grime left by the long submersion in the lake could diminish their splendor. The walls themselves were covered in the skeletal ancient text he had seen outside. There were more Hebrew passages too, but the other language occupied so much space that these were relegated to separate tablets laid out around the room's waterlogged perimeter.

It was obvious what the temple had been built to house. The wall opposite the entrance contained a niche a little over a foot high, more gold lining it. Above it was a faded painting, a stylized seven-branched menorah—a Hebrew lampstand—with several letters over it. Carvings resembling the sun's rays directed Rosemont's eyes to its contents.

A strange stone figure filled the nook. Its body was human—but the head was that of a lion. Wrapped tightly around the statuette's torso, shrouding it like wings, were several metal sheets embossed with a pattern resembling eyes.

Cross stood at the alcove, examining the artifact. "Do you see it?" he gasped. "Do you *see* it?"

"Yeah, I see it," Rosemont replied. There was a new edge to the other man's voice that he had never heard before, a breathless excitement—no, *wonderment*. "What is it?"

Cross gave his superior a glance that was somewhere between pity and disdain. "You *don't* see it, otherwise you'd know."

"Okay, then enlighten me."

"An apt choice of words." He leaned closer for a better look at the leonine head. "It's an angel."

"Yeah, I can see that, I guess. It does kinda look like an angel."

"No, you don't understand. It doesn't just *look* like an angel. It *is* an angel! Exactly as described in the Book of Revelation! Chapter four, verse six—'Four beasts full of eyes before and behind. And the first beast was like a lion.' And there's more: 'And the four beasts had each of them six wings about him.'" He crouched, the water sloshing up to his chest. "There's something written on its side. I know what it says."

"You can read it?" asked Rosemont, surprised.

"No—but I still know what it says. Revelation chapter four, verse eight—'And they rest not, day and night, saying "Holy, holy, holy, Lord God Almighty, which was, and is, and is to come."' They aren't *speaking* day and night—the words are written on them, always visible. That's what it means!"

"That's what *what* means?"

"Revelation! I understand it, it's all coming to me . . ." Cross stared at the angel, then turned to face Rosemont. The older agent was momentarily startled by his expression, an almost messianic light burning in his eyes. "You said this lake was a meteorite crater. Revelation chapter eight, verse ten—'There fell a great star from heaven, burning as if it were a lamp.' Wormwood, the falling star; it's describing a fireball, a meteor strike—and this is it, this is where it landed! It's the bottomless pit!" He faced the alcove once more. "The prophecy, it's true . . ."

"All right, so you've had a vision from God," said Rosemont, his discomfort replaced by impatience. "We've still got a mission to carry out. This is a job for archaeologists, not the CIA—let Indiana Jones take care of it. We need to get Kerim's intel on those Iraqi positions."

"You do that," Cross replied as he took out a compact digital camera. "This is more important."

"The hell it is." Rosemont stepped closer as Cross took a photo of the alcove and the surrounding text-covered wall. "You're coming with me, right now—"

"Mike!" Arnold's shout reached them from outside. "The chopper, it's coming back!"

"Shit," said Rosemont. The Iraqis had probably spotted the Toyota's tracks cutting across the dried-up marshlands. "Okay, Bible study's over—move out!"

He splashed back down the tunnel, readying his rifle. Cross hesitated, then almost reverently took the angel from its niche, finding it surprisingly heavy for its size, and followed.

The two men joined Arnold near the broken pillar. "They've turned out their nav lights," he warned.

Rosemont listened. The pulsing thunder again grew louder, coming from somewhere to the southeast. He couldn't see the aircraft, but with night-vision gear its pilot's view of the lake would be as clear as in daylight. "We need to get away from the ruins."

"You sure? The walls'll give us cover—"

"Not against rockets. The moment they see the truck, they'll assume we're inside and blow the hell out of the place! Spread out and try to reach Kerim's people." He started to move, then caught sight of what Cross was carrying. "What the hell are you doing?"

"I can't leave it behind," Cross replied.

"Put it down and take up your weapon! That's an order, Cross!"

The two men glared at each other, neither willing to back down . . . then the deadlock was broken by Arnold's cry. *"Incoming!"*

A flash of fiery light in the sky—and something streaked overhead. The CIA agents threw themselves flat—

The rocket hit the Toyota, the truck exploding in a dazzling fireball. Two more missiles hit the temple itself, shattering stonework and causing the roof to collapse with a crash that shook the surrounding sands. Then the gunship blasted over the ruin, swinging into a wide loop above the lake.

"Is everyone okay?" Rosemont called. His two companions responded in the affirmative.

"We lost the truck," said Arnold unhappily, looking back at the burning wreck. "How are we gonna get out of here?"

"We'll walk if we have to," said Rosemont, "but let's worry about staying alive first." He glanced toward Kerim's position. "We've still got two LAWs over there. We might be able to bring down that chopper."

Arnold was not convinced. "It'd take a miracle."

"God's on our side," said Cross, unshakable conviction in his voice. He held up the angel. "We found this for a reason. The Lord won't let us die now."

"We need firepower, not faith!" said Rosemont. "Leave that damn thing here—we've got to get those rockets." Cross gave him an affronted look, then reluctantly placed the angel at the foot of the pillar. "Okay, Gabe, find Kerim. Cross, with me."

The agents set off at a run. Rosemont searched for the Hind over the dark water but saw nothing. He could tell from the changing pitch of its engine note that it was turning around, though—another attack could come at any moment—

More fire in the sky—and dusty geysers erupted as cannon fire ripped across the shoreline. The gunner had spotted the Ma'dan and opened up as the Mi-24 swept in. The Marsh Arabs returned fire, muzzle flashes bursting from the reeds, but the AKs were useless against the Hind's thick armor. Tracer rounds homed in on the gunmen and hit home, screams rising over the helicopter's clamor as bodies were shredded by a storm of explosive shells.

Cross and Rosemont dived to the ground. The gun-ship roared over the shore, then vanished into the black-ness once again. Kalashnikovs crackled after it in futile rage.

Rosemont raised his head. "Jesus Christ!" He felt Cross bristle at the blasphemy, but he had no time or inclination to consider anyone's religious sensitivities. "We've got to get those LAWs before these bastards cut us to pieces."

They ran again, men racing past them in the other di-rection; fear of whatever haunted the temple had been overpowered by an instinctive urge to seek cover behind solid stone. The two agents vaulted the torn remains of several Ma'dan. "There!" said Cross, spotting the camp-fire's still-glowing embers.

Rosemont picked out the two crates in the moonlight. "We only get one chance at this."

"We'll do it." Cross snatched up the LAW from the open case as Rosemont retrieved the second weapon from the other. Both tugged out the pins to release their launchers' rear covers, then pulled hard to extend the firing tubes—

"*Incoming!*" Arnold cried.

The agents dropped again as the Hind swept in along the lake's edge. Rockets lanced from its wing pods, ex-plosions ripping down the shore. More screams, some abruptly cut off as another fusillade scattered mangled bodies.

"*No!*" Cross cried as the line of detonations reached the ruins—

The sawtoothed pillar disintegrated in a flash of flame. More rockets hammered what remained of the temple into rubble, then the Mi-24 veered back out over the lake.

Rosemont jumped up, raising the LAW to his shoul-der. He peered through the sight, fingers resting on the rubber trigger bar. "Cross! It's coming back around— get ready!"

But the other man was staring in horror toward the

ruins. "No," he whispered. "The angel can't have been destroyed. It *can't*!"

"Worry about your damn angel later. We've got—" Rosemont broke off as a new sight was picked out by the flickering light of burning reeds.

Something was swelling on the shore, a dirty mustard-yellow mass. It took a moment for the CIA leader to realize that it was a *cloud,* some sort of gas boiling up from the edge of the ruins. But it was like nothing he had ever seen before; far thicker and heavier than the smoke from the vegetation, almost like a liquid as it churned and spread outward.

It reached a dazed Ma'dan, roiled around him—and the man screamed. Clutching at his face, he tried to run but could only manage a drunken stagger before collapsing. The still-expanding cloud swallowed him, and his cries became a gurgling wail of agony before abruptly falling silent. Other men nearby joined the terrifying chorus as the gas reached them.

Rosemont's eyes widened in fear. "Holy shit, they're using *chemical weapons*! MOPP gear—suit up! *Suit up!*"

The United States had long accused Saddam's regime of possessing weapons of mass destruction, and now it appeared that the proof was rolling toward them as the deadly cloud kept growing. The CIA agents had come prepared, their webbing holding a pack containing Mission-Oriented Protective Posture clothing—an oversuit, gloves, and mask to protect against nuclear, chemical, and biological agents—but they had not expected to need it.

Panic rose in both men as they dropped the LAWs, shrugged off their gear, and tore open the pouches. More sounds of terror and death reached them as the sulfurous fog spread, swamping the fleeing tribesmen. Cross worked his arms into the thick nylon overalls and tugged them up over his shoulders, then hurriedly pulled on the gas mask before zipping up the garment and drawing the hood over his head. Rosemont sealed his own outer covering a few seconds later, closing the hood tightly around his mask before starting to don his gloves. He looked back down the shore—

"Gabe!" he cried, seeing a familiar figure in the fire-light.

Arnold was thirty yards away, desperately trying to secure his gas mask as he ran. Its straps were twisted, costing valuable seconds as he attempted to straighten them. At last he managed it and raised the hood, but his hands were still uncovered.

He pulled on one glove, fumbling with the other as the cloud reached him—

Contact with exposed skin was enough to kill, Rosemont saw with horror. Arnold suddenly grabbed at his unprotected hand, clawing it as if being bitten by a million insects. His shriek was clearly audible even through the mask. Then he dropped, writhing in the sand before the yellow haze consumed him.

The Marsh Arabs all suffered the same fate as the wind carried the cloud along the lake's edge. Kerim was among the last to fall, firing his AK-47 into the malevolent yellow mass in a final act of defiance before he too succumbed.

His second glove secured, Rosemont was about to run from the approaching miasma when he remembered that there were still other threats to deal with. The Hind's roar grew louder. "The rockets!" he yelled to the fully suited Cross. "Get the rockets!"

They retrieved the LAWs. There was nothing to aim at in the black sky, and with their thickly lined hoods up, it was hard to pinpoint the source of the noise. Rosemont took his best guess and stared down the sights, the mask's eyepiece smearing his vision. "Wait for it," he told his companion. "Wait . . ."

Staccato bursts of flame as the Mil's cannon fired—

"*Now!*"

Rosemont squeezed the trigger bar. The rocket shot from the launcher with a loud bang, the backblast smacking up a rooster tail of dust behind him.

But Cross hadn't moved. "Fire, *now*!" Rosemont

shouted, watching the orange spot of the rocket's motor race toward the gunship—

The Hind suddenly banked hard. The pilot had seen the incoming missile and was taking evasive action. Rosemont cursed as he realized his shot was going to miss . . .

Cross finally fired—and Rosemont realized why he had hesitated for a crucial moment. The Hind had swerved away from the first missile . . . but would fly right into the path of the second.

The cannon fire ceased, the Hind disappearing against the black sky. The first rocket continued pointlessly along its course, but the second was still angling to meet the aircraft. The engine note changed, the pilot applying full power as he tried to climb away from the incoming missile—

A flash—and for a split second the Hind was fully illuminated as the LAW struck home.

It exploded against the helicopter's tail boom. The Mil's heaviest armor was concentrated around the cockpit and engines, but even if it had covered the entire fuselage it would not have been enough to stop a dedicated anti-tank round. The warhead ripped a jagged hole through the chopper's flank, severing the mechanical linkage to the tail rotor.

The result was instantaneous.

Without the smaller rotor to counteract the enormous torque of the main blades, the Hind was hurled into an uncontrollable spin. Engines screaming, the helicopter cartwheeled overhead, Cross and Rosemont both ducking as it hurtled past. It smashed into the ground barely fifty yards beyond them, the mangled remains tumbling through the sand in a searing ball of flaming aviation fuel.

Rosemont lifted his head, heart pounding at the close call—only to freeze in fear as the yellow cloud rolled over the two men.

Everything went dark. He didn't dare move, or even breathe, terrified that doing so would open up a gap in

his hastily donned protective gear and let in the poisonous fog . . .

Seconds passed. No pain. He risked a breath. The
mysterious chemical agent had not found a way to his
lungs. "Cross!" he gasped. "Are you okay?"

No reply. Worry rose at the thought of being trapped
far behind enemy lines, alone—then he heard a voice.
"Yeah. I'm fine."

Another gasp, this time of relief. "That was a hell of a
shot."

"I was a hunter before I joined the marines. I hit what
I aim at."

"Good to know. Your suit's holding?"

"So far."

"Whatever this stuff is, MOPP-1 can resist it."
He carefully moved in the direction of the other man's
voice until his fingertips made contact with Cross's suit.
"I guess we've got our smoking gun. Saddam *has* got
chemical weapons, and is willing to use them. We have
to call this in." He reached for his radio before remembering that it had been attached to his discarded webbing.

"I don't think this was anything to do with Saddam,"
said Cross thoughtfully.

"What do you mean? You saw it—one of that copter's
rockets blew up and released it."

"No, it blew up, but the gas came from something
else." Cross suddenly gripped his wrist. "It came from
the angel! We've got to find it."

"If it got hit by a rocket, there won't be anything left
bigger than your pinkie," Rosemont pointed out. He
made out the other man's shape as visibility started to
return. "Help me find the radio."

"This is more important. Don't you see? Revelation
chapter nine, verse two—'And there arose a smoke out
of the pit—' "

"I don't give a damn what the Book of Revelations
says!" Rosemont barked. "This isn't Sunday school;
this is a Special Activities Division operation. You're an

agent, not a preacher; now shut the hell up and carry out the mission!"

Cross regarded him for a moment, his face unreadable behind the mask, then he turned away. "Don't you walk away from—son of a bitch!" Rosemont yelled after him. "You're finished, you hear me?"

* * *

Cross ignored Rosemont's angry shouts as he jogged back toward the ruins. The wind had shifted, wafting the yellow mass off the shore and out over the lake. The fires from the crashed helicopter and the burning reed beds cast a hellish glow across the landscape.

Appropriate, he thought. From the moment he first saw the angel inside the temple, he was absolutely sure, more than he had ever been about anything, that he knew what he had found—and what it meant.

But there had been only one angel. According to the Book of Revelation, there were three more. So where were they?

He approached the spot where the broken pillar had stood. The only thing there now was a rubble-strewn crater.

From which the gas was still rising.

He reached the edge of the gouge in the earth. A shallow pool of dark water was at the bottom. Among the debris around it, his light picked out a shape that was clearly not natural. Part of the statue. One of its wings was still attached, but the embossed metal that had been wrapped around the angel's body was now twisted and torn where the figure had been smashed by the explosion, exposing a darker core hidden inside.

The strange gas was belching from this black stone. The wind was enough to blow it clear, though he resisted the temptation to remove his mask for a better look. The sight put him in mind of a smoke grenade, but . . .

"Where's it all coming from?" he whispered. Smoke grenades contained enough chemicals to produce a screen for ninety seconds at most, but this was pumping out a colossal volume, and showed no signs of stopping.

He stepped down cautiously into the pit. A sound became audible even through his hood's charcoal-impregnated lining, a sizzling like fatty bacon on a grill. The dark material at the statue's heart almost appeared to be boiling, blistering with countless tiny bubbles, each releasing more gas as it burst.

Another wisp of the gas to one side caught his eye. A chunk of the broken statue, smaller than his little finger, had landed at the very edge of the pool. He crouched to examine it. There was a sliver of the dark material embedded in the cracked ceramic shell, partially beneath the water's surface. The exposed section was burning away just like its larger counterpart, consuming itself in some reaction with the air. As he watched, the top of the splinter spat and bubbled to nothingness . . . and the thin line of yellow smoke died away.

Intrigued, Cross gently lifted the fragment from the water. It was warm, even through his glove. After a moment, the strange substance fizzed and puffed a new strand of yellow fumes into the wind. He dipped it back into the puddle. The reaction stopped.

A light swept over him. "Cross!" called Rosemont from the crater's lip. "What the hell are you doing?"

"I found the angel," Cross replied, climbing out to meet him and indicating the larger hunk of the statue. "That's where the smoke's coming from. It wasn't a chemical weapon; it was here all along, hidden in the temple. Waiting for us to find it. Waiting for *me* to find it."

Rosemont shone his flashlight over the broken figure. It was still belching out its seemingly endless plume of oily yellow gas. "Damn. What the hell *is* that?"

"It's a messenger from God. Look." Cross illuminated the little pool. The dark water was revealed as a bloody red, the discoloration spreading outward from the fragment like ink across damp paper. " 'And the third part of the sea became blood . . .' "

The lead agent snapped his light at Cross's face. "I don't want to hear one more goddamn Bible quote out of you, okay? This whole situation has gotten way out of control."

"I know what we have to do. We have to take the angel out of here."

"Are you out of your mind?" Rosemont protested. "It killed Gabe, it killed Kerim and all his men! We're not taking it anywhere."

"Putting it in water stops the smoke. If we find a container, we can transport it—"

"Water, huh?" Rosemont jumped into the crater. Before Cross could intervene, he had hauled the remains of the angel from the ground. The toxic gas swirled around him as he stomped back out of the pit, heading to the lake's edge.

"What are you doing?" Cross demanded as he followed.

"Making this safe." He drew back his arm—and hurled the statue out into the water.

"No!" yelled Cross, but it was too late. The broken figure spun through the air, a poisonous vortex spiraling in its wake, before it splashed down some sixty feet from the shoreline. Both men stared at the water until the ripples subsided.

Rosemont turned back to Cross. "Right. Now we radio in and—"

He froze. Cross had raised his gun and was pointing it at his chest. "You shouldn't have done that," said the Virginian in a voice that, while level, was straining with anger. "You've just interfered with God's plan."

"God's plan?" said Rosemont, trying to control his fear. "What the hell are you talking about?"

"The Day of Judgment. It's coming. The first angel bound at the Euphrates has been released. The seals will be broken, the seven trumpets will sound, and . . ." He paused, new realization filling him with greedy wonder. "And the mystery of God should be finished . . ."

Rosemont shook his head. "You're crazy. Lower your weapon, right now, or—"

Cross pulled the trigger.

A single bullet ripped through Rosemont's heart and exploded out from his back. Eyes wide in shock behind his mask, he crumpled to the ground.

Cross stared at the dead man, his face unreadable, then bent to take his radio. He set it to an emergency frequency. "Wintergreen, Wintergreen, this is Maven," he said, using the operation's code names. "Wintergreen, this is Maven. Come in."

A female voice responded. "This is Wintergreen. We read you, Maven. Sitrep."

"Mission failure, I repeat, mission failure. We were ambushed—the Iraqis had a gunship on patrol. Rosemont and Arnold are dead. So are our contacts."

A pause. When the woman replied, it was with clear concern even through the fuzz of the scrambled transmission. "Everyone's dead?"

"Yes, everyone but me. Our transport was destroyed. I need immediate evac."

"We can't give you evac with a gunship in the air."

"It's been shot down. I need to get out of here before they come to see what happened to it."

A long silence as the controller conferred with a superior. Finally, she responded: "Okay, Maven, can you reach Point Charlie?" A backup rendezvous point some miles to the south. "If you hole up there, we'll get an extraction team to you asap."

"I'll make it," Cross answered. "I'll contact you when I arrive."

"Roger that, Maven. Good luck." She paused again, then added in a softer voice: "I'm sorry about Mike and Gabe."

"So am I," said Cross, giving Rosemont's corpse an emotionless glance. "Maven out."

He switched off the radio, then surveyed the area. The cloud had now mostly dispersed, but he didn't risk removing his MOPP gear; there were still drifting patches of haze in the air. Instead he returned to where he had donned the suit to retrieve his equipment webbing.

There was a water flask attached; he took it, then went back to the crater.

The small sliver of the angel was still submerged in the blood-red water. He removed the flask's cap, then carefully picked up the shard and dropped it inside before it started to smoke again. The thought occurred that he should find one of the dead agents' canteens, as there was no way of knowing how long it would be before he was rescued, but he dismissed it. He knew he would find what he needed to survive. " 'For the Lamb which is in the midst of the throne shall lead them unto living fountains of waters . . . ,' " he said quietly as he firmly refastened the cap.

His cargo secured, he set out into the wilderness.

1

New York City

Twelve Years Later

"Has everything I've done in my life been worth it?"
Nina Wilde sat facing Dr. Elaine Senzer, but her
eyes were lowered, avoiding the psychotherapist's gaze.
Instead she fixated on small, irrelevant details—a scuff
on the other woman's shoe, indentations on the carpet
where her chair had been moved—as she tried to put her
fears into words. "That's the question I've been asking
myself recently," she went on. "And the thing that's
worrying me is . . . is that I'm not sure it has."

Elaine leaned forward, adjusting her glasses. "I'm curious why you'd say that. You've already achieved more
in your life than most people—I mean, it's fair to say
that you're the most famous archaeologist in the world.
You found Atlantis, you discovered the lost city of El
Dorado, a hidden Egyptian pyramid, and all those other
amazing things. That's something to be proud of,
surely?"

"Is it?" Nina caught herself leaning back in her seat,
as if subconsciously trying to maintain the distance between them. "Yeah, I found all those things—and I got
a lot of people killed in the process. Too many people."

"You didn't kill them personally."

"Some of them I did." Even without looking directly

at Elaine, she could sense the psychotherapist's shock at the revelation. "They were trying to kill *me*, it was always in self-defense . . . but yeah, I've killed people. And you know what's really scary? I've lost count of how many."

Elaine hurriedly scribbled a note. "I see."

Nina gave her a grim smile. "You're not going to have me committed to Bellevue, are you?"

"No, no," the dark-haired woman hastily assured her. "I actually think it's good that you feel able to tell me about it at this relatively early stage. If you remember, when we started these sessions last month, it was quite a challenge for you to open up about anything at all. The very nature of post-traumatic stress causes sufferers to try to internalize it—there's a great deal of anger, guilt—"

"Tell me about it," Nina muttered.

"I'm afraid it doesn't work that way," said Elaine, with sympathy. "You have to tell me."

"You want me to tell you about my guilt?" Nina snapped. "Okay—about four months ago, one of my friends was murdered right in front of me. And it was all my fault! Macy wouldn't have been there if not for me . . ." Her voice faded to inaudibility.

A long silence was eventually broken by the psychotherapist. "Nina . . . are you okay?"

"If I was okay, I wouldn't be seeing a shrink, would I?" the redhead replied, wiping her eyes. "What kind of a stupid question is that?"

Elaine shrugged off the insult with professional calm. "Tell me about Macy. I know you're reluctant, but I really think it would help. Please," she added, seeing her patient clench her fists. "In your own time; you don't have to say anything if you don't want to."

"For a hundred and fifty bucks an hour, I'm not going to sit here in silence. I could do that for free at Starbucks, and the coffee would be better." Nina took a deep breath, then a second, before continuing. "Macy . . . she was an archaeology student when I first met her. She had a case of"—a brief smile at the memory—"hero worship." Her expression darkened once more. "Spending time with me soon cured her of that."

"But she *was* your friend," Elaine said.

"Yes. She could be annoying—God, she could be annoying!—but yeah, she was. She was young, that was all. And she thought life was there to be enjoyed, so she went all out to enjoy it."

"Whereas you . . . ?"

A wry shake of the head, her shoulder-length hair swinging. "I'm not exactly a party animal. Never have been. But Macy threw herself headfirst into everything. And that . . ." Her voice broke. "That got her killed."

"How so?"

"She invited herself along on my last job for the International Heritage Agency. I could have said no, sent her home. But I didn't. I don't know why, maybe because . . . maybe because I was afraid it might be the last chance I had to spend time with her."

Elaine flicked back through her notebook. "Your illness—you thought it was terminal at that point?"

Nina nodded. She had been under a slow death sentence, poisoned by a toxin from deep within the earth. "Yeah. There was a treatment, but I didn't know about it then." She kept the full truth to herself: that the "treatment" was nothing less than the legendary fountain of immortality sought by Alexander the Great. After the horrors she had been through to find it, she'd vowed to keep its location a secret, to prevent the inevitable further bloodshed if others fought to control it. "So I let Macy come with us, and . . ." She choked up.

"Are you all right?" Elaine asked. "Do you need a Kleenex or something?"

Nina rubbed away a tear. "No, no. I'm okay. It's just, talking about it . . ."

"I understand."

"It's . . ." Nina sat sharply upright, looking Elaine straight in the eye for the first time. "It's not *fair*! She was so young, she was practically still a kid! And this man, this *bastard*, killed her like she was nothing—just to get to me. If I hadn't gotten involved, or if I'd done what I should have done and told Macy to go home, she'd still be alive! I got her *killed*!"

She slumped forward, head in her hands, trying to hold in her sobs. Elaine looked on with concern. "Nina, I'm so, so sorry. But you must know deep down that's not true. You didn't kill your friend. Someone else did."

Nina forced out a reply. "If it weren't for me, she'd still be alive. The same goes for Rowan Sharpe, and Jim McCrimmon, and Ismail Assad and Hector Amoros and Chloe Lamb and—and so many others I can't even remember all their names!" She looked up in despair. "This is what I mean, Elaine. Yes, I made all those discoveries—but this was the cost. Hundreds of people have died because of me."

"It can't be that many," Elaine said, though with uncertainty.

"Trust me, I was there. My whole career, everything I've accomplished, has been surrounded by death and destruction. Even when I was still a kid, my parents died—were murdered—while they were hunting for Atlantis. Which is why I've been asking: Was it all worth it?" She looked down at her abdomen, where a small but distinct swelling revealed the presence of her unborn child. "Do I want to bring a kid into my world? What right have I got to put a baby at that kind of risk?"

"But you're not working for the IHA anymore," Elaine pointed out.

"Maybe, but you know what?" Nina said with another flare of anger. "Last month, a Nazi tried to kill me, right here in New York!"

The therapist's eyes widened. "A . . . Nazi?"

"Yeah, an actual goddamn Nazi. You see? I can't get away from this shit! I tried to, I just wanted to stay out of trouble and write my book, but it keeps finding me!"

"Your book," said Elaine, relieved at a chance to change the subject. "How's that going? You told me last time that you'd been having difficulty maintaining focus . . ."

Nina huffed sarcastically. "Oh, it's going super fine,

better than ever. No, I'm now almost completely blocked. My publishers are gonna be thrilled that they've paid over half a million dollars for three and a quarter chapters. Some people I know in Hollywood want to buy the screen rights." Macy's boyfriend, the film star Grant Thorn, had unsurprisingly withdrawn from the idea after the young woman's funeral, but his business partner had since made tentative inquiries about reopening negotiations. "Right now, though, it'd make a really short movie."

"Why are you blocked?"

"Why? Because every time I start trying to write about what I've discovered, it makes me think of the people who died in the process. It's . . ." She sagged, feeling emotionally drained. "I can't move forward."

"In what way?"

"In every way. With my life. All I keep thinking about is whether it's all been worth it, and I don't know the answer, and . . . and I'm stuck. Going nowhere."

"But you are going somewhere," said Elaine. "You've made progress over just the last month—you realized you were in denial over Macy's death, and the fact that you sought help from a therapist shows that you're able to start moving on."

"I might be *able* to start, but that doesn't mean I *have* started. On that, or anything else. The book's stalled, I can't even do something as simple as come up with baby names . . ."

"Do you know the sex?"

"Yeah. I had an ultrasound last week, and they could tell what it was. My husband, Eddie, told them not to say anything—he wants it to be a surprise—but I sneaked back in and asked. It's a—"

Elaine held up her hands. "No, no. I'm like your husband, I like surprises too. I didn't know what either of my kids was going to be until they were born."

"I guess I prefer to plan everything in advance. He's more the make-it-up-as-you-go type."

"So how have things been between you since you

learned you were pregnant? Has he been showing any tension, or . . ."

"No, no." Nina shook her head. "*He's* been great—he's absolutely thrilled at the prospect of having a kid, and he's been doing everything he can to help me. No, it's . . . it's me." She sighed. "I'm angry, I'm depressed, I'm confused—I'm a hundred and one negative things, and I'm taking all of them out on him."

"Why?"

"Because there isn't anyone else. Since I left the IHA, it's just been me and him. I've been horrible, and I know it, but . . . but I can't help it."

A sympathetic nod. "Pregnancy hormones can really affect your mood. It's often a lot harder with a first pregnancy, because you don't know what to expect. It's good that he's been so supportive."

"Maybe, but . . ." A lengthy pause as she struggled to make a terrible admission. "I can't help thinking that he's putting up with it for the baby rather than for me."

"But do you really believe that, Nina? Deep down, I mean?"

"I don't know. I don't know what I believe about *anything* right now." She stared back at the marks on the carpet.

The therapist made more notes before speaking again. "I don't know your husband, but from what you've told me, it certainly seems that he loves you. He wants to help you, but you're reluctant to allow it. That's understandable—you've been through a traumatic experience, and you've put up barriers to protect yourself from further harm. The problem is that you're not letting anyone through them, even the person who cares about you the most."

Nina managed a sarcastic grin. "Well, duh. I didn't need a psychiatrist to figure that out. I need one to tell me how to *deal* with it."

"I can't tell you to do anything, Nina. I can suggest, and advise, but in the end only you can come up with the answer. Although one thing I would suggest is couples therapy. If you both came in together, we could address some of these issues."

Another mocking little smile. "Eddie seeing a shrink? I can't imagine that ever happening. He has his own ways of dealing with things . . ."

* * *

The helicopter dived toward the Statue of Liberty. Eddie Chase gripped the controls, trying to regain height—

"Little advice, Eddie? Remember that thing I showed you called the stick? You might wanna pull it back."

"Oh. Yeah." Grimacing, Eddie brought the cyclic control joystick toward him. The Bell 206L LongRanger's nose came up, and the aircraft unsteadily leveled out. "That okay?"

"You didn't crash into Lady Liberty's face, so yeah. But we oughta go back out over open water. I'm havin' some bad flashbacks to when I first met you!" Harvey Zampelli took the controls, bringing the red, white, and blue helicopter around across the great expanse of New York Bay. The spires of Manhattan rolled into view as he notified air traffic control of his course.

"Well, it's only my second lesson," said the stocky, balding Yorkshireman once the exchange in his headphones had concluded. "And I haven't crashed it yet, so I'm not doing too bad."

Harvey quickly touched the cross hanging from his neck on a chunky gold chain. "Jeez, don't say things like that! It's bad luck."

Eddie decided not to tell him how many plane crashes he'd been involved in. "Thanks again for letting me do this," he said instead. "I've been meaning to learn to fly for ages."

"Hey, no problem," the black-haired pilot replied. "I mean, jeez, you saved my life! That's gotta be worth the price of some avgas. I sure as hell hope so, anyway! Right? Right?" He laughed, then added, with a hint of insecurity: "Right?"

"Right," Eddie told him with a grin that revealed the

gap between his front teeth. "But it's not a problem for you, is it? Doing this in the middle of the day, I mean."

"Nah, I had an empty slot, and if there ain't any paying customers, I gotta leave her sitting on the pad with the engine running anyway." The LongRanger's flight had begun from the heliport at Manhattan's southern tip; Harvey's aircraft was one of the many offering tourist tours around New York.

"Isn't that expensive?"

"Not as expensive as having to do a full check every time I shut down and restart the engine. Quicker too. Besides, I'm a pilot. Any chance to fly, I'm gonna take it!" He laughed again, then surveyed the surrounding airspace. "Okay, take the controls. Remember what I told you—keep the cyclic tipped forward to maintain airspeed, but don't push it too far or we'll lose height. We wanna stay between a thousand and fifteen hundred feet. Got it?"

Eddie checked the altimeter, then closed his hands around the two control sticks. "Yeah."

Harvey raised his own hands. "Okay, all yours."

The Englishman gingerly edged the cyclic forward. He had flown as a passenger in numerous helicopters during his military career with the elite Special Air Service, and in many more since, but his only attempts to fly an aircraft himself had been when the pilot was incapacitated or dead. Which, he mused, had happened alarmingly often.

Today nobody was trying to kill him. Operating a chopper even in peaceful conditions was still tricky, however. The Bell twitched and squirmed with every shift in the wind, and the fuselage felt as if it were swinging from the rotor hub like a hanging basket. But he held it steady, making slight adjustments to balance the airspeed indicator and altimeter.

"You're doing fine," said Harvey. "Okay, we're gonna follow the land." He indicated the shores of New Jersey and Staten Island. "Use the pedals like I showed you before, real easy."

Eddie carefully depressed one of the anti-torque pedals,

adjusting the power being fed to the tail rotor. The helicopter slowly turned. "That okay?"

"Yeah, that's great—whoa, hold on." A new voice came through Eddie's headphones: one of the heliport's staff, telling Harvey that he had a phone call. "Eddie, I gotta take this. Just keep doing what you're doing."

The Englishman gave him an okay as the call came through. "Lena, hey hey!" said Harvey, his Bronx accent becoming even more rapid-fire. "How you doin'? Great night last night, huh?"

Eddie tried not to be distracted by what very quickly became a personal conversation, concentrating on following the shoreline. The huge jetties of the New Jersey container terminal rolled by. He glanced down at them, only to realize with alarm when he looked back at the instruments that the altimeter was falling toward the thousand-foot mark. He moved the cyclic, but the descent continued. "Oh bollocks."

"Babe, I gotta call you back," said Harvey over the headset. "I got a slight altitude deficiency situation here." He laughed, then ended the call. "All right, man, I got this." He retook the controls, bringing the Long-Ranger back into a climb. "Sorry 'bout that. Women, huh? Gotta love 'em, but . . ." He briefly took one hand off the throttle to mime a duck quacking. "Damn, that reminds me, I gotta make another call."

There was a cellphone connected to the cabin's communication system by a cable; he thumbed through its contacts list. "Lana, hey, it's Harv," he said after connecting. Eddie was again an unwilling eavesdropper. "Yeah, sorry about last night. I had to stay late at the hangar to deal with some FAA paperwork. How 'bout I make it up to you tonight, huh? Yeah, that place on Leland. Nine o'clock? Epic. See you then. Bye, babe."

"Lena and Lana, eh?" said Eddie.

Harvey nodded. "Yeah. I gotta be *so* careful not to get their names mixed up! That might cause problems."

A sardonic smile. "You're not kidding."

"You ever been a juggler like that?"

Eddie shook his head. "Not me. One woman's always been enough for me. More than enough sometimes."

"You've had problems?"

"Well, my first wife wanted to kill me. And I mean she literally tried to murder me."

Harvey made a face. "Yow!"

"Yeah. Nina . . . well, at the moment it sometimes seems like she wants to as well."

"You want my advice? First hint of bunny-boiling, run, run, run! Life's too short to be dealing with psychos."

Eddie chuckled. "It's nothing like that. It's just . . ." He became more serious. "She's been pretty hard to get through to lately. And when I try, she . . ."

"Bites your head off?"

"Actually, yeah. She's a redhead; I'm used to a bit of mardiness, but this is different."

Harvey gave him a quizzical glance. "Mardiness? I guess that's British slang?"

"Yeah. Use it in conversation with Lana—or Lena— and she'll think you're all cultured and refined, just like me."

"No offense, man, but your accent? Not even slightly *Downton Abbey.*" The pilot grinned, then nodded at the duplicate controls in front of Eddie. "Okay, you're on the stick. Take us around the Narrows, then back toward the city."

The LongRanger was now cruising parallel to the shoreline of Staten Island, the great span of the Verrazano–Narrows Bridge straddling the mouth of the bay ahead. Eddie pushed the pedal again, and the helicopter swung into a lazy turn across the water. Brooklyn spread out before them, Manhattan coming back into view beyond. "Doin' good," Harvey assured him before checking his watch and making another call to air traffic control. "Okay, gotta start heading back now. My next tour group'll be waiting."

"Damn, and I was just starting to get the hang of this," Eddie replied. He still felt as if he were trying to balance a carton of eggs on a fingertip, but at least now he could maintain a constant height and speed.

"Stick with me and you'll be an expert in no time. I told you I'm a licensed instructor, right?"

"Several times," said Eddie, grinning. "How long can I stay in control?"

"Until we get to Governors Island. I'll take over when we're in the East River VFR corridor."

"The what?"

"Something you'll have to know about if you wanna be a proper pilot! Visual flight rules—basically, flying by eye. If you're in a copter, you don't need to tell ATC what you're doing in the Hudson and East River corridors, although it's kinda good sense to let 'em know. Although they'll be making the East River into controlled airspace soon for some UN summit. Pain in the ass."

"Yeah, I know what it's like dealing with the UN," Eddie told him with amusement.

He continued flying until the flat pear of Governors Island loomed ahead. "I got it from here," said Harvey as he took control once more. He reported to ATC that he was returning to the heliport, then pointed to the right, up the East River. "You seen that?"

"It's a bit hard to miss," said Eddie. The object of their attention was a huge Airlander airship, slowly cruising down the length of the waterway. The enormous twin-lobed craft, dwarfing even the largest airliner, was a new addition to New York's long list of tourist attractions, having arrived a month earlier to act as a mammoth advertising billboard. With the Airlander presently head-on to them, though, the commercials on its flanks were invisible. "It looks like a massive arse from the front."

"I always thought it looked like boobs myself. Whatever turns you on, man!" Harvey snickered. "I'll be glad when it's gone—it's a pain in the butt. Even in VFR you're supposed to maintain spacing with other aircraft, but that damn thing moves so slow, you've gotta go wide to keep clear of it. Airships, jeez." He shook his head. "What is this, the 1930s?"

"Oh, the humanity," Eddie joked. He sat back to watch the skyscrapers of Manhattan's financial district grow larger as the helicopter descended. "Thanks for the flight."

"No trouble," said Harvey, guiding the LongRanger toward the jetty where the helipads were located. "Like I said, anytime you want a lesson, I'll tell you when my next free slot is. Hopefully there won't be too many—if I'm not carrying passengers, I'm not making money!—but I owe you."

He brought the aircraft in to land at a vacant pad. "I'll be in touch," Eddie told him as he removed his headphones. "Try to remember which girlfriend's which!"

Harvey smiled and gave him a thumbs-up. A member of the heliport's ground crew opened the cabin door, and Eddie hopped down, keeping his head low as he moved away from the chopper. Another guide waited nearby with the next passengers, who were led aboard as soon as he was clear.

The first man took him back to the terminal building. He walked through it and emerged on South Street. Heading along the waterfront, he took out his phone and found Nina's number. "Okay, brace yourself . . . ," he muttered as he made the call.

Behind him, unnoticed, a man who had been waiting outside the terminal followed at a discreet distance, making a call of his own.

Nina looked up as her iPhone buzzed. Her laptop was open, her notes and manuscript on the screen . . . but the cursor had remained in the same spot for twenty minutes. She checked the phone: Eddie. "Hi."

"Hi, love," came the gruff reply. "You back from the shrink's?"

"Yeah, about half an hour ago."

"How was it?"

"I think it helped," she said, not even certain if she was being truthful. "Did you do your helicopter thing?"

"Just landed. Good fun—we went around the harbor, buzzed the Statue of Liberty. I flew it for about ten minutes. Didn't crash once!"

Nina tried to inject some enthusiasm, however ersatz, into her voice. "That's great."

She knew at once that she had failed. "Is everything okay?" her husband asked cautiously.

"Fine," she said flatly. "Where are you?"

"South Street, on my way to the subway."

"Can you stop off at the Soupman's and get me that jambalaya soup I like?"

"What? That's all the way over by Eighth Avenue—it's a bit out of my way."

"I'm pregnant, I get to decide what I eat and where it comes from!" She had meant it as a joke, but it came out more shrill than intended.

"Soup for you, then," said Eddie. "You want anything else?"

Was there a hint of sullenness? "No, that's okay. Although, wait—you could get me my favorite sandwich."

"The ones from Aldo's Deli back across in the East Village?" *That* was definitely tinged with exasperation.

"Okay, forget the sandwich." She sighed. "Just the soup."

"Just the soup. No problem."

"Thanks, Eddie." Silence on the line. "Are you all right?"

"Yeah, of course," he replied, still sounding downcast before suddenly becoming more enthusiastic—forcedly so, she couldn't help but think. "Oh, I came up with some more baby names!"

Considering his past suggestions, that immediately put her on alert. "Go on . . ."

"For a girl, I'm thinking Pandemonium. For a boy, Arbuthnot. Pandemonium Chase, that works, doesn't it?"

"Arbuthnot," she repeated. "That's not even a real name."

"Yeah, it is! It's a good, honest Yorkshire name. You can't go into a pub where I grew up without meeting a couple of Arbuthnots."

Nina knew that in other circumstances she would have been amused, but right now even Eddie's best efforts were failing to breach her prison of gloom. "I think we need to keep thinking."

"It'll be hard to top Arbuthnot."

Something snapped. "Stop saying Arbuthnot! That's the stupidest name I've ever heard. God! If you can't even take seriously something as simple as choosing a name, how are you going to manage being a father?"

The silence that followed was broken only by her own exasperated breathing. Finally he spoke. "I'll figure it out when it happens. I'll get your soup, then."

"Eddie, I—" But he had disconnected. "God*damm*it,"

she muttered, already annoyed at herself. He was, as always, just trying to help—in his own unique, occasionally infuriating way—and she had overreacted and blown her top. She glowered at the fetus. "You and your frickin' hormones."

She headed to the kitchen for a drink. Along the way she passed a shelf of memories. Beside her husband's hideous pottery cigar holder in the shape of a caricatured Fidel Castro—which she had by now despairingly accepted she would never find a believable excuse to smash—was a collection of photographs. The majority were Eddie's, pictures of himself with friends now gone: his SAS mentor Jim "Mac" McCrimmon, Belgian military comrade Hugo Castille, and others she knew only from stories.

But Nina had her memorials too. Macy in one, dressed up as Lara Croft from the *Tomb Raider* videogames for a magazine photo shoot; and in another, her own parents.

Henry and Laura Wilde beamed at her from the picture, a quarter-century-younger version of herself between them. She remembered the time and place: an archaeological dig near Celsus in Turkey. It had been a hot, dry day, making their descent into the partially excavated Roman tombs both a relief and a thrill. The memory made her smile . . .

It froze on her face.

Her parents were gone, killed by their obsession, which their daughter had then taken on herself. The question she had posed at the therapist's office returned: Had everything she'd achieved been worth it?

Another question from the session joined it. Was it right to bring a baby into her world? She knew herself well enough to be fully aware that her own obsession, her *need* to uncover the past, would never be sated. Was it fair to subject her own child to that mania, to continue the cycle?

What kind of mother would she be?

Nina was forced to admit she had no idea.

She broke out of her trance, leaving her nine-year-old

self behind and fetching a glass of water before returning to the study to find the cursor still blinking mockingly from its parking spot. She slumped huffily back in her chair, feeling trapped by her guilt and fear and uncertainty. She had to do something to break free, but what?

Elaine had been right, she decided. Clearing the air with her husband would be a good way to start. She reached for her phone, but then withdrew her hand. Eddie would be on the subway by now, and she knew *him* well enough to guess that he would still be pissed at her behavior. *Wait until he gets home,* she decided. *Until I've had my soup.*

* * *

Eddie emerged from the 77th Street subway station and headed north up Lexington Avenue, holding a cardboard cup of hot soup and a bag of crusty bread. He had considered getting a cab back to the apartment, the subway journey from the soup store being a pain requiring two changes of train, but in the end he decided the longer trip might give Nina a chance to calm down about whatever had pissed her off this time.

Still, the fact that he had gone out of his way would hopefully show her that he wasn't mad about how she'd treated him. Well, not anymore. His initial irritation had faded, replaced by a resigned amusement. She had endured so much in the past months, and surviving everything the world had thrown at them only to face an unexpected—though far from unwelcome—pregnancy would stress anybody out.

He still wanted the old Nina back, though. And it would take more than fancy soup to do that. He'd done everything he could to be supportive and helpful and loving, but what if that still wasn't enough?

He tried to put the depressing thought aside as he turned onto East 78th Street and headed for their building. Maybe the combination of time and food would calm her down . . .

Something triggered an alert in his mind.

It took a moment to work out what; all he initially had was a feeling of wrongness. But why? He was only a few hundred yards from home. Then he realized the cause.

A young man with dusty-blond hair stood not far ahead, talking on a phone. Nothing unusual about that—except that when he had glanced in Eddie's direction, his eyes had met the Englishman's and displayed *recognition*, an involuntary split-second confirmation that somebody he was expecting had arrived. Then he'd looked away, but too quickly.

The mystery man wasn't a mugger. He was waiting specifically for Eddie. And he had an oddly clean-cut air that felt out of place for a street criminal, a neat, conservative haircut and casual clothes that looked brand-new.

Eddie didn't know him, but the face was somehow familiar. He had seen him before, though couldn't place when or where. He kept walking, but tensed, ready to respond to anything that might happen.

The man seemed to pick up on his wariness. He pocketed his phone and stepped to the center of the sidewalk. There was a parked van to one side, a wall to the other. If Eddie got closer, he would be caught in a channel, the only escape routes being either to retreat the way he had come—or to go through his adversary.

He chose the latter. The man was younger than him—late twenties—and taller, but the former SAS soldier was confident he could handle him.

The other man's eyes locked on to him as he reached the van—then flicked to something behind him.

Eddie spun as he heard the sudden scuff of someone breaking into a run, seeing another young man charging at him. The first ambusher rushed to catch him in a pincer—

The Englishman dropped the bag and swiped the top off the cup—then flung its contents into the running man's face. "No soup for you!"

The jambalaya was still hot enough to hurt. The second man let out a yelp as he wiped his eyes—only for the sound to become a choked screech as Eddie's foot slammed firmly into his groin. He collapsed on the pavement.

Eddie whirled to face the blond, but a lunging fist caught the side of his face. He reeled as the blow jarred his skull, recovering just in time to intercept a second blow with his arm.

He straightened and faced his opponent, who shifted his stance. The younger man had clearly expected an easy victory, but now that he had a real fight on his hands, he was stepping up his game.

One of the man's feet lanced at Eddie's kneecap. He jinked away, an elbow barking against the van's side. Fists shot at him, left high then right low; he swatted away the first, but the second punch caught his side. He let out a grunt of pain. Satisfaction on his attacker's face, then he darted forward to deliver another blow—

Eddie caught his arm with both hands. Before the younger man could react, he forced it downward and twisted the elbow, hard. The joint crackled. The man started to cry out—but was silenced as Eddie headbutted him in the face, mashing the cartilage in his nose with a gushing squirt of blood.

The Englishman threw him against the wall. The second man tried to stand. Eddie kicked his head, then turned to run—

Something stabbed into the back of his leg—and a searing pain tore through his body as all his muscles locked solid.

He fell, paralyzed and helpless as a Taser's agonizing charge burned into his thigh. Through clenched eyes he saw a third, older man emerge from the van's side door and stand over him, shouting orders to his companions. They dragged him across the sidewalk and threw him into the vehicle. The stun gun shut off, the pain fading, but Eddie had no time to move before his attackers delivered several brutal revenge-fueled kicks, then secured his wrists and ankles with zip-ties.

The third man slammed the door and jumped into the driver's seat. The van peeled away with a skirl of overstressed tires.

Eddie struggled to break loose, but the plastic strips were unyielding. "Get off me, you fuckers!"

"Shut him up," ordered the driver, looking back. Late forties, American, narrow eyes and a small, mean mouth.

"*You* come and shut me up, you fucking shithead! I'll—" The words choked in his throat as the first man reactivated the Taser, another excruciating jolt of electricity blazing through him. A piece of rag was forced into his mouth, then a length of duct tape slapped roughly across his cheeks to hold it in place. The blond glared down at him. Eddie realized where he had seen him before—Little Italy, a month earlier, mistaking him for the Nazi who had attacked Nina. Whatever the men wanted, they had been following him for some time.

The current ceased, but all Eddie could do was scream muffled obscenities as the van disappeared into the crowded streets of New York.

* * *

The cursor continued to blink relentlessly, still fixed in place on the laptop's screen.

Nina stared at it, then sighed. Maybe she would feel more productive after lunch. Which reminded her: Where *was* her lunch?

She looked at the clock on the menu bar. Even allowing for the detour to the soup store, Eddie was late. That wasn't like him; as an ex-military man, timekeeping was ingrained into him at almost a cellular level, and if there had been some problem en route he would have phoned. So where was he?

A knock at the front door. "Speak of the devil," she said, going to answer it.

She reached for the lock—then hesitated. Why would Eddie knock? He had keys. It was possible that his hands were full . . . but the New Yorker's innate security consciousness prompted her to look through the peephole.

It wasn't Eddie.

Standing in the hallway were a tall, short-haired black

man and a white woman with a dark bob and unflatter-
ing thick-framed glasses, both smartly dressed in pale
clothing. She didn't recognize either. "Yeah?" she called.
"Who is it?"

"Dr. Wilde?" said the woman. "We need to talk to
you about your husband."

Worry filled her. "What about my husband? Is he
okay?" Were they cops? Had they come to tell her that
something had happened to Eddie?

"Can we talk to you, please?"

Again, she was about to release the lock when caution
returned. If they were cops, they would have identified
themselves by now. She put the chain on the door and
opened it a crack. "Who are you? What's—"

Nina leapt away in fright as the door was kicked open,
the chain ripping from the wood. The man advanced on
her, drawing a gun. The woman followed him inside.
"Stay where you are, Dr. Wilde," she snapped. "Shut up
and you won't get hurt."

Another two men filed into the apartment behind
them. "What the hell is this?" Nina managed to say,
outrage pushing through her fear. "What do you want?"

"Come with us," said the man with the gun.

"I'm not going anywhere," she replied. "Get the fuck
out of my house!"

One of the other men twitched in distaste at the obscenity. The woman ignored it, producing a tablet computer. "You *will* come with us, or your husband suffers.
Look." She switched on the device.

Ice ran through Nina's veins as she saw the image on
the screen. It was Eddie, pinned to the floor by two men,
his hands bound behind his back and tape covering his
mouth.

"Hit him," said the woman. In response, the men
punched their prisoner in the stomach. There was no
sound, but Nina could almost hear the impacts. Eddie
writhed in pain, cheeks blowing out as he struggled to
breathe behind his gag.

"No!" she cried, horrified. "Let him go!"

"If you come with us and do what you're told, he'll be

safe," said the gunman. He gestured toward the open door. "Let's go."

"Not until you—"

The woman cut her off. "Hit him again." The screen displayed another blow, this one to Eddie's face. Blood oozed from his nostrils.

Nina stared at him, terror rising. "Oh God! Stop!"

"Then come with us," the man repeated. "*Now.*"

It was a command that she had to obey. The two other men went back into the hall to form an escort. She stepped out after them, the man and woman falling into place behind. The latter pulled the door shut as they left.

They took her down to the street. She thought about yelling for help, but while the man had concealed his gun between himself and the woman, he was still pointing it at her back. And even if she did get help, their comrades had Eddie at their mercy. She gave the oblivious passersby a last despairing look before being ushered into the rear of a van.

A large box, worryingly close in form to a coffin, occupied most of the space. Its lid was open to reveal a padded interior. "Get inside," said the woman as her partner closed the doors.

Nina stared fearfully at the confined space. "Are you insane? I'll suffocate! I'm not getting in there."

"You'll be okay," said the black man. The woman opened a small plastic case, revealing an ampoule of some colorless liquid—and a syringe. "We're going to put you out for the journey."

"Fuck you!" Nina spat. "You're not injecting me with that!"

The woman's mouth tightened, and she nodded to her companions. The two other men seized Nina by her arms, the African American tugging up her sleeve. "Clean it," the woman told him. "We can't risk infection." He rubbed a sterile wipe over Nina's pale forearm.

"No, no!" she cried, panic rising. "Don't drug me, please! I'm *pregnant*!"

Her kidnappers froze. The woman looked at Nina's belly, almost doing a double take when she saw the small bulge. She examined it in profile, then straight-ened with an expression of dismay. "Simeon, I think she really is. We can't drug her; we can't risk killing an in-nocent. What do we do?"

"I'll call him," he replied, taking out a phone.

The two other men kept hold of Nina, tightly enough that she knew she couldn't break free. Instead she used the unexpected pause to try to calm herself and assess her captors. They were appalled at the thought of harming an unborn child—yet were more than willing to torture Eddie to force her to cooperate. And as she watched the man wait for his call to be answered, she realized that there was something very odd about his clothes. The woman's too. The style was modern, but the material was extremely coarse, as if they were made from burlap. That couldn't be remotely comfortable, but they were ap-parently enduring it by choice. Who the hell were they?

Simeon finally got an answer. "Prophet," he said, the reverence in his voice suggesting to Nina that it was more than a code name, "we've got Dr. Wilde, but there's a problem. She's pregnant. Anna thinks we can't risk drugging her for the journey. What should we do?"

A man replied, his tone both thoughtful and authori-tative, but Nina couldn't make out what he was saying. "Yes . . . yes, we will," Simeon said when he'd finished. "Thank you."

"What did he say?" asked Anna.

"He agrees that harming an unborn child would be a sin, so we can't drug her. But he doesn't want her to know the Mission's location." He gave the casket a meaning-ful look.

"I am *not* getting in that box," Nina warned him.

"You're coming with us, no matter what." He raised his gun. "You don't need your kneecaps to give birth."

She felt a jolt of fear. His deadly earnestness warned her that he would have no compunction about carrying out the threat. But Anna spoke before he could do so. "We only need to blindfold her."

Simeon nodded. He took off his tie and put it over Nina's eyes, knotting it behind her head. It was made of the same rough, scratchy material as the rest of his clothing. She fidgeted but was unable to shift it, her vision completely blocked.

"Now what?" she demanded, trying to hide her returning fear.

She heard movement as Simeon climbed into the front of the van and started it. "We're taking you to the Prophet," said Anna. There was a *thump* as the coffin's lid was closed, then hands pushed her to sit upon it. "Get comfortable—it's going to take a while."

Anna was not lying.

The journey to their final destination took several hours. The van headed out of New York to an airport; Nina had no idea which, but guessed it was a smaller satellite terminal rather than a major hub like JFK or LaGuardia, as they drove right up to a waiting private jet. She was quickly hustled aboard, and within minutes they were airborne.

Even in flight, she was not allowed to remove the blindfold. She lost track of time, only able to estimate that four or five more hours passed before the plane eventually landed.

The first thing she felt when she was escorted from the aircraft was heat—wherever she was, it was much closer to the equator than New York. The concrete had been baked by the sun, the only relief a wind blowing in from . . . the sea? There was a salty tang to the air. She was either on the coast or very close to it.

She was also at a commercial airport, not a private field. The whine of idling airliner engines was audible over her own plane. But any hope of attracting attention was immediately dashed as she was bundled into a car and driven a short distance to a waiting helicopter.

Squeezed between Simeon and Anna during the flight, she still had no opportunity to see where she was, although this leg of the journey was much shorter, barely fifteen minutes.

At last the helicopter touched down, ending the nightmare odyssey. It was searingly hot, and the ground underfoot felt like gritty sand. She heard the low crash of waves. Definitely on the coast—but where?

Gravel gave way to paved slabs as her captors guided her from the helicopter and up a slope. She entered shade. The rattle of a door being opened, then she was pushed into a building, the coolness of the air-conditioned interior like going from an oven into a fridge. "Wait here," ordered Simeon. The door closed behind her.

Nina stood still, listening. As far as she could tell, she was alone. She cautiously reached up to the blindfold and, when nobody challenged her, took it off.

After the increasingly frightening scenarios her mind had conjured up, the reality was almost disappointing. Her surroundings looked like any business traveler's hotel suite, neat and comfortable but utterly characterless. The lights were off, the only illumination slits of daylight leaking through shutters outside the single window. But even this was dazzling after hours of darkness. Nina squinted as her eyes adjusted, then tried the door.

Locked.

She was unsurprised to find herself a prisoner. Going to the window, she discovered that it too was sealed. Even if she broke the glass, the metal shutter outside would keep her trapped. She turned . . .

And froze.

Hung on the rear wall was something that would definitely not have been found in a chain hotel. Instead of generic prints of landscapes and cities, she saw a tall cross, the wood raw and chipped. Crude iron nails jutted from its arms and base. The stylized symbol of an eye, six feet across, was painted on the wall behind it.

"What the hell *is* this place?" she whispered. The small relief on finding that the nails were speckled with rust and not blood did nothing to counter her unease and disorientation. Prophets, crosses, followers dressed in sackcloth—her kidnappers were clearly members of some religious sect, but what did they want from her?

She found a wall switch and turned on the lights, then checked the rest of the suite. Another door led to a bathroom, as anonymously business-like as the main room, while a counter in one corner demarcated a small kitchen area. Cupboards contained an assortment of boxed and fresh ingredients, as well as pots and pans. Hunger pangs rose in her stomach, but she resisted the temptation to eat. First she wanted answers.

Nina went back into the main room. Two single beds, couch, armchair, desk. No television. The cross was the focus of attention—or contemplation.

A small box was mounted high in one corner. A red LED blinked as she moved: a security system with a motion sensor and camera. She was being watched. The eye behind the cross was more than merely symbolic.

Another box overlooked the kitchen. She was not surprised to discover a third surveying the bathroom. Every inch of the suite was under observation.

She returned to the first camera and put her hands on her hips as she glared up at it. "Okay, you can see me. When do I get to see you? I know you're watching— what, are you afraid to show yourself? You're scared of a pregnant woman?"

Clack.

The noise came from the door. She went to it and tried the handle. This time, it opened. She stepped outside.

Heat rolled around her again. The sun was low, the view ahead lit by a dazzling golden glow. She was in a village, numerous small white buildings spread out before her. It had the same artificial, too-clean feeling as her room, a carefully maintained holiday resort rather than a place where people lived and worked. Or some kind of private gated community? A religious one, apparently; the tallest structure was a church rising up beyond the houses, a cross atop its spire. The symbol of the eye was affixed behind this too, an outline in wood or metal.

Nina stepped out of the shade. She was near the village's perimeter, seeing a dense swath of palm trees beyond a chest-high wire fence with a barbed top strand. There to keep people in, or out?

Where *were* the people? Nobody was in sight, even though the weird little village looked large enough to house several dozen. But she knew *someone* was here, observing her. A high white pole nearby was topped by a grape-like cluster of glossy black spheres. CCTV cameras, pointing in every direction to give her mysterious hosts 360-degree video coverage. More such posts dotted the settlement. As she regarded the cameras, one of them rotated to stare back at her.

Not only was she being watched, but it was being made unavoidably obvious. God's eye—or that of a follower, at least—was upon her wherever she went.

She considered running into the trees, but instead advanced into the village. Right now, she needed to find out what was going on—and for all she knew, the jungle was also under surveillance.

There was still no sign of life as she moved between the pristine houses. Some had their shutters raised; she peered through a window. The interior was as neat and as impersonal as her suite, with another large cross and eye on the far wall. Increasingly unsettled, she reached the end of the street.

A path led to the helicopter landing pad, now empty, near the edge of a low, rocky cliff. Beyond it stretched the ocean. A brisk wind kicked up whitecaps as waves struck the stony shore below. She was facing away from the lowering sun, looking east—across the Atlantic, most likely. Was she on one of the Caribbean islands? Given the length of the journey, that seemed a safe bet. But which one?

She looked to her right. The church was fully visible from here, atop a little hill. Steps led up to it. If nothing else, she decided, it would give her a better view of the surrounding landscape.

She was halfway up the steps when a bell rang loudly from the steeple—and suddenly the village burst into life.

The church doors were thrown open. A throng of people poured out, hurrying toward her. All wore white clothing. Fearful, Nina tried to retreat, but they swarmed around her. There was no hostility, the group merely blocking her way, and everybody was smiling, but the silent uniformity of expression was somehow more disturbing than if they had been aggressive.

"Welcome, Dr. Wilde!" a voice boomed. Nina searched for its source, seeing loudspeakers above the church door. "Welcome to the Mission. My friends, bring her to me." The words echoed from other speakers throughout the village.

A plump middle-aged woman gestured toward the entrance. "This way, please." Others moved aside to form a clear path up the steps. "The Prophet is waiting for you."

"The Prophet?" Nina asked, but the only response was a polite nod. Smiling faces watched her expectantly. Feeling increasingly unnerved, she went through the human corral to enter the church.

The interior was clean, white, and devoid of any warmth or comfort, a place of worship that was entirely about the act rather than the feelings behind it. Even the tall, thin stained-glass windows were less inspiring than forbidding, the same eye motif topping simple grids of colored squares.

At the far end of the central aisle was a raised pulpit, in which stood a man dressed in white robes. Simeon and Anna flanked it. The former slipped a hand into his jacket to make it clear to Nina that he could draw his gun in a moment if necessary.

She retreated, only to find that the people behind her had closed ranks to block her exit. "Let me through!" she protested, trying to push between them. "I've been kidnapped! Let me out!"

"The Prophet wants to see you," said the woman amiably. Then, with a sterner undertone: "Don't keep him waiting."

The figure in the pulpit signaled that Nina should approach. Realizing that she would not find any support from the cultists—that was the only way she could think of the smiling white-clad crowd—she reluctantly started down the aisle.

The voice resounded from more speakers inside the church. "Dr. Wilde, I'm glad you decided to see me."

"Did I have a choice?" she called angrily.

"God granted you free will. Of course you had a choice. But making any other one might have had consequences. Something I hope you'll remember."

Nina approached the pulpit. "So you're Number One. Who are you? Or do I just call you Mr. Prophet?"

The man appeared to be in his late forties, with dark hair that was graying at the temples. His eyes, an extremely pale blue that appeared almost glowing, fixed unblinkingly upon her. "That's the title my followers gave me," he said. She was now close enough to hear his unamplified voice. "Their choice, not mine. My real name is Ezekiel Cross."

"Appropriate," Nina replied, indicating the symbol dominating the wall behind him.

"Yes. When I realized I'd been chosen as an agent of God's will on earth, everything about my life made sense."

"And when was that?" she said, mocking. "Did an angel appear before you?"

Simeon scowled, but Cross gave her a thin smile. "As a matter of fact, yes." He descended from the pulpit. "Come with me."

He led the way through a door at the rear of the church. Nina followed, Anna and Simeon falling in behind her. The robed man walked down a short passage, opening another door and ushering his guest inside.

Nina stopped in surprise. She had expected a study, but what she found was more like the control room of a television studio. The entire opposite end was a wall of monitor screens, curving around a large white leather swivel chair. The seat had touch screens at the end of each armrest, which she guessed Cross used to operate the system.

But what had brought her to a startled halt was not the digital panopticon, but its subject.

Herself.

Every screen displayed a different picture, but all had one thing in common: They were following her. Literally, in some cases, as the camera tracked her movements. Most of the footage had been shot in the last few minutes, showing her blindfolded arrival in the Mission, her search of the suite and subsequent exploration of the settlement, right up to her entering the church.

But, she realized with increasing alarm, there was older material too, recordings of her on the streets of New York. Entering and leaving her apartment building, visiting stores, her therapist—even the medical center where her obstetrician was based. That meant Cross's people had been watching her for some time, as her last appointment had been a month ago.

Eddie featured in some of the spy shots. The sight of her husband reignited her anger—and her fear for his safety. "Where's Eddie?" she demanded. "What have you done with him?"

Cross faced her. "I've had him kidnapped to force you to do what I want." On seeing her surprise at his blunt answer, he went on: "I used to work in intelligence, for the CIA. For a job that was supposedly about finding facts, there was far too much hiding of the truth behind walls of lies and evasion. And then, one day, I had . . . a revelation." A faint smile. "Since then, I've dedicated myself to truth, to clarity. Which is why I'm not going to waste time with veiled threats." He stepped closer, staring coldly at the redhead. "You're going to help me find something. If you don't cooperate, your husband will be tortured. Clarity, as I said."

It took Nina a few seconds to stammer out a reply. "And if I do cooperate? What happens to us?"

"That's up to God's judgment."

Fury rose inside her. "That's not *clarity*, you son of a

bitch! That's evasion—" She broke off with a gasp as Anna seized her by the hair.

Cross raised a hand. "I'm not being evasive, Dr. Wilde." Anna let go, and Nina drew away from her with a hate-filled glare. "You'll see what I mean when I get what I want."

"What *do* you want?" she growled. "Why do you need me—and why kidnap me and torture Eddie rather than just, y'know, asking nicely?"

"I have my reasons. One of which is that I had to be certain you would help me."

"I still might not."

His cold eyes flicked toward one particular screen. "You will."

Nina followed his gaze to see a slumped Eddie sitting in—no, secured to—a chair in a darkened room, apparently unconscious. Her blood froze. Somehow she knew it was a live image.

"What do you want?" she asked again, this time pleading. "Whatever it is, just tell me, and I'll try to find it for you."

Cross moved to survey the wall of screens. "Do you believe in God, Dr. Wilde?"

Being in a church, she should have been prepared for the question, but it still caught her off guard. "Not . . . no, not particularly."

"Then you're an *atheist*?" There was a venomous undercurrent behind the word.

"No."

He frowned. "Belief in God doesn't work on a sliding scale. You either do, or you don't. You're a believer, or you're not."

"Then I guess I don't share your belief."

"I thought so." His eyes returned to the screens. "My people have been watching you for some time. You've been to a lot of places, but not one was a church. And even a cesspool of sin like New York has churches."

Despite her fear, Nina still felt annoyance at the slur on her hometown. "I don't have an opinion on whether or not God exists, because it's not an issue that comes up a great deal in my everyday life. God might be real, or not, but either way the subway still runs late."

"Ah, an agnostic, then," said Cross in a patronizing tone. "In some ways that's worse than an atheist, because at least they have conviction. You don't believe in the Lord because you can't be bothered."

"I suppose you're going to tell me that sloth is a deadly sin?"

He shook his head. "Nowhere in the Bible says so directly. Proverbs eighteen, verse nine comes close—'He also that is slothful in his work is brother to him that is a great waster'—but the idea of the Seven Deadly Sins is an invention of the Catholic Church." His obvious disdain for that institution was almost as great as that for atheists. "Only what's written in the Bible itself matters. Which brings me to why you're here."

"Which is?"

Cross came back to stand before her. "Are you familiar with the Book of Revelation, Dr. Wilde?"

"If you're asking me if I can quote chapter and verse, then no—but yeah, of course I'm *familiar* with it. The last book of the New Testament, also known as the Apocalypse of John, written in exile by John of Patmos—who may or may not be John the Apostle, depending on which school of thought you follow—accepted into biblical canon at the third Council of Carthage in AD 397 over considerable opposition . . . and argued about ever since."

The white-robed man seemed almost impressed. "More familiar than I expected given that you claim you can't be bothered to believe."

"I'm an archaeologist—ancient history's kind of my thing."

"Then you accept the Bible as a historical document?"

"I accept *some* of it as a historical document—the parts that can be corroborated with other contemporary accounts. Revelation definitely isn't one of those parts, though."

"Why not?" His gaze became challenging. "Have you read it?"

"When I was a student, for historical context. It reads like something you'd hear from a crazy guy living in a dumpster." Cross and his two followers showed irritation at the criticism, but she pressed on: "Visitations by angels, stars falling from the sky, plagues, a pregnant woman being chased by a dragon, the four horsemen of the apocalypse . . . and the end of the world. It's completely at odds with the rest of the New Testament. There were other equally crazy apocalyptic gospels that were rejected from canon—Paul, Ezra—so why this one got through is a mystery."

Cross shook his head. "It's not a mystery. The reason is because the Book of Revelation is *true*." He leaned closer, a new and frightening intensity in his eyes. "And I'll prove it to you."

4

Cross led Nina across the control room to a vault-like metal door, using a thumbprint scanner to unlock it. Beyond was something even more incongruous within a church: a chamber that appeared to be a laboratory. Walls, floor, and ceiling were all tiled in gleaming white, a stainless-steel bench standing before a glass-and-metal cabinet. A laptop on the countertop was the only loose item.

Nina felt a new unease. She had been in a similar lab before, part of a Russian biological warfare center. Whatever Cross kept in here, he considered dangerous.

He went to the cabinet. "Do you know what that is?" he asked, pointing at its contents.

She peered through the toughened glass. On top of a small pedestal sat a fragment of pottery or ceramic. It seemed to have been burned, a dark charcoal smear on the surface. "It looks like . . . a piece of a statue?"

"It is," said Cross, nodding. "But it's also something else. I told you I'd seen an angel, Dr. Wilde. There it is."

"You mean you saw a *statue* of an angel?"

"Yes. But I believe—as firmly as I believe in the word of God and Jesus—that they're the same thing." On her questioning look, he went on: "The Book of Revelation talks of four angels, bound by God. Chapter nine, verse thirteen: 'And the sixth angel sounded, and I heard a voice from the four horns of the golden altar which is before God, saying to the sixth angel which had the trumpet, "Loose the four angels which are bound in the great river Euphrates." ' And I've seen one of them with my own eyes. This was it!"

Nina held back the more scathing of her immediate thoughts. "What do you mean?"

"I was on a mission for the CIA in Iraq, before the invasion. There's a lake between the Euphrates and the Tigris called Umm al Binni—we had a rendezvous with a group of Marsh Arabs there. Saddam had drained the marshes to drive them out, and because of that, the water level had dropped enough to reveal something in the lake. A temple. I went inside, and found the angel. The *unbroken* angel." He held one hand about twelve inches above the other. "It was this tall, and looked exactly as John described in Revelation—the body of a man but with the head of a lion, wrapped in six wings full of eyes."

"If you say so," said Nina warily.

He rounded on her. "I don't need to *say* so!" he barked. "I can show you!" He flipped up the laptop's lid. "Here!"

The screen came to life, displaying a photograph of the interior of the temple. The resolution was relatively low, but still clear enough for her to realize that whatever else she thought of her captor, he had made an impressive discovery.

He had also accurately described the angel, which rested inside a gold-lined nook. It did indeed have a lion's head on a man's body, metal wing-like shapes tightly encircling it. But she found herself more intrigued by the surroundings than the centerpiece. The walls were covered in inscribed text—she recognized it as Akkadian, a long-extinct language of ancient Mesopotamia. It wasn't one she could translate, though, those words visible through the dirt and shadows remaining indecipherable.

She also recognized another language: ancient Hebrew, carved into stone tablets propped against the wall. Their lower halves were lost beneath the flooded temple's murky waters, leaving only a few lines visible. Again she couldn't read the language; Latin and Greek had been her specialties.

"This was under the lake?" she asked, intrigued. She knew she was falling prey to her own weakness, her obsession with learning more about lost treasures of the past, but couldn't help wanting to know more.

Cross nodded. "It had been under twenty feet of water until Saddam drained the region. The Marsh Arabs avoided the area even before then; they thought it was a place of death."

"And was it?"

"I was the only person who got out alive after the Iraqis attacked, so yes. The temple was blown up by a helicopter gunship." He gestured at the sliver inside the cabinet. "That was the only piece of the angel I recovered."

Nina was still examining the photograph. "I don't know what you expect me to do with this. I can't translate Akkadian, and I only know a small amount of ancient Hebrew. I don't have a clue what this says."

"You don't need to. This was taken twelve years ago. I've had it translated since then. In pieces, so that no outsider would know what it all meant." Cross brought up another picture.

Words had been overlaid upon a copy of the original image. But they were positioned almost randomly across the wall, a scattershot translation. Nina frowned. "These are only fragments. Is there even a complete sentence there?"

"Only a few," he replied, with clear frustration at the fact. He pointed them out. She read them: *The guidance of God led His chosen through the desert and showed them water when they thirsted; Three times shall it be said, seven is the number of God, and man is always lesser; And the Elders sent their people into the lands around.* "They were all we could find, even after the picture was enhanced. But it told me enough."

"Which was?"

"That this place was used by the twenty-four Elders—the ancient Hebrew leaders who sit around God's throne in His temple, just as Revelation says." Cross indicated some of the translated text. "You see? The Akkadian symbols for the number twenty-four—and here in the Hebrew text," he added, pointing out one of the half-submerged slabs, "it actually uses the word *Elders.*"

Nina shook her head. "So it was an important religious site. That doesn't prove that God personally stockpiled His angels there. The ancient Hebrews spread out over a wide area, including into Mesopotamia."

"There's more." Cross's finger moved to other snatches of translation. "These Hebrew sections say that the Elders sent the other three angels away for safety, dispersing them as more tribes came into the region. And the older text, the Akkadian, describes how the angels were bound in the first place—or rather, what was bound *inside* them."

"And what would that be?" said Nina, her cynicism muted by the fact that she now genuinely wanted to know. She had no intention of taking Cross's deductions at face value, but at the same time she couldn't deny that his find deserved proper archaeological study.

"Do you know what the Umm al Binni lake is, Dr. Wilde?" Before she could speak, he provided the answer. "It's a meteorite crater. A meteorite hit Mesopotamia around 2200 BC. The destruction it caused led to the downfall of the Sumerian civilization—the Sumerians being replaced by the Akkadians."

"That's conjecture," Nina corrected. "It's a *possible* cause for the fall of Sumeria, but there are others. And yeah, I *have* heard of Umm al Binni. It might be a meteorite crater, but considering the state of things in Iraq since the war, nobody's been in a big hurry to check it out."

"I believe it *was* a meteorite. And you will too." Cross

went back to the cabinet, gazing down at the chunk of stone within. "Let me quote from Revelation again."

"Oh, I doubt I'm gonna be able to stop you," she sneered.

Anna strode right up to her. "Don't talk back to the Prophet again. Understand? I can hurt you without hurting your baby."

"Anna, that's enough. For now," said Cross. "Revelation chapter eight, verse ten: 'And there fell a great star from heaven, burning as if it were a lamp.' Now, what does that describe, in modern terms?"

"A meteorite," Nina had to admit—then her mind made a connection to another ancient story. "Wait . . . there's a section in the *Epic of Gilgamesh,* I think the eleventh tablet, that could be interpreted the same way. It describes the Anunakki—a group of Sumerian sky gods—'setting the land ablaze with their torch' and 'shattering the land like a pot.' That's followed by a great flood, maybe the same one from Genesis, but the timing of the Gilgamesh legend roughly coincides with a date of around 2200 BC."

Cross exchanged glances with Anna and Simeon. "You know your subject, Dr. Wilde," he told Nina. "That proves you're the right person to find what I'm looking for. But I'm curious. You're willing to accept *Gilgamesh* as a source of truth. So why not the Book of Revelation?"

"Because some of the events in *Gilgamesh* can be corroborated by other sources. Revelation can't. It's a completely stand-alone piece of work, and to be frank it reads like some sort of drug trip."

She expected an angry response. Cross's reply, however, surprised her. "Have you ever taken hallucinogenic drugs, Dr. Wilde?"

"What? Of course not."

"I have." Her surprise grew at the admission. "Part of my training with the CIA's Special Activities Division. It lets them judge if an operative's likely to give up information under truth agents. I passed the test, by the way."

Nina gave him a thin smile. "Congratulations."

"But I discovered something about hallucinations, which I've since corroborated from other sources." A glance at Simeon; had he been another CIA agent who'd undergone the same training? "Anything you see while under the influence is taken from your own subconscious mind—it's something you've already encountered, but reflected back at you in a distorted way, like a funhouse mirror. You can't hallucinate something you've never encountered before, because there's nothing for your mind to work with. So if you've never heard of an elephant, say, it would be impossible for you to hallucinate an elephant."

She regarded him dubiously, unsure where the sudden divergence of topic was heading. "I'll . . . take your word for it."

"So when I got back from Iraq and started researching—*really* researching—the Book of Revelation," he went on, "I realized that John's visions were very much like my experiences under drugs. The intensity, the *reality* of what you're seeing, the way your perception of time skips backward and forward, how all your senses are engaged—it made me think that John underwent a similar experience."

"Wait, wait a second," said Nina. "One minute you're telling me you believe the Book of Revelation is true, that you take it literally—and the next you say that nope, the guy who wrote it was tripping?"

"I never said I took Revelation *literally*. I said I believe it's true—that it *contains* the truth."

"I don't understand," she was forced to admit.

He clasped his hands together as if about to deliver a sermon. "I quit the CIA and went on a pilgrimage—to Patmos. There's a monastery there, the Monastery of St. John, marking where John wrote the Book of Revelation."

"The Cave of the Apocalypse."

"You know it?"

"I know *of* it. John supposedly lived in the cave during his exile, and that's where he wrote Revelation. I've never been there, though."

"You should."

"Let me go, and maybe I will."

That prompted a mocking snort from Simeon. Cross gave him a stern look, making him lower his head in penance, then continued: "I visited the cave, and saw the crack in the ceiling through which John heard the voice of God telling him to write down his visions. I also saw that water comes down through it from above. Now, the land around the monastery is private, but that never stopped me before. And you know what I found growing in the woods? Psilocybin mushrooms. Hallucinogens. It looked like the monks had tried to clear them, but there were still patches hiding away. And if they're growing naturally there now, there's no reason to think they wouldn't have been there two thousand years ago."

"So . . . you really *do* think that John was tripping when he wrote Revelation?"

Cross nodded. "The water might have been contaminated. Or he could even have eaten the mushrooms, not knowing what they were. But yes, I believe that his visions were psychoactive hallucinations." His gaze intensified. "So I had to find out where they came from."

"What do you mean?"

"I told you—you can't hallucinate something you haven't experienced. Yet John described mountains falling from the sky, the sea turning to blood, cities being destroyed—and he also described the twenty-four Elders, and the angels bound at the Euphrates." He returned to the laptop and pointed at the statue in the center of the image. "He described this!"

She frowned. "But he couldn't possibly have seen it."

"No. But someone could have described all those things to him. Or, more likely, he read about them, and all the other things that came from his subconscious when he had his vision. They were described so vividly, with such detail, that his mind was able to visualize them perfectly."

"So where did he read about them?"

"The answer's in Revelation. Chapters two and three are the letters that the Lord told John to send to the seven churches: Ephesus, Smyrna, Pergamum, Thyatira, Sardis, Philadelphia, and Laodicea."

"All in modern-day Turkey," said Nina.

"And all places that John must have visited to know so much about them. The Ephesians hated the Nicolaitans, the Smyrnans were rich, the Thyatirans tolerated the presence of the false prophet Jezebel—and he also knew that Antipas the bishop, his friend, was martyred in Pergamum." He watched Nina expectantly, as if waiting for her to make a connection.

One came almost immediately. "Pergamum is another name for Pergamon," she said. "And Pergamon had one of the largest libraries of the ancient world." His expression confirmed that she had guessed correctly. "Is that what you're saying? You think John read something there that formed his visions in Patmos?"

"That's exactly what I think, Dr. Wilde," Cross replied. "The library contained the ancient texts of the Elders—a record of the meteorite strike and the binding of the four angels at the Euphrates."

"Well, I can tell you a big problem with your theory right away," she said. "Mark Antony took everything from the Library of Pergamon to give to Cleopatra as a gift. He cleared the place out, every last scroll. There's no exact date for that, but he died in 30 BC—long before Jesus was born, never mind John. And Antipas died in AD 92, so Revelation couldn't have been written until after then."

"The Library of Pergamon still existed for centuries after John wrote Revelation," Cross told her dismissively. "Either Mark Antony didn't really take its entire contents, or some were hidden from him. John was still able to visit and read what he found there."

"That's just supposition, though," she objected. "You're making things up and presenting them as facts to fit your theory."

"It's not a *theory*!" he barked, making her flinch. "It's the truth! I know it's the truth, because God led me to it!" Another stab of his forefinger at the image of the angel on the laptop. "I found the angel! I witnessed its power with my own eyes!"

Nina tried to control her returning fear. Cross was revealing himself as a zealot, and she knew from experience that such people were most dangerous when their beliefs were directly challenged. "What power?" she asked, hoping to calm him by bringing him back to his pet subject.

He ignored her. "I found the truth on Patmos. I know what caused John to write the Book of Revelation—and I know it holds something real. I came here and established the Mission away from the corruption and sin of the world, and it gave me clarity. I've seen the truth. I believe it, my followers believe it, and you'll believe it too. You won't be able to deny it when I find the other angels!"

"That's what this is about?" she said. "Finding the rest of the angels from Revelation?"

Cross nodded. "The Elders kept one of them at the temple in Iraq, but hid the other three for safety. I believe they wrote down where they hid them, and that this text ended up in the Library of Pergamon, where John read it." He stared at the remains of the statue once more. "He might not have realized its significance, at least consciously, but when he had his visions it all came back to him. He wrote down everything he saw during the visions. It was all mixed up, scrambled, surrounded by other hallucinations, but it was still based on what he'd read about the Elders and the angels."

He whirled back to face Nina, white robes swirling. "*That's* what I believe the Book of Revelation is, Dr. Wilde. It's a code. And I've spent twelve years reading it, uncovering its secrets—cracking that code. The texts I found in the temple gave me the clues I needed to decipher it."

"This?" Nina protested, waving at the laptop's screen. "This is gibberish!"

"You don't need to read every word in a book to understand the story. It told me enough. I know where to find the angels—at least, I know which parts of Revelation contain the clues leading to them. What I don't know yet is where these locations are in the real world."

Realization dawned. "And that's why you need an archaeologist."

"Exactly," Cross replied. "Someone with the knowledge and experience to join the dots, to make the connections between the places John saw in his visions and where they are today."

"But why *me*?" objected Nina. "Your followers have obviously given you plenty of money if you've been able to build all this. You could have just hired somebody to work it out. Why kidnap me and Eddie?"

"I didn't want to involve an archaeologist until now, because they have their own biases that would have made them deny the truth. Just like all scientists. But you don't have the *option* to deny it. And . . ." The cult leader smiled. For the first time, the sense of malevolence lurking beneath the surface came out into the open. "You were highly recommended by an associate of mine."

The words sent a chill through her. That suggested Cross was working with someone with a personal grudge against her—but who? She and Eddie had made a lot of enemies . . .

She didn't have time to worry further about it as Cross spoke again. "Three locations are given special significance in the text of Revelation: 'the Synagogue of Satan,' 'the Throne of Satan,' and 'the Place in the Wilderness.' I think they're where the other angels are hidden." He closed the laptop and gestured toward the door. "Your job, Dr. Wilde, is to find them."

Nina suddenly realized that she already knew the true identity of one of the locations—but managed to hide her recognition of the fact, not wanting to give anything to her kidnapper. Instead she summoned up resistance. "I'm not doing a damn thing until I know Eddie's okay."

Simeon advanced on her. "You were warned—"

"Wait, Simeon," said Cross. "I was always going to

let you see your husband, Dr. Wilde. This way. Please."
The unpleasant smile returned.

That alone made Nina feel more worried than ever,
but she followed him back into the control room, Anna
and Simeon again shadowing her. The screens were still
cycling through clips of her at the Mission and in New
York, but her eyes went straight to the single monitor
showing the live feed of Eddie.

Cross went to his chair and tapped at a touch screen.
The dizzying display before him faded to black. Another
command, and the curved video wall came back to life,
the image of Eddie bound to the chair spread across it.
The camera was offset to his right, looking down at
him. "Mr. Irton," said Cross. "Can you hear me?"

"Yes, sir, I can hear you," came the reply. The new
voice was American, like Cross and his lieutenants, the
accent suggesting that the speaker was from one of the
southwestern states.

"Dr. Wilde is with me. Could you wake her husband,
please?"

"I sure can." Nothing happened for several seconds—
then a plume of water lanced in from the bottom of the
screen and hit the Englishman in the face.

Nina gasped as he thrashed and coughed. *"Eddie!"*

Eddie slammed painfully back to wakefulness as the frigid water hit him. He struggled to breathe, the sudden cold squeezing his chest tight—then realized he couldn't move. His arms were pinned painfully behind his back. Still straining to draw in air, he shook and writhed, trying to get loose.

No joy. Something was biting into his wrists. Handcuffs. No way to break them, but if there was enough slack in the chain, he might be able to bring his hands in front of him . . .

He couldn't. He was in a chair, a single metal pole supporting its broad back, and couldn't spread his arms far enough apart to lift them up around it. His ankles were secured too, tied to the chair's legs.

But he felt the whole seat flex slightly as he struggled. If he kept going, he might be able to crack a weld or strip a screw—

Movement nearby. He looked up, shaking icy water from his eyes, and knew he wouldn't get the chance.

Three men stared stonily back at him. The same bastards who'd attacked him on the street, shooting him with a Taser and bundling him into a van to be gagged . . . and drugged. They'd stuck him with something to knock him out. He had no idea how long he'd been unconscious, but he was both hungry and thirsty, with a groggy headache and raw, gritty eyes.

His surroundings came into focus beyond the trio. A warehouse or factory, derelict, gray daylight leaking in through grubby windows high above. Dirty crates and unidentifiable rusting machinery glinted with cobwebs. Closer by were some metal cases, their cleanliness telling him they had been brought by his kidnappers. His leather jacket lay crumpled on the floor nearby.

He also saw a video camera mounted on a tripod, connected to a laptop on a wooden bench. The red light by the lens suggested that he had an audience—

A voice cut through his fear. *"Eddie!"*

"Nina!" he yelled back. "Nina, where are you?"

"She's not here," said the older man mockingly. "Prophet? He's awake."

"Yes, I can see," came another disembodied voice from the laptop, an American man. "Dr. Wilde, you can talk to your husband. Briefly."

"Eddie!" Nina cried over the speakers. "Are you okay?"

"I've been better," he replied, blowing more dripping water off his face. "And I'm fucking freezing. These twats just woke me up with a bucket of ice water!"

"Watch your mouth," said the blond man, a plaster across his broken nose.

"Fuck off."

The man's face twisted with anger. Eddie saw the punch coming, but was completely unable to resist. It hit his stomach, hard, leaving him breathless.

"No, stop!" Nina shouted. "Leave him alone!"

"Mr. Chase," said the man with Nina, "I'd advise you to watch your language. Go on, Dr. Wilde."

"You son of a bitch," she muttered, before raising her voice again. "Are you all right, Eddie?"

"Like I said," he wheezed through gritted teeth, "been better. Where are you?"

"I don't know—somewhere in the tropics, I think.

They took me from the apartment and brought me here."

Worry gripped him. "Is the baby okay?"

"Yeah, as far as I can tell. They were going to drug me, but when I told them I was pregnant, they backed off."

"Oh, so they're the *caring* kind of kidnappers. Good to know. What the hell do they want with us?"

"They're . . . they're using you to force me to cooperate. Eddie, they say they'll torture you if I don't do what they want."

A different cold ran through him as he guessed what was in the cases. "Why? What are they after?"

"It's about the Book of Revelation, they—"

Sudden silence as the call was muted. "Nina?" Eddie shouted. "Nina! Put her back on, you fucking shithead!"

The blond man punched him again as the unknown voice returned. "You've seen that your husband is still alive, Dr. Wilde. Now I want you to see what'll happen to him if you don't do as you're told. Mr. Irton?"

The Taser man opened one of the cases. "Oh, *fuck*," Eddie gasped as Irton produced a cattle prod, a black baton two feet long with a pair of stubby electrodes protruding from one end.

"No!" cried Nina over the speakers. "I'll do what you want; you don't have to hurt him! Please, don't!"

But Eddie knew from the look in Irton's eyes that nothing she said would stop the shock from coming. The thin-mouthed man wasn't being sadistic or taking sick joy from inflicting pain on another human being—it was just business, part of the job, the professional detachment of the slaughterhouse worker. This was something he had done before, many times. He pushed a button. The electrodes crackled.

The Englishman set his jaw. "I'm going to kill you and all your mates," he growled. "That's a promise."

"They all say that," Irton replied dismissively—as he activated the cattle prod and shoved it against Eddie's soaked chest.

* * *

Nina's scream almost drowned out her husband's. "*No!* No, you bastard!" She threw herself at Cross, but Simeon easily intercepted her. "Stop him, *stop*! Please! Let him go!"

She looked back at the screens as Simeon dragged her away from the cult leader. Eddie convulsed in the chair, face twisted in agony as Irton moved the sparking rod up and down his body. "Why are you *doing* this?" she shrieked. "You're insane!"

Cross spun to face her, a sudden anger behind his piercing gaze. "I've never *been* more sane, Dr. Wilde! God Himself has set out this path for me, for His Witnesses"—he indicated Anna and Simeon—"for all of us. We will follow it to the end, and you're going to light the way."

He turned back to the screens. "Enough."

Irton retreated, the prod's high-voltage sizzle cutting off. Eddie slumped, wisps of smoke still rising from his T-shirt. Another man, younger than Irton, checked his pulse. "He's okay," he announced.

"Good," said Cross. He tapped the touch screen, and the video wall went blank. "Dr. Wilde, your husband's safety is now entirely up to you. If you locate the other angels, he'll be released."

Nina was unable to answer at first, shaking with fear and fury. "I don't . . . I don't know what I'm supposed to do," she finally said, voice quavering. "I'm not a biblical expert, it's not my field. Why me? Why do you think I can do it?"

"Because you have a talent for finding truth where others only see myths. Atlantis, Valhalla, the Garden of Eden. You found them. And you'll find the angels of Revelation too."

It took a moment for the full significance of his words to strike her, but when it did, it felt almost like a physical impact. "Wait—you believe I found the Garden of Eden?"

"Yes."

"But the way the media spun the story, it made me look like a kook. The whole thing was deliberately done to discredit me." It had taken her discovery of the lost Pyramid of Osiris in Egypt to restore her reputation.

"I know you found it. In Sudan. And I know it was destroyed by an American stealth bomber." Lines of disapproval formed around his eyes; he was as angered at its obliteration as Nina had been, though she imagined for very different reasons.

"How do you know that? I never told any of that to the IHA—and I sure as hell wasn't going to put it in my book."

"I have friends in the US government," Cross replied. "There are plenty who believe in the Lord and His plan as strongly as I do. And there are others whose faith is . . . weaker," he said, with another frown, "but who are willing to work with us. Yes, I know what you found."

"And you also know that what I found in Eden contradicts the Book of Genesis? That humans weren't created in God's image—that we weren't even the first intelligent species on the planet?"

Nina knew that challenging his core beliefs could go badly for her—and Eddie. But while Simeon and Anna were affronted, it did not trigger Cross's anger. "Yes, I know," he said. "About the Veteres—the race that walked the earth before us."

That revelation was even more startling, as her discovery of the Veteres was something known only to a handful of people. "And you accept it?" she asked. "But if you know that the first book of the Bible doesn't match reality, why are you so certain about the last book?"

"I told you, the Bible isn't to be taken literally. It was written by men, and men are fallible. It has to be studied and interpreted to find God's truth. It's not easy, but it's not *supposed* to be easy. Only people who've proven themselves worthy of God's truth will get to see His plan."

"And you think you're worthy?"

"I know I'm worthy. God has chosen me, Dr. Wilde.

He led me to the angel hidden in the temple in Iraq, and it's now my job to find the others."

"Seems like it's more *my* job," Nina said, acerbic.

"Then you should get started. Simeon, Anna, take her back to her house. You'll have everything you need, Dr. Wilde—biblical texts, historical reference material, maps, and limited Internet access. You'll be monitored at all times," he added, raising a warning finger. "You'll be cut off immediately if you try to contact anyone or access a site that might give away your location—such as by trying to log in to the IHA's servers."

"I quit the IHA over six months ago," she protested. "Why would I have access?"

"Because you've still got friends there. I know that your UN liaison, Oswald Seretse, gave you clearance even after you left. I also have friends in the intelligence services. We weren't only observing you on the streets."

"You've been monitoring our Internet too? Oh great, now you know all Eddie's favorite websites."

Anna's face creased as if she had just smelled a dead animal. "Yes, and they're disgusting." Her offense gave Nina an odd feeling of pride.

"Enough," said Cross impatiently. "Now, Dr. Wilde, it's up to you to find where the Elders hid the other three angels. Or your husband will suffer."

Fear returned, though this time with a sense of determination, a refusal to let Eddie's torturers win. "If they really exist, I'll find them," Nina told him.

"If you're as good as I've been told, I don't doubt it." Cross turned away.

Anna and Simeon escorted Nina from the room. Her mind was already working, but not on the task she had been given. The foremost question was: Told by *whom*?

*   *   *

An answer had not come by the time Simeon and Anna brought her back to the little house. The Mission's residents had dispersed from the church to their own homes, a few giving her friendly greetings.

Nina ignored them. However cheery the inhabitants

seemed, the fact remained that she was a prisoner, and nobody was willing to help her escape. And she was being watched every step of the way, cameras pivoting to track her. Even if she broke away from her escort, the alarm would be raised in seconds. How far could she get?

Simeon ushered her inside. "So housekeeping's visited," she said, seeing that a number of books and a laptop computer had been placed on the desk. "Any chance of some room service?"

Her companions were not amused. "Get to work," said Simeon.

"Get bent," Nina shot back. "I haven't eaten since breakfast. Do you know how cranky pregnant women get when they're hungry?"

The sorrowful look Anna gave Simeon made it clear to Nina that they were a couple. "We haven't been blessed with a child," she said.

"Maybe you don't deserve one."

"Maybe *you* don't." Simeon took a step closer to Nina, his glare ice-cold.

"Simeon," Anna said. His angry scowl deepened, but he retreated. "There's plenty of food. But if you want to cook, do it yourself. We're not your personal wait staff."

"I'm gonna give this place *such* a bad review on TripAdvisor," Nina snarked as they left. The door closed behind them, and as she'd expected the lock clicked. Even so, she tried to open it, with no success. "Shit."

She was in no mood to cook, so made do with throwing together a salad sandwich and devouring it before moving on to a box of crackers. Munching on the dry biscuits, she looked through the cupboards again. Her captors had at least stocked her prison with a decent selection of provisions.

A small bottle among various packaged ingredients and condiments caught her eye. Spirit vinegar. That jogged a memory, something Eddie had once told her. She looked back through the fresh vegetables. Corn, green peppers, chili, onions, some bulbs of garlic . . .

She glanced up at the camera silently watching her

from the corner. An idea had come to her, but she would have to be extremely careful and patient to carry it out—if she even could. If it worked, though, it might give her the chance she needed to run for the Mission's boundary.

For now, she had to at least make the pretense of working on Cross's assignment. If her watchers thought she was wasting time, Eddie would pay the price. Delaying tactics had caused Macy's death; she couldn't allow the same thing to happen again.

Another thought. Cross was insistent that she find the angels as soon as possible. Was he working to a deadline? And if so, why? The angels, if they existed, had been hidden for thousands of years. Why the rush?

She turned toward the desk. Sitting atop the stack of books was a copy of the Bible. The Old and New Testaments; Genesis to Revelation. Maybe the answer really *was* in there . . .

"Let's see what John of Patmos saw in his visions," she said to herself as she thumbed to its final book.

A faint knocking woke Nina. She frowned and raised her head, eyes still half closed. "Eddie, get the door, will you . . ."

Memory slammed back into place. She jerked upright in fear and confusion. Books and papers fell to the floor. She had fallen asleep fully clothed, her research scattered around her. How long she'd been out, she had no idea, but the daylight beyond the shutters was back; it had faded into night long before she dropped into an uneasy slumber.

Another knock at the door. "What?" she shouted, scrambling to her feet.

"Dr. Wilde?" came a female voice. "My name's Miriam. The Prophet asked me to bring you to him."

"He did, huh?" she said, crossing to the door. Red lights blinked on the cameras as she moved. She flipped them the bird. "Well, he can wait until I've had a shower and some breakfast."

A pause, then the voice hesitantly returned. "Uh . . . he wants to see you right now."

Nina tried the door; this time, it wasn't locked. Standing outside in the morning sun was a slim, pretty woman in her early twenties, wavy rust-brown hair dropping to her shoulders. Her clothing, a knee-length dress and a pair of sandals, was all white. "You pregnant, Miriam?"

Her visitor was startled. "Ah . . . no?" she said uncertainly.

Nina opened the door wider and pointed at her own bump. "Well I am, and let me give you some useful advice for if you ever are: Pregnant ladies always get to choose when they meet people. Okay? Tell your Prophet I'll see him when I'm good and ready. Which might be in ten minutes, it might be ten hours. Later, tater." She gave the freckle-cheeked woman a mocking wave, then slammed the door before going to the kitchen to search for food.

Another knock came a few minutes later. "Yeah, what?" shouted Nina through a mouthful of cereal.

Miriam peered around the door. "I'm sorry, I . . . I don't want to intrude, but . . . but the Prophet sent me to bring you, and—and I don't know what'll happen if I go back to him without you."

Nina spotted the glistening line of a tear on her cheek. "Are you crying?"

Miriam hurriedly wiped her face. "I didn't mean to, I'm sorry . . ."

The redhead's annoyance changed to concern. Her visitor was upset, even afraid. Nina went to her. "Are you okay? Your Prophet, Cross—will he hurt you if I don't go with you?"

She was genuinely shocked at the suggestion. "No, no, of course not! It's just . . . I don't want to let him down."

"Were you standing outside the door this whole time?"

Miriam nodded. "I didn't want to make you mad, especially as you're with child."

"Trust me, you're *way* down the list of things that have spiked my cortisol levels in the past twenty-four hours." She glared at the nearest camera. "So, what," she told her watchers, "you send this poor girl to get me as part of some emotional blackmail plan? Jesus!"

Miriam's mouth fell open in shock, this time at the blasphemy. Nina gave her an irritated look. "I'm guessing you're not from New York if something that mild upsets you. All right, okay, I'm coming," she told the camera with a frustrated shrug. "First things first, though."

"What?" asked Miriam.

"I need to pee. Maybe that's oversharing, but I really don't care." She disappeared into the bathroom, leaving the blushing woman staring after her.

After an unrushed break, Nina reemerged to find her guest still waiting. She gathered her papers. "Okay, let's go."

Miriam led her out of the house and through the Mission. She was silent to begin with, only piping up very quietly about halfway down the street of little houses. "Ulysses."

"What?" said Nina.

"Ulysses, Kansas. That's where I'm from. Well, not the actual town—I grew up on a farm about ten miles away. So no, I'm not from New York."

"Yeah, I'd guessed."

"But I always wanted to see it. It looks amazing. Scary, though. Isn't there a lot of crime?"

Nina made a sarcastic sound. "Sure, if you hop in your time machine and go back to the '70s. You aren't going to get stabbed in the middle of Times Square in broad daylight. Probably."

"Okay . . ." was the uncertain reply. "I'd still like to go one day, though."

"What's stopping you? You're not a prisoner here, are you?"

"Of course not! I came here by my own choice, to follow the Prophet." She smiled and gestured at their sunny surroundings. "It's lovely here. And I'm with friends who think the same way I do. Why would I want to leave?"

"I can think of a few reasons," said Nina, regarding the nearest set of security cameras. "So where *is* here?"

Miriam opened her mouth to reply, then clapped it shut. "I, uh . . . I'm sorry, but I was told not to tell you anything about the Mission."

"But we're somewhere in the Caribbean, right?"

She clenched her hands in agitation. "I'm sorry, really I am, but I can't tell you."

"You do know that I *didn't* come here by my own choice? I was kidnapped, Miriam—that's a federal offense, and every country in the Caribbean, even Cuba, has an extradition treaty with the US. Anyone who's involved in keeping me a prisoner here will be counted as an accessory. That'll get you a minimum thirty years in a federal prison." She had no idea if that was true, but she could tell from Miriam's alarm that she had made her point. "You realize that, don't you? But if you help me get out of here . . ."

Conflict was clear on the young woman's face. "I . . . I'm sorry, but I can't, I really can't," she said at last. "I can't go against the Prophet. I just can't! I'm sorry."

Nina held back her anger. Miriam was genuinely upset at not being able to help, but also unwilling—or unable—to disobey her leader. "This Prophet," she said instead, changing tack, "why do you follow him? What's he offering you?"

Miriam's smile returned as if a switch had been flipped. "He's going to lead us to the new Jerusalem! God's dwelling place will come down out of heaven to the earth, and He will live among us and wipe away all the tears from our eyes."

"And there'll be no more pain or sorrow, right?" Nina recognized her words as part of Revelation, which she had read several times the previous night.

"That's right!"

"And how exactly is he going to do this?"

"I don't know. But I trust him," she quickly added. "Everything the Prophet says makes sense. Revelation will come to pass, and God's kingdom on earth will begin."

"So you think your Prophet's a good man?"

"Of course he is!"

Nina's expression hardened. "Good men don't kidnap pregnant women, Miriam. And they don't torture people to force them to cooperate."

She shook her head. "He wouldn't do that."

"He *has* done that! He made me watch my husband being electrocuted with a cattle prod!" Seeing the other woman's dismay, she pressed on: "He's no prophet; he's an ex-CIA agent who went nuts. Whatever Cross really wants, it's not peace on earth and everyone singing 'Kumbaya.' You've got to help me!"

Miriam scowled. Nina realized she'd pushed too hard and put her on the defensive. "He's not nuts," she protested. "You'll see. When the angels are all released and the seventh trumpet blows, you'll see!"

"What will I see?"

"The truth," said a new voice. They had almost reached the church, and Nina looked up to see Cross at the top of the steps. "God's truth will be revealed." His eyes flicked toward the papers Nina was holding. "Soon, I hope. Very soon."

Miriam curtsied. "Prophet, I've brought her, like you asked."

"Thank you, Miriam. You can go back to your studies now."

She nodded, giving the archaeologist an uncertain look before departing. Nina glowered at her host. "Hope you're not expecting *me* to curtsy."

"Come inside, Dr. Wilde," he said. "I hope we've got a lot to talk about."

Nina followed Cross into the church. With him was a large young man she didn't recognize, hard-faced and with a distinctly military-style mustache. "Replacement bodyguard?" she asked. "What happened to the charmers who brought me here?"

"The Witnesses are preparing for a mission," Cross replied. "They flew out last night; I want them ready to move as soon as you find the location of the first angel."

"They're the two Witnesses?" Nina asked, picking up on another Revelation reference.

"Yes."

"That explains the outfits, then."

Cross nodded. "Chapter eleven, verse three—'And I will give power unto my two witnesses, and they shall prophesy a thousand two hundred and threescore days, clothed in sackcloth.' "

"Must be itchy for them. Especially in this heat." Even early in the day, the temperature was already well over seventy degrees Fahrenheit.

"They can endure it. They'll endure anything to get the job done."

They went through to the control room. It had acquired a table and chairs since her previous visit. Cross's imposing high-tech throne was at its head; he took his seat and gestured for Nina to join him. She sat at the opposite end, making a point of sliding her chair as far away from him as possible. The other man took up a somewhat intimidating position close behind her. "Now," said Cross, "the Synagogue of Satan, the Throne of Satan, and the Place in the Wilderness. Do you know where they are?"

"Not yet," she lied. "I might have some ideas—but I'm not doing anything until I see that Eddie's okay."

The cult leader let out an irritated breath. "All right. You can see him." His hand went to one of the touch screens.

"And talk to him."

His eyes narrowed. "Don't push me, Dr. Wilde. My patience isn't infinite."

"Mine's hanging by a frickin' thread. I want to talk to Eddie before I do anything else."

"You want to talk to him? All right." There was a nasty undertone that immediately put her on alert, but he tapped at the pad. The wall of screens lit up, showing the same elevated angle of Eddie as before. He was either asleep or unconscious, his arms and legs still secured. "There he is."

"Eddie!" she called. "Eddie, are you okay? Eddie!"

"He can't hear you," Cross said. "I haven't turned on the microphone yet."

"Then do that. You want me to cooperate, you want me to find your damn angels? Then let me talk to him."

He sneered, then ran his finger over a slider. "Okay."

"Eddie, can you hear me?" she said.

For a moment there was no response, then her husband raised his head. "Nina?" he croaked.

"Oh, thank God. Are you all right?"

He tried to move, only to let out a sharp gasp. "Ow! No, my arms are fucking killing me. These bastards left me cuffed to this fucking chair all night." He rolled both shoulders, trying to ease the pain in his stiff muscles. "Are you okay?"

"Yeah."

"And the baby?"

"Fine, it's fine. They haven't done anything to hurt me—yet."

"Wish I could say the same."

"Me too. But I'm going to do everything I can to get you out of there. They're trying to find the angels in the Throne and Synagogue of Satan—"

Cross stabbed at the pad again, cutting her off. Only one end of the link had been muted, though. "Nina?" said Eddie with growing anger and alarm. "Nina, what's happening?"

"You've spoken to him," Cross said to Nina. "Now, this is what happens if you make another demand of me." Another swipe at the slider. "Mr. Irton? Proceed."

"No!" cried Nina, but he had already cut the mike. Irton stepped into the frame, holding a couple of large, thick cloths.

Eddie struggled uselessly against his bonds. "You get away from me, you fucking—"

Irton punched him in the stomach, leaving him gasping. Two more men came into view. One went behind the chair, releasing a chain that was holding it to a metal ring on the floor, while Irton wrapped both cloths tightly around the Englishman's head.

Nina realized what they were about to do. "God, no!" she cried, jumping to her feet, but the bodyguard pushed her roughly back down. "Don't, please!" She grabbed her notes and waved them at Cross. "I'll tell you what I've found out!"

His response was a look of cold dismissal. "I warned

you, Dr. Wilde." He worked the volume control again. "Do it."

The cloths were secured. Eddie jerked in the seat, straining to draw in air through the stifling material. The two other men hauled the chair and its occupant a foot off the floor, then tipped it until the back of Eddie's head thumped against the concrete. Nina cringed, knowing that he was about to suffer even more—and that she was utterly helpless to prevent it.

Irton had moved out of sight while his companions lifted the chair; he now returned holding a bucket of water, which he held over Eddie's head . . .

And started to pour.

The water splashed onto the wrapped cloth. The weight of the sodden material pressed it down onto Eddie's face, revealing its contours—and his mouth opening wide as water filled his nostrils. He tried to cry out, but all that emerged was a gargling moan as Irton kept pouring.

Nina stood again, but was shoved back into her chair. "Stop it! Stop! Let him go!" she screamed at Cross. "You bastard, you're killing him!"

"He'll live," he replied. "British special forces, wasn't he? He'll have had SERE training; he can withstand being waterboarded. For a while, at least. Nobody can hold out forever." He looked back at the screens, where Eddie was squirming as the water flowed over his head. "The CIA didn't teach us these techniques so we could resist them. They taught them so we know how to use them."

She stared at him, appalled. "You're insane."

"Insanity is seeing all the evils in this world and refusing to do anything to stop them. I'm going to stop them, Dr. Wilde. And you'll help me." His intense eyes locked on to hers. "Are we in agreement?"

"Just stop hurting him," she said, defeated. "Please."

Cross was still for several seconds, then nodded. "That's enough, Mr. Irton. Bring him back up."

Irton retreated. His companions hauled their prisoner upright, one securing the chair back to the floor while the other peeled away the soaking fabric. Eddie retched, blowing water from his nose.

"Mr. Irton is an expert in enhanced interrogation techniques," Cross told Nina. "He can keep a man in a state where he thinks he's about to die for days at a time, if he has to. But he won't have to, will he?"

Nina's heart raced, fear and shock pumping through her. "No. He won't."

"Good. That'll be all for now, Mr. Irton. I'll contact you if you're needed again."

Irton looked up at the camera. "We'll be here, Prophet." He regarded his slumped captive. "So will he."

"So, Dr. Wilde," said Cross. "Tell me what you've learned so far."

"Give me a minute. Please." She raised a shaking hand to her head, trying to calm herself. It wasn't only Eddie she was worried about; high stress levels in a mother could cause tremendous harm to a developing baby.

"Norvin, get her something to drink," Cross told the other man. The bodyguard went to a cabinet, returning with a bottle of water.

Nina took it and gulped down its contents. She paused for breath, looking at the table rather than meeting Cross's gaze. Her notes were spread out before her. She took them in, her pulse slowing as her mind almost involuntarily resumed work on the challenge.

One page in particular brought an answer. She looked back at the image of her husband, then engaged in a silent debate with herself as she weighed various factors: her safety, the baby's health, Eddie's life, the danger that Cross posed to all of them . . . and made a decision.

"Okay. I think I have an idea where one of the angels is," she announced. "That's assuming you're absolutely one hundred percent convinced that the three places you gave me are where they've been hidden. You don't want me to look at other possibilities, just in case?"

Cross clasped his hands together. "I'm sure. I've been studying Revelation for twelve years. I *know* those are the places God wants me to find. The clues all point to them; the emphasis given to them in the text, the repetition of their names, makes me absolutely certain."

"So I'm only looking for them, nowhere else?"

"Nowhere else. What have you found?"

Another glance at Eddie, still lolling in the chair. "If I help you, you won't hurt him again?"

"If you help me, I won't need to."

Nina took a deep breath. "All right. I'll do what you want."

With an expression of satisfaction, Cross shut off the screens. "Good. Talk."

She sorted through her papers. "Okay. I read Revelation last night. It's not an easy read, especially since you only gave me the King James Version, but I came up with a possible link to the so-called Synagogue of Satan."

"You know where it is?"

"I know where it might be. In Rome."

Cross didn't seem surprised by her deduction. "That makes sense. There are several parts of Revelation that refer to Rome. The description of the Beast: 'The seven heads are seven mountains' means the seven hills on which the city was built. The *accepted*"—there was more than a hint of cynicism behind the word—"interpretation of Revelation is that John described Rome in riddles to hide that he was making a direct attack on the Romans who were persecuting the Christians."

"It's not exactly the Enigma code, though," said Nina. "And the Romans weren't dumb. They were always watching for signs of sedition or rebellion. One of the reasons John might have been exiled to Patmos in the first place was for being critical of Emperor Domitian, but if he'd been *too* critical, he would have been executed, not exiled. Saying that Rome was a whore and the emperor a demonic beast would have put him on the fast track to a crucifixion."

"Then the references to Rome in Revelation came from John's visions of the Elders' writings," said Cross thoughtfully. "They're part of the code to finding the angels." He looked back at Nina. "So where in Rome?"

"I'm not sure yet," she said. "But I think the mere fact that John made a direct association between a synagogue and Satan is significant." She flicked back through her notes, at the same time searching her knowledge of Roman and early Christian history. "Jewish Christians were a fairly major part of the Christian movement immediately following Jesus's death, but it didn't take long for them to be marginalized and later demonized—in John's case literally, since he flat-out accused them of being in league with Satan—by the religion's leadership. Both religions, actually; the Jewish leaders didn't want them around any more than the orthodox Christians did. By the end of the first century, they'd demanded a clear split—you were either Christian or Jewish; you couldn't be both."

"Understandable. You have to fully accept Christ and His teachings to be saved. There are no half measures."

"But before then," she went on, not wanting to be dragged into a debate about the fate of her eternal soul, "around the time Domitian took power in AD 81, there was still a degree of crossover. The weird thing was that Rome was actually one of the safest places for Jewish Christians. Nero scapegoated Christians following the Great Fire of Rome, and from that point on they were widely persecuted by the Romans, but Jews were tolerated in the empire. But at some point, the Christian leaders decided enough was enough, and they declared Jewish Christianity a false church. They risked coming into Rome itself to lay down the law about which version of Christianity they had to follow."

"The apostle Paul," said Cross, nodding. "He came to Rome after his third missionary journey. Acts chapter twenty-eight—he summons the chiefs of the Jews to try to convince them to follow Christ's teachings. 'Be it known therefore unto you that the salvation of God is sent unto the Gentiles, and that they will hear it. And when he had said these words, the Jews departed, and had great reasoning among themselves.' Verses twenty-eight and twenty-nine."

Nina raised a disbelieving eyebrow. "Have you memorized the entire Bible? Wait, don't answer that. But yeah, Paul came to Rome—or was brought to Rome, since he was there to stand trial for his alleged crimes against the empire. And it didn't go well for him, as he was executed."

"But he was there," Cross insisted. "And he spoke to the leaders of the Jews."

"*Where* did he speak to them? Does the Bible say anything?"

He thought for a moment. "Yes. 'And when they had appointed him a day, there came many to him into his lodging.' Acts chapter twenty-eight, verse twenty-three."

She was almost disappointed. "So they went to him. Damn. I'd thought that if Paul had wanted to speak to all the Jewish leaders, they would have chosen to meet him somewhere they had home advantage. A synagogue, in other words. They weren't specifically buildings as they are now—the word just means a meeting place."

"The Synagogue of Satan," said Cross, nodding slowly—then suddenly widening his eyes. "No, wait! There was another meeting, before they came to Paul's lodging. Verse seventeen: 'And it came to pass, that after three days Paul called the chief of the Jews together, and when they were come together, he said unto them . . .' They *did* assemble somewhere."

"Where?"

"That's what you have to find out. You're the archaeologist." Ignoring her dirty look, he addressed Norvin. "Take her back to her room. If she needs anything, get it for her."

"How about a plane ticket out of here?" Nina asked as she stood. She saw Cross's unamused expression. "Jeez, you fundies have no sense of humor. I told you I'd find your angels."

"Just remember that your husband is counting on you," he said as Norvin escorted her to the door.

Nina regarded the monitors behind Cross with a look as dark as the empty screens. "I hadn't forgotten."

* * *

The laptop's browser had several tabs open, Nina flicking between them as she scribbled down more notes. The blocks Cross had put in place were frustrating, as some of the primary sources of information she normally would have used were linked to the IHA or other United Nations agencies and were therefore verboten.

The active tab was not displaying the website of any official organization, however. It had taken some time to discover it: an obscure blog detailing the journeys of a Jewish traveler with an interest in her people's history. One such trip had taken her to Rome, where she had been lucky enough to visit a site not generally accessible to the public . . .

"That could be it," Nina whispered, scrolling through the traveler's pictures. They didn't contain the proof she was after, only an implication, a suggestion, but so far it was the best she had.

She clicked another tab. A map appeared, a twisting network of tunnels. The scale revealed that they were confined within a relatively small area, only a few hundred yards along each edge, but the numerous tiers of underground passages meant that there were several miles of them. It would take some time to explore them all.

Which was exactly what she had hoped.

She collated her notes and was about to stand when there came a timid knock at the door. "Saw me finish, did you?" she asked the nearest camera as she crossed the room.

Miriam was outside. "Dr. Wilde?"

"I'm guessing you've been sent to come and get me?"

She nodded. "The Prophet wants to see you."

"I thought he might. Okay, let's go."

They headed through the Mission, receiving greetings from residents along the way. The sun was high overhead; Nina could feel the heat prickling her scalp. Miriam noticed her discomfort. "Are you okay?"

"It's too hot."

The young woman's concern was genuine. "Oh! I'm sorry. You've got such pale skin, I should have thought . . . I could find you a hat?"

Nina felt ironic amusement that a prisoner was being treated like a VIP guest. "That's okay, I'll survive."

"I'm sorry," Miriam repeated.

"For what?"

"For not being able to get you everything you want."

Nina couldn't help but warm to the young ingénue. "What I *want* is to get out of here."

"I know." Miriam gave her another look of sincere apology. "I'd help you if I could, but the Prophet needs you."

"Do you do everything the Prophet tells you?"

"Of course. We're his followers, he's going to lead us to—"

"To God's new kingdom, heaven on earth; yeah, I know." Nina regarded her with sudden concern. "He doesn't . . . take advantage of you, does he?"

Miriam flapped her hands in dismay. "No, no! He doesn't do anything like that! Nor do any of the men here. It's written in the Book of Revelation. Chapter fourteen, verse four: 'These are they who were not defiled with women.'"

"No wonder they're all so uptight," muttered Nina. "And 'defiled'? John had some serious issues." She surveyed the village—and its inhabitants. "There aren't any kids here, are there?"

"No."

"So this new Jerusalem that Cross says he's leading you to—what happens when you get there? 'Be fruitful and multiply' was one of God's commands all the way back in Genesis, but if nobody's having children . . ."

"I don't know," Miriam admitted. "But the Prophet does. He's following God's plan, and when the time's right, we'll all be told what it is. It says so in Revelation."

Nina couldn't recall reading anything that suggested that, but memorizing every verse hadn't been her priority. Dismissing it as another of Cross's crackpot beliefs, she followed the younger woman up to the church. Cross was again waiting at the door, Norvin at his side. "Dr. Wilde, welcome back," the cult leader said.

"Thrilled to be here," she answered through a thin, sarcastic smile. "I think I've found what you wanted."

"I know. God is always watching here at the Mission."

"My idea of God never had him as a Peeping Tom."

"Eternal vigilance is the price of liberty."

Nina eyed him. "*That's* not a Bible quote."

"No, but it's practically the motto of the CIA. The best way to protect your people is to know everything."

"About their enemies, or about them?"

"In this case, about you." He regarded her notes. "You've found the Synagogue of Satan." It was not a question.

"I *think* I've found it," she replied. "I'll explain everything to you inside. Assuming you haven't already read it over my shoulder."

Cross nodded to Nina's guide. "I'll call you if I need you again."

"Thank you, Prophet," Miriam replied. She curtsied before departing, this time giving Nina a happy smile as she passed.

"So how did you persuade her to join your little cult?" Nina asked Cross as they entered the church. "Tour the Midwest to spread the word?"

"I'm not a preacher, Dr. Wilde," he said. "I'm just a seeker of the truth, by trade and by nature. When people seek the truth, others naturally join their quest. You should know that. You don't work alone either."

"No, but I've never managed to get my co-workers to pay for *my* tropical retreat."

"My followers donate to the Mission entirely of their own free will. All I ask from them is their belief in what we do, and their labor for our community. Beyond that, they're here to study Revelation and wait for its prophecies to come true." They reached the control room. "Which I'm hoping will happen soon." He took his seat and gestured for her to sit at the table.

Nina noticed that her chair had been moved closer to him, and pushed it away again as she sat, to his minor but obvious annoyance. "Okay," she said after laying out her notes. "Ancient Rome, according to historical texts, had between seven and sixteen major synagogues at various times. Most of their locations have been lost; they would have been demolished and built over as the city grew. But some left archaeological traces, from their catacombs—their burial chambers."

"How many?" asked Cross.

"Three major ones. There have been some smaller hypogea—underground chambers—discovered since the nineteenth century, but none of them are anywhere near as expansive as the ones at Monteverde, Vigna Randanini, and the Villa Torlonia."

"You think it's one of those? Which one?"

Nina had intended to explain her reasoning in full, but Cross's impatience was clear—and besides, he probably already knew to which she had devoted the most attention. "Villa Torlonia."

"Why?"

"Partly because of its size; it's the largest network of Jewish and early Christian catacombs in the city. The fact that it *is* both Jewish and Christian also made it look promising, because it lands right in that crossover period when the Jewish Christians of Rome were still enough of a threat to the orthodox Christian leadership that the apostle Paul went to them in person. Which made me think about that Bible verse you quoted about Paul calling the Jewish leadership together."

She had definitely caught his attention, any lingering irritation replaced by intrigue. "What about it?"

"Like I said, the Jewish Christians would probably choose the initial meeting place. It'd be somewhere they knew, and large enough to accommodate a lot of people, from the sound of it. So the most likely location would be at Rome's main synagogue."

"And was that the Villa Torlonia?"

"The excavations there uncovered a large area that had once been an open-air meeting place. In other words, a synagogue. Although . . ." She hesitated. "Nobody knows for certain."

"What do you mean?"

"It seems *likely* to have been a synagogue, but maybe it was just a courtyard—or maybe it was nothing to do with the catacombs at all. There are even some arguments about the age of the catacombs themselves; some of the more recent surveys suggest they predate Christianity by a couple of centuries, but quite a few people still insist that they're from the first century AD, which would probably be far too late for these Elders of yours to have hidden anything down there." A nervous shuffle of her papers. "Which is why I'm warning you right now that I can't be sure I'm correct. I've given it my best shot, but I can't guarantee anything."

Cross leaned forward, his cold eyes regarding her intently. "Then convince me that you've done the absolute best you can."

Nina paused, realizing her mouth had gone dry. Her captor had been a CIA agent, trained in intelligence gathering, and also in determining if that intelligence were true. That almost certainly meant he was experienced in questioning his sources . . . and interrogating them, if necessary.

If he didn't accept her assurance or, worse, thought that she was stalling, or lying . . .

"You've got my husband. You've got me. You've got my *baby.*" She pushed the chair back, rising to show him the swelling below her stomach. "The only way we're all going to get out of this alive is if I do everything I can to help you. You've made that pretty damn clear. Well, I want to be back home and safe with my family. I want—" Sudden emotion made the words catch in her throat. "I want to have my baby. And I want Eddie to be there with me. *That's* how you can be sure I'm doing the best I can."

Her hands were shaking; she clenched her fists to

cover it. Cross maintained his icy stare for a long moment . . . then sat back. "I believe you, Dr. Wilde. For now. So," he said, slightly more casually, "you think the angel is in the catacombs of the Villa Torlonia. Where? And how do we find it?"

Nina didn't answer him immediately, struggling to settle herself. "I don't know yet," she finally told him. "The catacombs aren't open to the public because of the levels of radon gas. They very occasionally run tours, but only for limited periods. Anyone going down there would need specialist equipment—masks, breathing gear."

Cross typed something on a touch screen. "Okay, noted. How big are the tunnels?"

"There are more than five miles of catacombs. And nothing resembling your angel has ever been found there, so it's not at the villa's museum. If it's down there, it's hidden."

He ran his finger down the pad, then tapped at it. The video wall flicked into life, showing a somewhat pixilated copy of the catacomb map she had consulted on the laptop. "These are the tunnels?"

"Yes." She realized that he had called up a list of all the webpages she had checked in her research. "The burial chambers are predominantly Jewish, although some Christian epitaphs have been found down there too. Depending on which dating scheme you accept, they were in use for between three and six centuries, so there's a lot of ground to cover."

Cross stared at the map as if studying a battle plan. "Nothing's been discovered that looks anything like the temple I found in Iraq?"

"No. Although I saw some photos that'll give you an idea of what it's like down there."

He swiped back through the menu. The map disappeared, replaced by a photograph of the catacombs. Narrow, damp tunnels wound through the earth, burial niches—loculi—carved into the walls. Some of the rectangular nooks were surrounded by decorative frescoes.

These in particular caught Cross's attention. "The paintings. Are there more like them?"

"There are more photos; see for yourself," Nina told him. "Most of the tunnels are plain, but some of the larger chambers are quite ornate."

More images flashed up, the seemingly endless passages disappearing into darkness—then Cross abruptly straightened. "What's that?"

Nina examined the new picture. It showed part of a ceiling, an image inside a circle picked out in gray and reddish-brown painted lines. "It's a menorah. You know, a Jewish candlestick? Don't tell me they didn't have Hanukkah where you grew up."

"I know what it is," he snapped. "Is that the only one down there?"

"No, there are quite a few of them. There should be pictures of a pair of menorahs on a wall—it's the most famous part of the place."

Cross flicked impatiently through more photographs to find them. An arched wall bore two large circular paintings of the seven-branched candleholders, a wide mouth-like split in the stonework beneath them making the whole scene resemble a cartoon ghost.

"Why is that important?" asked Nina, seeing his intense interest in the scene.

"The temple in Iraq—there was the symbol of a menorah right above the angel. Wait, look." He stabbed at the pad. The picture he had showed to Nina on her arrival filled the screens. He zoomed in on the niche. "There."

It was hard to make out clearly through the dirt, but there did indeed appear to be the image of a menorah inscribed on the gilded wall. "You think it's a marker?" she asked. "The menorah's a symbol showing the statue's location?"

Cross stared at the picture, then swiped back to the photos of the catacombs. "It could be," he said, almost to himself, before turning to Nina and saying more forcefully: "It is! I'm sure of it! It tells you where to find the angel; the Elders hid it somewhere in the cata-combs."

"Where, though? There were half a dozen menorahs just in those photos, and they were only from a small part of the whole system."

"We'll have to search. We need to find the one with the Akkadian and Hebrew symbols for the twenty-four Elders above it. The angel's wings are made of metal—once we locate the right menorah, we can use detectors to find it."

"Assuming someone hasn't already."

"You said it yourself: Nobody's found anything re-sembling it before."

"The catacombs have been there for a long time," Nina cautioned. "Someone could have taken it two thousand years ago."

Cross shook his head. "No. It's there, somewhere. I know it. I *know.*"

Alarm rose within her. Her captor had made his deci-sion based on nothing more than her educated guess—which with the limited time and research materials available was practically only a hunch. "And what if it's not there? What happens to me—and to Eddie?"

He didn't respond, which unnerved her all the more. Instead he brought up a new app on one of the pads. After a few seconds, the sound of a dialing phone came over the speakers.

The call was quickly answered. "Prophet?" came Simeon's voice.

"Where are you?" Cross asked.

"We arrived in Athens about an hour ago and met the others."

"Is the jet still there?"

"It's ready whenever we need it."

"You need it. Tell the pilot to arrange a flight plan for Rome, as soon as possible."

"The angel's in Rome?" said Simeon, with clear ex-citement.

"In the catacombs of a place called the Villa Torlonia.

I'll send you the intel. You'll need metal detectors and breath masks as well as the usual gear."

Anna chipped in. "I've got contacts in Europe who can arrange that."

"Good. We need to move quickly," Cross went on. "What time is it there?"

"Almost twenty hundred hours," Simeon told him.

A moment's thought. "It'll be around midnight, local time, by the time you're onsite," said Cross. "That should work for us—security ought to be minimal by then."

"We won't have much time to reconnoiter."

"You'll have to improvise. I want the angel found—tonight."

"Yes, Prophet." The line went silent.

"Why the rush?" Nina asked. "If the angel's there today, it'll still be there tomorrow, or a week from now."

Again he didn't answer. "Norvin, take her back to her house," he ordered. "Dr. Wilde, I want you to find out everything you can about the catacombs. My people need an efficient search pattern, and they need to know what to expect down there."

"What? It's a *tomb*," Nina replied as she stood. "It's literally as quiet as a grave. You're making it sound like it's going to be a military operation."

His silence this time was distinctly unnerving.

Nina was rinsing a plate in the kitchen when someone knocked on the door. Norvin had paid visits
throughout the afternoon to check the progress of her
research, but from the sound's hesitancy she guessed
that this time it was Miriam. "Come in!"

She had been right. "Dr. Wilde?" said the young
woman. "The Prophet asked me—"

"Yeah, yeah, bring me to him. I know the drill."

Miriam lowered her head, abashed, then sniffed the
air. "Oh, that smells delicious! What is it?"

"Nothing special," Nina told her. "I just fried up some
peppers and onions and things. I know fried food isn't
something you're supposed to have while you're pregnant, but screw it—sometimes you just have to obey
your cravings. And hey, at least it's not coal or something crazy like live goldfish."

"It's making me hungry, that's for sure." Miriam
looked at the countertop. "I'll clean all that up for you."

Nina held up her hands. "No, it's okay. I can take care
of it."

"Are you sure? At least let me put that in the gar-
bage." She indicated a wooden board on which were the
finely chopped remains of several peppers.

"No, I'm going to dry them out and use them as seasoning." Seeing Miriam's uncertainty, Nina smiled and went on: "Really, it's okay. I'm going to be here for a while, so I at least want to be able to cook my way, y'know?"

"If you're sure . . ."

"I'm sure. Okay, let me wash my hands and we'll go see what His Prophetness wants."

They left the little house, Miriam striking up a conversation about cookery. Nina had to bluff her way through it; she was far from a culinary expert, Eddie generally handling anything more complicated than scrambled eggs. They passed one of the poles topped by the black spheres of the security cameras, and she realized that she not only had a chance to change the subject, but that it was the only time she would be able to talk without being overheard. "Listen, Miriam," she said in a low voice, "you told me before that you wanted to help me."

The young woman nodded. "What can I do?"

Nina chose her words carefully. Their earlier exchanges had made it clear that she would not be able to persuade Miriam to act directly against Cross, but if she could appeal to her caring nature . . . "Miriam, I like you—you're a sweet girl, and I know that you care about what happens to me."

She smiled. "Thank you."

"Then you care about my baby too. Don't you?"

The smile became a little laugh. "Of course I do!"

"Because the thing is, I was brought here against my will. That's put me under a lot of pressure, a lot of stress—and that's not good for the baby. It can really hurt it. Do you hear what I'm saying, Miriam?"

Miriam's expression became one of concern, but conflict was also clear on her face. "I . . . I know that you want to go home, but I can't help you do that. I'm sorry. I really am."

"I'm not asking you to get me on the next flight back to New York. All I want you to do is phone my obstetrician and ask her the best way that I can keep my baby safe. I'll give you her number." She had other numbers in mind; friends, former work colleagues, anyone who could realize the significance of the message and pass it on to the authorities . . .

But it was not to be. "I'm sorry," Miriam repeated unhappily. "But I'm not allowed to make any phone calls without the Prophet's permission. I really, really want to do everything I can to help your baby," she added, eyes wide in reassurance. "But . . . I just can't do that. I'm sorry."

"Then you're not really any help at all, are you?" Nina snapped. But despite the situation, she couldn't feel any anger toward the shy, sincere young woman. In a lot of ways Miriam couldn't have been any more different from Macy, but she shared the same openness of personality, her heart right there on her sleeve. "Hey, it's okay, I didn't mean it," she said, seeing the stricken look on her companion's face. "You've done fine, you really have. I just wish you could do more."

"So do I," Miriam replied.

They arrived at the church. Norvin was waiting at the door. "What, I don't get a personal greeting this time?" Nina said in mock complaint.

"The Prophet's been busy. He's waiting for you" was the big man's reply.

Nina shrugged and followed him inside. "See you later," she said to Miriam, receiving a smile in return.

Cross really had been busy, she saw as she entered the control room. The two touch screens on his chair apparently weren't powerful enough for whatever he had planned, as a pair of laptops were set up on the table before him, a large printout of the catacomb map mounted on a stand nearby. The entrance to the system had been circled in red. Beside it was a smaller map of the Villa Torlonia's grounds. "Wow," she said. "Looks like you're set up for a really intense session of Dungeons and Dragons."

He gestured impatiently for her to sit as he adjusted a headset. "Comms check," he said into the mike. "Come in, Simeon."

Nina heard Simeon reply through his earphones but

couldn't make out the words. "Do I get to listen, or are you going to have subtitles?"

"Norvin, get her some headphones," Cross said with annoyance. The other man gave her a wireless headset. "Your mike is switched off, Dr. Wilde. I don't need you distracting my people with chatter and"—a sidelong glare—"snide comments."

"As *if* I would!" she replied with paint-stripping sarcasm.

"You're trying my patience" was his warning response before he turned his attention to the laptops. He typed commands, reading the results with satisfaction, then said: "All team members. Camera check."

The video wall lit up, individual screens showing different images as they had when Nina first saw it. But instead of CCTV footage of herself, this time unfamiliar faces appeared in the sickly green glow of night vision. All had small cameras mounted on their headsets, the images twitching with every slight movement.

Wait; not everyone was unfamiliar. She saw Anna on one monitor, Simeon on another, facing each other. Surnames were superimposed over the corner of each screen; theirs both read FISHER. The two Witnesses were indeed married.

Cross ran through a list, each of the ten team members responding in turn. "Okay, we're ready," he said at last. "Are you clear to move in?"

Anna stood, revealing that the group was in the rear of a truck as she clambered through to the cab. A narrow street was visible through the windshield, cars parked on both sides. A taxi went past, but there were no pedestrians in sight. "Nobody around. I think we're set."

"Go when clear," Cross ordered.

The screens erupted into bewildering movement, the effect almost nauseating. Nina forced herself to focus on the view from a single camera, the name at its corner TRANT. The group moved quickly out of the van's rear doors and ran to a nearby wall. It was higher than head height, but still proved little obstacle as they scrambled over it.

Beyond lay the expansive grounds of the Villa Torlonia. Nina knew from her research that the villa itself had once been Mussolini's residence, commandeered by the dictator from its owners for the far-from-princely rent of one lira a year. However, the imposing building was some distance from the team's destination: the Jewish catacombs.

The intruders dropped flat to the ground, checking their surroundings for guards. "All clear," Nina heard Simeon say. "Okay, we're heading for the entrance. Stay in the trees."

She glanced at the map. "Where did they come in?"

"The south wall, off the Via Siracusa. Here." Cross indicated a point.

"That's about as far as they could get from the catacombs."

"It also has the lowest pedestrian traffic and surveillance coverage. I know what I'm doing." He watched as his people scurried through the grounds. Lights flared in the distance, illuminating the estate's various palatial buildings. Smaller ones moved between them: the torches of security guards making their rounds.

Nina found herself torn between hoping the raiders would get caught and an almost perverse involvement in the game of hide-and-seek. Simeon and Anna led the way, the others stringing out behind them as they wove between the trees, occasionally ducking and freezing as the guards patrolled. But none of the wandering figures came close, sticking to the well-lit paths. Ever since its most famous former resident had been strung up outside a gas station, the Villa Torlonia had no longer needed high security.

"He's gone," said Simeon as another guard disappeared behind a building. "Move."

Nina's seasickness returned as the cameras jolted. She fixed her gaze back on Trant's screen, seeing Anna and Simeon ahead of him. The couple came to a stop in a small stand of trees. "I can see the entrance," Simeon reported.

"Got it," replied Cross. Two sets of fences surrounded a depression in the ground, a simple inner guardrail encircled by a taller chain-link barrier. "Can you climb it?"

"Not easily, but I can see a gate." Simeon's hand blocked the view from his camera as he peered through a set of compact binoculars. "It's padlocked."

"Go through it. Watch for security, though."

"Got it." Whispered orders, then the team ran to the outer fence. Someone produced a set of bolt cutters and snipped the padlock's shackle. Everyone hurried through the gate, Anna closing it again behind them.

A gap in the second fence led to steps descending to the bottom of the excavation. A wrought-iron gate blocked an opening in a stone wall, but its padlock fared no better than the one above. Simeon shone a flashlight inside. A gloomy tunnel led into darkness.

"Masks on," Cross ordered. The team members donned half-face respirators. "Move in. Start your search patterns."

Nina looked at the catacomb map. The ancient network of tombs was spread out over seven levels, its branching paths forming a genuine labyrinth. "How long are you going to have them searching down there?"

"As long as it takes," Cross replied.

The Fishers led the way, Trant and another man peeling off down a side passage behind them. The entire team quickly spread out into the maze, casting their flashlights over the loculi carved into the walls. The beams found dirt and debris, along with bone fragments. "You're looking for symbols of menorahs," Cross told them. "They might be on the walls or the ceiling—maybe even the floor. If you see one, check the area around it with your metal detector." He watched the screens as the group moved deeper. "Whelan, slow down. You need to check the ceiling too."

"Sorry, Prophet," said one of the men. He shone his light back the way he had come. "It's clear," he said with relief.

"Good. We *have* to find the angel. We can't leave without it."

"If it's not there, what will you do?" Nina asked.

Cross regarded her coldly. "It's down there." He tapped his chest, his heart. "I *know*."

"So long as you remember what I told you," she muttered—just as she caught something on one of the screens. "Wait, there!"

"I see it," said Cross. "Simeon, to your left."

Simeon's camera fixed upon a painted wall. It was decorated mostly with repeating patterns of interconnected lines and circles, but within the circles themselves were more detailed friezes. Nina saw a flower, a tree, a large tent in a desert . . .

And a menorah.

She glanced at Cross, to see him regarding the image of the ceremonial candlestick with almost predatory eyes. "Check it, now!" he snapped.

Simeon took something from his belt. He brought it up to the wall, revealing it as a metal detector, but a much more compact and sophisticated type than those used by beachcombers. He switched it on, then swept it over the picture of the menorah. Nina heard a faint warbling through her headphones, but nothing that suggested there was anything hidden behind the cracked plaster façade. He widened his search pattern, running the detector outward in an expanding spiral, but found nothing. "All right, it's not there," said Cross, disappointed. "Keep looking."

"There's another one here," said a man. Nina spotted a second menorah in the view of someone called Overton. This was more ornate than the first, but it soon turned out that it too concealed nothing metallic behind it.

She leaned back. "This could take a while. Glad I ate first."

Cross's impatience was plain, but he said nothing, alternately watching the video wall and checking the laptops. Nina realized that one of them was showing a tracker displaying his team's progress through the catacomb network. They were using extremely high-tech equipment; beyond the occasional video glitch, there hadn't been any communications dropouts, even underground. Whatever they were using, it was better than that available to civilians. Military gear? Or, considering Cross's background, intelligence-grade?

The search continued. Lights flicked over more burial chambers; the sight of a skull amid the dirt gave Nina a brief chill. The tunnels became narrower the deeper the team progressed. Ancient artwork still adorned the walls in places. She glimpsed images of animals, fish, people standing in temples—even something that she took to be the Ark of the Covenant.

And more menorahs. Each was checked, but the only metal found was worthless detritus. Nina took another look at the tracker. The paths that Cross's team had taken were marked in red—but there were still many more passages to be explored. "I told you this could take a while."

"We've got the whole night," Cross replied.

"And what happens when morning comes? Or if a security guard sees that the padlock's been cut and calls the cops?"

He frowned, then spoke into his headset. "Everyone listen." The bobbing cameras all steadied as their wearers stopped. "We need to pick up the pace. Set your detectors to maximum gain, and sweep the tunnels as you move—if you get a reading, see if there's a menorah painted there. We've got to move faster."

"Understood," Simeon replied. The other team members all responded in kind.

"You'll get a hell of a lot of false alarms," Nina pointed out.

"Better that than missing the real thing." The metal detectors were adjusted, then everyone set off again, moving at a quicker pace.

Nina soon heard an electronic squeal. Someone called Ellison swept his flashlight around the tunnel before zeroing in on the source of the signal. It turned out to be nothing more than a rusted nail.

"Warned you," she reminded Cross as she took off her headphones. "You might wanna send out for snacks."

It took all his restraint not to react to her barb. "Keep searching," he said instead, frustration evident.

Time trudged by. Hardly a couple of minutes passed without one of the searchers picking up a trace of metal, but each time it turned out to be junk. Nina walked around the room, under Norvin's watchful eye, to relieve the stiffness in her legs, while Cross remained fixated on the screens. She glanced into the church to see that day had turned to night outside. Returning to her seat, she saw on the laptop that barely a quarter of the tunnel network had been searched. The Fishers and their companions had been scouring the catacombs for over two hours and still come up with nothing.

"Do you actually need me here for this?" she said acerbically as she sat. "I'm four months pregnant, remember. I need sleep, I need food—and I need to pee. Seriously, you have no idea how often I need to pee."

Cross said something under his breath. Nina didn't catch it, but was fairly sure the second word was "woman," and doubted the one preceding it was complimentary. "Jerkoff," she muttered. She was about to get up and leave whether he granted permission or not when he sat bolt-upright, staring intently at one particular monitor. "There! Anna, get closer," he barked.

Anna's screen showed a painted menorah pinned in her flashlight beam—and from her discarded headphones, Nina heard an insistent whine. She donned them again. "Strong reading . . . very strong," Anna announced.

"Dr. Wilde, look at this," Cross said with urgency, and anticipation. "Do you see it?" He tapped his touch pad, and Anna's viewpoint expanded to fill the entire video wall.

Her metal detector rose into the frame. The whine became a screech each time it passed in front of the menorah. "There's definitely something behind it," said Nina.

"It's the angel." Cross spoke with total conviction. "Anna! Show me that marking above it."

Anna moved closer, the painting swelling to fill the screens. "Can you see it?" she asked.

"Yes. Can you, Dr. Wilde?"

"Yeah, I can . . . ," Nina replied quietly, almost unwilling to accept the evidence of her own eyes. Above the menorah were symbols—ones she had seen before.

The Akkadian and Hebrew that had also been present above the menorah in the sunken temple in Iraq.

She faced Cross. "Is it the same?"

"Yes. It is."

Nina was so astonished by the possibility that there could actually be some truth behind what she had dismissed as the insane theories of a religious crank that she didn't fully register the orders Cross was giving—until the point of a pickax slammed into the wall beside the painted menorah. A sharp crack of stone in her earphones made her flinch. "No! What are you *doing*?"

"I have to see," Cross replied. "We've got to get it out of there."

"But you're destroying the site!"

"I don't care." He watched as the attack on the wall continued. "The only thing that matters—There!" he cried. "There it is!"

Simeon levered away a crumbling slab to reveal an opening concealed behind the surface. Metal glinted within. "Careful, careful!" said Cross as the niche was fully exposed. "Let me see it!"

Anna brought her light nearer. The beam shone over a statue: a humanoid figure that Nina estimated to be a foot tall. Sheets of thin dimpled metal were wrapped around its body. But it was the head that caught her attention—not human, but animal, an ox.

"The second beast . . . ," Cross announced in awe. "The four beasts, the 'living creatures' from God's temple—they're the four angels bound at the Euphrates. I knew it—I was right. I found the code hidden in Revelation, and it was *true*!"

The statue was carefully lifted from its resting place. From Simeon's muted grunt of effort, it was heavier than it looked. He blew off dust, then turned it in Anna's light. Nina got a clearer view of the effigy. She was forced to admit that it did indeed resemble the description given in Revelation. But that wasn't enough to make her imagine—to *believe,* as Cross did—that they were one and the same. "So you've got it," she said. "Now what?"

"Now we get it back here. Trant," he said, "Simeon and Anna have found the angel. You've got the case—get to their location. Everyone else, return to the entrance. Move out as soon as the angel's secured."

Trant began to traverse the labyrinth to meet the Fishers. In the meantime, Nina watched as Cross gave instructions to Simeon so he could view the angel by proxy. The statue was turned to show every aspect to the camera. Three sets of wings, as he had said, the dimpling in the metal giving it the impression of eyes all around . . .

Something caught *her* eye. Not on the angel, but in the empty recess behind it. "Whoa, whoa!" she said. "There's something in the niche—written on the wall."

Cross saw it. "Anna! Show me the back of the opening!"

The green haze of the night-vision camera rendered the scene flat and lacking in contrast, but it was still clear enough for Nina to make out the text carved into the stone. "It's ancient Hebrew," she told Cross, "but I don't know the language well enough to translate it."

"You don't need to," he replied, working the touch screens. The footage on the video wall froze. A square box was superimposed over the image, which he manipulated to close in around the lettering. "This is a translation program."

"Yeah, I've used them before," she said, watching as the application identified the Hebrew letters, then ran the words they formed through a database to come up with an English equivalent. It did not take long, though as she'd learned to expect from such software, the end result was awkwardly phrased. Even so, it gave her a faint chill. "Okay, that's a little bit ominous . . ."

For the first time, Cross's expression revealed a degree

of trepidation. "'It is three times spoken,'" he read. "'The dragon number is of man. Have this wisdom to enter the temple of God.' The dragon . . ."

"The dragon?" Nina echoed, remembering her recent research. "You mean the Beast—Satan?" Several sections of Revelation were dedicated to the final battles between the forces of God and His enemies, led by the fallen angel.

Cross nodded, quoting another Bible verse. "'The dragon, that old serpent, which is the Devil, and Satan . . .'" He rounded on her with an air of triumph. "This is more proof that I'm right. Don't you see? The Elders wrote that inscription when they hid the angel in the catacombs—and John read it in the Library of Pergamon. It's all in the Book of Revelation!"

She was still far from convinced, but could tell that nothing she said would dissuade him. Instead she mulled over what she had seen as Cross put his team's cameras back on the monitors. The others gathered at the entrance and removed their breath masks as Trant reached the Fishers. He was carrying a rectangular case, opening it to reveal a lining of impact-cushioning foam rubber. Simeon laid the angel carefully inside and shut the lid.

"Okay," Cross said as Trant picked up the container. "Get back to the entrance."

More minutes passed as the trio hurried through the passages. "The Witnesses will bring the angel back to the Mission," Cross told Nina. "They have a private jet standing by."

"Expensive," Nina noted.

"Any price is worth paying for God's work."

"And how are you going to get a relic like that through customs?"

"The same way we got you through. I told you, I have friends." He returned his attention to the monitors as the trio reached the entrance. "Anna, lead the way out. Simeon, guard Trant and the angel."

Anna squeezed past the waiting men and opened the gate, making her way up to the top of the excavated pit. She surveyed her surroundings. "Nobody in sight. Move out, back the way we came." She went to the chain-link fence and swung the gate open. The first group of men ran past her and headed into the trees.

Trant left the tunnel, Simeon behind him. They reached the top of the steps—

"Back, get back!" Anna suddenly whispered. Her monitor became a blur of movement as she scrambled behind a tree outside the fence. "Guards coming, northeast!"

"The gate—close the gate!" Cross shouted, but it was too late for her to turn back without being spotted. Trant and Simeon retreated into the pit.

Anna leaned around the tree. Two uniformed security guards were walking down a path toward the fenced-off area. Their ambling pace showed that they hadn't yet seen anything amiss, but if they caught sight of the gate . . .

Nina felt a rising tension. Unlike the moments when the raiders had been sneaking through the Villa Torlonia's grounds, this time her concern was entirely for the unsuspecting men as they drew closer. "Get out of there," she whispered. "Just turn around, don't look at the padlock . . ."

Too late. One guard stopped, his body language expressing momentary confusion before he spoke to his companion. Then the image went dark as Anna ducked behind the tree; by the time she crept around the other side, the pair had reached the gate. One saw the severed padlock, then shone a flashlight over the surrounding area.

Movement on Simeon's monitor. The breath caught in Nina's throat as she saw him draw a silenced automatic and thumb off the safety. "No, don't," she said to Cross, pleading. "Don't let him kill them!"

"Their fate is in God's hands," he replied.

"No it isn't—it's in yours! Tell Simeon to—"

She broke off as Anna's camera showed the two guards going through the gate. "They're armed," Cross warned as one of the uniformed men drew a pistol. "Anna!"

She was already moving, making her way across the grass toward the gate. Simeon raised his gun. The camera on his headset made the view suddenly resemble a videogame, turning into a first-person shooter as Nina found herself looking down the sights.

But it was no game. Real people were the targets. "No, don't!" she cried, but they couldn't hear her.

The guard appeared on Simeon's monitor, flashlight flaring. He directed it down into the pit—and shouted in alarm as he saw the figures skulking in the darkness. He raised his gun—

Simeon fired first. A puff of blood exploded from the guard's chest, red turned greenish gray by the night vision. He spun and collapsed to the ground. Simultaneously Anna rushed up behind the other man, snapping a hidden blade out from her sleeve and stabbing it deep into the side of his throat. Another gush of discolored liquid fountained from the gaping wound as he fell.

"Jesus Christ!" Nina wailed, jumping from her seat. She had seen people die before—far, far too many times—but watching the deaths play out through the killers' eyes was appalling in a whole new way. "You fucking psychopaths!"

Cross's jaw clenched in anger. "Sit down! Sit down and shut up!"

"No! You're—"

Norvin shoved her forcefully down onto the chair. She gasped at a sharp pain through her lower body. Fear filled her—*the baby!*—but the stabbing sensation quickly subsided.

Breathing shakily, she looked back at Cross. "You murdering bastard. You say you're a man of God, but you're just a killer."

"I'm doing the Lord's work," he replied. " 'Thrust in thy sickle and reap, for the time is come for thee to reap, for the harvest of the earth is ripe.' Judgment is coming, and all worshippers of the Beast will be cast into the lake of fire."

"You don't know that they worship any beast."

"They're Italian. They're almost certainly followers of the false prophet."

It took her a second to get his meaning. "The pope? You mean because they're Catholics, they deserve to die?"

"'They were judged each man according to their works.' We all will be, when the last day comes—even me. But God has chosen me to do His will, so my name is written in the Book of Life, along with all my followers."

"You're insane" was all she could say.

On the screens, Anna, Simeon, and Trant hurried through the darkened grounds after the rest of the team. "Simeon, you and Anna get the angel to the jet," Cross ordered. "I want it here at the Mission as soon as possible. Paxton will be waiting with the chopper as soon as you arrive. The rest of you, hole up and wait for further instructions. As soon as the next angel is located, I want you ready to move out." He faced Nina. "You still have work to do, Dr. Wilde. The Place in the Wilderness and the Throne of Satan . . ." He tapped at one of the pads, the monitors flicking to show Eddie still trapped in the chair. "Your husband's life depends on your finding them."

"I'll find them," Nina growled, her glare at the cult leader filled with loathing. "Not for you. For him. But I'll find them."

New York City

A voice brought Eddie out of an exhausted but restless slumber. ". . . went over there earlier. Normally they have twenty or thirty people working, but there'll hardly be anyone there on those days."

The speaker's identity came to him: Irton, his torturer, talking on a phone. A spike of fear-fueled adrenaline instantly snapped him to full wakefulness. He was still tied to the chair, arms pinned painfully behind his back. His body cried out for him to move to ease the discomfort, but he resisted. The longer his captors thought he was still unconscious, the more he might overhear.

The respect, even deference, in Irton's voice told Eddie he was talking to his boss. "No, I wouldn't think so," the American went on. "Is that still the plan? Okay, yes. No, the security's only light."

A crunch of footsteps on the dirty floor nearby. "Hey," said another man. Eddie now knew that his name was Berman; the blond who had been waiting for him near the apartment. "I think he's awake." A hand slapped him hard across the cheek. "Open your eyes," said Berman. "I know you're faking it."

"Aw, but I was having such a shitty dream," Eddie

rasped, seeing the third man, Raddick, behind Berman. "And *you* were there, and *you* were there . . ."

"Cute," said Raddick with a mocking smirk. "Mr. Irton, sir! He's awake."

Eddie turned his head to see Irton standing by one of the pieces of abandoned machinery. "Chase just woke up," he said into his phone before moving away and resuming his discussion out of earshot. Night had arrived, only darkness visible through the skylights. Illumination inside the warehouse was limited to a lamplit circle around the torture chair.

"Thought you could play dead and listen in, huh?" said Berman. "What, you think we're idiots?"

"That's one thing on a bloody long list, yeah," Eddie replied. He had already braced himself for another blow, and sure enough it arrived a moment later. Wincing from the sting, he looked up at Berman. "An' I just added 'Slaps like a little girl' to it."

That earned him a full-blown punch to the face. "How was that?"

"*Fucker!*" He jerked against his bonds, making the chair rattle.

"Enough!" called the irritated Irton.

"Oh, sorry, am I interrupting your call?" shouted the Englishman. "I'll leave if you want!"

Irton scowled, then stalked through an exterior door, closing it behind him. Eddie looked back at the other two men. "Now he's gone, you can play with your dollies in peace."

Berman raised a fist, but Raddick patted his comrade's shoulder. "Hey, hey, he's just trying to yank your chain."

"Yeah, I guess." Berman moved reluctantly away, but gave Eddie a nasty look as he retreated. "You and me, we're not finished."

"Can't wait," Eddie replied, trying not to let his concern show. He had managed to withstand everything Irton and the others had inflicted upon him so far, but it had taken all his reserves of strength and willpower, and after more than a full day in painful captivity, he honestly didn't know how much more he could take. So far he hadn't been subjected to anything that would cause permanent injury, but if his kidnappers took things up a level to force Nina to cooperate . . .

That was possibly the only thing keeping him alive. They needed him to make Nina do something for them. Without him, they would lose their hold on her. Was there any way he could turn that to his advantage?

Before he could think any more about it, Raddick checked his watch. "I'm gonna get something to eat. You want anything?"

"Chicken wings and fries," Berman answered.

"I'll have a burger if you're going," Eddie piped up.

Raddick ignored him and headed for the exterior door. He had a brief exchange with the man outside, then a car started up and drove away.

Irton still seemed to be on the phone. If he kept talking . . .

"Chicken, eh?" Eddie said to Berman. "Isn't that cannibalism? You're kind of a chickenshit yourself."

The blond rounded on him. "What did you say?"

"You heard me. Fucking coward. You'll slap someone who's tied to a chair, but when it comes to an actual fight, you'd shit yourself so hard your rib cage'd implode."

Berman stepped up to him angrily. "Screw you, limey. I was in the United States Army. I'm no coward, I've seen action."

Eddie snorted sarcastically. "Yeah, right. I bet it's a nonstop adrenaline rush in the fucking typing pool." He put on a bad, nasal American accent. "If we don't get that toner cartridge changed in the next five minutes, there'll be hell to pay!"

"Shut up."

"I got a paper cut, give me a Purple Heart!"

"Shut up!" Berman's hand cracked across his face.

"That the best you've got?" said Eddie, giving him a sneering grin. "My niece could hit me harder than that. When she was six."

The hand clenched into a fist. "You wanna see the best

I've got?" growled the American, slamming it against Eddie's jaw.

The Englishman's head snapped back, blood squirting from a split lip—then he convulsed, mouth gaping as choking gurgles came from it. Berman stared dismissively down at him, only for his expression to change to concern as he realized his captive couldn't breathe.

"Oh, shit. Dammit, shit, *shit*!" he hissed, panic rising at the thought that he might have killed a vital prisoner. He glanced at the door but didn't call to Irton, instead pulling the struggling man upright in a desperate effort to clear his airway.

It had no effect. Eyes wide, Eddie shuddered, tongue squirming . . . then fell limp in his seat, head lolling to one side.

"Shit!" Berman hesitated, then checked Eddie's neck for a pulse. He moved his fingertips across the skin, not sure of the result. Another look toward the door in fear that Irton might choose this moment to return, then he leaned closer to listen for the other man's breath—

Eddie lunged at him and sank his teeth into his throat.

Berman tried to scream, but the Englishman had clamped his jaw around his Adam's apple with the frenzied determination of a terrier, crushing his windpipe shut. He lashed and clawed at his attacker's face, but the teeth only dug in harder—

With a final growl of fury, Eddie forced his jaw shut. A horrible crunch came from Berman's neck, and he lurched backward, a ragged, gore-spouting hole where his larynx had been. Eddie spat out a revolting hunk of torn tissue as Berman fell to the filthy floor, blood gushing down his chest.

The wounded man opened his mouth to cry out, but the only sound that emerged was a wet wheeze. He rolled onto his front, dragging himself toward Irton's torture equipment.

Eddie realized his intention. Berman wasn't trying to find a weapon, but something he could use to make a loud noise and alert his boss.

He threw himself from side to side, the chair's frame

creaking in protest. His previous attempts to break loose had been halted by his captors, but with nobody to stop him it only took seconds before metal cracked. The frame shifted beneath him, but the chair was still chained to the floor.

Eddie rocked forward to put his weight onto his feet. He strained with all his might, trying to stand. The underside of the chair's back dug into his bound arms. He felt something give, a bolt or screw breaking loose . . .

Berman reached one of the cases—

The seatback ripped away.

Eddie sprang upright. But his ankles were still tied to the chair's legs. All he could do was fall bodily onto the other man.

The landing knocked the breath from him—but Berman came off worse, his face pounded against the dirty concrete. Eddie twisted, kicking at the broken chair as it strained against the chain. One of the ties slipped from the bottom of the tubular leg. Partially freed, the Englishman rolled and scrambled to his feet.

Berman raised his head, spitting blood. His fingers clawed at the case of torture gear—

Eddie's foot slammed against the side of his skull. Berman fell limp as a last bubbling exhalation gurgled from the gruesome rent in his throat.

Regaining his balance, Eddie slid the other restraint loose and booted the chair away. His hands remained cuffed behind his back. He had to get free, fast; if Irton had heard the scuffle . . .

He still had blood in his mouth. Hoping it was all Berman's, he brought his arms to his right side as he leaned his head back over that shoulder and spat the liquid over the cuffs. Then he pulled them as far apart as he could and bent down, straining to force them over his hips.

The metal bracelets bit savagely into his wrists. But the pain was nothing compared with what Irton had already put him through. His blood-slicked forearms slithered over his jeans as he writhed to work them lower, every millimeter of progress a battle. The handcuff chain reached his hip bone, but his arms were stretched to their limit.

He pushed harder. A burst of pain—then suddenly the chain jerked past the obstruction. He breathed hard, but he knew the worst was over. His military training had taught him how to escape from numerous forms of restraint, although he found himself wishing for the flexibility of his younger self.

He dropped to a crouch, then rolled onto his back, drawing up one leg to bring his foot over the chain. The metal links rasped over the ridged sole of his boot, catching for a moment . . . then popping free. Eddie gasped in relief. Getting his other foot out was considerably easier. He jumped upright. His wrists were still cuffed, but he was almost infinitely more capable—and dangerous—now that they were no longer pinned behind his back.

Berman had stopped breathing. Eddie gave him a cursory glance that contained zero sympathy, then checked the case. The unnerving collection of CIA-approved torture implements shone in the cold lamplight. None were of any use to him right now.

But one of the rusty machines had what he needed.

He hurried to it and pulled loose a handle; a hefty corrosion-scabbed metal bar about two feet long. Wielding it like a baseball bat, he ran to the entrance and took up position to one side. A faint electrical hum reached him from outside, but he couldn't hear any voices. Had Irton finished his call?

Footsteps, frighteningly close, told him that he had.

The door opened. Irton stepped through, phone still in his hand. Shock crossed his face as he saw that the room was not as he had left it—

Eddie swung the metal bar.

Irton's reactions were good, his right arm snapping up to ward off the blow—but not good enough. The crack of the phone's screen shattering and the dull thud of the club striking first his hand and then his abdomen were almost simultaneous. He collapsed to his knees, winded.

"Ay up!" Eddie snarled as he slammed the bar down

on the other man's shoulders, knocking him flat. "Remember me, you bastard?" He kicked the fallen American hard in the side, then crouched to search his pockets.

Wallet, loose change, key ring. Eddie examined the keys. The smallest was for the handcuffs. He unlocked the bracelets and with huge relief tossed them aside, kneading the deep red grooves in his skin.

He checked the wallet. It contained a Nevada driver's license in the name of Walter Jefferson Irton, a credit card in the same name, about two hundred dollars in banknotes, and a small wad of receipts. "So you're a torturer who claims expenses?" he asked. Irton made no reply.

A flick through the tabs showed that most of them were for convenience stores and fast-food joints in Brooklyn. There was also a parking receipt for the Brooklyn Navy Yard. Was that where he was, across the East River from Manhattan? Eddie glanced at the door, considering making a run for it before Raddick returned, but changed his mind. He might be free, but whoever these people were, they still had Nina.

He hauled Irton bodily back into the illuminated circle and slammed him against the dirty wooden bench, knocking the laptop to the floor and toppling the camera's tripod. "Oi! Wake up!" Irton opened his pain-filled eyes. "Where's Nina, and what do you lot want with her?"

His only response was a malevolent glare. "Okay, so you're not going to tell me anything," said the Yorkshireman. "Good job there's all this stuff I can use to make you talk." He gestured at the equipment cases.

The American's face betrayed a moment of fear, but it was immediately replaced by defiance. "You won't break me," he growled. "I can withstand pain for days if I have to. I was trained by the best."

"Funny, so was I, and I don't remember seeing you at Hereford." He made as if to turn away—then smashed a fist into Irton's face before ramming his head down onto the table. "How's the withstanding going?"

Irton spat out blood and a broken tooth. "Fuck you!"

"Oh, you're using rude words now? Guess that must have hurt." He stood behind the other man. "Where's Nina?"

"Go to hell!"

Eddie kicked him hard behind one knee. Irton cried out as his leg buckled, hands splayed across the wooden surface to hold himself up. "See, the thing is," the Englishman said, "you've been trained in all this enhanced interrogation bollocks—waterboarding, electrics, stress positions, psych stuff. Break the mind, not the body, that's the idea, right? Now, me, I'm not that subtle." He again regarded the equipment in the cases, then spotted something better among the debris on the floor and picked it up. "This is more my style. Last chance: Where's my wife?"

Breath hissing through his clenched and bloodied teeth, Irton glared at him over one shoulder. "Go fuck yourself, Chase. You think you can break me? Not a—"

A grimy hammer smashed down claw-first on his left hand with such force that it dug into the wood under his palm. Irton screamed and flailed, but was pinned in place. "I can break *that*," Eddie said coldly. "Tell me where Nina is, *now*."

He twisted the hammer. Irton made a keening sound, face clenched in pain, but said nothing. Eddie frowned—then grabbed Irton's left wrist before yanking the tool free and flipping it around. The torturer tried to pull away, but the Englishman held him in place and pounded the hammer down onto each of his knuckles. Bone cracked. Irton wailed in agony.

"Where is she?" Eddie yelled, letting go. The American crumpled to the floor, clutching his mangled hand. "Talk to me!" He stood over Irton, waving the bloodied hammer in his face. "Tell me why you've kidnapped Nina, or I'll take your other fucking hand off!"

"All right! All right!" Irton gasped. "Stop, stop, oh God! I'll tell you!"

Eddie gave him two seconds to compose himself. "Come on, then."

"God!" He strained to force out the words. "Our

leader, the Prophet—he needs her to find the angels from the Book of Revelation."

"What do you mean, angels? The guys with wings and trumpets?"

"No, they're . . . they're statues, hidden away. The Prophet found one of them, and he's trying to find the other three. The clues are in the Book of Revelation. He knows what to look for, but he needs an archaeologist to tell him *where* to look."

Eddie frowned. "Why Nina? He could have just paid someone to do that. Why kidnap her?"

"I don't know. I don't!" Irton protested as the Englishman raised the hammer. "The Prophet chose your wife for a reason, but he didn't share it with us."

"He'll share it with *me* if I get my fucking hands on him. Where is he?"

"At the Mission."

"And where's that?"

Irton took another breath, eyes turning defiant once more. He was willing to endure more pain rather than give up the location. Eddie hefted the hammer again—

A bang from the entrance. Eddie spun. Raddick was back, arms laden with bags of take-out food. "Okay, I got your—"

He froze as he took in the scene. "Shit!" he gasped, throwing down the food and fumbling inside his coat for a gun—

Eddie hurled the hammer.

Raddick had just gotten the gun clear of its holster when the steel claws smacked into his forehead with a sickening crack. He fell backward, the tool embedded in his skull.

Eddie whirled back toward Irton—as the American leapt up and shoulder-barged him, sending him stumbling into one of the lamps and falling painfully onto his side. He scrambled upright, readying himself for an attack, but instead saw Irton run into the darkness of the empty building.

"Shit!" He hurried after him. The American was limping from the kick to his knee, but after more than a day tied to a chair, Eddie was little faster, muscles stiff and aching.

Yet he had to catch him. With both Berman and Raddick dead, Irton was his only link to Nina.

He followed the noise of the American's footsteps. Dim light appeared ahead through grimy windows high on the walls. A new sound reached him, a frantic clatter. Irton was climbing a metal staircase. Eddie made out the structure rising diagonally across the back wall and hurried to it, vaulting up the steps two at a time.

His quarry reached the top. A door was kicked open. Eddie saw Irton briefly outlined by the stark pinkish-orange glow of industrial sodium lights before he ducked out of sight.

He got to the door a few seconds later. Would Irton attack him as he came through? A split-second judgment: No, he was fleeing—flight, not fight. He booted the door and rushed outside.

Cold wind hit him as he emerged on a rooftop. Grim industrial blocks rose ahead. Where was Irton?

Off to the left, hobbling for the roof's nearest edge. Eddie raced after him. There was an electrical substation below, the dull hum of transformers growing louder. He had to be heading for a fire escape . . .

Shock as Eddie realized that he wasn't. There was nothing but a sheer fifty-foot drop. Irton wasn't just willing to suffer to protect his boss; he would make the ultimate sacrifice.

"No you bloody don't!" gasped Eddie, fighting through his own pain to run faster. Irton was twenty feet from the edge, ten . . .

He reached it just as Eddie dived at him.

The Englishman landed hard at the very lip of the roof, grabbing at Irton, but only managing to catch his left arm as he fell toward the substation. The torturer's sleeve slithered through his fingers—

One hand locked around Irton's wrist.

The American shrieked as smashed bones ground together, crushing nerves. Eddie tried to get a hold with his other hand, but Irton's weight was dragging him over the edge. He had no choice but to use it instead to brace himself . . . and the thrashing man started to slip through his grip.

"*Where is she?*" he yelled. Irton looked back at him, fear in his eyes behind the pain. Another nauseating crunch, and Eddie felt his opponent's mutilated hand slipping farther through his own. He squeezed harder, but knew it was a losing battle. "Tell me where Nina is, and I'll help you—"

Snap!

Bone broke, skin tearing with a hot gush of blood— and Eddie found himself holding nothing but a severed finger.

Irton plunged, screaming, to be impaled on the prongs of a transformer below. Sparks exploded from it, searing electrical discharges lancing out as the high-voltage current set his body aflame. Eddie jerked back as something overloaded and blew apart with a detonation that shook the building. The substation's lights flickered, then died, along with those of all the other nearby buildings.

"He went out with a bang," Eddie muttered, furious as much with himself for not maintaining his hold as with Irton for taking Nina's whereabouts to the grave. Still clutching the finger, he stood and turned back toward the door . . . and for the first time saw where he was.

The skyscrapers of Manhattan glittered like cubic galaxies across the dark waters of the East River. His guess that he was in Brooklyn had been right. A bridge loomed to his left behind buildings; he had lived in New York City long enough to recognize it immediately as the Manhattan Bridge. That put him somewhere in Brooklyn's Vinegar Hill district.

He looked to the right along the river. The lights of the Williamsburg Bridge spanned the waters about a mile away. A moment of surprise at an unexpected yet impressive sight closer by: the massive airship that he had seen from Harvey Zampelli's helicopter was coming in to land for the night. Its temporary home was the nearby Brooklyn Navy Yard, the decommissioned military facility that was now an industrial park and movie studio. Advertising slogans flashed across its bulbous side, their very mundanity giving him a bizarre sense of relief. Whatever was going on, he had survived it, and returned to the real world.

The feeling lasted barely a moment. He was free, but the mysterious Prophet still had Nina—and he had absolutely no idea where. *Somewhere in the tropics* was all she had been able to tell him. That didn't really narrow it down.

Another retort from the substation. He had to get away from what would very soon become a crime scene; the explosion would bring first the fire department, then the cops. Whatever Irton and the others were doing, they had given the definite impression that it was on the clock. He couldn't afford to waste time being arrested and interrogated by the NYPD.

Fortunately, he had friends in the police.

* * *

"Eddie?"

"Down here," he said, cautiously stepping out from behind a dumpster to greet the woman. "Hi, Amy."

Detective Amy Martin of the New York Police Department brought up her flashlight to regard him with shock. "Jesus, Eddie! What the hell happened to you?"

He had retrieved his leather jacket and other belongings including his phone from the abandoned warehouse, but the garment couldn't disguise that he was covered in blood. "Don't worry, it's not mine. Most of it."

"That's what I'm scared of!" The dark-haired young cop came down the alley for a better look at him. "Are you okay? What's going on?"

"I'm not sure myself. But you know there was an explosion a couple of blocks from here?"

"Yeah, I heard about it over the radio just after you phoned—" She broke off in dismay. "Oh man. Don't tell me that was you."

"Not . . . directly."

" 'Cause they found a body."

"Yeah, and they'll find another two in the factory next to it."

Amy shook her head and sighed. "God. What *is* it with you? What happened?"

"Short version: I was kidnapped, but got away. But Nina was kidnapped too, and they've still got her."

Her eyes went wide. "Kidnapped?"

"Off the street outside our apartment. I was tied up in a warehouse being tortured until about half an hour ago." He pulled up his shirt to reveal lurid bruises. "I need your help, Amy. I've got to find Nina, but I can't do that if the cops take me in for questioning. I need you to cover for me."

"Cover for you! People have *died*, Eddie—it's kinda hard to sweep that under the rug." She eyed him. "Did *you* kill them?"

"Yeah, but in self-defense. And the third one, I was trying to *save* him—he jumped off the roof rather than give up where they'd taken Nina." He saw that she was still struggling to process his first admission. "Come on, Amy! You *know* me. And you know the kind of stuff I keep getting dragged into."

"But you don't even work for the IHA anymore!"

"I bloody know! But whoever these arseholes were, it won't be long before their boss realizes his torture team isn't answering his calls. Soon as he knows I've escaped . . ."

"They might hurt Nina," she finished for him.

"Yeah. She's pregnant, Amy—I'm not going to let them do anything to her or our baby."

Her eyes widened. "She's pregnant?"

"Yeah."

"Congratulations! And thanks for telling me when I saw you last," she added with considerable sarcasm.

"I was busy chasing a Nazi!" he protested. "Anyway, look—I promise you that as soon as Nina's safe, I'll tell the NYPD everything that happened." He glanced down the alley as an emergency vehicle swept past, lights strobing. "But right now, I need you to run interference."

"Interference!" she hooted. "This is going to turn into a murder investigation. If I interfere, I could do more than lose my job—I could go to jail!"

"Amy, please!" He fixed his eyes on hers. "You trust me, don't you?"

"Oh, please, don't pull that card, Eddie," she cried. "You know I do! You saved the whole damn city." It had taken his drastic physical intervention to prevent a nuclear device from being detonated at the end of Wall Street, his arm still scarred as a result. "Everyone in New York owes you, and . . . and I just talked myself into helping you, didn't I?" She tipped her head back and let out a groan to the sky.

He grinned. "Thanks."

"Don't thank me yet. There's only so much I can do, even as a detective—and," she warned, "only so much I'm *willing* to do. I'm not going to lie for you."

"I'm not asking you to." They started back down the alley toward her car. "For now, just get me to the UN— no, wait, take me home first. I want to check the apartment. And see if there's been anything reported about Nina or me being kidnapped. If someone saw me get Tasered and dragged into a van, that should be enough to tell the cops I was the victim. And if there isn't a report on Nina's kidnapping, start one!"

They reached the car. More flashing lights were visible down the street outside the derelict building. "Okay, get in," Amy said unhappily. He climbed inside as she took the wheel. "These kidnappers—do you have any idea who they are?"

"No, but you can check if their prints are on file."

A confused look. "How?"

Eddie held up the severed digit. "I'll give you the finger."

A trip to the Upper East Side confirmed Eddie's fears. The apartment was empty, Nina's laptop still open in her study. She always closed it if leaving the room for more than brief periods. He hurriedly washed and changed his clothes, returning to Amy's car to learn that there had indeed been reports of an incident on the street. "What, nobody recognized me?" he complained. "Bloody snobby neighborhood."

"This helps you, though," Amy pointed out. "One of the witness statements said that someone was Tasered and taken away. That confirms you as the victim." She gave him a rueful look. "I'm still not sure how it'll balance against you killing all three of them, though."

"Worry about that when I have to," Eddie replied. "Okay, we need to get to the UN." As Amy started the car, he took out his phone and dialed a number—one that he had hoped never to need again.

* * * *

By the time they arrived at the United Nations, the man Eddie had called was waiting for him at the security gate, his long overcoat flapping in the cold wind. "Eddie," said Oswald Seretse, the Gambian official pointedly rubbing his hands together for warmth before shaking the Englishman's. "This is quite a surprise."

"Yeah, for me too. Thanks, Amy." He waved her off, then went with Seretse through the checkpoint. "Glad I caught you. I didn't know if you'd still be working this late."

"The world's leaders are meeting at the General Assembly soon," Seretse replied, gesturing at a stack of crowd-control barriers piled ready for deployment nearby. "That means long hours for everybody involved. Especially long-suffering departmental liaisons like myself—all the more so when working two jobs at once."

"You're still the IHA's acting boss?"

"After Bill Schofield was killed, the other candidate for the director's position withdrew. It has gained a reputation as a remarkably dangerous post."

"Tell me about it." Eddie gave him a small smile, then looked up at the glass tower of the Secretariat Building as they approached the entrance. "God, back here again. I can't seem to bloody escape it."

"Yes, for someone who no longer works for the United Nations, you certainly seem to visit us quite frequently." There was amusement in the diplomat's rich Cambridge-educated tones. "So, what can I do for you this time?"

"Nina's been kidnapped."

Seretse halted, the humor instantly evaporating. "I see."

"You don't sound too shocked."

He sighed. "I am long past the point where I can be surprised by anything that involves you or Nina. But why come to me rather than the police?"

Eddie decided to spare him the gruesome details of his recent captivity. "Because whatever the people who've taken Nina want her for, it's something to do with her work at the IHA."

"But Nina left the IHA at the same time as you."

"I don't think they care. I know what they're after, but I've got no idea what it means or why they need Nina to find it. Which is why I came to you."

Seretse nodded. "Come inside."

They entered the Secretariat Building, Seretse vouching for Eddie at another security check, and took an elevator up to the tall diplomat's office. The Englishman gazed out the window overlooking the East River as his host sat at his desk. "I couldn't help but notice," said Seretse, "that you appear to have been in the wars."

Eddie turned toward him, showing off the cuts and bruises on his face. "Nina wasn't the only one who was kidnapped. They took me to force her to find what they're after."

"Which is what?"

"Angels."

The African's eyebrows rose. "Angels?"

"Yeah. I told you, I don't know what that means. They let Nina talk to me, and before they cut her off, she managed to tell me what they were after; turns out these angels are from the Book of Revelations." The eyebrows went higher still. "Some kind of statues. One of the guys who kidnapped me said that the clues to finding them are hidden in the Bible, and his boss needs an archaeologist to help decode them."

"Why Nina? There must be other archaeologists who could do that. Why risk kidnapping her?"

"That's what I want to know." He looked back out the window. In the distance downriver, beyond the Williamsburg Bridge, the giant spotlit eggshell of the now moored airship marked the Navy Yard; he had been held prisoner not far from it. "But she's not even in the country now—she said she was in the tropics. Someplace called the Mission, apparently."

Seretse typed on his laptop, then shook his head. "I just searched for 'tropics' and 'Mission,' but there are almost a million results."

"I'm pretty sure if you Google 'angels' and 'Book of Revelations,' you'll get even more," Eddie said glumly. "We're not going to find these statues that way. That's why I want to get the IHA involved."

"You want to find the *angels*?" said Seretse, surprised. "Not Nina?"

Eddie faced him again. " 'Course I bloody want to find

Nina. But I've got nothing to go on, and as long as they're holding her I've got no leverage either. But if I can get these angels before they do . . ."

"It gives you bargaining power. Nina for the angels."

"Exactly. Whoever's behind this—some nut calling himself the Prophet—seems to want to find them as soon as possible, so there's probably a deadline, something that'll make him more desperate the closer it gets. If I reach 'em first, then he'll have to let Nina go if he wants them."

"If he truly is desperate, that might put Nina in more danger," Seretse warned.

Eddie regarded him grimly. "Yeah, I know. But it's all I've got right now." He sat facing Seretse. "So I need another archaeologist to help me. Someone who's as good as Nina, and who knows about the Bible." A small frown. "Bible stuff isn't even Nina's specialty. I mean, she knows way too much about pretty much bloody everything to do with archaeology, but there must be people who've spent their entire *careers* on it. Why'd they need her?"

"I can't answer that," said Seretse, typing again, "but I can tell you who is currently working for the IHA and their areas of expertise." He scanned the list on his screen. "Dr. Ari Ornstein is a specialist in ancient Hebrew civilization . . ."

"Wrong half of the Bible," Eddie said. "Even I know that Revelations is New Testament, not Old."

"Indeed." He resumed his search. "Colette Seigner's doctoral thesis was about the conversion of the Roman Empire to Christianity. Perhaps she might be able to help?"

"I know Colette, but . . . I dunno. Christianity didn't really take off with the Romans until a few centuries after Jesus died, did it?" A huff of frustration. "I don't know when the Book of Revelations was written, but I don't think it was that late."

"The first century AD, I believe. And no, the Roman Empire did not adopt Christianity as its official religion until AD 380, under the Edict of Thessalonica."

Eddie shot him a wry grin. "Maybe you should help me."

"The by-product of a classical education, nothing more. My specialty has always been international law. Unfortunately, I doubt that will be much help to you." Seretse read on—then leaned forward with sudden intrigue. "Ah . . ."

"You've found someone?"

"Perhaps. She is no longer connected with the IHA—she resigned a few years ago—but among her many areas of expertise is New Testament archaeology, and she even still lives here in New York."

"Sounds good to me," Eddie proclaimed. "Give her a call."

Seretse seemed faintly pained. "There is one small issue."

"What is it?"

"She . . . dislikes you. And she *especially* dislikes Nina."

"Why would anyone from the IHA dislike me? Don't you bloody even . . . ," he added, catching Seretse's expression. "And who hates Nina that much?"

The diplomat turned the laptop to face him, revealing a personnel file, complete with photograph. Eddie recognized the pinched-faced elderly woman immediately. "Oh for fuck's sake. Why'd it have to be *her*?"

* * *

"Ah, Oswald," said Professor Maureen Rothschild, welcoming the United Nations official into her apartment. "A pleasure to see you again. It's been, what, three years?"

"The reception at the Egyptian consulate, I believe," Seretse replied, kissing her cheek.

"Yes, I think it was." She moved to close the door, but her visitor remained in front of it. With a quizzical look, she continued: "So what brings you here this late?"

He hesitated before answering. "It is a . . . delicate matter. We need your help."

"We? Do you mean the United Nations, or the IHA?"

"Actually, this is more a personal request. From myself, as a friend, but also from . . . someone you know." He moved aside—to reveal Eddie as he stepped through the door.

"Ay up, Maureen," said the Englishman, faking a smile. "Remember me?"

The elderly academic had long been a thorn in Nina's side, their mutual dislike dating back even before his wife's discovery of Atlantis. Rothschild had a few years earlier been appointed as director of the IHA—whereupon her first act had been to shut down Nina's work. Her disdain for Eddie was simply through association, although from the way she regarded him, he couldn't help wondering if he had just tracked something unpleasant onto her carpet. "Yes, I remember Mr. Chase," said Rothschild dismissively. "What does he want?"

"Your help," Seretse told her.

"My help?" she scoffed. "Why should I help him? He and his wife were the main reason why I had to resign from the IHA after that fiasco in Egypt. You know, being forced to leave a high-profile organization under a cloud does *not* do wonders for your résumé. If I hadn't already had tenure, I'm sure the university would have loved to shuffle me into early retirement—"

"Nina's been kidnapped," Eddie cut in.

That silenced her, if only for a moment. "That's . . . terrible," she said, with a marked lack of conviction. "I hope she's recovered safe and well."

"So do I. That's why I'm here. The people who've got her are religious nuts who think she can take them to something mentioned in the Book of Revelations. Ozzy"—a glance at Seretse, who held in a weary sigh at the diminutive—"reckons you're the best person to work out how to beat 'em to it. At short notice," he added. "Who lives right here in New York."

"How wonderful to get such a glowing recommendation," Rothschild said acidly.

"But you *are* the best," said Seretse, smoothly moving to soothe her ego. "There are surely few people who could match your knowledge of the Bible from both an archaeological and a mythological perspective."

Rothschild regarded him through narrowed eyes, but his appeal to her professional vanity had worked. "I can at least hear you out, I suppose," she said. "Come in."

She led the way into a lounge. It wasn't what Eddie had pictured; his past dealings with her had led him to expect the domain of a mean-spirited Victorian schoolmistress, but the furnishings had more of a bohemian feel, with lots of plump cushions. A large black-and-gray dog of indeterminate breed was sprawled on the floral carpet like a shaggy rug, its tail giving the new arrivals a single lazy wag before it settled back into sleep.

"Nice dog," said Eddie.

"Horrible, smelly old thing," Rothschild replied, with evident affection. "Now, what's this biblical mystery I can apparently help you solve?" She sat in an armchair, directing the two men to a sofa.

Eddie stepped over the dog to reach it. "It's in the Book of Revelations—"

"Revelation," she interrupted, with heavy emphasis on the last letter. "It's a singular revelation, not plural. Not that I would expect the uneducated or ignorant to care about the importance of a single *s*."

"You're right, I don't give a hit. But whatever it's called, these nutters really believe in it. They're making Nina find the angels of Revelation*nnnuhhh*," he said with mocking exaggeration.

Rothschild ignored his sarcasm, deep thought already evident on her brow. "Revelation is full of angels. 'Thousands upon thousands,' to quote it, and then specifically the four standing at the corners of the earth, the seven who blow the trumpets, another four bound at the Euphrates who are sent to wipe out a third of mankind . . ."

"Those last four sound like something people might want to get hold of. The kind of people me and Nina have dealt with before, anyway."

Her scathing tone returned. "Yes, you two do seem to

be an almost magnetic draw for megalomaniacs, murderers, and terrorists."

"But if there is potentially some kind of threat to the world," Seretse pointed out, "then it does become the responsibility of the IHA's experts. Even those who no longer work for the agency."

"I suppose you're right," she said begrudgingly. "But what are they?"

"Some sort of statues," Eddie told her. "They're making Nina look for places mentioned in Revelation. The Throne and Synagogue of Satan, she said."

Rothschild sat up. "The Throne of Satan?"

"You have heard of it?" Seretse asked. "You know where it is?"

"Of course I do!" She sounded almost affronted. "It's an early Christian name for the Altar of Zeus, from Pergamon in modern-day Turkey. Every archaeologist worth their salt would figure that out in five minutes or less. I don't know what it says about Nina if she couldn't."

"She *did* work it out," Eddie realized. "Of course she bloody did. She just didn't tell them—she started looking for the other ones first!"

"Why would she do that?" said the diplomat.

"To buy time. The longer she can keep these arseholes from finding the angels, the longer she'll stay alive. I didn't believe for a minute that the guys who tortured me were going to let me go home afterward, and I bet Nina thinks the same."

"You were tortured?" Rothschild asked, shocked.

Eddie pointed at the cuts on his face. "I didn't get these shaving. But this altar—is there anything on it about angels?"

She shook her head. "No, not that I know of. It's a pre-Christian relic; all the gods on it are Greek."

"It's definitely the same thing from Revelation, though?"

"Absolutely. Pergamon, or Pergamum, is mentioned several times in the text, and the altar itself is a major archaeological treasure. I'm actually a good friend of the man overseeing its restoration, Dr. Markus Derrick."

Eddie turned to Seretse. "Looks like I need to get to Turkey, then."

"Turkey?" Rothschild laughed. "The altar isn't in Turkey anymore, Mr. Chase. It was taken to Berlin in the late nineteenth century. It's the centerpiece of a whole museum."

"Berlin? Even better, it's nearer. Ozzy, can you sort me out a flight?"

"I think," Seretse said carefully, "it may be a good idea for you to accompany Mr. Chase, Maureen."

"Me?" she exclaimed, startled.

"After all, you know Dr. Derrick, I believe you speak German . . . and as an archaeologist, you should be able to help locate this mysterious angel."

"What, you're suggesting that I drop everything and fly to Europe first thing tomorrow morning with"—a disapproving stab of her finger at Eddie—"*him*?"

"I wasn't thinking first thing tomorrow," said Eddie. "I was thinking, pull strings to get on the next flight out tonight. Or a private flight, even. I know the IHA can set them up at short notice—Nina did all the time when she was running it."

Rothschild seemed about to make a biting comment, but Seretse headed her off with more diplomacy. "Yes, the UN's accountants and I remember very well."

The Yorkshireman glared at him. "This is *important*, Ozzy. Nina's life depends on it. And the baby's."

"Baby's?" the old woman echoed. "You have a baby?"

"Nina's pregnant," Eddie told her. "Four months. You didn't know?"

"I haven't exactly been following her on Twitter. But no, I didn't. My God." She appeared genuinely shaken. "Kidnapping a pregnant woman? That's . . . that's *evil*, is the only way to describe it. I'm sorry."

Despite the expression of sympathy, Eddie still couldn't let her abrupt change of heart pass without comment. "If she hadn't been pregnant, though, you wouldn't have been bothered?"

Rothschild straightened, regarding him down her thin nose. "Let me be clear, Mr. Chase. I don't like you, and I especially don't like your wife. In my opinion, you've cost the field of archaeology far more than you've brought to it, with all the death and destruction you've caused."

"Oh, is that right?" Eddie replied, bristling.

"But," she went on, "I don't believe that a child should suffer for the sins of the parents. Especially not an . . . an unborn child." Her voice quavered for a moment, but then she recovered. "I want to ask you a question, and I expect—no, I *demand*—an honest answer. If I help you find this angel, do you really believe you'll be able to use it to bring Nina and her child home safely?"

"Yeah, I do," he said without hesitation. "I'm not an archaeologist, but this kind of thing? It's what I do best."

"Everyone has one talent, I suppose . . . Very well. I'll help you." She turned to Seretse. "Although I would like something in return."

The diplomat tensed at being put on the spot. "And what would that be?"

"Nothing major. Just some consultancy work for the IHA. With a stipend, of course. I'm getting on in life, and extra income is always welcome."

Seretse looked at Eddie, who gave him a *do it!* nod. "I will see what I can arrange," he said wearily.

"And what about a plane?" Eddie asked.

"It will take a few hours, but I can get a private jet to take you to Germany. Exactly how I will explain it to the accountants, I am not yet sure."

"You're a diplomat, you can justify anything." Eddie stood. "We'd better get going."

"What about my dog?" said Rothschild, waving at the animal, which sleepily got to its feet and padded to her. "Someone needs to look after him."

"I will take care of that too," Seretse assured her with an air of resignation. "Now, you will both need your passports."

"I'll have to go home for mine," said Eddie. "Where'll this jet fly out of?"

"LaGuardia."

"Okay, I'll meet you there. Both of you."

Rothschild finished petting the dog, then stood. "Going on a mission with you, Mr. Chase. I would never have imagined it."

"Yeah, over eight hours on a plane together?" Eddie said sarcastically. "Can't wait."

*   *   *

Even with Seretse's best efforts to expedite the process of chartering a private flight, it was still well after two o'clock in the morning by the time all the arrangements had been made. But finally he led Eddie and Rothschild across the damp concrete of LaGuardia airport toward a Gulfstream G550 business jet. "You will be landing at Berlin Tegel," the official told the two travelers over the whine of its idling engines. "With the flight duration and the time difference, it will be late afternoon by the time you arrive."

"Hope the seats recline, then," said Eddie. "We'll need some kip on the way. What about when we get there?"

"I've already spoken to Markus," Rothschild said. "We can go from the airport directly to the museum, and he's arranged for us to stay after hours to examine the altar. I should warn you, though," she added, "I mentioned that we were looking for some sort of angel or Christian symbol, and he's absolutely certain there isn't any such thing on the altar itself, or on any of the pieces awaiting restoration. He's been overseeing the work for almost a decade, so if there were anything, he would already have seen it."

"Yeah, I was afraid of that," replied Eddie. "Can't imagine there'd be many places to hide something in an altar."

"Have you learned anything more about the men who kidnapped you?" asked Seretse. "You told me your friend in the NYPD was investigating."

Eddie shook his head. "She ran his fingerprint, and it came up blocked. Not unknown; restricted. So did the other dead guys'. That means they were all US intelligence or special forces. Past or present, it doesn't matter—spooks always cover each others' arses."

Rothschild gave him a nervous look. "And these are the people who've kidnapped Nina?"

A sardonic grin. "Welcome to our world."

They reached the plane, a uniformed attendant waving them to the cabin steps. "This is where I leave you," said Seretse. "I hope you find what you are looking for. And that you recover Nina safely," he added to Eddie.

"Thanks, Oswald," the Yorkshireman said, offering his hand. The diplomat shook it. "See you when we get back."

"If I still have my job," he answered with a sigh, followed by a faint smile. "Good luck, Eddie. And to you, Maureen."

Eddie hopped up the steps. "Okay, then. Let's go." He ducked through the entrance, Rothschild exchanging a polite kiss on the cheek with Seretse before following. The attendant pulled in the steps, then sealed the hatch.

Ten minutes later, the Gulfstream left the runway. It climbed into the sky, leaving the lights of New York behind as it headed east into the night.

10

The Mission

Nina slowly emerged from a troubled sleep. The room was already uncomfortably warm, even early in the morning. She pushed the sheet down her body, shifting to find a cooler patch on the mattress—

Someone was standing over her.

"Jesus!" Nina shrieked, sitting bolt-upright. Her unexpected guest was Miriam. The young woman squealed and jumped backward. "What the *hell*, Miriam? Why didn't you knock?"

"I did, I did!" she replied, hands flapping. "You didn't answer, and I was worried, so the Prophet unlocked the door."

"I was fine until you scared the crap out of me! God-*damm*it!" Nina pulled the sheet back up to her shoulders as she got out of bed. "Never frighten a pregnant woman, it's not good for the baby."

"I'm sorry, really I am." Miriam turned her back.

"Dunno why I'm bothering covering myself; your creepy voyeur boss is watching me from six different angles," Nina muttered with a glare at the nearest camera as she found her clothes. "What are you doing here?"

"The Prophet sent me to get you. The angel's here."

That caught Nina's attention. She paused, half dressed. "Already?"

"Yes. The Witnesses arrived by helicopter about thirty minutes ago."

The archaeologist's expression hardened. "You know that Simeon and Anna killed people to get it, don't you? They murdered two security guards in Rome." Seeing Miriam's shock, she pushed on: "And those two men are dead because your Prophet forced me to find this angel by torturing my husband."

She shook her head. "No, no, I . . . I don't believe . . ."

"This place has got nothing to do with God, or Jesus," Nina insisted. "The people in charge are *murderers*. You're complicit in that just by being here. But if you help me get away, or just tell the authorities where I am, I can—"

"Good morning, Dr. Wilde," came a new voice, seemingly from all around her. Cross. There were loudspeakers as well as cameras inside the house. "Miriam, I think you should return home. Norvin is on his way to bring Dr. Wilde to me."

Miriam bobbed her head obediently and went to the door. "Yes, Prophet."

"How many of them know?" Nina demanded loudly as she exited. "Huh? How many of the people here know what you're doing in their name? You murdering bastard!"

"Everyone here believes in my cause," said Cross as the door closed. "They believe that the prophecies in Revelation will soon be fulfilled. I am God's instrument on earth; any actions I take in His name are justified."

"So said every despot, wack-job, and psycho for the past ten thousand years. I've met people who believed they had a hotline to God before, but they were all just lunatics. What makes you so different?"

"The difference, Dr. Wilde, is that I really do."

There was unshakable conviction behind his words. "Jesus," whispered Nina, shaking her head. "You're worse than I thought."

"You'll soon see the truth. You won't be able to deny

it once you've seen the angel. Now get dressed. Norvin is here." A sharp rap came from the door.

"*He'd* better not come in while I'm naked." Cross did not reply, but neither did the door open, though Nina still finished dressing as quickly as she could.

Once she was ready, Norvin escorted her through the Mission. The helicopter pad was empty, she noticed, so the pilot had not stuck around after delivering the Fishers and their cargo. At the church, he took her to the control room. The vault-like door was open, Cross inside. As well as his usual pristine white robes, he also wore a pair of fine cotton gloves of the kind she had sometimes used herself to handle delicate artifacts. "Dr. Wilde," he called. "Good to see you."

"The feeling's about as unmutual as it could get," she said.

Not even insults could dampen his smug elation. "Come in. I want you to see what you've helped bring us."

She entered the laboratory, Norvin at her back. Within, Simeon and Anna Fisher regarded her with unfriendly eyes. Beside them on the stainless-steel bench was a metal case—the same one Trant had carried the previous night.

Cross saw her flash of recognition. "Yes, this is it. The second angel." He opened the case.

The angel was revealed within, cleaned and polished, its metal wings glinting under the lights. It was made from a smooth gray material, cast rather than carved: pottery or ceramic fired in a kiln.

That was consistent with how Cross had described the artifact from Iraq. She glanced at the fragment of the first angel, still sitting inside its protective glass case, then back at the new arrival. "Is it the same as the one you found?"

"Apart from the head, yes. That was a lion; this is an ox. Or a calf, depending which translation of the Bible you use."

"It looks more like an ox to me," Nina noted.

"I know. The King James Version seems closer so far."

She peered more closely at the statue, spotting something inscribed into the surface. "There's something written on it. Have you had it translated?"

"I don't need to. I already know what it says. The angel I found in Iraq had the same words." Cross carefully lifted the statue with his gloved hands, turning it to follow the text around its body. "Revelation chapter four, verse eight: 'And they rest not day and night, saying "Holy, holy, holy, Lord God Almighty, which was, and is, and is to come."' It doesn't literally mean that they're talking nonstop, but that the words written upon them are an eternal statement of God's greatness. Another of John's hallucinogenic interpretations of what he'd read."

"You should put all this stuff in a book," said Nina, not willing to be convinced, even though she couldn't fault his logic. "There's always a huge market for explanations of the Bible. Call it *The Revelation Code* or something. I'm sure it'll be a bestseller."

He shook his head. "I'm not interested in money, Dr. Wilde. I'm only interested in the truth, God's truth. Which is now one step closer to being revealed."

"Well, it *is* called Revelation," she said, but he was distracted from her facetious comment by a noise from outside—the roar of a helicopter coming in to land. "Expecting company?" she asked.

"A . . . friend," he replied. "Norvin! Go and meet him." The big man nodded and hurried from the lab.

Cross returned the angel to the case. Nina eyed it, but the close proximity of Simeon—and his gun—deterred her from getting nearer. "So that's two angels accounted for," she said instead. "What about the others?"

"That's up to you," said Cross. "The Throne of Satan, and the Place in the Wilderness—we still have to figure out where they are. But since you found the Synagogue of Satan so quickly, I'm sure you won't have any problems."

Nina forced herself not to show any reaction to the first undiscovered location. She had known where it was from the moment Cross had initially mentioned it: The only thing it possibly could be was the Pergamon

altar in Berlin. If the former CIA man or any of his followers had possessed an archaeological background,
they would have worked that out already. Fortunately,
fundamentalists—of any stripe—were prone to sticking
solely to their existing beliefs rather than exploring anything that might challenge them. "To be honest, I'm
amazed that actually paid off," she told him. "My picking the Villa Torlonia was just a guess."

"Not just a guess," Cross replied. "You were *guided*."

"By whom?"

"God, of course."

"*God* guided me?" she exclaimed. "I don't think so! If
God were giving me a helping hand, He wouldn't have
let you kidnap me and torture Eddie."

Something about her words briefly affected the others, glances—unsettled? concerned?—flicking between
Simeon and Cross, but whatever the cause, it quickly
passed. "He's not guiding you," said Cross. "He's guiding *me*—but as part of that guidance, He brought you
to me. Everything you've been through, everything
you've survived, that was all His will."

"Really," Nina said flatly.

"Really! You've fallen out of airplanes, escaped sinking ships, gotten through death traps—and you've had
so many people try to kill you that you've probably lost
count. Divine intervention is the only possible explanation for your survival. Wouldn't you say?"

"No, I wouldn't," she insisted. "I'd put knowledge,
determination, desperation, and sheer dumb luck above
God keeping me safe so you could use me for your crazy
plan."

"It's not just His plan," said a new voice from behind
her. "It's mine."

Nina spun toward the entrance—only to freeze as she
saw a horribly familiar face. "Son of a *bitch* . . ."

Victor Dalton, the disgraced former leader of the free
world, regarded her mockingly. "If you don't mind, Dr.
Wilde, I prefer to be called *Mr. President*."

11

" I can think of plenty of other things to call you," said Nina, struggling to hide her shock. While in the White House, Dalton had collaborated with religious extremists to try to kill her and Eddie to suppress their discovery of the Garden of Eden. He had then been forced to resign after Eddie leaked online a graphic video of his affair with the woman who had plotted the nuclear attack on New York, only to resurface seeking revenge on the couple and a cabal of the world's wealthiest people, whom he considered to have betrayed and abandoned him.

The last she had seen of him was on television, being arrested by the FBI. "So you didn't end up in a supermax prison? Damn."

"People like me don't *go* to prison," Dalton replied, his smile becoming caustic around the edges. "You can't jail the president of the United States, even a former holder of the office. It would be a national embarrassment."

"You *were* a national embarrassment!"

Any trace of good humor vanished. "I was a better president than the idiot who replaced me. But in America, anyone can be rehabilitated—and actually, I have *you* to thank for giving me my chance."

"How?"

"I don't know what you and your psycho husband did, but the Group went chasing after you into Ethiopia . . . and never came back. You did, though, so I assume you killed them." She didn't reply, not wanting to give him any leverage against her. "Hey, no need to be coy—I'm happy about it! Those bastards set me up, but after they disappeared, nobody at Justice had the balls to push the charges. So everything was quietly dropped."

"Everyone still remembers that you were busted for security violations, though."

He shrugged. "The American public has a *really* short memory. There's always some rock star doing drugs or an actor making an ass of himself to distract them. Once the media stops pushing a story, it becomes a footnote."

Nina smiled a little. "Like your political career."

"It's not over yet!" he snapped. "That's why I'm here. I knew Mr. Cross"—a brief look at the robed man— "from my time on the Senate Intelligence Committee; our paths had crossed, no pun intended. And I knew he shared my views about the state of America, and the state of the world." His tone became more oratorical. "I've joined with him to continue what I started in office . . . and soon, I'll *regain* that office. I was hounded out of the White House as a philanderer. But I'll be voted back into it as a savior."

Nina treated him to slow, sarcastic applause. "Nice stump speech. Who's it aimed at—adulterers and snake-handlers?"

"It's aimed at *everyone*, Dr. Wilde," Dalton said, with a flash of anger. "Everyone in America. And they *will* all support me." He moved to examine the statue, brushing past her. "So this is it?"

"That's it," Cross told him. "One of the angels of Revelation. The clues to finding it were in the Apocalypse of John all along, but it took me to crack the code."

"And me to find the statue for you," Nina said, cutting.

"For which we're both very grateful," said Dalton, politician's smarm back at full intensity. "But the angels will let me finish what I started in office. Once they're . . . used"—he glanced at Cross again, as if to check that he wasn't giving away some secret—"religious conflict around the world will reach new highs. All those jihadist groups, all those terrorists, they'll be targeting America like never before—and that will create the unstoppable desire at home to unify behind a single banner. One religion: *our* religion. This won't be some fake populism backed by billionaires who want tax cuts and the EPA disbanded. This will be real, and you'll either be with it or against it."

"Sounds like my idea of hell," she said with distaste.

"Then get out." There was a sudden vehemence to his words. "You don't like America? Leave. We don't need you, or want you."

"I guess you don't need or want the Constitution or the Bill of Rights either. The First Amendment ring any bells?"

"We'll be taking them back to their true intent. The next election isn't far off, and by then, the world will be in chaos. America will be crying out for strong leadership, and that's what I'll give them. I'll be standing as an independent against that jackass Leo Cole, and whoever the other side puts up against him—and I'll win. Once I'm back in power, I'll secure the homeland and kick out anyone who's a threat to it. Including your friends at the UN," he added. "America shouldn't kowtow to anyone else's laws. We *make* the laws. And enforce them."

Nina could hardly contain her disbelief at his newfound megalomania. "America has treaties with the United Nations—are you just going to ignore them?"

"The United Nations!" Both turned at Cross's outburst. "The most corrupt and evil organization in history. It shouldn't be kicked out of America, it should be destroyed!" He gazed reverently at the angel, then stepped away and spread his arms to make a proclamation. "The kings of the world will witness God's judgment soon enough. Babylon will fall. And then the kingdom of God will be founded here on earth!"

Both the Fishers and Norvin watched their Prophet, enraptured, while Dalton, clearly surprised, could only stare. But Nina was looking not at Cross, rather at the statue, exposed and unattended just a few feet away.

Her chance—

She shoved the startled Dalton aside and snatched up the figure. The others all whirled, Simeon drawing his gun, but she had already raised the statue above her head. "Back off or I'll smash it!" she cried.

They froze—but from the fear on Dalton's face and Anna's expression of horror, they were scared of something more than the destruction of a religious artifact. "I mean it," Nina continued, trying to cover her anxiety.

"Don't!" said Dalton, holding up both hands. "That would be a—a very bad idea. For all of us."

"Why?" she demanded. "Is it dangerous?"

"Yes. It's dangerous," said Cross. He indicated the glass case. "I keep that piece of the first angel in there for a reason. It shouldn't pose a threat, not anymore, but I'm not willing to take chances."

"What kind of threat?"

He gestured at the artifact above her head. "Will you put it down?"

"Nope," she said defiantly. "If anyone tries anything . . ."

"If you break open the angel," said Cross, "we'll all die. Not just us in this room, but everyone in the Mission. Please. Put it down."

Nina looked up at the statue. It didn't appear deadly, but it was unusually heavy for its size. "Is there something inside it? Is that what you're all so scared of?"

Cross nodded. "You remember I told you the Umm al Binni lake was a meteor crater? The meteorite that hit there wasn't just a rock. There was something more to it—something deadly. 'And I saw a star fall from heaven unto the earth, and to him was given the key to the bottomless pit. And he opened the bottomless pit; and there arose a smoke out of the pit, as the smoke of a great furnace. And there came out of the smoke locusts upon the earth.' Revelation chapter nine, verse one. The pit was the impact crater, and I saw the smoke myself, in Iraq. When the first angel was broken."

"Smoke came out of it?"

"Not smoke; *gas*. There was something inside the meteorite, a substance that doesn't occur naturally on earth, that reacted with the air." He turned to Anna. "Anna was a chemist and biochemist for the CIA—she can explain it."

"It was a pyrophoric material," said Anna. "Something that ignites spontaneously when it comes into contact with oxygen. It burns at a high temperature, judging from the effect it had on the ceramic containing it"—she indicated the fragment inside the cabinet—"until it's completely consumed. But as it burns, it gives off an extremely toxic by-product."

"A yellow cloud, like sulfur," said Cross solemnly. "It kills almost instantly. I had protective gear, but the Arab rebels didn't. They all died in agony, as if they were being eaten alive by insects, after just a few seconds."

Nina gave the statue another look, this time considerably more nervous. "So this material, part of the meteorite . . . it's *inside* the angel?"

"Yes. The twenty-four Elders managed to contain pieces of it."

"How? If it burns on contact with air . . ."

"Water stops the reaction," Anna told her. "Or at least slows it."

"It poisons the water, though," said Cross. "Exactly as Revelation said in chapter eight. 'The sea became blood,' and then three verses later, 'and many men died of the waters, because they were made bitter.' The fragments must have poisoned the water supply around the crater. But the Elders figured out a way to make them safe."

"Seal them in clay while they're still in the water, then harden the outer shell in a kiln, I'd guess. The wings were a way to reinforce it?" Nina said, lowering the statue slightly for a better look. Cross nodded in confirmation. "And over time . . . the story of what happened turned into folklore," she realized. "The meteorite became a burning mountain, the locusts were the toxic gas, all inflicted on humanity by an angry God—and the statues became angels, based on existing mythology. I've seen the same four heads representing angelic beings before, in the Garden of Eden."

Cross stepped closer, holding out his hands. "Put the angel down, Dr. Wilde," he said. "If you destroy it, we won't be the only ones who'll die. The cloud will spread over the entire Mission. There are almost a hundred people here—do you want to be responsible for their deaths?"

"Whatever you're planning, they're in it with you," said Nina, but with uncertainty.

The former CIA agent picked up on it at once. "You think Miriam's in on it? She's a sweet, innocent young girl who's following her heart. She's never hurt anyone in her life." A firmer tone. "Just like Macy."

Nina's jaw clenched at her friend's name. "You son of a bitch. Don't you talk about her."

"I know what you think—that it's your fault she died," he pressed on. "And the guilt over that's been eating away at you ever since, hasn't it? That's why you went into therapy. Because of the guilt."

Tears stung the corners of Nina's eyes. She angrily blinked them away. "Screw you."

Another step nearer. "If you smash the angel, you'll murder a lot of innocent people. Including Miriam."

She looked at the heavy steel door. "Not if you close that. The only people who'll die will be in here."

"Mr. President?"

"Yeah?" said the sweating Dalton.

"Leave the room, please. Norvin, Anna, Simeon—you too."

Nina hefted the statue again. "I'm warning you!" But Dalton made a hurried exit, Cross's followers doing so more reluctantly to leave the pair alone.

"I know you won't do it," said the cult leader. "You can't accept more innocent people getting hurt because of you. Especially not the most innocent of all." He looked down at the bump marking the presence of the new life inside her.

She felt a hot tear run down one cheek. "Son of a *bitch*," she hissed. But the statue remained in her raised hands.

"Give it to me."

Nina drew in several angry breaths . . . then slowly lowered her arms. Cross reached out to take the statue. He had to pull it from her grip, her fingers refusing to surrender, but then it was his. "I should have done it," she whispered, but she knew he was right.

"I'm glad you didn't." He placed the angel in the case and closed the lid. "But it proves what I told you. God kept you alive as part of His plan." The statue secure, he called out: "Simeon! It's okay. You can come back in."

Simeon hurried into the lab. He aimed his gun at Nina, but Cross signaled for him to lower it. The others followed, Dalton last to enter after peering nervously around the door. "Is everything safe?" he asked.

"It's safe," Cross replied.

Nina wiped away another tear. "So you got your precious angel," she said bitterly. "Is that your plan? You're going to break it open and claim that all the victims died because it was God's will? Poison Mecca or somewhere to start a religious war?"

Dalton looked momentarily startled, but Cross shook his head. "This isn't about war, Dr. Wilde. It's about fulfilling a prophecy—and it's about *knowledge*."

"What do you mean?"

"I was a CIA operative—a spy. It was my job to find out information about America's enemies, to discover their secrets. But when I went to Iraq, when I found the temple and the first angel, I realized there was a way to discover *the* secrets, the most important ones in all creation. The secrets of God Himself!"

Nina stared at him, unsure how to respond to his sudden messianic shift. "God's secrets? What . . ."

"It's written in the Book of Revelation!" Cross continued, as if offended that she didn't know. "Chapter ten, verse seven—'But in the days of the voice of the seventh angel, when he shall begin to sound, the mystery of God should be finished, as he hath declared to his servants the prophets.' Do you know what that means? It means that as the seventh angel sounds his trumpet, all of God's secrets will be revealed to His prophets. And I *am* one of those prophets!"

He turned to his followers, who watched enraptured even as Dalton seemed faintly uncomfortable. "Seven angels are given a task in turn by God. The sixth angel is ordered to loose the four angels that were bound at the Euphrates. *These* are those angels!" He stabbed one hand at the fragment behind glass, the other at the closed case. "One has already been released, in Iraq. We've found the second angel—so there are only two more to locate." He whirled back to face Nina, his pale eyes wide and terrifyingly intense. "Two more for *you* to locate. When we have them, they'll be released. President Dalton will get his war, but I'll get something more important. Once all the statues have been loosed and the sixth angel's task is completed, the seventh angel will sound—and God will reveal everything to me. His plan, His secrets, the meaning of everything. I'll know it all."

Nina was speechless for several seconds, the sheer madness of his plan almost too much to process rationally. "So you think," she finally said, "that loosing the angels, releasing this gas, and killing who knows how many people will persuade God to let you into His inner circle? You're *insane*!"

Both the Fishers reacted angrily, Simeon advancing with his fists balled, but Cross waved him back. The cult leader was also furious, but contained it—just. "Unbelievers throughout history have accused God's prophets of being mad," he growled. "Noah, Moses, even Jesus Christ—they've all faced mockery. But you'll see the truth once all four angels are loosed. The army of the horsemen will be unleashed upon the earth, just as Revelation says—and as Babylon falls, I will know God's plan." His voice rose to a shout. "I *will* know!"

Appalled, Nina turned to Dalton. "*You* can't believe

any of this? You're a politician—you're in this for your-self, not to fulfill some biblical prophecy!"

"Thank you for that vote of confidence, Dr. Wilde," Dalton said sarcastically. "But you're wrong. I *do* believe; I believe that finding and unleashing the rest of the angels will make America stronger. That's my duty to my country, as a true patriot."

"Patriot, my ass," Nina snarled. "You're so crooked, you make Nixon look like Mother Teresa."

It was Dalton's turn to be angered, but before he could reply, Cross, his composure now recovered, cut in. "I'm not asking you to believe, Dr. Wilde. I'm asking you to *obey*. There are still two more angels out there. The Throne of Satan, and the Place in the Wilderness—where are they?"

"I don't know. And even if I *did* know, now that you've told me what you're planning, there's no way I'm going to help you find them."

"I didn't *only* suggest using you to find the angels out of revenge—although I have to admit, that was a bonus after everything you and Chase did to me," said Dalton. "I genuinely believed you were the person most likely to succeed. But if you're not going to cooperate, then you're . . . surplus to requirements."

"No, no," said Cross, holding up a hand. "She *will* find them for us."

"Did God tell you that?" Nina said with a sneer.

"No. You did." His gaze intensified. "I was an intelligence officer, Dr. Wilde. I know people—how they think, how they'll respond to specific situations. And I know that you'll do what I ask to protect your husband." He led the group back into the control room and went to the video wall. "I'll demonstrate."

A tap on the controls, and the screens blinked on—showing Eddie still secured to the chair. The camera had changed position, now staring down at him from his left side. He looked around, mouth moving as he responded to someone out of frame, but the audio was muted.

"Waterboard him," said Cross. "Don't hold back this time." Irton appeared, a towel in his hands.

"Goddamn you," Nina gasped as Eddie tried in vain to break loose. A silent shout at Irton, who responded by punching him in the stomach. The torturer's two assistants prepared to tip the chair backward as their boss swaddled the Englishman's head in the thick cloth. "Don't do it, please!"

Cross was unmoved. "It's up to you how long this goes on. A minute, an hour . . . all day. He won't die, but he'll wish he could." The chair was lifted and tilted back until its occupant's head hit the floor. "All you have to do to stop it is tell me where one of the other angels is."

"But I don't know," she protested.

Irton brought a bucket to the chair. "I think you do," said Cross. "You already know something, and you're keeping it from me. Do you think I'm an idiot? I know when someone's hiding the truth. Finding it is what I do. Irton!"

The bucket tipped, sending a gush of water over Eddie's cocooned head. He convulsed, mouth open in a silent scream beneath the sodden material. Nina gasped in sickened, helpless fear.

"I really think you ought to do what you're told," said Dalton, tone patronizing.

"Your choice, Dr. Wilde," Cross added. "There's only one way to stop this."

She stared in anguish at the man she loved, the father of her child choking as more water filled his airways. She tried to resist, but felt surrender swelling inside her as his torment continued, unable to contain it—

"Berlin," she whispered.

Cross jabbed at a control, the monitors going black. "What?"

"Berlin," Nina repeated. "The Throne of Satan from Revelation—there's only one thing it can be, and that's the Altar of Zeus from Pergamon. John had obviously been there, because he knew Antipas the martyr, so he would have known about the altar as well."

"Isn't Pergamon in Turkey?" demanded Dalton.

"The whole thing was transported to Germany in the

late nineteenth century. It's a Greek relic, though—I don't know of any connection to ancient Judaism or Christianity."

"But there must be one," said Cross. He touched the control pad. "Irton, let him go. For now." He turned to Nina. "Get back to work. Research this altar, find anything that might link it to the angel or the twenty-four Elders."

She nodded, despondent. "I'll do what I can."

"What about the Place in the Wilderness?" he added. "Are you keeping that from me too? Because if you are . . ."

"I don't know anything about that," she insisted, truthfully.

His unsettling eyes stared into hers, then he nodded. "Okay. Focus on the altar for now."

"Do you want us to fly to Germany?" asked Simeon.

"No, Trant can handle it. Tell him to get the team to Berlin. You work out a plan to extract the angel once we find it."

"*If* we find it," said Dalton. "If this altar's been moved, the angel might already have been discovered when it was dismantled."

Cross shook his head. "No. It's waiting to be found. I have faith. In God's plan . . . and in Dr. Wilde's love for her husband. She won't let him suffer."

"Go to hell," Nina muttered, filled with shame for having capitulated. She looked at the case containing the angel. "I should have smashed that thing when I had the chance."

"I'm glad you didn't," said Dalton. "You're doing what's best for America. You'll see."

"Anything that involves you can't be what's best for America." But there was almost no defiance left in her, just sullen resignation.

"Norvin, take Dr. Wilde back to her house," ordered Cross. "She has a lot of work to do." The bodyguard escorted Nina out.

* * *

Dalton waited until she was gone before speaking again. "Two angels found already? I knew she was good, much as I hate to admit it, but I'm surprised she located them so quickly. Mind you," he added, gesturing toward the empty screens, "you did give her an incentive."

"We got lucky," Cross said quietly.

"What do you mean?"

"I mean this." He tapped the touch pad again. The image of the warehouse reappeared—but this time it was a freeze-framed scene of chaos.

Dalton flinched as he saw a body at the end of a smeared trail of gore. "What the hell happened?"

"Chase happened" came the reply.

"Chase?" The ex-politician rounded on Cross with a sudden flash of fear, which he had to fight to keep under control. "You mean he's *escaped*?"

"He broke out late last night. I don't know what happened after he killed Berman—this was the last image before the video link was cut off—but since I can't contact Irton or Raddick, I have to assume they're dead too. What I just showed Wilde was a recording, flipped so she wouldn't realize it was the same thing she saw before. If she hadn't caved in when she did, I would have run out of footage, and she would have realized we don't have Chase anymore."

"But—but he could bring this whole thing down!" Dalton's words rose in pitch despite his best efforts to maintain a calm front. "If he finds this place, if he rescues Wilde, it'll all point back to me!"

"Irton's tracks are covered," said Cross, with more than a hint of impatience. "Chase won't find the Mission."

"Chase once found his way into my *house,* into my goddamn *bedroom,* and that was when I still had Secret Service protection! You underestimated him, Ezekiel. That's a big mistake."

"I know what I'm doing, *Mr. President.*" Dalton was taken aback by Cross's warning tone, but the cult leader ignored his reaction. "If Chase tries to interfere with the plan . . . we'll kill him."

Berlin

"Nice day for it," Eddie sighed, watching the rain-drenched outskirts of the German capital crawl past beyond the clogged autobahn. He and Rothschild had unluckily landed at Tegel airport just in time to catch the evening rush hour. "Everyone's drowning in Berlin."

His companion didn't get the reference to the old pop song; either that, or she was simply ignoring him. "Why are we going this way?" she complained instead. "The Saatwinkler Damm would be much more direct."

"Calm down, the IHA's paid for the ride." The Mercedes had picked them up at the terminal. "It's not like the driver's trying to rip you off by taking us via Poland."

Rothschild's pinched little mouth shrank further, but rather than make a sarcastic rejoinder, she instead spoke in German to the driver. "There's been a car crash," she told Eddie. "So we're having to go a longer way around. But at least this way we'll see more of the city."

Eddie peered at the heavy slate-gray sky and the wet tower blocks silhouetted against it. "Terrific, I'll get my camera ready. So you know Berlin pretty well?"

"It's been a while since I was last here, but yes. I even

lived here for several months after I got my master's in archaeology."

"Yeah? Did you meet the kaiser?"

"No, of course not, that was a long time before—" She finally got the joke and treated him to a withering glare. "I'm no fan of Nina's, but I always thought she was at least intelligent. Her seeing *anything* in you makes me question that, though."

Eddie shrugged, grinning. After putting up with the elderly woman's barbs on the long journey across the Atlantic, he'd been unable to resist getting in one of his own. "Is that how you know the bloke at this museum?" he asked, changing the subject.

"Markus? Yes. We've been friends for a long time. And by that, I mean since the 1970s, not the 1910s," she added peevishly.

The Englishman smiled again, then turned his attention back to the city. His only prior visits to Germany had been brief, and he had never been to Berlin itself. What he'd seen of it so far was what he had expected, however: lots of postwar tower blocks, though with more green space around them than similar developments in London or Paris. The car crossed over a river— or given its straightness, a canal—and continued toward the capital's heart, more unappealing concrete buildings rolling by before the visitors passed over another bridge and before long entered a large swath of parkland.

"That's the Siegessäule," said Rothschild, pointing ahead.

"The what?"

"The Victory Column. There." Eddie looked past the driver and saw a tall pillar at the end of the road, a winged golden figure at its top. "It used to be in front of the Reichstag, but Hitler and Albert Speer had it moved. A good thing, otherwise it would have been flattened by Allied bombers. This park leads all the way to the Reichstag and the Brandenburg Gate, actually."

"Uh-huh," said Eddie, not particularly interested. Monuments to the common soldiers who had fallen in wars meant more to him than extravagant celebrations of the politicians who claimed to have won them. But as the Mercedes negotiated the large roundabout circling the edifice, he had to admit that it was quite impressive, floodlights making the statue at its summit gleam even in the rain. "The Brandenburg Gate's where the Berlin Wall was, right?"

"Yes, and it was the site of the signing of German re-unification. So you know *some* history, then."

"Military history I'm pretty good on. I even surprise Nina sometimes." He looked ahead as the car turned onto a long, broad tree-lined avenue, but saw nothing through the traffic and the dull haze of rain. "How far is it?" he asked, peering at the driver's satnav to get an idea of the city's layout. A winding river bisected the capital, its wide, snaking curves running north of their current position.

"Over a mile," Rothschild told him.

"Glad we're driving, then. Don't fancy getting wet—I had way too much of that recently." His expression darkened as he briefly thought back to his waterboarding ordeal. Rothschild gave him a curious look but decided not to voice any questions.

The Mercedes continued down the long avenue. Eventually the towering triumphal arch of the Brandenburg Gate came into sight, though to Eddie's slight disappointment the road didn't go through it, traffic instead diverting around a broad pedestrianized area. Even in the bad weather, there were still plenty of tourists at the monument. "Not far now," said Rothschild as the gate passed out of sight behind a building.

"Great," Eddie replied. "This friend of yours, Dr. Derrick—he's an expert on this altar, right?"

"It's been his life's work, and he's in charge of overseeing its restoration, so you could say that, yes."

"Good. 'Cause I've been thinking—"

Flat sarcasm. "Really."

"A hardy har. I've been *wondering* how this angel could be hidden in it without anyone having found it already, even if it's behind a secret panel or something."

Rothschild smiled patronizingly. "Do you know how big the Altar of Zeus is, Mr. Chase?"

"I dunno. But an altar's basically a fancy table, so . . . ten feet long and six wide?" he guessed. "Twelve feet?"

She could barely hide her amusement. "A little bigger."

The Brandenburg Gate reappeared behind them as the car turned onto a wide boulevard and headed east for roughly half a mile, then picked its way north through smaller streets before finally stopping. "This is it?" Eddie asked. Another glance at the satnav told him that their destination was actually on an island.

"That's it," Rothschild replied. "The Pergamon Museum."

A footbridge spanned a waterway in front of the imposing classical building, steps leading up to a plaza between the two long wings of the museum. A far more modern structure, a cylindrical tower, occupied most of the space. "Big place just for an altar."

"The Altar of Zeus isn't the only exhibit; there's also the Museum of Islamic Art, the Near East Museum, and the antiquity collection. But Markus can show you . . . Ah, here he comes." A tall figure beneath a large black umbrella scuttled down the steps and crossed the bridge to meet them.

The driver opened the door for Rothschild, Eddie following her out. "Markus, hello!" she trilled, embracing then kissing the new arrival. "It's so good to see you again!"

"You too, after all these years," said the square-jawed German. Eddie guessed him to be in his sixties, although his hair was a chestnut brown suspiciously rich for someone of that age. "Ah, Maureen. *Willkommen zurück,* welcome back. Come, come inside, out of this rain."

Rothschild took shelter under his umbrella and was about to go with him when Eddie cleared his throat. "Oh. Yes," she said, with faint irritation. "Markus, this is Eddie Chase. Mr. Chase, Dr. Markus Derrick."

"Nice to meet you," said Eddie, offering his hand.

Derrick shook it with enthusiasm. "Mr. Chase." He

gave Rothschild an expectant look, awaiting a more detailed introduction, but none came. "Okay! Please,
come with me." The group headed across the bridge,
Eddie getting wet as his traveling companion stayed beneath the umbrella. "So, you have come all this way to
see the Pergamon altar, yes? It is a good thing Maureen
is my friend; that wing of the museum will be closed to
the public for some years as we build a new roof. But I
can get you in. As the director of the altar's restoration,
it is a perk of the job!" He chuckled.

They reached the glass doors leading into the cylindrical structure, which housed a lobby and visitor center.
The museum was still open, though the tourists were
now mostly leaving. Derrick nodded in greeting to a security guard, who let the group through a side gate, and
they headed into the building proper.

"Now, what is this about?" he asked. "Your phone
call was very mysterious, Maureen. You want to examine the altar for . . . angels? Christian symbols? You can
be sure there are none. I have looked very carefully at it
for over twenty years!"

"It might not be *on* it," said Eddie. "It might be hidden
inside it, we don't know. All we do know is that these
angels are something to do with the Book of Revelation—
and somebody's kidnapped my wife to try to get hold of
them."

Derrick stopped in surprise. "Kidnapped your wife?"

Rothschild anticipated his next question. "He's married to Nina Wilde."

"Nina Wilde? *The* Nina Wilde?"

"You know her?" Eddie asked.

"Of course I do! We have never met, but I know of
her, naturally. *Menschenskind!* Married to Nina Wilde.
A remarkable career she has had, yes."

Eddie took a moment of pleasure from Rothschild's
visible jealousy—whatever her issues with Nina, Derrick didn't share them—but had more important concerns. "They're forcing her to look for these angels. And
we think they've already found one."

"In Rome," added Rothschild. Seretse had given them

the news during the flight. "Someone broke into the Jewish catacombs in the Villa Torlonia last night. Nobody knows what they took, but they smashed a hole in a wall to get it. And murdered two security guards as they escaped."

Derrick was shocked. "Murdered! Who are these people?"

"Some sort of religious cult," said Eddie. "Their leader reckons he's a prophet."

"Since they seem obsessed by the Book of Revelation, it's reasonable to assume that the prophecies they're interested in are of the doomsday kind," Rothschild said.

"Okay," said Derrick, perturbed. They set off again. "Then you are here because the altar—or the Throne of Satan—is mentioned in Revelation?"

"That's right," Eddie replied. "Soon as I told the prof about it, she knew what it meant."

"Mr. Chase thinks Dr. Wilde had already made the connection but was deliberately holding it back to buy time," said Rothschild. "Whether she did or not, she still apparently identified another site, possibly the Synagogue of Satan from Revelation—and because of that, two innocent people were killed."

"Don't you bloody dare," Eddie warned her. "She'd have done everything she could to slow them down. If she hadn't, they might already be here." He glanced at the museum's visitors. "And even more people could get hurt."

Derrick was becoming more alarmed by the moment. "There could be a danger to the public? I shall arrange more security."

"If we find this angel, you might not need to," the Englishman told him. "Once I've got it, I'm going to use it to make them let Nina go."

"Two points," said Rothschild. "First: Even if we do find it, it's not yours to take—it's the property of the German government, and I doubt they'll let you simply hand it over to some murderous cult. Second: How will you let these people know you have it? You don't have any way to contact them."

"I'll find 'em. Or they'll find me. Either way, they'll know I've got the thing. Once we figure out where it is."

Derrick led them to a set of glass double doors with a barrier in front. He moved the obstacle aside. "I do not know if there really is an angel hidden inside the altar, but"—he opened the doors wide—"you are welcome to look."

Eddie followed the avuncular German through—and stopped in astonishment.

The room was a cavernous space in its own right, but its contents were what had impressed him. The far side was occupied by what he assumed was a Greek temple, wide stairs leading up between the two arms of the inspiration for the museum's exterior. Elegant columns supported a roof bearing several statues, an opening beyond the top of the steps leading to a display room.

There was more to the temple than sheer size, though. Around its base was an elaborate frieze, larger-than-life carved figures of gods and heroes locked in combat with monstrous creatures. Sections were missing, however, pale blank stone filling the gaps.

"Okay, wasn't expecting this," Eddie said. "It's pretty good." Rothschild made a faintly exasperated sound.

Derrick was apparently more used to British understatement. "It is, yes?" He swept an arm from one side of the frieze to the other as they approached. "That is the Gigantomachy, the battle of the gods of Olympus—Apollo, Athena, Hecate, and others—against the giants. There are more panels along both the sides."

"Lot of gaps in 'em," Eddie observed.

"Yes, unfortunately. But there are many more pieces that we are reassembling. Someday we hope to finish the whole display."

"So where's this altar, then?" Eddie looked up the steps, assuming it would be at the top, but saw nothing.

Derrick gave him a confused look before laughing, while Rothschild struggled to contain a mocking snigger.

"All right, what's the joke?" Eddie demanded.

"This *is* the altar," said the German. He waved his

hand again to encompass the whole of the massive structure. "All of it! The Altar of Zeus, moved brick by brick from Turkey."

Eddie stared up at the building in dismay. "Buggeration. This might take longer than I thought . . ."

13

Eddie reached the end of the Gigantomachy frieze on the altar's right wing, gazing up at the final panels—displaying a warrior with his face and one arm missing beside an equally incomplete horse—before turning and retracing his steps around the structure to the same position on the left side. A tall mirror was mounted on the back wall to create the illusion that the building continued deeper into the museum; his reflection regarded him disconsolately.

There were numerous winged figures among the carved combatants, which he had immediately thought were angels, but Rothschild and Derrick explained during the group's examination of the ancient temple that they were actually Greek gods such as Nike and Uranus. It was a sign of his growing concern that he hadn't made a joke about either name. The German had assured him that the sculptures were solid slabs of marble, with nothing concealed either inside or behind them, and that they long predated the birth of Christ.

"So where is this bloody thing?" he asked himself. The balding mirror image had no answer. With a sigh, he went back the way he had come.

The two archaeologists were at the top of the stairs, in

the display room behind the façade. Eddie ascended to find them examining another frieze set out along the walls. "Have you found anything?"

"No, I'm sorry," Derrick replied. "There is nothing I know of on the altar that could possibly be any kind of Christian symbol, not even in the unrestored pieces in storage."

"Damn. And there's no way the gods with wings might have been seen as angels?"

Rothschild shook her head. "The early Christians explicitly rejected the Greek and Roman pantheon—they called this place the Altar of Satan for a reason. And the modern image of an angel, a man with wings on his back, doesn't match the biblical descriptions of them. They generally look indistinguishable from ordinary people, but they can also be beings of fire, or lightning, or even resemble some sort of machine—'a wheel intersecting a wheel' is I think how it's worded. The angels in Revelation are just as varied, but none are described as men with wings."

"How *are* they described?" Eddie asked. "Anything that matches these guys?" He indicated the frieze.

"Not that I can think of."

He turned away in frustration, trying to think of anything to help him locate the angel—and his wife. "These arseholes found something in Italy. Nina worked out where it was . . . but *what* was it? How did they know what to look for?"

"I don't know," said Rothschild. "But according to Oswald, they went to a specific spot in the catacombs and smashed a wall open to reveal a cavity. Presumably they took whatever was inside."

"The angel?" asked Derrick.

"Maybe. But nothing else appeared to have been damaged."

"So why did they go to that spot?" wondered Eddie. "This catacomb—is there anything on the walls? Paintings, inscriptions, that kind of thing?"

"Some paintings, yes," said Derrick. "I have not been

there, but I have seen photographs. Most are decorative, but there are some Hebrew religious symbols . . ."

He broke off, lips pursed. "What is it?" Eddie asked.

"Hebrew symbols," the German replied. "I did not think about it earlier, because you told me you were looking for *Christian* symbols. But there is a piece in storage . . ." He searched his memory, then his eyes widened. "Yes, I know which one. Come with me."

He strode from the antechamber, Eddie and Rothschild hurrying down the stairs after him. "What is it, Markus?" asked Rothschild.

"There is a panel that we have not yet managed to match to a specific location on the altar," said Derrick, leading them into a side room. This was also closed to the public, plastic sheets covering some of the exhibits and scaffolding rising up one wall. Eddie had been married to an archaeologist long enough to recognize that the treasures in this room were Roman rather than Greek. The columned front of a pale marble structure rose almost to the high ceiling. "The Market Gate of Miletus," the German remarked as he headed up a ramp and through a doorway at its center. Another barrier beyond blocked the way; he moved it.

"God, it's like I've stepped through a time portal," Eddie exclaimed as he took in his new surroundings on the far side. Roman history had given way to Arabian, the gateway through which they had come a towering blue arch topped by elaborate castellations. "What's this?"

"The Ishtar Gate," Derrick told him, replacing the barrier. "Part of the walls of Babylon. We are now in the Vorderasiatisches Museum—the Museum of the Near East."

Eddie looked down a corridor ahead, the walls of which were lined with more relics. "I'm almost glad Nina's not here," he said with a grim smile. "She'd never leave the bloody place."

"This way." Derrick brought them to a flight of stairs. The museum had now closed, Eddie realized; there were no other visitors. He went up the steps after the other man, who opened a side door and led them down a passage. "This is where we are restoring the Gigantomachy frieze."

The German showed Eddie and Rothschild into a large room. A faint smell of dust and plaster hung in the air. Lights flicked on to reveal a pair of long workbenches running across the room, upon them adjustable lamps and freestanding easels bearing photographs. Beyond the benches was a large piece of machinery that Eddie didn't recognize, though a sticker displaying the international warning symbol for a laser—a starburst at the end of a horizontal line—gave him a clue as to its function. Past that, running along both long walls, were the movable, track-mounted shelving banks of an archival storage system.

"How are the restorations going?" Rothschild asked.

"Very well. We have a new high-resolution laser scanner." Derrick rounded the benches and stopped beside the machine, opening a large semicircular shield to reveal a steel platform within. A gleaming mirror on a rotating base was mounted behind a glazed vertical slot in the scanner's casing beside it. "We can scan a piece over two meters long to a precision of less than half a millimeter. Once we have the scan, we can either send it to the milling machine"—he pointed out another piece of hardware at the room's far end—"to make a copy, or we can give it to the computer to find a match with other pieces automatically. Like a jigsaw puzzle in three dimensions," he added to the Englishman. "The computer is much faster than a human being at putting the broken pieces together."

Eddie regarded one of the easels, which held photos of various sculpture fragments. "So it's worked out that these fit together, and now you're going to rebuild 'em?"

"Yes, that is right. Of course, that does not mean that they *will* fit, only that they should. That is why we make the copies, to test them, so we do not damage the original pieces." He went to a table by the storage units, on which was a large, heavy book. "Now, let me try to find this piece."

Derrick leafed through the tome. Each page had a picture of a fragment of the frieze, along with a description, and there seemed to be several hundred pages. "Hope that thing's got an index," said Eddie.

"It could take some time," Derrick admitted. "There is a machine outside if you would like a drink."

"You want something?" Eddie asked Rothschild with a shrug.

"Coffee," she replied. "White. Two sugars."

"Hemlock or no hemlock?"

Her only reply was a scowl. Grinning, Eddie headed for the door.

. . .

He had not only returned with drinks but also finished his by the time Derrick called to his guests. "Here, see," he said, tapping at a picture.

Eddie and Rothschild joined him. The image showed a ragged-edged marble slab bearing the carved relief of a robed man with one hand held out from his side. A ruler beside it provided scale; the piece was about two feet tall and a foot wide.

"That's it?" asked the Yorkshireman.

"Yes," Derrick replied. "When I told you about the Hebrew symbols, I remembered this." He indicated a marking beside the figure, but it was too small to make out clearly. "Now I shall find it." He checked a number at the bottom of the page, then went to one of the storage units.

Rothschild put on her glasses and peered at the photo. "The sculpting is crude compared with the rest of the frieze. Where on the altar did it come from?"

"We do not know," Derrick told her. He took hold of a wheel on the end of the rack and spun it effortlessly. The shelf unit silently rolled apart from its neighbor, revealing banks of large drawers. "There are many pieces that we have not yet found a place for."

"So this might not have come from the altar at all?"

"No, no," the German insisted. "Everything was brought from the site at Pergamon. The original excavation by Carl Humann was very thorough. Ah! This is it."

He slid open a drawer. Inside was a bulky wooden box. He carefully lifted it out and brought it to one of the workbenches. "Here," he said, lifting the lid.

Eddie immediately saw that Rothschild had been right. It was obvious even to a layman like himself that the sculpture was of a far lower quality than those around the Altar of Zeus. The stone was roughly carved, even chipped in places, and the figure's face was crude and almost amateurish compared with the perfection of the Greek gods. "Looks like someone palmed it off on their apprentice. Or their kid."

"I can't imagine that it was made at the same time as the rest of the frieze," agreed Rothschild. "Where's the Hebrew symbol?"

Derrick pointed. "There."

The visitors leaned closer. Inscribed next to the standing figure was a coarse but recognizable representation of a menorah. Above it Eddie saw letters less than half an inch in height. "What does that say?"

"Some of the characters are Akkadian—not my specialty, I'm afraid," said Rothschild. "But these others are Hebrew letters, *dalet* and *kaf*—although they can also represent numbers. These would mean twenty-four."

"So this guy's the Jewish Jack Bauer?" Eddie said with a smirk.

Neither archaeologist responded to the joke, both deep in thought—and reaching the same conclusion. "The twenty-four Elders?" said Derrick.

"It could be," Rothschild replied, intrigued. "We should find out if the spot that was broken open at the Villa Torlonia had the same symbols. If it does, this might also be a marker."

"A marker for what?" asked Eddie. "One of these angels?"

"Maybe. But if it is," she went on, "we still won't be able to figure out where it's hidden unless we can identify where this piece of the frieze belongs." She turned to

Derrick. "Markus, you don't have *any* idea where it should fit?"

The German shook his head. "No. We have not yet matched it to any part of the altar."

"So maybe it *isn't* part of the altar," Eddie suggested. "Can you stand it up? Let's see the rest of it."

"There is nothing on the other sides," Derrick assured him.

"Humor me."

"What are you thinking?" Rothschild asked as the German started to lift the piece. "I know that attitude—I'd expect it from Nina." Her own attitude was not exactly approving.

"Guess I've picked up bad habits from her. But you know what one of her other bad habits is? Usually being right. About archaeology, anyway. Kids' names, not so much." A brief smile, which vanished in a flare of anger at the thought of her still being a prisoner.

That in turn hardened his resolve to do whatever it took to get her back. Derrick had by now stood the thick block on its end; Eddie took hold of it. "Wait, you should not—" the archaeologist protested, but he had already pulled it around a half turn. "This is a valuable artifact! Only museum staff are allowed to touch it."

"Report me to the boss. Oh, wait, that's you," Eddie replied, switching on the bench's lamps. "Hey, look at this."

The back of the block appeared plain. "Look at what?" said Rothschild.

Eddie ran a fingertip over the surface. Large parts felt rough to the touch, like a fine sandpaper—not at all like marble, even though it was the same color as the rest of the piece. "The front and sides are all lumpy, like the sculptor was a bit cack-handed—but this is almost flat. And it feels different."

Derrick gave it an experimental stroke with a fingertip. "He is right," he told Rothschild. "It is like . . . like a *patch*, where a flaw was repaired." His hand moved back across the blank face. "But this is too big to be a simple fix. I think . . ." He trailed off.

"You think there's something inside it?" Eddie finished for him. "Like this block's hollow—they chiseled it out, stuck the angel in the hole, then filled it in again?"

"It can't be," said Rothschild, though with some uncertainty.

Derrick bent down to scrutinize the surface. "It is possible," he admitted. "Look, here—with the light at the right angle, you can see where the repairs were made."

He withdrew, letting the woman take his place. "Yes, I see it," she said, almost reluctantly.

"If this angel's inside, we've got to get it out," Eddie said.

"And how do you suggest we do that?" demanded Rothschild.

"I know a way—worked fine last time I tried it." He hefted the lump of stone, turning as if to dash it on the floor.

Both archaeologists simultaneously shrieked, *"No!"* Derrick darted to clap his hands around it before Eddie could let go. "You cannot do that!" he yelled.

"We've got to find the angel or they'll kill Nina!" the Englishman replied.

"There are better ways than smashing it to bits!" protested Derrick. "We have an ultrasound scanner. I can see if there really is something hidden inside. If there is, then I will consider—*consider*—drilling into it. But this is a valuable piece!"

"The patch is at the back," Eddie pointed out. "Even if you open it, the bloke on the front won't be damaged. Once you work out which part of the altar it comes from, you can stick it where it belongs and nobody'll know anything happened to it. That's if it's even actually part of the altar," he added.

"The style really doesn't match any other part of the Gigantomachy," Rothschild reluctantly reminded Derrick.

The German scowled, but finally nodded. "Okay. I will use the ultrasound. But we will not damage it unless we are sure this angel is there. Agreed?"

"Agreed," said Eddie, nodding. He released his hold.

Derrick reclaimed the block with relief. He returned it to the box, then opened a cabinet and took out a piece of equipment. "Now, this will take a few minutes to set up. But we will soon see what is inside."

* * *

Outside, the rain continued to fall, spraying off a tram as it rumbled past the museum. Night had arrived, the darkness deepened by the thick clouds. A guard looked through the lobby's glass doors, glad he did not have to go out into the deluge.

He was not, he mused, even supposed to be on duty tonight. But there had been some sort of security scare, extra staff called in to keep watch. Being summoned on very short notice was inconvenient, but the overtime pay would make up for it.

The guard was about to continue his rounds when something drew his attention. The parking spaces immediately in front of the museum were reserved for buses, but whoever was driving the black van that had just arrived in a hurry clearly didn't care about such restrictions. The driver and passenger emerged, as did another four men from the vehicle's rear.

All wore peaked uniform caps, glimpses of dark clothing visible under rain capes. One was carrying what looked like a small suitcase. "Hey, I think the cops are here," the guard called to a colleague stationed at the front desk.

The older man looked up from his Sudoku puzzle. "What do they want?"

"Don't know." The six figures made their way across the bridge. "Must be something to do with this security alert."

The second guard huffed, then joined his comrade as the new arrivals reached the door. The lead cop, face hidden in shadow beneath his hat's dripping visor, rapped sharply on the glass. "Police!" he barked.

"What's going on?" asked the first guard.

"Police!" He gestured for the door to be opened.

The pair swapped looks, then the older guard unlocked the doors. "Come in, then," he said sarcastically as the cops bundled into the lobby, shaking off water. "What do you want?"

The lead cop threw back his rain cape—revealing a compact MP7 submachine gun, a bulky suppressor attached to its barrel. "Sorry, I don't speak German," said Trant as he fired.

The guard fell backward, blood spouting from three tightly spaced bullet wounds in his chest. His companion fumbled for his holstered handgun, but another man had already brought up his own MP7. A second trio of rounds tore into the younger guard's rib cage.

Trant gave both bodies a brief glance to confirm that they were dead, then marched across the lobby. "There'll be more guards. Spread out and find them." He tossed away his cap, then donned the camera headset he had worn in Rome. "We're in," he announced.

"Good," said Cross through the earpiece. "Secure the building, then find the angel."

* * *

Eddie watched as an image formed on the monitor. "God, I thought it was hard to work out what I was looking at on *Nina's* ultrasound," he said. All he could see was a shimmering gray fuzz.

"This will not give such a clear picture as a medical ultrasound," Derrick told him as he edged a pencil-like probe across the rear of the carved stone block. "Marble is hard to penetrate. But if this is hollow, we will soon know."

Rothschild looked on, fascinated. "This is a much more advanced model than anything I've seen before."

"It is German, of course," he replied, smiling. "I am not the expert, but I have used it to look for cracks and flaws inside pieces of the frieze. And . . . there *is* a flaw." He pointed at the monitor.

Eddie saw only a slightly different shade of gray. "What is it?"

"That is where someone used another material to patch a hole. It is probably marble dust mixed with pitch." He adjusted a dial. "Now we are looking deeper inside. The patch is still there; this flaw also goes deep. But . . . yes, there!"

A dark smudge appeared amid the electronic haze. "Is that a hole?" asked Eddie.

"Yes, it *is* hollow," confirmed Derrick. More movements of the probe expanded the shadowy gap in the image. He muttered in German as he tweaked the scanner's settings again and something far brighter leapt into view. "That is not stone," he said. "That is metal!"

"Metal?" echoed Rothschild. "The Gigantomachy frieze doesn't have any metal pieces, does it?"

"No, it does not."

"Then this isn't part of it," Eddie concluded. "It's like you said," he told Rothschild, "this sculpture was made by somebody else. Whoever they were, they did it to hide this angel—and they hid it inside the Throne of Satan. Maybe they liked the idea of giving the Greek gods a kick in the nuts by putting a symbol of their own religion right in the middle of them."

"That is an interesting way of putting it," said Derrick, amused, "but yes, there may be something to it." He turned his attention back to the monitor. "These white areas are definitely metal, surrounding . . . I am not sure. Pottery, perhaps, but there is something else—something very dense. Lead? I cannot tell."

"So get out the hammer and chisel," said Eddie.

He shook his head. "No, no. We have to study it, decide how to proceed—"

The Englishman's patience was wearing thin. "I *know* how to proceed. Get the bloody thing out of there! The longer we piss about arguing, the more chance the bad guys'll force Nina to tell them that it's here."

Derrick was still not convinced. "This is a priceless historical relic! There are procedures that must be followed. I shall have to—"

"The same people who kidnapped Nina kidnapped me

too," Eddie said. He indicated his bruised face. "They did this to me, and more—and they killed two people in Rome. They might kill more here. Please, open it up."

Support came from an unexpected source. "This *is* an IHA investigation, Markus," Rothschild said quietly. "It's what the agency was created to do—find and protect archaeological finds that may have global security implications."

The German put down the probe and stared at the stone block for several long seconds. "If the IHA wants to take charge," he said at last, his displeasure plain, "then the IHA can take responsibility for any damage. The German government supports the agency, so I am sure it will back you. But I will not let this fall on me, Maureen. I am sorry."

"I'll call Oswald Seretse to confirm," Rothschild told him. She took out her phone.

"While she's doing that," said Eddie, "how about you get started?"

Derrick gave him a dirty look, but stood. "I will get the tools."

* * *

"Dr. Wilde," said Cross as Norvin brought Nina into the control room. "My team has entered the Pergamon Museum in Berlin. Now: Where is the angel?"

Nina didn't reply at once, gazing in mortified sadness at the monitor screens. Several showed live headset feeds—one looking down at a uniformed man sprawled on the floor. She had no doubt at all that he was dead. "You bastards," she finally said. "You didn't need to kill anyone." She glared at Dalton, who had an unsettled expression. "You're just as guilty as he is."

"If they're worthy, they'll sit with God in heaven on the Day of Judgment." Cross turned back to the video wall. "The angel. Where will it be?"

"I have absolutely no idea," she said. "I've never been to the Pergamon Museum, and I've never studied the Altar of Zeus, so I don't know." Simeon, standing to

Cross's right, glared at her. "Really! I *don't know*. Just because I'm an archaeologist doesn't mean I have total knowledge of every artifact from every period of history."

Anna was on her leader's left. "Then what use are you, *Doctor*?" she demanded, sneering.

"Anna," Cross warned, before addressing Nina again. "You found the first angel. I'm sure you can find the second, if only to save your husband any more pain. Think! What do you know about the altar that we haven't already found out online?"

Nina blew out a frustrated breath. "I don't . . . Okay, let me think. Built in the early second century BC, surrounded by a frieze showing the war between the Olympian gods and their enemies the giants . . ."

"Giants could be a reference to the giants in Genesis," suggested Simeon. "Or the Nephilim?"

"It's not the Nephilim," Nina countered. "I've met them. Okay, not 'met'—they were long-dead—but . . . anyway, that doesn't matter," she said on seeing the questioning looks aimed at her. "The altar's been on display in Berlin for over a century. If there was anything obviously non-Greek about it, we'd already know—it would be mentioned in every piece of literature about the altar, and probably the subject of a dozen Discovery Channel specials linking it to ghosts and UFOs and Bigfoot."

"Then what about the parts that *aren't* on display?" said Dalton.

"It's still being restored, so yeah, something might have been overlooked. But I can't tell you what, because I just. Don't. *Know*. Okay?"

Cross regarded her with cold annoyance, but nodded. "All right. So where would they keep these other pieces?"

"I don't have a floor plan!" she cried. "They probably have storage and archives somewhere off-limits to the public."

He turned back to the screens. One of his men was still in the lobby, having dragged the two corpses out of sight of the main doors. "Ellison, check the security station. See if there's a plan of the building."

Ellison's camera darted around as he searched before locking on to a display board for the fire alarms. "Found it" came a voice from the speakers.

"Good. Are there any archives?"

"Second floor, there's a section marked 'Archivieren.' I think that means archives?"

Cross glanced at Anna, who nodded. "Okay, that's where we'll start the search. Trant, leave two men to cover the entrances and get the rest up there." The various monitors broke into dizzying motion. "Dr. Wilde, if you see anything, tell me immediately. Or—"

"Or you'll torture Eddie—yes, I know." Defeated, all Nina could do was watch as Cross's men moved through the museum.

* * *

Eddie peered over Derrick's shoulder as the archaeologist worked. Breaking into the hidden cavity inside the stone block had not taken long; the substance used to seal the hole was relatively fragile, splitting after just a few taps with a small chisel. Once the first crack had appeared, Derrick's reluctance to damage the artifact quickly gave way to professional curiosity about what was hidden inside.

"Careful," warned Rothschild as the German made his final delicate strikes.

"I know what I am doing," he replied testily. Eddie smiled at her getting a taste of her own medicine, then watched as Derrick gently used the chisel's tip to lever the freed section upward.

The interior was revealed beneath, light reflecting dully off copper.

"There is definitely something inside," he announced with rising excitement. He lifted the piece away.

"So that's an angel, is it?" said Eddie, gazing at what lay within.

The figure had the body of a man but the head of an eagle, several metal wings wrapped tightly around its torso. It fit the space inside the block almost perfectly, the gaps filled by fine dry sand to act as a cushion. Whoever had concealed it had also wanted to protect it.

Rothschild adjusted one of the lamps. "There's some text on the body. It looks like Akkadian."

"Will you be able to translate it?" Eddie asked.

"I can, of course," said Derrick. "It is hardly Linear A!" He and Rothschild shared a chuckle.

"Archaeology jokes, always hilarious," said the Englishman, straight-faced. "But it *is* an angel, right?"

"I think so," Rothschild replied. "Although by the letter of Revelation, the eagle head would actually make it one of the 'living creatures'—or 'beasts,' depending which translation of the Bible you choose—before God's throne. They summoned and released the four horsemen."

"What, as in the horsemen of the apocalypse?"

"Yes, although they're never called that in Revelation. Markus, can you get it out of there?"

Derrick blew sand off the figure and lifted it from its resting place. "It is very heavy," he noted, surprised. He set it down on the table. "Hmm. The wings, they seem to have been pressed into the clay before it was fired. But they are only thin; I wonder how they kept them from melting? Perhaps—"

A loud bang echoed down the corridor outside. Eddie's head snapped up. "What was that?"

"It is just the security guards," Derrick replied. "But they know they are not supposed to slam the doors—the vibrations can damage the exhibits." He stood at another *thump*. "I will talk to them."

Eddie and Rothschild looked back at the statue as he crossed the room. "I must admit," said the elderly woman, "I honestly didn't believe anything would come of this. Revelation is open to a great deal of interpretation, to put it mildly. But whoever kidnapped Nina was right about where to look."

"And now they're making her tell them what to look for," Eddie reminded her grimly. "But we beat 'em to this. If I can persuade your friend to let me use it to get her back ..." He glanced at Derrick as the German reached the door—

Someone outside kicked it open.

Derrick staggered back. A man dressed in black burst into the room—a submachine gun in his hands, laser sight dancing over its targets.

14

"Nobody move!" the intruder yelled.

Eddie's first instinct was to grab Rothschild and duck behind the workbench, but the laser spot had already locked on to his chest—

Derrick reeled back in front of the gunman. "*Was ist—*"

The man in black's finger tightened on the trigger— then, at a command through his headset loud enough for Eddie to hear, he changed his attack to a physical blow, striking the German's head with his weapon. Derrick crumpled to the floor.

Eddie shoved the fear-frozen Rothschild down, then grabbed the angel and dived after her as the man spun back toward him—

Bullets ripped into the workbench, cracking off the stone block, which exploded into pieces. Rothschild shrieked as fragments rained down on them. "For fuck's sake!" Eddie cried. "Just once, just fucking *once*, I'd like to find the thing and get out *before* the bad guys turn up!"

Running footsteps from outside—the attacker was not alone. Someone shouted an order as three more men rushed through the doorway. Eddie looked around. There was another exit at the room's far end, but they would never reach it before being cut down.

Trapped.

Unless—

Eddie felt the weight of the statue—and realized he had one chance of survival. "Any closer an' I'll smash your fucking angel!" he yelled.

The sounds of movement stopped abruptly, replaced by muttered discussion. Eddie shuffled backward to take shelter behind the laser scanner. He raised his head just enough to see that the nearest gunman had a compact camera—night-vision, from the LED illuminator beneath the lens—mounted on a headset. Somebody was observing the operation. The mysterious Prophet?

Whoever it was, he had Nina. "All right," said Eddie loudly, the thought of his wife strengthening his resolve, "Everyone put down your guns. Otherwise bird-face here gets his wings clipped."

Another brief exchange, the first gunman responding to a message over his headset; then, with his gun still in one hand, he reached into a belt pouch and pulled out a gas mask. "Okay, not quite what I was hoping for . . . ," Eddie muttered in dismay as he donned it.

The other men followed suit. "Mr. Chase!" called one, voice muffled by the mask's filters. "If you break the angel, it'll release a deadly gas. You'll die, but we'll be safe."

"You still won't get what you're after!" Eddie shouted back.

"Yes we will! The Prophet *wants* to release the angel. He'd rather not do it here, but if it's the will of God that it happens, then it happens."

"Bollocks! You're bluffing."

"Then smash it, Mr. Chase. You'll see. For your last few seconds on earth. Ellison, move in."

"Shit," Eddie hissed. His own bluff had been called—and now the first gunman was advancing again, his suppressed MP7 raised.

* * *

Nina stared at the screen, elation rapidly overcome by terror. Eddie had somehow escaped from his torturers—only to fall back into the hands of their collaborators. The lead gunman, Ellison, moved through the room, his camera picking out Eddie hunched behind a large piece of equipment.

"They're not in full MOPP gear," Anna warned Cross. "If he drops the angel—"

"I know," the cult leader replied. That told Nina that he wasn't as blasé about the angel's destruction as Trant had informed Eddie, but her husband was still in grave danger.

Ellison rounded a large workbench. Nina glimpsed someone else hiding behind it at the edge of the screen, but he continued to advance. His gun rose into the frame, its laser spot a dazzling flare as it fixed on the Englishman—

"Ellison, wait," said Cross sharply. "I don't want the angel damaged if we can help it." He turned toward Nina. "Remind him that we have his wife!"

* * *

Eddie tensed, retreating farther behind the open scanner as Ellison drew level with the tracked shelves. He would have a clear line of fire within seconds . . .

Ellison suddenly stopped, head tipping quizzically as he listened to another order via his headset. He looked back at the other intruders for confirmation. "Do it," said the leader.

"We've got your wife," the gunman called to Eddie. "Give up the angel and she won't get hurt."

They weren't willing to let the statue be destroyed, then. That gave him an edge, however small. "Let me talk to her," he replied. "To prove you've got her."

Another brief exchange through the earpiece, then Ellison took off the headset and held it out as he edged closer. Eddie warily watched the other armed men as he shifted the statue to his left hand. All were alert, staring back at him, but while their guns were up, their forefingers were off the triggers. They were obeying the order to let him talk to Nina . . . but it would only take them a fraction of a second to fire.

He had to make the fullest possible use of that moment.

Impatient, Ellison twitched the headset to prompt Eddie to take it. Eddie raised his left hand to make it clear that the statue would be dropped if anything happened to him, then reached out with his right. Ellison leaned closer—

Eddie lunged—grabbing not the proffered gadget but the hand holding it. He bent the other man's fingers backward, hard, as he yanked him nearer. Ellison's little finger snapped at its first joint.

His scream of pain jolted his comrades into life, laser sights flashing onto their target. But Eddie had already pulled Ellison to him, turning the gunman into a human shield.

His prisoner overcame his initial shock and tried to slam an elbow into Eddie's chest, but the Englishman easily absorbed the blow and savagely wrenched the broken finger around by almost ninety degrees. Ellison let out a bloodcurdling shriek. "All right, let's try this again!" Eddie shouted. "Guns down, back off, all the rest."

The other attackers briefly remained still, but instructions soon came over their radios. They spread out to round the first workbench, keeping their guns fixed on the whimpering Ellison, ready to shoot the man behind him the moment they had the chance . . .

Rothschild's eyes were still closed—

"Oi! Prof!" Eddie called to Rothschild, still curled behind the second bench. "Can you catch?"

"Wh-what?" she asked, blinking up at him.

"Can you catch this?" He waved the statue.

"I . . . I don't know. I can try."

"Good, 'cause here it comes!" He lobbed it at her.

She gasped, flinging out both arms to catch it—more by luck than judgment, as her eyes were squeezed tightly shut.

Trant and the other masked men flinched, but when it became clear the statue had survived, they resumed their advance, MP7s raised and locked as Eddie backed behind the scanner. They would soon reach Rothschild—and the angel.

He stabbed the button.

The scanner hummed—and a swath of brilliant green light lanced from the laser.

The intruders instantly fell into disarray as the dazzling beam overpowered their optic nerves. Eddie took advantage, slamming Ellison face-first against the shelves, then shoving the stunned gunman's head into the gap between two of the storage units and spinning the nearest wheel.

The units rolled smoothly along their tracks—and a splintering crunch came from the shrinking space between them as Ellison's skull suddenly became a few inches narrower.

The laser continued its sweep, but even blinded, most of the attackers had dropped into cover. One man was still standing, though, reeling with a hand over his eyes—

Eddie grabbed Ellison's gun and felled the man with a three-round burst, then hurried to Rothschild and pulled her to her feet. "Come on!"

He directed her past the scanner to the second exit. "My God!" she shrilled, opening her eyes to see Ellison's limp corpse slumped between the shelves.

"Don't look at it, just get to the door. And keep hold of the angel!" He backed up behind her with his gun ready.

Nobody poked their head above the workbenches. Rothschild opened the door, Eddie following her into a corridor. "Which way?" she cried.

He spotted a green sign, an arrow beside a running stick-man. "There!" They ran to the emergency exit as furious orders were shouted behind them.

Eddie kicked the door open to find a narrow stairwell. He descended two at a time. "What about Markus?" Rothschild wailed.

"They just knocked him down. He'll be okay," Eddie replied, hoping he was right.

He reached the foot of the steps and barged through another door to find himself back in the museum proper. They were in the long hallway he had seen earlier, the walls decorated with gleaming tiles displaying paintings of stalking lions. At its far end he recognized the Ishtar Gate, but his only concern now was getting out of the building. The gunmen had made no attempt at stealth; that meant the museum's security staff were either prisoners or dead, and after what had happened in Rome, more likely the latter.

The restoration work had blocked off the nearest apparent exit, but he spotted another emergency evacuation sign. "Down here," he told Rothschild, going right at a run. Past the stairs they had ascended with Derrick was the marked door. "Okay, through this," Eddie said as he reached it—

He flinched back as if the handle were electrified, hearing noises beyond, getting closer. Not all of the Prophet's men had gone to the upper floor. "Or not," he amended, rushing to a smaller door across the corridor only to find it locked. The only way out was through the Ishtar Gate. "Hurry up!"

"I'm sixty-seven years old!" gasped Rothschild. "I can't go any faster!"

"You'll have to if you want to be sixty-eight!" He reached the great arch, throwing aside the barrier and charging through.

They emerged from the Miletus Gate on the other side. Eddie looked back as another black-clad gunman burst through the emergency exit. A moment later, Trant appeared from the stairwell, his surviving companion behind him. The Englishman fired another three-round burst to force them into cover, then caught up with Rothschild as she reached the doors to the room containing the Altar of Zeus.

Nobody was waiting for them in the cavernous space. The entrance through which Derrick had brought them was in the center of the long wall to the left, facing the temple. He glanced at Rothschild as they ran toward it. The old woman still held the statue, and despite her heavy breathing was maintaining her pace—fear was a great driver. They might get out alive after all—

A shadow stabbed along the floor from beyond the glass doors.

"Shit!" Eddie cried, pulling back and firing a wild burst as a man appeared at the entrance. One of the doors exploded into fragments, the gunman hurriedly jerking back.

Shouts from behind. Trant and the others were in the Roman room, cutting them off, and if they tried to reach the other exit in the far wall, the man at the shattered door would have a clear shot—

"Up there!" yelled Eddie, swinging Rothschild toward the towering altar.

"There's no way out!" she protested.

"I bloody know!" They reached the broad marble steps. "Set off the fire alarm—I'll try to hold 'em off until the cops arrive!" He turned, trying to cover both the entrances from which their enemies would come.

The man at the glass door leaned into view. Eddie loosed another burst. All three rounds went wide, smacking against the wall, but it forced the gunman to retreat. The Englishman reached the top of the stairs and darted behind a column. Rothschild still had several steps to go. "Quick! Get—"

Trant appeared at the other entrance, firing wildly on full auto.

Bullets ripped into the marble stairs, a line of dust-spitting impacts chasing after Rothschild. Splinters hit her legs. She screamed and tripped just short of the top. The statue was jolted from her grip—and rolled back down the steps, loud *clunk*s echoing around the room.

Trant had taken off his gas mask; his expression was a flash of pure panic as he watched the angel's clattering descent. "Back, get back!"

Eddie also watched the stone figure with alarm. The

attackers' fear confirmed that they hadn't been lying about the danger . . .

Clunk, clunk—and the angel finally reached the floor, skittering across the polished wood before coming to a halt. For a moment, all eyes were upon it, tension rising . . . then Trant spoke. "It's safe! I'm gonna get it— cover me!"

Gun raised, Eddie whipped around the pillar—but he held his fire, conflicted. The doorway was a choke point, meaning he might be able to hold the gunmen back while he made a desperate run for the angel . . . but doing so would leave Rothschild unprotected in the open.

His indecision lasted only a split second, but that was enough for Trant to run into the great hall—and for the two men with him to aim up at the altar from the doorway.

Eddie grabbed Rothschild and dived with her over the top of the stairs as they opened fire. Chunks of pale stone exploded from the columns, ricochets twanging and screaming across the room. "Jesus!" he gasped.

"I've got it!" Trant shouted. "Get to the sluice channel!"

More guns blazed with suppressing fire as the others followed their leader. Eddie crawled to cover Rothschild as debris pummeled them, then raised his gun to catch anyone climbing the stairs to finish off the two fugitives . . .

Nobody came for them. The gunfire stopped. Eddie waited for a moment, then cautiously lifted his head. There was no one below—and the statue had gone. "Shit!" he growled, standing.

"What's happening?" Rothschild asked plaintively.

"They've got the angel. Stay there." He raced down the steps and went to the glass doors. Nobody was in sight, though he heard a door bang from the direction of the lobby.

He ran after them. They would be heading for a getaway vehicle; if he caught up, he might be able to shoot the driver or a tire, or at the very least get its license plate for the police.

He reached the lobby. No rear guard—the gunmen were in a hurry to escape with their prize. He went to the main doors, spotting a couple of corpses behind the security station. The rain was still streaking down outside, a large black van parked in front of the bridge.

The raiders weren't in it. They had instead gone to the bridge's side, climbing onto its wall . . . and jumping off.

Eddie barreled into the open just as the last man dropped out of sight. The roar of engines came from the waterway below. Rather than risk being hemmed in on Berlin's roads, the raiders were making their getaway by boat along the Spree, the river bisecting the city. He ran to the wall, seeing the lead craft with Trant and two others aboard already powering away under a railway bridge to the northwest. Another picked up speed behind it, a man in the backseat sealing the angel inside a case—

The Englishman flicked the MP7 to full auto and unleashed a long burst after the trailing speedboat. The man flailed and fell over the side, but then the compact weapon's magazine ran dry. "Fuck!" Eddie roared, watching helplessly as the two craft surged away into the darkness with their prize.

"Eddie!" He looked back to see Rothschild hurrying toward him.

"I told you to stay put!"

"I know where they're going! That man told the others to get to the sluice channel—he means the *Schleusenkanal,* along the river. We passed it on the way from the airport."

"They must have a car waiting," Eddie realized. Using the river would make it easy for the robbers to evade pursuit, and once they reached their rendezvous, they could quickly reach Tegel and leave the country. "You know how to get there?"

"Yes, but—"

"Okay, come on. We might be able to catch 'em." He ran to the street. Rothschild hesitated, then followed.

He guessed that the van belonged to the raiders, but doubted that the driver had left the keys in the ignition. Besides, the boats were doing at least forty miles per hour; he needed something much faster . . .

"And there it is," he said as he saw the very thing approaching.

A sleek silver Porsche 911 was cruising through the rain. Eddie ran out into its path, waving his arms. The driver swerved to go around him—then jammed on the brakes as Eddie pointed the gun at his car. *"Achtung!"* shouted the Englishman. "Outta ze *Auto*!"

The middle-aged man might have been confused by the words, but he couldn't mistake the message. He scrambled out, hands up as he stared in fear at the man marching toward him.

"Here, present for you," said Eddie, handing the weapon to the startled driver. "Prof, get in!"

Rothschild ran to the Porsche. Its owner looked in confusion between his car and the gun, then took a couple of panicked steps backward and pointed the MP7 at the Yorkshireman. "You—you are not taking my car!"

"It's empty, you dozy twat," Eddie replied. The driver gawped at him. "I'll try not to smash your Porsche to fuck, but if anything happens, send the bill to Oswald Seretse at the United Nations in New York. Okay?"

"Oswald Seretse," the German replied slowly. "Okay. Yes."

"Great. Thanks!" Eddie dropped into the bucket seat and slammed the door. Rothschild swung herself awkwardly into the passenger seat beside him. "All right, never driven one of these before. Hope *Top Gear* was exaggerating about how hard they are to control!"

He depressed the clutch, slotted the gear stick into first, then rocketed into the night at the head of a huge trail of spray.

15

Even from a wet standing start, the speedometer needle surged past ninety in mere seconds. "Whoa, bloody hell!" Eddie cried, struggling to hold the Porsche in a straight line as the wheel squirmed in his hands. "Guess this one's a turbo."

Rothschild clutched the door handle with one hand and the center console with the other, fingernails digging into both like claws. "Oh my God!" she screamed. "Slow down, slow down!"

"I'm chasing them—going fast is the whole fucking point!" The one-way street became two-way at a junction. He swung to avoid the flaring headlights of an oncoming car, then slammed the power back on to whip around another vehicle ahead. The road ran along the riverbank, the long façade of another museum rising across the water to the right. "Can you see them?"

"Not yet—and what exactly are you planning to do? They're in boats, we're in a car! And you don't have a gun anymore; how are you going to stop them?"

"Not a clue. But if they get away with the angel, I've got no chance of finding Nina. So that's not going to happen, whatever I have to fucking do." The clenched fury behind his words deterred her from asking further questions.

The channel curved, the road following it. "There!" Eddie said, spotting churning wakes on the dark water. As the Spree widened, the boats had moved out into its center. The Porsche was gaining rapidly, but as Rothschild had pointed out, there was no way of reaching them. "This sluice canal—how far away is it?"

"Four or five—Ah!" She gasped in fright as the Porsche swerved to overtake another car. "Four or five miles," she concluded, her voice noticeably higher in pitch.

"We should be able to beat 'em there, but . . ."

"But what?"

"Exactly. They've got guns, and we don't. And the rate they're going, they'll still arrive before the cops sort themselves out, especially as we haven't even *called* the cops yet!"

"I'm sure the poor man whose car you stole will have done that by now."

"Yeah, which means they'll be chasing *us,* not the bad guys! Shit, and Derrick needs an ambulance an' all," he remembered. "Why didn't you stay and help him? He's your friend!"

Rothschild bristled. "You told me he'd be all right! And if I hadn't come with you, you wouldn't have known where they were going. They've stolen a priceless artifact—we can't let them get away with it."

"Fuck's sake," Eddie muttered. "You're as bad as Nina!"

Ahead, the boats went under a bridge. "Which way?" he demanded. "Stay on this side or go across?"

"I don't know!" she protested. An intersection was coming up fast, a long tram trundling toward the bridge blocking their view of what lay beyond. "I . . . This side, stay on this side!"

Eddie jammed the wheel to the left, stabbing at the brakes to send the Porsche around the tram's rear. He felt the car's heavy back end threaten to snap out on the wet road; even with decades of development and technological aids, the 911's rear-mounted engine was still a trap for the unprepared driver. A punch of adrenaline as he caught the slide, then straightened—only for the headlights to reveal that the road along the river was blocked by building work, signs warning that it was for pedestrians only. "Shit!"

He braked hard, debating what to do. The sight of the boats pulling away made his mind up in an instant. He accelerated again, sounding the horn as he plowed through the signs and traffic cones.

"No, no, oh my *God*!" Rothschild wailed. Shocked Berliners dived out of the way, one man vaulting the railing and hanging above the edge of the Spree as the 911 thundered past. "You're going to *kill* someone!"

"You bloody told me to go this way!"

"I haven't lived in Berlin for forty years! It's changed a lot!"

Eddie shot her an angry glare, then returned his full attention to negotiating the waterfront. The Porsche's left flank clipped a couple of construction barriers as he jinked to avoid a dumbfounded young couple, then its right side took a greater pounding as the Englishman was forced to grind against the metal railings along the river to dodge an oblivious headphone-wearing man. Rothschild shrieked as sparks flew past her window.

The construction zone ended just before the street passed under a large bridge, a train rumbling over the Spree above the boats. Eddie crashed through more barriers back onto the road and shot across an intersection— only to realize he was now going the wrong way down a one-way street. "Jesus!" he gasped, flinging the car onto the curb as a truck rushed at him. His passenger closed her eyes in terror.

He dropped back onto the street with a bang. Even with all the obstacles, they were still gaining on the boats. Eddie had no idea what he was going to do when he caught up with them, but as long as he could keep them in sight, he had a chance of recovering the angel, and bargaining for Nina's release—

He dodged an oncoming car—and saw a new problem ahead.

A road bridge crossed the Spree on the right. Ahead, the street continued along the river—but it was barricaded, steel pillars allowing pedestrians and cyclists through while blocking cars. "Which way?" he shouted. Rothschild's eyes remained firmly squeezed shut. "Oi! Prof! Which fucking way do we go? Do I cross the bridge?"

She risked a look. "No, it'll take you away from the river." With no other options, Eddie flung the Porsche into a slithering left turn. "And don't you dare swear at me again!"

"Then bloody help me!" he snarled back. The new street was also leading him away from the Spree. "How do we catch up with the boats?"

"If you can get onto 17th June Street, you'll be able to get back to the river."

"Where's that?"

"The long road through the park that we came down when we arrived." She looked at the modern apartment buildings around them. "I don't recognize where we are. If you can find the Reichstag, I can direct you from there. Go right!"

The next road in that direction was another one-way street, two cars at traffic lights blocking it, with more bollards preventing Eddie from taking to the pavement. "Have to try this next one," he said, peering ahead. The Porsche rapidly closed the distance to an intersection with a broad boulevard. More traffic waited at the lights; he pulled into the wrong lane to overtake. "Okay, hold on!"

Rothschild flinched as her memory finally caught up with the speeding car. "No, wait!" she cried, but Eddie had already hurled the 911 into another wildly fishtailing turn—onto the broad pedestrian plaza leading to the Brandenburg Gate.

Even on a rainy night, there were still plenty of tourists milling around the Pariser Platz, forcing him to resume his symphony on the horn as he swerved to avoid knots of people and dawdling bicycle rickshaws. Making matters worse were the numerous uniformed men and women around the square's periphery; it was home to both the French and American embassies, ensuring the constant presence of the Berlin police. "Like we weren't in enough bloody trouble already!" he complained as the cops ran to try to block him.

"They have guns!" Rothschild said in alarm. "Perhaps we should—"

"We're not stopping," Eddie growled. He fixed his gaze on the illuminated arch of the Brandenburg Gate at the plaza's far end and dropped down the gears, foot to the floor.

The Porsche's acceleration punched them back into the seats. Eddie's continuous shrilling of the horn finally had an effect, the tourists clearing the 911's path as it raced toward the central archway. He saw a cop beside the monument draw his gun, but was now committed. "Duck!" he warned Rothschild.

The car blasted through the gate at over seventy miles per hour, emerging on a wide semicircular plaza. A single gunshot cracked after it, but the bullet glanced off the Porsche's sloping rear. Rothschild squealed at the impact. "They're *shooting* at us!"

"Welcome to my bloody life!" Eddie responded as he rounded another stand of bicycle rickshaws and brought the 911 thumping back down onto asphalt. He now knew where he was, seeing the long tree-lined avenue receding ahead. "How do we get back to the river?"

She reluctantly peered over the dashboard as the Porsche began its sprint down 17th June Street. "Go to the Victory Column," she said, pointing at the distant floodlit statue. "Then back over the bridge we took this afternoon. Will we be ahead of them?"

The speedometer needle surged upward, Eddie weaving across all three westbound lanes through the traffic. "Damn well better be."

Rothschild pushed herself back upright. "Why are you so angry with me? If I wasn't helping you, you wouldn't be able to follow those boats at all. You wouldn't even have known to come to Berlin!"

"I'm mad because you dropped the bloody statue," he

said. "I had to save you rather than get the angel—and if I don't have the angel, I've got no way of finding Nina!"

"You don't even like me! And I know Nina certainly doesn't. I'm surprised you didn't go after the angel instead."

"Don't think I wasn't bloody tempted."

"Then why didn't you?"

"Because . . . because I couldn't let another innocent person die for getting mixed up in our lives," he admitted. "Speaking of which, shut up and let me try to drive without killing anyone!" Rothschild fell silent, but her surprise at his revelation was clear.

The speeding Porsche ate up the distance to the Victory Column in well under a minute. Eddie made a last jink around a bus before flinging the car into a power slide through the roundabout. Other vehicles skidded in panic around him, but he was already clear and racing up the next avenue.

A few more lunges around slower-moving cars and he saw the bridge ahead. He braked hard, bringing the Porsche down to an almost legal speed as he reached the crossing. Railings ran along its sides, giving him a view of the river below—

Movement on the water to his right. Both boats came into sight, still holding course along the center of the channel. He had beaten them here, but now what? "How far to this sluice canal?" he asked.

"Still two or three miles," Rothschild replied.

Eddie swore under his breath. He remembered the roads ahead from his journey into the city, and knew he wouldn't be able to go nearly as quickly as through the park. He needed a new plan, fast.

The boats would pass under the bridge in about twenty seconds. He stopped the car, staring at them, judging their courses . . . "Get out! Now!"

The elderly woman opened her mouth to protest, but Eddie's expression warned her that it was in her best interests to obey. She clambered out. He waited until she was clear, then slotted the 911 into reverse and pulled hard on the wheel as he depressed the accelerator.

The Porsche swung backward through ninety degrees to block the oncoming lane, a couple of cars skidding to a standstill. Eddie ignored the blare of horns, his eyes fixed on the approaching boats. The second, carrying two men and the angel, was still lagging behind the leader, off to one side to stay clear of its wake.

He drummed his fingers on the steering wheel, bracing himself—then put the car into gear and stamped on the accelerator.

The 911 leapt forward, all four wheels clawing for grip on the wet road. Rothschild clapped her hands to her face in shock as it sprang over the curb, hit the railing—

And smashed through, arcing down toward the water as the first boat raced by.

Eddie was hurled forward in his seat as the car's nose hit the water—only to be brought to an equally abrupt halt as the air bag fired. The 911 floated almost vertically for the briefest moment, then the weight of the engine slammed its tail down into the river.

The air bag had already deflated. Eddie dizzily opened his eyes as water gushed into the cabin—to see the second boat racing straight at him, its shocked driver unable to change course in time—

The speedboat's keel hit the Porsche's hood, flinging it upward over the windshield and roof as if jumping a ramp. It left the water, lancing at the bridge . . .

And slammed into the arched girders beneath the crossing.

The men aboard were thrown headlong against the unyielding steel, blood raining down over the churning waters below. The boat's mangled remains dropped back into the Spree, its prow crushed like an eggshell.

The Porsche had fared little better. Its windshield had shattered as the craft ran over it, an explosive wave rushing in. Eddie choked and gasped, pinned in his seat by the weight of water.

The torrent finally eased as the cabin was completely

filled, but now the Yorkshireman faced a new threat as cold hit him like a train. The temperature of the Spree on this miserable night was barely above freezing. He fought through the initial shock and clawed for the broken windshield's frame. The Porsche was dropping backward into the dark depths; he kicked free of the jellyfish mass of the expended air bag and squirmed upward through the opening. A dull boom from below told him that the car had hit bottom, bubbles surging past him. He followed them to the surface.

He breached the waves, gasping as cold air hit his wet skin, and looked around. The wrecked boat was floating beneath the bridge. Pieces of bodies bobbed around it. Someone on the bridge shouted in German. He tipped his head back painfully to see people staring down over the railings.

Eddie started swimming—not for the shore, but the boat. An echoing engine note warned that the first speedboat was slowing and coming around. A crushed and bloodied face sprang at him from the lapping waves; he shoved the corpse aside, searching in the low light for the destroyed vessel's cargo.

A case floated nearby—the one containing the angel. He grabbed it, then swam for the river's north bank, seeing a flight of concrete steps leading up from the water.

The engine noise grew louder, angrier. The first boat was racing back toward him. Onlookers above urged him on, but he ignored them, expecting gunfire at any moment.

He reached the steps and scrambled up them, cold water streaming from his clothes. Running footsteps; he turned to see a Berliner hurrying along the footpath— and on the river, the boat arriving, Trant standing up—

"Down, get down!" he yelled, diving flat. The man on the footpath hesitated, needing a moment to translate the warning.

The tiny delay cost him his life. A submachine gun roared from beneath the bridge, Trant having removed the suppressor before spraying the bank with bullets.

The running man took several to his torso and tumbled to the ground.

Screams came from the bridge, the onlookers fleeing. Still clutching the case, Eddie rolled clear of the river's edge, then jumped up and ran. Another burst of fire slashed through the air behind him.

He hared up a second set of steps to street level, finding himself at an intersection on the bridge's northern side. Concrete apartment blocks lined the waterfront, no shelter in sight among the tightly packed buildings. Instead he cut diagonally across the main road from the bridge, spotting an alley between more drab, graffiti-spattered towers.

The gunfire had cleared the streets with shocking speed, cars peeling away. A loud *thump* came from the river as the second speedboat bashed against the bank. More shouts, these in English. "Get after him!"

Muscles aching from exertion and exposure, Eddie reached the alley, glancing back to see Trant and his two companions pounding up the second flight of steps. The leader saw him and whipped up his MP7, but the Englishman ran between the buildings before he could fire.

At the alley's end was a square within a complex of apartment blocks, trees standing over a little park. Bushes and hedges dotted the lawns, a brick-and-concrete spiral at the center some sort of children's play area.

The nearest way out was diagonally opposite where he had entered—too far for him to reach before his pursuers entered the square. They would have a clear shot at his back. The only visible entrance to any of the buildings was just as distant.

"Shit," he gasped, searching desperately for a hiding place—and finding none.

16

Trant led his two remaining men, Overton and Whelan, at a sprint down the alley. They reached the end of the passage, guns raised—but there was no sign of their target, just rain drenching a dimly lit garden area. The only apparent exits were a door into one of the apartment buildings and a gap between two blocks to the north. Trant knew his quarry couldn't have reached either in the short time he had been out of sight. That meant . . .

"He's still here," he warned his companions. "Find him."

"Careful," said Simeon through his headset. "This guy's a pro."

Sirens wailed in the distance. "Cops coming," said Overton.

"We've got a minute or two," Trant replied. "Move fast." He directed Overton to the left and Whelan into the center of the small park, then angled right toward the gap.

A line of hedges, reaching to his thighs, ran along a lawn's edge. Trant readied his gun, then hurdled it.

Nobody there. He checked behind a nearby tree with

the same lack of result. "Clear here," he announced, continuing across the grass.

Overton followed a path into the garden, checking behind the hedges and bushes. No sign of the Englishman, or the case containing the angel. He moved under a large tree, glad of the brief respite from the downpour. The speedboat's driver was cold and thoroughly damp despite his rain cape. "Anything?" he whispered, peering into the shadows. He had not gone into the museum, so his headset had not needed a camera—something he was now regretting, as those observing at the Mission could have warned him if the Brit was skulking in the darkness.

"Not yet," Whelan reported.

"Me neither. Pick up the pace," ordered Trant.

Overton continued under the trees. He glanced to his right to see Whelan investigating another patch of bushes, while beyond him Trant checked behind a low brick wall. Their quarry was still nowhere to be seen. He kept going, scanning ahead.

Something caught his eye, a low, blocky shape among some plants.

The case. He started toward it, about to alert the others—when water streamed over him from above.

Overton hesitated. He was still under a tree, so the foliage must have thinned out. Or—

*　*　*

The other explanation hit him at the same time as Eddie did.

The sodden Yorkshireman had climbed up onto one of the lower branches, hoping simply to stay out of sight, but when the black-clad man passed almost directly beneath him, he knew he couldn't miss the opportunity. He dropped on top of him, smashing his elbow down hard against the back of his skull and slamming him face-first to the ground.

The American went limp beneath him. Taking no chances, Eddie grabbed his hair and yanked his head up before driving a vicious knuckle-punch into his exposed throat. Cartilage crunched. The man spasmed, faint choking noises from his gaping mouth barely audible over the hiss of the rain.

Eddie rose to a crouch, searching for his pursuer's MP7—only to realize that the man had landed on top of it. He was about to roll him away when some instinct made him check on the positions of the other raiders—

The nearest turned toward him.

* * *

Nina realized she was breathing heavily as she watched events in Germany play out on the video wall, Trant investigating the park's far end while Whelan searched its center. The latter had just reached an open paved area containing benches, night vision turning the rainy gloom as bright as day. He turned his head, the view panning back in Overton's direction—

"Whelan, stop!" Cross shouted. The image stabilized. "There, under the tree—there's something on the grass."

Simeon stepped closer to the monitors, trying to make out the crumpled shape. "Is that a man?"

"It's Overton," said Cross grimly. "Trant! Man down, south end of the park." The other screens blurred as the team leader whipped around.

"What's going on?" said Dalton, agitated. "Is he *dead*?"

"Don't screw with my husband," Nina said quietly.

Whelan moved cautiously toward the slumped figure. "It's definitely Overton," he said, his camera darting from side to side as he scanned the park. Nothing moved except the falling rain.

"Whelan, look to your right," ordered Cross. "There's something in that flower bed—there!"

The screens revealed a blocky shape in the undergrowth. "It's the case," said Anna.

"It's open," Cross growled. "Check it out, but be careful. He's around there somewhere."

"Cops are getting closer," said Trant as he headed in a crouch back along the edge of the park. Sirens became audible over the background noise.

Whelan reached Overton. He nudged the motionless figure with a foot, then crossed the grass to the case and reached down to raise the half-open lid . . .

A dull *thump* came over the speakers.

"What was that?" said Cross, but Whelan was already turning to find the source. The camera fixed upon something on the wet grass—an object that had not been there seconds earlier.

"It's the angel!" exclaimed Dalton.

The stone figure lay on its side, raindrops bursting against the metal and clay. "It's intact," Whelan said, relieved.

Sudden realization made Cross sit bolt upright as Whelan went to retrieve the statue. "No, wait, it's a decoy—check behind you!" he cried—

The image whipped around through 180 degrees with a sickening snap of bone. Then the monitors filled with an extreme close-up . . . of Eddie Chase.

He released his neck-breaking hold. The camera flopped, looking down Whelan's back. Then Eddie stepped away and the dead man crumpled to the ground.

"*Definitely* don't screw with my husband," said Nina.

Simeon and Anna both shot her angry looks, but Cross remained focused on the view from the remaining camera. Trant had reacted to his warning by dropping behind a hedge. He peered warily over it to see Eddie crouched by Whelan's corpse, collecting his MP7 before picking up the statue.

"Careful," snapped Cross into his headset as Trant's own gun rose into the camera's field of view and lined up on the Englishman's back. "You might hit the angel. Move in closer."

The team leader sidestepped along the hedge to a gap, then began a cautious, measured advance. "No, wait," said Nina in alarm. Eddie still had his back to Trant, the angel under one arm as he cleaned mud off the weapon. "Don't kill him!"

"Too late for that now," snarled Simeon.

She rushed to the cult leader's side. "If you kill him, I'll never help you find the last angel!"

"You will," Cross replied, his cold certainty far more menacing than any of Simeon's threats.

Nina looked back in desperation at the monitors. Trant was now directly behind Eddie, closing with each step. The MP7 was fixed on the Englishman's back.

"Aim for the head," said Cross. The gun's muzzle rose slightly. "Ready—"

Nina snatched the headset off him—and jammed its microphone against the earpiece. Trant flinched at a squall of nerve-scraping feedback—

Eddie heard the shriek from the other man's headphones and spun, firing a burst from his MP7 squarely into the cultist's chest.

The camera's view blurred as Trant was flung backward, ending up pointing skyward. The image rippled as rain landed on it.

Dalton gawped at the screens. "What just happened?"

"Eddie just happened," said Nina with triumph, even as Simeon hauled her away from Cross.

The cult leader jumped up, facing her with an expression of rage, but before he could speak, a voice boomed from the speakers. "Ay up. You at the other end of this camera—can you hear me?"

Eddie reappeared, pulling the headset from the dead man and peering into the lens. "Anyone there?" he asked, tapping the microphone with a loud *whump*. "Come on, speak up."

"Eddie, I'm here!" Nina shouted into the headset before Simeon snatched it from her.

The Englishman's face broke into a strained smile. "Nina! Thank God."

"Mr. Chase!" said Cross as he put the headset back on. "Can you hear me?"

Eddie frowned. "Who's that? You this Prophet bloke?"

"Yes, I am. Do you have the angel, Mr. Chase?"

Eddie drew the camera back and lifted the statue into view. "Here. Say hello to everyone at home, angel. *Hello, everyone!*" he added in a squeaky voice. Nina couldn't help but smile.

"You know how dangerous it is," said Cross. "If you want to see your wife again, you'll—"

"No, no, no," Eddie cut in, shaking his head sarcastically. "Here's the deal. You tell me where you are, I turn up, you let Nina go unharmed and *then* I give you this little fella here. Otherwise, I'll put it somewhere nobody will ever, *ever* get their hands on it again. There's a lot of construction sites in Berlin—a lot of concrete being poured, if you know what I mean. Your man Irton told me you're pretty desperate to have the full set of these things. So without this, I guess your plan's fucked, right?"

Cross's jaw muscles drew tight with anger. Simeon gripped Nina harder, making her gasp in pain. "Nobody dictates terms to us!" he told his leader. "If we hurt her, he'll back down—"

Eddie interrupted him. "Cops are almost here." The sirens were now much closer. "You want me to leave it for them?"

"Antigua," said Cross, the word forcing its way free of his mouth. "We're in Antigua. Bring the angel to the island, and we'll make the exchange."

"Antigua, eh? Me and Nina'd been thinking about having a holiday there. Let me talk to her."

Cross reluctantly returned the headset to Nina. "Eddie!" she said. "You're okay?"

"Bit wet. What about you? Have they hurt you?"

"Not yet." She gave Simeon a sidelong look. "There have been some threats, though."

Eddie's glare through the screen seemed to be aimed directly at Cross. "And the baby?"

"Safe, as far as I know. And Eddie . . . I've decided on a name."

"Oh you have, have you? Don't I get a say?"

"Nope. That's what happens when you don't want to know the sex in advance."

"Nowt wrong with Arbuthnot, for a boy *or* a girl," he muttered before glancing back at the alley. "Okay, gotta go. I'll see you soon, love—trust me."

"You know I do," she replied. He grinned, then dropped the headset onto the grass and ran.

Dalton whirled to face Cross. "You're giving in to him?" he asked incredulously. "You're letting him come *here*?" A faint edge of hysteria entered his voice before he glanced almost in embarrassment at Nina and hurriedly regained his composure.

"No, I'm not, Mr. President," Cross replied, holding in his anger. "There's only one international airport in Antigua, so he has to come through it. We know him; he doesn't know us. We'll take the angel from him when he arrives—by force if necessary."

"It'll be necessary," rumbled Simeon. Anna nodded in agreement.

"He'll be ready for you," said Nina.

"And we'll be ready for him," Cross replied. "Norvin, take her back to the house. Dr. Wilde," he added, as the bodyguard led her away, "you're still going to find the last angel for me, no matter what happens with your husband. You can trust *me* on that."

Again the threat was perfectly clear. But Nina also felt a new sense of hope. Not only had Eddie survived; right now he had the upper hand—and the angel.

And now that she knew where she was, she had options too. Without the threat of Eddie's suffering to force her cooperation, she could risk an escape attempt. She knew from her vacation research that the Caribbean island was not large, and was certain she would not have to go far to find help.

There was the problem that she was under constant surveillance, of course, both electronically as well as by guards like Norvin. She had already started preparations to deal with the latter, though. Even if she was successful, it wouldn't buy her much time—but it might be enough to let her make a run for the jungle beyond the Mission's boundary.

With the baby's well-being to consider as well as her own, though, she couldn't afford to take the chances she would have in the past. The moment had to be right.

But she was sure it would come.

* * *

Eddie took a circuitous route back to the bridge, tossing the gun into the river along the way. He saw police cars at the intersection, and Maureen Rothschild among a small crowd of onlookers.

He moved up behind her. "Ay up, Prof."

"Oh my God, Eddie!" gasped Rothschild. "You're alive!"

He huffed with dark humor as he ushered her away from the gawpers. "Don't sound so horrified."

"That—that's not what I meant. I thought they'd killed you! I heard gunshots—"

"That was me."

"But you didn't have a gun."

"Took one of theirs."

She sucked in her thin lips. "I . . . don't want to know how, do I?"

"Probably not. But," he went on, opening his sodden leather jacket to show her what he was holding inside, "I got the angel."

She regarded the statue with amazement—and concern. "Is it intact?"

"If it wasn't, I get the feeling I'd be dead already, and so would a lot of other people." He closed his jacket again, suppressing a shiver.

"My God," she said, this time with sympathy. "You're freezing! You've got to get indoors and dry off."

"I can do that back at the museum." He took out his phone. "Nina thought I was mad for paying so much, but I'm really glad now I shelled out for a waterproof case."

"Who are you calling?"

"Seretse, for one; we'll need him to fix things up with the Germans." He looked down the street at the police cordon. "Last thing I need is to get arrested on a murder charge. It was self-defense, but stuff like that can take days to sort out, and Nina doesn't have that long. I've got to get to her, fast."

"You know where she is?"

Eddie nodded. "Antigua."

"In the Caribbean?"

"No, in Siberia." He gave a halfhearted smile. "Yeah, the Caribbean. I've got a mate who moved there, so that's another call I need to make. But I managed to talk to Nina, and the arsehole who kidnapped her. We're making an exchange, the angel for her."

"Do you think you can trust this person?"

"Nope. Which is why I want to go back to the museum."

"Oh, I hope poor Markus is all right," Rothschild said.

"So do I. I need his help with something." He looked across the river at the city beyond, then asked a question that left his companion puzzled. "You know what time the shops open in Berlin?"

17

Antigua

Maps and notes covered the desk, the laptop open and displaying a chapter from the Bible, but Nina was not reading it. Instead she was in the kitchen making herself breakfast, having forced herself away from her work.

She hadn't planned to continue Cross's task, but she found herself being drawn back in, first by boredom and then by her own insatiable curiosity. She kept telling herself that she wasn't helping her captor by doing so—certainly there had been no blinding flashes of inspiration revealing the last angel's location—and that with Eddie now free and on the way to her, even if she did discover a secret hidden within Revelation, Cross would never hear it. But a small voice kept warning her that she was falling into a familiar trap . . .

"I know, dammit!" she whispered to herself, annoyed by the chidings of her own personal Jiminy Cricket. A glance at the nearest camera, then at the small glass jar beside the sink, containing a cloudy liquid in which a few of the chopped and mashed ingredients were faintly visible. While Norvin had taken over the task of escorting her, Miriam had still been acting as housekeeper; to Nina's relief, she had left her recipe untouched.

She quickly looked away, suddenly concerned that the attention would somehow alert the watchers to her plan, and took her breakfast to the desk. The Bible text was still waiting on the screen. She munched her toast, trying to ignore it, but her inquisitive side was already drawing her gaze back to the words. They were not from Revelation, but a part of the Old Testament, Exodus, which she had come to suspect was an important piece of the puzzle laid out by John of Patmos almost two millennia earlier. Exactly how, she didn't know, but the references in Revelation to specific numbers and people and places now seemed unlikely to be coincidences—

"Mommy's doing it *again*," she told her bump as she caught herself. As irresistible as she had always found an unsolved puzzle, this time she had to fight the urge to discover the solution.

She finished her meal, battling tedium as she pretended to be working. Even then, part of her mind was still trying to fit the pieces together for real. Finally, she caved in and checked one of the reference books. A map showed the ancient Near East, Egypt to one side and the lands that were now Israel, Jordan, and Syria on the other, with the possible routes of the Exodus winding across the arid desert. Landmarks mentioned in the Bible stood out: towns, mountains, oases . . .

Nina looked back through her notes, frowning as an idea gently brushed her thoughts like a passing moth. There was something important, if not on this map then in another she had seen in her research, but she couldn't quite make the connection—

The answer came to her.

It almost *did* feel like a blinding flash, so clear that she couldn't believe she had missed it before. Excited, she peered more closely at the map, about to trace one of the lines with a fingertip before remembering that she was being watched. Instead, she forced herself to follow the path with her eyes alone until it reached a particular named spot.

Could that be it? The clues were in keeping with those

that had led to the angels hidden in the catacombs of Rome and the Altar of Zeus. And however insane Cross might be, the fact remained that he *had* broken the code in Revelation, lacking only the archaeological knowledge to pin down the actual locations. If he was also correct about the third clue, then she might just have identified the Place in the Wilderness . . .

The sound of the door lock snapped her back to the present. "Dr. Wilde!" said Norvin, entering before she could answer. "The Prophet wants to see you."

She tried to conceal her sudden nervousness. This was her chance—the only one she would get. "Okay, let me wash these," she said, quickly tying her hair into a ponytail before standing and collecting her plate and cup.

He folded his arms. "Now."

"It'll only take a second." Nina went to the sink and ran the crockery under the faucet. "Can you pass me that dishcloth?" She nodded over her shoulder.

Norvin grudgingly picked up the cloth. "Here," he said, stepping up behind her—

Nina whirled and threw the jar's contents into his face.

The big man staggered back, trying to cry out, but could only manage a strangled gasp. The recipe was something Eddie had once taught her: a makeshift chemical agent of dried chilis and garlic and vinegar, weak compared with commercial pepper sprays . . . but still more than potent enough to blind and choke an assailant.

Nina took full advantage and smashed the plate against his head. Norvin collapsed, clawing at his burning eyes. She ran for the door, hoping her observers had been frozen by the shock of the attack—

She pulled it open just as a *clack* came from the lock. The watchers had recovered and tried to seal her in, but too late. She rushed out into the sunlight, alone on the grounds of the Mission.

Waving trees beckoned beyond the fence. She ran to it, grabbing the barbed topmost wire and pulling it upward before forcing herself through the gap. Her clothing snagged; she tore free, pregnant belly sliding over the steel line below before she almost fell out on the other side.

Her back and one thigh were bleeding from stinging cuts, but tetanus was currently the least of her worries. She looked over the fence. The nearest CCTV camera turned to track her. Cross's voice barked from the loudspeakers: "Dr. Wilde! Come back, right now!"

She ran into the trees. The cult leader's tone became more strident as he issued orders to his followers. "Dr. Wilde has escaped! Everyone—hunt her down!"

His wording sent a chill through Nina. Another glance over her shoulder, and she saw white-clad figures pouring from the houses. They ran toward the fence after her.

"Shit!" she gasped, fear driving her on. One hand outstretched to protect the baby from low branches, she used the other to swat foliage aside as she hurried deeper into the jungle.

It took only seconds before the Mission was lost to sight among the greenery, but she could see nothing except plants in every direction. Which way? Following the coastline either north or south would probably bring her to somebody else's seafront property, but she might end up trapped on a promontory.

Inland. She adjusted her course, hoping she was heading due west. The country's eastern, Atlantic side was less developed than the calmer Caribbean west, but on such a small island, she couldn't imagine being more than a mile at most from any settlement.

Running a mile while pregnant presented new problems, though. At this stage, it was not a danger in itself to the baby, but nor was it actively encouraged. And she had let herself slack off in recent months, the combination of reduced exercise and occasional binge eating now combining with the heat to sap her energy.

No choice. This was her only chance to escape.

The ground began to slope more steeply as she weaved between the trees. She angled upward, breath starting to burn her throat. There might be a viewpoint at the top of the hill, letting her see which way to go instead of trusting to blind chance.

If she could reach it. Shouts came from behind. The cultists were spreading out through the trees after her. The dense layers of wet fallen leaves masked her footprints to an extent, but she had already been through patches of mud, leaving clear tracks. Could she risk trying to decoy them in the wrong direction?

Another shout, this time clear enough for her to make out. "Over here!" She hadn't been seen directly, but her path had been spotted. They were on her, closing fast.

No time to decoy them—and she couldn't outrun them for much longer either, already tiring. Once they were close enough to see her, her flight was over. That would happen in a minute, less. Nowhere to run—

Hide. But where? All she could see were trees and shrubs . . .

A large rock jutted from the ground higher up the slope. She ran to it. Could she hide behind it, under it, inside it?

No—but it had a smaller neighbor, and there was a gap between them. Would she fit?

She would have to. The hunters were closing, calling to one another as they swept the hillside.

Nina crouched and backed into the hole feetfirst. Stone barked against her heels even before her waist was under cover; the opening was shallow.

She twisted to fold herself almost into a fetal position as she squirmed backward, then on some desperate instinct grabbed the broken fronds of a palm from the ground and spread them like a fan, holding them up in front of her. It was a pathetic ruse, she knew. Anyone giving it more than the most casual glance would see through it.

The flat *thump* of footsteps warned her that her time was up. She froze, hardly daring to breathe.

A middle-aged man with a graying beard came into view past the rock, moving at a rapid jog. He cast a brief sidelong look at the stones to make sure nobody was skulking behind them . . . then continued on.

Nina felt a moment of relief—which was instantly consumed by fear as a second white-clad man rounded the other side of her hiding place. "Anything?" he called.

The first man slowed. "Not yet."

"I definitely saw footprints. Try down the hill."

"No," said someone else. Nina recognized the voice: Simeon. "Maintain spacing. If you spread out too far or bunch up, we could miss her." The Witness came into view, his rough clothing instantly recognizable. He stopped to gaze into the trees ahead, his back to her.

More people passed, some of them panting. Not all Cross's followers were super-fit ex-military or -CIA, it seemed. "Are you sure she came this way?" someone gasped.

Simeon turned toward the unseen speaker. Even though he was not looking directly at Nina, merely seeing his eyes filled her with terror. The slightest movement at the edge of his vision could draw his attention . . .

"I'm sure," he replied, glowering at the unseen man—then setting off again. "Okay, remember she's pregnant!" he called as he ran. "She'll get tired long before we do!"

He disappeared into the trees. More figures in white flitted between the palms, then were lost to sight deeper in the jungle.

Nina let out an exhausted breath. She waited for a minute to be sure her pursuers had moved away before hesitantly lowering the frond and emerging.

No voices, no flickers of white clothing among the trees. As far as she could tell, the hunters had gone.

How long before they came back, she couldn't guess. All she could do was keep going. She regained her breath, then resumed her ascent.

It did not take long to reach the summit. The trees thinned out, the sun's position high above helping her get her bearings. She finally cleared the undergrowth, looking west to see . . .

"No!" she gasped, heart sinking in despair.

She was looking at Antigua—*in the distance.* Between

the mainland's coast and the jungle below was a stretch
of open ocean, the Atlantic's winds kicking up churning
whitecaps. The two shores were well over a mile apart,
far beyond her ability to swim. She had escaped one
prison only to find that it was nested within another.

Nina closed her eyes as the hopelessness of the situation rose to swallow her . . . then snapped them open
again. "No," she said again, this time with determination. "Not happening." She had come this far; no way
was she giving up now.

She turned, taking in the entirety of the island. It was
an elongated rough triangle, about a mile in length. Its
westernmost tip pointed toward the mainland; the Mission, the church spire rising above the trees, was near
the southeastern corner. Nothing was visible beyond it
except the empty Atlantic. Trapped . . .

Wait, she told herself. There had to be *some* way on
and off the island other than by helicopter; it would be
insanely expensive to ship everything by air. That meant
boats. The shoreline at the enclave itself was a wave-
pounded cliff, so nobody would be able to land there.
They would need somewhere more sheltered . . .

There. A small cove southwest of the Mission, almost
perfectly circular behind its narrow entrance—and visible within was what looked like a jetty. Any boats would
be there.

She judged the distance. Not much more than a quarter of a mile. Even moving through the jungle it would
not take long to reach—if she didn't get caught.

No sign of any pursuers below. Resolute, Nina set
off downhill. Occasionally she paused on hearing calls
and shouts on the wind, but none were close by. She
pressed on.

The terrain flattened out. She crossed faint paths
through the woods—the Mission's residents were not
forced to stay within its boundaries, then—but still nobody was in sight. Crashing waves gradually became
audible. She hurried through the undergrowth toward
the sound, emerging at the edge of a low cliff overlooking the cove.

A pounding *whump* and *whoosh* to her right. Some quirk of geology was forcing incoming waves into the western corner of the little bay, where they hit a narrow ridge and surged upward before erupting like a geyser. Given time, the sea would eventually gnaw entirely through the barrier to join up with the coastline on the far side, but for now the Atlantic was still dashing itself against a near-vertical wall rising ten feet above the frothing waters. Nina had read about a similar feature on the Antiguan mainland called Devil's Bridge; this was less impressive, but both had been carved by the same almost metronomic blasts of spray.

The ragged spit arced out to form one side of the cove. The curving cliff on which she stood made up the other, a stony beach at its foot. The wooden jetty extended out from it; a boat was tied to its end.

She ran along the cliff until the slope to the beach became shallow enough to traverse, then scrambled down and headed for the jetty. The boat had an outboard motor; if she could start it, she should be able to reach the mainland in minutes—

"Down there!"

Nina glanced back at the shout with renewed fear. Simeon and a couple of others were on the clifftop. They ran after her, Simeon leaping down to the shingle as his companions rounded the cove's perimeter. There was an open-walled shed near a path that she guessed led to the Mission, a couple more boats inside. The cultists could pursue her, but they would have to carry their craft to the water, giving her a head start—if she could launch before being caught.

She hurried along the jetty. The bobbing boat was secured by two ropes. She unfurled the one at the prow, then ran back to the second at the stern—seeing Simeon sprinting across the beach toward her.

She struggled with the coils of wet rope. A knot snagged on the metal cleat. She tugged at it, for a moment unable to pull it free; then it popped loose. The final loops came away, and she leapt into the boat.

Simeon reached the jetty and pounded along it. Nina

grabbed the outboard's starter rope. The motor grumbled as she pulled, but didn't turn over. "Come on!" she cried, tugging again. *"Come on!"* Another pull, Simeon's feet banging on the planks as he sprinted at her—

The motor caught, coughing out blue smoke before fully turning over. Nina twisted the throttle on the tiller as far as it would go, and the boat surged out into the little bay.

She looked back—as Simeon made a flying leap from the jetty's end, slamming down onto the stern beside the outboard.

The extra weight pitched the boat's nose upward. Legs dragging in the water, he clawed at the hull, trying to pull himself fully aboard.

Nina hit him in the face. "Get off my boat!"

The African American slipped backward, dropping into the water up to his hips. He scrabbled to keep his grip as she drew back her arm to strike again—

Simeon grabbed the tiller and yanked it hard.

The sudden turn threw Nina against him. Before she could regain her balance, he clamped his left arm around her throat. "If I go in, you go in!" he snarled. "Slow it down."

She struggled, but his hold tightened, cutting off her air. "Slow down *now*," he ordered. "Or I'll choke you out. You don't wanna know what that might do to your baby."

"Son of a bitch . . ." Nina croaked, but she had no choice except to comply. She reduced the throttle. The boat slowed and settled into the water.

Simeon levered himself aboard, releasing Nina, then pushing her away. "You're lucky you're pregnant," he told her, breathing heavily. "If you weren't . . ."

He left the threat unspoken, but it was enough to send a chill through her. She hunched up in one of the front seats, defeated, as Simeon brought the boat back toward shore.

18

Cross was waiting when Simeon brought Nina back to the Mission: not in the control room, but in the church, glaring down at her from the pulpit. The light shining through the stained-glass windows cast a malevolent red tint over his face. "Did you really think you could escape, Dr. Wilde?" he asked. "There are cameras all around the island, not just at the Mission—we saw you as soon as you came out into the open."

"Yeah, I should have guessed" was Nina's sullen reply. "A control freak like you wouldn't stop at watching people in the bathroom."

"So what do we do with her?" demanded Simeon.

"She should be punished," added Anna. Norvin, the skin around his eyes a blotchy red, nodded in agreement.

Dalton, sitting in the front row of pews, spoke up. "As much as I'd like to see her suffer, we need her. Even if we get the angel from her thug of a husband, she still has to find the last one."

Anna gave him a cold look. "If you hadn't insisted on getting revenge on them, we could have *paid* another archaeologist. Chase being at the museum in Berlin proves that someone else could have worked it out."

The ex-president glowered at her, displeased that anyone would challenge him, but was interrupted by Nina before he could reply. "The Altar of Zeus was the easiest to connect to what John wrote in Revelation," she said. "Finding the one in the catacombs in Rome was much harder—and there was a hell of a lot of luck involved as well."

Simeon's unfriendly gaze turned upon her. "I *knew* she was sandbagging us. If she'd told us about Berlin first, we would have gotten the angel without our entire team being wiped out!"

"You think the statue in Berlin would have been sitting on a desk waiting for you if Eddie hadn't gone there?" she countered. "Someone with a great deal of knowledge of the altar found it for him, and you don't get that by waving guns around."

Cross raised a hand to silence the argument. "Her husband's on the way with the angel now."

"You're sure?" asked Dalton.

"I checked with a contact of mine at Langley. He left Berlin on a United Nations flight this morning; it lands at V. C. Bird this afternoon." He looked to his right-hand man. "We'll be there to meet him—with backup."

"If you hurt him, I'll never cooperate with you," said Nina.

"That's up to him," Cross replied. "But I get the feeling Mr. Chase isn't the type to give up without a fight."

"You're goddamn right about that," muttered Dalton.

"If he fights us, he dies," Simeon said flatly.

Again Cross waved for silence. "I'm not worried about the third angel. It's the fourth one that concerns me—the one hidden in the Place in the Wilderness. We need to find it, soon."

"Why?" Nina demanded. "Are you on a timetable?"

He gave her a patronizing shake of the head. "You've read Revelation, but you haven't taken it in. So many things in it happen according to a schedule set by God."

"Yeah, I remember." She indicated the Fishers. "How long have your Witnesses been prophesying? They only get one thousand, two hundred and sixty days of walking around in sackcloth before people get fed up with their yammering and kill them."

"And then they are reborn." Cross lifted his head, looking up not at the ceiling but at the heavens beyond. "After that . . . the seventh angel shall sound."

Nina could only respond with sarcasm. "And God lets you in on all his secrets." She turned to Dalton. "And you get cheered back into the White House, and Charlie Brown finally kicks that football. I know which *I* think's most likely to happen. Hint: It involves a cartoon kid with a big head."

"There's something else you know, isn't there, Dr. Wilde?" said Cross. The change in his tone made her suddenly uneasy; he sounded extremely confident. "The location of the last angel." His pale eyes fixed on hers, as if drilling into her soul for the truth.

"There's nothing to find," she replied, trying to conceal her nervousness. "Even if you're right about it being in the Place in the Wilderness—which you might well be, considering you're two for two so far—the clues are too vague to pin down. You could be looking at practically anywhere in the Middle East, from Egypt all the way over to Iraq."

"But your research suggests that you've narrowed it down to the route of the Exodus."

Nina felt even more unsettled. Everything about Cross's attitude implied that he somehow knew about her own personal revelation before the escape attempt. But that was impossible. Her notes, her Internet usage, even the pages of the reference books she had checked—none could have given it away. "That was just a possibility, and it's not as if I'm the only person to have thought of it."

Cross stared down at the redhead for a moment, then descended from the pulpit to stand in front of her. "Then explain why, at ten thirteen this morning, you had a sudden surge of adrenaline."

She looked back in confusion. "I . . . what?"

"Those aren't just video cameras in your house. We monitor your heartbeat, respiration, temperature, perspiration, even involuntary eye response, all remotely. It's the same gear the CIA uses. I can track every tiny physical fluctuation of your body and know what you're feeling even before you're consciously aware of it." An unpleasant smile, then he took a single step closer. Nina tried to back away, but Norvin moved to block her. "Now. The response you had was exactly consistent with that of somebody who's just made a great discovery . . . and then immediately tried to hide it."

"The CIA's been doing this for a long time," Dalton chipped in. "They really can tell what you're thinking."

"It's not mind reading," continued Cross, "not yet. But it's the next best thing. So what did you find?"

"I didn't find anything," Nina insisted.

He loomed closer, their faces just a few inches apart, then abruptly drew away to walk across the church. "My mission in life has always been about seeking the truth, Dr. Wilde. The truth of individuals, of nations, of God. So I find it almost personally offensive when someone tries to keep that truth from me. Don't insult me by trying to deny it," he snapped as she opened her mouth to do just that. "Even if you don't know exactly where the angel is, you know which area to search." He turned to face her. "And now you're going to tell me."

"I can't tell you what I don't know."

He came back toward her, eyes narrowing to threatening slits. "But you *do* know. So I'm going to give you a very simple choice. Either you tell me . . ." His right hand slipped inside his robes—and drew a slim steel dagger. "Or I'll kill your baby."

The room closed in around Nina as he held up the knife. She looked to the others, but found no support. Only Dalton was anything other than stone-faced, the former president clearly shocked. "You—you wouldn't," she gasped.

"I will if I have to," he told her, advancing slowly. She tried to flee, but Norvin grabbed her. "I don't want to. I consider the murder of the unborn a sin against the Lord. But the mission God has given me is more important than one innocent life. I'll make it quick and painless for the child. One stab will do it. You won't need more than minor treatment to survive."

"You're *insane*!" Nina cried, desperately trying to pull free of Norvin's hold. "You're out of your fucking mind! Dalton—Mr. President!" she wailed. "You can't possibly agree with this!"

Dalton stared back, for once at a loss for words. "I—this shouldn't, but . . . ," he stammered before jumping to his feet. "For God's sake, Nina! Tell him!"

Cross stopped in front of her. He lowered the dagger toward her belly—

"All right!" she screamed. "Okay, I'll tell you, I'll *tell* you! Just don't hurt my baby, please!"

He blinked, almost as if emerging from a trance, then retreated and passed the knife to Simeon. "I'm glad you did that, Dr. Wilde."

"For God's sake, Ezekiel!" said Dalton, appalled.

"I'm not proud of myself, but it had to be done," Cross told him. He looked back at the trembling Nina. "Now. Where is the fourth angel?"

She still wanted to resist, but knew he had no compunctions about carrying out his threat. "The woman . . . ," she croaked, mouth bone-dry. She struggled to draw saliva, then spoke again. "From Revelation—the woman with the moon under her feet . . ."

"Chapter twelve, verse one," said Cross, nodding. "'And there appeared a great wonder in heaven; a woman clothed with the sun, and the moon under her feet, and upon her head a crown of twelve stars.'"

"I realized what the part about the moon is referring to. The Wilderness of Sin."

"Sin?" Dalton echoed. He had returned to his seat, visibly disturbed by what had just happened. The former politician had been more than willing to order the use of violence by others, but the prospect of actually witnessing it in person had shaken him.

"A region the Israelites passed through during the Exodus," Cross told him.

"It's nothing to do with sinfulness," continued Nina. "Sin was the name of a Semitic deity—one of the gods worshipped by the ancient Jews before they became monotheistic followers of Yahweh. That's God, if you didn't know."

"Yes, I know. I'm not *completely* ignorant," Dalton growled.

"Sin was a moon god; what was written in Revelation is sometimes interpreted as a reference to the other gods being trampled underfoot as Yahweh became dominant, but it could *literally* mean walking over the desert named after him. Now, there's also a mention of this woman—the Woman of the Apocalypse, as she's known—going to a place prepared by God."

" 'And the woman fled into the wilderness, where she hath a place prepared of God,' " said Cross.

"Yeah. But I thought about what that might actually *mean*. It could be that God picked a spot and made it safe for her to stay. Or, more likely, that it was already an important religious site, which at some earlier point had been prepared, sanctified, whatever. Somewhere the Israelites had set up camp during the Exodus. I think that's what the reference to the twelve stars means—the twelve wells they found as they traveled across the desert."

The cult leader nodded. "That's a fairly common interpretation."

"So the angel is in some sort of temple in this Wilderness of Sin?" asked Dalton. "How hard will that be to find?"

Cross gave him a patronizing smile. "Quite hard, Mr. President. Nobody actually knows where the Wilderness of Sin *is*."

"It's generally considered to be the region between Elim—the location of the twelve wells—and Mount Sinai, where Moses received the tablets containing the Ten Commandments from God," Nina explained. "Except nobody knows which mountain that is anymore. It's extremely unlikely that it's the modern-day Mount Sinai in Egypt, because that location doesn't fit any of the descriptions of the journey in Exodus or other books of the Torah or the Bible."

"So how does that help us?" Dalton demanded.

"I think she knows something more, Mr. President." Cross turned back to Nina, awaiting an answer.

"It's only a theory," she insisted.

"A theory you thought was important enough to hide. So tell us."

She took a deep breath. "Okay. There's a list in the Old Testament of the places the Israelites visited during the Exodus."

"The Book of Numbers," said Cross.

"Right. I think there are forty-two stations?" Another nod. "They start out in Egypt, and after forty years in the wilderness end up on the Moab plains, in modern-day Jordan. But the part that caught my attention is the journey from the Wilderness of Sin to a place called Dophkah."

"Numbers chapter thirty-three, verse twelve: 'And they took their journey out of the Wilderness of Sin, and encamped in Dophkah.'"

"Dophkah is in the Timna Valley, in southern Israel," said Nina. "Part of the Arabah desert. It's an archaeological site—copper's been mined there since at least the tenth century BC. That gives us a specific location to use as a starting point."

Cross gestured toward the doors behind the pulpit. "Show me."

The group went into the control room. He brought up a map on the video wall, zooming in on Israel to center upon the Timna Valley. "There's your starting point, Dr. Wilde," he said. "Now where do we look?"

"That's a whole lot of nothing," Dalton remarked. Highways ran parallel to Israel's eastern and western borders, heading to the country's southern tip at the Red Sea, but between them the map was almost empty.

Cross tapped at a touch pad. The view changed to a satellite image. Features appeared, but they were all natural: rugged desert hills and mountains, their colors a universally arid sandy brown. "Numbers thirty-three eleven tells us that the Israelites came from the Red Sea, so this"—he swept a hand over the area south of Timna—"must be the Wilderness of Sin."

"Big area to cover," said Simeon. "Even if we stick inside the Israeli borders, that's got to be a hundred square miles of desert."

"But it's there somewhere," Cross said to Nina. "It's all in Revelation. The moon is a reference to Sin; the twelve stars tie it to the Exodus. It makes sense. And following your line of thinking about an important religious site, the 'place prepared of God' is most likely somewhere that the Israelites set up the Tabernacle. Yes?"

"I hadn't thought of it like that, but yes," she replied. The Tabernacle was a portable shrine carried by the Israelites on their journey, containing their holiest treasures, including the Ark of the Covenant. "If they stayed at this place for some time, they could have set up a semi-permanent place of worship."

Dalton took a closer look at the satellite view. "Why would anyone stay in that godforsaken hellhole?"

"Because God gave them what they needed to survive," said Cross. "He provided water to drink, and manna to eat."

"There's been water there in the past," Nina added. She pointed out channels cut into the mountains. "And that's how I know what to look for."

All eyes turned to her. "Well?" said Dalton impatiently. "Tell us!"

"It's all there in Revelation," she answered. "Distorted as usual, coded, but John's still telling us what he learned in Pergamon. The Woman of the Apocalypse was pursued into the wilderness by a dragon—one of the guises of Satan. God protected her, helped her reach the place prepared for her—"

" 'And to the woman were given two wings of a great eagle, that she might fly into the wilderness, into her place,' " Cross cut in.

"But he also defended her while she was there," Nina went on. "She was pregnant, and the dragon wanted to devour her child right after it was born. He failed, but sent a flood to kill her in revenge. And I'm sure you're about to give me the relevant quote," she said to Cross.

"Chapter twelve, verse fifteen," he said. "But I'll spare you the full text."

"Good. Because it's the *next* verse that holds the answer. You can quote *that* to everyone if you like."

He frowned, but recited the words. "'And the earth helped the woman, and the earth opened her mouth, and swallowed up the flood which the dragon cast out of his mouth.'" A long pause, during which Cross and his followers exchanged glances, as if waiting for their own revelations. None came. "How does that help us?" he demanded.

Nina gave him a faint but cutting smile. "It helps a lot, if you know something about geology as well as archaeology. Remember that John is describing his hallucinogenic interpretations of the Elders' writings. They wrote about a flood—possibly a flash flood, which in the desert can happen miles from where any rain actually fell. But the earth opened up and swallowed it before it reached the Place in the Wilderness." She paused, waiting for a response. "Seriously? Did nobody do Geology 101. The only thing that could be is a sinkhole! A sinkhole swallowed the flood—and those things don't just disappear. It'll still be there!"

Realization filled Cross's eyes. "The sinkhole will mark the angel's location!"

"Finally!" said Nina. "Yeah, that's right. *That's* what I worked out this morning. Somewhere in that desert"—she gestured at the screens—"is a sinkhole, either near or actually in a water channel. And somewhere very close to that . . . is your last angel."

Everyone regarded the satellite map. "So how do we find it?" asked Dalton.

"Hell if I know," she snorted. "If there are any more clues in Revelation, I haven't figured them out. I don't know who the Woman of the Apocalypse is meant to represent, or what the reference to her being 'clothed with the sun' means. She's pregnant—for all I know, it's a prophecy about me." She indicated her bulge, before remembering Cross's threat and putting her arms protectively over it.

"We don't need any more clues," Cross decided. "We can locate all the sinkholes in the region from the satellite imagery, then find any archaeological traces near them from the air."

"Oh, you can, can you?" Nina said scathingly. "Maybe I should have traded my PhD for a pilot's license."

He ignored the comment. "We know we're looking at waterways, so that'll cut down the area we need to check." He turned to Dalton. "I know people in Israel who can get us free access to their airspace, and hopefully even provide military assistance if we need it. If you can call on your diplomatic contacts to get us into the country without drawing attention . . ."

"No problem," he replied. "But that's the fourth angel—what about the third one?"

"We'll have it soon. Simeon? Get some people and meet Mr. Chase at the airport." He faced Nina again. "If your husband's sensible and hands over the angel, I'll let him live." Simeon clearly did not approve, but said nothing. "I can be magnanimous."

"I can't," she replied with cold anger. "You were going to kill my baby. That's not something I'm willing to forgive. If I ever get the chance . . . I'll kill *you*."

She couldn't tell if the threat had affected Cross or not. "Take her away" was all he said.

19

Eddie emerged from the arrivals gate at V. C. Bird airport to see his name in crooked marker pen on a piece of cardboard. He had expected a reception committee, but at the back of his mind throughout his flight was the thought that it might not be friendly. However, he knew this one had been arranged by a friend simply because he had acquired some extra initials: E.B.G. CHASE. "Cheeky bastard," he said under his breath, grinning.

The man holding the card was not the one he had called, but a middle-aged Antiguan wearing a battered baseball hat and a long baggy shirt bearing patterns of shells and starfish. Eddie approached him. "I'm Eddie Chase. Are you Nelson?"

"Thas right," the man drawled, giving him a broad, lazy smile. "Nelson Lightwood, at your service. At your service," he repeated, for no reason the Englishman could determine. "Tom ask me to take you to Jolly Harbour. Jolly Harbour."

"That's great. That's great," Eddie replied, unable to resist gently ribbing him.

Nelson either didn't notice or didn't care. "You wan' me to take your luggage?"

Eddie had only a carry-on bag and wasn't planning to relinquish it—for the moment. "No, that's okay. You've got a cab?"

"Outside. The white Toyota." He jabbed a thumb in the general direction of the exit. "The Toyota."

Eddie saw as he stepped into the humid heat outside the terminal that while Nelson was being accurate, he was not being specific; about a dozen taxis were lined up at a stand, all white Toyota vans. He wondered why there were no American vehicles, the United States being much closer, before realizing the answer: The former British colony, like Japan, drove on the left. "The one with the flower," his driver offered.

"Tell you what, just show me." He followed the nodding Nelson down the rank, glancing back to see if anyone was paying him undue attention.

A tall black man with a close-cropped haircut looked away just a little too quickly, while one of the three Caucasian men near him was almost giving a master class in how to look suspicious. All four wore similar white outfits, feebly disguised under jackets. Eddie remembered seeing the black guy lurking near the exit when he'd met Nelson. He had company, then, but he would have been surprised if he hadn't.

"This one, my friend," said Nelson. The dented Toyota HiAce minibus looked little different from its neighbors, though Eddie was amused when he spotted its identifying feature: a fake sunflower on the dashboard. "Step inside." He pulled back the sliding side door.

Eddie took a place on the rear bench seat. The interior had seen a lot of use but otherwise appeared to be a perfectly normal island taxi. Of more concern was the object beneath the driver's seat—a half-empty bottle of vodka. Hoping it was only enjoyed *after* its owner finished his shift, he waited for Nelson to amble around the vehicle and climb aboard. "Okay, my friend," said the Antiguan. "Jolly Harbour."

He pulled away. They passed the four waiting men, all of whom watched them go. Eddie looked back as the cab cleared the end of the rank to see the whole group make a beeline for a parked car.

The taxi left the airport grounds and headed south-west around the outskirts of the capital, St. John's. "How long will it take to get there?" he asked.

Nelson shrugged. "Who can tell? This is rush hour." The traffic didn't look to Eddie any heavier than he would expect on a quiet Sunday afternoon in England, but the squealing brakes and sudden swerves of other drivers suggested that the Antiguan attitude toward road discipline was a lot more lackadaisical.

"Well, there's no hurry." He looked at the bag on his lap, then over his shoulder. The silver Honda his tails were driving was a few cars behind. "You got a map of the island?"

"Sure, man." Nelson passed him a brochure. St. John's was in the island's northwest quarter; Jolly Harbour, his destination, was down on the southwestern Caribbean coast. The distance between the two was only about seven miles, but he doubted that any part of the trip would be on a motorway.

Of more concern was that once they were past the southern fringes of St. John's, there appeared to be only a few small villages dotted along the route, nothing but green between them. "The way we're going—does it go through open countryside?"

Nelson nodded. "Oh yeah, man," he said, turning to peer back at him. "We goin' along Valley Road, very pretty along there, very pretty. You get a good view of Mount Obama there, yeah."

"You might want to get a good view *here*," Eddie suggested, seeing a stationary bus looming in the taxi's path.

Nelson gave him another languid smile and looked ahead, slowing just in time to avoid a collision. "No problem, man. I been driving here thirty-three years, thirty-three years. Not dead yet."

The Honda was still holding position not far behind. "You ever had any trouble in that time?" asked the

Yorkshireman. "I don't mean with cars, but with their drivers. Or anyone else."

An amused grunt. "You think we in paradise? Ha! We got some not very nice folks here, same as anywhere. I can take care of myself, my friend."

"Good. 'Cause you might need to."

Nelson used the mirror to meet his eyes, for the first time showing a hint of steel behind the sleepy front. "Tom told me why you come here. Don' worry. I don' lose a passenger yet."

"Glad to hear it." Eddie settled back, occasionally glancing through the rear window to check on their tail.

The taxi made its way around the periphery of St. John's. The brightly painted houses became smaller and more basic as they moved away from the capital's center, before finally petering out. "Valley Road," Nelson announced. "Valley Road."

Eddie saw lumpen tree-covered hills rising in the distance beyond a rippled plain of farmland and forests. According to the map, the road was the main route to the various villages and resorts in the southwest. It was hardly an interstate, though, the bumpy highway only two lanes wide. What little traffic there was seemed content to amble along at no more than thirty miles per hour, Nelson giving a toot of the horn to warn the driver of an old pickup doing half that speed that he was about to overtake.

The Antiguan glanced at the truck as he passed and chuckled. "That guy, he smokin'. Say, you smoke? I get you all hooked up, man. All hooked up."

"No thanks," said Eddie. "Not my thing." Another look back. With fewer cars on the road, the Honda was running out of cover. Its driver held position behind the dawdling pickup before seeing that his quarry was pulling away and making a hasty pass. They were now in open countryside. "How far to the next village?"

"Jennings, about a mile and a quarter," Nelson told him. "Then another half mile to Bolans. Bolans."

Bolans was not far from their destination. If something was going to happen, it would be here, as far as possible from any witnesses. "Stay sharp," said Eddie. "I think we're going to have company—"

The words had barely emerged when the Honda surged forward, catching up with the taxi in seconds. It drew alongside—and the black man in the passenger seat pointed a pistol from his open window, waving for the cab to turn down a track to the left. Nelson yelped a Creole curse. "Better do it," Eddie told him.

The Toyota pulled off the road, stopping a short way down the muddy track. The car halted behind it, angling to block both the view of anyone passing by and the cab's escape route. "This all fucked up!" Nelson protested as the four men climbed from their vehicle. "*Fucked* up!"

"Just stay calm," said Eddie. He shifted to the middle of the rear seat, putting the bag next to the sliding door, and picked up the vodka bottle. As the men advanced, he slipped it under his right arm, holding it in place by the neck.

The door was hauled open. The black man leaned in and pointed the gun at the Yorkshireman, who raised both hands to chest height. "Toss away the keys," he ordered Nelson. His accent was American. The wide-eyed driver obeyed, dropping the keys from his window. "Okay, Chase. Keep your hands where I can see them. Where's the angel?"

"In the bag," Eddie replied.

The gunman's gaze flicked to the duffel bag. "Bring it out. Slowly."

Eddie picked it up with his left hand and carefully clambered from the taxi, keeping his other arm against his side to conceal the bottle behind him. The three white guys, to his relief, didn't have guns, but the biggest held a tire iron, repeatedly slapping it against his open palm.

"Okay, put it down." The Englishman lowered the bag to the ground. "Washburn, open it. Make sure the angel's inside."

One of the other men squatted by the duffel and pulled back the zip. Inside was a thick roll of bubble wrap surrounding an object about a foot long. "I brought your precious bloody angel," said Eddie as the man tugged at the plastic cocoon. "Where's Nina?"

"Safe. Until we don't need her anymore," the black man replied dismissively.

"And I suppose that now you've got the angel, you don't need me either?"

"You got that right." He scowled. "You killed a lot of good men in Berlin, Chase. That makes you a threat to our plan—*God's* plan."

Eddie eyed the gun, which was fixed unwaveringly on his chest. "What, you're just going to shoot me in the street?"

"This isn't New York. By the time the cops respond, we'll be long gone. We're leaving this island soon anyway—"

"Simeon!" said Washburn. He had peeled open one end of the thick wrapping to reveal the head of an eagle. "It's the angel!"

Simeon glanced down to see for himself—

Eddie brought his elbow outward, dropping the bottle—and whipped his hand down to catch it.

The gunman was transfixed by the sight of the statue for a split second too long. His eyes snapped back to Eddie—as the bottle smashed against his gun hand, shards lacerating his skin.

He screamed as the alcohol seared the wounds and reflexively pulled the trigger—but the impact had knocked the pistol away from his target, the bullet whipping past the Yorkshireman to clunk into the taxi's bodywork.

Eddie swept one leg up and kicked Simeon's bleeding hand. The gun was sent spinning into the tall bushes beside the track. The American let out another cry.

Washburn jumped up, fists balled, only to reel away with a shriek as jagged glass slashed his cheek. Holding the bloodied bottle like a knife, Eddie backed up past the taxi to give himself more room to maneuver.

"The angel! Get the angel!" Simeon barked, clutching his injured hand. One of the other men snatched up the bag, while his companion with the tire iron moved past him toward the Englishman, whipping the length of metal from side to side.

Eddie retreated, watching the bar flick before him. The man holding it was built powerfully enough to break bone if a blow landed. Behind him, the other three attackers were hurriedly returning to the Honda with the bag.

The big man lunged. Eddie jerked aside as the tire iron stabbed past his head, glimpsing Nelson scrambling from the taxi behind his attacker. Another strike, this a savage horizontal swipe that whooshed past just inches from his nose.

He flinched back—and staggered as his heel dropped into a deep rut.

The man bared his teeth in a malevolent smile, raising the bar to smash Eddie's skull—

And screamed, one leg giving way as Nelson stabbed a long serrated knife into his thigh.

Eddie punched the hulking thug hard in the face, sending a gush of blood from his nostrils. He toppled backward into the mud, weapon forgotten as he clutched the stab wound. The Englishman grabbed the tool, about to finish the fight permanently before deciding that a murder would not endear him to the Antiguan authorities. He settled instead for viciously kicking his opponent's crotch. The big man convulsed, every muscle in his body drawn tight, before slumping unconscious.

The Honda's engine roared. Eddie scrambled for cover, expecting his attackers to mow him down, but instead it reversed sharply before skidding back onto the main road. Within seconds it was out of sight behind the bushes, heading back toward St. John's.

He turned to Nelson. "You okay?" The Antiguan nodded, staring almost in bewilderment at the blood on his blade before hurriedly wiping it on the downed man's shirt. "Thanks for that—I'm glad you had that knife."

"Mos' taxi drivers do. I tell you, you only *think* this place is paradise." He regarded the motionless figure with dismay. "They were gonna kill you!"

"They'd have killed both of us." Eddie spotted a glint of metal in the undergrowth and retrieved the gun. "Come on, let's go. Somebody might have heard that shot, and I don't have time to piss around dealing with the police."

The taxi driver didn't move. "What we gonna do with this guy?"

Eddie snorted. "He started it—and I bet he won't go to the cops. You didn't hit the artery, so he's not going to die. Leave the bastard there and let him limp home when he wakes up. You coming?" He went to the cab.

Nelson examined his vehicle. "Look at this! Look at this!" he complained, poking a fingertip into the bullet hole. "How I gon' explain that to me wife?"

"Just remind her that this place isn't paradise," Eddie said with a grim smile.

Nelson frowned, then recovered the keys. "I come get you as a favor to Tom. Now he better do *me* a favor!" He got back into the taxi. "They took your bag, man," he said, regarding the empty rear bench. "Took your bag!"

"Yeah, I know," said Eddie as he returned to his seat, then leaned back—with an expression almost of satisfaction. "Real shame, that . . ."

Nelson gave him a disbelieving look, then, muttering under his breath, reversed the cab to the road and set off again for Jolly Harbour, leaving the dazed man lying in the mud.

20

" Ee bah gum," said Tom Harkaway in an exaggerated attempt at a northern accent. "It's Eddie Chase!"

"That's Lancashire, not Yorkshire, you thick southern bastard," Eddie replied, grinning up at the large bearded man on the deck of the motor yacht. "We say 'Ay up!' not 'Ee bah gum'!" He shook his head. "E.B.G. Chase? You daft twat."

"Whatever, you're all bloody barbarians as far as I'm concerned." Tom tramped down the gangway to the wooden dock, shaking his fellow Englishman's hand before clasping him in a bear hug. "So, how's things?"

"Right now? Been better," Eddie replied as he extricated himself. "In the past few days I've been Tasered, waterboarded, and shot at, I've driven a Porsche off a bridge, and just since I arrived on this island someone's tried to kill me. Oh, and my wife's been kidnapped by a bunch of religious nuts."

Tom cocked his head to one side. "Business as usual, then."

"Yeah, more's the fucking pity. Thanks for agreeing to help me out."

"Us SAS boys have to stick together," replied his old

squad mate. He gave Nelson a concerned look. "Someone tried to kill him? You okay?"

"Fine, both fine," said Nelson, sounding aggrieved. "But my taxi got a bullet hole! Who gon' pay to fix that?"

Tom's eyes went to Eddie. "Don't look at me," he said. "You're the one with the yacht."

"Yeah, and you arrived on a private jet!" The older man sighed, then told Nelson: "I'll sort it out. Take it to Viv at the boatyard." He gestured across the harbor at a cluster of industrial buildings. "He'll patch it up for you. Elena doesn't have to know anything about it."

The taxi driver looked relieved. "Thanks, Tom."

"Cheers for the lift," Eddie said as Nelson departed, before turning to take in the moored yacht beside them. The name FLIRTY LADY was painted on the hull of the seventy-foot white-and-blue vessel; he was no nautical expert, but from its decided lack of sleekness compared with the other craft nearby, he guessed it was a good few decades old. "Never imagined you as a navy man. Go cruising with Seaman Staines and Master Bates, do you?"

"Ha ha. Fuck off, Eddie. This is how I make a living now—tourist trips. We go out around the island, drop anchor off some of the nicer beaches, and let 'em go snorkeling before partying on the way back."

"Sounds like really hard work," Eddie joked, surveying his surroundings. Jolly Harbour was an attractive and clearly wealthy enclave with rows of houses right on the waterline, many having their own docks. Steep little hills rose around the bay, providing a backdrop of lush tropical vegetation. "Nice place. My mum always wanted to come here. You've got a tough life."

"You can joke, but you try keeping up with the payments on a ship this size, even a third-hand one," Tom told him as he ascended the gangplank. "Then there's the insurance, fuel, berthing fees, all that crap. It's not exactly a license to print money."

Eddie followed him into the main cabin. "So," said Tom, with a penetrating look. "You ring me last night, tell me you're coming to Antigua on some kind of urgent mission for the UN, I agree to help you . . . and now I find out that your wife's been kidnapped and someone wants you dead. Kept *that* part quiet, didn't you? What the bloody hell's going on?"

"I'm not exactly sure myself," Eddie admitted.

"Okay. And do you know who these people are?"

"Nope."

Tom pursed his lips. "Riiiight. Do you even know where they're keeping your wife?"

"Nope again. Although," he added, taking out his phone, "if I'm lucky, I'll find that out soon . . ."

⁂

Even locked in her house with a pair of guards posted outside the door, Nina couldn't miss the clatter of a helicopter coming in to land. Soon afterward, Cross's disembodied voice summoned her. A *clack* from the door lock, and two men entered to escort her through the compound.

Some of the Mission's white-clad residents were rushing about, excitedly passing on news to their neighbors. Nina saw someone familiar. "Miriam?" she called. "What's going on?"

The young woman hesitated, nervousness plain on her open face. The current news wasn't the only gossip; Nina's attack on Norvin had also done the rounds. But whatever had happened was so exciting, she couldn't hold it in. "They've found the third angel!"

"It's here?" The redhead looked toward the helipad in alarm. If Cross's people had taken it from Eddie already . . .

"Yes! One of the Witnesses just delivered it to the Prophet."

"I guess I'm going to see for myself," said Nina as her guards directed her onward.

"It's wonderful!" Miriam called after her. "There's only one more angel to find, and then the seventh trumpet will sound!"

"You say that like it's a good thing," she offered in

parting. She had now studied Revelation enough to know what followed the last trumpet: war, destruction, and death on a colossal scale.

She tried to hide her foreboding as she was brought to the church. The Fishers emerged in a rush as she arrived. Simeon's left hand was clamped tightly around his right, blood oozing between his fingers. Anna ushered him along, face full of concern for her husband. Both glared at Nina as they passed.

Their anger gave her a perverse feeling of hope. Even if they had taken the angel from Eddie, he had certainly put up a fight.

The cult leader was waiting inside with Dalton. The two men smiled when they saw her, though in the former president's case it was decidedly gloating. Cross, however, was almost ecstatic. "Dr. Wilde! This is one of the most important days in the history of the world—and it wouldn't have happened without you."

"I'm absolutely *thrilled* to have helped," she replied, in a tone acidic enough to peel paint.

Dalton's smile slid into a smirk. "Cynicism's so unbecoming in a mother-to-be."

"Oh, cram it up your ass, Mr. President." Nina reached them, seeing a carry-on bag on the front pew. "Where's Eddie?"

"Still alive, unfortunately." She wasn't sure which gave her more pleasure: the news itself, or the former politician's discomfiture at announcing it.

"It doesn't matter," said Cross. "What does matter is that three angels are now accounted for. The one destroyed in Iraq, the second from the catacombs in Rome, and now the third." He indicated the bag. "There's only one more to find—and we know where to look. We're already making preparations for the search. You'll join us, of course," he added. "You're right: We might still need an archaeologist on the ground."

"Trekking around a desert while pregnant? Boy, I can't wait."

"You won't have to wait long. We'll be leaving tonight." Cross opened the bag. "But first I wanted you to see this."

He donned white gloves, then carefully lifted out an object cocooned in bubble wrap. One end had been pulled open, revealing a hint of what was inside. "The third angel—the eagle," he said, showing it to her.

Nina couldn't help but feel a thrill at the sight. However dangerous it might be, the angel was still an incredible find. But the feeling passed almost immediately at the thought of how Cross intended to misuse it—for devastation, not discovery. "Is it intact?" she asked. "After everything it went through, you were damn lucky it didn't get broken in Berlin."

"You can blame your husband for that," said Dalton.

"If it had broken, it would have been God's will," Cross said as he started to peel away the wrapping. "It doesn't matter *where* the angels are released, just that they *are*."

"Although some locations are better than others, obviously." The ex-president seemed to be enjoying some private joke.

Cross paid no attention, fixated on freeing the statue. "Here," he said with reverence as the last wrapping came away. "At last."

Dalton came to see for himself. "Three down, one to go." He turned to Nina. "What do you think, Dr. Wilde?"

Nina didn't answer, her attention fixed on the statue. Something was *wrong*, she realized. Compared with the second angel, it was different—the way it caught the light, the tint of the ceramic, the arrangement of the metal wings surrounding the body . . .

Cross caught her confusion. "What are—" he began, before looking sharply back at the relic. He ran his gloved fingertips over its surface, then turned it to examine the inscribed text, almost squinting as he tried to make out details.

"What's the matter?" Dalton demanded.

"It's . . . it's not real," whispered Cross. He gave Nina a frenzied glare, as if it were her fault. "It's a fake!

Look at the lettering! It's *stepped*—like a low-resolution copy!" He tugged off one glove to scratch the statue with his fingernail. Tiny flecks of the surface broke away.

Nina almost laughed. "I think you've been scammed. Or *scanned*, rather. Eddie must have put the real angel into that laser scanner at the museum and three-D-printed an exact copy. It's nice work, though. Somebody's even gilded the wings to make them look like real metal."

"But . . . but why?" asked Dalton. "He must have known we'd realize it was fake, so he couldn't have exchanged it for you."

"He wasn't going to exchange it," said Cross. He turned the statue upside down, examining its base. A small length of metal was set into the flat surface—something that had not been present on the angel taken from Rome. "It's an *antenna*!" Fury filled his voice. "It's a tracker, a GPS beacon. He *wanted* Simeon to take it from him. Now he knows where we are!"

He raised the statue as if about to smash it on the marble floor, then forced back his anger, regarding the replica for a moment before lowering it again. "We need to move up our schedule," he said more quietly, calculating.

"Wait—where's the real angel?" said Dalton.

"Chase must still have it, or has gotten someone to bring it to Antigua for him. He needs it to get his wife back." Cross looked at Nina. "He'll be coming here. But we'll be ready for him."

* * *

Eddie zoomed in on the map on his phone to a small island off Antigua's eastern coast. "That's where they are—where Nina is." He had bought the GPS tracker and its phone app from a spy shop in Berlin that morning, getting the bruised but otherwise unharmed Derrick to conceal it inside the replica. "You know it?"

Tom nodded. "Elliot Island. Never landed there, though—it's private property. You get too close, and the residents turn up and wave you away. Not a big deal; its beaches aren't great, so it's not a prime tourist spot."

"Know anything about the people who own it?"

"Some religious commune, I think. There's a church. Apart from that . . ." He shrugged.

"I need to get out there without them seeing me. It won't take 'em long to realize that wasn't the real statue—oh, and there we go." The tracker's dot vanished, a message popping up to announce that the signal had been lost. "Still, it told me what I needed."

"When you say you need to get out there," said Tom warily, "I'm assuming you want me to take you?"

Eddie smiled. "That'd be helpful, yeah."

"I told you, they'll see us coming. The *Flirty*'s not exactly a stealth boat."

"That's why it's perfect. How quick can it get out there?"

"At full pelt? An hour and a half, maybe." He looked through a porthole at a call from the dock. "Who's this?"

"That's for me," said Eddie. He went out onto the deck to find Maureen Rothschild at the bottom of the gangway. "Hi, Prof! You made it, then."

"Yes, I did," she replied, with a distinct lack of enthusiasm. "I waited in the plane for ten minutes before going through customs, as you asked, and by that time a jumbo jet full of tourists had arrived! I had to wait in line behind three hundred people. And when I finally got out, it took an age to find a cab. Why couldn't I have come with you?"

"Trust me, you wouldn't have wanted to be in my taxi," he told her, marching down the walkway to pick up her travel case. "I had a reception committee. And they weren't there to give me cocktails in a hollowed-out pineapple."

Rothschild's eyes went wide. "You were ambushed? Are you all right?"

"I didn't know you cared." He ascended the gangway.

"I'm displaying simple human decency, Mr. Chase," she replied tartly as she followed. "Something in which you apparently still need lessons. What about the statue? Did they take it?"

"Yeah, just like I'd hoped. So now I know where they are." He helped her onto the yacht. "You've got the real one?"

Rothschild huffed. "No, I left it on the plane. Of course I brought it!"

"Sarcastic, snappy . . . you're more like Nina than either of you'd want to admit." Eddie put down the case. "Tom, this is Maureen Rothschild. Prof, this is Tom Harkaway, an old mate of mine."

"Nice to meet you," said Tom, extending his hand.

She shook it dubiously, eyeing a pouting pinup girl painted on a bulkhead beside the vessel's name. "Thank you. This is a . . . nice boat."

He chuckled. "It's seen a fair few parties."

"Speaking of which," said Eddie, "how fast can you drum up some passengers? A party boat without partiers'll look a bit suspicious."

Tom pointed beyond the houses along the harbor's western edge. "There are two big resort hotels just over there, the Tranquility Bay and the Jolly Beach. It shouldn't be too hard to find some people who want a cruise." He paused. "You want me to give them a *free* cruise, don't you?"

"Quickest way to fill up the boat, innit?"

"And who's going to pay for all this?"

"There's a bloke at the United Nations called Oswald Seretse . . ."

Rothschild shook her head. "Poor Oswald. He's in for a shock."

"Not as much as the arseholes who took Nina." Eddie took the gun from inside his jacket and checked the magazine.

"Jesus, put it away!" cried Tom, eyes wide. "You don't want to get caught with that. The Antiguans had a big crackdown on guns after some tourists were murdered a few years ago. Shoot someone and you'll get anything from twenty-five years to the death penalty."

"Didn't seem to worry the bloke who took the statue,"

Eddie replied, slipping it back out of sight. "You know any local cops?"

Tom nodded. "I've got some friends."

"Could be worth bringing 'em in. Pretty sure I'll need backup."

"But the police won't land on a private island without a good reason."

"They've kidnapped Nina, for fuck's sake!"

"They don't have proof that she's there," Rothschild pointed out.

"She's right," said Tom. "They'd need a warrant or probable cause to go and look."

"All right, then they can fucking come and arrest me for trespassing!" The Yorkshireman frowned, then an idea came to him. "You've got distress flares, haven't you?" His friend nodded. "Okay, if I fire off a flare, that means either I've found Nina, in which case they can come ashore and arrest 'em for kidnapping, or I'm being shot at, in which case they can come ashore and kill the bastards! How does that sound?"

Rothschild and Tom exchanged looks. "I've heard better," the latter admitted.

"This is how you come up with all your plans?" exclaimed the elderly woman, incredulous. "Random improvisation? It's amazing that you're still alive!"

"I'm not hearing anything better, and the clock's ticking." Eddie regarded the case. "All right, Prof, I need the angel. Tom, we need to set things up."

"I'm going to regret this, aren't I?" muttered the older man, but he nevertheless went back into the cabin to search for a flare.

"You're really going to do this?" asked Rothschild as she opened the case. "You're going to give them the statue, even though they want it for something dangerous?"

"Yep." Eddie took out another bubble-wrapped item; this time, it was the real angel.

"You are insane, you know."

"You're not the first person to say that. But I'm not planning on letting them keep it. Why do you think I want to get the cops involved? I'll talk to Ozzy too, see if we can bring Interpol and the State Department into it. Pretty sure a US citizen being kidnapped should get their attention, especially when it's someone famous like Nina."

"Nina," she echoed, with a wistful nod. "You really do love her, don't you?"

"'Course I bloody do," said Eddie, surprised by the question. "I'm married to her, she still puts up with me even after all the crap we've been through—and she's having our baby. Why would you even have to ask?"

Her eyes couldn't quite meet his. "No reason."

He was sure there *was* one, but he had neither the time nor the inclination to discover it. "Right," he said, removing the angel from its padding. "Let's get this party started."

21

The journey around the island showed Eddie two very different sides of Antigua. The waters of the western shore, facing the Caribbean, were a calm and incredibly clear turquoise. By the time the *Flirty Lady* had made her way along the southern coast and turned north into the Atlantic, however, things had become considerably more choppy.

The dancers on the main deck were coping with the swaying floor with surprising ease. Tom had rounded up a group of young, mostly German vacationers. The promise of unlimited alcohol magically ended any questions about why the free cruise was being offered, and after one of the revelers connected an iPhone to the yacht's speaker system to pump out an endless succession of Euro dance tracks, further conversation became impossible anyway.

The bridge provided only a modest amount of sound-proofing. "I must be getting old," Eddie complained loudly after closing the door, deciding that Rothschild had made a very sensible decision by staying ashore. "Modern music all sounds the bloody same!"

Tom, at the wheel, grinned in agreement. "If they'd

just stuck one track on repeat, I doubt I'd know the difference." He pointed ahead. "There it is."

"That's Elliot Island?" From this distance, only trees were visible above the rocky shoreline. "Where's this place with the church?"

"Eastern side. You can't see it from here." He turned the wheel to the left. "We'll go up its west coast and around to the north, then head back south past the village. That should bring them out to keep an eye on us, and give you your distraction."

"Did you talk to the police?"

"Had a word with one of my mates. He says they'll be ready for us, but they won't come out unless something actually happens. I asked him about the people who own the island; apparently they keep well in with one of the local politicians, so he's a bit cagey about going onto private property without a damn good reason." Tom nodded at a ship-to-shore radio. "Once you fire a flare, I'll call them in, but it could take them a while to get here from Nelson's Dockyard."

"Hope they've got something faster than a pedalo. All right, I'd better get changed."

A few minutes later, Eddie had stripped down to a pair of swimming shorts. Tom gave him a wolf whistle. "Fuck off," said the Yorkshireman with a grin as he donned a scuba tank, then put everything he was taking with him in a bag that he clipped to the cylinder. "Okay, where's the best place to drop me?"

The *Flirty Lady* was now circling the island's northwestern shoreline. Tom indicated a small bay. "That should put you about three-quarters of a mile from the village. I'll time it so we go past when you get there."

Eddie surveyed the coast. "What're the waters like?"

"This side of the island's shielded from the really big waves coming in from the Atlantic. Shouldn't be any trouble to swim."

"Sharks?"

"Sometimes."

"Yeah, that's helpful."

"They don't work to a timetable. But you're more

likely to see stingrays than sharks. They're generally friendly—don't bother them and they won't bother you."

"Me, bother anyone?"

They both chuckled, then Tom opened the bridge door and called to a white-shirted crewman keeping an eye on the partygoers. "Melvin! Take the wheel for a minute." The Antiguan hurried up to the bridge. "Right, let's get you into the water."

He helped Eddie down the stairs. "Hey, are we going swimming?" asked a cheerfully drunk blond German.

"Just me," Eddie replied. "Lost a contact lens overboard."

"Ah." The young man regarded him with owlish curiosity before smiling. "Ah! That is English humor, yes? Monty Python, Mr. Bean? I get it!"

"That's the one," Eddie replied, impatient. "You know there's free beer over there, right?"

The youth danced unsteadily away between his friends. Eddie shook his head. "Kids. Who'd have 'em? Oh, wait. Me." He sat on the boat's port side and put on a pair of flippers.

Tom stood in front of him to block the view of anybody on shore. "Looks clear to go."

Eddie peered past him. There was no sign of any human activity on this side of the island, but that didn't mean it was deserted. He tested the scuba regulator, then pulled a diving mask over his eyes. "I'm ready."

His friend nodded. "Melvin! Reduce to eight knots!" He waited until the chug of the diesel engine slowed, then turned back to Eddie. "Good luck."

"See you soon." He put the regulator into his mouth, gave Tom a thumbs-up, then rolled backward into the ocean.

Even in the subtropical warmth, the water briefly felt like ice. He flinched, then the initial shock passed and he kicked to move away from the yacht. Its swirling wake briefly pounded him, fading as the *Flirty Lady* continued on its way.

He turned onto his front and started swimming. Small

fish glided past, paying little attention to the intruder in their realm, but to his relief nothing larger—friendly or not—appeared in the crystalline depths.

It took only a few minutes before the seabed became visible, gradually rising to meet him. The currents became stronger as the water shallowed. He plowed on, waves buffeting him, until his fins brushed the ground.

If anyone was watching, they would be able to see him by now. Eddie breached the surface and stood, water streaming down his mask before clearing to give him a view of the little bay.

Nobody in sight.

He waded ashore, kicking off his fins. The stony beach was deserted. He looked along the tree line but saw nothing. A glance back out to sea: The *Flirty Lady* was out of sight, though he could still hear the faint rumble of its engine and the pulse of Europop.

He removed the scuba tank and opened the bag, taking out a loose shirt and a pair of deck shoes with thick rubber soles. Both were soaked but would dry out quickly enough in the heat. The distress flare and gun went into his pockets.

The final item was the angel. He picked it up, then hurried across the beach into the trees beyond.

Fifty yards away, a camera mounted on the trunk of a palm tracked him until he was lost to sight amid the greenery.

* * *

"This is getting tiresome," said Nina as her two guards escorted her into the control room. "Bring me here, send me back, bring me again . . . you might as well set me up a bed in the corner."

"I wanted you to see this," Cross replied from his chair. "And you too, Mr. President," he added as Dalton entered, looking as annoyed as Nina at the summons.

"See what?" Dalton demanded.

The cult leader activated the video wall. "This was filmed a few minutes ago."

Nina took in the surveillance footage. The camera overlooked a small beach, the Antiguan mainland visible on the horizon. It slowly panned across the vista—then abruptly zoomed in on something in the water.

A figure emerged from the ocean, plodding through the breaking waves and discarding a pair of flippers. She recognized him instantly.

"Your husband's here," said Cross.

Nina's delight was mirrored by Dalton's alarm. "Chase is *here*?" he squawked. Learning that the Englishman had escaped from his kidnappers in New York had unsettled the former politician; his being only a short walk away brought outright horror. "Here on the island? Oh my God!"

"Hope you've got space in your baggage for your ass, because he's about to hand it to you," said Nina, unable to contain a smirk.

Dalton went to Cross, grabbing the swivel chair and pulling its occupant around to face him. "You've got to stop him! That man's a maniac, a psycho! You have no idea how many people he's killed—and now he's coming for *me*!"

"He's not coming for *us*," Cross corrected, his annoyance clear. "He's coming for her. Look." He paused the playback, zooming in on Eddie as he took something from a bag. "He's brought the angel. The real one."

"You're sure it's real?"

"Of course I'm sure. The fake was a decoy so he could locate the Mission, but now that he's bargaining for the lives of his wife and child, he'll have to use the actual angel."

Dalton withdrew, still agitated. "So where is he? Why aren't you tracking him?"

"The cameras only cover the shoreline. Don't worry, though," he added as the ex-president shot him a look of dismay. "Once he gets close to the Mission's perimeter, we'll pick him up again." He tapped another control. "Paxton? Get the chopper ready. We move out as soon as the angel's secured." He waited for an acknowledgment, then made another announcement. Nina heard it echo over the public address speakers outside. "This is Ezekiel. A visitor is about to bring us the third angel. Everyone be ready for him."

He stood, turning to Nina. "Come on, Dr. Wilde. Let's meet your husband."

* * *

The sound of a voice over loudspeakers in the distance made Eddie crouch behind a tree and draw the gun, checking the vegetation for threats. Nobody was there, but he was now on full alert.

Cautious, he continued through the jungle. Before long he saw faint paths. Rather than follow them, he moved parallel to one, keeping in the undergrowth as he advanced.

Something man-made ahead, a straight line standing out among the curves of nature: a wooden post about fifteen feet tall at the intersection of two paths. He looked at its top. A black sphere was mounted upon it. A camera. Had it seen him?

"Mr. Chase!" The voice he had heard earlier, now perfectly clear and audible. "My name is Ezekiel Cross. Welcome to the Mission."

"Oh, *bollocks*," Eddie muttered. That answered his question.

"We saw you the moment you set foot on the beach," the unseen man continued. "And we know you've brought the angel—the *real* angel. Your wife is here with me."

"Let me talk to her!" he yelled at the camera.

He didn't expect a response, but after a moment he heard a new voice: Nina's. "Eddie! It's me, I'm okay. They're—"

She was cut off, Cross speaking again. "Follow the path if you want to see her."

Eddie glared at the camera, then continued onward. Before long, he saw a wire fence ahead. "Keep going, Mr. Chase," said the voice. "Head to your right. There's a gate."

He reached the fence. Through it he saw the village spread out before him. Small wooden houses led his eye to the Mission's centerpiece: a church, its spire rising high above its surroundings.

Also visible were three men dressed in white, coming up the slope toward him. The sight of more cameras overseeing the entire village explained how they knew his position. "All right, I get it—you've got the whole Big Brother thing going on," he shouted at the nearest. "You can see me, but I can't see Nina. Where is she?"

"She's outside the church, with me," said Cross. "You have my word that you won't be harmed as long as you bring me the angel."

Eddie eyed the approaching men. None appeared armed, though he didn't accept his mysterious host's assurances for a moment. Keeping the gun trained on them, he went along the barrier until he reached the gate and entered the compound.

The men came closer. "Back off," he warned them, waving the gun.

"Let him through," said the amplified voice. The white-clad reception committee moved back. Eddie started toward the church, the men following at a discreet distance.

The houses he passed were all pristine and tidy, almost to the point of sterility. "I'm in fucking Toytown," he muttered, wondering where the residents were. Apart from the men behind him, there was no sign of anyone.

That changed as the church came into full view ahead. A crowd waited outside—he guessed eighty or ninety people. All were dressed in white.

Except one.

"Nina!" he yelled, seeing his wife at the front of the congregation.

"Eddie!" she cried back, joy in her voice as well as tension. Two men, Simeon one of them, stopped her from running to him. "I'm okay, the baby's okay!"

"You can see she's alive and well," said the voice. For the first time, Eddie laid eyes on the man responsible for everything that had happened; the robed Cross stood close to Nina, speaking into a small headset microphone. A black case was at his feet. "You came to make a trade."

"Yeah," Eddie replied. "But first . . ." Holding the statue under one arm, he took out the flare and popped off the plastic cap. Pointing it upward, he used his thumb to hook the pull-tab on its base. The projectile rocketed from the tube with a flat bang and a trail of smoke, arcing into the sky. Its parachute deployed after a few seconds, the bright-white star drifting out to sea.

People in the crowd exchanged anxious looks. "That was to tell the Antiguan police that you're holding a kidnap victim!" Eddie called as he resumed his march toward the church, aiming his gun at Cross. Simeon angrily drew a pistol in his bandaged hand. "They know I'm here too, dickhead. So killing me'd be a really bad idea. I'm told Antigua has the death penalty for gun crimes."

Cross waved for his henchman to lower the weapon. "Only God will take any lives here."

There was a commotion at the church doors. Eddie looked toward them—and was shocked to see Victor Dalton pushing through the crowd to reach Cross. "He's called the *cops*?" the former politician said. "We've got to get out of here! If I'm still here when they arrive, I'll be linked to a federal crime!"

The Yorkshireman neared the group. "You!" he barked at Dalton, who flinched. "*You're* behind all this? I should have fucking killed you when I had the chance!"

"Paxton's ready with the chopper," Cross told his partner, unconcerned.

Eddie looked around at the whine of a turbine engine starting up, seeing a helicopter on a pad near the cliffs. Beyond it he spotted the *Flirty Lady* cruising southward past the village, its passengers waving to those on shore. "Going somewhere?"

"We have a plane to catch," replied Cross. "But first, Mr. Chase, we had a deal. The angel for your wife."

"Eddie, you can't let them take it," protested Nina. "They'll use it to kill hundreds, maybe even thousands of people!"

Simeon raised his gun again. "We're doing God's will. Now hand it over."

Eddie kept his own weapon and gaze fixed on Cross. "You're right, we made a deal. I'll honor my side, if you honor yours." Dalton's gaze flicked nervously between the two men.

Cross was silent for a long moment, then he nodded. "Let her go."

"*What?*" barked Simeon. Anna was equally shocked.

The cult leader turned his cold gaze upon them. "Do you trust me?" he asked.

The question caught them both off guard. "Yes, of course," said Anna. "But—"

"Then don't question me. We can find the last angel without her."

She nodded. Simeon was more reluctant, but he lowered his gun. Cross looked back at Eddie. "The angel?"

The Englishman put the statue on the ground, then warily stepped closer to Nina, holding out his free hand. She reached for it, then stopped. "Don't give it to them, Eddie," she pleaded.

"You trust *me*, don't you?" he asked.

"Yes, but . . ." Another moment's hesitation, then she took a firm hold of him. "There *aren't* any buts."

"That'll upset Sir Mix-a-Lot. Okay, let's do this." The couple backed away, Eddie keeping the gun raised. "There's your statue."

"Hold it," said Simeon. "How do we know this isn't another fake?"

Cross picked up the figure. He turned it over in his hands, holding it up to the sunlight to examine the fine details. "It's real," he announced. "It's real!" He faced his congregation, holding the figure above his head. "The third angel of the apocalypse is ours!" Joyous awe spread through the crowd, some of his followers bursting into tears.

Eddie was less enthused. "The angel of what?"

"I *told* you not to give it to him!" said Nina. "They've got some insane plan to bring about the apocalypse so Dalton can get back into power."

"Wouldn't the end of the world kind of screw up his political career?" he asked as they retreated farther. "Hard to get out and vote if it's raining fire and brimstone."

"They didn't let me in on their endgame. But I know it involves loosing the angels—breaking open the statues to let out what's inside, something that reacts with air and turns into toxic gas."

"That'd explain the gas masks they had in Berlin, then." Eddie flicked the gun at the three men who had followed him to the church; they let him and Nina pass. "But don't worry, they'll never get a chance to do it. Like I said, the cops are on the way. Even if they leave in the chopper, they'll still get stopped at Antigua airport, or whichever other island they try to fly out from." He winked at her. "See? Trust me. I know what I'm doing. More or less."

Cross returned to the black case and reverently placed the statue inside next to its fellow from Rome, then closed it. "My friends," he said, his voice still coming from the loudspeakers, "my faithful followers, I must leave you now. Three of the angels bound at the Euphrates have now been found, and I know where the last one is hidden. I'll find it, I promise, and I *will* fulfill the prophecy of the Book of Revelation. When the angels have been released, the seventh trumpet will sound—and then Babylon will fall and Satan will be cast down into the lake of fire. When that is done, nothing can stop God's kingdom on earth from becoming a reality."

Eddie looked askance at Nina. "Is this bloke for real?"

"Unfortunately, yes," she replied. "He believes every word he's saying."

He twirled a forefinger at his temple. "Wibble."

"The problem is, he's been *right*." At Eddie's look of surprise, she went on: "About some of it, at least. The clues hidden in Revelation really did lead to the angels. And now he knows how to find the last one. I told him where to look."

"You did?"

"I didn't have a choice. Eddie, he . . . he threatened to kill the baby."

He stopped abruptly, his face turning utterly cold and blank. Nina had seen the frightening look before, after the murder of his friend "Mac" McCrimmon, and knew what it meant: He had targeted someone for death, and would be both relentless and merciless in carrying out that mission. "Then I'll kill *him*," he said simply.

"No, wait," Nina gasped. But he was already taking aim. She grabbed his arm, trying to force him off target—

Simeon whipped up his own weapon—but before either man could fire, screams and cries came from the crowd as they too realized the danger. Several people rushed to put themselves between Cross and the Yorkshireman.

Nina recognized one of them. "Miriam!" The young woman was terrified, but she held her position, arms spread wide in a desperate attempt to shield her prophet. "Eddie, don't shoot!"

"Nobody shoot," said Cross. "Simeon, stand down. That's an order!" Simeon bared his teeth in frustration but obeyed.

Eddie jerked his wrist from Nina's grip, his chilling mask replaced by anger. "What're you *doing*?"

"You called in the cops! If you kill him in front of all these people, it'll be cold-blooded murder—and you said Antigua has the death penalty. I'm not going to let you throw your life away. Our baby's not going to grow up without a father."

He glowered at her, but then a shout caught everyone's attention. "Boats!" called a man on a small parapet at the base of the church spire. "Boats are coming!" He pointed south. "The police and the coast guard!"

"Thank you, Tom," Eddie muttered. For the cops to have arrived so quickly, his friend must have decided *what the hell* and radioed them long before the flare was launched.

"See?" said Nina, pulling her husband's gun hand firmly downward. "They can handle everything from here." The pair of them resumed their retreat up the hill.

"It's time to go," Cross said, still speaking over the PA system. He picked up the case. "Mr. President, if you'll come to the helicopter?"

Eddie and Nina were now out of Dalton's earshot, but his agitated body language told them he was still worried. "It doesn't matter," Cross's amplified voice assured the politician as he, Dalton, and their entourage, including the human shields, started toward the helipad. "We won't be stopped at the airport."

Eddie watched them with growing suspicion. "Why's he so fucking confident?"

"I don't know," Nina replied, her own unease growing. "But I think we should get out of here."

"We need to tell the cops what's going on."

"The only place they can land is over there." She pointed toward the cove to the southwest. "If we meet them, they can contact the airport and stop Cross from leaving, can't they?"

"Yeah, that was the plan. But . . ." Eddie stared after the cult leader as his group reached the helipad. "Something's not right."

Norvin opened the helicopter's doors. Dalton was first to scramble aboard, Anna and Simeon following. But Cross remained, signaling for his white-clad guardians to face him. "My followers," he said, "my friends: You have all had faith in me, faith in the word of the Lord and in the prophecy of the Book of Revelation. I *will* find the fourth angel, I *will* see that Babylon falls. But another prophecy must be fulfilled, here, today, right now. Revelation chapter six, verse ten: 'And they cried with a loud voice, saying, How long, O Lord, holy and true, dost thou not judge and avenge our blood on them that dwell on the earth?'"

"Doesn't he ever shut up?" complained Eddie.

Nina waved for him to be quiet, trying to remember what followed. "I don't like this . . ."

Cross continued his recital. "'And it was said unto them, that they should rest yet for a little season, until their fellow servants also and their brethren, that should

be killed as they were, should be fulfilled.' " He opened
the case. "Miriam. Will you take the second angel?"

Nina watched with rising concern. "What's he doing?
Why's he giving it to Miriam?"

"Who's she?" Eddie asked.

"One of his followers—she's just a kid, an innocent.
Why is he . . ." A horrible possibility occurred. "Oh my
God."

"What?"

She looked at him in alarm. "The angels—Cross thinks
that for him to learn God's secrets, all four angels have
to be released. But one was *already* released, in Iraq, so
they don't have to be broken at the same time." Possibility became certainty, and as her gaze snapped back to
the helicopter, it seemed that Cross was looking past
Miriam directly at her, almost taunting. "He's going to
do it *here*! Miriam, don't!"

She was drowned out by Cross's amplified voice.
"Miriam has taken the angel," he announced, kissing
her on both cheeks before entering the helicopter. Norvin was last aboard, closing the door. Some of the other
villagers were filing toward the helipad with a clear mix
of emotions from worry to near-rapture. "Now may
God's will be done!" The aircraft took off, rising vertically at full power before heading west.

"Miriam!" Nina cried again, as futilely as before. The
young woman, tears glistening on her cheeks, raised the
statue high above her head. The other cultists cleared a
space around her.

"And God shall wipe away all tears from their eyes,"
boomed Cross. The helicopter was rapidly disappearing, but his voice remained. "And there shall be no more
death, neither sorrow, nor crying . . ."

He paused. Nina used the moment of silence to scream
Miriam's name again, begging her to stop—

"Neither shall there be any more pain."

Miriam's mouth opened in a silent cry . . . then she
threw the statue to the ground.

22

"*No!*" shrieked Nina. But it was too late.

The angel shattered against a rock—and a sickly yellow gas erupted from the meteorite fragments exposed at its core. Miriam screamed as the glutinous vapor swallowed her, the cloud expanding with frightening speed.

Some of the cultists at the helipad stood their ground, while the nerve of others broke and they fled. It made no difference. The gas consumed them in moments, people flailing in agony before vanishing into the opaque mass.

Eddie and Nina broke through their shock and ran. Behind them, panic spread through the congregation at the church, faith wavering and breaking at the sight of death rolling toward them.

The cloud reached the houses, swirling and slithering around them like a liquid snake. An elderly woman tried to run but tripped and fell; her husband hesitated, then went back to help her, only for both to succumb to the toxic gas as it swept over them. Some followers ran into the church in the desperate hope that its walls would provide sanctuary. Seconds later, all were dead. Others raced for the jungle, but anguished screams cut through the air as they were caught one by one.

"What the fuck *is* that stuff?" Eddie gasped.

"Something you don't wanna get near!" Nina replied. "Through that gate, there!"

They sprinted for the opening. One final choked wail reached them, then the Mission fell silent.

Eddie threw open the gate, letting Nina through. She was already short of breath, clutching at her abdomen. "Are you okay?" he asked as he caught up.

"No!" she snapped. "I'm pregnant and running from a huge poisonous cloud! I am *not* okay!"

"Love you too," he said, managing a brief grin, which vanished as he looked back. The looming mustard-yellow miasma was still rising behind them. "How far's this dock?"

"Just down here!" Nina saw water between the palms ahead.

"And there *is* a boat, right?"

"Yes, there's a boat! What, did you think I was planning to *swim* out of here?"

"Five more months of this, just five more months . . . ," Eddie told the jungle. She glared at him, but forgot her anger as they cleared the trees and saw the jetty. The boat was still there. "I'll get it started!" He ran ahead to the jetty, quickly unknotting the mooring rope and jumping aboard.

Nina reached the dock. "Eddie, look!" She pointed at the bay's entrance. Two boats were carving through the sea toward it. "It's the police!"

Eddie spotted them—then with alarm saw something closer. The death cloud had broken through the trees and was roiling along the edge of the bay, toward its mouth. "Shit! It's going to cut us off!" He looked around, finding that the cove had no other exits to the ocean.

Nina clambered into the boat as Eddie tugged at the starter cord. The engine clattered, then roared. He shoved the prow away from the jetty, then revved to full power, swinging out into open water.

The police boats were almost at the cove's mouth—but so was the gas. Oozing across the shore, it rolled the last few dozen yards over the rocks and dropped lazily down to the incoming waves. "The water!" Nina exclaimed, seeing a change in its movement. The thick, oily mass appeared to be reacting on contact with the sea, becoming thinner. "Cross said water stopped the reaction—it might absorb the gas too!"

"Not quick enough," Eddie realized. He had already judged how long it would take their boat to clear the bay, and unless the cloud completely vanished, they wouldn't make it.

The two police vessels reached the opening. "No, get back!" Nina shouted, waving her arms to warn them off; the cops probably thought it was nothing more dangerous than smoke. "Turn around!"

Too late. The cloud drifted across their path, blocking them from view . . .

Both boats burst from the dense fog, yellow vortices streaming out behind them. The men aboard thrashed and screamed. One vessel veered sharply away as its pilot hit the steering wheel in his blind panic. It rolled in a tight turn, engine still at full throttle, then flipped over, hurling its dying occupants into the water.

The other craft charged onward, holding course—

Straight at Eddie and Nina.

"Whoa, *fuck*!" Eddie yelped. He jammed the tiller to its limit, leaning into the turn to keep from capsizing. The coast guard powerboat surged past barely a foot behind them, bounding over their wake before smacking back into the water. It kept going, heading for the jetty.

"Turn, *turn*!" Nina cried after it, but there was nobody alive on board to hear. The boat rammed into one of the jetty's pilings, wood and fiberglass disintegrating in a huge shower of smashed fragments. Its ruptured fuel tanks exploded, sending a black mushroom cloud boiling into the sky.

But a different cloud dominated the couple's thoughts. Even though the water seemed to be affecting it, the sulfurous mass had still engulfed the bay's entrance and was now spreading across its interior after them. "We'll have to get back on shore," Eddie said, "and hope it doesn't cover the whole fucking island!" He turned the boat toward land, beyond the burning jetty.

"Eddie, wait!" Nina pointed at the rock spit. "There's a blowhole or something where the waves hit the rocks." Right on cue, a great burst of spray erupted from the corner of the cove. "The cliff's only narrow, and the sea's right on the other side—we might be able to ride a wave over it!"

He shot her a disbelieving look. "Those pregnancy hormones must've screwed up your brain. It's *me* who's supposed to come up with the insane plans, not you!"

"It's the only way out!"

Eddie grimaced, but knew she was right. The deadly cloud would soon cover the entire bay. "Let's hope I time it right," he said, revving the engine.

The boom of water striking the rocks grew louder as they approached. Spray was being flung high into the air over the barrier, but most of the frothing waves stopped a couple of feet short of its top. Some managed to clear it, but there was no way to predict which ones.

Eddie slowed, watching the waves roll in—then twisted the throttle to full. A large breaker had already passed beneath them, and they rapidly caught up with it. "Come on, come on—*Shit!*"

He had mistimed it, the crest smashing against the wall and reaching almost to its top, then falling just as they angled up its rising shoulder. He turned away hard, but momentum carried them onward—

The backwash as the wave retreated saved them from a catastrophic crash, but the boat's side still slammed against the rocks, throwing its passengers sideways before being pulled clear. Water sluiced into the hull as the craft lurched upright and careered back into the cove.

The Yorkshireman shook foam off his face. "Jesus!" he gasped, regaining control. "Are you okay?"

Nina sat up, clutching a bruised arm. "Yeah. I think." She flicked wet strands of red hair from her eyes, then flinched as she saw what lay ahead. "Oh, crap!"

The cloud now covered more than half the bay, consuming the jetty, and was still advancing on them. If they had made landfall, they would never have been able to outrun the vaporous juggernaut.

Eddie hurriedly turned away, but the boat was rapidly running out of space to maneuver. He looked back at the cliff. "We'll have to go for it," he said reluctantly, "but we'll only get one more chance. You ready?"

Nina braced herself. "No, but do it anyway!"

He half smiled, then turned his attention back to the water. He had no choice but to follow the first large wave that came along, and hope it would propel them over the ridge.

None was coming. The sickly cloud roiled ever closer.

A deeper trough—then a new wave broke through the deadly fog.

Eddie didn't know if it would be strong enough, but he had to use it. He waited for it to pass beneath the boat, then—as the first yellow tendrils stretched out toward him—jammed the throttle to full power.

The boat leapt forward, following the wave. One last tweak of the tiller, aiming for the spot where the impacts were focused, then he gripped Nina with his free arm and held on for dear life—

The wave struck, surging upward before exploding against the cliff and sending a broad spout of water and spray skyward . . .

Carrying the boat with it.

It tipped back almost vertically, riding up the wave to be flung off its top into a blinding mass of spume. The keel hit the rock with a hideous raw crunch, the boat teetering atop the ridge like a seesaw for a nerve-shredding moment . . . then the weight of the water falling back into the hull pulled the prow downward. It rasped over the summit and dropped into the sea on the far side with a pounding smack.

The landing flung Nina and Eddie from their seats. The Englishman spat out seawater, then scrambled back to the motor. He looked up—to see the deadly cloud spill over the clifftop and drop toward them like a slow-motion avalanche.

"For fuck's *sake*!" he yelled, grabbing the throttle.

The propeller clashed against rock, making the tiller jar painfully in his grip, then finally bit into clear water. The boat surged away as the malevolent mass silently fell down behind it.

He swung away from the shore, only looking back once he was sure they were at a safe distance. "Christ . . ."

Nina was just as shocked. The cloud was draped over the island's eastern side like a monstrous jellyfish, still swallowing up the jungle tree by tree. Its advance did appear to have been slowed over the water, but at a price: The azure sea around it had turned a bloody red. "My God. I can't believe how big it is!"

"All of that from one little statue? What the bloody hell was in it?"

"Part of a meteor, according to Cross. Something that fell to earth in ancient history and became part of apocalyptic mythology."

"Yeah, I can see why." He glanced toward Antigua. "Shit, we've got to warn somebody! If that stuff reaches the mainland . . ."

Nina looked more intently at Elliot Island. "I don't think it will. Look, over by the Mission. It doesn't seem to be pumping out any more gas, and the wind's starting to push the cloud out to sea. Cross told me that whatever creates it gets burned up when it reacts with air; maybe it's all been consumed."

"Along with everyone in the village," Eddie reminded her.

"Oh God, yes . . ." She nodded sadly. "I don't think most of them were bad, just . . . just misguided. Cross found people who could be persuaded to follow his beliefs, used them to build his organization, then left them to die once they'd served their purpose. Poor Miriam . . ."

Eddie was less sympathetic, but kept his opinions to himself. "Over there," he said instead, pointing. The *Flirty Lady* was visible in the distance, having moved well clear of the island. "That's my mate's ship. We can radio the mainland from it and tell 'em what's happened. Hopefully we'll be able to stop Cross and Dalton from taking off."

"Hopefully," said Nina, though with little confidence. The damaged propeller was slowing them; it would take a while to reach the ship. She looked back toward the Mission. The gas cloud was indeed dispersing in places, the church spire now visible through the yellow haze, but a good third of the island was covered. "Because they've got another angel. If they release it in a city . . ."

She didn't need to say more. Eddie shared her grim look, then guided their vessel toward the yacht.

23

" So they got *away*?" Eddie barked at the speakerphone.
"I am afraid so, yes," came the voice of Oswald
Seretse. It was now dusk; Tom Harkaway had brought
the *Flirty Lady* into the nearer port of Nelson's Dockyard rather than returning to Jolly Harbour. He had
alerted the authorities about the events on Elliot Island
by radio after Eddie and Nina boarded, but by the time
word reached the airport, a private jet had already taken
off. "The aircraft filed a flight plan to Geneva, but it
now seems unlikely it is actually going there."

Eddie shook his head. "Black flights. Fucking CIA."
He turned to Nina. "That must be how they got you out
of the States without anyone asking questions. The CIA's
got a whole fleet of planes they use to whip people
around the world, as passengers—or prisoners. Cross
and Dalton must still have mates there."

"But we know where they're going," she replied. "Israel. It'll take them at least twelve hours to arrive, so
that gives us plenty of time to alert the Israelis and get
them to arrest them when they land."

Even over the phone, Seretse was clearly uncomfortable. "There are two problems, Nina. The first is that
we have no proof of Victor Dalton's involvement other

than your word. He was not seen by customs officials at Antigua airport, and there is so far no evidence to suggest that he was even on the island. Without such proof, making direct accusations against him would be . . . unwise. He may have been forced out of office, but he still has supporters."

"I didn't *imagine* seeing him, Oswald," she snapped.

"I am sure you did not. But the second is that when he was president, Dalton was a great supporter of the Israeli government; the US representative on the United Nations Security Council while he was in office had a one hundred percent record of voting in favor of Israel or vetoing resolutions that were against its interests. If he really is going there, he will have many friends in high places."

The couple had been brought by helicopter to Government House in St. John's; in the room with them were the island's governor general and the prime minister, James Jefferson, the latter responding with a burst of indignation. "Whether President Dalton was here or not, the man who owned Elliot Island, this Ezekiel Cross, has committed an act of terrorism against my country!" he snapped. "He released a chemical weapon! We don't know how long it will be before the island is safe to visit, and even though the gas cloud has gone, the sea has been poisoned—we have already had reports of dead fish and birds." He glared at his companion. "You have to do something, Calvin. You're the queen's representative here. Even if the British government is too afraid of the Americans to act, we must still issue a formal protest to the United States, and tell them to find this CIA plane!"

The governor general, an elderly Antiguan named Sir Calvin Woodman, had the expression of someone who had expected a relaxing day in paradise only to find the beach littered with land mines. "We cannot do anything until we know exactly what has happened," he protested. "The Americans are sending experts to check the island."

"And when will they be here?" Nina demanded.

Seretse gave her the answer. "Both USAMRICD and the CDC have been alerted about the release of a possible chemical agent. Specialists will be arriving overnight."

"Yeah, but they won't be able to do anything until morning," said Eddie. "And the people who caused it'll be halfway around the world!"

"I have done all I can," Woodman offered feebly. "The experts are on their way, and we must wait to see what they find. As for this allegation about President Dalton, I find it extremely hard to believe." Ignoring Nina's angry look, he went on: "We must wait for absolute proof of his involvement before demanding further action."

"So fuck-all's going to get done, then," said Eddie. It was now the governor general's turn to look indignant.

There was a quiet rap on the door. An Antiguan woman entered at the prime minister's response to announce that the chief of the country's defense forces had arrived. "I'll see him in my office," the politician told her. Woodman left with him.

"Mr. Chase?" the woman added. "Professor Rothschild is here."

Eddie nodded. "Show her in, thanks."

Nina gave her husband an unhappy look. "Professor Rothschild?"

"Yeah."

"As in Professor *Maureen* Rothschild?"

"Uh-huh."

"The bane of my professional existence? The woman who spent years undermining my career? The miserable old bag I *absolutely cannot stand*?"

"That's the one. Unless there's another Professor Maureen Rothschild who decided to drop in for no particular reason."

"God*damm*it, Eddie!" cried Nina, jumping up—then whirling as the door opened again. "Maureen," she said, with a fixed, icy smile of greeting. "What an unexpected surprise."

"Surprises usually are, Nina," Rothschild replied as she entered.

"Hey, Prof," said Eddie, standing. "No trouble getting here, then?"

"Your friend Tom arranged a cab for me. I'm glad you made it back in one piece, Eddie."

Nina eyed him. "You two are on first-name terms now, huh?"

"He saved my life," Rothschild told her. "That *is* usually something of an icebreaker. Although unlike you, I don't intend to marry him."

Eddie clapped a hand to his chest. "Ow! I'm heartbroken."

"We needed someone with extensive archaeological knowledge to find the angel statue in Berlin," Seretse said over the speakerphone. "Maureen kindly agreed to help us."

Rothschild smiled. "In return for some IHA consultancy work."

"*What?*" demanded Nina.

"Now, love," Eddie said, putting his hands on her shoulders, "you remember that you don't even work for the IHA anymore, right?"

"That's not the . . . Oh, shut up." She huffed and pouted.

"I did overhear what you said just before I arrived," revealed the elderly woman, to Nina's slight mortification, "and while I would never be so rude as to voice my own feelings about you in public, I have to admit it's not exactly a dream reunion. But I'm honestly relieved that you're still here to be as charming as ever. And," she added, "I understand congratulations are in order. Do you know if it's a boy or a girl?"

"Uh . . . no, no, not yet," Nina mumbled, caught off guard. Eddie gave her a curious look.

"Well, I'm happy for you both. But anyway, what happened to you?"

It took several minutes to describe everything that had transpired, and by the time Nina and Eddie finished, Rothschild's face was pale. "My God," she said quietly. "Nearly a hundred people dead? That's . . . that's appalling."

"There'll be a lot more joining them if these arseholes get what they're after," Eddie reminded her.

"Victor Dalton, though? I've met the man; I can't believe he's involved in this."

"He'll do whatever it takes to get back into power," said Nina. "And I was dragged into this specifically because he wanted revenge on me and Eddie. He made it personal—and so did Cross when he threatened my baby."

Seretse broke the uncomfortable silence. "Nina, you said Cross will be going to Israel to search for the angel near a sinkhole. Do you know exactly where?"

"Somewhere in the southern desert," she replied. "The clues in Revelation point to the route of the Exodus."

"Which clues?" asked Rothschild.

"The ones relating to the Woman of the Apocalypse. The reference to 'the moon under her feet' I think meant the Wilderness of Sin, because Sin was—"

"A Semitic moon god, yes," Rothschild interrupted. She went to the door and called to the aide. "Excuse me? Do you have a Bible?"

A copy was quickly procured. "Thank you," she said as the woman left. "Most Caribbean nations are extremely Christian, so I thought there would be one on hand. Now, let's have a look at Revelation." She opened the book to its final section. "Chapter twelve, let's see . . . 'a woman clothed with the sun, with the moon under her feet and a crown of twelve stars upon her head.'"

Nina nodded. "The twelve stars are probably the wells of—"

"The wells of Elim, yes. Nobody has identified the precise location yet, but the most likely possibilities are in the Sinai peninsula, which fits in perfectly with the following station of the Exodus on the coast of the Red Sea, most likely at the tip of the Gulf of Aqaba."

"And then," Nina pressed on, irritated, "they headed north toward the next station, Dophkah, which is—"

"Timna, of course."

"Will you *stop* doing that?"

Rothschild looked down her nose at the younger

woman. "I'm only trying to help, Nina. I thought my experience might be useful to you."

"She did work out that the statue was in that temple in Berlin," Eddie pointed out to his wife.

"Anyone could have figured that out," she replied.

"Cross didn't."

"Anyone who isn't an insane religious nut, then! But . . ." Her expression softened slightly as she looked back at Rothschild. "If you hadn't done it, Cross would have gotten the third angel—and Eddie wouldn't have found me. I'd be on my way to Israel at gunpoint by now. So . . . thank you, Maureen."

Rothschild was surprised, but pleased. "Perhaps if your baby's a girl, you might consider naming her after me?"

"All right," said Eddie, seeing Nina's eye twitch even at the humorous suggestion, "let's get back to stopping this psycho, eh? The last angel's somewhere in Israel—but where?"

"There must be more of a clue to the location than simply being near a sinkhole," said Rothschild, checking the Bible passages again. "They're not uncommon."

"I know," Nina said. "I'm sure there's something more to the symbolism, but I don't know what."

The elderly woman tapped the page. "The whole section with the Woman of the Apocalypse is cloaked in symbolism. The moon under her feet, the twelve stars . . . so what about the sun? 'Clothed with the sun'—what could that mean?" She read on. "And then there's verse fourteen: 'The woman was given the two wings of a great eagle, so that she might fly to the place prepared for her in the wilderness.'"

Nina remembered the verse. "Cross told me the repetition of the reference to a location is what made him think the woman is the key to finding the angel. It appears in verse six as well as fourteen."

"So the whole thing is a clue . . ." Rothschild put down the book, she and Nina both staring intently at the text. "The wings of an eagle. That has to be relevant . . . the wings of an eagle."

"What about 'em?" Eddie asked.

"She's given wings to reach the place prepared for her . . . Nina, which version of the Bible was he using?"

"The King James," Nina told her.

"This one's the New International, so there are differences in the translation. If I remember, the King James says that she goes into 'her place' rather than 'the place prepared for her.' "

Eddie cocked his head. "Is there a difference?"

"There's a *huge* difference," Rothschild replied. "The location is hidden behind symbolism, remember. It's the same place as in verse six, but this time it's referred to specifically as *her* place, the woman's place. But where is that?"

He smirked. "I'd say the kitchen, but I know Nina'd hit me."

"So hard you'd wish you felt as good as the last time you got shot," his wife confirmed. "But yes, that has to be symbolic. What would be a woman's place that could also represent a physical location?"

The two women were briefly silent, deep in thought—then, to Eddie's surprise, Nina's cheeks flushed. "What's up?" he asked.

Her expression was one of distinct embarrassment. "Well, it could be something a woman has that, ah, a man doesn't. A kind of, um, sacred passage." Her face became even rosier.

Rothschild arched her eyebrows. "Really, Nina, you're such a prude. She means a vagina," she explained for Eddie and Seretse.

Eddie laughed. "Yeah, I know. But thanks for saying it out loud!"

"Indeed," Seretse added.

"Yes, okay, we've all had our little joke," Nina snapped, not amused. "But that could be what the symbolism represents. The angel is in a place prepared by God, somewhere holy, sacred, that's reached through the so-called woman's place. A passage leading to somewhere safe from where her child emerges, but also where the dragon is forced to wait outside."

Rothschild read from the Bible. " 'The dragon stood in front of the woman who was about to give birth, so that it might devour her child the moment he was born.' "

"Yeah. You can interpret the dragon however you like—Satan, the armies facing the Israelites, whoever—but for whatever reason, he can't get into this place. Why not?"

"The wings of an eagle," said Rothschild. "The wings are symbolic too. This passage or canyon, whatever it is—it might seem that it can only be *reached* by an eagle. It's high up."

"Easy to defend," Eddie added. "If you've got an army after you—or a dragon—you want to be above them and make them come through somewhere narrow. If you've got a good defensive position, you can hold off a much bigger force for ages."

"If it's high up," said Nina with sudden excitement, "then Cross'll be looking in the wrong place!"

"How so?" Seretse asked.

"Because he's looking for sinkholes, based on the verse about the dragon releasing a river and the earth swallowing it. He thought—*I* thought—that meant the Place in the Wilderness must be in a river valley. But if Maureen's right, it would be higher up. Possibly much higher, if you need wings to reach it."

"So how did the Israelites reach it?" said Eddie.

"It's only symbolic. The Castle of the Eagles in your favorite movie isn't literally full of eagles, is it?" Ignoring his amusement at how the plot of *Where Eagles Dare* would change if that were the case, she addressed the phone. "Oswald, Eddie told me he came over here on a UN-chartered jet—can you get one to take us to southern Israel?"

What sounded suspiciously like a resigned sigh came over the speaker. "I thought you might ask. I had already arranged for it to be refueled for you."

"Thank you, Oswald. And we'll need access to the IHA's databases en route—maps, terrain, all the archaeological and historical files we have."

"We?" echoed Rothschild. "I thought you'd resigned from the IHA, Nina."

"I just keep getting dragged back there, don't I?"

"I shall arrange for whatever you need," said the United Nations official.

"You might not be able to get *everything* we need," said Eddie. "But I've got a mate in Israel who can sort out the rest."

"If by 'the rest' you mean weapons, I would rather not know," Seretse said with another sigh.

"I appreciate it, Oswald," Nina told him. "I don't know if we'll be able to find the place, though. There's still an awful lot of ground to cover."

"I might be able to narrow it down," said Rothschild, looking up from the Bible.

Nina went to her. "What have you found?"

"The line describing the Woman of the Apocalypse as being 'clothed by the sun.' I just had an idea about what that might mean."

"What is it?" Eddie asked.

"Dophkah—Timna, as it's now known—has been a source of copper for millennia. In some places, the copper veins were so rich, they were even visible on the surface."

"Like the old silver mines we saw in Egypt on the way to the Pyramid of Osiris," Nina said to Eddie, remembering a similar find.

"Accessibility is also an issue with mining, though," Rothschild went on. "There are places high up where the copper can be seen in the rock but it would be almost impossible to mine, so it's still there. I've seen examples myself, and they're quite spectacular in the right lighting. Such as at sunrise," she concluded, with meaning. "The copper seams reflect the dawn light, and the rock seems to glow like the sun itself."

"'Clothed with the sun,'" Nina said quietly. "You think that could be what Revelation means?"

"I personally wouldn't want to commit an expedition merely on a possibility, but"—she gave Nina a look of grudging admiration—"your career has been built on wild, crazy gambles, and I have to admit that it's more than paid off for you."

"Why, *thank* you, Maureen," replied Nina thinly. "But if you *were* to take a wild, crazy gamble, would you suggest looking for sites facing either due east or due west to catch the sun?"

"Due east is more likely," said Rothschild. "The dawn has far more symbolic importance to ancient religions than sunset. But I'm sure you knew that already."

"Yes. I did."

The two archaeologists exchanged frosty smiles, then Rothschild nodded. "But . . . good luck anyway, Nina."

"Thanks," she replied, before giving the older woman a quizzical look. "Can I ask you something, Maureen?"

"What?"

"You still don't like me. So why *did* you agree to help Eddie find me?"

Rothschild seemed reluctant to answer, so Eddie stepped in. "For the baby," he told Nina. "A baby shouldn't suffer because of its parents. That's what you said, right, Maureen? Especially an unborn one."

His wife was taken by surprise. "That's . . . Maureen, thank you so much," she said, this time with genuine gratitude.

Rothschild hesitated again before speaking. "There was a little more to it, actually," she admitted. "You're having a child. It's a great gift, maybe the greatest. I, ah . . ." Her voice lowered. "I was going to have one, once. But . . . he never came to term."

"My God," said Nina. "I'm sorry. I had no idea."

"It was a long time ago. But I still think about what might have been . . ." A moment of sad reflection, then she looked back at the couple. "I wish you all the best with the baby—and with what you're about to do. I hope you find the last angel."

"So do I," said Nina. "Because I've seen what'll happen if we don't."

24

Israel

"Colonel Brik," said Cross with a smile, shaking hands with the Israeli officer. "Meshulam, my old friend."

"Ezekiel," Brik replied. "It is good to see you again." He looked up as a second passenger emerged from the jet—another man he recognized, though in this case not from any personal encounters. "Wait, that is—"

"President Dalton is not officially here," the former CIA operative told him. "This visit is . . . off the record."

The Israeli nodded. "Our mutual friend in Tel Aviv said you were traveling with someone important. But this I did not expect!"

Dalton stepped down onto the concrete, already looking uncomfortable. The temperature at Ovda airport—a small civilian terminal that shared runways with the sprawling military base to the east—was not excessively hot at this time of year, but the morning air was extremely dry and dusty, stinging his eyes.

"Mr. President, this is Colonel Meshulam Brik," Cross told him. "Colonel, it's my honor to introduce President Victor Dalton."

Brik offered his hand. "Pleasure to meet you, Colonel," said Dalton, giving him a firm but brief shake. He surveyed his surroundings. The air base was located on a long plain, crumpled mountains rising to the east and west. "Kind of an isolated facility you have here."

"We do not mind," Brik replied. "When your country has enemies on all sides, it is best to keep your defenses far from their eyes."

"I guess so," said Dalton, nodding politely. "Although Egypt"—he waved to the west—"and Jordan"—another flick of the hand in the opposite direction—"aren't your enemies right now."

The Israeli gave him a somewhat patronizing smile. "Mr. President, Israel has only one true friend in the world—the United States. Everyone else either is or could be our enemy. We are prepared for all possibilities."

"Well, we're glad to be Israel's friend. And I promise you I'll do everything in my power to make our relationship even stronger."

"Thank you, Mr. President," said Brik. He glanced at the plane as more people emerged, Simeon and Anna leading the group. Cross had already sent a team to Antigua's airport before evacuating the Mission; the expedition now numbered ten in total. "There is a helicopter ready for you, as requested. The facilities of my base are at your disposal—if you need food or sleep, we can give you whatever you need."

Dalton looked about to take him up on the offer of sleep, but Cross spoke first. "Thanks, but we're ready to go. We've got a lot of ground to cover."

"Of course." Brik nodded. "Still dedicated to duty and secrets, Ezekiel? You have not changed." He raised his voice to be heard over the roar of a helicopter gunship taking off from the base. "You will have free access to Israeli airspace in this region, along with complete discretion from myself and all my men. You also have my personal assurance that you will receive whatever help you need."

"That's much appreciated, Colonel," said Dalton.

Cross shook Brik's hand again. "Thanks for this, Meshulam."

Brik shrugged. "I owe you a favor, my friend. All I ask is that one day, you tell me what all this is about."

The American smiled. "Don't worry. I guarantee you'll know soon."

. . .

A few hours later, and some twenty miles to the south, another business jet landed in Israel, this one at the commercial airport of Eilat at the northernmost tip of the Gulf of Aqaba. Its occupants were as tired following the lengthy transatlantic flight as Dalton had been, but their journey had been more productive.

"So we know where to look," Nina said with a yawn as the flight attendant opened the hatch and lowered the stairs. "We've got four possible locations for the Place in the Wilderness." She had used the IHA's extensive databases en route to search for places where the terrain matched her theory: an area of high, inaccessible land featuring both a narrow passage and a sinkhole, with current or exhausted copper deposits. Even with the assistance of a computer program, it had been a tiring task.

"Assuming you and Rothschild were right," Eddie said, donning his battered black leather jacket.

"I found the other two angels, didn't I?"

"*Cross* found 'em," he reminded her. "He did all the groundwork, anyway. But that doesn't mean he got the last one right too."

"We can't take that chance. Not after seeing what that gas does to people."

They descended the steps, harsh sunlight striking them. "Ay up," said Eddie on seeing the tall, lean young man waiting for them. "Hope Mossad sent you to take care of us and not *take care of us,* if you know what I mean."

Jared Zane gave the Englishman a mocking smile. "If I were going to kill you, you wouldn't even have known I was here." He was an agent of the Mossad, the Israeli intelligence agency, who had worked with Eddie and Nina to hunt down a group of escaped Nazi war criminals—the last survivor of whom had sought revenge on the couple only a month earlier.

"Ah, but you might be saying that to lull us into a false sense of security!"

"Oh, shut up, *alter kocker*." The Yiddish insult roughly translated as "old fart."

"Cheeky little bastard." Both men grinned.

"Ah, boys," said Nina with an exaggerated sigh. "Have you finished shaking your peacock feathers at each other?"

Jared smiled. "Hi, Nina. Good to see you again."

"You too! And thank you."

It was more heartfelt than simply meeting them at the airport warranted. Jared regarded her curiously. "What for?"

"For saving my life—again. If you hadn't warned Eddie that one of the Nazis from Argentina had survived and was out for revenge . . ."

He dipped his head modestly. "You and Eddie saved *my* life, so it was the least I could do." He glanced down at her baby bump. "I'd heard you were pregnant. Congratulations!"

"Don't remember telling you," said Eddie.

"I'm from the Mossad. We know everything." Another grin, then he became more business-like. "Although in this case, we *don't* know everything—or at least, I don't. It seems I don't have a high enough security clearance. After you phoned," he said to Eddie, "I tried to find out if this Ezekiel Cross and ex-president Dalton were coming to Israel. It wasn't long before I was called into my superior's office and told to stop asking questions."

"So someone's covering it up?" Nina asked.

The young man nodded. "It must be somebody high up. Whether in the Mossad or the government, I don't know. Dalton was very popular here in Israel."

"Surprised Mossad let you help us," said Eddie.

A small grimace. "Actually, I'm not technically on duty right now. My superior let me take a leave of absence on short notice—*very* short notice—so I could show some visiting friends around the country."

"Very generous of him," Nina remarked knowingly.

"Even bosses get called into *their* boss's office sometimes. And they don't like it either."

Eddie smiled. "Good to know spooks have office politics too."

"It's not all hanging from cliffs and car chases. Anyway, I've got a jeep waiting, and all the gear you'll need. Including something for you, Eddie. I know you need to compensate for your inadequacies with big guns, so I brought you a fifty-caliber Desert Eagle."

Eddie pulled a sarcastic face. "So what did you bring for yourself, a bazooka?"

Jared laughed. "Don't worry about the customs check; I've dealt with it," he said as the attendant brought out the couple's luggage. "Nina, let me take that." He picked up Nina's travel bag.

"You can take mine an' all if you want," Eddie suggested.

"Carry it yourself," Jared replied cheekily. "You're an old man, but not *that* old."

"Fucking kids!" Eddie mock-grumbled, picking up his bag. He and Nina followed the curly-haired Israeli to the terminal.

"So," said Jared, "since you didn't want to tell me the details over the phone, what's this all about?"

*   *   *

Twenty minutes later, Nina and Eddie finally finished their explanation. "Okay," Jared said unhappily as he drove a Land Rover Discovery north into the Israeli desert, "what *is* it with you two? Everyone else's archaeology involves carefully digging junk out of the dirt, but with you it's always maniacs trying to destroy the world!"

"You think I *want* that?" Nina hooted. "I'd love nothing more than to spend three months excavating a site with only a trowel and a sieve."

"Me, not so much," said Eddie from the seat behind her. "I'll be on the beach with the kid while you're doing that."

"No you won't, you'll both be with me. And enjoying it."

"You need to do more research on what kids actually like."

"I liked it when I was a kid!" she protested.

"Yeah, but you're weird."

Nina glared over her shoulder at him. "You're lucky I needed the space up front, or you would *so* be slapped right now."

Jared smiled. "Okay, so: crazy ex-CIA guy with chemical weapons, here in my country to look for more. How do we make sure he doesn't get them?"

Nina took out a map of southern Israel. "I found four places where the last angel might be. If Cross is still working from the theory that it's near a sinkhole in a river valley, then he shouldn't go near them."

Jared glanced at the map. "If he's searching in this area, he'll never be far away. Israel is only about twelve miles east to west at the Timna Valley, and it gets narrower the farther south you go." He gestured to the right. "The border with Jordan is less than a mile away."

"He'll still have almost a hundred square miles to cover," Nina insisted. "And he'll be looking at the valleys when he should be searching the highlands. We can beat him."

"Assuming *your* theory is right."

Her face became rueful. "If it's not, then a lot of people could die. So I have to hope that it is."

They drove on. The highway stretched north through a sandy plain, small settlements and sparse patches of irrigated farmland soon surrendering to the desolation of the desert. Barren mountains rose on the horizon to each side. Eventually they neared a turnoff, a side road heading west toward a small village. "Okay, that's . . . Be'er Ora," said Nina, struggling with the pronunciation. "We go past it and head up into the mountains. The first site is about three miles from here."

Jared made the turn. "How accessible is it?"

"We should be able to see it from the ground. We may

need to climb to check it, though. You brought climbing gear, didn't you?"

"Everything you need." The Israeli indicated the equipment in the four-by-four's cargo bed. "You shouldn't climb when you're pregnant, though."

"I shouldn't be kidnapped or chased or jump over cliffs in speedboats when I'm pregnant either," she snapped.

"But it could be—"

Eddie leaned forward and put a hand on Jared's shoulder. "When you hear that tone of voice, trust me, mate, that's when you shut up." He added in a stage whisper: "Then you do what you were going to do anyway without telling her—Ow!"

Nina swatted the side of his head. "Warned you." He withdrew, amused.

Jared drew in a breath. "My mother keeps pushing for me to get married. I think I might wait a while longer . . ."

The Discovery headed through the little village, the road rising into the parched peaks beyond. Asphalt quickly gave way to a stony track. Jared switched the four-by-four's terrain mode to maintain grip. "This could be rough," he said. "How far do we follow the road?"

"Until it runs out," said Nina, examining the map. "It'll take us over this range and into a valley—we go south down it and then turn west again."

"I don't think this first one'll be it," Eddie said dubiously. "It's too close to that village. Somebody would have found it already—I mean, this whole area's a national park, isn't it?" Jared nodded.

"We still have to check, though," said Nina.

The Land Rover picked its way between the peaks, scrabbling up a steep pass before dropping back into a flat, sandy valley. Had Nina stuck with her original theory of the angel's location, this would have been one of the places to search. It was bone-dry at the moment, but alluvial channels carved into the ground proved that when water did flow through this part of the desert, it did so with force.

They headed south. "There should be a smaller valley

about half a mile away," she told Jared. "It leads into a canyon; the place we're looking for is another half mile along it."

"Let me see the map," said Eddie. Nina passed it to him. "Still don't think this can be it. It's too easy to get to. If we turn off and follow this ridge here"—he pointed to it—"we could *drive* to the bloody place. There's probably a falafel stand there for tourists."

"Soon find out," she replied. But he had already convinced her that they were unlikely to find anything on their first try.

That turned out to be the case. Jared took Eddie's advice and, rather than continue along the canyon floor, ascended a steep rise to the top of one of its sides. From there they had a clear view of their intended destination. Nina was the first to look through a pair of powerful binoculars. "You were right, Eddie," she admitted. "There are no signs of any copper deposits. I can see a sinkhole in the canyon, but it's not very deep, and the passage in the rock above it is too wide and too shallow to look like, ah . . ." Her cheeks flushed as she glanced at the young man beside her. "Like what we think it should look like," she concluded lamely.

"She means a woman's bits," Eddie informed him, failing completely to hide a smirk.

Now it was Jared's turn to look faintly embarrassed. "You mean like, uh . . . breasts?"

"No, kid," said the Englishman, trying not to crack up. "The *other* bits." Even Nina couldn't help but laugh.

"Okay, okay," huffed the Israeli.

"You do know what I mean, right?"

"Yes, I do! *Tahat.*"

"Don't worry about it, Jared," said Nina, unable to resist a little teasing of her own. "I think it's sweet."

"I should leave you two here," he muttered. "But this isn't the place, is it?"

She shook her head. "It doesn't match the clues hidden in Revelation. We should move on to the next one."

"I've got an idea," said Eddie. "How about we go straight to the one that's the farthest from anywhere, and work backward? Like I said, if this place were too easy to find, somebody would have done it by now."

Nina opened the map. "We're here"—she tapped one of the marked spots—"and the one deepest into the desert is . . . here. About five miles northwest."

Eddie examined the contour lines around it. "Steep cliffs. Looks like that mountain from *Close Encounters.*"

"It's joined to the rest of this higher range to the north, so it might be reachable that way." She looked at the two men. "Shall we do it back-to-front, then?"

"If we'd done that four months ago, you wouldn't be pregnant," said Eddie. It took her a moment to figure it out, and when she did, he hurriedly ducked away from another swat of her hand. "But yeah, I'm up for it."

"It'll take us a few hours to get there," Jared warned. "There isn't a direct route—we'll have to follow these valleys and cut through this pass." He traced the path with his fingertip.

"So long as we *can* get there, that's the important thing." Nina folded the chart back up. "Okay, let's get started."

She looked toward the distant peaks, catching a glint of light in the cloudless sky. A helicopter, crossing the desert. She watched it for a moment, wondering if her enemies might be aboard conducting their own search, before deciding it didn't matter. If it *was* Cross and Dalton, they were some distance from any of her potential sites.

* * *

Victor Dalton shifted in his seat, uncomfortable and annoyed. The Bell 430 helicopter was large enough to accommodate all the members of Cross's expedition, but the window seats were occupied by those scouring the ground below through binoculars. With Paxton piloting and Cross in the copilot's seat beside him, the ex-president had ended up sandwiched between two of the cult leader's men, without much of a view. "It's too damn hot back here," he growled into his headset's mike. "Can you turn on the air-con?"

"It's already on, Victor," Cross told him dismissively. "This isn't Marine One; you'll have to manage."

"There's a big fan right above us," added Simeon, with a mocking glance up at the main rotor. Anna chuckled.

"Damn right it isn't Marine One," Dalton muttered. He tried to look over the pilot's shoulder at the desert below. "Any sign of what we're after?"

"Not yet," Cross told him. "But we've only checked three sites so far. We'll find it, though. Have faith."

"Right now, I'd rather have legroom."

"I see a sinkhole," Simeon reported. "Ten o'clock, thirty degrees down." Other binoculars turned to locate it. Paxton slowed the chopper and began to circle.

"Well?" Dalton demanded impatiently after a couple of minutes. "Is that it?"

"We're still checking," said Cross. "But there's nothing nearby that might be ruins, or a cave system, and the sinkhole itself is empty, so . . . I don't think so," he decided, crossing off another marker from the map. "Okay, Paxton, take us to the next site. Four down."

"Too damn many to go," Dalton grumbled as the helicopter wheeled about to begin the next leg of its laborious search.

◆ ◆ ◆

The other group of explorers were enduring an equally laborious, and considerably less comfortable, journey. Even for a vehicle of the Discovery's off-road prowess it was hard going, with no roads to follow, nor even tracks.

Eddie had taken over navigation duties from Nina, having much more experience from his military career. Despite this, the map's lack of fine detail meant they were sometimes forced to backtrack from terrain beyond the Land Rover's abilities. "Shit," he exclaimed as he looked ahead, seeing that what on the chart was an open, if narrow, valley was in reality blocked by a near-vertical ridge of rock taller than a man. "Okay, Jared, turn us around. We'll have to head back to that big boulder and try to get up the hill."

"It might be too steep," the Israeli said as he reversed.

"If we don't try, we'll need to go all the way back around this fucking mountain." Eddie glared out of the side window at the offending peak.

Jared retraced their tracks to a large sand-weathered rock, then turned north to face a steep incline. "I don't know if we'll be able to get up this."

Eddie assessed it. "So long as you put it in low range and keep moving, you'll make it. And for Christ's sake don't go at an angle, or we'll roll over."

"We will? Wow! I'd never know these things without you to tell me. All that time the Mossad spent teaching me how to drive off-road . . ."

"All right, don't be a cheeky twat," said the Yorkshireman. "Just go for it."

Jared aligned the Discovery with the shallowest route up the incline, then started his ascent. The big four-by-four managed a reasonable pace at first, before its wheels began to slip and scrabble. "There's more grip over there," Eddie suggested, pointing to where the rock had less of a covering of sand.

"I know, I've seen it!" the younger man replied testily as he turned the wheel. "Did the SAS give you training in stating the obvious?"

"No, just in taking the piss out of kids who think they know everything."

Nina was more interested in something to one side. "Look, over there," she said. Jared kept his eyes on the climb, but Eddie followed her gaze. A cluster of loose stones had built up in a dip: stones of a very distinctive tint. "Those rocks—you see the greenish color on them? That's copper, oxidized copper. There must be deposits higher up."

Eddie peered up the hillside. "Can't see anything. They might have rolled half a mile to end up here, though."

"It's still a promising sign. Let me see the map again." Eddie handed it to her; she perused it, so deep in thought that she was oblivious to the Land Rover's lurches as it clawed its way up the hill.

The slope finally eased. "I wouldn't relax yet," Jared told Nina as she looked up from the map. "We still have to get back down."

"But we've found it," she said. "This is the valley!"

Spread out before them was a winding gorge. Its walls grew higher in the distance, the pale sandstone cliffs almost vertical as they passed out of sight around a bend. "If my theory's right, that the line 'clothed with the sun' from Revelation refers to somewhere with copper deposits facing east, then it should be at the top of a cliff down there," said Nina. "Come on, let's go."

The Discovery set off again. They headed along the canyon, before long rounding the bend to see . . .

"There!" exclaimed Nina. "It's up there!"

The valley opened out before them, creating a broad natural amphitheater several hundred feet long. It forked at the far end, one leg turning northeast and the other almost due south, closing off the western end of the great open space with a towering cliff. A couple of taller peaks rose beyond it, forming a massif surrounded by ravines.

Jared stopped the four-by-four. Its occupants got out, Nina scanning the barrier through binoculars. A vertical cleft in the rock was obvious even to the naked eye, and under magnification she glimpsed beyond it a narrow, twisting passage cutting deep into the sandstone, blue sky visible at its top. The channel was about sixty feet deep, the base of its entrance almost two hundred feet above the canyon's floor.

But it was not the shape that had caught her attention; it was the *color*. Patches of shimmering turquoise-green stood out clearly on the surrounding rock where veins of copper had been exposed to the elements. There were also streaks and spots of a darker golden hue. The soft stone was being relentlessly scoured by the desert winds, gradually revealing new deposits of raw, unoxidized copper as the surface layers fell away. Even with the sun high in the sky they shone with a warm light; at dawn,

Nina imagined, the reflected glow would be quite spectacular.

"Is that what we're after?" Eddie asked.

"Looks like it," she said. "A narrow passage—the, ah, woman's place—high up where someone would need wings to reach it, surrounded by copper that would catch the dawn light. It fits what John of Patmos wrote in Revelation, after being filtered through his hallucinogenic visions."

Jared squinted up at the opening. "Where does it go?"

"There was definitely a sinkhole on its far side in the satellite photos," said Nina. "Let's get a closer look."

They drove the rest of the way down the valley. Reaching the cliff, they found that a steep pile of scree had built up along its foot, reducing the distance to the bottom of the crevice by some forty feet. "Still a fair old climb," said Eddie.

"A hundred fifty feet? No worse than that cliff we climbed in Italy," Jared said.

"The one you almost got killed on when you slipped and fell?"

"I caught myself."

"*I* caught you."

The young man frowned, then reluctantly admitted: "Huh. Yeah. You did." Eddie gave him a smug look.

"But you can get up there?" asked Nina.

"Looks straightforward enough," her husband assured her. "Although we'll need to use ropes if the rock's that crumbly." He looked at Jared. "You up for it?"

"Anytime, old man," the Mossad agent replied. He opened the Discovery's tailgate and began to take out the climbing gear.

25

"Nothing here either," reported Cross, marking another site off his map. "Okay, Paxton, let's move on."

Behind him, Dalton had by now abandoned any attempt to disguise his irritation. "All this time, and nothing down there but sand and potholes. I should have gotten out when we went back to Ovda to refuel. How long before we have to gas up again?"

Paxton checked the gauges. "Another two hours, sir."

"Two hours! Christ." The exclamation brought disapproving glances from Simeon and Anna. "How about we refuel early so I can get out?"

"We're not going to disrupt the search because you're uncomfortable, Victor," said Cross. "We have work to do—God's work."

He spoke politely, but it was perfectly clear to all that a challenge had been issued. "Now wait one damn minute, Cross," Dalton rumbled. "I don't intend to be jolted around in this sweatbox for another two hours just because it interferes with your schedule. And my title is still 'Mr. President,' thank you very much."

"Of course . . . Mr. President." Cross managed to keep all but a tinge of disdain from his voice. "But it's your schedule too. And considering how the timing has worked out perfectly for us, we need to stick to it." He looked back at the former politician. "It's in both our best interests. Don't you agree, Mr. President?"

Dalton became acutely aware that he was surrounded by his partner's most loyal disciples, and that all of them were armed. "I suppose so, yes," he said, trying to salvage some decorum. "But if I can't even look out of a window, I'm not contributing much."

"That you're not, Mr. President. That you're not." Dalton glared at him, but the cult leader had already turned away.

* * *

With a loud grunt, Eddie pulled himself up into the cleft in the rock face. He caught his breath, then stood. The passage was narrow, about six feet wide at its entrance and barely half that deeper within.

Huffs and scrapes from behind. He turned to see Jared's head appear over the edge. "Need a hand?" the Englishman asked.

"No, I'm fine." The Mossad agent hauled himself onto level ground and shrugged off the long coil of rope he was carrying before detaching his climbing harness from the line. "That wasn't hard."

"I believe you. Thousands wouldn't," Eddie replied as he removed his own gear, then took a walkie-talkie from his belt. "Nina? We're both up here and safe."

Nina's voice crackled from the radio. "What can you see?"

"So far, nothing. The passage twists too much."

"According to the satellite, it should go back a couple of hundred feet before opening out at the sinkhole." A mix of eagerness and anxiety entered her voice. "You *will* be able to get me up there, won't you?"

"Oh, I dunno, might be too risky," Eddie told her, knowing full well that he and Jared would be able to bring her up the cliff with no risk to the baby. He smiled at the yelp of complaint that was audible from below even without the radio, then went on: "Yeah, we'll be able to. We'll see what's back there first, though. No point hauling you all the way up here for nothing."

"Okay," she said reluctantly. "Tell me what you see the whole way, though."

"Rock, rock, rock, rock . . ."

"You're a funny man, Eddie."

"Yeah, that's why you love me. Don't worry. If we find anything, I'll tell you." He lowered the radio. "Jared, you ready?"

"Always," the Israeli replied.

"Good. Let's go."

The two men started down the passage, boots crunching over the gritty sand. They rounded the first turn, losing sight of the entrance but seeing something new ahead. "That's tight," said Jared. The walls narrowed still further to a point where they were less than two feet apart. He had to turn slightly sideways to pass through. "Hey, will you even be able to fit?"

"You calling me fat?" Eddie replied. "Just 'cause you're built like a fucking beanpole . . ." But the obstruction presented no difficulty, the crevice widening out again after a short distance. "Okay, there's a narrow section, but you'll be able to get through," he said into the walkie-talkie. "Good job you're only four months pregnant and not eight."

Nina was already becoming impatient. "Have you reached the sinkhole yet?"

"No, I'll tell you when we do. It's nice in here, though." Beneath the snaking line of blue sky directly overhead, the rock walls were banded in different shades of brown, glinting seams of copper running through them. "Like being in a tiramisu mine."

"Great, now I've got a craving for some. Thanks, hon!"

Eddie smiled, then followed Jared up the passage. It occasionally narrowed, but was still navigable. Presenting more of a problem were fallen rocks, some almost blocking the way. The Israeli looked up after climbing over one, seeing a ragged gap high above from where the stone had fallen. "I don't think these cliffs are safe."

"Well, we don't have to climb 'em," Eddie replied as he traversed the blockage. "But if you hear a big cracking noise from above, don't look up to see what it is—just leg it!"

Jared chuckled, then looked ahead. "Hey, it's opening out."

"Nina, we're almost at the end," Eddie reported. "I'll tell you what we see." The pair continued on, the passage gradually widening—until they emerged in the open.

"What is it?" Nina demanded. "Have you found the sinkhole?"

"Yeah—and more besides."

He and Jared stepped out into a roughly egg-shaped depression in the mountain, the far wall of the bowl rising up to flatter ground about fifty feet above. The sinkhole Nina had seen on the satellite imagery was indeed here, an almost perfectly circular opening near the hollow's center. Eddie peered down into it. Blue-green water rippled gently around ten feet below him. Small pieces of debris floated on its surface. He couldn't see the bottom.

Just above the pool, a cave was cut into the shaft's wall, forming a ledge. He didn't need a doctorate in archaeology to know instantly that it was not a natural feature. Beneath the shelter of the overhang were several small archways, tunnels leading into the mountain. Inscribed around each were blocks of text.

The Englishman didn't recognize the language, but his companion did. "It's Hebrew," said Jared, eyes widening.

They hurried around the sinkhole and climbed down for a closer look. "Can you read it?" Eddie asked.

The Israeli examined one of the carved sections. "Some of it," he replied. "It's ancient Hebrew, not modern. There are a lot of differences."

"But you know what this is?"

Jared perused some of the other writings. "I think it's a temple. This word here"—he pointed it out—"is definitely *Yahweh*. God."

Nina was almost at bursting point with her radioed

demands for an update. Eddie told her what they had seen, then added: "I'm assuming you want to come up here and look for yourself?"

"No, no, I'll just stand around in the baking sun while you two poke around" came the sarcastic reply. "Of *course* I want to come up there!"

Jared pretended to wince. "So that's what being married is like? I think I'll have to disappoint my mom for a few more years."

"Nah," said Eddie with a grin, "I'm sure you'll go on disappointing her for the rest of your life."

The younger man now winced for real at having left himself wide open for the joke. "*Hamor,*" he muttered, before looking back at the tunnels. "Should we check what's inside before we bring her up?"

"Only if you want her to kill you," Eddie replied breezily. "Come on, let's go back and rig up a belay."

* * *

Less than thirty minutes later, Nina had been brought up to the passage. "That was only about half as terrifying as I'd expected," she said as Eddie helped unclip her harness from the rope. "Are you sure the baby will be okay?"

"Little Arbuthnot'll be fine," he assured her.

"More like Arbuth-*not*." She turned to Jared. "I'm glad you waited for me rather than rushing in. Exploring those tunnels on your own probably isn't a good idea."

"You think it might be dangerous?" he asked. "Booby-trapped, like the Spring of Immortality?"

"It's possible. If the last angel is here, it could be protected."

"The other angels weren't," Eddie pointed out.

"No, but this site's different—Revelation suggested it was a place of great religious importance, some kind of redoubt for the Israelites. The angel might not be the only thing here."

"Let's see, then." Eddie led the way through the twisting cleft, helping Nina over the fallen rocks.

"Oh, wow," she gasped as they emerged in the bowl beyond. "Definitely a place prepared in the wilderness. I want to go down to that cave."

"What's the magic word?" Eddie asked with a smirk.

She glowered at him. "*Now.*"

He laughed. "Near enough. We'll set up a rope to make it easier for you."

Nina overcame her impatience long enough to wait for the two men to put down the climbing equipment, then tie a line around a boulder and hang it over the edge. Eddie went first, supporting her from below as Jared helped her descend. She found her footing on the ledge, taking in the ancient inscriptions before her, then looked back at the pool. "What are those things in the water?"

Eddie scooped up the nearest floating piece of detritus as Jared swung down. "Fungus, it looks like. Some sort of mushrooms."

"Probably best not to drink the water, then, or we might end up having our own hallucinogenic visions. Let's take a look inside."

"Which tunnel?" asked the Israeli. There were four entrances before them.

"You tell us," said Eddie. "You can read the language."

"I can only read *parts* of it," he protested. "I'm a Mossad agent, not a rabbi."

"This one," said Nina, indicating the left-most.

"How do you know?"

"Because I can't read ancient Hebrew, but I *can* read symbols. I've seen this one before." She went to the archway, pointing at something carved above it: a menorah, accompanied by the characters that she and Cross had identified as representing the twenty-four Elders. "It was in the temple in Iraq and the catacombs in Rome. I'm guessing it was also on the piece of the Altar of Zeus where you found the angel in Berlin."

Eddie nodded. "So it's the way to the last angel?"

"Most likely." She went to the neighboring opening, taking a flashlight from her backpack and shining it inside. A short tunnel opened out into a chamber, but it appeared empty. "This was an important religious site, but it was also a shelter where the Israelites could hold out against their enemies. They supposedly wandered in the wilderness for forty years, but the desert's not *that* big. The Old Testament books concerning the Exodus are very vague about the timescale. They probably established settlements at various points along the way—or fortifications, in this case. There was a water supply here, so they took advantage of it."

Jared checked another archway. "This one's empty too," he announced, disappointed.

"It's a big find, though. Even if there isn't anything else here, I think this is definitely one of the stations of the Exodus. That'll keep the archaeologists busy— and the theologians arguing." Nina returned to the left-hand tunnel and cautiously entered it, taking off her sunglasses and shining her light around the walls and ceiling. Faded paintings were revealed on the stone, images of people and animals framed by elaborate patterns. "These are a lot like the ones in the catacombs."

"No traps?" Eddie asked, joining her.

"Not yet. But look, the tunnel slants upward." The beam fell upon a steeply sloping floor.

"Great," said Jared gloomily. "It really *is* like the Spring of Immortality."

"I don't think there'll be any killer statues or giant crabs," said Nina as she started up the passage. "But let's be careful, huh?"

They proceeded deeper into the mountain. The tunnel's walls had been smoothed by both hand and time, giving the undulating passage an unsettlingly organic feeling. Its color changed as they climbed through different strata. Stubs of side passages occasionally branched off, copper deposits having been grubbed from the rock, though more often than not the valuable metal had been left in situ. Eddie paused to rub one of the seams. "Wonder why they stopped mining it?"

"Out of reverence, I'd imagine," said Nina, examining a wall painting. Unlike those at the entrance, which showed general scenes of the Israelites' lives, this was clearly religious in nature: robed figures standing with their heads bowed before a tent in the desert. "This tunnel seems to be going somewhere important—maybe a temple. Once it was established, mining was probably considered disrespectful."

Jared peered at the image as Nina moved away. "What is it?" Eddie asked.

"The tent . . . I think it's the Tabernacle. The shrine to God that the Israelites carried with them," he explained, seeing the Yorkshireman's quizzical look.

"The Tabernacle of the Covenant," said Nina. "Where they kept the Ark."

"What, like the *lost* Ark?" Eddie asked. "As in, *Raiders of the*?"

"That's right. The actual one."

"Wow. If you found that, it might finally make you more famous than Indiana Jones."

"I've had more than enough of being famous, thanks!" she said firmly.

They continued upward. "It's getting damp," Nina observed before long. In places, the walls had a faint sheen, some of the painted scenes smeared by water and mold.

Eddie sniffed. "Something smells a bit dodgy."

"It might be these." She played her light over something low on the wall. A small patch of bulbous white mushrooms was growing on the glistening stone. "Fungi."

"Yeah, I know I am."

"What? Oh God," she added with rolled eyes as she got the pun. Eddie chuckled. "There are more up ahead."

The walls were indeed home to other colonies of the fungal growths. They were so pale in color that they almost seemed to glow in the reflected light. But Jared was already looking past them. "Hey, I can see something." He moved to investigate.

Eddie and Nina followed. "Okay, we found where the smell's coming from," the Englishman announced, wrinkling his nose.

A vertical shaft thirty feet in diameter opened out before them, dropping into darkness below. The walls were home to more mushrooms, the largest bigger than a clenched fist. A faint light came from what Nina at first thought were small holes in the ragged ceiling high above, before closer inspection revealed that the milky glow was actually being refracted through veins of some type of translucent crystal.

But the most arresting feature was man-made.

A narrow bridge of blackened wood led across the chasm to an archway flush with the wall on the far side, the opening barricaded by a heavy door. A now familiar symbol was marked upon it: the menorah of the twenty-four Elders. Beside the entrance, a large nook had been carved from the rock, numerous small objects sitting within. "Careful," Nina warned. "That doesn't look safe."

Eddie moved to get a look at the crossing's supports. "No kidding."

He retreated so Nina could see. The near end of the rickety bridge was supported by what she could only think of as a hinge; the whole thing seemed designed to plunge intruders into the pit below.

She dropped a loose stone over the edge. A faint splash echoed back up the shaft after a couple of seconds. "It must be a cenote," she mused. "There's a reservoir at the bottom; it might even join up with the sinkhole outside. And this"—she waved her hand at the bridge—"is a trap to tip people into it."

"I'll go back and get some rope," said Eddie.

"No, wait a minute. Look at that." She shone her flashlight at the nook. Set into its back was a piece of glinting metal: a bronze slab almost a foot wide and several inches deep. There was a slit in the rock beneath it, through which a rod protruded to support the shelf. "We've seen something like that before, in the Atlantean temple in Brazil. It's a weighing scale."

"To weigh what?" asked Jared.

"Those." She shifted the beam to pick out the objects below the scale: stones of various sizes. "There's more text by the door. It's some sort of test; a puzzle. It probably tells you what you have to do to get in."

"Which you've got to cross the bridge to read," Eddie said dubiously.

"Yeah, that's kinda worrying. But I don't think it automatically throws everybody who tries to cross down the shaft. It's more likely that it only catches people who fail the test. The people who knew the answer, the ones who built this place, could come and go as they wanted."

Jared conducted his own examination of the bridge. "That may have been true when they built it. But look at it! It's falling apart. If it really was made by the Israelites, then it's over three thousand years old."

"It might not be as old as you think," Nina countered. "The people who hid the angels, the Elders, did so a long time after the Exodus. John of Patmos discovered their writings in the Library of Pergamon, and that wasn't founded until around 350 BC."

Eddie made a sarcastic sound. "Oh, so it's only over *two* thousand years old. That makes it *completely* safe."

"The site may have still been used for a long time after that, though."

"Or it might not. Seriously, don't even think about crossing it until we get some ropes."

"I'll go back for them," said Jared. "Wait here for me."

"Don't bloody worry, we're not going anywhere!" the Englishman told him. Jared smiled and headed back down the tunnel.

Nina watched him go, then moved to the bridge. "Oi," said Eddie.

"What?"

"You're thinking about putting a foot on it, aren't you? Just to test your theory."

"No I wasn't," she said, not entirely convincingly.

He shook his head. "I dunno. You say you're done with all this stuff, but give you half a chance and you're back climbing cliffs to reach ancient temples. Even when you're pregnant."

The words had been spoken with humor, but Nina's

expression revealed that she had taken them very seriously indeed. "What is it?" he asked.

"I'm worried that . . . that I'm going to be a bad mom," she admitted in a quiet voice.

Eddie was surprised. "Why would you think that?"

"Isn't it obvious?" She held out both hands to encompass their surroundings. "I'm four months pregnant, and I'm in a cave halfway up a mountain in the middle of a desert looking for an ancient relic with the power to kill thousands of people! I should be going to Lamaze classes or pigging out with a big tub of chocolate fudge ice cream."

"Just because you're having a baby doesn't make you an invalid. And it doesn't mean you have to give up everything else, either."

"That's the thing, though," she said. "I don't *want* to give this up. Not now; not at all. And that's why I'm worried about becoming a mother—because I'll *have* to give it up. Which makes me . . . selfish. We're having a child, but I just keep thinking about how that'll stop me from . . . from doing what I *do*."

She turned away from him, looking down into the darkness of the cenote. "You know what's weird? We were both dragged into this in the worst way possible, but now that we're free . . . I'm almost glad I'm here. I could have told Oswald to hand this over to someone at the IHA, but I wanted to do it. I *wanted* to do it," she repeated, with emphasis. "I deliberately chose to do something that could be dangerous, even though I'm pregnant. What the hell kind of mother does that?"

"But . . . you do still want a child?" Eddie asked hesitantly.

"Yes, I do—of course I do!" She looked down at the slight swell of her abdomen. "I want us to have a baby together. But it's kind of scary, and I hadn't realized just how scary because I had other issues going on. First I was in denial about how much Macy's death had affected me, and because of that I was hyper-obsessed with working on the book—and then I was blocked because I was depressed and not sure if everything I'd done in my life was actually worth it."

"You were?" he asked, surprised.

"I wasn't seeing a shrink to get over my fear of public speaking. And I know I should have told you exactly why I was having therapy, but I couldn't. I didn't want to burden you with my psychological problems."

"Yeah, you should have," he said, though with sympathy rather than in remonstration. "We're married. Being burdened with your problems is sort of my job! But just because we're having a kid doesn't mean you have to give up everything important to you. It just means you need to change how you do it. You can still write your book, for a start." He moved up behind her. "And since you're not at the IHA anymore, maybe you can do some of that 'proper' archaeology you go on about, and dig little bits of junk out of the dirt instead of being surrounded by gunfire and explosions."

"I could definitely live with that," she said, managing a small smile, albeit brief.

Eddie wrapped his arms around her waist. "You can do anything you put your mind to; I know you, you're too bloody stubborn to give up! Trust me, you'll be a great mum."

"I don't know," said Nina glumly. "I really don't know if I will . . ."

Echoing footsteps signaled Jared's return. "I brought the rope and some gear," the Israeli called as he reappeared.

"Good lad," said Eddie. "Okay, let's set this up."

Nina watched as they pounded a pair of pitons into the rock wall, then fixed the rope to them. "You do realize that if the bridge collapses when you cross it, you'll swing back and slam into the wall, right?"

"'Course I do," her husband replied. "That's why I'm sending the kid!"

Jared gave him a startled look, which quickly became one of smug superiority. "Actually, I was going to volunteer anyway. You can't leave something like this to an unsteady old man."

"You keep thinking that," said Eddie. He secured the rope to the younger man's harness. "You sure you want to do this?" he asked, more concerned.

Jared looked down into the pit's inky depths. "No . . . but somebody has to, and my mom really *would* be disappointed in me if I let a pregnant woman risk it!"

"Thank you, Jared," said Nina, with an appreciative nod.

"I'll play out the rope to you," said Eddie, picking up the coil of nylon line. "If the bridge looks like it's going to give way, run right back. If you fall, I'll catch you."

Now the Israeli was the appreciative one, although he couldn't resist making a crack. "Hope your withered arms can take the weight, *alter kocker*."

"Or I could fucking *kick* you over there . . . Ready?"

Jared steeled himself. "Yeah."

"Okay. Watch yourself."

The Israeli cautiously put one foot on the narrow bridge. The old wooden beams had been dried out over flames to harden them; even so, they creaked. He edged forward. "Seems solid so far."

"Your weight's still being taken by that hinge," Nina reminded him, her nervousness growing. "Please be careful."

"Don't worry, I will!" He aimed his flashlight down at the bridge, then advanced until he was clear of the support. The creaks grew in volume as he shuffled along . . . then eased.

Nina let out a relieved breath. "Thank God."

"You're doing fine," Eddie called, carefully letting out more rope. "Just take it easy. You're about a third of the way there."

Jared moved on—then abruptly stopped. "Some of the planks are missing."

"Then don't step on the holes!"

The advice drew a glare, but he adjusted his step to traverse the gap. The next intact board held, though with a raspy protest. A second space, wider, but this too he successfully crossed. "It's holding."

"Great," said Eddie, trying not to let his concern

show. He knew that a loss of confidence could be as dangerous as any broken plank. "You're almost halfway across. Just keep going, nice and steady."

Jared used his torch to check the remainder of the bridge. "There aren't any more gaps," he said as he took another careful step. "I should be able—"

Crack!

Nina shrieked as the gunshot snap of breaking wood echoed around the cenote. Jared staggered, trying to regain his balance . . .

He failed. Arms flailing, he toppled toward the abyss.

26

Eddie yanked the rope, pulling Jared onto his back just before he plunged. The whole bridge shook. The Israeli's flashlight spun away into the darkness below as he grabbed at the crossing. "Jared!" yelled the Yorkshireman, reeling in the line. "Hold on, I've got you!"

Jared secured himself. "It's okay, it's okay!"

Eddie held the line taut. "You sure?"

The younger man waited until the bridge stopped shuddering, then very slowly sat up. More moans came from the supports, but the structure held. "Yes! Let it out again so I can get up."

Reluctantly, Eddie did so. Jared cautiously rose to a crouch. Nina aimed her flashlight to illuminate the bridge ahead of him. He surveyed the dusty wood, then continued onward with great care. Eddie played the rope out in his wake.

The Mossad agent passed the three-quarters mark—then froze, as did Nina and Eddie, as a pole cracked beneath him. The structure swayed . . . then steadied. Nina shone her light at the supports. "I think it's okay," she said.

"How does the bridge feel?" Eddie asked Jared.

The Israeli glanced back. "About two thousand years old! Nina, can you give me more light?"

She brought the beam to the top side of the crossing. Jared composed himself, then set off again. Five feet to go, three . . . "There," he said with a gasp of relief. "Okay, I'm going to secure the rope."

It did not take long to hammer another two pitons into place and fasten the line to them. Eddie tested that it was firmly secured by hanging beneath it. "All right," he said, "we can get across without worrying about falling into the lair of the white worm."

Nina raised an eyebrow. "Okay, your movie references keep getting more obscure."

"Now we need to get that door open. I'm guessing the dynamite method isn't going to be approved."

"Nope," she told him. "Jared, come back over so I can look at the scale. We shouldn't risk having two people on the bridge at once."

"Or even one person," Eddie said.

Jared remained in place, examining the alcove beside the door. "No, you'll need my help. There's more ancient Hebrew here."

"Okay," Nina decided reluctantly. "Translate as much of it as you can and tell me what it says."

He nodded. "I need a light."

Eddie held up his own torch. "Hope you can catch better than you can walk across bridges."

"Yeah, yeah, old man. Just throw it to me."

Eddie tossed the torch across the gap; Jared caught it with one hand. "Show-off."

The Israeli grinned, then directed the light at the alcove. "What do you see?" Nina asked.

"There are about thirty stones, all different sizes," he reported. "Each one has a letter carved into it . . . No, wait, they must be numbers. I can read parts of the text. It says that God's number is seven, and then something about . . . wisdom, needing wisdom?" He was silent for a long moment, scanning the ancient words. "Okay, I think it says that you have to prove your wisdom, I guess, to get through the door. You were right about it being a test. You have to know the . . . the number of a man?"

An idea had already formed in Nina's mind at the mention of the word *wisdom,* and now it came to her in a flash of—appropriately enough—revelation. "That's right!" she called, excited. "It *is* the number of a man. I don't remember the exact chapter and verse from Revelation, but I know what it says: 'Let him that hath understanding'—or wisdom in some translations—'count the number of the beast: for it is the number of a man.' "

"That sounds familiar," said Eddie. "You're about to quote some Iron Maiden lyrics, aren't you?"

"Not quite. The King James Version isn't as catchy. But according to John of Patmos, the number of the Beast is 'six hundred threescore and six.' "

"Six! Hundred threescore! And six! The number of the Beast!" he sang tunelessly. "Yeah, definitely not as catchy."

"What was that noise?" demanded Jared.

"Tchah! Kids today don't appreciate the classics. So are you supposed to put three stones with sixes on them onto the scale?"

"Seems like it," Nina told him . . . though with a hint of doubt.

"I can do that right now," Jared called out. "It's using the Hebrew system, so the symbols we need are *tav resh,* six hundred . . ." He plucked a pebble from the group, then located a second. "*Samekh* for sixty, and then . . . here—*vav,* six. Six hundred plus sixty plus six. So I put these on the scale and the door should open, yes?" He picked them up, about to deposit them on the bronze slab—

"No, no!" Nina suddenly yelled. "Don't do anything!"

"What's wrong?" Eddie asked, alarmed—though not nearly as much as Jared, who froze with one hand above the scale.

"Give me a second. I need to think." She closed her eyes for a moment. "The number might not *be* six-six-six. That's the generally accepted version today, but there are several ancient copies of Revelation where it's written as six-*one*-six. The Codex Ephraemi Rescriptus, Papyrus 115 from the Oxyrhynchus excavation in Egypt . . . they predate the King James Bible by over a thousand years."

"Both versions can't be right," said Eddie.

"No, they can't. One of them is a transcription error . . . but there's no way to know which."

Jared put the stones back in the niche. "So should I change the second number to *yud*, ten?"

"I don't know," admitted Nina.

"It's a fifty–fifty chance," Eddie pointed out.

"I don't want to risk Jared's life on a coin toss."

"What should I do?" asked Jared. "Shall I come back over?"

"Hold on." Nina stared at the alcove, then redirected her flashlight. "Jared, can you move sideways so I can see the door?"

The Israeli reluctantly leaned aside, holding the rope for support. "What is it?" asked Eddie. "You found something?"

"Maybe." The light shone upon the symbol of the menorah. "That's the sign of the twenty-four Elders—the people who contained the meteorite fragments in the angels, then dispersed them for safekeeping. Cross showed me a photo he took inside the ruins—the same symbol was there too." She frowned, trying to tease out a memory. "There was some writing with it, something about numbers . . . Jared, what exactly does it say there about the number of God?"

Jared checked the text upon the door. "As near as I can tell, it reads, 'The number that is Yahweh is seven.'"

"That's what it said in the temple Cross found," Nina said thoughtfully. "Seven is the number of God . . . and man is always less than God."

"So the number of a man would be six?" suggested Eddie.

The truth came to her as she finally remembered the rest of the translation the cult leader had shown her at the Mission. "Yes—but the Elders said more than that.

'Three times shall it be said' was how they put it. And in the catacomb in Rome, they said it again: 'It is three times spoken, the dragon's number is that of man.' It's not just the number six on its own, and it's not six hundred sixty-six—it's six, repeated three times for emphasis. Just like in your song," she added with a smile. "Six! Six! Six! *That's* the number of man—and that's the answer to the test."

She called out across the cenote. "Jared! The stone that represents the number six—put it on the scale three times."

"You mean, put it on, take it off, then put it back again twice more?" he asked, puzzled.

"That's it exactly. But for God's sake, keep hold of the rope in case I'm wrong!"

Jared took a firm hold of the line as he used his other hand to pick up one particular stone. With a nervous look back at Nina, he placed it on the scale.

The metal shelf dropped slightly under its weight. Everyone held their breath . . .

The bridge remained intact. "Well, that's a start," said Eddie, exhaling.

"It made a noise," the Israeli reported. "There was a clank from behind it, like two pieces of metal hitting each other."

"Do it again," Nina said.

Jared picked up the stone. The scale rose back to its original position. He repeated the process. Another faint sound came from whatever mechanism was hidden behind the wall. A third time; a much louder bang resounded through the shaft. Jared grabbed the rope with both hands—but the bridge stayed in place.

"Look!" cried Nina. "It's opening!" The door swung slowly inward. It stopped after moving only a foot, but that was enough for Jared to step onto a solid floor. He pushed it wider. "What can you see?"

"Another tunnel," he replied.

"Wait for me. I'm coming over."

"*We're* coming over," Eddie corrected. "And you're not taking any risks, either. Hold on." He hooked Nina's climbing harness to the rope. "Right, now you can go. But take it easy."

"Okay, *Dad*," she huffed.

"Hey, I actually *am* going to be a dad, so I'm allowed to be overprotective."

"Point taken." They smiled at each other, then Nina set off, sidestepping across the bridge with both hands on the rope. A moment of worry as she reached the broken plank, but she picked her way over without incident. Once clear, she hurried to the doorway, standing on the step before detaching the harness.

"You okay?" Jared asked as he helped her through.

"Fine, thanks." She panned her light around the new passage. It had the same rounded cross section as on the other side of the shaft, but its decorations were far more elaborate, gold leaf and precious stones set around the paintings of religious scenes. The door was not merely a barrier; it also marked the boundary of an inner sanctum, a place of great importance to the ancient Israelites.

Eddie made his way across behind them. "All right, so what have we got?"

"This must be the entrance to their temple," Nina said, pointing the flashlight along the tunnel. The ornate walls curved away out of sight. There was no sign here of the mushrooms growing around the cenote; the door had apparently acted as a seal, keeping the air inside dry. "Come on."

"Will there be any more traps?" asked Jared, eyeing the paintings with suspicion as they started down the tunnel.

"I don't think so. This place was protected by a combination of obscurity and inaccessibility, and probably had people defending it too. Revelation said it had been 'prepared,' so somebody had to be here to do that. That door was the final barrier, to make sure that only people who knew the true meaning of the Elders' texts would be able to get in."

"All the same," said Eddie to Jared, "keep an eye out, will you? Just in case anything pops out of the walls."

The younger man hurriedly redirected his flashlight beam to the sides of the passage.

No booby-traps interrupted their progress, however. Before long, something came into view ahead. "Ay up," said Eddie, surprised. "There's a light in there." The tunnel opened out into a larger chamber, where they could clearly see the gleam of gold even without their torches.

"It's not daylight," Nina noted. There was an almost rainbow-like iridescence to the illumination. She entered the room—and stopped in astonishment. "Oh . . ."

Eddie moved up beside her, equally amazed. "Christ, that's impressive. What *is* this place?"

She surveyed the wonders before her, almost unable to believe what she was seeing. "Based on the description in the Book of Revelation . . . I think we've just found God's temple."

The chamber was an expansive oval, an existing cave made much bigger by years, even decades of patient excavation. The walls were largely covered by drape-like hanging tapestries bearing Hebrew symbols. The dominant feature was a massive opal over two feet across embedded in the rock of the high ceiling. There was evidently a fissure in the mountain above that reached to the surface, letting in sunlight, which was then refracted by the great gemstone into a brilliant prismatic display.

The brightest spot was directly beneath the opal, a dazzling beam shining downward like a laser. It landed upon a large golden throne, which stood on a patch of highly polished quartz set into the floor. More thrones, similar in design but somewhat smaller, encircled it. Nina started counting them, but already knew how many there would be. "Twenty-four," she said, confirming her belief. "These are the thrones of the twenty-four Elders."

Eddie glanced at the central seat. "So whose is number twenty-five?"

"God's. He sits in the middle of everything, with His followers around him." Nina moved hesitantly into the ring. She was not religious by nature, but couldn't help feeling a reverential awe. "Everything matches John's description. The circle of thrones around God's seat, the rainbow surrounding it . . ." She indicated where the opal was casting a spectrum of light on the floor, catching the swath of quartz. "Even this; John described it as a 'sea of glass,' which considering that he was having a vision based on something he'd only read is pretty accurate. And then there's the altar, the seven lamps . . ." A large menorah stood before the throne, near a golden dais with a horn-like protrusion at each corner.

Jared nervously followed Nina and Eddie into the circle, having to force himself not to avert his eyes from the throne beneath the opal. "It feels like this is something I shouldn't be allowed to see."

Nina noticed something at the chamber's far end. "If you're worried about being struck down by God, then you really shouldn't get any closer to that."

Beyond the golden circle was something extremely incongruous in the splendor of their surroundings: a simple tent made from animal skins. It was rectangular, around fifteen feet wide and three times as long. Time had dried and decayed the hides in the stillness of the chamber, but they had clearly been exposed to the harsh elements of the desert beforehand. The entrance was draped in woven curtains, the faded remnants of once vibrant colors still showing after uncounted centuries.

"Okay, that doesn't really go with the other furniture," Eddie said.

"You don't know what it is?" she replied. "Oh, right; you always skipped Sunday school when you were a kid, didn't you?"

"I had better places to be. Like literally anywhere."

"I know what it is," gasped Jared. "It's . . . it's the Tabernacle, the communion tent!"

Eddie couldn't hold back a smile. "So the Ark of the Covenant is actually *here*? In your face, Indiana Jones!"

Nina started toward the tent. "Wait, wait," said Jared, suddenly worried. "Should we go in there?"

She gave him an incredulous look. "Are you going to

tell me that because we're not Levites, we'll be killed if we get too close?"

"No, but . . . it's a holy place. The *most* holy place."

"And this is why I didn't go to Sunday school," said Eddie, joining his wife. "So this kind of thing doesn't scare me off. If the angel's here at all, it must be in there or we would have seen it by now. We've got to find it."

The younger man nodded reluctantly. "Okay. But be careful. I don't want to be the one who destroys the Tabernacle!"

"You think *I* do?" Nina hooted.

They approached the entrance. The redhead shone her flashlight over the curtains, then removed her backpack before hesitantly moving them aside and slipping through. The two men followed.

The animal-skin walls were thick enough to block the glow from the crystal. Jared added his light to Nina's. The space they had entered occupied two thirds of the tent's total length, but was only sparsely furnished. A wooden table stood to one side, whatever offerings had been placed upon it long since turned to dust. Near it was a seven-branched menorah on a tall stand, dark smears of old oil upon the metal lamps. Beyond them, before a white curtain, was a golden altar, glinting in the torch beams.

"Is that the Ark?" Eddie asked.

Nina shook her head. "That must be the Altar of Incense. If the Ark's in here, it'll be beyond the veil." She indicated the curtain.

"That's where that saying comes from, is it? Huh. Learn something every day."

"Stick with me, kiddo," she told him with a smile, leading the way through the room. "On the other side of the veil is—"

"The Holy of Holies," said Jared. "*I* learned all this at school," he added to Eddie, who grinned.

"That's right," said Nina. She examined the altar, then turned her attention to the curtain. "Okay. If God *is* going to strike us dead, he'll do it about . . . now."

She parted the veil. Swaths of the material disintegrated like gossamer as her hand brushed it. She cringed in dismay at the damage, but pressed on through.

The last room was square. The only thing in it was a large box, coated in gold.

All three recognized it instantly.

They had found the Ark of the Covenant.

27

"God," whispered Nina, adding: "Literally."

Jared stared openmouthed. "It . . . it's the Ark," he managed to say. "It really is the Ark of the Covenant!"

Eddie whistled a few bars of "The Raiders March." "We need our own cool theme tune," he said. "This is it? The real thing?" Nina nodded. "Bloody hell! This is a massive find—and you weren't even looking for it!"

"No, but here it is." Awed, Nina circled the relic. It did not quite match the popular image from classical paintings and a certain Steven Spielberg movie, the smaller details differing, but it perfectly fit the description given in the biblical Book of Exodus. The main body of the gold-covered chest was a little under four feet long, finely detailed patterns similar to those in the Jewish catacombs and the tunnel outside inscribed into the plating. Rings of the precious metal supported two long poles on each side, covered in gold leaf.

Atop the Ark was the mercy seat. Despite what the name suggested, it was not a place of rest, rather an elaborate lid. A pair of cherubim stood upon it. Two of each of their four wings extended backward, meeting above the center of the chest. She peered at one of the cherubim, feeling a thrill of recognition as she saw the face of the angel—rather, the *faces,* plural. Both creatures had four positioned around their heads, each looking in a different direction: a lion, an ox, an eagle, and a man. She had seen the same arrangement on the mechanical guardians of the Garden of Eden. The image had been remembered and passed down over many millennia as a symbol of fearsome, godly power.

She stepped back, almost overcome by excitement at the magnificence of the find—before remembering that it was not why she was there. She reluctantly turned away to cast her light around the rest of the room. "There's nothing else in here?"

"It doesn't look like it," Jared confirmed.

"Then the angel must be in the Ark." She produced a camera and took several photos for the record, then returned to the chest, suppressing her professional disquiet at what she was about to do. "Can you lift the lid?"

Now it was Eddie's turn to hesitate. "You sure? You know what's supposed to happen if you open this thing. Lightning, firestorms, melting Nazis . . ."

"And I thought you weren't superstitious."

"No, but I'm movie-stitious."

"We don't have a choice—the clues to the angel's location in Revelation pointed here. Cross is already in Israel, and sooner or later he'll realize he needs to widen his search, so we've got to get it out of here before that happens. We can't leave it and hope that *he* gets melted when he opens it."

"Maybe I should close my eyes," Eddie grumbled, but he moved to one end of the chest. Jared gave Nina an uncertain look but went to the other. The Englishman warily tapped one of the poles before risking touching the lid itself. "Not struck dead on the spot. That's a start."

"Okay," said Nina, "now very carefully, lift it up."

The two men strained to raise the mercy seat. "It's heavy," grunted Jared. "The statues must be solid gold." They pulled harder.

With a scrape of metal, the Ark of the Covenant began to open.

* * *

The Bell 430 continued its monotonous search of the empty desert. Dalton made a show of checking his watch for the third time in as many minutes. "How much fuel has this damn thing got left?" he complained.

"We'll go back to Ovda after we check the next valley," Cross replied. "Then you can get out. I'm sure that'll be a relief." *For everyone,* he didn't need to add.

"Just remember that you wouldn't even be here without my help," Dalton snapped. "I was the one who told you Nina Wilde was the best person to find the angels, I got you into Israel without—"

"There's someone down there!" Simeon barked. The ex-politician was instantly forgotten as all eyes went to the windows. "I can see a truck." He raised his binoculars as Paxton slowed the helicopter. "No sign of anybody with it."

Cross brought up his own field glasses. Sunlight flashed off the windows of a four-by-four parked near the foot of a cliff. He looked up the sheer rock face, spotting the faint line of a rope. It led to a narrow yet tall cleft in the massif, a very thin pass snaking away to . . .

"A sinkhole," he said, seeing what lay at its end. "There's a sinkhole on that mountain."

Dalton craned his neck to peer at the landscape below. "It can't be the one we're looking for. I thought we were checking the valleys, not the hills."

"We were," said Cross with growing realization. "And we were wrong!" He snapped the binoculars back to the cliff. Faint sparkles in the rock marked where the intense sunlight glanced off copper deposits. "It reflects the sun. 'Clothed with the sun'—that's what John meant! And you'd need the wings of eagles to get up there . . ."

"Wilde lied to us?" said Anna.

"Maybe—or she hadn't figured it out when she told us where to look. But she has now. She's down there!"

"Wilde's *here*?" said Dalton, disbelieving. "Are you sure?"

"It's her. I'm certain." He turned to the pilot. "Paxton, bring us down as close to the sinkhole as possible."

Dalton became even more unhappy. "We're not going back to refuel?"

"We won't need to. The angel's down there."

"And so are Wilde and Chase," Simeon reminded him.

"Not for long," said Cross as the helicopter began its descent.

* * *

Nina watched with nervous anticipation as the mercy seat was inched upward.

"Almost there," Eddie told Jared. "Move it over on three."

Jared nodded. The Yorkshireman counted down, then with loud grunts they shuffled sideways to set it down on the stone floor with a heavy *clunk*.

Nina leaned over the chest to see what was inside. Her flashlight beam found the very items named by legend. A scroll, supposedly the first part of the Torah, written by Moses himself; a wooden staff, which she took to be the rod of Aaron, brother of Moses; an earthenware jar, which had contained some of the manna sent by God to feed the Israelites in the desert . . . and two flat slabs of stone, inscribed with ancient Hebrew text.

Her heart quickened. She was looking at the tablets holding the original Ten Commandments.

But she forced herself to ignore them for now. There was one more relic inside the Ark.

The fourth angel.

It was of the same design as the other two she had seen, a dense ceramic body shrouded by metallic wings. The head of this figure was that of a man, his brow creased in stern warning. She carefully lifted it out, feeling the weight of the deadly meteoric material trapped in its core. "That's what you're looking for?" Jared asked.

Nina nodded. "The last angel—the last harbinger of

the apocalypse, if you believe Cross. But we've beaten him to it. Whatever he had planned, he can't go ahead with it without this."

"Unless he decides, *You know what? Bollocks to it, I'm going to do it anyway,*" Eddie said grimly. "He's still got one angel he can release somewhere."

"I know." She held up the statue. "But at least we can secure this—"

She broke off as she saw dust motes falling through the flashlight beams, the first few specks quickly joined by more, and more, drifting from the tent's roof. "What's doing that?" Eddie demanded. He glanced at the Ark. "We haven't bloody brought down the fury of God and the wrath of sixty special-effects people, have we?"

"It's outside," said Jared. A deep rumbling sound gradually rose in intensity.

Still holding the statue, Nina hurried back through the veil. More dust was falling in the tent's outer room, scraps of rotted fabric dropping to the floor. She pushed through the curtain into the throne chamber. The noise grew louder—

The light coming through the giant opal in the ceiling suddenly flickered. A moment later, a shadow passing over the crack above briefly plunged the room into darkness. Then the illumination returned to its spectacular norm, but the bass rumble continued.

"It's a chopper!" Eddie said. The aircraft had gone right overhead, coming in to land on the mountain above them.

"Cross," said Nina. "It's Cross!"

"How do you know?" asked Jared.

"Because who *else* would it be? This always frickin' happens to us!"

Eddie drew the Desert Eagle. "Looks like I'll find out if this thing's as good as my Wildey."

Jared produced his own, smaller gun. "We need to get out of here."

"We'll never get clear," Nina realized. "There's no way we'll be able to climb down the cliff and back to the

jeep in time. And even if we could, they've got a helicopter! We can't outrun them."

"So what do we do?"

"Chuck that thing in the sinkhole," Eddie suggested,
nodding at the angel. "They won't have brought scuba
gear. It'll take 'em ages to find it, if they ever do."

"Yes, but we'll probably be dead!" the Israeli objected.

"And they might still find it," added Nina. "We don't
know how deep the sinkhole is—if it's only ten feet, it
won't take them long to search the bottom."

"Then drop it off the bridge down the big shaft,"
Eddie persisted.

"But if it breaks, then as far as Cross is concerned the
angel has been released, and he wins."

"What, then?" he demanded, exasperated. "We can't
run, there's nowhere to hide the thing, and if we smash
it, that's the same as letting him get it. What the bloody
hell are we supposed to do?"

"I don't know!" She turned her eyes to the refracted
daylight coming through the ceiling as the noise of the
helicopter settled . . . then began to die down. It had
landed, the pilot shutting off the engines. "You're SAS,"
she told Eddie, turning back to the two men, "and Jared,
you're Mossad—what would *you* do?"

The question galvanized the younger man. "They'll
have seen our truck—it's probably what made them
land—so they know we're here. They'll expect an ambush."

Eddie nodded in agreement. "We'll have to decoy
them."

"Yeah. But how?"

The Englishman looked back at the tent. "If Cross is
such a Bible-basher, he'll know what that is, and what's
inside. We need to keep his attention on it." A moment's
thought, then: "There's an app for that."

* * *

Simeon swung down from the lip of the sinkhole into
the sheltered cave beneath, whipping up his MP5 sub-

machine gun and sweeping it across the entrances. No-body moved within them. He brought his left forefinger to the trigger of the M203 grenade launcher mounted under the weapon's barrel, ready to fire a shrapnel-filled high-explosive round at any hint of activity.

Still nothing stirred. He took cover beside the right-most opening as more of his men dropped down and spread out to check the other archways. "Clear," one soon reported. The others gave the same message.

Simeon cast a wary eye into the underground cham-ber before moving to look up to the surface. "Nobody here."

Cross, Anna, and Dalton gazed back down at him. "Good," said the cult leader. He lowered himself to the cave, Anna following. "What have we got?"

"Four entrances. I don't know which they took."

Cross surveyed the arches, then pointed at the left-most. "That one, with the symbol of the twenty-four Elders. Prepare to move in."

"Hey!" came an aggrieved shout from above. "You going to leave me up here?"

"Simeon, Norvin, help Mr. Dalton down," said Cross, the upward flick of his eyes as much a disparaging roll as an indication of the disgraced politician's location. Simeon let out a sound of contempt, then he and the bodyguard took up positions to catch Dalton as he clum-sily clambered over the edge.

Even with their support, the ex-president touched down with a *thump*. He shook himself free of them. "All right, I'm here," he announced. "Now, what's the situation?"

"They're down there," Cross told him, going to the entrance. One of his men, a jut-jawed blond named Hatch, crouched to examine the floor; faint footsteps in the dust confirmed his leader's statement.

"And what else is down there?"

"The angel, is all I can say for sure. Other than that . . ." He regarded the symbol above the opening with intense curiosity, then signaled for his team to ad-vance.

Simeon took point, Norvin behind him. The others followed in single file. They cautiously made their way up the sloping passage, listening for sounds of activity. But they heard none. It wasn't until they reached the growths of mushrooms that Cross broke the silence. "Manna?" he wondered in a whisper, pausing for a closer look.

"Sir!" Simeon hissed. "I heard voices—and there's something up ahead."

The mushrooms forgotten, Cross made his way to the front of the group, joining Simeon at the edge of the cenote. The cult leader aimed his flashlight into the depths, revealing water a long way below. His right-hand man, meanwhile, used his own light to track the rope across the rickety bridge. "Through there," he said, seeing the open doorway.

"I hear them," Cross murmured. Two people were speaking; the words were indistinct, but one voice was male . . . and the other female. "It's Wilde."

Simeon raised his MP5, aiming the grenade launcher at the doorway, but Cross pushed it down. "No! You might damage the angel. We need it intact."

Anna listened to the voices. The discussion seemed casual, unworried. "They don't know we're here."

"It could still be an ambush," her husband warned. "And I don't like the look of this bridge."

"They got across it; so can we," said Cross. He tested the rope. It held.

Dalton squeezed past the other team members. "What's going on?"

"Keep your voice down," Simeon growled. Dalton twitched in anger, but the African American went on: "They're on the other side of this shaft. We've got to get across without letting them know we're here."

"Norvin, you go over first," Cross told his bodyguard. "If the tunnel on the far side is clear, cover it while the rest of us follow."

Norvin nodded, slinging his MP5 and taking hold of the rope. He sidestepped across the bridge. His companions watched with growing anxiety, a few stifled gasps escaping when the structure swayed under his weight, but after steadying himself he was able to continue to firm ground. He quickly readied his gun and checked the tunnel, then signaled that the way was clear.

"Maybe you should wait here," Cross suggested to Dalton.

"Like hell," Dalton replied. "I want to see the look on Wilde and Chase's faces when we take the angel from them."

"As you wish." The white-clad man turned his back on him, waiting for Simeon to cross before starting his own journey. "Come over after Anna. Hatch, watch out for him."

One by one the group traversed the cenote. By the time the last man made it, Cross had already instructed Simeon and Norvin to advance. They crept along the decorated passage, guns raised. The voices became louder as they neared its end. "I see lights," Simeon whispered.

"Careful," said Cross, but he was already almost unconsciously increasing his pace, glimpsing wonders waiting ahead. Gold glinted under a strange rainbow glow. He forced himself to slow and listen. "It's definitely them."

Nina's voice reached him. ". . . way beyond what I'd expected to find. I mean, we came looking for the angel, but to discover this as well? It's incredible."

"Yeah." The other speaker was Eddie Chase. Simeon's hands tightened on his weapon, while Dalton gulped faintly, his mouth suddenly dry.

"This will change biblical archaeology forever," Nina went on. "It's quite possibly the biggest thing I've ever discovered. The actual Ark of the Covenant, intact, and in God's temple as described in the Book of Revelation? Amazing!"

"Uh-huh," came the reply.

Simeon reached the entrance, silently panning his gun across the chamber. The voices were coming from a tent at the far end, lights glinting through thin patches in its ancient coverings. "They're in that," he said, his own voice barely above the volume of a breath. "Room's clear."

"The Tabernacle . . . ," Cross whispered, astounded. The cult leader entered the room, then stepped aside to let his armed followers past as Dalton stood beside him. He knew where he was, almost overcome by religious awe at the sight of God's throne beneath the shaft of spectral light, but managed to restrain his wonderment. His first priority was securing the angel.

Which would be easy. The archaeologist was still talking, her husband muttering the occasional reply. Cross issued an order: "Take them."

Simeon took command, using hand signals to direct the others toward the tent. The men spread out to surround it, while Anna hung back inside the circle of thrones to cover a wider area. The African American silently made his way to the entrance, reaching out to pull back the curtains . . .

"Ay up."

The voice came not from the tent—but from behind Cross and Dalton.

28

Both men whirled—to see Eddie and Jared emerge from behind the tapestries, guns raised. "Chase!" Dalton cried.

Simeon and the others spun, but the two ambushers had already moved to use Dalton and Cross as human shields. "Drop your guns!" Eddie commanded, grabbing the politician and spinning him around to shove the Desert Eagle's blocky muzzle hard into his back. Jared simultaneously jammed his own gun into Cross's face. "Do it, or they die!"

"Drop them!" shrieked Dalton. "He's a psycho!"

Cross was more restrained, but his face still creased with anger as Jared pulled him around. "Do what he says."

The team lowered their weapons to the floor—with the exception of Simeon, who brought up his MP5 and took careful aim at what he could see of Jared. "Let them go," he growled.

Cross raised a hand. "Put it down, Simeon. That's an order."

Confusion crossed Simeon's face. "But—"

"We're in God's temple. I won't allow it to be desecrated. Only God has the right to take a life in here."

When Simeon did not respond at once, he shouted, not in fear but anger: *"Do it!"*

With deep reluctance, Simeon placed his submachine gun on the floor. "Okay, hands up and kick 'em away," said Eddie. Guns skittered across the floor, Simeon's ending up between two of the thrones. "Nina? You can come out now."

Nina emerged from the tabernacle, even with Eddie's assurance nervous at the sight of Anna, Simeon, and five other men watching her. She gingerly slipped past them and crossed the chamber. In one hand she held the angel; in the other, Eddie's phone, its voice memo app playing a recording. "Right," said Eddie's voice from the speaker. She thumbed the screen to silence it, then pocketed the device.

"Clever," said Cross, almost approving. He looked at the tent. "So you found the angel, but . . . is the Ark of the Covenant *really* in there?"

"It is," said Nina, joining Eddie. She gave Dalton a scathing glare. "Oh, hey, Mr. President. You're a long way from the campaign trail, aren't you?"

"What are you going to do with us?" Dalton demanded. He had outwardly regained his composure after his near-panic at finding himself face-to-face with the Englishman, but there was still fear in his eyes.

"We're gonna leave you in here," Eddie told him. "The Israelis can pick you up once we've taken that statue somewhere safe."

"And how exactly are you planning on holding us?" asked Anna, sidling closer.

"Stay where you are," Jared warned. "Keep your hands up. All of you." The biochemist's hands were already half raised; she scowled, but brought them higher.

"We'll take out that bridge," said Eddie, answering her. He addressed Cross. "So you'll have plenty of time to spend with the Ark."

"What's inside the Ark?" Cross asked Nina. "Is it what the Bible described?"

There was no sense that he was trying to buy time to regain the advantage; he was genuinely desperate to know the truth. "It is," she replied. "The angel was in there, but so were Aaron's staff, a scroll of the Torah— and the Ten Commandments."

"I have to see them." He tried to move toward the Tabernacle.

Jared yanked him back. "Don't move!"

"Let him go!" Anna darted closer, halting only when the Israeli pushed his gun into the cult leader's cheek.

"It's okay," Cross told her. "Stay where you are."

"And you, back off," Eddie warned Simeon, seeing that he had used the moment of confusion to move closer to his gun. The black man scowled, but retreated. Jared lowered his weapon, pressing the muzzle into his prisoner's back.

"Consider it a trade," Nina said to Cross. "The Ark for the angel. Whatever you wanted the statue for, after what happened at the Mission there's no way we're going to let you take it."

Dalton shook his head in aggravation. "You got something to say?" asked Eddie.

"Only that you two have already caused great harm to America by refusing to see the big picture, and now you're going to do it again," he complained. "Yes, what's inside the statue is extremely dangerous, and yes, regrettably lives have been lost. But what I'm doing will strengthen the security of the entire nation, whether or not you're willing to realize that. That's what being president is all about: knowing when force *has* to be applied, and making hard decisions for the greater good."

"Nice speech," Nina said. "Just one minor point— you're not the president. And the reason you're not is that you proved you can't be trusted."

"The reason I'm not is because Travis Warden and those other cocksuckers in the Group threw me to the wolves rather than getting their media outlets to spin things my way!" Dalton exploded. Cross gave him a disapproving glare. "Oh, don't get up on your damn moral high horse, Ezekiel. Not with what you're going to do. A bit of bad language is nothing compared with—" He stopped abruptly.

"Compared with what?" Eddie prompted. "Come on, don't make this the one time in your life when you don't want to hear the sound of your own voice."

Nina stood before Dalton, holding up the angel. "You thought you'd have two angels, so I imagine you also had two targets for them. What are they?"

"Damned if I'm going to tell you," the former president growled.

"Damned if you don't."

"*Dead* if you don't," added Eddie.

Nina shook her head. "Face it, *Victor*, you're finished. You'll be directly linked to what happened in Antigua; the place was full of security cameras, so there'll be plenty of proof that you were there when Cross killed almost a hundred people." A flash of fear in the politician's eyes told her that was something he had either not considered or been fervently hoping nobody else had. "The best you can hope for is to plea-bargain your way into a minimum jail term, but there's no way you'll ever get so much as a sniff of power again."

For a moment Dalton seemed about to break . . . but then he summoned up a reserve of haughty defiance. "I'm not telling you a goddamn thing. And you, Chase," he snapped, looking back at Eddie, "get that damn gun off me, you limey son of a bitch!"

He tried to pull out of the Englishman's hold. Eddie responded by driving a knee into the back of his leg, making him cry out and stumble.

Jared instinctively glanced toward the scuffle to see if his friend needed help—

A sharp metallic *snick*—and Anna charged at him, brandishing a glinting switchblade that she had pulled from her sleeve.

Jared caught the movement, but his line of fire was blocked by Cross. He hesitated for an instant, not wanting to shoot a prisoner in the back—then shoved Cross aside—

His shot caught Anna's left arm, blowing a chunk of flesh from her biceps. She screamed—but had already dived at him, the blade held out before her like a lance.

It stabbed into Jared's thigh.

He yelled, leg buckling as she crashed against him. Eddie hauled Dalton around as he tried to aim at the wounded woman, but she was shielded behind the fallen Mossad agent.

"*Anna!*" cried Simeon. He hurled himself behind the circle of thrones and snatched up his fallen MP5. Eddie spun to face the new threat—

"Nobody shoot!" boomed Cross. "No one shoot!" He raised both hands, turning to address both Eddie and his own followers. "There won't be any killing in God's house."

"Don't bet on it," Eddie snarled, pulling Dalton closer as he kept the Desert Eagle locked on Simeon's cover. The metal of the throne was thick, but a .50-caliber round was more than capable of punching a hole right through it, and the man behind.

"He shot Anna!" Simeon shouted.

Cross glanced at her wound. "She'll live."

"You won't," gasped Jared, bringing up his gun—

Anna wrenched her blade around, tearing it deeper into his muscle. His cry this time was a full-blown scream of agony. But despite the pain, he swung the gun toward her . . .

She swiped it from his hand. The pistol clattered across the stone floor to end up near a tapestry.

"Nina, get the gun!" Eddie shouted.

She started forward, only for Cross to block her way. "Dr. Wilde," he said. "It seems we have a standoff."

"Like buggery we do," said Eddie.

Cross glanced toward his men, some of whom had recovered their weapons in the chaos. Washburn, his slashed cheek now home to a line of stitches, glared at Eddie. "We outgun you, over two to one," the cult leader said. "But I'm not willing to see a bloodbath in this holy place. Unless," he added, "you leave us with no choice."

Nina regarded him coldly. "Yeah, I was wondering how long it would take before you gave yourself a get-out clause."

"I don't want to do it. But I'm being completely honest; I'm willing to offer a deal. Let us leave with the angel, and I give you my word before God that as long as you remain in this temple, we won't kill you."

"Prophet!" protested Simeon. "Anna needs medical attention. We can't let these—"

Cross raised an angry hand, silencing him. "Those are my terms, Dr. Wilde," he continued. "They're non-negotiable. If you want to stay alive, hand over the angel."

Eddie drew Dalton closer, tapping the gun against the gray-haired man's head. "Aren't you forgetting something? You want me to go all Lee Harvey on your mate here?"

Cross gave his prisoner a dismissive look. "You can keep him. I don't need him anymore."

"What?" said Nina, shocked.

"*What?*" echoed Dalton, with considerably more anger.

"His political connections were useful, and he did suggest that you were the best person to find the angels," Cross explained. "But right now, the office of the president of the United States is a symbol, if not the embodiment, of the utter corruption of the so-called elites of this world. Do what you like with him."

Dalton shook with fury. "You slimy little son of a bitch!"

Eddie was barely more pleased. "We don't want him either!"

"Time to make a decision, Dr. Wilde," said Cross, ignoring him. "You can have a shootout that will leave you, your husband, and your friend dead—"

"And you too," Eddie warned, keeping behind Dalton as he shifted his aim to the cult leader.

"But we'll still have the angel. My followers will carry out the plan. Babylon *will* fall, even if I'm not there to witness it. Or you can give us the angel and we'll leave you to give this man first aid." He glanced at Jared, then nodded to Anna. "Which he'll need." The young Israeli screamed again as Anna ground the knife deeper into his thigh.

"Goddammit!" Nina cried. "You said we wouldn't be hurt!"

"I said you wouldn't be *killed*. Your choice, Dr. Wilde. The only way for all three of you to stay alive—all four of you," he added, gaze flicking to the apoplectic Dalton—"is to give me the angel."

Nina regarded the statue in her hand, then looked helplessly at her husband. "Eddie . . ."

"They're going to kill us anyway," he rumbled.

Cross shook his head. "No. I gave my word before God. I won't break it, and my followers won't either." He gestured to his men. They hesitated, then lowered their guns. Simeon held out, but a second, more forceful signal finally prompted him to obey.

Eddie rapidly reassessed the odds. If he was accurate with the Desert Eagle, he would kill or incapacitate anyone he hit, but he doubted he would get off more than two shots before being cut down. He was also certain that Dalton's presence wouldn't deter the gunmen in the slightest, the ex-president now nothing more than a meaty bullet sponge.

But he still wasn't willing to give Cross what he wanted. "If they take the angel, they'll kill a lot of people," he reminded Nina. "I don't want to say this, but the best thing to do is smash the fucking thing right now. Better twelve people die than twelve thousand."

"I know, but . . ." The numbers made sense in terms of cold logic, a small sacrifice to save countless lives . . . but there were more than twelve lives in the chamber. She brought her palm to the small swelling below her waist. "I can't," she whispered. "I can't do it. It's just . . . I can't," she repeated.

"Shit," said Eddie under his breath, though with full understanding and sympathy.

Nina looked back at Cross. "I absolutely have your word, before God, that you won't kill us?"

"We'll take the angel and leave," he replied. "As long as you stay in this throne room, we won't harm you. I've made you a promise, and my followers will keep it too." He locked eyes with each of his people in turn. All nodded, even Anna and Simeon. "Anna, let him go."

Anna tugged the blade out of Jared's leg. The Israeli let out a cry, clapping a hand over the wound as she stood painfully.

Cross held out a hand. "The angel?"

"Nina . . ." said Eddie.

"I have to," she told him, conflict clear in her voice. She placed the statue on the floor, then stepped back.

Cross crouched to examine it with reverence before picking it up. He turned it over in his hands, paying close attention to the fine details, before announcing: "It's real. It's the last angel. And," he said as he stood, "it's mine."

"You're really going to let them live?" demanded Simeon.

"Yes, we are. I gave my word to God." He bowed his head to the central throne, then started toward the exit. "Everyone move out."

Keeping his gun aimed in Eddie's direction, Simeon scurried to Anna, giving Jared a poisonous glare as he checked her wound. The other men went to the exit. Eddie stayed behind Dalton, Desert Eagle at the ready. "Nina, get behind me." She retreated, using one of the thrones as cover.

"You're letting them *go*?" Dalton asked Eddie with angry disbelief.

"You want me to start shooting?" he fired back. "'Cause you'll be my bulletproof vest!"

"Nobody needs to shoot anyone," said Cross, holding the statue up to the iridescent light coming through the opal. "Not in here. But if you leave the throne room before we're gone . . ."

"Knew there'd be a fucking catch," Eddie muttered.

Cross and Simeon exchanged whispered words, then the latter spoke to his troops. "Norvin, get the Prophet and the angel out of here. I'll take Anna; the rest of you, cover us." He glanced at Cross, then went on, trying to suppress his frustration: "Don't fire unless fired upon."

Hatch and the other men took up positions at the entrance as first Cross and Norvin, then Simeon and Anna left the room, the cult leader looking longingly at the Tabernacle before departing. "If there is a God, he'll make that fucking bridge collapse under them," said Eddie as the remaining gunmen retreated.

Dalton watched them go with dismay. "*Now* what do we do?"

"Oh, so when everything goes up shit creek, you ask *us* for advice? You fucking idiot." The Yorkshireman shoved Dalton away and moved to look down the tunnel, spotting Hatch backing away, gun raised. "That Bible-thumper promised God that we wouldn't be harmed in here, but I bet that promise ends the second we set foot outside the door."

Nina retrieved her backpack, then hurried to Jared. "Eddie, I'm sorry, but I couldn't do it," she said as she took out a first-aid kit. "I couldn't do that to our baby. I'm sorry."

"It's okay," he told her. "We'll figure something else out." Hatch disappeared from view; Eddie went to the tunnel entrance. "Jared, you okay?"

"I never realized being stabbed would hurt this bad," the Israeli replied through clenched teeth.

"Just wait until you try to walk on that leg."

"Thanks a lot, *alter kocker*." He gasped as Nina cut away the torn material to reveal the bloodied wound beneath. "How does it look?"

"I'm not an expert, but . . . not great." Blood was still pumping from the gash.

"Just do what you can to stop the bleeding," said Eddie. "I'll come and help you in a minute."

"Where are you going?" asked Nina.

"To stop that lot from leaving." There was no sign of anyone in the tunnel, though he could still hear activity in the cenote. Raising the Desert Eagle, he crept down the passage.

He soon saw the doorway ahead. The raiders had not left a rear guard—at least not on this side of the bridge. He moved closer.

The rope was still in place, pulled taut above the crossing. But he saw as he neared the door that it was moving, jiggling up and down—

He realized what was happening just as the person hacking away at the line with a combat knife finally severed the last few strands. The far end of the rope fell away to hang limply down into the cenote. Eddie held in an obscenity, hearing movement from the other side of the bridge.

He leaned around the edge of the opening . . .

And his eyes widened in fear as he saw Simeon aiming his grenade launcher.

Eddie sprinted back into the darkness as a shotgun-like *bam!* propelled a forty-millimeter grenade across the chasm.

It struck—but he wasn't the target.

Instead, it hit the end of the bridge. The explosion as the ancient wood was blasted into splinters blew Eddie off his feet. The shattered structure toppled into the abyss with a noise like the clattering of dried bones.

* * *

On the far side of the cenote, Simeon and Hatch, holding a flashlight, scrambled backward as the detonation sent broken stones flying at them. A deep crunching reverberated around the passage—then a great chunk of the cenote's wall sheared off and smashed down onto the end of the tunnel, almost completely blocking it.

Simeon regained his composure. "Don't think they'll get out of there," he said, as Hatch shone his light over the boulder. The two men shared a triumphant smile, then hurried to catch up with their leader.

* * *

Nina had just finished cleaning Jared's wound when the explosion ripped through the passageway. "Eddie!" she yelled, running down the tunnel to find him.

A choking cloud hit her, reducing her flashlight's beam to a haze. She buried her nose and mouth in the crook of her arm. "Eddie, can you hear me?" she called, voice muffled.

Coughing answered her. "Yeah, I'm okay," her husband rasped. "Just got knocked over. My ears are still ringing, though. Not that that's anything new."

She groped in the darkness, her hand finally touching leather. "Can you stand?"

He took her arm. "More or less." Another bout of coughing, then they headed back to the throne room. "Bastards took out the bridge with a grenade. They cut the rope, too."

"So how are we going to get out of here?" They cleared the wafting smoke, the sparking light of the temple beckoning them ahead.

"Dunno, but we'll have to—Oh, for fuck's sake."

Dalton stood inside the entrance, pointing Jared's pistol at them. "Stay where you are! Drop the gun, Chase."

"Sorry, Eddie," said the Israeli from the floor, one hand covering his wound. "I wasn't fast enough to stop him."

"No problem," Eddie replied, eyes fixed contemptuously on the older man's trembling hand. "The dozy twat's left the safety on."

Dalton frowned, but with a flicker of uncertainty. Eddie shrugged and advanced on him. The politician twisted his wrist to bring the safety lever into view, tipping the weapon away from its target—and the Englishman instantly snapped up the Desert Eagle and aimed it unwaveringly at his head. "Drop it."

Dalton flinched, then with a muted moan of defeat let the pistol fall to the floor. "Now that's what I call an executive decision," said Nina.

"Dickhead," said Eddie as he collected the weapon. "If someone you're pointing a gun at tells you the safety's on, you know how you test that? By pulling the fucking trigger!"

"Pardon me for not being a psychotic killer," Dalton replied, fuming.

"Oh, you're a killer," Nina told him as she returned to Jared. "Just not the kind who gets his hands dirty. Until now, at least. How does it feel to be out in the field, and on the wrong end of some blowback?"

The ex-president struggled to get his temper back under control. "Never mind that," he said. "If the bridge is gone, we're trapped in here! What are we going to do?"

"Shoot you if you don't stop whingeing," said Eddie. "Nina, you got my phone?" She passed it to him. He checked the screen. "No network. Can't say I'm surprised, but it was worth a try."

Nina bandaged the Mossad agent's leg. "You said they cut the rope. From this side?"

"No, the other side," Eddie replied.

"So we might be able to use it to get across the cenote?"

"Maybe, if that explosion didn't shred it or knock the pitons out of the wall."

"We need to check." She secured the bandage. "How does that feel?"

Jared sat up slowly, face drawn tight with pain. "Like I got stabbed in the leg."

Nina helped him up. "Can you walk?"

He took a couple of experimental steps. "Just about," he gasped.

"Guess you won't be winning this month's Mossad fun run," said Eddie.

Jared gave him a strained grin. "At least I'll be trying, old man."

"Yeah, you're bloody trying all right. Come on, let's see what's left of the bridge." He waved the Desert Eagle at Dalton. "Oi! Commander in Chief, lead from the front. Let's go."

The group made their way back down the decorated passage. Some of the paintings near the doorway had been damaged by flying debris, but to Nina's relief the majority were intact; even given their grim situation, part of her was still overjoyed that the temple and its contents had not been destroyed.

Whether she would ever tell anyone about her find was another matter. "That's . . . not ideal," she said, shining her light at the empty space where the bridge had been.

Eddie had reclaimed his own torch from Jared. "Nor's

that." He illuminated the rock blocking the tunnel across the shaft. "Looks pretty unstable, but I don't fancy trying to pull it loose from that hole."

"We could send Dalton over," suggested Nina jokingly. The politician was not amused.

Eddie redirected his torch at the rope. As he had feared, it had been damaged by the blast—the outer layers of strands closest to the grenade's point of impact were torn and ragged—but it was still in one piece. He pulled on it, testing both that the pitons were still fixed to the rock and that it would not snap under stress. "It'll hold. I think."

"What are you going to do?" Jared asked. "Run it around the shaft and try to pull that rock out of the way?"

"It won't reach." The length of line was just enough to span the shaft's diameter, but the smooth, curved walls forming the cenote's circumference were much longer.

"Then we're trapped here?" exclaimed Dalton.

"At least we'll have something to eat," said Nina, staring at him for just long enough to make him uncomfortable before indicating a clump of mushrooms that had survived the explosion. "Actually, we'd probably find some of these inside the jar in the Ark. It's supposed to contain manna, the food God sent to the Israelites, and the description of manna was like a kind of mushroom or fungus."

"These are in a cave, not out in the desert, though," Jared pointed out.

"Yes, but we saw them in—" An electric thought hit her. "The pool outside, the sinkhole. There were some floating in the water!"

"So?" asked Dalton. "They probably grow all over this place."

"But we've only seen them in the tunnels. So," she pressed on, "there's water at the bottom of this shaft, and we came up a slope for some distance to get here. What if it's the same water in both, at the same level, and they're connected? The mushrooms we saw outside might have come from here!"

Eddie looked down the shaft, seeing a glimmer of a reflection from his torch. "It's a long drop—seventy feet, easy."

"But the rope's about thirty feet long. If someone hung from the end before letting go, that would cut the drop to not much more than thirty feet. And they'd be landing in water."

"We don't know how deep it is," said Jared. "If it's shallow, they'd break their legs."

Eddie picked up a hunk of broken stone and lobbed it over the edge. The sound of a loud splash rolled up the shaft. "It's more than a foot deep," he said, "or we would've heard it hit the bottom. But that doesn't mean it'll be a soft landing for whoever tries it. Who, let's face it, will be me."

Jared hobbled to the edge. "No, I can do it."

Eddie snorted. "Stabbed," he told the Israeli. "Pregnant," he said to his wife. "Wanker," he concluded, jabbing a thumb at the affronted Dalton. "I'm the only one who *can* do it."

Nina was already having second thoughts. "If there isn't a way through to the sinkhole, or it's too narrow to fit through, you'll be trapped down there."

Jared looked back toward the throne room. "I'll probably be struck dead for suggesting this, but we could tear up the tapestries to make a longer rope. Or maybe take down the Tabernacle—"

"And how long'll that take?" Eddie cut in. "Cross'll be on the way back to his helicopter by now. Once he's gone, we've lost him—and the angel." He tested the hanging rope again. "Buggeration and fuckery. I'm actually going to have to do it, aren't I?"

Nina tried desperately to think of an alternative, but came up with nothing. "Eddie, just . . . don't die. Please. In fact," she continued, pleading giving way to determination, "you're not *allowed* to die. Your daughter needs you."

The torches weren't pointing at his face, but his smile still lit up the shaft. "We're having a little girl?" he exclaimed, delighted.

Nina beamed at him. "Yeah. I know you wanted it to be a surprise, but if there was ever a time when you should know . . ."

"We're having a girl!" he cried, embracing her. "Holy shit, we're having a daughter. That's amazing!" He kissed her.

"Well, it was that or a boy, a fifty–fifty chance," she reminded him with a grin.

Jared clapped him on the back. "Well done, old man."

"Congratulations," said Dalton, with considerable sarcasm. "Now maybe we can try to get out of here?"

Eddie released Nina. "Okay, you're right," he told her. "No fucking way am I going to die before I see her. And preferably not for a long time after that." He pocketed his gun and flashlight, then took a firm hold of the rope and moved to the edge. "We're getting out of here. I mean, I've got to be there to take her ice-skating at Rockefeller Center, intimidate her first boyfriend . . ."

"Be nice," Nina told him. "And be careful!"

"Always am. Usually. See you soon." He blew her a kiss, then stepped backward to begin his descent.

The damaged rope was rough to the touch, scraping his palms. He could feel the fibers straining under his weight. But he was now committed to the climb—either it would hold, or his drop would be even longer than expected.

He had made many such descents before, and this one was no more challenging than any other. The only complication was the sheer smoothness of the cenote's wall, forcing him to bring his feet up higher than he liked to maintain grip with his soles. But he made quick and steady progress, until . . .

"I'm out of rope!" he shouted. He took all his weight with his left hand as he wound the line's severed end around his right, then held himself in place as he took out the torch and directed it downward.

A black pool shimmered below. It filled the entire shaft. No protruding rocks broke the surface, or even debris from the destroyed bridge, but he couldn't tell how deep it was. He could judge the distance to the surface, though: It was still a thirty-foot drop, about as far as an Olympic high dive. A simple landing if the water was deep enough. If it wasn't, or he hit wreckage, his bones would shatter.

"Can you make it?" Nina called from above.

"Going to have to!" Eddie brought his feet up until he was almost perpendicular to the wall. Landing on his back would hurt, but it would bring him to a stop at a shallower depth than if he dropped vertically.

Assuming he didn't hit something first.

But it was either that or climb back up and remain trapped in the tunnels. "Okay," he said, taking a deep breath as he psyched himself up. "One, two—"

The rope snapped—and he fell.

29

A brief sickening feeling of free-fall and fear—
Impact.

Pain flared through Eddie's back—then the water crashed over his face, causing a moment of panic before he regained his senses. He thrashed his limbs. No sharp agony from broken bones. Relieved, he tipped himself upright and breached the surface to draw breath, probing with his feet. They touched an uneven floor about five feet below, strewn with debris. Landing flat had saved his life; if he had dropped straight down, he would have hit solid rock and broken both ankles.

"Eddie! Are you okay?" cried Nina.

"I'm fine!" he shouted, straightening to his full height and bringing the waterproof flashlight above the rippling surface. The water was littered with splintered wood and mushrooms stripped from the walls by the explosion.

The latter reminded him what he was looking for. He surveyed the walls. The cenote widened out at its base to form a bulbous, lopsided cavern, but there were no exits above water level. He lowered the torch under the surface and submerged again.

Nothing was visible. The falling wreckage had churned

up the pool, disturbing long-settled sediment. He resurfaced, swearing under his breath. He would have to search blind . . .

Or would he? "Nina! Switch off your light!" he called, clicking off his own torch.

"You sure?" she asked.

"If there's a way through to the sinkhole, I might be able to see daylight."

"Okay!" Her light went out. Eddie closed his eyes, letting them adjust to the darkness, then opened them again.

At first he saw only blackness. But then a vague cyan haze took on form to one side. He waded closer. The ghostly sheen gradually became more distinct. Dropping below the water, he saw a rough rectangle of dim light lower in the wall. "I think I've found a way out," he told the others after surfacing.

"Big enough to get through?" asked Jared.

"I'll find out in a minute!" He swam across the pool, then submerged again.

There *was* a passage through the rock, around five feet wide—but far shallower, two feet high at most. That he could see daylight on the far side suggested the tunnel was not long, but if he got caught on a jutting rock . . .

He resurfaced. "Okay, I'm going to try to reach the sinkhole. If I get through—"

"*When* you get through," Nina corrected. "Daughter waiting, remember?"

"*When* I get through, I'll fetch the rest of our gear, then try to push that rock out of the way so I can throw another rope across to you."

"See you soon," she said. He switched his torch back on and waved it at her, then took several deep breaths and plunged back under the water.

The passage took on form, a pale blue void in the surrounding darkness. He swam into it, finding the highest point. Even that was uncomfortably claustrophobic, and it quickly became even tighter as he advanced. Stone scraped his head. He angled downward, but within seconds felt rock brush his chest.

He switched tack, using his hands as much to pull himself forward as to swim. The light ahead grew brighter, but the ceiling and floor continued to close in. His heels struck the stone above, forcing him to slow and switch to a more frog-like kick.

The end of the underwater tunnel was now in sight, though. He kept kicking, dragging himself along—

An overhanging protrusion caught his shoulder. He tried to drop under it—only to find he had no more room to maneuver, his chest flat against the floor. He shoved himself sideways, but found his way blocked in that direction as well.

He backtracked, heart starting to race as the remaining oxygen in his lungs was consumed. A crab-like crawl across the passage, then he started forward again. This time the floor rose up to meet him, pushing him against the ceiling. Rock nudged his body from above and below.

He was running out of air! Clawing at the floor, he hauled himself through the fissure. The slabs of stone squeezed more tightly against him, his clothing catching on rough edges—

His other shoulder became wedged.

No time to back up and try another route. It was either onward—or nowhere. A fist clenched around his lungs. He dug his fingernails against the rough surface and pulled, writhing as he tried to break loose . . .

His pinned shoulder shifted slightly, jacket slipping against the rock—then with a jerk he pulled free. He squirmed past the obstacle and kicked out of the passage.

The sinkhole waited above, a near-perfect circle of blue. He swam to it, breaking the surface with a gasp—

And immediately clamped his mouth shut as he heard voices.

Heart thudding, breathing heavily through his nostrils, he eased himself to the pool's side. He had emerged near the cave dug out below ground level—and somebody was inside it.

Eddie brought his breath under control, then carefully

moved along the pool's edge until he could see into the cavern. Two of Cross's men, armed with MP5s, stood within. Both thankfully had their backs to him, watching the tunnel leading to the cenote. A rear guard.

He looked up at the lip of the sinkhole. Nobody else was there, as far as he could see. But he couldn't hear any engine noises either. For a moment he was worried that Cross had already left, but decided, based on the time between the helicopter's arrival and the bad guys entering the temple, that they had not yet made it back to their aircraft.

As much as he wanted to help Nina, she and the others would be safe where they were for now. If there was a chance to prevent Cross from leaving, he had to take it. But he would have to deal with the sentries first.

He held on to the ledge with his left hand, then quietly drew the Desert Eagle and brought it above the surface, tipping it to drain the water from its barrel and receiver. He knew he ought to eject the magazine and rack the slide to make sure the mechanism was fully cleared, but doing so would make a noise that the guards couldn't possibly miss.

He would just have to take his first shot—and hope the second didn't jam.

The two men were halfway between the pool and the tunnel entrance, both facing away from him, though the man on the left had turned his head toward his companion as they talked. He would be the quicker to react—which made him the first target.

The Englishman raised himself higher in the water, then aligned the Desert Eagle's sights on the man's back. A .50-cal shot would go right through him at this range, but it was the second guard who concerned Eddie. If the guy was quick, he might be able to spin around and retaliate before the Englishman could recover from the recoil of firing the huge gun one-handed . . .

Eddie steeled himself—and pulled the trigger.

The gun's boom was near-deafening, resounding like the striking of a massive bell. Even with his arm tensed, the recoil kicked it backward. But the impact on the first guard was far greater. A great burst of gore exploded from the exit wound, blood and viscera splashing over the walls. Already dead, he crumpled to the floor.

The second man jumped in shock, but recovered almost instantly, whirling to face the threat—

The Yorkshireman hauled the gun back down and unleashed a second ear-pounding gunshot. The bullet shattered the man's shoulder, almost severing his left arm. He was flung backward, sending a wild spray of fire against the cavern's ceiling.

Eddie pulled himself from the water. His opponent was down, but not out. The MP5 flailed toward him—

A third thunderous shot—and the man's head burst apart as if a bomb had detonated inside his skull, only his lower jaw and tongue remaining intact amid the carnage.

"Don't think I'll be telling my kid about this bit," Eddie said as he lowered the smoking Desert Eagle. He glanced at the tunnel leading back to Nina, then reluctantly collected the first dead man's MP5, slinging it over his shoulder before jumping to grab the lip of the cavern's overhanging roof. Water dripping from his clothes, he pulled himself up and looked around, spotting boot prints in the dust. He started uphill after them.

He had barely gone twenty yards before hearing the distant whine of an engine. Cross and the others had reached the helicopter. "No you fucking don't," he muttered, checking that the MP5 was ready for action as he ran.

The climb was steep and rocky, but he saw flatter ground some way above. He hurried up the slope, hearing the chop of rotor blades picking up speed. It would be at takeoff revolutions soon; once it left the ground, it would be out of his weapon's range very quickly.

Dust billowed over the edge of the rise as the noise reached a crescendo. A moment later, the red-and-white aircraft rose into view, already tipping into flight away from him . . .

Eddie whipped up the MP5 and fired on full auto.

A stream of bullets arced into the air after the chopper.

He was at the limit of the weapon's effective range, but sheer firepower was enough to score several hits. Sparks spat from the fuselage as rounds struck home, punching through the thin aluminum to strike more vital components beneath. A puff of smoke came from one of the exhausts. "Yeah!" he yelled as the helicopter lurched. "Get back down here!"

*   *   *

Cross grabbed his seat for support as the Bell jerked violently. Paxton wrestled with the controls, an alarm shrilling urgently in time with flashing warning lights. "I'm losing oil pressure in number two engine!" the pilot shouted. "I'll have to shut it down!"

"Can we still fly on one engine?" demanded Simeon, holding Anna in place.

"Yeah, but it'll be tricky. We should make it back to Ovda, though."

The landscape swung past the windshield as the helicopter slewed around. Cross spotted something on the hillside below—a figure in dark clothing. "It's Chase!"

"I *told* you I should have killed him!" Simeon snarled.

Cross shot him an angry look, but he had bigger concerns than insubordination. The Englishman fired another brief burst. Norvin flinched, but no more bullets came. "He's out of ammo!"

"Take us back around," said Simeon, grabbing his MP5. "I'll deal with that son of a bitch!"

"No, we need to get out of here!" Paxton countered, knuckles white as both hands gripped the shuddering controls.

"Take us back to the air base," Cross ordered, to Simeon's disappointment. He looked back at his right-hand man as the aircraft gained height. "Don't worry, they won't get out of there." He reached for the radio. "Time to call in a favor."

*   *   *

Eddie glared after the chopper as it stabilized and headed into the distance. "Bollocking fuck-nuts!" he said, discarding the empty MP5 and squishing back down the mountain. He didn't know where the helicopter was going, but Israel was a small country; Cross and his remaining people would probably be on a jet with the angel within the hour.

He dropped back down into the cavern, retrieving the climbing gear before returning to the cenote. The rock blocking the mouth of the passage proved to be as precariously balanced as he had thought; it only took a couple of minutes to force it over the edge. It fell to the foot of the shaft with a booming splash. "Eddie!" said Nina with relief from across the gap. "Are you okay?"

"Yeah, but Cross got away," he said glumly. "What about you?"

"I'm fine. Jared's stable, but from the way he's been acting, you'd think he was fit and ready to run a marathon." The Israeli, sitting against the open door, grinned. "And Dalton's been a moaning prick, but that's nothing new."

The politician was hunched against the tunnel wall. "You know, I'm getting really tired of your attitude."

"And I'm getting really tired of your continued existence. Now, Mr. President, kindly shut the fuck up." She put both hands to her bump. "Mommy doesn't normally use rude words, hon—that's Daddy's department—but sometimes they're justified. Don't you use them, though, okay?"

Dalton rolled his eyes. "Nauseating."

"Yeah, I bet you were a fun dad," Eddie snarked. "Okay, Jared? We'll rig up a Tyrolean traverse and use the harness to bring you over."

He pounded new pitons into the rock and fixed ropes to them, then threw the rest of the coils across the chasm. Jared and Nina caught them and pulled them in. The Englishman then lobbed over the hammer and more steel pegs. Once one rope was secured on both sides, the other was tied to Nina's climbing harness so it could be pulled back across, then she, Jared, and finally Dalton made their way over. "Thank God!" the latter gasped as his feet made contact with the floor.

"Thank Nina," said the Englishman. "I would've left you over there." He set about retrieving the climbing equipment. "We'll need this to get back down to the Landie."

"Great," grumbled Dalton. "It'll take us hours to drive out of this desert."

"If only we'd had access to the CIA's black funds for a helicopter," said Nina sarcastically. "You know, Mr. President, they really should have revoked your access to all that stuff when you resigned from office."

"And you don't work for the IHA anymore, yet they seem happy to fund your whims at the drop of a hat. It's high time the United Nations had its funding brought into check—"

Eddie jabbed a finger at his face. "Oi! Mr. Pussy-dent!" Nina let out an involuntary guffaw at the sheer childishness of the insult, and Dalton's outraged reaction to it. "You know how she told you to shut the fuck up? Shut the fuck up." Dalton seethed, but bit his lip at the Yorkshireman's menacing stare.

"The only thing we want to hear from you is what Cross intends to do with the angels," said Nina as Eddie finished gathering the gear. They started down the tunnel. "Where's he planning to release them?"

"I've got nothing to say," Dalton replied stiffly.

Nina blew out an incredulous breath. "Seriously? You don't get it, do you? Cross *betrayed* you! He got everything he needed from you and then left you here to die. You've got nothing to gain by protecting him." The ex-president stayed silent. "Maybe you think you're maintaining plausible deniability, and that somehow you'll be able to worm your way out of responsibility for what happened at the Mission. But trust me: You won't be celebrating your political comeback when you return to the States. You'll be in a federal prison on charges of conspiracy to kidnap and murder, if not outright terrorism."

"I told you, people like me don't go to jail," he retorted.

"Then maybe it's time for a bit of vigilante justice," said Eddie, making a show of checking the Desert Eagle. Dalton fell silent.

They emerged in the cavern. Eddie helped Nina out of the sinkhole, then Jared, before climbing out himself. The two men then pulled Dalton up. "Are you okay?" Nina asked Jared, seeing him grimace.

"Yeah, yeah," he replied, not with full conviction. "But you're right, I won't be doing much on this leg for a while."

"Hopefully you won't have to."

"Still got to climb down," Eddie reminded them. He started toward the passage through the cliffs, the others following. "How long'll it take before we can tell anyone what's happened?"

"I think going west rather than back the way we came will be the quickest route to a highway," Jared replied. "There's one running parallel to the Egyptian border. We should get cell reception there." They clambered over the fallen rocks and continued along the narrow, winding ravine.

"So what about it?" Nina asked Dalton. "Your only chance of staying out of prison is to tell us where Cross plans to release the angels. If you help stop the attacks, you might just save your sorry ass."

"If I'm going to say anything," he replied with disdain, "it'll be through my lawyer to the attorney general. It sure as hell won't be to the likes of you."

She shook her head. "You really *do* think you'll still be able to get back into the White House, don't you? Jeez. I know politicians have an inflated sense of self-belief, but you're outright delusional!"

"We'll see" was his reply.

"Twat," said Eddie, turning sideways to pass through the tight clench. "All right, we're almost at the cliff." The light ahead grew brighter as they neared the last twist in the chasm. "I'll rig the rope, and . . ."

He trailed off as he rounded the last corner—and

heard a rising noise. The others stopped behind him. "What's that?" Nina asked.

The answer came a moment later as an Apache helicopter gunship rose into view, its cannon swinging toward them.

30

Dalton pushed forward, waving at the helicopter's pilot—Colonel Brik. "Hey! It's me! Help me! I'm—"

Eddie seized him. "Back!" he yelled, driving the others into cover around the corner—

The gunship opened fire, its thirty-millimeter chain gun blazing. Shells tore into the chasm's walls, ripping out chunks of rock.

Eddie shoved Dalton away and grabbed Nina, shielding her with his body. Jared stumbled against a wall as he tried to run, while the politician fled before tripping in his panic.

Brik jinked the aircraft sideways to give his gunner a better angle down the narrow cleft. The curve of the walls still blocked their targets from view, but that didn't ease the trigger finger of the man in the forward seat. More shells screamed against the cliffs, fractured stone spalling in all directions.

"Move, move!" Eddie screamed, barely audible over the gun's thunder. A lump of rock smacked against his head as he pushed Nina onward. Just ahead of them, Jared managed to hobble around the next bend before his leg gave way.

The cannon fire stopped, a few last pieces of debris ricocheting past. Then the only movement was the dust blown through the ravine by the rotor downwash. "What the hell was *that*?" Nina demanded.

"That was one of our Petens!" Jared replied, shocked. The Apache—Peten, meaning "adder," was the Hebrew name for the American aircraft—was painted in the brown-and-gray camouflage pattern of the Israeli air force. "Why's it attacking *us*?"

"I bet *he* knows," Eddie growled, going to Dalton. He dragged him upright. "Hey! Where did that fucking chopper come from?"

The politician was wide-eyed with fear. "It's some old contact of Cross," he panted. "Colonel Brik, base commander at Ovda. Cross must have called him."

"Still think he's on your side?" said Nina angrily. "He just tried to kill us!"

"He hasn't stopped," Eddie warned. The Apache's engine note changed, the gunship pulling back from the cliff and descending. "Get in farther—go, go!"

They squeezed through the narrow clench, but Eddie knew they were still not safe. "Cover your ears!" he cried.

"Why, what's happ—" Dalton began, but the sight of the others pressing their palms firmly to their heads rapidly prompted him to do the same. Eddie hunched down, bracing himself against the wall as he again shielded Nina—

A sharp hiss—then the entire cliff shook with the impact of a rocket. Another *whoosh* and a second missile struck just inside the cleft. A gritty shock wave blasted pulverized fragments of stone down the passage, the blast knocking those within to the ground.

The echoes faded. Eddie coughed, spitting out dust. "Is everyone okay?"

"I . . . I think so," said Nina, wincing. Despite Eddie's efforts to protect her, pain coursed through her hip where a flying rock had struck her. "We were lucky."

"They haven't given up," Eddie said ominously. He stood, listening. Even with the ravine's strange acoustics, it was easy to tell that the gunship was on the move. Seconds later a hot wind stinking of burnt aviation fuel tore through their shelter as the gunship thundered directly overhead.

Dalton pushed himself back against the wall. "Oh God! They're going to shoot us from above!"

"They can't lower the gun that far," Eddie told him. "And this place is too twisty for them to get a clear shot . . . Shit!" Realization hit him. "They're going to the other end to seal us in!"

Nina looked after the aircraft with alarm. "How many rockets do they have?"

"Too fucking many." He had seen rocket pods beneath the Apache's stub wings; each could hold nineteen Hydra or CRV7 seventy-millimeter unguided missiles.

"*Do* something, Chase!" cried Dalton.

"Like what?" he snapped, drawing the Desert Eagle. "Shoot it down with this?"

"Why not? It's huge! I know those helicopters are armored, but—"

"The cockpit can take a hit from a fifty-cal round. I *might* get through the armor somewhere else, but I've only got a few bullets left. I fired an entire mag at Cross's chopper and didn't cause enough damage to bring it down—shit, incoming!" He heard the Apache's engine note change again and hurriedly put down the handgun to cover his ears. The others did the same—

More rockets pounded the far end of the cleft. This time Brik ordered his gunner to keep firing, missile after missile exploding against the cliffs. The ground shook with the man-made earthquake, then a deeper, more fearsome vibration flung everyone to the floor again as rock gave way under the onslaught.

An entire section of the massif collapsed into the hollow, hundreds of tons of debris plunging down the sinkhole, and more blocking the narrow passage through the cliffs. Another blinding, choking wave of dust rolled over the fugitives.

Eddie checked that Nina had not suffered any more

injuries, then looked through the haze to find Jared and Dalton. "Are you okay?"

"Yeah, but we're trapped in here!" the Israeli replied.

The dust swirled in the Apache's downdraft as the gunship passed back overhead. Dalton watched it in dismay. "So . . . so what are they going to do? Hover at the end of the ravine and pick us off if we show our faces?"

"Pretty much," Eddie told him, helping Nina up.

"There must be *something* you can do!"

"Oh, so now I'm the answer to all your problems? We can't get back to the temple, and if we try to climb down the cliff, they'll shoot us." The Englishman tipped his head, looking up between the sheer walls. "I could chimney-climb to the top, but there's no cover, so they'd only have to gain a bit of height to take a shot—"

He broke off. He had still been in the SAS when the Apache entered British military service, and had taken the opportunity to get a close look at the new machine that would be providing his fellow servicemen with air support. Now a memory returned from when he had actually sat inside one. The gunship's cockpit was indeed designed to resist bullets, but not from every angle. One part had been left unarmored to save weight, on the grounds that it would never normally be exposed to an enemy . . .

Nina realized that he was forming a plan. "What is it?" she asked.

"*I* might be able to take a shot," he said, ejecting the Desert Eagle's magazine to count the remaining rounds. Four, including the one already chambered. "If the Israeli Apache is like the British one, then the window right over the pilot's head is regular Perspex rather than bulletproof. I can shoot the bastard—if I can get to the right angle." He slapped the mag back into place, then gave his companions a grim look. "Problem is, to get to that angle, someone'll have to keep 'em busy." He quickly explained his idea.

"That's suicide!" Dalton objected.

"Then you'll be glad to know I wasn't expecting you

to volunteer." He turned to Jared. "Sorry, but you're the best bet."

The young man straightened, wincing as he put weight on his injured leg. "I'll get it done."

"Eddie, he can't," Nina protested. "He won't be able to move fast enough!"

"I can't get *him* to do it," said Eddie, with a contemptuous jerk of his thumb at Dalton, "and I'm not bloody letting you try. Not with our baby on board."

"I can do it, Nina," Jared assured her.

"And we need to do it now," Eddie said. The helicopter had moved back over the valley to watch the open end of the cleft. "Okay, Jared, wait until I'm almost at the top and then show yourself. Hopefully that'll keep 'em occupied long enough for me to get into position."

"And if it doesn't?" asked Dalton.

"Then I'll chuck you off the cliff into their rotors!" Ignoring the gray-haired man's outrage, he went to Nina. "Okay, love, I'll get going now. Whatever you do, stay safe." He kissed her, then gently placed one hand against the swell of her lower body. "Both of you."

He hurried back to the narrowest part of the passage and began his ascent, arms and legs spread to give himself support on each side of the fissure. The climb was quick at first, but before long the strain of holding his full weight started to slow him. He twisted to brace one shoulder against a wall, taking some of the pressure off his arms, and looked up. About thirty feet to go; halfway there.

He resumed his climb. Each step crunched against the limestone, dust and grit falling away from his feet. His breathing became heavier as he shuffled upward. A chimney climb would normally be made in a crack in the face of a cliff, giving him three walls where he could find handholds and support, but here there was nothing but air on two sides.

And the cleft was gradually widening the higher he went. He could no longer use his shoulders for support, instead having to push his palms against the wall behind him. If his arms weakened, or his feet slipped on the crumbling surface, he would plunge straight back down.

To his death, from this height.

Fifty feet. Just ten to go. He glanced down, seeing the others watching. "Jared, get ready!" he called.

Five feet. The rock, now fully exposed to the elements, became rougher. More grip, but it was also more fragile.

He looked toward the valley. A dark shape was visible through the rippling heat haze, the Apache drifting lazily sideways as its crew watched the entrance to the crevice. Shit! It was too high; they would spot him the moment he reached the clifftop. "Go now, *now*!"

＊ ＊ ＊

Jared heard the call. "Okay, wish me luck," he said, starting down the passage.

Nina watched his limp grow more pronounced with each step. "Jared, you can't," she said, hurrying after him.

"I can't let you do it," he replied.

"I can't let *you* do it! You can hardly walk, never mind run. You're about to deliberately put yourself in front of a machine gun—if you can't move fast enough, it'll kill you!"

"Nina, you're pregnant—"

"Yeah, I'm pregnant. But as Eddie reminded me, I'm not an invalid, and even with a baby inside me I'm still quicker than you." To prove her point, she darted past him. He tried to block her, but the mere effort of pivoting on his wounded leg caused him to gasp and stagger. "I'm not going to let you kill yourself just because you want to prove how tough you are."

"No, don't!" he cried, hobbling after her, only to clutch at the rock for support as he almost fell again. "I promised Eddie—"

"I promised him *more,* when I married him," Nina replied, glancing back up at her husband. "But I never promised that I'd always do exactly what he told me. Seriously, what's that all about?" She composed herself.

"Now get back and watch Dalton. I've got a feeling I'll need as much room to run as I can get."

Before Jared could object, she scurried on, a curve in the confined channel taking him—and Eddie—out of sight. The gunship's engines became louder as she crept to the final corner and peered around it.

The opening was no longer a vertical crack, a ragged chunk of rock having been blasted from one side as if a giant had taken a bite from the cliff. The helicopter was out of sight, but getting closer. From what Eddie had said, the gunner would have his sights fixed upon the cleft. She would only have a few seconds between making herself visible and the first shells landing—if she was lucky. If the man in the chopper had razor-sharp reactions, she might not even get *one* second.

The brutal aircraft drifted into view against the empty sky. It was higher than her position, the cannon under its nose pointed down at its target. She needed it to descend for Eddie's plan to work.

There was only one way to make that happen.

Nina steeled herself . . . then stepped into view.

*　*　*

Eddie was still straining to hold himself just below the top of the crevasse, his eyes locked on the gunship. He couldn't risk climbing out into the open, but neither could he stay where he was forever. "Come on, Jared," he whispered. "Give me my shot . . ."

The Apache continued its lazy motion—then suddenly the engine note changed.

*　*　*

Nina stared up at the helicopter for what felt like an eternity, the insectile machine's silhouette burning itself into her vision. Then movement from its gun turret snapped her back into the moment.

The chain gun's muzzle flashed with fire as she turned and ran back down the passage. The first shell hit the ground where she had been standing, the anti-armor round ripping deep into the limestone before exploding and showering her with fragments. She shrieked, but could no longer hear her own voice over the pounding of thirty-millimeter fire.

The gunner tracked her. Even though she was out of his direct line of sight, the shrapnel from the shells bursting on the walls was as dangerous as a direct hit. Terrified, she sprinted for the next bend—

Red-hot agony seared into her thigh as a metal shard tore through skin. She screamed, falling.

More shells blasted the walls, the detonations closing in—

The cannon fell silent.

* * *

"Cease fire, cease fire!" Brik ordered. He had slipped the Apache sideways to maintain a firing angle down the tight ravine, but the person he had briefly glimpsed had made it back into cover.

From gunfire, at least.

"Switch to rockets," he told the gunner. "I'll bring us to firing position." The gunship's missile pods were fixed, requiring the whole aircraft to be brought into line with their target.

"Two degrees to port," the gunner told him. Brik applied pressure to a rudder pedal, turning the aircraft. A vertical line superimposed down the center of the gun sight bisected the entrance. "Okay. Bring us closer, descend ten meters."

The colonel began the maneuver, the crosshairs slipping down toward the base of the cleft.

* * *

The moment the Apache fired, Eddie pulled himself onto the clifftop. If his plan had worked, Jared, acting as his decoy to draw the aircrew's attention, would have already retreated beyond the chain gun's line of fire, forcing the gunner to switch to rockets—and requiring the helicopter to come lower to line up its fixed weapons.

That would put him out of sight for the precious seconds he needed.

If the plan hadn't worked, his friend would already be dead.

The firing stopped. The gunship hung in the air . . . then descended.

Eddie ran for the cliff's edge. The Apache came back into sight. It was about a hundred yards away but drawing closer, still gradually losing height.

He could see the weak spot—the top window of the upper canopy, right in front of the main rotor head. But to his dismay he realized he didn't have a clear shot. The gunship was now too *low*, the spinning rotor in the way. A bullet might pass cleanly through and hit its target . . . or strike a carbon-fiber blade and be deflected away.

No matter what, he had to take the shot before the gunship fired its rockets. He lined up the Desert Eagle's sights—and pulled the trigger.

Sparks and paint flakes spat from behind the cockpit. His aim wasn't at fault; as he'd feared, the bullet had glanced off the rotor and been thrown off target. Now he only had three bullets left.

And the Apache's crew knew he was there.

* * *

Colonel Brik hadn't heard the gunshot, the Apache's roar and the insulation of his helmet blotting out most external sounds, but he couldn't miss the sharp clank of a large-caliber bullet impact less than a yard behind his head. He swore, looking up to see a figure on the cliff. "Hostile, above! Take him out!"

The gunner searched for the new threat. The chain gun, slaved to his head movements, followed his gaze— only to clunk to a stop with a warning buzz as it reached the limits of its travel. "Can't traverse!"

Brik was already increasing power. The Apache rose toward its prey.

* * *

Eddie took aim again as the gunship climbed. The chain gun was at maximum elevation; it would be able to target him in moments—

He fired. The second shot did no better than the first, the bullet twanging off the rotors. So did the third. Only one round left. The cockpit's upper canopy came into clear view beneath the whirling blades, but he was out of time.

The cannon strained against its restraints, then finally found its target—

The Englishman unleashed his last shot.

It struck home, punching through the acrylic window into the cockpit to hit Brik in the head.

His composite flight helmet was built to resist normal small-arms fire, but the Desert Eagle's half-inch-wide bullet was considerably more powerful. It shattered as it tore through the protective layers, but the individual fragments still carried enough momentum to rip into the top of the Israeli's skull. Bone splintered, hot metal churning through brain matter like mixer blades.

The gunner fired the chain gun—as Brik's spasming limbs sent the Apache lurching violently sideways. Eddie dived backward as the first few shells hit the cliff, but the rest of the shots went wide.

The helicopter spun toward the ground. The gunner screamed, hauling frantically at his duplicate flight controls, but Brik still had a death grip on his own sticks—

The main rotor smashed against the sheer cliff below the cleft. The blades disintegrated, and the airframe plunged as gravity eagerly reclaimed its hold. The Apache hit the ground hard, the stumps of the rotors digging into the earth and flipping it over before fuel and munitions ignited, blasting the tumbling wreck into a billion blazing fragments.

The rumble of the explosion faded. Eddie shook off grit and crawled to the edge. The gunship's burning remains were strewn below—along with those of the Land Rover, which had been parked beneath the passage. "Bollocks," he said as he recovered his breath. "Looks like we're in for a long walk."

He stood and went to the top of the ravine, looking into it with trepidation as he searched for Jared—only for his heart to freeze in fear. There was a figure lying unmoving below, but it wasn't the Israeli.

It was his wife.

31

Eddie ran back to the chasm's narrowest point and made a rapid descent. He dropped the last ten feet and shoved past Dalton, ignoring the politician's questions as he ran down the passage. The limping Jared was ahead; he quickly caught up. "What the fuck have you *done*?" he roared at the younger man.

"I tried to stop her!" Jared protested.

"Not fucking hard enough!"

"She got past me and ran off! I tried to catch up, but . . ." He regarded his wounded leg. More blood had soaked the bandage. "Then the chopper started shooting."

Eddie held in another curse and ran on, rounding a corner to see broken rocks strewn over the floor—and a dust-covered figure lying among them. He hurried to her. "Nina! Nina, are you okay? Can you hear me?"

No movement for agonizing seconds as he checked for a pulse . . . then she painfully turned her head, squinting up at him. "Did you get it?"

"Yeah, I got it."

"Hooray for us . . ." She tried to sit up, but cried out as she moved her leg. "Oh! Damn, that hurts!"

He saw blood on her thigh and examined the injury.

"Looks like shrapnel. Jared!" he said as the Israeli hobbled into view. "The first-aid kit's in the bag—get that useless shithead Dalton to bring it."

"Is she okay?" Jared asked, worried.

"No," he snarled, "'cause you let her do your job! Go!"

"Don't be angry at him," Nina told her husband as the shamefaced young man turned away. "He wanted to do it, but I stopped him." She gestured toward the entrance, the passage now pockmarked with ragged holes. "And I'm glad I did, because if I hadn't, he would have been killed."

"You're glad you got a piece of shrap in your leg?"

"Okay, maybe not *glad* exactly . . ." She shifted position as carefully as she could to look down at her stomach. "God, I hope she's all right."

"Me too. I'll get that bit of metal out, then check if she's okay."

"How? I don't think we brought an ultrasound scanner."

The corners of his mouth creased upward, just a little. "Getting sarky? You can't be that badly hurt, then."

"Yeah, you just keep telling me that and maybe I'll start to believe it." Nina too managed a small, pained smile.

Jared soon returned, Dalton following with the backpack. Eddie took out the first-aid kit and cleaned Nina's wound, then used tweezers to grip the protruding end of the metal shard. "Okay, this'll hurt," he warned.

Her sarcasm was now more overt. "Yeah, I'm *so* glad you told me that in advance."

"Well, I could've just yanked it out without warning while I was in the middle of talking to keep you distracted, but—" He yanked it out without warning.

She shrieked. "Aah! Son of a—Bastard—*Shit!*"

Dalton winced at the spurt of blood, but still found the time to be patronizing. "The world's most famous archaeologist, eloquent and classy as always."

"Shut the fuck up," the couple told him in unison. Dalton huffed.

While Eddie dressed the wound, Jared limped to the

end of the passage and peered at the wreckage below. "They took out the truck!" he said as he returned.

Dalton went in alarm to see for himself. "We're *stranded*?"

"Someone'll be along soon," Eddie replied, unworried.

"We're in the middle of a desert! How can you possibly know that?"

"Because when a twenty-million-dollar helicopter gunship crashes and explodes, the people who own it usually want to find out what happened pretty sharpish. And I doubt shooting at a pregnant archaeologist, a Mossad agent, and an ex-president was an officially sanctioned mission." He looked at Jared. "How far away's its base?"

"Ovda? About twenty miles," the Israeli replied.

"So I bet you there'll be another chopper here in the next ten minutes."

"Hopefully not another gunship," said Nina. She drew in a sharp breath as Eddie finished working on her wound, then carefully sat up and regarded Dalton. "So while we're waiting, *Mr. President,* I think we should talk about Cross. Now that he's tried to kill you, it's safe to assume you aren't best buddies anymore?"

"You've got that right," Dalton growled. "That son of a bitch! He *used* me!"

"Matthew chapter seven, verse fifteen: 'Beware of false prophets,'" said Nina, to his annoyance. "He doesn't care about your political rehabilitation, and he never did. He just saw you as a means to an end, a way to bring about the apocalypse. So maybe now you should stop thinking about how to protect him and start thinking about how to save your own ass."

"Not much point getting back into power if the world ends five minutes later," Eddie pointed out.

"If you tell us where Cross plans to release the angels, I'll do everything I can with the UN, Interpol, and the US and Antiguan governments to explain that you helped us try to stop him," Nina said. "If you don't, and Cross succeeds . . ." Her expression hardened. "I'll let you twist in the wind by your balls as you're brought up on charges of terrorism and mass murder. Good luck with your immunity deal, Mr. President."

Worry was clear in Dalton's eyes, but he still jutted his jaw in defiance. "I'm not going to be intimidated into making deals. I was the president of the United States, not some two-bit police informant!"

Eddie advanced upon him. "If I chucked him off the cliff, do you think anyone'd really care?"

Dalton took a worried step backward, but before he could respond, Jared looked around sharply. "Quiet," said the Israeli. "I can hear something."

Nina picked it up a moment later. "Sounds like a helicopter." In the distance, she heard the thrum of rotor blades.

Eddie gave Dalton a last threatening glare, then started toward the entrance. "Be careful," Nina called. "They might shoot first and ask questions later."

"I'll be ready to run, just in case!" He looked down the valley.

The burning Apache had left an unmissable marker of its position: a column of dirty black smoke. He leaned out of the ravaged chasm to scan the sky, quickly spotting the dark dot of an approaching helicopter. To his relief, it had the rounded profile of a transport aircraft rather than the narrow, angular shape of a gunship.

It took the chopper a few minutes to reach the crash site, circling overhead before descending into the valley. It was military, an Israeli Black Hawk in pale desert camouflage. It appeared unarmed, but all branches of Israel's military were ready for combat at a moment's notice, so Eddie decided to play things with care. He moved to the center of the opening, waving both arms above his head.

The Black Hawk slowed to a hover, one of its side doors sliding open. A man inside stared at him through binoculars. Eddie changed his signal, spreading both arms and holding them up in a Y-shape to indicate that he needed help—and also to make it plain that he was not holding a weapon. The helicopter's passenger looked back down at the wreckage, but it was obvious there was nobody alive in the flaming tangle of metal. Brief discussion with the pilot over his headset, then the man made an exaggerated thumbs-up gesture and the aircraft came about to head for the clifftop above.

The Englishman returned to the others. "They're landing," he announced. "Jared, you do the talking. It'll be better to have a Mossad agent tell 'em what's happened rather than the bloke who just shot down one of their Apaches with a handgun . . ."

* * *

Members of the Black Hawk's crew descended into the ravine on ropes to be given Jared's account of events; unsure how to take it, and especially confused by the presence of a former world leader, they settled for lifting the injured out on stretchers before taking them back to their base at Ovda. Even without knowing any Hebrew, Nina and Eddie could tell that the crew were deeply suspicious of their passengers and their involvement in the loss of their commander's aircraft, but it was also clear that the relatively junior military officers and men aboard did not want to tangle with the Mossad. One of Jared's first requests—or demands—was for a field telephone, which he used to contact his superior in Tel Aviv.

That same superior arrived at the base by helicopter as the sun set two hours later, meeting its new acting commander before both men strode into the hospital ward where the rescuees were being kept under guard. "Sir!" said Jared as they entered, jumping to his feet even with his injury and snapping to attention.

Eli Shalit was a small, thin man with prominent cheekbones and a bristling mustache. He waved a hand for the agent to sit back down, then cast his intense gaze over the room's other occupants. "Dr. Nina Wilde and Edward Chase," he said. "Welcome to Israel. And you too, Mr. President," he added, with a distinctly dismissive nod at Dalton.

"You know who we are?" Nina asked.

"Jared told me on the telephone, but I had also read his report on the events of four months ago, when he was seconded to the Criminal Sanctions Unit. Israel is very grateful to you both for helping to eliminate that nest of Nazis."

"Our pleasure," said Eddie, a little sarcastically.

Shalit gave him a cynical smile. "I know that you are not a great fan of the Mossad. But that does not lessen our gratitude. Now." He put his hands behind his back. "We have a situation, I believe."

"You could say that," Nina told him. "There's a religious maniac about to unleash chemical weapons because he thinks that bringing about the apocalypse will let him learn all of God's secrets. That's definitely situation-y."

"Indeed it is." The Mossad official's gaze went to Dalton. "Mr. President, your presence here is causing some . . . trouble, shall we say, in our government. You had important friends here—I mean, *have* friends, of course," he corrected, in a way that suggested the slip was by no means accidental—"who saw to it that you were able to enter our country incognito, who provided you with help, resources . . . Only now, I am told by one of my best men"—a nod at Jared—"it seems that you are connected to an act of terrorism in the Caribbean, and to the madman who intends to carry out more of these acts. What do you have to say, Mr. President?"

The color had visibly leached from Dalton's face; nevertheless, he drew himself up to stand tall and arrogant before the Israeli. "First, I would point out that I am in no way responsible for any of the acts carried out by an individual with whom I had the misfortune of being acquainted before I realized his true intentions—"

He paused at Nina's disbelieving cry of *"What?"* then continued: "Second, I would also point out that as soon as I realized these intentions, I disassociated myself with this individual and have done everything in my power to help track him down and prevent further loss of life."

Nina almost laughed at his sheer gall. "You are so full of shit! If it wasn't for you, none of this would ever have happened."

"We made an agreement, if you recall," Dalton pointed out. "I give you information about Cross's plans, and in return you make it unequivocally clear to all the relevant authorities that I helped you try to stop him. You were the one who offered that deal, Dr. Wilde. I agreed to it, so I expect you to honor it. And your husband too," he added, with a warning look at Eddie.

The Englishman glowered back at him, folding his arms. "Don't remember shaking on it."

"Eddie," said Nina reluctantly. "He's right, we need him. And we can't afford to waste time—Cross and the Fishers might be halfway to their targets already."

"Don't I even get to punch him in the face?" Eddie asked, clenching one hand into a fist. Dalton twitched.

"As much as I'd like that, no. Not this time."

"Next time, then," he muttered, then nodded to the politician. "Okay, we'll put in a word for you. Won't be the one I'm thinking of right now, though."

"You've got your deal," Nina told Dalton. "Now it's your turn. What's Cross's plan?"

Dalton took a couple of heavy breaths before answering, aware that whatever agreements were in place, he was still linking himself to the cult leader's plot. "All right," he said at last. "Simeon and Anna Fisher are going to take the statues to Mecca, and to the Vatican in Rome."

"As opposed to the Vatican in Hogfoot, Arkansas?" Nina said scathingly. "Yeah, I know where it is."

"Mecca. And Rome." Shalit turned from side to side as if looking toward each of the two cities. "I would not describe either as a close friend to Israel—though one is far less friendly than the other. I am sure you can guess which. But it is not in Israel's current interests to see it destroyed. We have enough enemies without arousing a billion and a half angry Muslims against us. And they *would* rise against us, even if we had nothing to do with it." Another edged smile at Eddie. "Those with no reason to hate us will still take any reason to fight us."

"They're going to release the gas there?" Nina asked.

"Obviously," Dalton snapped. "On the flight over, Cross kept saying how the timing was perfect. The hajj is on in Mecca right now, so there are Christ knows how many Muslims there on pilgrimage, and the pope has an audience in St. Peter's Square tomorrow, which will also have thousands, tens of thousands of people watching. That was what he wanted: maximum victims, maximum impact."

"It's also what *you* wanted," Eddie said, disgusted. "Typical fucking politician. You're already trying to distance yourself from it!"

"So that was how the two of you planned to set off a religious war?" asked Nina. "Attack Mecca and the Vatican, let it come out that American evangelical Christians were responsible, and watch the fireworks while you set up Fortress America?"

Eddie shook his head, speaking before the politician could issue another denial of his direct involvement. "That's what I get for missing Sunday school. I never read the bit of the Bible where Jesus says that mass murder is brilliant. Oh, wait, that's because it *doesn't fucking exist*!"

"You're not Christians any more than Jim Jones and his crazies were," Nina told Dalton.

"Don't lump me in with those loons," he replied. "I had nothing to do with Cross's followers. They joined him because they wanted him to bring about the end of the world."

"Which he did, for them."

"Yes, he did. And don't forget that you're a part of it too," Dalton went on, jabbing an accusatory finger at her. "You found the angels for him."

Nina gawped in sheer disbelief at his attempt to swing the blame back onto her. "Only because Eddie and I were kidnapped, *on your orders*! Jesus!"

Shalit held up a placatory hand. "Dr. Wilde, we have the information. The question now is: How shall we act upon it?"

"We've got to stop 'em, obviously," said Eddie.

"Yeah," agreed Nina, turning to Shalit. "You need to contact the authorities in Rome and Mecca, tell them to watch for Simeon and Anna."

The Israeli spymaster smiled mockingly. "I am sure

the Saudis will be happy to obey the Mossad." Even Dalton smirked.

"Okay, then contact the UN and get *them* to talk to the Saudis!" she pressed on, annoyed. "Call Oswald Seretse in New York."

"You've probably got his number," said Eddie, with a sly glance at Jared. "Someone once told me Mossad has *everyone's* number." The younger man grinned.

"I am sure we have," replied Shalit. "I shall make the call."

"What about the find?" Nina asked. "The temple of God, and the Ark of the Covenant—they need to be secured."

"They will be," he assured her. "I have already arranged for troops to guard the site until our archaeologists can reach it. And I shall also notify the IHA, of course. Such a discovery is of global importance, after all. Now, Dr. Wilde, Mr. Chase, if you will come with me?"

The couple followed him to the door. Dalton started after them, but Shalit held up a hand. "Mr. President, stay here, please."

Dalton was affronted. "This is a diplomatic matter; I should be involved—"

"I am *being* diplomatic when I say that you should stay here. For your own safety." There was an unmistakable hint of threat behind his politeness. "I have already spoken to officials from your State Department. They have requested that you be returned to the United States as soon as possible, on the orders of the White House."

"What?" said the politician, startled.

"I guess President Cole wants to discuss your immunity deal," Nina suggested, smiling coldly.

"Best of luck with that," added Eddie. "Jared, will you be okay?"

The young Israeli glanced dismissively at his injury. "It'll take more than this to keep me down, *alter kocker*. I'll be back."

The Englishman grinned. "Glad to hear it. See you later, kid. And you, Mr. President." The Israeli gave the couple a cheery wave as they departed with Shalit, leaving the sputtering Dalton behind.

* * *

Shalit commandeered what had been Colonel Brik's office to call Seretse in New York. Once through, Nina explained what they had found in the desert, and what had happened afterward. "I see," said the Gambian diplomat, speaking slowly and carefully, as if trying to process what he had just heard. "I shall of course immediately contact the Saudi and Italian ambassadors to the UN, and the Vatican's permanent observer. But the Fishers could be in Italy and Saudi Arabia already—a private flight there from Israel would not take long."

"I know, I know," Nina replied wearily. "Do the investigators in Antigua have any CCTV footage of Anna or Simeon they could send to the police and security forces?"

"Not yet, I am afraid," said Seretse. "Teams from the CDC and USAMRICD have entered the Mission to check the contamination levels, but their most recent report said the computers have been either wiped or encrypted."

"Might have known," Eddie complained. "Bloody spooks, they're all paranoid. We'll give you descriptions so you can put together e-fits, then."

"Digital facial reconstructions are not as useful as photographs," said Shalit with a small shake of the head. "The Mossad has run tests; even top agents failed forty percent of the time to recognize a suspect when trying to identify them from an e-fit alone. That number is much higher with ordinary law enforcement personnel."

"So what do you suggest?" Nina said with exasperation. "We've got to *try* to stop them!"

"There is something you can do," said Seretse. "If you go to the Vatican and Mecca in person, you will be able to confirm any possible sightings of the Fishers. I know it is a long shot, but we must try. Will you go?"

Eddie and Nina exchanged tired looks. "We don't

have much bloody choice, do we?" said the Yorkshireman.

"No, we don't," she agreed with a marked lack of enthusiasm. "Everyone does remember that I'm four months pregnant, right? I'm supposed to be eating crazy food and being waited on hand and foot, not rushing around the world and being shot at!" She took a long, deep breath. "Okay, rant over, I'm done."

"In that case, I will tell the ambassadors that you will assist with the search in person," said Seretse. "Nina, you should go to Rome; Eddie to Mecca. I am sure you understand why I did not suggest sending you to Saudi Arabia, Nina," he added.

"Countries that oppress women, flog bloggers, and behead people for sorcery aren't exactly high on my list of vacation destinations," she said scathingly. "I'll take Rome any day. But St. Peter's Square is huge! There'll be thousands of people there if the pope's giving an address. And I can't even begin to imagine how many people there'll be in Mecca during the hajj."

"Yeah, I know," said Eddie. "Just have to hope the cops are on the ball—and that we get lucky."

"I shall make the arrangements," Seretse told them. "It may take some time, but I will call you back as soon as everything is confirmed."

"Great," Nina muttered as he disconnected. She turned to her husband. "Oh God. How do we keep ending up in these situations? I tell you, after this is over, we're taking a three-year vacation."

He grinned. "You'd be bored out of your mind after a month."

"Probably. But we've got the baby to look forward to, so who knows? Motherhood might be the best thing ever to happen in my life. Apart from meeting you," she added.

"It will be, I'm sure of it," he said. "So you're feeling more confident about being a mum now, are you?"

It was her turn to grin. "I'm probably tempting fate by saying this, but after everything else I've been through since I met you, I should be able to handle a baby." They both looked around at a chuckle from Shalit. "Something to say?"

"Only that whether you are a soldier, a scientist, or a spy, nothing can prepare you," the Israeli replied, humor in his eyes.

"That's reassuring," Eddie said.

"I'm ready for it," Nina insisted. "Whatever it brings."

"Yeah?"

"Yeah."

"Good." He kissed her. " 'Cause so am I." A glance back at the phone. "Just a pain in the arse that we've got to save the world first."

"I know," she said with a sigh. "But we need to make sure our daughter's got a world to be born into, so . . . let's finish this."

32

Saudi Arabia

Even with his United Nations diplomatic status temporarily restored, Eddie still faced bureaucratic obstacles on his arrival at King Abdulaziz International Airport outside the city of Jeddah the following morning. The first came when a customs officer checked his passport and declared with a scowl that he had recently visited Israel; the fact that the jet chartered by the UN had *come* from Israel escaped the man's notice. Not even Eddie's diplomatic papers dissuaded the surly apparatchik from insisting he was not allowed to enter the country, and only the appearance of more senior figures silenced him.

However, this brought other problems. The newcomers, clad in traditional robes and ghutra headgear, were from the Mabahith, the Saudi domestic security agency: the country's secret police. This in itself made Eddie wary of them, as the Mabahith was infamous for human rights violations and its brutal treatment of anyone who spoke out against the repressive Saudi regime—and the first words from the younger of the two, a skinny, broadnosed man in his twenties, suggested they were not going to be helpful. "You have wasted your time coming here, Mr. Chase."

"Nice to meet you too," the Englishman replied sarcastically.

The second man, a craggy fifty-something, was more polite. "Welcome to Saudi Arabia, Mr. Chase. I am Abdul Rajhi of the General Investigation Directorate. This is my associate, Prince Saleh al Farhan."

"Prince?" said Eddie in surprise.

Rajhi did not respond, instead continuing: "We are grateful for your help in discovering a terrorist threat, but I am afraid that you will not be able to help us search for this man Fisher in person."

"Why not?"

His expression became patronizing. "Because you are not a Muslim, of course. Unbelievers are not permitted to enter the holy city of Mecca. We have the picture you provided; it is already being distributed to police, hotel staff, and officials at the Kaaba. We will find him without you."

"You still might not recognize him," Eddie objected. "There's a big difference between looking at a photofit and a real person. And he could be in disguise. I'm the only person who's actually seen the guy before—you need me there."

"We will easily be able to find a black American," said al Farhan haughtily. "We have records of everyone who has entered our country, and who is staying at every hotel."

"What, you think he'll be using his real name? He'll have a passport from Sudan or somewhere and be calling himself Muhammad."

"That may be so," al Farhan said, drawing himself to his full height, "but you will not be allowed into Mecca!"

Eddie was about to remind him of his diplomatic status, but one look at the brick wall of the Saudi's face told him it would be pointless; even with the threat of murder on a massive scale, rules and dogma still counted above all else. Instead he turned to the older man. "You've been in your job for a while, yes?" he asked.

Rajhi was surprised by the question. "Yes. Over twenty years."

"And you're pretty high up in the Mabahith?"

He nodded. "I am, yes."

"Then you must remember what happened two years ago. In Mecca. At the Kaaba." Rajhi frowned, not sure where he was heading. "With Pramesh Khoil?"

Now realization dawned, the official's eyes widening. "So how's the Black Stone these days?" Eddie pushed on.

"The Black Stone," Rajhi echoed, to his companion's puzzlement. "You are *that* Eddie Chase?"

"No, there's seventeen of us, we work different days. Of course it's bloody me!"

Al Farhan asked a question in Arabic, but his superior hurriedly shushed him. The older man thought for a moment, then said to Eddie: "May I speak with you in private?"

"Go ahead."

To al Farhan's consternation, Rajhi took Eddie aside for a whispered conversation. "The theft of the Black Stone is one of my country's most closely guarded secrets! If it was ever revealed to the masses that one of our holiest relics had been stolen—by infidels!—and replaced by a replica, there would be . . ." He didn't need to finish; his horrified shake of the head was enough to paint a picture of chaos.

"Yeah, but me and Nina got it back for you," Eddie reminded him. "Now, she's not likely to include that bit in her memoirs, and I won't be shouting about it on Twitter, but it'd be *really appreciated* if you'd let me help you."

Rajhi considered that, then waved al Farhan over. "Under exceptional circumstances, non-Muslims are allowed to enter Mecca," he announced. Now it was his companion's turn to be shocked. "I consider this threat to the hajj to be one of those times. Mr. Chase will help us find this terrorist." The younger man began a strenuous objection, but Rajhi made a firm gesture to silence him before turning back to the Yorkshireman. "As a representative of the United Nations, you will be expected to follow the highest standards of behavior."

"I'm always on my best," Eddie replied with a broad grin.

Rajhi did not seem convinced, clearly knowing Eddie's reputation, but had no choice but to accept his word. "Very well. I will have a helicopter take us to Mecca."

"Cool. I can play some bingo while I'm there." Both Saudis regarded him with vaguely offended bewilderment. "British humor," he told them. "Come on, let's find this guy."

* * *

The flight from Jeddah to Mecca took Eddie across the desert into the climbing sun. There was little between the two cities except sand and mountain ranges, but even from a distance of twenty miles he could pick out the gray sprawl of Islam's most holy settlement—and its most grandiose landmark.

"Is that the clock?" he asked, pointing at a dark, angular shape rising from the city's heart.

"The Abraj Al Bait tower," al Farhan told him via his headphones, with distinct pride. "The tallest building in Saudi Arabia—and one of the tallest in the world."

"Your mates in Dubai have still beaten you, though," said Eddie, taking a small amount of pleasure in the Saudi's annoyance at having his bubble pricked.

"The Kingdom Tower in Jeddah will soon be taller," al Farhan insisted. "But the clock tower is still bigger than anything in America. Or England."

"Size isn't everything."

Rajhi made a muted sound of amusement. "I can tell you do not know our country."

The helicopter passed over the rocky hills west of the city, heading for its center. The Grand Mosque, to which millions of Muslims made a pilgrimage each year, was clearly visible as a roughly circular complex of buildings surrounding the Kaaba, the cube-shaped structure that was home to the Black Stone. But it was overshadowed—at certain times of day, literally—by a mammoth piece of twenty-first-century engineering.

The Abraj Al Bait was a megastructure in every sense

of the word. Almost two thousand feet high, it dwarfed the likes of the Empire State Building and even One World Trade Center in New York not only in height but also by sheer bulk, its broad base sprouting several smaller—though still skyscraper-tall—towers. The complex was topped by the world's largest clock, four vast gold-slathered faces displaying the time to all points of the compass. Even from miles away, Eddie could read it clearly; London's Big Ben was a wristwatch in comparison. The whole structure was a combination of five-star hotels and vast shopping malls, a monument not so much to Allah as Mammon. Only the wealthiest pilgrims could afford to look down upon the Grand Mosque from their suites over a quarter mile above.

And it was the helicopter's destination. Rajhi concluded a brisk discussion over the radio, then addressed Eddie. "They think Fisher is at the Fairmont Hotel, in the clock tower," he said. "They have a copy of the passport he was using, and will have CCTV waiting so that you can identify him."

"If you think it's him, why don't you just arrest him?" Eddie asked.

The security official sucked in air through his teeth. "The Abraj Al Bait is owned by the government—by the royal family." He glanced surreptitiously at his partner. "The police do not want to cause a disturbance unless they are absolutely sure there is a threat."

"Nobody wants to kick up a stink, right?" Eddie shook his head. "If it's Fisher and he releases the gas, there really *will* be a stink." He gazed at the approaching colossus, then down to the Grand Mosque. The great courtyard was already filled with pilgrims, slowly circling the Kaaba. "If he's here, why hasn't he already done it? There are loads of people there—lots of targets. What's he waiting for?" He looked back at his companions. "What times are your prayers today?"

"The next *salat* is at nine minutes past noon," said al Farhan.

"I'd ask what time it is now, but, well . . ." He grinned and indicated the clock face, which told him it was ten past eleven, then became more serious. "That's what he's waiting for. These guys really, *really* don't like Islam, so killing a load of Muslims in the middle of praying on their pilgrimage to Mecca would be pretty big for them symbolically."

"That only gives us an hour to find him," said Rajhi. "But what if he has set the gas to be released on a timer?"

"When we catch him, we will make him tell us where it is," al Farhan said ominously.

"Simeon Fisher is ex–special forces," Eddie told him. "You won't break him—not in time. But he'll probably have the angel with him."

"How can you be sure?" asked Rajhi.

"He thinks he's one of the Witnesses from the Book of Revelation. They were killed before the seventh trumpet sounded—and since their boss wants that to happen, they're probably going to make it a suicide attack. They'll go out surrounded by their enemies . . . and take them with them."

The clock loomed ever larger as the helicopter swung toward a helipad atop one of the lower towers. Up close, the domineering structure was revealed as gaudy, even ugly, traditional Arabian design elements like arched windows simply enlarged and stretched to fit the enormous slab-like walls without any consideration of human scale. Eddie admitted—and had also been told on numerous occasions by his wife—that he lacked taste in matters aesthetic, but even he considered this as tacky and vulgar as the worst excesses of Las Vegas. He decided to keep his views on architecture from his hosts, however.

Dust blew from the pad as the chopper touched down— even almost fifty stories up, the desert still constantly reminded everyone of its presence—and several men ran to meet it, heads low. Al Farhan gripped Eddie's arm before he could leave his seat. "You are an unbeliever in our most holy city," he said, eyes narrowed. "Do not disrespect it, or us. Remember that."

"How about remembering that I'm trying to stop a

nutter killing thousands of people?" Eddie shot back, pulling free.

He stepped onto the helipad, feeling brief vertigo. The clock tower's summit was well over a thousand feet above him, more than the tallest building in London, but the sight of the surrounding horizon reminded him that he was already several hundred feet up. The disorientation passed, but all the same he fixed his eyes on the new arrivals: officers in the beige uniform and beret of the Saudi police, and two men in Western-style suits who engaged al Farhan in rapid conversation as the group headed for the building's entrance.

"This is Mr. Essa, the hotel manager," Rajhi told Eddie as they filed into an elevator. Essa was the older of the two suited men, a slim, elegant figure with a neatly trimmed gray beard. "And Mr. Nadhar, chief of security."

Eddie greeted them. "Have you found Simeon Fisher?"

"That was not the name he was using," said Essa. Although he was of Middle Eastern ancestry, he had a distinct French accent. "But he appears to be the man you are looking for. He checked in late last night. Mr. Nadhar has pictures." The elevator started its descent.

The other well-dressed man, somewhat bulkier than his boss, handed out sheets of paper to the visitors. Eddie took a close look. One was a color photocopy of a passport. The country of origin was Mozambique, the name Samora Costo, but even with the addition of a mustache and beard, Simeon's face was unmistakable.

Another picture was a still from a lobby security camera. The figure at the reception desk was small in the frame, but again Eddie recognized the Witness, the identification made easier by the bandage on his hand. "That's him," he said.

"Which room is he in?" asked al Farhan.

Nadhar checked a list. "Room 1416."

"Is he still there?"

"I checked the computer just before you arrived. He last used his keycard at around eight thirty this morning. But I do not know if he is still in his room."

Rajhi issued orders in Arabic, one of the cops relaying

them by radio. "We will use a SWAT team," he told Eddie.

"Risky," replied the Englishman. "You need to evacuate all the rooms around it—better yet, the whole floor. I've seen how fast this gas spreads; it's not like anything normal."

"We know what we are doing," sniffed al Farhan.

The elevator stopped at a lower floor. Essa briskly led the way through the hotel's corridors. Eddie took the opportunity to make a phone call to Nina. "Hey. Where are you?" he asked.

"Just coming in to land," she replied. "What's happening there?"

"I'm at Simeon's hotel, but we haven't found him yet. The Saudis are going to raid his room."

"Did you persuade them to evacuate the Grand Mosque?"

"I can't even get them to evacuate the hotel," he said with a sigh. "What about you?"

"Well, I managed to speak to the pope—"

"You know, I love that our conversations have 'I spoke to the pope' casually dropped into them."

She laughed, putting a smile on his face. "Yeah. I spoke to him by phone with Seretse, and tried to persuade him to call off today's audience. But he said no."

"Seriously?"

"He said that if it's canceled at such short notice, Anna will know we're on to her, and she might change her attack to an unpredictable time and place. In effect, he's acting as live bait to draw her out. I understand his reasoning, but I don't like it."

"Not even you get to tell the pope what to do, eh?"

"Sadly, no. And I've got so many good ideas!" Another laugh. "But the authorities in Rome and at the Vatican have agreed to cooperate fully to track her down."

"What time's his speech?"

"It's due to start at ten o'clock—that's noon, your time."

"Just before prayers here," Eddie noted grimly. "They're either doing a simultaneous attack, or close to." Ahead, he saw more uniformed cops waving away curious guests as a group in tactical gear hurried into the hotel. "Okay, I've got to go. Call me when you get to the Vatican."

"Will do. Love you."

"I love you," he replied. "See you soon." Hoping with all his heart that he would, he ended the call and followed the rest of his group into a conference room. The SWAT team members were already prepping their weapons. "What, you're just going to run up there and kick the door down?" he said. "No recon?"

"There is no time," al Farhan told him. "If this gas is as deadly as you say, then we have to stop him before he can use it. Essa?"

The hotel manager gave the cops a hurried briefing in Arabic, using a laptop and projector to show a plan of the hotel's fourteenth floor. Room 1416 was on the building's southern side, overlooking the city, not the Grand Mosque. "He won't be attacking from there, then," Eddie mused, as much to himself as to Rajhi beside him.

"Why not?" asked the Saudi.

"Not enough targets. There's only a big empty construction site behind the hotel—I saw it when we landed. If his room faced the mosque, he could just smash a window and let the gas blow out over the crowd."

"So where will he attack from?"

"Good question. Worst-case scenario is that he's already inside the mosque."

"There is security at all entrances. They have been given his picture."

"Yeah, but how many thousands of people go through every minute? Could you pick out one face from all that lot? You need to evacuate the place."

Rajhi shook his head. "I am afraid that is not possible," he said, his resignation showing that the decision had already been made by someone above him.

Eddie muttered an obscenity, then looked back at al Farhan as he finished giving instructions to the SWAT team. They rapidly donned one-piece coveralls, then put on full-face respirator masks and secured the hoods tightly around them. Al Farhan put on a headset as the masked force marched out of the room. "They know what to do," he told Rajhi.

"I hope so," said Eddie. "What's the plan?"

The younger official gave him a scornful look. "They are going to storm his room and capture or kill him, then secure the weapon. What else?"

"I dunno, maybe check if he's in there first? Fiber-optic camera, thermal scope, drone looking in through the window—hell, just knock on the door! And what about evacuating the other guests?"

"We do not have time to waste," al Farhan sniffed. "Now be silent. I need to listen." He turned away, press-ing his headphones to his ears for emphasis.

"I will tell you what is happening," Rajhi told Eddie as he found a headset of his own.

"Aren't you his boss?" Eddie asked. "He's putting lives at risk by rushing into this."

"I am his boss, yes," said Rajhi, with a heavy nod. "But he is a member of the House of Saud—the royal family."

Eddie raised an eyebrow. "So he really is a prince?"

"From one of the cadet branches, yes." He lowered his voice as al Farhan spoke to the SWAT commander. "There are thousands of princes. He is not in the line of succession, but he has the attention of those who are. It is . . . not in my best interest, shall we say, to get in his way. If he is successful today, it will be of great benefit to him politically."

"And if he fucks up, a lot of people'll die," Eddie coun-tered. Rajhi's only response was a tired shrug. "Great. Maybe I should've stayed at the airport after all."

Al Farhan listened intently to the reports over the radio, then issued an instruction. "They are on the four-teenth floor," Rajhi reported to Eddie. "Moving to the room . . . taking up positions."

The other official glanced at him, for a moment almost seeming to be seeking approval—then he turned sharply away, his expression becoming determined. *"Hejwem!"*

The loud bang that followed was audible to Eddie even from Rajhi's headphones, as was a hubbub of shouting voices. "They are in the room, searching, searching . . . ," said the older man, holding his breath, then exhaling in a mix of disappointment and relief. "He is not there."

"What about the statue?" Eddie demanded.

Al Farhan relayed the question. Seconds passed . . . then the answer came. "No. They cannot see it."

"That means he's got it with him—he's definitely going to attack. Look, you've *got* to evacuate the mosque."

The prince scowled at him. "You do not tell me what to do!"

"If he releases the gas in the middle of a crowd, it'll kill everyone. I've seen it!"

Al Farhan stormed over to him, his nose just inches from the Englishman's. "This is the hajj—the holy pilgrimage! Two million people make it each year, and there are tens of thousands of them down there right now. Some have waited their whole lives to be here, spent everything they have to make the journey. We cannot turn them away. There would be a riot!"

He spoke to Rajhi. "Get more men to the Grand Mosque. Guards at all entrances, and cameras and snipers on the roofs. We have Fisher's photograph—check all black men against it. We must find him!" A brief pause, remembering that he was technically addressing his superior. "That is my recommendation."

Rajhi nodded. "It is a good one. Carry it out."

The younger man departed, issuing more commands.

"You seriously think you'll be able to pick out one man in that crowd?" Eddie asked Rajhi, making his disapproval clear. "You've only got just over half an hour to find him."

"We will call in soldiers to help with the search," he replied. "You may not think so, but we do know what we are doing. We have dealt with threats to the hajj before. Now that we know what he looks like, we have very good spotters, facial recognition systems . . . If he is in the Grand Mosque, we will find him, I promise you."

"Let's hope." The Saudi seemed confident in his security forces, which improved the Englishman's mood slightly—and then prompted a thought. "The security at the mosque—is it visible? Are the guards out in the open?"

"At the entrances, yes. We want visitors to feel safe, and it also helps us control the crowds. There are other guards inside, though they are more discreet. And there are undercover men also, but we do not tell that to the public," he added with a sly smile.

"Simeon would know about them, though," said Eddie, "because Cross would know. He was in the CIA; intel's his business. So it's got high security?"

"As high as any place that is open to the public, yes." The security official recognized the growing concern on the other man's face. "What is it, Mr. Chase?"

"Something's wrong, but I'm not sure what . . ." He slowly paced across the room, trying to collate his thoughts. "Even if he thinks that me and Nina are dead, Cross would still know that after what happened in Antigua, people would be looking for him—and his Witnesses. So if the security at the Grand Mosque is as good as you reckon, Simeon would be taking a big risk by going in there. He might get caught before he can release the gas, and that'd wreck Cross's plan."

"So you think he might attack a different target?"

"What else is there, though? Where else could he . . ." Eddie stopped as an answer came. He tipped his head to look upward—not at the ceiling itself, but to take in the hulking structure beyond. "The clock tower's got an observation deck, hasn't it?"

"Yes . . ."

"Open-air?" Their eyes widened simultaneously. "Shit! He's not going to release the gas from the ground—he's going to drop it from the roof!"

"He may be up there already," Rajhi said in alarm.

They hurried for the exit, as did the two hotel representatives. There were still some uniformed police officers nearby; Rajhi summoned them, and the group ran through the corridors, eventually descending into the mall at the clock tower's base to reach the elevators serving the observation deck. There was a long line of tourists waiting; the arrival of the cops aroused consternation.

There was no sign of Simeon among the waiting visitors, though. "Give security down here his picture, just in case he hasn't turned up yet," Eddie told Essa and Nadhar. The hotel manager scurried away to the ticket booth.

An elevator disgorged returning tourists, who were startled to find several armed policemen waiting for them. A quick check that none was their target, then they boarded. Nadhar gave Eddie a dubious look as the elevator set off. "It is not safe for civilians to come with us."

"Trust me, I know what I'm doing," the Yorkshireman replied. "And I've seen the guy in person, not just photos."

"He has seen you too," Rajhi pointed out.

"Yeah, I know. And he's not a fan!"

The ascent in the high-speed elevator did not take long. "Where will he be?" asked Nadhar as the doors opened.

"He'll be on the side facing the mosque to make the attack," Eddie said, "but he might stay out of the way until it's time. Does the deck go all the way around the clock?" The answer was in the affirmative. "We'll need to spread out."

He made his way through a doorway into a covered gallery, to be met first by a rush of wind, then the glare of the desert sun.

But no desert. It was not until he passed through one of a line of arches and into the open air that the horizon came into view beyond the edge of the observation deck. All that stood between him and a very long drop was an ornate balustrade, a covering of netting supported by large metal hoops along the balcony's length preventing anyone from climbing over it.

The holes in the net were easily large enough to fit a hand through, however. And as Eddie squeezed between the tourists for a closer look, he saw that it was made from a nylon mesh. The lines were thick enough to resist being torn by hand, but would offer almost no resistance to a blade. It would only take Simeon seconds to cut a larger hole through which he could throw the statue.

If he was here. He turned away from the dizzying view of Mecca to the people staring down at it. The vast majority were of Arab descent, but with other ethnicities among them—Persian, African, Southeast Asian, Caucasian. He focused on the black faces. None were Simeon. "I don't see him here," he told Rajhi as he rejoined him.

"The men are moving around the balcony," the Saudi replied. "I have told one to watch the elevators, in case he tries to escape."

Eddie glanced up, seeing one of the colossal clock faces, 150 feet across, looming above the balcony. Its massive hands now read eleven thirty-six. There was still time to stop Simeon before the call to prayer. "We should go around too," he said. "I'll go that way." He pointed clockwise around the balcony. "You go the other, and we'll meet on the far side."

"Mr. Chase," said Rajhi as Eddie turned away.

"Yeah?"

A faint smile. "Please do not cause a diplomatic incident."

Eddie grinned. "Who, me?"

He set off through the crowd. Most people were jostling for the best view, though quite a few visitors had been struck by vertigo and retreated under cover through the archways. That meant the searchers would have to check more than just the balcony; Simeon could be lurking inside. Eddie looked back for Rajhi to make the suggestion, but the security official was already lost among the throng.

Hoping the idea had also occurred to his guide, he continued along the walkway. The clock tower was rectangular rather than square, its northern and southern sides considerably longer than the east and west. It took him a couple of minutes to reach the first corner, surreptitiously checking every dark-skinned face he passed.

Still no sign of the American. Was he even here? Maybe he was in the Grand Mosque after all . . .

He went through a covered section topped by a golden minaret at the observation deck's corner, then started

along the eastern balcony. The crowd here was thinner—
the view across Mecca's hotels and residential areas was
far less impressive than the mosque.

Ahead, he saw one of the cops. The man was only giving the visitors the most cursory checks, Eddie realized.
"Slow down, you daft sod," he muttered. Shalit, the
Mossad spymaster, had been right: For most people,
identifying someone in the flesh from only a photograph
was surprisingly hard—and that was assuming the subject hadn't changed their appearance. If Simeon had disguised himself, the cop might have walked right past
him . . .

The thought brought him to a sudden halt. What if
the cop *had* missed Simeon? He looked more closely at
every potential suspect nearby. Still no sign of him.
Maybe he was just being paranoid—

An internal warning bell sounded.

A black man dressed in a colorful striped robe and
matching hat was crouched near the outer wall. He appeared to be changing a camera's battery or memory
card . . . but it was not what he was doing, rather the
way he was doing it, that caught the former SAS soldier's attention. He had served in Afghanistan, and seen
firsthand the various ways that insurgents attempted to
camouflage their preparations for an ambush or placing
an IED by pretending to do something innocuous. But
however hard they tried, it was almost impossible for
them to conceal their tension, their rising adrenaline . . .

The robed man had betrayed that tension. Only for an
instant, a twitch of the head to check that the policeman
had gone by—but that was enough to tell Eddie he had
something to hide.

He couldn't tell if it was Simeon, though, the man facing away from him. It was possible he was a criminal
rather than a terrorist; a pickpocket relieving wealthy
tourists of their valuables. But he had to check, and do
so without alerting the suspect.

Eddie moved to the balustrade, positioning himself
beside an Arab family gawping at the scenery. He leaned
outward, head almost touching the taut netting as he

tried to peer past them. He still couldn't see the black man's face clearly, his features obscured by short dreadlocks protruding from beneath the hat. But he *could* see that his free hand was fiddling with something made of glossy white plastic inside a satchel. Whatever it was, it was no memory card.

The man gave the retreating cop another wary glance, then bent lower, putting down the camera to lift the white object out into the open—

Eddie's view was suddenly blocked by the face of a small boy as his father lifted him up to see the vista below. He frowned and tried to look past him, only to draw first surprised, then offended looks from both parents. "Sorry," he told them, retreating. The father eyed him with suspicion, then raised his child higher.

The Englishman sidestepped to peer behind them—and saw a bandage on the man's hand.

It *was* Simeon. He took the object out of the bag. Eddie felt a chill as he identified it.

A drone.

The satchel contained a compact quadcopter. And with it, he glimpsed a familiar stone shape. The angel.

Simeon's plan became clear. A drone that small would not have enough power to maintain flight with the statue hanging from it, but it would still be able to slow its fall. If he released it from the observation deck, the little aircraft could carry the angel far enough to reach the Grand Mosque.

And then detonate. There was a pale-yellow strip taped to the figure. Plastic explosive. Enough to shatter the angel and disperse its deadly contents across the crowded courtyard.

If that happened during the call to prayer, tens of thousands of worshippers would be killed—and far more outside the mosque and in the city beyond. Eddie fought a surge of fear. The cop was now too far away to call back without alerting Simeon, and he couldn't see any of the other officers nearby. But with the American about to make his attack, he couldn't risk letting him out of his sight to find backup. If he had been armed, he could have simply shot the cultist and ended the threat right there, but the Saudis had not allowed him to bring weapons into the country.

He would have to take him down with brute force.

Eddie moved out from behind the tourists. Simeon was twenty feet away, still concentrating on preparing the drone. The Yorkshireman closed on him. He needed to score a solid, brutal kick to the back of his head to knock him down, then put him in a choke hold and drag him away from the statue before he could set off the explosive—

Laughing, the father lifted his son higher, pretending to throw him. The little boy screamed in fear.

Simeon's head snapped around at the noise—and he saw Eddie.

33

The two men were still ten feet apart. Eddie started to charge—but Simeon snatched a gun from the satchel. The Englishman instantly changed direction, diving through an arch. A bullet cracked off the pillar behind him.

Tourists scattered in blind panic, people being knocked down and trampled. The policeman tried to fight through the crush, yelling for them to move as he drew his gun—

Simeon fired again. The bullet hit the cop's throat, blood splattering over the polished marble floor. He fell backward into the crowd, their screams growing louder.

Eddie glanced around the pillar. Simeon grabbed the satchel, leaving the little drone behind as he raced through an arch into the covered gallery. Another shot came from an entrance to the clock tower's interior.

The Englishman sprinted to the dead cop and grabbed his gun—a revolver rather than an automatic—then followed the American. Chaos met him inside, trapped visitors trying to flee and a second policeman down in a puddle of blood. "Where did he go?" he yelled.

"Down there!" shrilled a woman, pointing. "He went down there!" Eddie pushed through the crowd toward one side of the lobby.

A gunshot somewhere ahead. He ducked, but it had not been aimed at him. Two more retorts followed. He forced his way into an open space, seeing one of the tower's security staff dead on the floor. Where was Simeon?

"Chase!" Rajhi battled his way through the throng, gun drawn. One of the cops was with him. "Did you see him? Where did he go?"

"There!" Eddie replied. A door near the dead guard was ajar; from the way it was painted to match the walls, he guessed it was only meant for maintenance and emergency use. He hurried to it, the cop and Rajhi meeting him. The lock plate had a pair of bullet holes in it. "Cover me."

He readied his gun, then kicked the door wide. Nobody there. A metal staircase spiraled upward. The clank of hurried footsteps echoed down from above. Eddie aimed up the stairs, but all he could see of Simeon was his shadow against the railings.

"He's got the angel, and it's rigged with a bomb," he told Rajhi as Nadhar and another policeman arrived. "Come on!" He led the way after the American, the Saudis following. "He was going to use a drone to blow it up over the mosque. He can't do that now, so he's gone to Plan B."

"What is that?" Rajhi asked.

"I dunno—and maybe neither does he. Where do these stairs go?"

"To the machine floor for the clocks," Nadhar told him.

"Can he get outside from there?"

"Only through a hatch, and it can only be reached from a special lift."

"So either he's trapped—or he actually does have a Plan B." A door banged above. "He's off the stairs."

"The clock room," Nadhar confirmed, grim-faced.

Eddie reached the next landing, knowing Simeon would have had enough time to prepare an ambush. "Okay, Mr. Nadhar," he said. "You know what's in there—where's the nearest cover?"

Nadhar briefly closed his eyes to picture the room. "We will be in the northeastern corner," he said. "There is a display for VIP tourists to the left, and on the right there is some machinery."

"Which will give the most cover?"

"The machinery."

"That's probably where he'll be."

Rajhi issued orders to his men. "We are ready," he told the Englishman.

Eddie took hold of the door's handle. "Okay, on three. One, two, three—go!" He yanked the door open.

The first cop rushed through—and took three bullets to the chest. He crashed to the floor, lifeless limbs flailing. The second man was right behind him; he tried to retreat, but another two rounds caught him in the upper arm and shoulder. He fell back on the landing, a bullet splintering the doorframe behind him.

"Shit!" Eddie gasped, helping Rajhi pull the wounded man into cover. "Did you see him?"

Rajhi repeated the question in Arabic, getting a strained reply. "By the machine," he translated, glancing through the doorway. "It is about ten yards away."

Eddie looked for himself, spotting a large generator or transformer. "He's got a Glock 25," he said, remembering the glimpse of Simeon's gun as he took it from the satchel. "Nine mil, these wounds look like. And he's fired twelve shots, so he's got three left. If we can make him use 'em, that'll give us a chance to get into the room while he reloads."

"Unless he has reloaded already," warned Rajhi.

"Find out in a second," Eddie replied as he crouched beside the door. "Okay, I'll draw his fire; you run after the third shot."

"What if there is a fourth shot?"

"Then we're fucked!" He steeled himself, then leaned out, gun raised.

Simeon was lurking behind the machinery, watching the entrance. He saw the movement and instinctively fired—but he had been aiming higher, expecting someone to run through it. The bullet hit the doorframe just above the Yorkshireman's head. He adjusted his aim, but Eddie returned fire, his shot ricocheting off the transformer's side. Simeon flinched, his next attack going wide and blasting plaster from the wall.

One bullet left. Eddie sent a second round in his enemy's general direction, then sprang out into the open.

The tourist display Nadhar had mentioned was off to the left, closer than Simeon's cover. He raced for it, some sixth sense prompting him to dive as the American tracked him and fired again. The bullet seared over him, blowing out one of the display's flat-screens.

The third shot—and there was no fourth. The Glock's slide was locked back. The weapon was out of ammo . . . but Simeon was already ejecting the spent magazine.

"Now! Run, *run*!" Eddie yelled as he scrambled behind the display. Rajhi and Nadhar erupted from the doorway. The Saudi official followed Eddie, but the hotel's security chief headed straight for Simeon's position. "No, he's reloading—"

Too late. Simeon whipped his gun back up and fired. The bullet hit the running man squarely in the heart. Nadhar fell as the American drew back behind the humming machine.

Rajhi cursed. "What do we do now?"

"I don't know, but whatever we do, it's got to be fast." Eddie surveyed the machine room. It was a large, high-ceilinged space, dominated by the four giant clock mechanisms in the middle of each wall. Massive electric motors turned the hands outside, great brass gears slowly rotating to keep the time. Gray metal panels mostly covered the back of each clock, but around each hub was an opening to allow access to the mechanism. Beyond them were visible the complex webs of wiring feeding the millions of LEDs that illuminated the clock faces at night. More banks of machinery provided power, and additional cover was offered by a replica mechanism at the room's center, as well as further displays for visitors.

He looked back at Simeon's position. The American couldn't defend both sides of the large machine at once, but there was no cover along the most direct approach from either direction. "We'll have to get around him, use this stuff for protection," he said, indicating the chamber's contents. "If you get a shot, take it."

Rajhi nodded, then cocked his head at a sound. "What is he doing?"

Eddie strained to listen, hearing a faint tearing above the background noise. "Shit! The bomb taped to the statue—he's taking it off."

"Why?"

"So he can blow up something else. Maybe us . . ." His eyes went back to the exposed section of the northern clock face. "Or he might be trying to make a hole so he can chuck the statue out."

Rajhi looked dubious. "He will not reach the Grand Mosque from here."

"He doesn't need to—the gas'll still kill everyone outside the hotel." He moved around the rear of the display. "I'll get behind that model," he said, pointing at a scale replica of the clock tower in a glass case. "Cover me."

He brought up his gun—and ran.

Simeon broke off his task to swing out from behind the machine and fire. Eddie simultaneously unleashed a suppressing shot back at him. The Englishman felt a whipcrack of displaced air on the back of his neck as the round seared past, but his own bullet forced his attacker to retreat. He dropped down behind the model clock, then looked around its plinth—to see the American lean out from the other side of his hiding place.

Another exchange of fire, and broken glass showered Eddie as a round punched through the case. His own retaliatory shot hit the machine Simeon was using for shelter. This time it did not simply glance off; something sparked, its electrical hum turning into a menacing growl. A warning buzzer rasped on a control panel.

Simeon looked up at it in alarm before pulling back into cover. Eddie moved to the other side of the plinth. If he could force him into the open . . .

A yellow cover on the machine's side bore a warning symbol. He locked on to it and fired again. The plastic shield flew off, some component beneath shattering. There was a sharp crack of electricity and more sparks spewed out, followed by a spurt of smoke as the growl grew louder—

Simeon broke from hiding as flames spat from the transformer, running for the north clock with the statue held in his outstretched left hand. Eddie hesitated, not wanting to risk breaking the angel.

Rajhi opened fire, sending several shots after the running man. Simeon dived to the floor, his hat and the fake dreadlocks flying off. Eddie tracked him, but now his target was shielded behind a display of gleaming giant cogs.

The Saudi moved into the open and took aim—

Simeon was faster, unleashing a trio of shots. Only one hit, but that was enough. Rajhi fell with a cry of pain, blood staining his robes.

Eddie instinctively glanced to check if he was alive or dead. The former, for now, but in the split second his eyes were off Simeon, the American had burst back into motion. He recovered his aim and zeroed in—

The former marine had the same combat sixth sense as the Englishman, ducking and jinking just as Eddie fired. The bullet hit him, but only a graze, ripping the shoulder of his colorful robe. He gasped but kept running, disappearing behind the clock's hulking mechanism.

And now Eddie was out of ammunition, the revolver's six rounds gone. He looked back at Rajhi, but the security official's automatic was nowhere in sight. Searching for it would make him an easy target. "Maybe I can throw this at him," he muttered, glaring at his useless weapon.

There was another tourist display near the north clock's motor, more screens flashing up images of the tower. From there, he might be able to round the mechanism and tackle his opponent.

Might. Even at a sprint, it would still take him a few seconds to cover the distance, more than enough time for Simeon to put a bullet in him.

But he had to try. Sounds of activity reached him; he couldn't see what Simeon was doing, but knew it couldn't be anything good. Keeping the gun raised, he readied himself . . . and ran.

The crunch of glass underfoot gave him away the instant he moved. Simeon whipped into view. With a yell, Eddie pointed the revolver at him. The sight of the gun caused the American to flinch—but then he realized the bluff and opened fire.

The distraction had given Eddie the tiny advantage he needed, though. The shots passed behind him. Before Simeon could refine his aim, he flung himself headlong behind the display stand.

But he was not safe even there. More bullets tore across the room, revealing the display's backing as nothing more than painted plywood. Splinters stabbed at Eddie as he scrambled along on his hands and knees. One of the screens above him exploded as a round ripped through it, falling glass hitting his head.

The gunfire stopped. Eddie peered around the display. Simeon had moved back behind the mechanism. A shadow on the panels backing the clock revealed that he was placing the explosive beside the hub. Once he used the bomb to blow open the clock face, he would be able to hurl the angel into the crowds below . . .

The bomb. Simeon would have to move away from it or be caught in the blast. If Eddie could get close enough, he might be able to catch the American before he could throw the statue.

He stood—then sprinted for the clock.

Simeon lunged back into view, his gun coming up—

Eddie threw himself into a dive. Two shots tore past him as he hit the floor and rolled behind the clock's drive. Simeon ran toward him.

He jumped up—and hurled the empty gun at the cultist's head.

Simeon jerked back, snapping up both arms to deflect the spinning hunk of metal away from his face. A grunt of pain, then he recovered, advancing once more as Eddie ducked behind the giant motor.

A *bleep* from the hub. The gunman looked back in alarm, then dropped—

The bomb detonated.

The explosion was more powerful than either man expected. Metal panels blew from their supports as a ragged hole ripped open in the clock's face. Shrapnel flew across the machine room. A supporting beam tore loose, scything away more panels and crashing down on top of the hub. A fierce wind shrieked in through the rent.

Simeon, caught in the open, had been knocked over by the blast. Eddie saw his chance and rushed at him.

The gun came up again—

Eddie kicked it from his hand. The pistol glanced off the motor and disappeared through the opening into the emptiness beyond. Simeon cried out. His opponent drove another kick at his head.

The blow made contact, blood spurting from Simeon's burst lip, but the American still managed to grab Eddie's leg—and now he was off balance as Simeon tried to drag him down.

He staggered—and his hand slapped one of the giant cogs. He jerked it away just before it was crushed in the gears, but he was now past the point of no return and fell heavily to the floor.

Simeon clawed at him. Eddie lashed out with his other foot. A sharp *smack*—and the African American lurched back as the Yorkshireman's boot heel struck his eye socket.

Eddie dragged himself upright and pressed his attack, kicking the dazed man hard in the stomach before grabbing him and throwing him against the exposed gears.

Simeon's robe caught in the cogs. He tried to fight back, but was abruptly restrained as the material pulled tight around his neck, the mechanism slowly but remorselessly drawing his clothing between its teeth. Eddie hit him again, then looked around. Where was the angel?

Outside, he could see the clock's long hand, pointing toward the eight. It had been damaged by the explosion and flying debris, a long, jagged split along its length surrounded by shards of carbon fiber. Closer to him, the motor was making a deep, ominous buzzing noise. The broken girder had wedged against the shaft bearing the clock's massive hands, jamming the mechanism. It was at risk of overheating and catching fire, or even exploding as the electrical system overloaded.

But there was a greater threat. The statue lay under the hub, just inches from the gaping hole in the clock face.

And it was *moving*, creeping toward the precipice.

For a moment Eddie thought the wind was blowing it, until a vibration through his feet told him the true cause. The fallen beam had jammed the clock—but the motor was still trying to turn the gears. The entire mechanism was shuddering, transmitting the movement through the floor.

Ripping cloth. He looked back to see Simeon tear free from his robes. The American's eye was almost shut where Eddie had kicked it, but his other was open and blazing with rage.

Simeon was still a danger—but if the angel fell, the gas would kill thousands. He had to save it—

Eddie rushed to the hub. The shaft was not far above the floor, forcing him to crouch to reach the statue. The vibration became more pronounced as the overload built up. He ignored it, groping for the sculpture and pulling it from its hiding place.

Running footsteps behind him—

He jumped up, turning to face his opponent—as Simeon delivered a flying kick squarely to his chest.

Eddie spun backward . . . and toppled through the hole.

34

Mecca rolled far below the Englishman, the wind screaming in his ears as he fell—

He hit the clock's long hand and grabbed at it in terrified desperation. He jolted to a halt, the fifty-six-foot pointer digging hard against his armpits as he dangled from its upper edge.

But he was far from safe. The clock's hands were as elaborately decorated as the rest of the enormous timepiece, but the curlicued gold details were simply applied to the surface, offering no grip. And he could feel the whole thing shaking from both the impact of his landing and the vibrations of the overloading motor. He kicked backward, trying to brace himself against the clock, but managed only to break off LEDs set into the sheer face.

Still clutching the angel, Eddie strained to raise himself higher. If he could secure the statue inside his jacket, he might be able to climb back to the hole—

The clock hand jolted, almost shaking him loose. He squeezed both arms against it to pin himself in place. But he still began to slide sideways . . . and downward.

The minute hand was moving—and at a much faster rate than sixty seconds per minute. Loud cracks came from the gear mechanism at the hub's end as teeth were stripped from an overstressed cog—

An explosive bang of shearing metal, and the long hand swung freely from its axle, six tons of steel and composites sweeping down toward the vertical. Eddie slithered along its edge—until it dropped out from under him.

He plunged, both raised arms scrabbling helplessly for a hold—

His feet hit a jagged slab of carbon fiber. It snapped under his weight, but slowed him for the fraction of a second he needed to thrust his left arm into the crack down the clock hand's damaged rear.

Broken shards tore through his jacket and slashed his skin, making him scream, yet he still managed to grab a thick skein of wiring. Some of the LEDs embedded in the front of the huge pointer tore out, but more held. He jerked to a stop as the minute hand swung pendulously back and forth over the six o'clock position.

Eddie gasped for breath. Directly below him was the observation deck. He saw the curved supports of the protective netting, and considered letting go and dropping onto it, before realizing that would be suicide. The net was pulled drum-tight; falling on it from this height would be like landing on a trampoline, catapulting him over the edge.

But the hand's tip was less than fifteen feet above the netting. If he climbed down farther, he might make it . . .

A fierce jolt canceled all thought beyond holding on. He looked up. The entire axle assembly was visibly shaking, more fragments of the ruptured clock face falling past him. The wind drew a streamer of smoke out through the hole; it became darker and thicker as he watched, swirling away into the sky. The overloading motor was catching fire.

Simeon appeared at the opening. He looked down, expression changing to an almost offended anger as he saw Eddie still alive below. He ducked back inside with a barely suppressed obscenity, returning holding a broken metal spar—which he threw at the Englishman.

Eddie whipped his right arm above his head just fast enough to take the painful blow. If it had struck his skull, it would have knocked him senseless. The steel bar fell away, bouncing off the netting to be flung into the void.

Another violent shudder. He managed to jam the statue inside his jacket before taking hold of a carbon-fiber spearhead with his right hand, forcing himself to ignore the pain as it cut his palm.

Above him, the hour hand was now rocking violently against the axle like a ruler twanged on the edge of a desk. More panels in the clock face buckled outward. The smoke grew denser, and even over the wind he could hear a fearsome electrical growl. It wasn't just the clock's motor: the overload was feeding back into the transformers powering it, and he knew from experience that could have explosive results.

The same thought occurred to Simeon. A concerned glance back into the room, then he leaned out and gripped both edges of the minute hand. "You might as well let go!" he called down to Eddie as he held himself in place, then pressed the insteps of his boots hard against the pointer's sides. "Because it'll hurt a lot more if I have to come down there!"

"And I thought suicide was a sin!" Eddie shot back.

"Don't worry—you were always going to hell!" The American started a controlled descent toward him.

Eddie looked back at the netting. It now offered his only chance of survival, but he had to get to the bottom of the clock's hand before Simeon caught up. He shifted position, easing his grip on the wires—only to clamp his fingers tight again as the pointed carbon shard in his right hand creaked menacingly under his weight. Blood oozed as the sharp edges sliced his skin.

Simeon came closer, muscles visibly straining with the effort of holding on, but he showed no signs of slipping. He was now only six feet above the Englishman. Above him, the escaping smoke turned black. "Hey, how you hanging?" he said with a malevolent grin.

Eddie searched for a better handhold, but the only possibilities were either too fragile to support him, or even more razor-edged. And now Simeon was upon him—

One foot swiped down, grazing the back of his left hand. It was only an exploratory attack, the American unsure if he could maintain his hold—but the second strike, with his other foot, was more confident. The carbon shard Eddie was holding snapped off at the base as Simeon's heel stamped down on his knuckles. The Yorkshireman swung and fell a few inches as more wires in his left hand ripped away before the remaining ones again just barely caught his weight.

Simeon lowered himself farther, about to smash his foot down on the other man's head—

Eddie stabbed the composite spearhead deep into his calf.

Simeon screamed, almost losing his grip. Eddie twisted his makeshift dagger deeper into his flesh, then tugged at his ankle as hard as he could. The American's hands slipped down the pointer's edges. "Time's up!" Eddie yelled—

The cultist finally lost his hold and fell—only to slam to a stop after barely a foot. Another protruding carbon spike had caught him, impaling him up through his abdomen and behind his rib cage. He shrieked, blood and stomach fluids gushing from the wound.

A loud detonation from above. The whole clock shuddered as if kicked by a giant. Eddie looked past the flailing American to see flames belch out of the hole, dirty smoke spewing from the widening gaps between the panels. The machinery was on the verge of destroying itself, the hub about to rip away and take the long fall to the ground.

Still gripping Simeon's leg, Eddie released his hold on the wires and hurriedly clamped his hand around the pointer's edge. He followed the American's example, pressing his insteps against its sides, then let go of the other man—and dropped.

He managed to grab the edge with his right hand as he fell, but his palm was slick with blood. He squeezed harder, but wasn't slowing fast enough, the great pointer narrowing to just two feet wide at its tip . . . and then nothing.

Eddie plummeted toward the balcony—

The netting caught him—but it was drawn so tightly that it felt almost solid, pounding the breath from his lungs. He clawed at the nylon lines as the rebound threw him toward the edge, finding grip with one hand. Fingers clenched so tightly he could have crushed coal into diamond, he flipped over, landing hard on his back. Muscles and tendons strained to their limit, arm joints almost wrenching from their sockets . . .

But they held.

He bounced once, twice, then came to rest on top of the mesh. Gasping, he looked up. Simeon was still pinned gruesomely to the minute hand, his screams echoing down the building.

Another blast from the machine room—and the center of the clock face disintegrated as the hub was ripped out of the motor, dragging girders and lighting panels with it. Both hands toppled forward—then the tip of the minute hand hit the elaborate golden relief around the clock's circumference and flung the entire assembly outward, away from the tower's face.

Simeon was still screaming as he fell past Eddie. "I should've said, *Time's down!*" the Englishman yelled after him. Seconds passed—then a colossal crunching boom reached him as the clock hands smashed apart a quarter mile below, their unwilling passenger reduced to a bloody pulp amid the storm of carbon shards.

Eddie caught his breath, then groped inside his jacket. The statue was still there. "Thank God," he said, before looking at the Grand Mosque below. "Or thank Allah. Or Yahweh, or whatever he's called." He rolled over to get a hold on the netting with both hands—

Twang!

The tightly stretched net jerked beneath him—and he suddenly found himself slipping toward the balcony's edge. Falling debris had ripped the mesh, and now the rest of it was tearing free from the support posts, one strand after another breaking with an insistent *ping-ping-ping* of snapping nylon.

"Oh, come *on*!" he cried, pulling himself up hand over hand, but the netting was rolling toward the void faster than he could climb. The observation deck slithered past behind his outstretched arms, followed by the balustrade—

Hands locked around his wrists.

Eddie raised his head to see al Farhan braced against the low wall, teeth bared with the strain of holding him. He shouted in Arabic; several policemen ran over and raised the Yorkshireman onto the balcony.

"Thanks," he wheezed, looking around. The observation platform was strewn with debris, but he was relieved that the tourists had all been evacuated. He hoped the same was true at ground level.

"What happened?" al Farhan demanded. "Where is Rajhi—and did you get the statue?"

"I got it," Eddie replied wearily, producing it from his jacket. "Rajhi's in the clock's machine room; he's hurt. So are some other people. You need to get paramedics up there."

The Saudi prince issued orders, then regarded the figure in Eddie's hands. "So that is the angel? Is it safe?"

"I think so," he said, checking it for signs of damage and finding none. "That's one taken care of. I hope we can do the same for number two . . ."

35

Vatican City

"You've got the angel?" Nina said into her phone. "Thank God! What about Simeon? Did you catch him?"

"No, the ground did," her husband answered. "What about you? Don't suppose you convinced the pope to postpone his talk?"

"Ah . . . nope." She regarded the covered stage standing before the great façade of St. Peter's Basilica. A figure in white robes stood within, his words resounding from loudspeakers around the vast expanse of St. Peter's Square while his image was relayed to numerous giant screens for the benefit of the hundreds of thousands attending the papal audience. "He just started."

"Oh. Great. And I'm guessing you haven't found Anna yet?"

"No, we're still searching. Her picture's been put out to all the police and security personnel, but there are a *lot* of people here." She turned in the other direction to survey the square. In front of the stage was a large cordoned area with thousands of seats reserved for those who had either obtained tickets or been specially invited—most near the front were priests and nuns. Beyond it, the rest of the square was standing room only, a mass of faces watching the address. "But she might not even be this close. She could release the gas outside the square and still kill thousands of people."

"Yeah, I know," Eddie said gloomily. "She could be half a mile away. Simeon was going to use a drone."

"That might not work here. The cops have sharpshooters on the rooftops, and Massimo—he's in charge of security," she explained, glancing at the rangy Italian as he spoke with one of his officers—"told me they've been prepared for potential drone attacks for a few years now. So she's probably hiding in the crowd. But," she added with a sigh, "it's a big-ass crowd."

Massimo Rosetti gestured for her to join him, his expression suddenly excited—and tense. "Hold on," she told Eddie, going to the Italian. "What is it?"

"A guard saw her," he replied, pointing toward one of the checkpoints at the perimeter of the seating.

"What, she's in *here*?" Nina exclaimed.

"Yes, but that means she cannot get out."

"She doesn't *want* to get out. I told you, this'll be a suicide attack—she thinks she's one of the Witnesses from Revelation, who both have to die before the prophecy can come true. And the other one just did!"

Rosetti gave orders over a walkie-talkie. "I have told my men to look for her in the seats," he said, starting for the checkpoint. Nina followed, limping from her leg wound. "Quietly, so they do not alarm her—or anyone else. If a panic starts, many could be killed."

"Many could be killed anyway," she pointed out before returning her attention to the phone. "Okay, Eddie, I'll call you back. Love you."

"I love you too," he replied. "And the baby!"

She smiled, then pocketed the phone. "Do we know what she's wearing?"

The Italian shook his head. "That will not help us."

"But if he recognized her—"

"That is why we are going to talk to him."

They made their way down an aisle between the banks of seats. Nina became acutely aware that Anna knew her by sight. But if she had been spotted, there was no sign, the crowd watching the pope with rapt attention.

They reached the checkpoint, a booth with an airport-style scanner to check the personal items of those entering. Two uniformed guards manned it. Rosetti spoke to one, frowning before turning to Nina. "He remembers the statue on the X-ray, but not the woman carrying it," he said, annoyed.

"Why not?" she asked.

The young guard shrugged helplessly. "She was a nun."

"What did she look like?"

"A nun!"

Nina looked back, seeing more habits than she could count. "Well that's really useful!"

"We must find her," said Rosetti. "Dr. Wilde, you will recognize her if you see her?"

"Yeah, and she'll recognize me! If she realizes we're looking for her, she might release the gas."

"But you say she will release it anyway, so we must try." Transmitting more instructions, he led her back up the aisle.

Nina looked along each row as she passed, but the sheer number of people was visually overwhelming even when she tried to focus solely on the nuns. "Great, it's like finding one particular penguin in an entire colony."

Rosetti stopped to speak to a small group of his subordinates, who rapidly dispersed, giving orders through their own radios. "Every man I have here is now looking for her," he told Nina. "But if you could also help . . ."

"I'll do what I can." She scanned the crowd, wondering where to start.

From the front, she decided. Cross's cult considered the Catholic Church a heretical organization, which would make its leader practically the Antichrist in their eyes. While it made no difference in terms of the prophecy from Revelation whether he died or not, the pope would almost certainly be Anna's primary target: His murder would be a massive blow to the faith. Nina had seen how quickly the gas spread, but if Anna was too distant, the pontiff's staff could still get him to safety.

So where was she? The first five rows, ten? The stage was at the top of the broad steps outside the basilica, at least seventy feet from the front row of seats. Movement above caught her eye: fluttering flags atop the building . . .

The wind. It was blowing roughly southeast, away from the pope's position. If Anna was too far back, the breeze would slow the gas cloud, or even stop it from reaching him.

She tried to picture the square from above. When Miriam had broken the angel at the Mission, the initial release of gas had been extremely forceful, mushrooming outward for about a hundred feet before the wind finally caught it. The breeze was more gentle here, so assume a radius of 150 feet to be sure of reaching the stage . . .

The first twelve rows, she estimated, and in the sections of seating to either side of the broad central aisle. *If* her assumptions were correct. She could be wrong—about how the gas would expand, about Anna's plan.

But it was all she had. "I'm going to check these two blocks of seats," she told Rosetti, pointing them out.

"You think she is there?"

"Maybe. But it's just a guess."

"I will come with you," he said, following her.

"You do that," she said distractedly, her gaze already sweeping the ranks of visitors. The seating was divided into eight rectangular blocks across the width of the square, around twenty chairs to each of their twelve rows. That meant almost five hundred people in the two-block section to which she had narrowed her search. Even limiting it to nuns alone left over a hundred suspects. And would she pick out Anna? With her hair covered, a pair of glasses could be enough of a disguise . . .

She and Rosetti reached the front of the crowd and moved across it. Nina surveyed the guests, slowing to check each face beneath a headscarf or habit. Annoyed glares came back at her; some not welcoming the attention, others simply irritated that she was obstructing their view.

She crossed the first block to the central aisle. "Have you seen her?" Rosetti asked quietly.

"No, but I couldn't get a good look at all of them." Some nuns had been obscured behind taller audience members, or had their faces turned away.

They crossed the aisle, Nina glancing sideways to see the pope still delivering his sermon. A message crackled through the policeman's radio. "More men are coming from the rest of the square to help us," he said.

"Tell them to hurry up." Nina's nervousness was rising; the attack could happen at any time. She looked over the next sea of faces. It seemed that half of them were nuns. Young, old, fat, thin, white, black, and all points in between, but the one she wanted to find was nowhere to be seen . . .

Her eyes met a nun's, just for a moment—and the woman hurriedly turned away.

Nina flinched with a shock of adrenaline . . . and fear. "Have you seen her?" Rosetti asked urgently.

"I don't know." She looked back at the nun, but saw only the top of her head: she had leaned forward as if picking something up from the ground. "It could be her, about eight rows back."

The Italian stared into the crowd. "Which one? I can see ten nuns around there."

"The one who's trying to keep her face hidden!" Nina increased her pace, eyes locked on the hunched figure as she reached the aisle and turned down it. The woman in question was just under halfway along the row—and as Nina drew level, she saw that the nun was pulling something from a small bag.

The angel.

"Shit, it's her!" she cried. A few visitors reacted with offended shock at the obscenity, but she didn't have time to worry about wounded feelings. "She's got the statue! There, there!"

Rosetti pushed down the row, drawing his sidearm as he shouted a warning in Italian—

The statue was not the only thing Anna had taken from the bag.

Her arm whipped up—and Rosetti staggered, a slim black throwing knife jutting from his throat. He fell heavily onto an elderly man beside Anna. The other people nearby were momentarily stunned . . . then the screams started.

Nina was already forcing her way along the row. "Down, stay down!" she shouted, pushing a panicked nun back into her seat before she could block her path.

Anna had the statue in one hand, the other tugging the carbon-fiber blade from Rosetti's neck. "Back, bitch!" she yelled, stabbing it at the redhead.

Nina jerked away from the bloodied tip, then overcame her fear and lunged for Anna's arm. The blade caught her palm, making her gasp, but she managed to grab the cultist's wrist. "That's *Doctor* Bitch to you!" she yelled, twisting the knife away—

Her heart froze as she saw Anna's other arm draw back . . . and hurl the statue.

It flew over the front rows of the crowd. Time seemed to slow, the angel falling toward the base of the steps . . .

It hit the ground—and shattered. Nina stared at it, paralyzed with terror—

The broken pieces came to rest. She drew in a startled breath. There was no gas, no eruption of yellow poison. Anna was equally stunned, mouth open in disbelief. "But . . . it can't . . ."

"It can," Nina replied, realizing what had happened. It was not the real angel. Cross had given Anna the fake Eddie had used to locate the Mission—and it was clear that the biochemist knew nothing about the deception. "He lied to you. Your Prophet lied to you!"

"No!" Anna jerked her arm free and slashed the blade at Nina's face. The redhead jumped backward to avoid it, only to stumble against a chair. A burst of pain from her injured leg, and she fell.

Anna shoved past Rosetti and stood over Nina as others in the crowd fled. But she didn't stab her, instead holding the knife to her throat. "Back off!" she cried as a uniformed cop pointed a gun. "Back off or I'll kill her!"

The cop retreated, but kept his weapon raised. Shouts in Italian reached Nina as more officers closed in. "You've failed," she said breathlessly. "You *and* your husband. Neither angel has been released. We recovered the one in Mecca."

Anna stared at her, anger and panic in her eyes. "What happened to Sim—the other Witness?"

Nina hesitated, feeling the blade against her skin. But she knew she had to tell her. "He's dead."

The other woman did not react for a moment, as if she hadn't heard, then anguish joined the other emotions. "Dead?" she repeated, voice cracking. "He can't . . . No, he—" She broke off, her anger resurgent. "Killed by the minions of the Beast . . . so now the prophecy can be fulfilled!"

She pulled back the knife, about to stab it into Nina's neck—only to hesitate after a glance at the redhead's abdomen. Then she leapt onto the now empty seats, letting out a demented scream as she charged at the nearest cop.

He fired. The bullet hit her chest. More screams came from the crowd as she crashed to the ground.

The cop ran to her, kicking away the knife. Other armed men hurried to join him. "Wait, get back from her, get back!" Nina called, staggering to her feet. A brief glance told her that the pope was being rushed into the safety of the basilica. "Anna," she said, crouching beside the dying woman, "Cross lied to you—he *used* you. He always had three targets, because he thought he'd have three angels, but he had to change his plan when he destroyed one angel at the Mission, didn't he? He gave you a fake and kept one for himself, so he could attack the biggest target personally. He sent you to die as a decoy! Where is he? Where's the real angel?"

Anna turned her head weakly, coughing blood. Red speckled the white cloth of her habit. Despite her pain, she was almost smiling. "No, doesn't matter, he's . . .

succeeded. When the Witnesses . . . die, the second woe is past, and then the seventh angel sounds!"

"No it doesn't!" Nina protested. "The seventh angel doesn't sound until after the Witnesses are resurrected and taken to heaven in a cloud—and that's not going to happen because *this is the real world*! Cross himself thinks John was hallucinating when he wrote Revelation: There *is* no prophecy, it's all nonsense. You and Simeon have died for nothing!"

"If it's . . . nonsense, then how did you find . . . the angels?" The smile twisted into mocking disdain.

A policeman clambered over the seats to check on Rosetti, surprise and concern in his voice telling Nina he was still alive. But she had no time to be relieved—or to argue theology. "Where's the last angel?" she demanded, leaning closer. "What's Cross going to do with it?"

"Loose it," Anna gasped. "Of course . . . the Prophet will release the angel . . ." An expression almost of joy crossed her face. "And bring down . . . Babylon. The kings of the world . . . will witness . . ."

"What do you mean?" said Nina. "Tell me!"

But the other woman's eyes grew unfocused. One last sigh of escaping breath, then she fell still and silent. "God*damm*it," Nina whispered.

The cops closed in around her. "*É morta?*" asked one.

"Yeah, she's dead," Nina replied. "And so are our chances of finding the real angel."

36

"So Cross gave Anna the copy and took off with the real angel?" said the disbelieving Dalton over the conference call. "Where's he taken it?"

"That's kinda what I was hoping you could tell us," Nina said, exasperated. While paramedics tended to Rosetti, she had been taken to an office inside the Vatican to give the bad news to Seretse in New York and Eddie in Mecca, calling upon Dalton—now in transit to America in the company of a trio of US marshals—in the hope of learning the cult leader's true plans.

"I have no idea," the disgraced politician replied.

Her frustration grew. "Are you saying that because you don't want to incriminate yourself in front of law enforcement officials, or do you genuinely not know?"

"I genuinely don't know!" Dalton snapped. "Until that son of a bitch dumped me in the desert, I'd planned to go back to Tel Aviv and meet some Israeli friends. I don't know where he meant to go!"

"Wait, you have friends?" Eddie said sarcastically.

"Not helping," said his wife.

"I've still got plenty of friends in Washington, too," Dalton growled. "I can assure you that I'll be back in—"

"Just one moment, Mr. President," interrupted Seretse,

breaking off to speak to someone. When he returned, despondency was clear even in the diplomat's normally controlled voice. "I have had a message from the State Department."

"Doesn't sound like the one you were hoping for," noted Eddie.

"I am afraid not. They were able to reach out to the intelligence services and provide the flight plan of the jet Cross had been using, but after leaving Ovda air base yesterday, it flew to Jordan—and is still there. Anna and Simeon traveled on to their targets by commercial flights under false passports. It would appear that Cross also left the country under an assumed identity, but so far we have not been able to track him."

Nina put her head in her hands. "So he could be literally anywhere in the world by now? Great."

"How are we going to find him?" asked Seretse. "What is his target?"

"Babylon," she told him. "That's what Anna said: Babylon will fall. All part of Revelation, but somehow I doubt that Cross plans to attack the ruins of an ancient city in Iraq."

"Maybe he really hates sci-fi and he's going after the bloke who created *Babylon 5*," Eddie suggested.

"*Eddie!* This is serious."

"What, a terrorist attack that could kill thousands of people? No!"

"I don't know what's more terrifying," said Dalton. "That prospect, or the fact that you two are the best hope to stop it."

"At least we're *trying*," snarled Nina. "Rather than coming up with the idea in the first place, only to have it all blow up in your face!"

"I did not come up with—"

"Oh, shut up, Mr. President. Stop trying to cover your ass and *help* us! You know Cross, you know what motivates him and what he was trying to achieve. What's his endgame? His target could be anywhere in the world—but where?"

There was no immediate reply. Eddie was the first to break the downcast silence. "So he's not going to attack the original Babylon. What else could it be?"

"One theory about Revelation was that Babylon was code for Rome," said Nina.

"Rome was not the target today, though," said Seretse. "Not the real target."

"I know. But Babylon was the center of an ancient empire, Rome was the same in John's time, so now . . . Washington, DC?" she suggested.

"I wouldn't think so," Dalton replied. "Cross was many things, but he was definitely a patriot. His long-term goal was to bring about the creation of a unified Christian America—"

"You mean *your* goal," Eddie cut in.

Dalton ignored him. "But that was by using the attacks on Rome and Mecca to build up threats from outside the country, not to attack the country itself and kill US citizens."

"Maybe that's not his plan anymore," said Nina. "Maybe it never was. Learning God's secrets was always his ultimate goal. If people die, even Americans, it doesn't matter because the end of the world is imminent—they'll soon be judged by God no matter what."

"So there still is a possibility that he may attack Washington?" asked Seretse.

"Anything's a possibility with that maniac," replied Dalton. "But right now, the balance of power in DC is with people who would tend to side with him. Wiping out Congress wouldn't get him what he wants."

"It'd get a big cheer from everyone else in the country, though," said Eddie. Nina could tell he was grinning without needing to see him.

"You'll forgive me if I don't find jokes about killing political leaders amusing," Dalton snapped.

Nina sat up as his words prompted a thought. "Anna said something else before she died," she said. "It wasn't just that Babylon would fall. It was also that the kings of the world—the leaders—would witness it. But there's only one world leader in DC . . ."

She jerked bolt-upright as another possibility came to her. From the startled gasp over the speaker, the same thought had struck Seretse. "The General Assembly!" the diplomat cried. "The world's leaders are coming *here*, to New York."

"The UN is a tower where all the world's languages are spoken—just like the description of Babel in Genesis," said Nina. "Your Fortress America, Dalton—you said it wouldn't be subject to United Nations treaties. And Cross hates the UN even more than you do—he wants it removed from American soil. Gassing the place in the middle of a General Assembly would be one way to do that. And taking out most of the world's leaders would stand a pretty good chance of bringing about the apocalypse!"

"But he'll still be an angel short," Eddie noted. "The one he meant for Mecca's still in one piece."

"He doesn't care. He already justified scrambling and skipping over the parts of Revelation that didn't fit his time line as a result of John the Apostle's hallucinations, and I think he's jumping right to its end on the principle that if he brings about the fall of Babylon, everything else will come to pass as well—and then he'll learn all God's secrets. Oswald, is there anything you can do to increase security?"

"I am not sure if anything more *can* be done," Seretse told her. "I can warn the Secret Service and the police about Cross, but the streets around the United Nations complex are already cordoned off. The first of the world leaders have begun to arrive."

"What time does the assembly actually start?" Nina asked.

"Most of the delegates will be arriving over the course of the morning—President Cole is expected at one thirty. The session opens at three P.M."

"That'll be when Cross is most likely to do it," Eddie said. "When they're all in the same place at the same time."

Nina checked her watch, adding in the time difference between Rome and New York. "That's only just over eight hours from now! It's not even enough time to get us back to the States."

"You want to come back here?" Seretse asked.

"Absolutely I do! Eddie and I stopped the attacks in Mecca and Rome—well, okay, Eddie stopped one of the attacks, and the other one was a decoy," she admitted. "But we still might be able to help. At the very least, we've both seen Cross before. We spotted his Witnesses; we might be able to find him as well."

"But it's all academic, isn't it?" said Dalton in a biting tone. "Italy to New York is at least a nine-hour flight. Even if you chartered a business jet, there's no way you could make it before the session starts."

"There's one way," Eddie cut in. "Be hard to arrange, but you might actually be able to help with that, Mr. President. If you really do still have friends in Washington."

The politician was surprised, both at the suggestion and at the Englishman's sudden politeness, or at least lack of open hostility. "What do you mean?"

"Yeah, what *do* you mean, Eddie?" said Nina, curious.

"I mean, Mr. President, that if you still had enough pull with the CIA to get rides on their black flights, then maybe you've also still got some pull with your old mates at the Pentagon—like you did when you got us access to Silent Peak."

Dalton had once arranged security clearance for the couple to enter a top-secret government archive. But it had come with a price. "Uh, that didn't work out too well," Nina reminded him. "For any of us."

"He's not going to betray us *this* time, though, is he?" said Eddie. "Not since he wants to keep his arse out of jail, and out of the hands of his cellmate Bubba Manlove."

"I promised I would do everything in my power to find Cross and stop whatever he's planning," Dalton said stiffly. "What is it you want, Chase?"

"A lift."

"A lift?" said Nina, wondering what he meant.

*   *   *

She saw the answer for herself an hour later.

"Have you ever been in a fighter jet before, ma'am?" asked US Air Force captain Tyler Fox as he escorted her across the concrete apron of Rome's Ciampino airport.

"Can't say that I have," she replied with trepidation. Standing before her was a slate-gray aircraft, an F-15E Strike Eagle: her transport back to America. Whatever contacts Dalton had, they had come through in spectacular fashion.

"I'll go easy on you, then. Especially since you're pregnant. I've never had a baby on board my aircraft before! It sure isn't standard operating procedure, but I understand it's real important you get to New York asap."

"Yeah, it is." She looked down at her olive-drab flight suit and the helmet in one hand. "I feel like I should call myself Maverick or something."

"*Top Gun* is navy, ma'am," said Fox, with a hint of disdain. "The air force shows 'em how it's done."

She smiled. "What is it with you military guys? The air force can't stand the navy, and my husband's ex–army special forces with very strong views on flyboys. Or 'crabs,' as he calls them."

Fox grinned back. "Friendly competition, ma'am. Well, usually friendly. But we all pull together when it comes to the crunch." They reached the idling aircraft, where two uniformed ground crewmen were waiting. "You were lucky to get me, I gotta say. We're normally stationed in England, but we've been doing NATO exercises over Turkey and the Black Sea these past few days. I was kinda surprised to get called for taxi duty, but hey, if you need to get back home in a hurry, there ain't a faster way than riding in an Eagle."

The ground crew positioned ladders so Fox and Nina could climb into the cockpit. Her pilot took the front seat; she went to the weapon officer's position behind him, waiting nervously as her harness and oxygen system were secured. "You had the safety briefing, right, ma'am?" Fox called over his shoulder.

"Yeah, the CliffsNotes version."

"These things are very reliable, and tough—one of 'em once landed with an entire wing shot off! If anything does happen, just do what I tell you and you'll be fine. But I doubt there'll be any trouble."

The ground crew finished strapping her in, then descended and removed the ladders. Fox closed the canopy, running through a truncated series of preflight checks and communicating with air traffic control before addressing her again, this time through her helmet's earphones. "Okay, we have takeoff clearance. We'll be refueling three times over the Atlantic, but since we'll be going supersonic as much as possible, the total journey time should be under four hours."

"How fast will we be going?" she asked.

"Top speed of an F-15E is classified, I'm afraid," he said, humor in his voice, "so please try not to look at the airspeed indicator during flight. But I can tell you we'll be reaching speeds in excess of Mach Two. *Well* in excess." Another exchange with the control tower. "All right, here we go."

The whine of the idling twin engines rose in pitch, and the Eagle started to move, bumping along the taxiway. Nina flexed her hands nervously, trying—and failing—to relax. The impending takeoff was not her only worry. Four hours was less than half as long as a commercial flight would take, but it was still cutting things fine. By the time she arrived in New York, there would be under three hours before the General Assembly's first session began, and it was entirely possible that Cross planned to attack before then.

The main runway swung into view ahead. "Okay, Dr. Wilde," said Fox, "we're good to go. You might want to brace yourself."

She did not like the sound of that. "Is it going to be a fast takeoff?"

"You need to get to New York in a hurry! Are you ready?"

Nina gulped, crossing her arms protectively over her stomach. "Yeah," she said, dry-mouthed.

"Then hang on to your butt . . . I mean, your *hat*, ma'am."

The engines rose to a shriek, even through her helmet's soundproofing—then a thunderous crackling roar joined the cacophony as both afterburners ignited, raw fuel pumping into the jet exhausts and blasting out the twin nozzles in a spear of flame. The F-15 shot forward like a rocket. Nina gasped as she was thrust back into the seat. The acceleration of an airliner was nothing compared with the jet fighter's, and the g-forces kept building as the plane hurtled along the runway. Almost before she could register it, the Eagle was airborne, Ciampino dropping sharply away, and the pressure on her body grew even stronger as Fox pulled the nose up to what felt like the vertical. "Oh my *God*!" she squeaked.

"Are you okay?" Fox asked.

"I don't know! What are we doing, ten g?"

"Only about two, ma'am."

"Two!" she cried. "Is that all?"

"I deliberately kept it low on account of your condition. But I can ease off if it's too much."

"Please, be my guest. I'm not supposed to ride roller coasters while I'm pregnant, and this doesn't seem much different!"

"I guess I won't be showing off any barrel rolls for you, then."

Her glare bored through the rear of his seat into his skull. "No thanks."

Fox chuckled, then had another exchange with air traffic control. The F-15 eased out of its climb, Nina looking out of the cockpit's side to find with surprise that the fighter had not even gone steeper than forty-five degrees in its ascent, never mind vertical. Rome receded below, the Vatican clearly visible at its heart. "Okay," he told her, "we're going to a cruising altitude of forty-five thousand feet. I can't go supersonic until we clear the Italian coast, and I'll have to drop back below the sound barrier while we fly over France, but once we reach the Atlantic I'll put the hammer down."

"How about that," she said quietly, putting her hands on her bump and speaking to its resident. "Most people don't get to fly supersonic in a jet fighter in their entire lives, but you've done it before you're even born." A smile, mixed with a sigh. "I really, *really* hope your life isn't as interesting as mine."

She leaned back as the F-15 banked and headed west.

* * *

Traveling at supersonic speed turned out to be surprisingly unexciting. The Strike Eagle's breaching of the sound barrier was marked with a jolt and a split-second burst of vapor whisking past the cockpit, but the flight afterward felt no different from that preceding it. Their traversal of the Mediterranean seemed to take only minutes, then the plane slowed to make a high-altitude pass over southwestern France before the empty gray curve of the Atlantic appeared ahead. Fox accelerated again, continuing for twenty minutes at full speed before slowing once more to rendezvous with a hulking KC-135 tanker aircraft. The maneuvers required to link the two planes for refueling did nothing for Nina's stress levels, but Fox made the connection with practiced ease, and before long the F-15 was on its lonely way again.

With nothing but ocean far below, there was little sense of motion. The unchanging view and the constant rumble of the engines, added to Nina's general exhaustion, soon became soporific. She drifted into sleep, waking as the plane juddered. "What was that?" she said, blinking in alarm.

"Nothing to worry about," Fox replied. "We just caught some turbulence from the Extender." She leaned to look past him, seeing another KC-135 growing larger ahead. "We're about to gas up again. Once we're done, it's nonstop all the way to New York."

"How long will that take?" she asked, shocked that she had managed to sleep through the second refueling.

"Just under an hour. Oh," he added, "and if you look back and to your left, there's something I think you'll want to see."

She craned her neck to peer back over the F-15's wing. "There's another plane!" A sleek gray shape was approaching, its twin tails suggesting that it was a second Eagle.

"That's right. It's not one of ours; it's a Saudi bird. It set off before we did, and from what I've been told, it's hauled ass at the redline the whole way to catch up, on the direct orders of the Saudi king himself. I was actually ordered to slow down a bit, because you both need to land at the same time."

"And who's aboard it?" she asked, smiling because she already knew the answer.

"I'll switch radio channels so you can talk to them yourself."

Brief electronic chatter in her headphones, then she heard a familiar voice. "Ay up, love."

"Ay up yourself," Nina replied with a huge grin. "So I guess Dalton came through for you too."

"Most of this came from the Saudis," Eddie told her. "Funny how they roll out the red carpet when you save their holy city from being gassed. Are you okay?"

"Yeah. I just hope we can get to New York in time to do something—and that we actually *can* do something."

"Got to try, haven't we? Won't be setting much of an example for the kid if we don't."

"Maybe, though when most parents worry about being a good role model it's usually about whether they eat too much junk food, not how many terrorist attacks they've stopped!" She watched as the other fighter drew closer. "Huh, I just realized something."

"What?"

"What I'm doing—it actually fits with Revelation. The woman who took refuge high in the wilderness was pregnant, and according to the text she was given 'two wings of a great eagle.' I'm pregnant, this wilderness is about as high as you can get, and this plane *is* an Eagle! Maybe there's something to the prophecy after all."

"Hope not," Eddie said. "Wasn't she called the Woman of the Apocalypse? That's what we're trying to avoid!"

"Ah. Yeah. Good point. That's what I get for trying to be smart." The other F-15 was now near enough for her to make out the figure in its rear seat; she waved at him, getting the same gesture in return. The sight made her smile, before her mood fell again. "Do you think we'll be able to stop him?"

"'Course we will," said Eddie. Even over the radio, he had recognized the gloom in her voice and adopted a more upbeat tone to counter it. "We stopped Simeon and Anna; we can find Cross too."

"*You* stopped Simeon," she pointed out. "The only reason Anna didn't kill everybody in St. Peter's Square is because Cross tricked her. Yes, I found her, but I didn't reach her in time. If her statue hadn't been a fake . . ."

"Doesn't matter," he insisted. "It's the results that count. You know how you said you'd been seeing a shrink to figure out if everything you'd done was worth it? Well, this proves it is. We saved thousands of lives today—and Christ knows how many more in the past. We've stopped *wars,* Nina. *You've* stopped 'em. And yeah, I know we've both lost people we cared about because of it . . . but we might have lost a lot more if we hadn't. Like you told me in the tunnel, this is what you *do.* And it *is* all worth it."

Nina smiled, accepting his words as truth and feeling that a weight had been lifted from her. "Thanks, honey. I didn't need to pay for a shrink after all, did I?"

"Just call me Dr. Frasier Chase." She could almost see his grin even across the gap between the two fighters.

The aircraft moved into position behind the KC-135, Nina's the first to connect to the refueling boom extending from beneath its tail. The procedure was completed quickly and cleanly. The Saudi F-15 then took its place before both Eagles, now fully fueled, dropped away from the tanker. "You ready?" Eddie asked.

"Not entirely, but . . ." Nina took a deep breath, then gave him a thumbs-up. "Let's make everything worth it."

The F-15s ignited their afterburners. Side by side, they raced into the empty sky.

37

New York City

The two military jets touched down at LaGuardia airport, much to the surprise of observers and the infuriation of those waiting to land, as the airspace was cleared for their arrival. Nina and Eddie were quickly ushered to a waiting helicopter, taking a moment to embrace and kiss before boarding. Seretse was waiting inside the cabin. "Welcome home," he said, shaking their hands.

"Good to be back," Nina replied. "Although I really, *really* need to pee! Four hours strapped into a chair is no fun at all."

"Some people pay good money for that," Eddie said with a smirk as he took his seat. "Any news on Cross?"

Seretse shook his head. "Nothing yet."

Nina fastened her seatbelt as the chopper wound up to takeoff speed. "Are we going to the UN?"

"No, Brooklyn."

"Brooklyn? What the hell's in Brooklyn?"

"A surprising amount," Seretse replied with a faint smile. "I know that as a lifelong resident of Manhattan, you may find that difficult to comprehend."

She huffed. "Funny man."

"But the regional headquarters of the Secret Service is

located there," the diplomat went on, "and they are in charge of security outside the United Nations complex, so that is where we are going. Hopefully you will be able to provide them with useful information."

"Let's hope." She looked out of the window. The helicopter cleared the boundary of LaGuardia, heading southwest across the relatively low-rise sprawl of Queens toward Brooklyn. The towers of Manhattan rose on the far side of the East River. Her home; but it was again under threat.

The flight did not take long. The chopper touched down in Brooklyn Heights' Columbus Park, a convoy of black SUVs waiting to whisk them to the Secret Service offices a short distance away on Adams Street. Seretse took a phone call as they arrived. "Air Force One has just landed at JFK," he told Eddie and Nina as they went inside. "In light of the threat, President Cole will be taken to the United Nations by helicopter rather than in a motorcade."

"That's good," said Nina, relieved.

"A number of the world leaders are traveling there by road, though," he continued, dampening her mood. "They are still at risk."

Eddie shook his head. "If Cross hates the UN so much, he'll make the attack when they're all there. They'll be like his Pokémon—gotta catch 'em all." Seretse and Nina exchanged puzzled looks. "Oh, come on. Nina, you'll *have* to learn something about pop culture once the baby's born!"

"I can't wait," she lied. "You're right, though. He'll want all the kings of the world to witness the fall of Babylon—and if he can kill them afterward, so much the better to bring about the apocalypse. But he'll probably have a hard time getting close enough to do that."

"No probably about it," said a new voice. A broadshouldered, harried-looking bald man in his fifties marched to meet the group, the coiled cable behind one ear giving away that he was a member of the Secret Service. "Dr. Wilde, I'm John Talsorian, USSS special agent in charge of diplomatic security at the General Assembly."

"USSS SAIC?" said Eddie. "That's a lot of esses."

Talsorian gave him the briefest of dismissive glances. "Mr. Seretse, good to see you again. If you'll come to the briefing room?"

"You sound confident about your security," said Nina as they headed through the building.

"The place is locked down," he replied firmly. "We were already on high alert even before this threat warning, and now it's been taken to maximum. Nobody can get within three blocks of the UN without being checked by either the Secret Service or the NYPD. The FDR Drive is closed, NYPD river patrol has the East River fully covered, and we've got helicopters flying circuits watching all the rooftops. Beyond that, if anything tries to breach the city's airspace, there are Air National Guard F-16s ready to scramble from Atlantic City; they can intercept in six minutes."

"What about submarines?" Eddie asked him, deadpan. "A minisub could get into the UN basement through the old fire hydrant pipes. I know, 'cause I was there when it did."

Talsorian's expression was now one of outright contempt. "Who are you again?"

"This is my husband, Eddie Chase," Nina said. "And you should listen to what he has to say—well, most of it. He's already saved thousands of lives just this morning, so he knows what he's talking about."

The Secret Service agent seemed unconvinced, but he said nothing, instead bringing the group into a crowded room. Roughly half its occupants were in conservative dark suits, the others in tactical gear. A pair of large screens mounted on one wall displayed a map of the area around the United Nations complex—and a photograph of Ezekiel Cross. "All right, listen up," said Talsorian as he stood before the screens, facing his agents. "This is Nina Wilde; you may have heard of her, she's a famous archaeologist, but right now that's not important. What matters is that she has information about the man we're looking for. Dr. Wilde?"

Nina was taken aback by the brusqueness of his introduction, but the agent was clearly already under pressure, and there *was* a time factor involved. She regarded the image of Cross, which she estimated was at least ten years old, possibly from his CIA file, before turning to her expectant audience. "Okay, I'll tell you what I know. This man is called Ezekiel Cross; he's an ex-CIA agent turned religious fundamentalist, who was responsible for the gas attack in Antigua that killed almost a hundred people. He tried and failed to carry out an attack on a much larger scale in Mecca earlier today. He also used a similar attack on the Vatican as a decoy; I believe that his real target is the United Nations."

Talsorian cleared his throat impatiently. "Dr. Wilde, my people have already been briefed—we know all this. We need you to tell us something we *don't* know. Like: Where is he now? How is he planning to make the attack?"

"I . . . don't know," she admitted, his tone immediately putting her on the defensive. "I can tell you that even though he has associates, at least four other people, I think he'll try to carry it out personally. He wants to watch Babylon fall, see the biblical prophecy he's obsessed with come true—"

The agent interrupted her. "You *think*? Do you know for sure? You're not a profiler."

"No, I'm an archaeologist—"

"This isn't ancient history. This is happening right now, and we need concrete information."

"The only concrete in here's inside your skull," Eddie snapped.

Talsorian didn't even look at him, merely pointing in his direction. "Remove him." A pair of burly men in tactical gear advanced on the Englishman.

Eddie raised a hand in warning. "I wouldn't."

"Agent Talsorian," said Seretse placatingly. "Mr. Chase may also have useful information. If you could please hear them out?"

Talsorian scowled, but gestured for the two agents to return to their seats. "Okay, then. Let's have it. What can you tell me about Cross's associates?"

"Ah . . . not much, I'm afraid," Nina said. "He has a bodyguard, a big guy called Norvin; his pilot, Paxton—"

"Norvin? Is that a first or last name?"

"I don't know. But they're all American, and I can't imagine it's a common name. And there was another man called Hatch, I think." She described them as best she could, Eddie adding his own recollections.

"Got a hit on Paxton," said a female agent, tapping on a laptop. The pilot's photograph flashed up on the big screen beside Cross. "Daniel Aldo Paxton, age thirty-nine, ex-USAF, qualified to fly pretty much anything."

"That's him," Nina confirmed.

The agent kept typing. "Not enough info to narrow down the others."

"Is that all you've got?" Talsorian asked Nina. "Well, it's something, I guess. Okay, get Paxton's picture out there alongside Cross's, and see if you can find a link between them and those other names. All right, let's get back to it." The agents stood and began to file from the room. "Mr. Seretse, Dr. Wilde . . . Chase, thanks for your help."

"Wait, that's it?" said Eddie. "That's all you want from us?"

"That's all you've got," he replied. "Unless you've any other insights? Some sort of *Da Vinci Code* thing from the Bible telling us where he's going to strike?"

"I'm afraid not," Nina told him.

"That's what I thought. Okay, I've got work to do. Mr. Seretse, I'm heading back to the UN—you're welcome to join me."

Seretse gave Nina and Eddie an apologetic look before replying. "Thank you. That would be most helpful." He turned to the couple. "I am sorry. After all the effort involved in bringing you back here . . ."

"It's okay, Oswald," said Nina. "We did what we could."

Eddie gave Talsorian an annoyed glare as the Secret Service man spoke to the agent with the laptop. "Even if some dickheads apparently don't want our help. So now what do we do?"

"We could go to the UN and help look for Cross," suggested Nina. "I know it's a long shot, but . . ."

Seretse shook his head. "I am afraid that will not be possible. You do not have security clearance. After all," he reminded the archaeologist on seeing her surprise, "you no longer work for the United Nations."

"So there's nothing else we can do?" said Eddie.

"Unfortunately not. Hopefully you have done enough already. You foiled the attack in Mecca, and from the failed attack in Rome realized that Cross's true target was the UN. That may be enough."

"Only if you find him," Nina said unhappily.

"I have to have confidence that we will," said the diplomat, drawing in a weary breath, "because the alternative is too terrible to contemplate." Talsorian called his name. "I must go. All I can suggest for now is that you return home. Although I would also suggest taking a route that gives the United Nations as wide a berth as possible. The traffic in Manhattan will be quite appalling."

"Don't suppose we could hitch a lift in your helicopter?" Eddie asked. "Just land in Central Park at the end of our road, nobody'll mind."

Seretse smiled. "I suspect that would not be the case. Nina, Eddie, goodbye, and thank you for all you have done. I hope that when I next speak to you, I will have good news." He shook their hands, then departed with Talsorian and several other Secret Service agents.

"Bloody idiot," Eddie said, glowering after the departing SAIC.

"I can kinda see his point," Nina had to admit. "He's got his hands full trying to protect over a hundred world leaders in one of the busiest cities on the planet, and then we turn up and tell him there's a new threat, but don't actually give him anything that could help. I mean,

he was right: I *don't* know if Norvin was that guy's first
or last name."

"Got to be his last name. Who the hell would call
their kid Norvin?"

"You wanted to call ours Arbuthnot," she reminded
him with a grin.

"That was if it was a boy. Now I know it's not . . .
although actually, it would still work." He rubbed his
chin thoughtfully.

"No it wouldn't," she insisted. "Come on. Let's get
out of here."

* * *

That was easier said than done. Even outside Manhattan, the gridlock caused by the closure of roads around
the United Nations had worked back through the
bridges and tunnels to the island. Traffic was moving at
a crawl, or not at all. "This is going to take ages," Nina
sighed, looking out from their cab at the East River
below. The driver had taken the Manhattan Bridge, assuring them it would be the quickest route, but they had
been forced to a halt only a short way over the crossing.

Eddie peered past her. "So they did ground that thing
for the summit." He pointed at the river's eastern bank
about a mile away. The great twin-humped shape of the
advertising airship was now moored at the Brooklyn
Navy Yard rather than plying up and down the East
River. "Harvey told me they would."

"Harvey?"

"You know, the chopper pilot. I got kidnapped just
after having a flying lesson with him." He indicated the
buildings closer along the shoreline. "That airship was
one of the first things I saw when I escaped—the place
they were holding me was just down there. When I went
up on the roof, I saw it landing at the Navy Yard."

"It's a hard landmark to miss," said Nina. She returned her gaze to Manhattan, and the unmoving traffic. "Maybe we should have stayed in Brooklyn until the
roads quiet down. Whatever Oswald might think, I do
know the place isn't *entirely* uncivilized."

She looked back at her husband, only to find that he hadn't heard her joke, instead frowning in puzzlement. "What is it?"

"The guy who tortured me, Irton—he'd *been* to the Navy Yard, he had a parking receipt or something in his wallet. And when he was talking to Cross . . . what did he say?" His forehead scrunched as he dug into his memories. "Something about there not being much security on certain days."

"What did he mean?" Nina asked.

"I dunno. But . . ." He stared back at the airship. "Cross won't be able to get near the UN on the ground or by water, at least if that arse from the Secret Service was right about his security. And the air's covered by the NYPD"—he indicated a couple of helicopters circling midge-like in the distance—"and the National Guard, so anything that tries to get close'll be shot down. But that airship, I read about it: The whole thing was designed so it *can't* be shot down, not easily. It's massive, and it's got loads of different compartments for the helium, so even if you blow holes in some of them, it'll stay in the air. But it can fly at something like sixty miles an hour, so it could reach the UN in a couple of minutes— the National Guard's planes wouldn't be able to catch it in time."

Nina cocked an incredulous eyebrow. "You think he might be planning to attack using an *airship*? Who is he, Count von Zeppelin?"

"Yeah, I know, it sounds like the ending of *A View to a Kill*. But if he stole the thing, he could fly right over the UN and drop the angel on it—and nobody would be able to stop him."

"The Secret Service did say Paxton could fly practically anything," she recalled. "Would that include airships?"

"It's a big balloon with propellers on it. Can't be too hard. We should check it out."

"Or we could tell the Secret Service to check it."

"You think Talsillybugger'd pay any attention to us?

It's just a theory, and a pretty fucking daft one at that. But . . ."

"But it's just insane enough to be true?" she finished for him. They exchanged looks. "Just when I thought it was all over . . ."

"We need to hire a fat lady to sing for us," Eddie said with a grin. "Okay, so how the hell are we going to get off this bridge?" He checked the road. They were on the upper deck, two narrow Manhattan-bound lanes with concrete barriers hemming them in on both sides, and no sidewalks. Nor was there any easy way to climb down to the walkway on the lower deck. "Huh. Might have to rethink this."

Nina looked ahead. The traffic was still stationary. "God knows how long it'll take us to get across the river. And then we've still got to come back the other way." She reached for the door handle. "We'll have to do it on foot."

The driver turned in alarm. "Hey, hey! You can't get out on the bridge."

"No, you can't," Eddie added. "Seriously! It's at least a quarter of a mile back to ground level."

"It'll be a lot faster than driving across and then turning around. And you were the one who wanted to check out the airship. If Cross really is planning to use it—"

"That was just a theory! And like I said, a daft one at that. How often am I right about this stuff?"

"Way too often. Come on." She opened the door and hopped out.

"No, lady, wait!" the driver yelled. "Get back inside!"

"Nina—Oh, for Christ's sake," Eddie said in exasperation. He thrust some banknotes through the cab's pay slot, then slid across the rear seat to follow her.

She had emerged on the roadway's right, beside one of the barriers. A railing behind it meant that she was in no danger of falling over the edge, but there was very little space between the concrete wall and the oncoming vehicles. "Nina, wait!" he shouted as she hurried toward Brooklyn. She didn't stop; with a dismayed shake of his head, he ran after her. People in the stationary cars regarded them boggle-eyed as they passed.

He quickly caught up with his limping wife. "Are you fucking insane?"

"I'm pregnant," she shot back. "If anyone asks, I'll tell them it's hormones!"

"At least let me go in front of you." He squeezed past. "I'm not having you use the baby as a bumper!"

They crossed the shoreline, descending the bridge's long ramp until they were finally able to climb over the barrier to a footpath below. "You okay?" asked the Yorkshireman as he helped Nina down.

"Yeah, just winded," she replied.

"And the baby?"

She gave him a strained grin. "She's survived gunfights, explosions, and jumping over cliffs in boats in the past few days. Jogging for a quarter mile's the least of what she's been through."

"You're bloody mad. You know that, don't you?"

"Must be why we work so well together." Another smile, this time filled with genuine warmth, then she looked eastward. "We're only a few blocks from the Navy Yard here, aren't we?"

"Yeah, but it's a big place, and the airship's on the far side," Eddie reminded her. "We need another cab." They followed the path to a road passing beneath the Manhattan Bridge's lower end, soon spotting a yellow taxi and hailing it. They climbed in and set off for the north gate of the Brooklyn Navy Yard.

*　*　*

From the bridge, the airship had appeared huge; from the ground, it was like a mother ship from another world. The conjoined helium envelopes of the Airlander dwarfed even the largest passenger airliners. The mere sight of the gargantuan craft caused Nina a moment of cognitive dissonance, her brain's gears grinding as they tried to process the existence of something that seemed impossible. "Damn, that's . . . *big*" was all she could say as their cab pulled up at the gate. There were buildings between her and the airship, but its sheer scale made them appear no more than shoe boxes.

A security guard leaned out of a booth. "Where ya goin'?"

"There," Nina said, pointing at the behemoth. "We've got an appointment."

The guard didn't seem interested in her cover story. "Yeah, yeah. Take the second right onto Gee Avenue, you can't miss it." The gate rose.

"Has anyone else been to see it today?" Eddie asked him.

"Loadsa people wanna see it," he replied with a shrug. "Some guys went to the company offices maybe half an hour ago."

"How many guys?"

Another shrug. "Four, five? I dunno, I wasn't really payin' attention."

"Keep up the good work," the Englishman told him sarcastically as the cab pulled away and made a right turn.

"You think it could be Cross?" said Nina, peering anxiously ahead.

"Maybe. Or maybe not. A lot of people come here; like he said, it's kind of a tourist attraction."

The taxi drove past docks on the river's edge. Ahead was a low building, and rising behind it, moored on an expanse of open ground, was the vast beetle-like airship, its broad stern toward them. Their driver stopped in the parking lot. "You want me to wait?" he asked.

"No, that's okay," Nina answered. The couple paid him and got out, then regarded the building. A sign reading SKY SCREEN INC. was affixed to the wall, an arrow directing visitors around to the structure's other side. They followed it. The airship came into full uninterrupted view, an almost comically small gondola mounted under its centerline seeming as if it were about to be squashed flat beneath the elephantine mass. The whole vessel was so large that one of the roads to the piers beyond had been blocked off to give it room to land. Its flanks were covered with a grid of LEDs that in flight turned it into a colossal *Blade Runner*-style animated billboard, but today they were dark.

Eddie looked up at the craft. "This thing's not supposed to be flying," he said. "So why're the engines going?"

Nina saw that the propellers were slowly turning, diesel engines rumbling. "Maintenance?" she offered, not convinced.

"Let's ask." They headed cautiously for a door. Eddie opened it, flinching as an electronic bell made a loud *beep-boop* noise. "So much for the element of surprise," he muttered before raising his voice. "Hello?"

No response for a few seconds, then: "Yo! Come on in."

"Wait here," Eddie told Nina, wary. He entered a reception area. It was empty, but a large photograph behind the desk of the airship at night told him he was in the right place. Another doorway went through to an office area overlooking the airship's landing pad.

"Anyone here?" he said. The office was apparently shared by the airship's flight and ground crews and those who sold advertising space on the giant craft's sides, a nest of cubicles surrounded by whiteboards and flip charts showing sales figures and targets. But there was still no sign of any staff.

He rounded a battered couch, noticing an overturned coffee cup on it. A faint rush of cold air told him that an exterior door had been opened. In the far corner, a fire exit swung shut—

He froze. Poking out from behind one of the cubicle dividers was a foot, a man lying on the floor. There was a dark, glistening stain on the cheap carpet tiles nearby. Eddie instantly knew it wasn't spilled coffee.

Another door opened, this one behind him—

He dived behind the couch as Washburn burst out of a back room, gun in hand. Bullets punched through the sofa's back, spewing shredded foam stuffing over him as he scrambled toward a small desk bearing thick ring binders of paperwork.

The scar-faced man skirted the couch after him, seeing

the Englishman go underneath the table. He bent lower
to take a shot—

Eddie jumped up—bringing the desk with him. He
hurled it at the gunman. Washburn fired, but the round
hit only wood and paper. An instant later wood and paper
hit *him*, the table knocking him to the floor and landing
on top of him.

The gun was still in his hand. Eddie rushed over and
stamped a heel down hard on his wrist. A pained gasp,
and the pistol thumped to the carpet. The Yorkshireman
snatched it up. Washburn shoved the table away—only
to take a bullet to the head from his own weapon.

Shouts from outside, Nina's voice among them. Eddie
ran back through the reception area, checking for further enemies before emerging.

His wife had gone.

But he could still hear her. He hurried to the corner of
the building and looked across the landing field—

To see Cross dragging the struggling Nina with him as
he and Norvin headed for the airship.

The cult leader had a gun to her head, using her as a
shield. Eddie whipped up his own weapon, but knew he
couldn't shoot at Cross without risking hitting her. He
aimed instead at Norvin, but before he could fire was
forced to jerk back as the bodyguard sent several shots
at him.

Another man sprinted toward the airship's cabin. Eddie
recognized him: Hatch. He had released the mooring
lines, the cables now hanging limply from the bulbous
envelope. Paxton was visible at the controls in the gondola.

Norvin fired again, forcing Eddie to retreat farther
as bullets smacked off the wall. When he looked back
around it, Hatch had reached the cabin, Norvin following him aboard. He saw Nina shout, but couldn't hear
her over the noise as the propellers revved. Cross pulled
her inside, and the door closed.

Eddie ran into the open, raising his gun. He knew it
wouldn't deflate the airship, but the envelope wasn't his
target. Instead he took aim at one of the engines. There

were two pusher propellers mounted on the stern, and he opened up on the nearer. The fiberglass cowling cracked apart.

The gondola's door slid open again, Cross leaning out—with a sniper rifle.

Eddie immediately abandoned his attack and sprinted for cover. A bullet tore the air barely a foot behind him with a supersonic crack. He threw himself behind a parked van as another shot exploded brickwork in his wake. Before Cross could fire again, he hunched into a tight ball behind the front wheels. The whole vehicle jolted as a third round struck the engine block.

The airship's propellers grew louder. Eddie looked up to see it pulling away from him. He fired his remaining rounds at the second engine, but this time caused no visible damage, and even with its cowling broken the port engine was still running.

The airship gained altitude, slowly at first but with increasing speed as its forward engine nacelles tilted downward to provide extra lift. It cleared the landing field, turning north over the East River toward the United Nations.

With Nina trapped aboard.

38

"Watch her," ordered Cross as he went to the front of the cabin. It was equipped for sightseeing, ranks of aluminum seats on each side of the central aisle. Norvin and Hatch shoved Nina into a window seat opposite the door, the hulking bodyguard squeezing beside her to block her in as the other man took the place directly behind.

"So this is your plan?" Nina said over the buzz of the engines. "You're going to drop the angel on the UN and kill the 'kings of the world'?"

"Babylon will fall, Dr. Wilde," Cross replied. He put down his rifle and took the eagle-headed statue from a bag. "The prophecy will come true."

"But it *can't* come true," she insisted. "We stopped Simeon's attack in Mecca, and his statue's been secured. It'll never be loosed, which means the sixth angel's instructions can't be carried out. Until that happens, it's impossible to fulfill the prophecy."

Cross glared at her, eyes wide in mania. "It doesn't matter! The Witnesses are dead. That means the seventh angel is about to sound—and when I destroy Babylon"— he held up the figurine—"the end time will come!"

"No it won't!" Nina shot back. She realized how dangerous he now was, clinging to his delusion even as it crumbled in the face of the evidence, but she couldn't help challenging him. "You're picking and choosing pieces of Revelation to suit yourself! What happened to the seven angels who pour out their vials of plague over the earth? What about the Beast, and the dragon? Where are they? You're ignoring anything that doesn't fit your interpretation!"

"I found the angels!" he shouted. "That proves my interpretation is *right*. I saw through all the layers of hallucination and metaphor in John's writing—I saw the *truth*. The only truth! God's word was revealed to me, and now I'll reveal it to the world!"

"You're insane" was the only response she could manage.

Fury clenched his face. "You'll soon see," he growled. The airship was now passing over the Williamsburg Bridge, the United Nations complex visible on the west bank a few miles ahead. "The gas will kill everyone at the UN. 'And the kings of the earth, who have committed fornication and lived deliciously with her, shall bewail her, and lament for her, when they shall see the smoke of her burning.'"

"And how are they going to do that if they're all dead?" Nina demanded. Cross did not reply, instead regarding the view ahead with growing anticipation. "You can't answer that, can you? You've lost it."

He stalked back down the aisle, getting in Nina's face to snarl: "After Babylon falls, so will you, Dr. Wilde." His gaze flicked toward the cabin door. "Right onto its ruins from five thousand feet up!"

◆ ◆ ◆

"Look, just get everyone out of there!" Eddie yelled into the phone at Seretse. "The airship'll be there in a few minutes!"

"A full evacuation in such a short time will be impossible," the alarmed diplomat protested. "There are thousands of people here; even if we get the leaders out first—"

"Just do what you can," Eddie snapped before ending the call. He stared helplessly at the receding Airlander, which was still gaining height, then had an idea. He found another number in his contacts and hurriedly dialed it.

Infuriating seconds passed. He watched the airship retreat—then a shrill of engine noise told him that he was through. "Harvey! Harvey, it's Eddie Chase—can you hear me?"

"Eddie? Yeah, sure," Harvey Zampelli replied, sounding puzzled. "Where you been? I phoned you a coupla days ago, but—"

"Harvey, we've got trouble," the Yorkshireman interrupted. "Where are you?"

"Right now? Just comin' back from a tour of Liberty Island."

"I need you to pick me up. I'm at Brooklyn Navy Yard, the airship landing field."

"Pick you up?" the helicopter pilot exclaimed. "Eddie, I got passengers, I can't—"

"Can you see the airship?"

A moment's pause. "Yeah. Hey, I thought it was supposed to be grounded 'cause of that thing at the United Nations."

"It was, but someone's stolen it to *attack* the UN. Harvey, they've got Nina, my wife, aboard. I've got to get after them!" When there was no immediate reply, he went on: "You said you owed me a favor. Forget flying lessons—this is it. A lot of people will *die* if I can't stop this!"

"You're not kiddin', are you?" said Harvey, worried. "Okay, I'll come find you. Not sure how I'm gonna break it to my passengers, though."

"Just get here," Eddie said. He stared upriver once more. The airship was still heading relentlessly toward its destination—but had now been noticed by the forces guarding it, helicopters changing course to intercept.

* * *

Paxton listened to a message through his headphones, then turned to Cross. "They're ordering us to turn back to the Navy Yard and set down."

"Of course they are," Cross replied, surveying his target through binoculars. The United Nations was now only two miles away, and the Airlander had reached its cruising speed: two minutes' flight time. "There's a lot of activity on the ground. They know we're coming."

"They're evacuating," Nina told him. "The VIPs'll be out of there before you can drop the angel."

"In two minutes? No, they won't. There are one hundred and sixty-five world leaders attending the General Assembly, and they'll all be fighting over who gets to escape first. I know how these things work. The Secret Service won't let anyone else leave until President Cole's been secured, and they don't even have a *police* helicopter on the ground, never mind Marine One." He raised the binoculars to check the sky ahead. "Paxton, NYPD choppers coming in." He indicated a white-and-blue Jet Ranger heading toward them.

"I see them," Paxton replied. "What do you want me to do?"

"Stay on course. I'll deal with them."

"I'll have to slow down," the pilot warned. "The wind at this speed'll throw your aim off."

"I can handle it. Just hold us steady." Cross went to the port-side door and opened it. Wind rushed into the cabin, the rasp of the propellers rising to earsplitting volume. He squinted into the slipstream. "Come right five degrees so I can get a clear shot!"

Paxton obeyed, turning the Airlander slightly to starboard. Cross leaned against the doorframe as he aimed the rifle through the opening at the nearer of the approaching helicopters. "Steady, hold it steady," he called, fixing the crosshairs in the telescopic sight on his target. "Steady, and . . . *now*!"

He fired. Even over the roaring engines, the retort made Nina jump. For a moment, it seemed that he had missed—then the leading helicopter slewed around, dropping into a corkscrewing descent.

Cross hurried to the front of the cabin to watch as its fall picked up speed, spinning like a sycamore leaf until it smacked down on the river. The rotors sliced into the water's surface and kicked up a great swath of spray before the downed aircraft rolled over and began to sink. "You got it!" Paxton crowed.

"There's still another one."

The second helicopter started a sharp climb, taking a course that would pass directly over the airship. Paxton leaned forward to follow it, then turned in alarm to Cross. "He's going to use his rotor downwash to force us down!"

"Will that work?"

"Against a ship this big? Probably not, but it'll throw us around and make it almost impossible to steer."

Cross returned to the door with his rifle, but the Jet Ranger was now out of sight above the airship's bulbous twin prows. The cabin shook, forcing its occupants to brace themselves. Nina held on tightly to the seat in front as the Airlander rocked despite Paxton's best efforts to stay level—

She felt something protruding from the aluminum frame. A latch. The lightweight seats were designed to be easily disassembled and removed . . .

The idea that formed was quashed as the Airlander wallowed, pitching sickeningly like a ship on stormy seas as the chopper's downdraft pounded it. Cross grabbed a ceiling strap. "Up, take us up!" he roared.

* * *

Eddie shielded his eyes from flying dust as the red, white, and blue tour helicopter swept in to land. He scurried beneath the whirling rotor blades. "Come on, everyone out!" he yelled to the passengers. Even after Harvey had explained the situation, they were still bewildered and frightened. "You'll be a lot safer on the ground, trust me!" He helped them down. "Sorry about this, but I'm sure Harvey'll give you a refund."

"Refund?" said the pilot as Eddie clambered into the front seat and donned a headset. "They got a longer flight than they booked—they should be payin' me!" He checked that the passengers were clear, then applied throttle and raised the collective control. The Long-Ranger left the ground and turned up the East River.

"There's the airship!" said Eddie.

"It's kinda hard to miss," Harvey replied sarcastically. Even from almost two miles away, the Airlander still loomed like a floating football stadium. He frowned, spotting something above it. "The hell's that guy doing?"

Eddie saw an NYPD helicopter flying directly over the enormous airship. "Must be trying to force them down."

The pilot grimaced. "Hell of a chance he's taking. If the airship comes up underneath him, the displaced air'll maybe cause a vortex ring!" The Yorkshireman gave him a blank look. "That's a bad thing."

"What about the airship? Can he make it crash?"

"Only if he completely wipes out on it, and hopefully he ain't that stupid. Probably the most he'll do is slow it down."

"Good enough for me. The longer it takes it to get to the UN, the more chance there is of evacuating everyone." The LongRanger cleared the Williamsburg Bridge, rapidly closing the gap to the airship as the huge craft veered right, its nose tilting upward—toward the buzzing fly above it. "Oh shit! They're going to hit each other!"

Harvey stared at the police helicopter in horror. "Move, you asshole, *move*!"

* * *

"Full power!" screamed Cross. "Ram him!"

Paxton shoved the throttle levers to maximum. The engine noise rose to a scream, the airship forcing its way through the downdraft—

A muffled *whump* reverberated through the vessel as it hit the police helicopter's skids. The impact threw everyone around in their seats. Paxton struggled to maintain control, wrestling with the joystick.

Nina pulled herself upright, her hand again finding the latch. This time, she tugged it. It opened with a *clack*, but the noise was drowned out by the roar of the propellers. The seatback came loose, aluminum tubing sliding freely inside its frame. If she raised it, it would detach.

But she kept it in place as Norvin levered himself up beside her. She now had a weapon, however improvised; what she needed was the right time to use it.

Paxton pulled back the joystick. The Airlander pitched upward once more—and another blow shook the cabin.

. . .

"That guy's crazy!" said Harvey, unable to look away from the slow-motion collision.

"The chopper pilot, or the airship pilot?" Eddie asked.

"Both!"

The police helicopter reeled drunkenly as it bounced off the Airlander's upper hull, the tips of its main rotor coming perilously close to the envelope's Kevlar skin. It leveled off, trying to climb out of trouble, but the airship rose after it like a killer whale. The pilot finally decided that discretion was the better part of valor, accelerating away before turning to flank the enormous craft from a safe distance.

The Jet Ranger's rear door opened and a cop leaned out—holding a submachine gun. He opened fire, shots spraying the airship's port lobe. The envelope was tough, but it was designed to resist impacts from birds and hailstones rather than bullets. It puckered and ripped, helium gushing out with a piercing shrill.

Yet the airship was not slowed. Only one of its internal compartments had been violated, and the others provided more than enough buoyancy to keep it afloat. Magazine empty, the cop withdrew.

"Now what's he doing?" Harvey asked as the helicopter descended.

Eddie saw the cop return to view, holding a different weapon. "He can't shoot down the airship—so he's going to shoot the pilot!"

• • •

A red light flashed insistently upon the instrument panel. "We're losing helium," Paxton warned.

"How bad?" Cross demanded.

The pilot checked the display. "Only looks like one cell."

Cross looked to port, seeing the helicopter drop back into sight. He hefted the rifle and went back to the door. "Hatch, give me cover fire. I'll take him out."

The cult leader braced himself against the bulkhead. Hatch unslung his gun and crouched alongside him to take aim at the helicopter—

The police sniper saw them and fired first. The round ripped through Hatch's thigh. He screamed and fell through the opening, tumbling into empty space.

But Cross had now locked on to a target of his own— and pulled the trigger.

The sniper lurched, then toppled out of the Jet Ranger. Nina gasped in shock, flinching as he jerked to a stop in midair, hanging from a safety line. The helicopter jolted violently with the abrupt shift of weight. It peeled away from the airship, the wounded cop throwing the aircraft off balance as he swung back and forth.

Cross tracked the chopper as if about to shoot the pilot, then drew back inside the cabin, returning his attention to the view ahead. Nina lifted the loose seatback slightly. He was barely six feet from her, beside the open door. If she could reach him, she was certain she could push him out . . . but Norvin was a wall of flesh obstructing her. "Don't try anything," the bodyguard rumbled, as if reading her mind.

She looked away, seeing that the airship had been knocked from its flight path by the helicopter. Roosevelt Island bisected the river ahead, the UN complex off to one side. "Bring us back on course!" Cross called to Paxton.

The pilot adjusted the rudders, the behemoth angling to the left. "We'll be overhead in a minute," he announced.

"Excellent." Cross returned to the front of the cabin, putting down the rifle and collecting the angel. He gazed down at the approaching tower of the Secretariat Building and the broad domed sweep of the General Assembly beyond, the ground around it a seething mass of people. "'Thus with violence shall that great city Babylon be thrown down . . .'"

Norvin glanced back through the rearmost window as the airship turned. "Prophet!" he cried in sudden alarm. "There's another chopper coming in behind us!"

* * *

Harvey's helicopter was gaining fast on the airship. Eddie picked out the mooring lines hanging over its sides. "Get above it," he said. "I'll jump down on its top!"

"You'll *what*?" said the Bronxite in disbelief.

"Those cables—I can climb down one and get to the cabin." The lines were affixed to the upper part of the hull; Eddie was sure he could reach one before the envelope's curvature became too steep for him to keep his footing.

"The hell you can! There must be an eighty-foot overhang between the side of the blimp and the cabin."

"I can swing that far. I've done it from bridges—"

"That ain't a bridge! It's a floating bag of gas doin' sixty knots! Eddie, I know you've done some wild shit—I've *seen* you do some of it—but there's no way you can swing from the side of that thing like Spider-Man and jump into the cockpit. You try it, you'll be killed. Hell, even just *thinking* about trying it'll probably tempt fate!" Harvey briefly took his left hand off the collective control to finger the gold cross around his neck.

"I've got to do something," Eddie protested. "How about slicing it open with the rotors?" Harvey's expression told him that was a very bad idea. "Okay, maybe not—*Shit!*"

He saw movement in the cabin's open door: Cross aiming his rifle—

A hole exploded in the windshield—and Harvey jerked

back with an agonized shriek as a bullet tore through his upper left arm. "Jesus!" Eddie cried, feeling hot blood on his face and neck.

The pilot's wounded limb flopped nervelessly to his side. He clapped his other hand over the torn flesh, trying to contain the gush of blood . . . and the LongRanger pitched sharply toward the river.

Eddie grabbed the copilot's controls. "What do I do, what do I *do*?" he yelled. But Harvey's only response was a keening moan. "Shit! Two fucking lessons! That's all I've had!" he shouted at the universe in general. "Two fucking lessons and I have to fly a fucking helicopter that's—that's about to crash into the United fucking Nations!"

The LongRanger had overtaken the airship, heading straight for the Secretariat Building. Eddie increased power and tried to gain height, pushing hard on the rudder pedals—but they refused to move, Harvey's feet wedged against his own set in his pained paralysis. The green glass tower loomed ahead; even at its maximum rate of climb, the chopper would still hit its upper floors. "Harvey! Move your feet! Move your fucking—"

He changed tack, leaning over to deliver a solid punch to Harvey's jaw. The pilot fell limp. "Sorry," Eddie told him, cringing, but the duplicate pedals were now free to move as the other man's feet slid off the main set. The LongRanger's tail swung around—and the helicopter veered away from the skyscraper, the rotor tips slicing within mere feet of the windows.

* * *

Cross watched the LongRanger begin its uncontrolled descent, then put his rifle on a seat near the door and reclaimed the statue as the Airlander approached the United Nations. " 'And the earth was reaped,' " he said, returning to the opening ready to throw the angel out at the crowds below—then he froze as the chopper swung crazily back toward the airship.

* * *

Eddie gasped in relief at having avoided the crash, only to realize he still had no idea what he was doing. "Okay, okay," he said, desperately trying to remember what Harvey had taught him. "Center the stick, level out, keep the throttle at . . . at something, fuck knows what." The East River and Brooklyn beyond blurred across his view as the helicopter continued its sharp turn. "Stop spinning, that'd be a good start! Okay, level the rudder pedals, and—*Fuuuuuuck!*"

The Airlander's swollen hulls loomed in front of him.

He jammed the chopper into a dive. Nausea rose in his stomach as it plunged, the rotors whisking just below the port lobe—

A sound like a concrete block being thrown into a wood chipper—and he was flung hard against the door as the helicopter whirled like a top.

The LongRanger had hit one of the airship's mooring cables.

Squeals of rending metal sounded behind Eddie as parts of the overstressed rotor assembly disintegrated. The steel-reinforced line had tangled and jammed the rotor head—and the engine's torque was instantly transferred back to the fuselage. The dangling aircraft spun around, its forward momentum swinging it upward behind the Airlander's stern before gravity pulled it back down like a pendulum.

But the airship was also affected. Even with its huge lift capacity, it still had to be properly stabilized in flight, and the sudden addition to one side of almost a ton of corkscrewing metal threw it wildly off balance.

• • •

The savage lurch as the helicopter snagged the mooring line sent the airship's occupants flying. Paxton was hurled over the instrument panel, his flailing foot kicking the throttles to full power, while Norvin crashed to the floor in the central aisle. Nina ended up on her side in the bodyguard's seat, clutching the now detached seatback.

Cross came off worst. The impact flung him against

the thin Plexiglas window in front of the door, smashing it. He dropped the statue, which skittered under the seats. The cult leader lunged after it—only to reel as the swinging helicopter jerked the dirigible sideways.

He fell backward through the open door, barely catching the sides of the frame with his fingertips. The Secretariat Building rolled past behind him as the craft overflew the United Nations complex. "Norvin!" he screamed. "Help me!"

"Prophet!" Norvin yelled, scrambling to the door. "I'm coming, hold on!" He gripped his leader's arms and hauled him back inside.

Cross collapsed on the seats behind the door, eyes wide with shock—then his expression became one of alarm as he saw something behind his bodyguard. Norvin turned—

Nina smashed the seatback into the big man's face. He stumbled over Cross's sprawled legs—and fell through the open doorway, plummeting over seven hundred feet with a terrible scream.

Cross jumped up at Nina—only to crash back into the chair as her makeshift club swung again and hit with a bang. "Fasten your seatbelt, asshole!" she yelled, snatching up his rifle.

He froze as she pointed it at his chest. "Put it down, Dr. Wilde."

"The hell I will," she replied, glancing over her shoulder to see Paxton pushing himself off the console. "Tell your man to land this thing, or I'll shoot you."

"You're not a murderer."

"No, but you are. And you're a direct threat to the world's security." The United Nations complex dropped out of sight beyond the open door as the airship continued into the city. "I'll do whatever I have to in order to protect it."

"*Protect* it?" he spat. "Corruption, decadence, blasphemy—evil and ungodliness everywhere? This is the world you want to protect?"

"It's the only one we have!"

"It needs to be cleansed! Babylon must be destroyed

to bring about God's kingdom on earth! The prophecy will come true—I'll *make* it come true!"

"You're not God's prophet," Nina shouted back. "You're a delusional lunatic!"

Hatred glinted in Cross's eyes. " 'The fearful, and unbelieving, and all liars, shall have their part in the lake which burneth with fire and brimstone . . .' "

"Shutteth the hell up," she snapped. Paxton finally dropped into his seat; she glanced back at him. "Hey, pilot guy! Take this thing down right now, or I'll shoot your boss—"

Paxton gasped in fear, but not at her threat. Nina looked back—to see the black glass monolith of the Trump World Tower looming directly in the airship's path. "Shit!" she gasped, grabbing the nearest seat.

The pilot yanked back the joystick. The Airlander pitched upward, the forward engine nacelles pivoting to speed its ascent. It swept over the corner of the seventy-two-story tower's roof, narrowly clearing it—but still demolishing a couple of communications masts as it climbed. Nina gripped the chair more tightly, holding her breath as the building's edge passed barely a foot beneath the gondola . . . then they were clear.

Paxton reduced power and put the airship into a hard turn back toward the river. "Hey!" she yelled at him. "I told you to set us down! If you don't, I'm gonna—"

She was thrown to the floor as the vessel slammed to an abrupt stop.

39

The crippled LongRanger's engine cut out: whether through some safety mechanism or simply because it had been destroyed, Eddie neither knew nor cared. But the helicopter's insane whirl was slowing, the blur through the windows resolving itself into the skyscrapers of New York.

A tall black one whipped past, and again, and again, closer each time—

"Shit!" he yelped, seeing the helicopter's reflection in the dark glass growing ever larger. He grabbed Harvey—as the aircraft smashed into a penthouse apartment like a wrecking ball.

Its tail was ripped off and fell away, but the main fuselage plowed through the condo's windows, scattering ultra-expensive furniture as it bowled across the living room. The mooring line snapped taut as the airship pulled away from the tower, dragging it backward—but the remains of the rotors wedged against a freshly exposed steel girder above the demolished windows. The cable strained, but held, the makeshift anchor yanking the Airlander to a sudden halt.

Eddie opened his eyes . . . to find himself looking straight down at a sheer drop through the broken windshield. Only his seatbelt kept him from plunging to the sidewalk over eight hundred feet below.

And his position was far from secure. The mooring line rasped against the girder as the airship tried to pull free, rocking the cockpit. "Oh, *arse*," he gasped, securing one foot against the column supporting the instrument console. "Harvey, are you okay? Harvey!"

The pilot stirred weakly. "Oh man, what . . . what happened?"

"My third flying lesson didn't go too well. Harvey, we've got to move—this thing's going to fall any second."

"Fall? Whaddya—Whoa, *shit*!" Harvey cried as he opened his eyes. "Jesus Christ!"

"Yeah, you'll meet him in a minute if you don't get out! Go!" Eddie unbuckled his seatbelt, balancing precariously on the support column as the other man frantically released his own restraints and barged the door open. Harvey piled out—and the helicopter lurched with the shift of weight.

The Englishman scrambled across the cockpit, batting aside dangling headset cords and diving after the American—

A shrill of buckling metal—and the fuselage toppled over the edge behind him as he hit the carpet.

Heart racing, Eddie looked up to see a stylishly dressed woman in her fifties staring at him in stunned amazement. "Hi," he said. "Sorry about the mess. There's a bloke called Oswald Seretse at the UN, he'll pay for the damage . . ."

Her gaze went back to the gaping hole in the wall as a shadow fell over the room. Eddie turned to see the airship drawing closer. Without the lift from the engines at full power, the craft was being pulled downward—and back toward the building—by the helicopter wreckage.

* * *

Nina grabbed a seat just in time to arrest her slide as the cabin pitched backward. But she had dropped the rifle, and it was now slithering down the aisle.

Toward Cross.

She caught it with one hand—as Cross lunged at her. He landed on her legs, catching her shrapnel wound. She cried out in pain as he clutched at the gun. "Give it to me!" he roared.

"Go to hell!" she snarled, pulling one leg free and thrashing at his chest. He grunted in pain, but still managed to grip the rifle. He forced the barrel toward her head and clawed at the trigger—

She let go of the seat.

They both skidded down the central aisle, slamming against the seats behind the open door as the swinging helicopter made the airship roll sideways. Nina grabbed the rifle with her free hand, pushing it away from her—as Cross found the trigger.

The boom of the rifle at close range was agonizingly loud. Nina felt the muzzle flash scorch her hair as she screamed—but it was Paxton who was hit, the bullet striking him squarely in the back of the skull and exploding his face across the windshield.

⁘ ⁘ ⁘

Eddie watched in horror as the airship reeled toward the tower. If it hit the roof's edge side-on, multiple buoyancy cells would be slashed open at once and it would fall out of the sky like an airborne *Titanic* as the helium escaped, taking Nina with it—

The behemoth rolled, a whale turning onto its other side. The wreck of the LongRanger had swung away from the tower as it fell, but it was now coming back, changing the airship's center of gravity.

The helicopter would smash into the building several floors directly below him. And the Airlander was still approaching, blotting out the sky . . .

"Get back!" he told Harvey and the penthouse's occupant as he judged the movement of the mooring cable, waiting for the impact—

What was left of the chopper pounded against the featureless black glass face of the Trump World Tower. The fuselage was flattened by the blow—and the rotor assembly disintegrated, the central shaft tearing loose. The cable whipped free as the heavy debris fell away.

Eddie burst into a run—and leapt out the window at the quivering line.

He seized it with both hands, swinging away from the building as the airship, shorn of the helicopter's weight, shot upward. Pulling the cable to his chest, he used his feet to secure himself in place, passing it under one foot and back over the other.

First Avenue rolled past far beneath him as the Airlander angled back toward the United Nations. "Okay, maybe Harvey was right about this being a fucking stupid idea . . . ," muttered Eddie as he started to climb.

* * *

Cross pulled himself over Nina, using his weight and greater strength to shove the rifle down to the deck with one arm, then clamped the other hand around her throat. "'True and righteous are his judgments, for he hath judged the great whore!'" he snarled.

"Don't you . . . call me a . . . whore!" she gasped as he squeezed, clawing at his arm with her fingernails. "You Bible-thumping prick!" She drew blood, making him flinch. He leaned away from her, trying to force the rifle out of her grip.

Realizing there was no way she could keep hold of the weapon, she instead let go of it, lashing her now free hand at his eyes. Cross gasped, reflexively jerking back to save his sight.

But his hand was still wrapped around her throat. He pulled her upward—then slammed her head back down against the deck, once, twice. Nina's vision blurred, pain overwhelming her. Cross squeezed harder, forcing a choked rasp from her mouth . . . then he let go.

A thin line of blood running from the corner of his eye, he collected the rifle and stood. Terror surged through the breathless Nina as she thought he was going to shoot her, but instead he hurried past her to the controls. The engines' roar grew louder as he increased power, aiming the craft back toward the United Nations.

* * *

Eddie was still climbing the mooring line when he heard the propellers speed up. He looked ahead. The airship was heading for the plaza outside the General Assembly. The crowd was spreading, people running for the exits to First Avenue, but it seemed that for every person who had fled, at least two more had replaced them as politicians and diplomats and officials spilled from the complex's buildings. Several helicopters were hovering nearby, one a heavily modified Black Hawk in green-and-white livery: Marine One, the transport of the president of the United States. But despite the efforts of the Secret Service and UN security to clear a landing space, the panic at ground level was making it impossible.

Aware that he was rapidly running out of time, he brought himself a few last feet higher and secured himself. He was not far below the gondola; from this low angle, he had a partial view of its interior through the large windows and open door. No sign of Nina, but he saw movement at the front—

Cross! He was at the controls, looking down through a gruesome film of blood on the windshield as he lined up the airship with the plaza. Then he stood and moved down the cabin. The Englishman felt a brief fear that he was going to throw the statue from the doorway, but instead he went past the opening, turning from side to side as if searching for something.

There was only one thing it could be. The last angel.

Time was up.

Eddie kicked his legs back, then thrust them forward, building up momentum as he started to swing from the line. His original plan had been to reach the gondola's door, but Cross was armed, and would shoot him before he could recover from the landing. Instead he aimed at the cult leader himself. One of the windows was broken, revealing it as flimsy Plexiglas; if he had built up enough of a swing to reach the cabin, he would be moving fast enough to smash straight through another thin acrylic panel and hit the man behind it.

He hoped.

Another sweep brought him closer to his target. Two more would do it. He fell back, the wind whistling in his ears as he swept backward, then in again toward the airship's underside. The boundary of United Nations territory passed below. One more swing to go, the gondola just feet away as he reached the top of his arc . . .

* * *

Nina clutched at Cross's leg as he moved back down the aisle, but he pulled away without even seeming to notice. She struggled to roll onto her side, feeling a new wave of pain as she raised her head.

The cult leader was looking for the fallen angel. She could see under the seats from her position on the floor, spotting the statue a few rows back from the open hatch. Breathing heavily, she started to pull herself up, feeling dizzy as her head throbbed again . . .

A dark shape moved past the doorway, just for a moment, before falling away. Nina blinked, not sure what she had seen. It hadn't been another helicopter—it was much too close, only a few feet from the gondola.

But the mystery object vanished from her mind as Cross finally found the object of his search. He bent down—and grabbed the angel.

* * *

Eddie kept his eyes fixed upon the American as he dropped away. Out as far as he could go, the Airlander's bloated flank hanging above him like a solid cloud . . . then he whooshed back at the gondola, bringing up both legs as he hurtled toward the window.

The cult leader stood, holding the angel in one hand. He turned—and saw the Englishman rushing at him like a cannon shell—

Eddie hit the window—but it didn't break.

The entire panel popped out of the frame with a crack of ripping rivets, the impact propelling it across the cabin to hit Cross like a transparent bulldozer blade. He flew backward, the rifle spinning from his hand.

But Eddie's swing came to a premature halt when he slammed against the window. The cable jerked from his grip. He dropped, the backs of his thighs hitting the edge of the opening—and pitching him backward out of the cabin.

Pure instinct saved him from a long and fatal fall as he bent his knees to slam his heels back against the inside of the wall, hooking his legs over the sill. He jolted to a stop, hanging upside down from the gondola's side.

He was anything but secure, however. Pain burned through his hamstring tendons as the angular metal edge ground against them. He flailed his arms, searching desperately for a handhold, but found only smooth aluminum and empty air—and he could no longer hold his position, his own weight pulling him downward—

Someone grabbed his ankles. He squinted up at the window—seeing a familiar face with a halo of wind-blown red hair looking back.

"Eddie!" Nina cried. She pressed herself against his legs to hold them in place and stretched an arm out to him. "Eddie, grab my hand!"

"No, get back!" he shouted. "It's too dangerous, you'll fall out!"

She took a firm hold of the window frame with her other hand and leaned out, determination clear in her voice. "I'm not letting you go. You've got diapers to change, mister!"

Somehow Eddie managed a crooked smile. He strained to bend at the waist, raising his arms toward her waiting hand. "Come on, come on!" Nina cried, stretching out farther. Their fingertips brushed . . . then hooked together, husband and wife gripping each other as hard as they could.

She leaned back, pulling him upward. He managed to get hold of the window's sill with his free hand and hauled himself upright, his legs finally sliding down into the cabin. There was a red-painted handle set into a recess above the window where the gondola was attached to the envelope. He reached for it, wanting a firmer handhold as he lowered himself inside, but then made out some warning text above it: PORT-SIDE ENVELOPE RIP—DO NOT PULL EXCEPT IN EMERGENCY. He hurriedly reconsidered and gripped the top side of the window frame instead.

With both hands now secured, he worked his lower body through the opening. "Are you okay?" Nina asked as his feet touched down.

"Yeah," he gasped. "Thanks."

"If I'm going to be a good mom, I want support from a good dad!"

They both smiled, then Eddie looked back outside. They were now directly over the crowded plaza, the Secretariat Building looming ahead. "We'll turn this thing out over the river—"

"No!"

They both looked around at the shout to see Cross back on his feet. He was clutching the angel—and had retrieved the rifle, pointing it at them. He sidestepped to the door, raising the statue ready to hurl it to the ground. " 'There will be no more delay!' "

His finger tightened around the trigger—

Eddie's hand snapped up—and pulled the emergency handle.

The results were literally explosive.

On a smaller airship, the envelope would have been ripped by physically tearing away a cable embedded in the material; a craft the size of the Airlander, however, required something more powerful. A line of detonation cord ran the length of the port lobe—and it took only a split second for the controlled explosion to slice open a gash in all the helium compartments.

A hurricane of escaping gas blasted out, the airship rolling as it lost buoyancy on one side. Eddie was flung back through the window, swinging from the handle with only the grip of his fingers keeping him from falling. Nina shrieked as she was thrown against the wall, one hand snatching a ceiling strap as her other stretched out to grab her husband's legs.

Cross staggered as the floor tilted beneath him. He dropped the rifle and tried to catch a seat, but too late—

He hit the bulkhead beside the door. The statue flew from his hand. He clawed at the doorframe as he toppled out of the cabin and managed to halt his plunge, hanging on by his fingertips.

The airship's roll worsened, venting helium gusting over Eddie as he hooked his ankles back over the window frame. Below, the Secret Service had finally created a cordon large enough for Marine One to land, the helicopter touching down to pick up President Cole. Cross's target was still in danger, Nina realized. "The angel!" she cried, pulling her husband in as she tried to spot the statue. "If it falls—"

It was on the floor—and rolling toward the opening.

"Eddie, hold on!" she cried, releasing him and diving for the angel. She snatched it up just before it tumbled out into the void—

A hand grabbed her wrist.

Nina shrieked as Cross tugged at her arm, his right hand in a death grip on the doorframe as he tried to drag her through the opening. The plaza circled beneath him, the deflating airship banking into a turn. "Give me the angel!" he snarled.

"No!" She jammed a foot against the bulkhead, but Cross's weight was drawing her inexorably toward the open door.

"Why?" he shouted over the wind. "Why are you protecting this corrupt world?" Another tug, and her foot slipped back, only her toes holding her in place. "What's in it that's worth saving?"

Nina tried to pull away, looking down at him over her stomach. The sight of the small bump gave her a sudden surge of strength . . . and an answer. *"My daughter!"* she replied, smacking the statue down hard on his right hand.

Bone broke with a flat crack. Cross yelled, losing his grip and swinging away—but he still had a firm hold on Nina's arm, dragging her after him—

Eddie grabbed her, pulling her back. She gasped in

pain as her shoulder joint took the cult leader's full weight.

But Cross did not give up, still struggling as he tried to dislodge her. " 'The hour of judgment is come!' " he roared. " 'Blessed are the dead which die in the Lord!' "

"You want blessing?" Nina yelled back. "Bless *this*!"

She slammed the statue back down against his clutching hand.

The force of the blow hurt her wrist—but the pain Cross felt was far worse. He cried out, straining to maintain his hold . . .

And failing.

His hand slipped over hers. One last desperate grab at her fingers, then he was gone, reduced to a dot in moments as he plunged toward the plaza. He screamed all the way down, people below scattering as they saw him fall—

Onto Marine One.

The helicopter was on the ground while President Cole and his closest staff were bundled aboard, its main rotor spinning just below takeoff speed. Cross plummeted into the whirling blades—and was reduced to a wet haze, what little remained of him spraying out over the aircraft and across the plaza.

Nina grimaced as she saw Marine One's white livery turn crimson. "Jesus!"

Eddie drew her away from the door. "Red, white, and goo," he said—in a high, duck-like voice. He had inhaled some of the escaping helium, affecting his vocal cords. "Buggeration and quackery! That's not right."

She embraced him. "Are you okay? Apart from the voice, I mean."

"I'll live. What about you?"

"Same. For both of us." She put a hand on her belly. "This has *so* not been good for my cortisol levels."

Eddie squeezed her, then looked outside. The crippled airship was spiraling down toward the plaza at an increasing rate. "We need to get this thing under control. And stop grinning, this is serious."

"I can't help it," Nina replied, finding his high-pitched voice incongruously amusing.

He huffed, then clambered to the front of the cabin. A tug at Paxton's seatbelt buckle released the dead man, who fell sideways from his chair. "Okay, how hard can this be?" Eddie asked himself as he took the pilot's place and examined the controls. Joystick, rudder pedals, throttle levers; the basics, at least, were much simpler than a helicopter's. He looked through the blood-streaked windshield, the Secretariat Building coming into view as the Airlander circled.

Nina joined him, keeping a tight hold of the angel. A monitor revealed that the port lobe had now lost most of its gas, and what remained was venting fast. "The helium's almost gone on that whole side."

"We'll hit the ground pretty hard at this rate," he warned. "I'll try to get us to the UN's roof before we lose it all."

He took the joystick. The airship turned sluggishly toward the green glass tower. Nina judged their speed and the distance they still had to travel against the rate at which the Airlander was descending. "We won't make it—we're falling too fast!"

Eddie shoved the throttles to full power. "That's the best we can do." He pulled the stick back in an attempt to gain height, but to no avail. "Fuck!"

Another smile, despite the situation. "That's not what ducks say."

"They do in Yorkshire!" The rooftop passed above the level of the cabin. "Shit, we're going to hit it!" He forced the stick and rudders hard over, trying to turn away from the building—

The gondola swung clear—but even largely deflated, the airship's port lobe still overhung its side. It caught the roof's edge, the torn composite fabric scraping along it and tearing away antennas and satellite dishes. Eddie and Nina clung to their seats as the Airlander lurched to a stop, debris cascading down the face of the Secretariat Building.

The cabin tipped back toward the horizontal . . . and

continued past it, rolling in the other direction as the starboard lobe, unable to support the trapped craft's weight on its own, continued to wallow toward the ground. "Now what do we do?" Nina cried.

Eddie saw a glossy green wall rushing toward them. *"Hang on!"*

The gondola hit the tower's side. Glass shattered, flying shards spraying in through the airship's doorway and missing windows. The airship creaked and moaned as it settled, then everything fell silent as Eddie shut down the engines.

"We need to get out before this thing falls," he said, voice starting to drop to its usual deep timbre. He helped Nina from her seat, and the couple made their unsteady way along the tilted cabin. It had come to rest practically inside one of the UN building's offices, the glass broken and the window frames buckled by the gondola's lower edge. "Hop up."

Nina pulled herself out of the door as her husband pushed from behind—and was startled to recognize her surroundings. Eddie emerged behind her to react with similar shock. "Bloody hell. We just can't get away from here, can we?"

They were in the office of the director of the International Heritage Agency, which until six months earlier Nina herself had occupied. "Stepping right back into my old office? You think that's an omen?"

"It'd better not be," Eddie rumbled, clearing his throat as his voice returned to normal. Feet crunching over glass, he led her away from the windows. "We've got other stuff to do. More important stuff." He switched on a lamp and checked his wife for injuries. She had acquired new cuts and bruises, but internal damage was his greatest fear. He put a hand on her lower body, feeling the small swelling within. "God, I hope she's okay . . ."

"She is," Nina told him.

He looked up at her. "You sure?"

"Yeah, I am." She smiled. "Mother's intuition."

He grinned. "It took all of this to finally make you realize you were cut out to be a mum?"

"What can I say? We don't lead a normal life." She kissed him. "But yeah, I can be a mom, I know it for sure now. I even picked a name for our little girl."

Eddie nodded. "What is it?" he asked.

Nina hesitated, then said the name that had dominated her mind for what seemed like an eon. "Macy."

Simply saying it out loud made her feel as if a tightness around her chest and heart had been released. She drew in a nervous breath, awaiting his response . . .

It was a gentle smile. "I thought it might be."

"Yeah?"

"Yeah. I know how you've been feeling—and I know you must have been worried sick that naming our baby after Macy would be . . . disrespectful. But it isn't. I think it's honoring her." He put his hands on her arms, the smile widening. "And Macy would have been chuffed as nuts to know we'd named our kid after her."

Nina glanced heavenward. "Maybe she still is. Who knows?"

"Who knows," he echoed. "I know one thing, though."

"What's that?"

"We should start now if we want to reach the apartment before it gets dark." He looked back at the window, the view of Manhattan blocked by the hanging mass of the crashed airship. "Traffic'll be a nightmare."

Nina laughed. "And I get the feeling a lot of people will want to talk to us." She kissed him again. "Come on then. Let's go home."

New York City

Five Months Later

"Welcome home," said Eddie, unlocking and opening the door. "Both of you."

"Thanks," said Nina with relief as she entered the apartment, her newborn baby in a sling against her chest. The little girl—*impossibly* little considering the size of her bump after nine months of pregnancy, she still couldn't help thinking—had been asleep during the ride from the hospital, but was now starting to stir again. "Hey, honey," she cooed. "This is where we live! It's Mommy and Daddy's home—and now it's yours too."

"Mummy," said Eddie with a grin as he followed her in.

"*Mommy.*"

"Mummy!"

"Am I wrapped in bandages? Then it's Mommy. Although *you'll* be wrapped in bandages if you say it again," she warned him jokingly.

He leaned in closer to his daughter. "Mummy's bad-tempered and violent because she's got red hair," he said in a stage whisper. "You want to be more like Daddy."

"What, going bald?" In fact, they weren't sure what color the baby's hair would eventually become, as it somehow managed the feat of seeming blond, dark, or even red depending on the light. "Don't listen to Daddy—he's British, he talks in a weird way. And he's from Yorkshire, so that makes him even weirder."

"Tchah!"

"See what I mean?"

Eddie took off his leather jacket. "Okay, then. Let's show the little one her room."

They went through the living room, pausing en route at the shelf of mementos. Nina gently shifted the baby to see one photograph in particular: that of Macy Sharif. "Macy . . . meet Macy." She didn't know which Macy she was addressing, but decided it didn't matter. Macy Laura Wilde Chase blinked her wide green eyes in response, then made a soft mumbling sound that her mother decided meant *hello*.

Eddie smiled. "Macy would have loved that. Big Macy, I mean."

"I know." A moment of sadness as she regarded the picture of her friend, then she looked back at her namesake. "When you're older, I'll tell you all about her." Her gaze moved again, this time to the photograph of herself with her parents. "And I'll tell you all about my mommy and daddy too. They would have been so happy to meet you . . ."

"You okay?" Eddie said softly, after a moment.

"Yeah." There was a hint of sadness to her voice, but it vanished as she regarded her daughter once more. "But that can wait for another day. Let's get you into your bed."

They continued to another room. What had previously been the study was now a nursery, the desk replaced by a crib containing a Moses basket. Nina went to it, taking a deep breath. "Okay, I practiced this with a doll, so hopefully I'll manage the real thing," she said, gingerly unfastening the sling with one hand while supporting the baby with the other.

"You'll do it," Eddie assured her. "Trust me, you're not going to drop the baby. You could be juggling hand grenades and you *still* wouldn't drop the baby!"

"I hope you're right . . ." The sling came free, and she

took Macy's weight with both hands, carefully lifting her out and lowering her into the cot. "Yes! I did it! I actually did it—and she didn't even cry!" Macy squirmed in her new bed but didn't make a sound. "Oh my God, Eddie. Look at her. Isn't she beautiful?" She felt tears swelling in her eyes.

"Yeah, she is," he agreed. "My baby girl. Wow." He made a sound that was half chuckle and half disbelieving gasp. "I'm a dad. I'm a bloody dad!"

"That only just sank in, huh? I *thought* you looked a bit spaced out at the birth."

A grin. "Having her here at home is what did it. We're an actual *family* now." He reached down to stroke his daughter's cheek; she wriggled in response. "So are you ready to be a mum?" he asked Nina. "Or a mom, even."

"Yes," she replied. "I'm ready—I really am." The admission was entirely truthful, and it felt good. "Though I know it's going to be hard work. She's quiet now, but . . . well, you heard her at the hospital before I fed her! I don't know how she fits such big lungs into such a tiny body."

"At least we can concentrate on her. Your book's finished, and you've optioned the movie rights to Grant, so we don't need to worry about money. You don't have to go chasing after any more archaeological bollocks for a while."

Nina laughed. "Just because I've become a mother doesn't mean I'm going to stop doing what I do."

"Yeah, I was afraid you'd say that. Oh well . . ." He let out an exaggerated sigh, then wrapped his arms around her, looking down at their sleeping baby. "It doesn't matter right now, does it?"

"No, it doesn't." She smiled, then kissed him. "We've just started a whole new adventure."

Don't miss the twelfth explosive
Nina Wilde and Eddie Chase adventure

THE
Midas
Legacy

Coming soon from Dell Books

Nina and Eddie emerged from the auditorium, to be immediately greeted by several journalists. "Dr. Wilde!" said one, recorder raised. "So, *The Hunt for Atlantis,* the movie based on your life story—what did you think of it?"

Nina was about to let them know her true feelings, how her hopes for a serious, sober account of archaeological discovery had been quickly dashed by a parade of gunfights, train crashes, and exploding helicopters, but the sight of the movie's producer nearby—and the thought that she had signed a contract that specifically forbade her from criticizing the film before release—persuaded her to be more diplomatic. "It was . . . interesting," she managed. "A lot was changed from my book, which was what actually happened, but it was all still very . . . exciting."

"Hey, I thought it was great," said Eddie. "Some of the stuff in the movie was different from real life, but you can never have too many explosions, right? And the gist of the story was the same."

"Insofar as Atlantis was being hunted for, yes . . ."

To Nina's relief, some of the stars of the movie chose that moment to appear, immediately drawing the journalists away with the promise of more famous prey. "Thank God," she said "Can we go now?"

They headed for the exit. Nobody tried to catch them, Nina giving silent thanks that archaeologists were low on the celebrity totem pole—

"Dr. Wilde? Nina?"

"Goddamn it," she muttered before turning to see who had called her name.

To her surprise, it wasn't a member of the press but an elegantly dressed old lady with a VIP guest badge. Despite her age, the woman's green eyes were bright and intelligent, regarding the redhead with a contemplative, almost approving air. "Hello?" Nina said after an uncomfortable silence.

"I'm sorry," the woman said. "It's just that . . . I hadn't been prepared for how much you look like Laura."

At hearing her mother's name, spoken by a complete stranger, Nina felt unsettled. And as she looked back at the woman, the feeling grew—because she was now also experiencing an odd sense of recognition. Something about the elderly lady was familiar, almost disturbingly so. "Do I know you?"

"No, I'm afraid you don't. But I did know your mother—and we need to talk about her."

"What about my mother?" Nina demanded. "Who are you?"

The woman smiled. "My name is Olivia Garde. I'm your grandmother."

PRAISE FOR STEPHEN KING AND
ON WRITING: A Memoir of the Craft

"[An] elegant volume. . . . *ON WRITING* opens with a mini-memoir so finely seasoned that it whets your appetite for a full-scale autobiography."

—*Entertainment Weekly*

"Wonderful moments."

—*USA Today*

"Monstrous as it was, [King's being struck by a car] turned *ON WRITING* into a much stronger, more meaningful book than it might have been. Halfway through this project, when he was hurt, Mr. King incorporated his revivifying return to work into this book's narrative in ways that will make readers realize just how vital it has been for him. And the accident is eloquently described here, as a sterling illustration of all the writing guidelines that have come before. For once, less is more in Mr. King's storytelling, and the horror needs no help from his imagination."

—Janet Maslin, *The New York Times*

"An unexpected gift to writers and readers."

—*Sunday Patriot-News* (Harrisburg, PA)

"Remarkable and revealing. . . . Memoir, style manual, autobiography—the inspiring *ON WRITING* seems almost unclassifiable."

—*The Wall Street Journal*

"Generous, lucid, and passionate, King . . . offers lessons and encouragement to the beginning writer, along with a warts-and-all account of a less-than-carefree life. . . . A useful book for any young writer, and a must for fans, this is unmistakably King: friendly, sharply perceptive, cheerfully vulgar, sometimes adolescent in his humor, sometimes impatient with fools, but always sincere in his love of language and writing."

—*Kirkus Reviews*

"We who climb aboard for this ride with the master spend a few pleasant hours under the impression that we know what it's like to think like Stephen King. Recommended for anyone who wants to write and everyone who loves to read."

—*Library Journal*

"[King] imbues each snapshot with wisdom and advice for writers."

—*Book* magazine

"Exerts a potent fascination and embodies important lessons and truths. . . . [A] triumphant vindication of the popular writer, including the genre author, as a *writer*. King refuses to draw, and makes a strong case for the abolition of, the usual critical lines between Carver and Chandler, Greene and Grisham, DeLillo and Dickens."

—*Publishers Weekly*

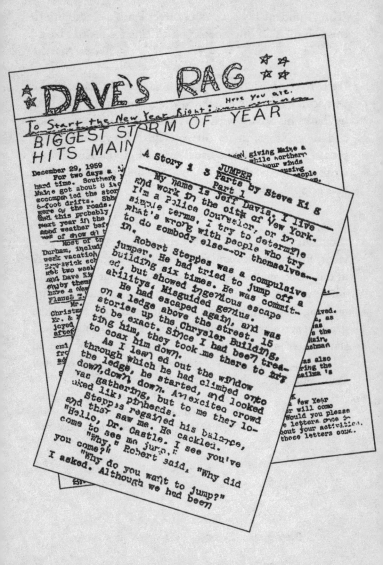

★ DAVE'S RAG ★★ ★★

To Start the New Year Right: Here you are.

BIGGEST STORM OF YEAR
HITS MAIN...

December 29, 1959
For two days a ...
hard time. Southern ...
Maine got about 8 inc...
accompanied the stor...
6-foot drifts. Sbb...
were on the roads. ...
and this probably ...
next year in the ...
good weather bef...
ves of snow on th...

Most of tr...
Durham, includi...
week vacation...
Brunswick sch...
got two week...
and Dave Kid...
enjoy themselv...
have a New...
Flavs? Th...

Mr. ...
Christm...
Mr. & ...
joyed ...
after...

...giving Maine a
...while northern
...hour winds
...people...

...ived,
...as
...the
...Main
...shman
...was also
...ring the
...mailma's

...a few Year
...er will come
...Would you please
...e letters once in
...bout your activities.
...these letters come.

A Story 1 · 3   JUMPER
Part 1   Parts by Steve Ki 8

My name is Jeff Davis; I live
and work in the city of New York.
I'm a Police Counselor, or in
simple terms, I try to determine
what's wrong with people who try
to do somebody else—or themselves—
in.

Robert Steppes was a compulsive
jumper. He had tried to jump off a
building six times. He was commit-
ed, but showed ingenious escape
abilitys, but showed ingenious escape
He had escaped again, and was
on a ledge above the street. 15
stories up the Chrysler Building,
to be exact. Since I had been tred-
ting him, they took me there to try
to coax him down.

As I leaned out the window
through which he had climbed onto
the ledge, he started, and looked
down, down, down. An excited crowd
was gathering, but to me they looked lik; pinheads.
Steppes regained his balance,
and then saw me. He cackled,
"Hello, Dr. Castle. I see you've
come to see me jump. I
"Why," Robert said, "Why did
you come?"
"Why do you want to jump?"
I asked. Although we had been

STEPHEN KING

On Writing

A MEMOIR OF THE CRAFT

POCKET BOOKS
New York   London   Toronto   Sydney

POCKET BOOKS, a division of Simon & Schuster, Inc.
1230 Avenue of the Americas, New York, NY 10020

ISBN-13: 978-0-7434-5596-1
ISBN-10:   0-7434-5596-7

First Pocket Books paperback printing July 2002

20   19   18   17   16   15   14   13

POCKET and colophon are registered trademarks of Simon & Schuster, Inc.

Front cover illustration by Lisa Litwack
Photo credits: Kathleen Campbell/GettyImages, Susie Cushner/Graphistock, Tom Francisco/Graphistock

Manufactured in the United States of America

For information regarding special discounts for bulk purchases, please contact Simon & Schuster Special Sales at 1-800-456-6798 or business@simonandschuster.com

Permissions

Honesty's the best policy.
—Miguel de Cervantes

Liars prosper.
—Anonymous

First Foreword

In the early nineties (it might have been 1992, but it's hard to remember when you're having a good time) I joined a rock-and-roll band composed mostly of writers. The Rock Bottom Remainders were the brainchild of Kathi Kamen Goldmark, a book publicist and musician from San Francisco. The group included Dave Barry on lead guitar, Ridley Pearson on bass, Barbara Kingsolver on keyboards, Robert Fulghum on mandolin, and me on rhythm guitar. There was also a trio of "chick singers," *à la* the Dixie Cups, made up (usually) of Kathi, Tad Bartimus, and Amy Tan.

The group was intended as a one-shot deal—we would play two shows at the American Booksellers Convention, get a few laughs, recapture our misspent youth for three or four hours, then go our separate ways.

It didn't happen that way, because the group never quite broke up. We found that we liked playing together too much to quit, and with a couple of "ringer" musicians on sax and drums (plus, in the early days, our musical guru, Al Kooper, at the heart of the group), we sounded pretty good. You'd pay to hear us. Not a lot, not U2 or E Street Band prices, but maybe what the oldtimers call "roadhouse money." We took the group on tour, wrote a book about it (my wife took the photos and danced whenever the spirit took her, which was quite often), and continue to play now and then, sometimes as The Remainders, sometimes as Raymond Burr's Legs. The personnel comes and goes—columnist Mitch Albom has replaced Barbara on keyboards, and Al doesn't play with the group anymore 'cause he and Kathi don't get along—but the core has remained Kathi, Amy, Ridley, Dave, Mitch Albom, and me . . . plus Josh Kelly on drums and Erasmo Paolo on sax.

We do it for the music, but we also do it for the companionship. We like each other, and we like having a chance to talk sometimes about the real job, the day job people are always telling us not to quit. We are writers, and we never ask one another where we get our ideas; we know we don't know.

One night while we were eating Chinese before a gig in Miami Beach, I asked Amy if there was any one question she was *never* asked during the Q-and-A that follows almost every writer's talk—that question you never get to answer when you're standing in front of a group of author-struck fans and pretending you don't put your pants on one leg at a time like everyone else. Amy paused, thinking it over very carefully, and then said: "No one ever asks about the language."

I owe an immense debt of gratitude to her for saying that. I had been playing with the idea of writing a little book about writing for a year or more at that time, but had held back because I didn't trust my own motivations—*why* did I want to write about writing? What made me think I had anything worth saying?

The easy answer is that someone who has sold as many

books of fiction as I have must have *something* worthwhile to say about writing it, but the easy answer isn't always the truth. Colonel Sanders sold a hell of a lot of fried chicken, but I'm not sure anyone wants to know how he made it. If I was going to be presumptuous enough to tell people how to write, I felt there had to be a better reason than my popular success. Put another way, I didn't want to write a book, even a short one like this, that would leave me feeling like either a literary gasbag or a transcendental asshole. There are enough of those books—and those writers—on the market already, thanks.

But Amy was right: nobody ever asks about the language. They ask the DeLillos and the Updikes and the Styrons, but they don't ask popular novelists. Yet many of us proles also care about the language, in our humble way, and care passionately about the art and craft of telling stories on paper. What follows is an attempt to put down, briefly and simply, how I came to the craft, what I know about it now, and how it's done. It's about the day job; it's about the language.

This book is dedicated to Amy Tan, who told me in a very simple and direct way that it was okay to write it.

Second Foreword

This is a short book because most books about writing are filled with bullshit. Fiction writers, present company included, don't understand very much about what they do—not why it works when it's good, not why it doesn't when it's bad. I figured the shorter the book, the less the bullshit.

One notable exception to the bullshit rule is *The Elements of Style,* by William Strunk Jr. and E. B. White. There is little or no detectable bullshit in that book. (Of course it's short; at eighty-five pages it's much shorter than this one.) I'll tell you right now that every aspiring writer should read *The Elements of Style.* Rule 17 in the chapter titled Principles of Composition is "Omit needless words." I will try to do that here.

Third Foreword

One rule of the road not directly stated elsewhere in this book: "The editor is always right." The corollary is that no writer will take all of his or her editor's advice; for all have sinned and fallen short of editorial perfection. Put another way, to write is human, to edit is divine. Chuck Verrill edited this book, as he has so many of my novels. And as usual, Chuck, you were divine.

—Steve

C.V.

I was stunned by Mary Karr's memoir, *The Liars' Club*. Not just by its ferocity, its beauty, and by her delightful grasp of the vernacular, but by its *totality*—she is a woman who remembers *everything* about her early years.

I'm not that way. I lived an odd, herky-jerky childhood, raised by a single parent who moved around a lot in my earliest years and who—I am not completely sure of this—may have farmed my brother and me out to one of her sisters for awhile because she was economically or emotionally unable to cope with us for a time. Perhaps she was only chasing our father, who piled up all sorts of bills and then did a runout when I was two and my brother David was four. If so, she never succeeded in finding him. My mom, Nellie Ruth Pillsbury King, was one of America's early liberated women, but not by choice.

Mary Karr presents her childhood in an almost unbroken panorama. Mine is a fogged-out landscape from which occasional memories appear like isolated trees . . . the kind that look as if they might like to grab and eat you.

What follows are some of those memories, plus

assorted snapshots from the somewhat more coherent days of my adolescence and young manhood. This is not an autobiography. It is, rather, a kind of *curriculum vitae*—my attempt to show how one writer was formed. Not how one writer was *made;* I don't believe writers *can* be made, either by circumstances or by self-will (although I did believe those things once). The equipment comes with the original package. Yet it is by no means unusual equipment; I believe large numbers of people have at least some talent as writers and storytellers, and that those talents can be strengthened and sharpened. If I didn't believe that, writing a book like this would be a waste of time.

This is how it was for me, that's all—a disjointed growth process in which ambition, desire, luck, and a little talent all played a part. Don't bother trying to read between the lines, and don't look for a through-line. There are *no* lines—only snapshots, most out of focus.

– 1 –

My earliest memory is of imagining I was someone else—imagining that I was, in fact, the Ringling Brothers Circus Strongboy. This was at my Aunt Ethelyn and Uncle Oren's house in Durham, Maine. My aunt remembers this quite clearly, and says I was two and a half or maybe three years old.

I had found a cement cinderblock in a corner of the garage and had managed to pick it up. I carried it slowly across the garage's smooth cement floor, except in my mind I was dressed in an animal skin singlet (probably a leopard skin) and carrying the cinderblock across the center ring. The vast crowd was silent. A brilliant blue-white spotlight marked my remarkable progress. Their wondering faces told the story: never had they seen such an incredibly strong kid. "And he's only *two!*" someone muttered in disbelief.

Unknown to me, wasps had constructed a small nest in the lower half of the cinderblock. One of them, perhaps pissed off at being relocated, flew out and stung me on the ear. The pain was brilliant, like a poisonous inspiration. It was the worst pain I had ever suffered in my short life, but it only held the top spot for a few seconds. When I dropped the cinderblock on one bare foot, mashing all five toes, I forgot all about the wasp. I can't remember if I was taken to the doctor, and neither can my Aunt Ethelyn (Uncle Oren, to whom the Evil Cinderblock surely belonged, is almost twenty years dead), but she remembers the sting, the mashed toes, and my reaction. "How you howled, Stephen!" she said. "You were certainly in fine voice that day."

– 2 –

A year or so later, my mother, my brother, and I were in West De Pere, Wisconsin. I don't know why. Another of my mother's sisters, Cal (a WAAC beauty queen during World War II), lived in Wisconsin with her convivial beer-drinking husband, and maybe Mom had moved to be near them. If so, I don't remember seeing much of the Weimers. *Any* of them, actually. My mother was working, but I can't remember what her job was, either. I want to say it was a bakery she worked in, but I think that came later, when we moved to Connecticut to live near her sister Lois and *her* husband (no beer for Fred, and not much in the way of conviviality, either; he was a crewcut daddy who was proud of driving his convertible with the top *up*, God knows why).

There was a stream of babysitters during our Wisconsin period. I don't know if they left because David and I were a handful, or because they found better-paying jobs, or because my mother insisted on higher standards than they were willing to rise to; all I know is that there were a lot of them. The only one I remember with any clarity is Eula, or maybe she was Beulah. She was a teenager, she was as big as a house, and she laughed a lot. Eula-Beulah had a wonderful sense of humor, even at four I could recognize that, but it was a *dangerous* sense of humor—there seemed to be a potential thunderclap hidden inside each hand-patting, butt-rocking, head-tossing outburst of glee. When I see those hidden-camera sequences where real-life babysitters and nannies just all of a sudden wind up and clout the kids, it's my days with Eula-Beulah I always think of.

Was she as hard on my brother David as she was on me? I don't know. He's not in any of these pictures. Besides, he would have been less at risk from Hurricane Eula-Beulah's dangerous winds; at six, he would have been in the first grade and off the gunnery range for most of the day.

Eula-Beulah would be on the phone, laughing with someone, and beckon me over. She would hug me, tickle me, get me laughing, and then, still laughing, go upside my head hard enough to knock me down. Then she would tickle me with her bare feet until we were both laughing again.

Eula-Beulah was prone to farts—the kind that are both loud and smelly. Sometimes when she was so afflicted, she would throw me on the couch, drop her wool-skirted butt on my face, and let loose. "Pow!" she'd cry in high glee. It was like being buried in marsh-gas fireworks. I remember the dark, the sense that I was suffocating, and I remember laughing. Because, while what was happening was sort of horrible, it was also sort of funny. In many ways, Eula-Beulah prepared me for literary criticism. After having a two-hundred-pound babysitter fart on your face and yell *Pow!*, *The Village Voice* holds few terrors.

I don't know what happened to the other sitters, but Eula-Beulah was fired. It was because of the eggs. One morning Eula-Beulah fried me an egg for breakfast. I ate it and asked for another one. Eula-Beulah fried me a second egg, then asked if I wanted another one. She had a look in her eye that said, "You don't *dare* eat another one, Stevie." So I asked for another one. And another one. And so on. I stopped after seven, I think—seven is the number that sticks in my mind, and quite clearly. Maybe we ran out of eggs. Maybe I cried off. Or maybe Eula-Beulah got scared. I don't know, but probably it was good that the game ended at seven. Seven eggs is quite a few for a four-year-old.

I felt all right for awhile, and then I yarked all over the floor. Eula-Beulah laughed, then went upside my head, then shoved me into the closet and locked the door. Pow. If she'd locked me in the bathroom, she might have saved her job, but she didn't. As for me, I didn't really mind being in the closet. It was dark, but it smelled of my mother's Coty perfume, and there was a comforting line of light under the door.

I crawled to the back of the closet, Mom's coats and dresses brushing along my back. I began to belch—long loud belches that burned like fire. I don't remember being sick to my stomach but I must have been, because when I opened my mouth to let out another burning belch, I yarked again instead. All over my mother's shoes. That was the end for Eula-Beulah. When my mother came home from work that day, the babysitter was fast asleep on the couch and little Stevie was locked in the closet, fast asleep with half-digested fried eggs drying in his hair.

– 3 –

Our stay in West De Pere was neither long nor successful. We were evicted from our third-floor apartment when a neighbor spotted my six-year-old brother crawling around on the roof and called the police. I don't know where my mother was when this happened. I don't know where the babysitter of the week was, either. I only know that I was in the bathroom, standing with my bare feet on the heater, watching to see if my brother would fall off the roof or make it back into the bathroom okay. He made it back. He is now fifty-five and living in New Hampshire.

– 4 –

When I was five or six, I asked my mother if she had ever seen anyone die. Yes, she said, she had seen one person die and had heard another one. I asked how you could hear a person die and she told me that it was a girl who had drowned off Prout's Neck in the 1920s. She said the girl swam out past the rip, couldn't get back in, and began screaming for help. Several men tried to reach her, but that day's rip had developed a vicious undertow, and they were all forced back. In the end they could only stand around, tourists and townies, the teenager who became my mother among them, waiting for a rescue boat that never came and listening to that girl scream until her strength gave out and she went under. Her body washed up in New Hampshire, my mother said. I asked how old the girl was. Mom said she was fourteen, then read me a comic book and packed me off to bed. On some other day she told me about the one she saw—a sailor who jumped off the roof of the Graymore Hotel in Portland, Maine, and landed in the street.

"He splattered," my mother said in her most matter-of-fact tone. She paused, then added, "The stuff that came out of him was green. I have never forgotten it."

That makes two of us, Mom.

– 5 –

Most of the nine months I should have spent in the first grade I spent in bed. My problems started with the measles—a perfectly ordinary case—and then got steadily worse. I had bout after bout of what I mistakenly thought was called "stripe throat"; I lay in bed drinking cold water and imagining my throat in alternating stripes of red and white (this was probably not so far wrong).

At some point my ears became involved, and one day my mother called a taxi (she did not drive) and took me to a doctor too important to make house calls—an ear specialist. (For some reason I got the idea that this sort of doctor was called an otiologist.) I didn't care whether he specialized in ears or assholes. I had a fever of a hundred and four degrees, and each time I swallowed, pain lit up the sides of my face like a jukebox.

The doctor looked in my ears, spending most of his time (I think) on the left one. Then he laid me down on his examining table. "Lift up a minute, Stevie," his nurse said, and put a large absorbent cloth—it might have been a diaper—under my head, so that my cheek rested on it when I lay back down. I should have guessed that something was rotten in Denmark. Who knows, maybe I did.

There was a sharp smell of alcohol. A clank as the ear doctor opened his sterilizer. I saw the needle in his hand—it looked as long as the ruler in my school pencil-box—and tensed. The ear doctor smiled reassuringly and spoke the lie for which doctors should be immediately jailed (time of incarceration to be doubled when the lie is told to a child): "Relax, Stevie, this won't hurt." I believed him.

He slid the needle into my ear and punctured my eardrum with it. The pain was beyond anything I have ever felt since—the only thing close was the first month of recovery after being struck by a van in the summer of 1999. That pain was longer in duration but not so intense. The puncturing of my eardrum was pain beyond the world. I screamed. There was a sound inside my head—a loud kissing sound. Hot fluid ran out of my ear—it was as if I had started to cry out of the wrong hole. God knows I was crying enough out of the right ones by then. I raised my streaming face and looked unbelieving at the ear doctor and the ear doctor's nurse. Then I looked at the cloth the nurse had spread over the top third of the exam table. It had a big wet patch on it. There were fine tendrils of yellow pus on it as well.

"There," the ear doctor said, patting my shoulder. "You were very brave, Stevie, and it's all over."

The next week my mother called another taxi, we went back to the ear doctor's, and I found myself once more lying on my side with the absorbent square of cloth under my head. The ear doctor once again produced the smell of alcohol—a smell I still associate, as I suppose many people do, with pain and sickness and terror—and with it, the long needle. He once more assured me that it wouldn't hurt, and I once more believed him. Not completely, but enough to be quiet while the needle slid into my ear.

It *did* hurt. Almost as much as the first time, in fact. The smooching sound in my head was louder, too; this time it was giants kissing ("suckin' face and rotatin' tongues," as we used to say). "There," the ear doctor's nurse said when it was over and I lay there crying in a puddle of watery pus. "It only hurts a little, and you don't want to be deaf, do you? Besides, it's all over."

I believed that for about five days, and then another taxi came. We went back to the ear doctor's. I remember the cab driver telling my mother that he was going to pull over and let us out if she couldn't shut that kid up.

Once again it was me on the exam table with the diaper under my head and my mom out in the waiting room with a magazine she was probably incapable of reading (or so I like to imagine). Once again the pungent smell of alcohol and the doctor turning to me with a needle that looked as long as my school ruler. Once more the smile, the approach, the assurance that *this* time it wouldn't hurt.

Since the repeated eardrum-lancings when I was six, one of my life's firmest principles has been this: Fool me once, shame on you. Fool me twice, shame on me. Fool me three times, shame on both of us. The third time on the ear doctor's table I struggled and screamed and thrashed and fought. Each time the needle came near the side of my face, I knocked it away. Finally the nurse called my mother in from the waiting room, and the two of them managed to hold me long enough for the doctor to get his needle in. I screamed so long and so loud that I can still hear it. In fact, I think that in some deep valley of my head that last scream is still echoing.

– 6 –

In a dull cold month not too long after that—it would have been January or February of 1954, if I've got the sequence right—the taxi came again. This time the specialist wasn't the ear doctor but a throat doctor. Once again my mother sat in the waiting room, once again I sat on the examining table with a nurse hovering nearby, and once again there was that sharp smell of alcohol, an aroma that still has the power to double my heartbeat in the space of five seconds.

All that appeared this time, however, was some sort of throat swab. It stung, and it tasted awful, but after the ear doctor's long needle it was a walk in the park. The throat doctor donned an interesting gadget that went around his head on a strap. It had a mirror in the middle, and a bright fierce light that shone out of it like a third eye. He looked down my gullet for a long time, urging me to open wider until my jaws creaked, but he did not put needles into me and so I loved him. After awhile he allowed me to close my mouth and summoned my mother.

"The problem is his tonsils," the doctor said. "They look like a cat clawed them. They'll have to come out."

At some point after that, I remember being wheeled under bright lights. A man in a white mask bent over me. He was standing at the head of the table I was lying on (1953 and 1954 were my years for lying on tables), and to me he looked upside down.

"Stephen," he said. "Can you hear me?"

I said I could.

"I want you to breathe deep," he said. "When you wake up, you can have all the ice cream you want."

He lowered a gadget over my face. In the eye of my memory, it looks like an outboard motor. I took a deep breath, and everything went black. When I woke up I was indeed allowed all the ice cream I wanted, which was a fine joke on me because I didn't want any. My throat felt swollen and fat. But it was better than the old needle-in-the-ear trick. Oh yes. *Anything* would have been better than the old needle-in-the-ear trick. Take my tonsils if you have to, put a steel birdcage on my leg if you must, but God save me from the otiologist.

– 7 –

That year my brother David jumped ahead to the fourth grade and I was pulled out of school entirely. I had missed too much of the first grade, my mother and the school agreed; I could start it fresh in the fall of the year, if my health was good.

Most of that year I spent either in bed or housebound. I read my way through approximately six tons of comic books, progressed to Tom Swift and Dave Dawson (a heroic World War II pilot whose various planes were always "prop-clawing for altitude"), then moved on to Jack London's bloodcurdling animal tales. At some point I began to write my own stories. Imitation preceded creation; I would copy *Combat Casey* comics word for word in my Blue Horse tablet, sometimes adding my own descriptions where they seemed appropriate. "They were camped in a big dratty farmhouse room," I might write; it was another year or two before I discovered that *drat* and *draft* were different words. During that same period I remember believing that *details* were *dentals* and that a bitch was an extremely tall woman. A son of a bitch was apt to be a basketball player. When you're six, most of your Bingo balls are still floating around in the draw-tank.

Eventually I showed one of these copycat hybrids to my mother, and she was charmed—I remember her slightly amazed smile, as if she was unable to believe a kid of hers could be so smart—practically a damned prodigy, for God's sake. I had never seen that look on her face before—not on my account, anyway—and I absolutely loved it.

She asked me if I had made the story up myself, and I was forced to admit that I had copied most of it out of a funnybook. She seemed disappointed, and that drained away much of my pleasure. At last she handed back my tablet. "Write one of your own, Stevie," she said. "Those *Combat Casey* funnybooks are just junk—he's always knocking someone's teeth out. I bet you could do better. Write one of your own."

– 8 –

I remember an immense feeling of *possibility* at the idea, as if I had been ushered into a vast building filled with closed doors and had been given leave to open any I liked. There were more doors than one person could ever open in a lifetime, I thought (and still think).

I eventually wrote a story about four magic animals who rode around in an old car, helping out little kids. Their leader was a large white bunny named Mr. Rabbit Trick. He got to drive the car. The story was four pages long, laboriously printed in pencil. No one in it, so far as I can remember, jumped from the roof of the Graymore Hotel. When I finished, I gave it to my mother, who sat down in the living room, put her

pocketbook on the floor beside her, and read it all at
once. I could tell she liked it—she laughed in all the
right places—but I couldn't tell if that was because she
liked me and wanted me to feel good or because it
really *was* good.

"You didn't copy this one?" she asked when she had
finished. I said no, I hadn't. She said it was good enough
to be in a book. Nothing anyone has said to me since has
made me feel any happier. I wrote four more stories
about Mr. Rabbit Trick and his friends. She gave me a
quarter apiece for them and sent them around to her four
sisters, who pitied her a little, I think. *They* were all still
married, after all; their men had stuck. It was true that
Uncle Fred didn't have much sense of humor and was
stubborn about keeping the top of his convertible up, it
was also true that Uncle Oren drank quite a bit and
had dark theories about how the Jews were running the
world, but they were *there*. Ruth, on the other hand,
had been left holding the baby when Don ran out. She
wanted them to see that he was a talented baby, at least.

Four stories. A quarter apiece. That was the first
buck I made in this business.

– 9 –

We moved to Stratford, Connecticut. By then I was in
the second grade and stone in love with the pretty
teenage girl who lived next door. She never looked
twice at me in the daytime, but at night, as I lay in bed
and drifted toward sleep, we ran away from the cruel
world of reality again and again. My new teacher was

Mrs. Taylor, a kind lady with gray Elsa Lan-
chester—*Bride of Frankenstein* hair and protruding eyes.
"When we're talking I always want to cup my hands
under Mrs. Taylor's peepers in case they fall out," my
mom said.

Our new third-floor apartment was on West Broad
Street. A block down the hill, not far from Teddy's Market and across from Burrets Building Materials, was a
huge tangled wilderness area with a junkyard on the far
side and a train track running through the middle. This
is one of the places I keep returning to in my imagination; it turns up in my books and stories again and
again, under a variety of names. The kids in *It* called it
the Barrens; we called it the jungle. Dave and I explored
it for the first time not long after we had moved into our
new place. It was summer. It was hot. It was great. We
were deep into the green mysteries of this cool new
playground when I was struck by an urgent need to
move my bowels.

"Dave," I said. "Take me home! I have to push!"
(This was the word we were given for this particular
function.)

David didn't want to hear it. "Go do it in the
woods," he said. It would take at least half an hour to
walk me home, and he had no intention of giving up
such a shining stretch of time just because his little
brother had to take a dump.

"I can't!" I said, shocked by the idea. "I won't be
able to wipe!"

"Sure you will," Dave said. "Wipe yourself with some
leaves. That's how the cowboys and Indians did it."

By then it was probably too late to get home, anyway; I have an idea I was out of options. Besides, I was enchanted by the idea of shitting like a cowboy. I pretended I was Hopalong Cassidy, squatting in the underbrush with my gun drawn, not to be caught unawares even at such a personal moment. I did my business, and took care of the cleanup as my older brother had suggested, carefully wiping my ass with big handfuls of shiny green leaves. These turned out to be poison ivy.

Two days later I was bright red from the backs of my knees to my shoulderblades. My penis was spared, but my testicles turned into stoplights. My ass itched all the way up to my ribcage, it seemed. Yet worst of all was the hand I had wiped with; it swelled to the size of Mickey Mouse's after Donald Duck has bopped it with a hammer, and gigantic blisters formed at the places where the fingers rubbed together. When they burst they left deep divots of raw pink flesh. For six weeks I sat in lukewarm starch baths, feeling miserable and humiliated and stupid, listening through the open door as my mother and brother laughed and listened to Peter Tripp's countdown on the radio and played Crazy Eights.

– 10 –

Dave was a great brother, but too smart for a ten-year-old. His brains were always getting him in trouble, and he learned at some point (probably after I had wiped my ass with poison ivy) that it was usually possible to get Brother Stevie to join him in the point position when trouble was in the wind. Dave never asked me to shoulder *all* the blame for his often brilliant fuck-ups—he was neither a sneak nor a coward—but on several occasions I was asked to share it. Which was, I think, why we both got in trouble when Dave dammed up the stream running through the jungle and flooded much of lower West Broad Street. Sharing the blame was also the reason we both ran the risk of getting killed while implementing his potentially lethal school science project.

This was probably 1958. I was at Center Grammar School; Dave was at Stratford Junior High. Mom was working at the Stratford Laundry, where she was the only white lady on the mangle crew. That's what she was doing—feeding sheets into the mangle—while Dave constructed his Science Fair project. My big brother wasn't the sort of boy to content himself drawing frog-diagrams on construction paper or making The House of the Future out of plastic Tyco bricks and painted toilet-tissue rolls; Dave aimed for the stars. His project that year was Dave's Super Duper Electromagnet. My brother had great affection for things which were super duper and things which began with his own name; this latter habit culminated with *Dave's Rag,* which we will come to shortly.

His first stab at the Super Duper Electromagnet wasn't very super duper; in fact, it may not have worked at all—I don't remember for sure. It *did* come out of an actual book, rather than Dave's head, however. The idea was this: you magnetized a spike nail by rubbing it against a regular magnet. The magnetic charge imparted to the spike would be weak, the book said, but enough to pick up a few iron filings. After trying this, you were supposed to wrap a length of copper wire around the barrel of the spike, and attach the ends of the wire to the terminals of a dry-cell battery. According to the book, the electricity would strengthen the magnetism, and you could pick up a lot more iron filings.

Dave didn't just want to pick up a stupid pile of metal flakes, though; Dave wanted to pick up Buicks, railroad boxcars, possibly Army transport planes. Dave wanted to turn on the juice and move the world in its orbit.

Pow! Super!

We each had our part to play in creating the Super Duper Electromagnet. Dave's part was to build it. My part would be to test it. Little Stevie King, Stratford's answer to Chuck Yeager.

Dave's new version of the experiment bypassed the pokey old dry cell (which was probably flat anyway when we bought it at the hardware store, he reasoned) in favor of actual wall-current. Dave cut the electrical cord off an old lamp someone had put out on the curb with the trash, stripped the coating all the way down to the plug, then wrapped his magnetized spike in spirals of bare wire. Then, sitting on the floor in the kitchen of our West Broad Street apartment, he offered me the Super Duper Electromagnet and bade me do my part and plug it in.

I hesitated—give me at least that much credit—but in the end, Dave's manic enthusiasm was too much to withstand. I plugged it in. There was no noticeable magnetism, but the gadget *did* blow out every light and electrical appliance in our apartment, every light and electrical appliance in the building, and every light and electrical appliance in the building next door (where my dream-girl lived in the ground-floor apartment). Something popped in the electrical transformer out front, and some cops came. Dave and I spent a horrible hour watching from our mother's bedroom window, the only one that looked out on the street (all the others had a good view of the grassless, turd-studded yard behind us, where the only living thing was a mangy canine named Roop-Roop). When the cops left, a power truck arrived. A man in spiked shoes climbed the pole between the two apartment houses to examine the transformer. Under other circumstances, this would have absorbed us completely, but not that day. That day we could only wonder if our mother would come and see us in reform school. Eventually, the lights came back on and the power truck went away. We were not caught and lived to fight another day. Dave decided he might build a Super Duper Glider instead of a Super Duper Electromagnet for his science project. I, he told me, would get to take the first ride. Wouldn't that be great?

– 11 –

I was born in 1947 and we didn't get our first television until 1958. The first thing I remember watching on it was *Robot Monster,* a film in which a guy dressed in an ape-suit with a goldfish bowl on his head—Ro-Man, he was called—ran around trying to kill the last survivors of a nuclear war. I felt this was art of quite a high nature.

I also watched *Highway Patrol* with Broderick

Crawford as the fearless Dan Matthews, and *One Step Beyond,* hosted by John Newland, the man with the world's spookiest eyes. There was *Cheyenne* and *Sea Hunt, Your Hit Parade* and *Annie Oakley;* there was Tommy Rettig as the first of Lassie's many friends, Jock Mahoney as *The Range Rider,* and Andy Devine yowling, "Hey, Wild Bill, wait for me!" in his odd, high voice. There was a whole world of vicarious adventure which came packaged in black-and-white, fourteen inches across and sponsored by brand names which still sound like poetry to me. I loved it all.

But TV came relatively late to the King household, and I'm glad. I am, when you stop to think of it, a member of a fairly select group: the final handful of American novelists who learned to read and write before they learned to eat a daily helping of video bull- shit. This might not be important. On the other hand, if you're just starting out as a writer, you could do worse than strip your television's electric plug-wire, wrap a spike around it, and then stick it back into the wall. See what blows, and how far.

Just an idea.

– 12 –

In the late 1950s, a literary agent and compulsive sci- ence fiction memorabilia collector named Forrest J. Ackerman changed the lives of thousands of kids—I was one—when he began editing a magazine called *Famous Monsters of Filmland.* Ask anyone who has been associated with the fantasy–horror–science fiction genres in the last thirty years about this magazine, and you'll get a laugh, a flash of the eyes, and a stream of bright memories—I practically guarantee it.

Around 1960, Forry (who sometimes referred to himself as "the Ackermonster") spun off the short-lived but interesting *Spacemen,* a magazine which covered science fiction films. In 1960, I sent a story to *Spacemen.* It was, as well as I can remember, the first story I ever submitted for publication. I don't recall the title, but I was still in the Ro-Man phase of my development, and this particular tale undoubtedly owed a great deal to the killer ape with the goldfish bowl on his head.

My story was rejected, but Forry kept it. (Forry keeps *everything,* which anyone who has ever toured his house—the Ackermansion—will tell you.) About twenty years later, while I was signing autographs at a Los Angeles bookstore, Forry turned up in line . . . with my story, single-spaced and typed with the long-vanished Royal typewriter my mom gave me for Christmas the year I was eleven. He wanted me to sign it to him, and I guess I did, although the whole encounter was so surreal I can't be completely sure. Talk about your ghosts. Man oh man.

– 13 –

The first story I did actually publish was in a horror fanzine issued by Mike Garrett of Birmingham, Alabama (Mike is still around, and still in the biz). He published this novella under the title "In a Half-World of Terror," but I still like my title much better. Mine was "I Was a Teen-Age Graverobber." Super Duper! Pow!

– 14 –

My first really original story idea—you always know the
first one, I think—came near the end of Ike's eight-year
reign of benignity. I was sitting at the kitchen table of
our house in Durham, Maine, and watching my mother
stick sheets of S&H Green Stamps into a book. (For
more colorful stories about Green Stamps, see *The Liars'
Club.*) Our little family troika had moved back to Maine
so our mom could take care of her parents in their
declining years. Mama was about eighty at that time,
obese and hypertensive and mostly blind; Daddy Guy
was eighty-two, scrawny, morose, and prone to the occasional Donald Duck outburst which only my mother
could understand. Mom called Daddy Guy "Fazza."

My mother's sisters had gotten my mom this job,
perhaps thinking they could kill two birds with one
stone—the aged Ps would be taken care of in a homey
environment by a loving daughter, and The Nagging
Problem of Ruth would be solved. She would no longer
be adrift, trying to take care of two boys while she
floated almost aimlessly from Indiana to Wisconsin to
Connecticut, baking cookies at five in the morning or
pressing sheets in a laundry where the temperatures
often soared to a hundred and ten in the summer and
the foreman gave out salt pills at one and three every
afternoon from July to the end of September.

She hated her new job, I think—in their effort to
take care of her, her sisters turned our self-sufficient,
funny, slightly nutty mother into a sharecropper living a
largely cashless existence. The money the sisters sent her
each month covered the groceries but little else. They

sent boxes of clothes for us. Toward the end of each summer, Uncle Clayt and Aunt Ella (who were not, I think, real relatives at all) would bring cartons of canned vegetables and preserves. The house we lived in belonged to Aunt Ethelyn and Uncle Oren. And once she was there, Mom was caught. She got another actual job after the old folks died, but she lived in that house until the cancer got her. When she left Durham for the last time—David and his wife Linda cared for her during the final weeks of her final illness—I have an idea she was probably more than ready to go.

– 15 –

Let's get one thing clear right now, shall we? There is no Idea Dump, no Story Central, no Island of the Buried Bestsellers; good story ideas seem to come quite literally from nowhere, sailing at you right out of the empty sky: two previously unrelated ideas come together and make something new under the sun. Your job isn't to find these ideas but to recognize them when they show up.

On the day this particular idea—the first really good one—came sailing at me, my mother remarked that she needed six more books of stamps to get a lamp she wanted to give her sister Molly for Christmas, and she didn't think she would make it in time. "I guess it will have to be for her birthday, instead," she said. "These cussed things always look like a lot until you stick them in a book." Then she crossed her eyes and ran her tongue out at me. When she did, I saw her tongue was S&H green. I thought how nice it would be if you could make those damned stamps in your basement, and in that instant a story called "Happy Stamps" was born. The concept of counterfeiting Green Stamps and the sight of my mother's green tongue created it in an instant.

The hero of my story was your classic Poor Schmuck, a guy named Roger who had done jail time twice for counterfeiting money—one more bust would make him a three-time loser. Instead of money, he began to counterfeit Happy Stamps . . . except, he discovered, the design of Happy Stamps was so moronically simple that he wasn't really counterfeiting at all; he was creating reams of the actual article. In a funny scene—probably the first really competent scene I ever wrote—Roger sits in the living room with his old mom, the two of them mooning over the Happy Stamps catalogue while the printing press runs downstairs, ejecting bale after bale of those same trading stamps.

"Great Scott!" Mom says. "According to the fine print, you can get *anything* with Happy Stamps, Roger—you tell them what you want, and they figure out how many books you need to get it. Why, for six or seven million books, we could probably get a Happy Stamps house in the suburbs!"

Roger discovers, however, that although the *stamps* are perfect, the *glue* is defective. If you lap the stamps and stick them in the book they're fine, but if you send them through a mechanical licker, the pink Happy Stamps turn blue. At the end of the story, Roger is in the basement, standing in front of a mirror. Behind him, on the table, are roughly ninety books of Happy Stamps, each book filled with individually licked sheets of stamps. Our hero's lips are pink. He runs out his tongue; that's even pinker. Even his teeth are turning pink. Mom calls cheerily down the stairs, saying she has just gotten off the phone with the Happy Stamps National Redemption Center in Terre Haute, and the lady said they could probably get a nice Tudor home in Weston for only eleven million, six hundred thousand books of Happy Stamps.

"That's nice, Mom," Roger says. He looks at himself a moment longer in the mirror, lips pink and eyes bleak, then slowly returns to the table. Behind him, billions of Happy Stamps are stuffed into basement storage bins. Slowly, our hero opens a fresh stamp-book, then begins to lick sheets and stick them in. Only eleven million, five hundred and ninety thousand books to go, he thinks as the story ends, and Mom can have her Tudor.

There were things wrong with this story (the biggest hole was probably Roger's failure simply to start over with a different glue), but it was cute, it was fairly original, and I knew I had done some pretty good writing. After a long time spent studying the markets in my beat-up *Writer's Digest,* I sent "Happy Stamps" off to *Alfred Hitchcock's Mystery Magazine.* It came back three weeks later with a form rejection slip attached. This slip bore Alfred Hitchcock's unmistakable profile in red ink and wished me good luck with my story. At the bottom was an unsigned jotted message, the only personal response I got from *AHMM* over eight years of periodic submissions. "Don't staple manuscripts," the postscript read. "Loose pages plus paperclip equal correct way to submit copy." This was pretty cold advice, I thought, but useful in its way. I have never stapled a manuscript since.

– 16 –

My room in our Durham house was upstairs, under the eaves. At night I could lie in bed beneath one of these eaves—if I sat up suddenly, I was apt to whack my head a good one—and read by the light of a gooseneck lamp that put an amusing boa constrictor of shadow on the ceiling. Sometimes the house was quiet except for the whoosh of the furnace and the patter of rats in the attic; sometimes my grandmother would spend an hour or so around midnight yelling for someone to check Dick—she was afraid he hadn't been fed. Dick, a horse she'd had in her days as a schoolteacher, was at least forty years dead. I had a desk beneath the room's other eave, my old Royal typewriter, and a hundred or so paperback books, mostly science fiction, which I lined up along the baseboard. On my bureau was a Bible won for memorizing verses in Methodist Youth Fellowship and a Webcor phonograph with an automatic changer and a turntable covered in soft green velvet. On it I played my records, mostly 45s by Elvis, Chuck Berry, Freddy Cannon, and Fats Domino. I liked Fats; he knew how to rock, and you could tell he was having fun.

When I got the rejection slip from *AHMM,* I pounded a nail into the wall above the Webcor, wrote "Happy Stamps" on the rejection slip, and poked it onto the nail. Then I sat on my bed and listened to Fats sing "I'm Ready." I felt pretty good, actually. When you're still too young to shave, optimism is a perfectly legitimate response to failure.

By the time I was fourteen (and shaving twice a week whether I needed to or not) the nail in my wall would no longer support the weight of the rejection slips impaled upon it. I replaced the nail with a spike and went on writing. By the time I was sixteen I'd begun to get rejection slips with handwritten notes a little more encouraging than the advice to stop using staples and start using paperclips. The first of these hopeful notes was from Algis Budrys, then the editor of *Fantasy and Science Fiction,* who read a story of mine called "The Night of the Tiger" (the inspiration was, I think, an episode of *The Fugitive* in which Dr. Richard Kimble worked as an attendant cleaning out cages in a zoo or a circus) and wrote: "This is good. Not for us, but good. You have talent. Submit again."

Those four brief sentences, scribbled by a fountain pen that left big ragged blotches in its wake, brightened the dismal winter of my sixteenth year. Ten years or so later, after I'd sold a couple of novels, I discovered "The Night of the Tiger" in a box of old manuscripts and thought it was still a perfectly respectable tale, albeit one obviously written by a guy who had only begun to learn his chops. I rewrote it and on a whim resubmitted it to *F&SF.* This time they bought it. One thing I've noticed is that when you've had a little success, magazines are a lot less apt to use that phrase, "Not for us."

– 17 –

Although he was a year younger than his classmates, my big brother was bored with high school. Some of this had to do with his intellect—Dave's IQ tested in the 150s or 160s—but I think it was mostly his restless nature. For Dave, high school just wasn't super duper enough—there was no pow, no wham, no *fun*. He solved the problem, at least temporarily, by creating a newspaper which he called *Dave's Rag*.

The *Rag*'s office was a table located in the dirt-floored, rock-walled, spider-infested confines of our basement, somewhere north of the furnace and east of the root-cellar, where Clayt and Ella's endless cartons of preserves and canned vegetables were kept. The *Rag* was an odd combination of family newsletter and small-town bi-weekly. Sometimes it was a monthly, if Dave got sidetracked by other interests (maple-sugaring, cider-making, rocket-building, and car-customizing, just to name a few), and then there would be jokes I didn't understand about how Dave's *Rag* was a little late this month or how we shouldn't bother Dave, because he was down in the basement, on the *Rag*.

Jokes or no jokes, circulation rose slowly from about five copies per issue (sold to nearby family members) to something like fifty or sixty, with our relatives and the relatives of neighbors in our small town (Durham's population in 1962 was about nine hundred) eagerly awaiting each new edition. A typical number would let people know how Charley Harrington's broken leg was mending, what guest speakers might be coming to the West Durham Methodist Church, how much water the

King boys were hauling from the town pump to keep from draining the well behind the house (of course it went dry every fucking summer no matter how much water we hauled), who was visiting the Browns or the Halls on the other side of Methodist Corners, and whose relatives were due to hit town each summer. Dave also included sports, word-games, weather reports ("It's been pretty dry, but local farmer Harold Davis says if we don't have at least one good rain in August he will smile and kiss a pig"), recipes, a continuing story (I wrote that), and Dave's Jokes and Humor, which included nuggets like these:

Stan: "What did the beaver say to the oak tree?"
Jan: "It was nice gnawing you!"

1st Beatnik: "How do you get to Carnegie Hall?"
2nd Beatnik: "Practice man practice!"

During the *Rag*'s first year, the print was purple—those issues were produced on a flat plate of jelly called a hectograph. My brother quickly decided the hectograph was a pain in the butt. It was just too slow for him. Even as a kid in short pants, Dave hated to be halted. Whenever Milt, our mom's boyfriend ("Sweeter than smart," Mom said to me one day a few months after she dropped him), got stuck in traffic or at a stoplight, Dave would lean over from the back seat of Milt's Buick and yell, "Drive over em, Uncle Milt! Drive over em!"

As a teenager, waiting for the hectograph to "freshen" between pages printed (while "freshening," the print would melt into a vague purple membrane which hung in the jelly like a manatee's shadow) drove David all but insane with impatience. Also, he badly wanted to add photographs to the newspaper. He took good ones, and by age sixteen he was developing them, as well. He rigged a darkroom in a closet and from its tiny, chemical-stinking confines produced pictures which were often startling in their clarity and composition (the photo on the back of *The Regulators,* showing me with a copy of the magazine containing my first published story, was taken by Dave with an old Kodak and developed in his closet darkroom).

In addition to these frustrations, the flats of hectograph jelly had a tendency to incubate and support colonies of strange, sporelike growths in the unsavory atmosphere of our basement, no matter how meticulous we were about covering the damned old slow-coach thing once the day's printing chores were done. What looked fairly ordinary on Monday sometimes looked like something out of an H. P. Lovecraft horror tale by the weekend.

In Brunswick, where he went to high school, Dave found a shop with a small drum printing press for sale. It worked—barely. You typed up your copy on stencils which could be purchased in a local office-supply store for nineteen cents apiece—my brother called this chore "cutting stencil," and it was usually my job, as I was less prone to make typing errors. The stencils were attached to the drum of the press, lathered up with the world's stinkiest, oogiest ink, and then you were off to the races—crank 'til your arm falls off, son. We were able to put together in two nights what had previously taken a week with the hectograph, and while the drum-press was messy, it did not look infected with a potentially fatal disease. *Dave's Rag* entered its brief golden age.

– 18 –

I wasn't much interested in the printing process, and I wasn't interested at all in the arcana of first developing and then reproducing photographs. I didn't care about putting Hurst shifters in cars, making cider, or seeing if a certain formula would send a plastic rocket into the stratosphere (usually they didn't even make it over the house). What I cared about most between 1958 and 1966 was movies.

As the fifties gave way to the sixties, there were only two movie theaters in the area, both in Lewiston. The Empire was the first-run house, showing Disney pictures, Bible epics, and musicals in which widescreen ensembles of well-scrubbed folks danced and sang. I went to these if I had a ride—a movie was a movie, after all—but I didn't like them very much. They were boringly wholesome. They were predictable. During *The Parent Trap,* I kept hoping Hayley Mills would run into Vic Morrow from *The Blackboard Jungle.* That would have livened things up a little, by God. I felt that one look at Vic's switchblade knife and gimlet gaze would have put Hayley's piddling domestic problems in some kind of reasonable perspective. And when I lay in bed at night under my eave, listening to the wind in the trees or the rats in the attic, it was not Debbie Reynolds as

Tammy or Sandra Dee as Gidget that I dreamed of, but Yvette Vickers from *Attack of the Giant Leeches* or Luana Anders from *Dementia 13*. Never mind sweet; never mind uplifting; never mind Snow White and the Seven Goddam Dwarfs. At thirteen I wanted monsters that ate whole cities, radioactive corpses that came out of the ocean and ate surfers, and girls in black bras who looked like trailer trash.

Horror movies, science fiction movies, movies about teenage gangs on the prowl, movies about losers on motorcycles—this was the stuff that turned my dials up to ten. The place to get all of this was not at the Empire, on the upper end of Lisbon Street, but at the Ritz, down at the lower end, amid the pawnshops and not far from Louie's Clothing, where in 1964 I bought my first pair of Beatle boots. The distance from my house to the Ritz was fourteen miles, and I hitchhiked there almost every weekend during the eight years between 1958 and 1966, when I finally got my driver's license. Sometimes I went with my friend Chris Chesley, sometimes I went alone, but unless I was sick or something, I always went. It was at the Ritz that I saw *I Married a Monster from Outer Space,* with Tom Tryon; *The Haunting,* with Claire Bloom and Julie Harris; *The Wild Angels,* with Peter Fonda and Nancy Sinatra. I saw Olivia de Havilland put out James Caan's eyes with makeshift knives in *Lady in a Cage,* saw Joseph Cotten come back from the dead in *Hush . . . Hush, Sweet Charlotte,* and watched with held breath (and not a little prurient interest) to see if Allison Hayes would grow all the way out of her clothes in *Attack of the 50 Ft. Woman.* At the Ritz, all the finer things in life were available . . . or *might be* available, if you only sat in the third row, paid close attention, and did not blink at the wrong moment.

Chris and I liked just about any horror movie, but our faves were the string of American-International films, most directed by Roger Corman, with titles cribbed from Edgar Allan Poe. I wouldn't say *based upon* the works of Edgar Allan Poe, because there is little in any of them which has anything to do with Poe's actual stories and poems (*The Raven* was filmed as a comedy—no kidding). And yet the best of them—*The Haunted Palace, The Conqueror Worm, The Masque of the Red Death*— achieved a hallucinatory eeriness that made them special. Chris and I had our own name for these films, one that made them into a separate genre. There were westerns, there were love stories, there were war stories . . . and there were Poepictures.

"Wanna hitch to the show Saturday afternoon?" Chris would ask. "Go to the Ritz?"

"What's on?" I'd ask.

"A motorcycle picture and a Poepicture," he'd say. I, of course, was on that combo like white on rice. Bruce Dern going batshit on a Harley and Vincent Price going batshit in a haunted castle overlooking a restless ocean: who could ask for more? You might even get Hazel Court wandering around in a lacy low-cut night-gown, if you were lucky.

Of all the Poepictures, the one that affected Chris and me the most deeply was *The Pit and the Pendulum*. Written by Richard Matheson and filmed in both widescreen and Technicolor (color horror pictures were still a rarity in 1961, when this one came out), *Pit* took a bunch of standard gothic ingredients and turned them into something special. It might have been the last really great studio horror picture before George Romero's ferocious indie *The Night of the Living Dead* came along and changed everything forever (in some few cases for the better, in most for the worse). The best scene—the one which froze Chris and me into our seats—depicted John Kerr digging into a castle wall and discovering the corpse of his sister, who was obviously buried alive. I have never forgotten the corpse's close-up, shot through a red filter and a distorting lens which elongated the face into a huge silent scream.

On the long hitch home that night (if rides were slow in coming, you might end up walking four or five miles and not get home until well after dark) I had a wonderful idea: I would turn *The Pit and the Pendulum* into a book! Would novelize it, as Monarch Books had novelized such undying film classics as *Jack the Ripper, Gorgo,* and *Konga.* But I wouldn't just write this masterpiece; I would also print it, using the drum-press in our basement, and sell copies at school! Zap! Ka-pow!

As it was conceived, so was it done. Working with the care and deliberation for which I would later be critically acclaimed, I turned out my "novel version" of *The Pit and the Pendulum* in two days, composing directly onto the stencils from which I'd print. Although no copies of that particular masterpiece survive (at least to my knowledge), I believe it was eight pages long, each page single-spaced and paragraph breaks kept to an absolute minimum (each stencil cost nineteen cents, remember). I printed sheets on both sides, just as in a standard book, and added a title page on which I drew a rudimentary pendulum dripping small black blotches which

I hoped would look like blood. At the last moment I realized I had forgotten to identify the publishing house. After a half-hour or so of pleasant mulling, I typed the words A V.I.B. BOOK in the upper right corner of my title page. V.I.B. stood for Very Important Book.

I ran off about forty copies of *The Pit and the Pendulum,* blissfully unaware that I was in violation of every plagiarism and copyright statute in the history of the world; my thoughts were focused almost entirely on how much money I might make if my story was a hit at school. The stencils had cost me $1.71 (having to use up one whole stencil for the title page seemed a hideous waste of money, but you had to look good, I'd reluctantly decided; you had to go out there with a bit of the old attitude), the paper had cost another two bits or so, the staples were free, cribbed from my brother (you might have to paperclip stories you were sending out to magazines, but this was a *book,* this was the bigtime). After some further thought, I priced V.I.B. #1, *The Pit and the Pendulum* by Steve King, at a quarter a copy. I thought I might be able to sell ten (my mother would buy one to get me started; she could always be counted on), and that would add up to $2.50. I'd make about forty cents, which would be enough to finance another educational trip to the Ritz. If I sold two more, I could get a big sack of popcorn and a Coke, as well.

The Pit and the Pendulum turned out to be my first best-seller. I took the entire print-run to school in my book-bag (in 1961 I would have been an eighth-grader at Durham's newly built four-room elementary school), and by noon that day I had sold two dozen. By the end of lunch hour, when word had gotten around about the lady buried in the wall ("They stared with horror at the bones sticking out from the ends of her fingers, realizing she had died scratcheing madley for escape"), I had sold three dozen. I had nine dollars in change weighing down the bottom of my book-bag (upon which Durham's answer to Daddy Cool had carefully printed most of the lyrics to "The Lion Sleeps Tonight") and was walking around in a kind of dream, unable to believe my sudden ascension to previously unsuspected realms of wealth. It all seemed too good to be true.

It was. When the school day ended at two o'clock, I was summoned to the principal's office, where I was told I couldn't turn the school into a marketplace, especially not, Miss Hisler said, to sell such trash as *The Pit and the Pendulum.* Her attitude didn't much surprise me. Miss Hisler had been the teacher at my previous school, the one-roomer at Methodist Corners, where I went to the fifth and sixth grades. During that time she had spied me reading a rather sensational "teenage rumble" novel (*The Amboy Dukes,* by Irving Shulman), and had taken it away. This was just more of the same, and I was disgusted with myself for not seeing the outcome in advance. In those days we called someone who did an idiotic thing a dubber (pronounced *dubba* if you were from Maine). I had just dubbed up bigtime.

"What I don't understand, Stevie," she said, "is why you'd write junk like this in the first place. You're talented. Why do you want to waste your abilities?" She had rolled up a copy of V.I.B. #1 and was brandishing it at me the way a person might brandish a rolled-up newspaper at a dog that has piddled on the rug. She waited for me to answer—to her credit, the question was not entirely rhetorical—but I had no answer to give. I was ashamed. I have spent a good many years since—too many, I think—being ashamed about what I write. I think I was forty before I realized that almost every writer of fiction and poetry who has ever published a line has been accused by someone of wasting his or her God-given talent. If you write (or paint or dance or sculpt or sing, I suppose), someone will try to make you feel lousy about it, that's all. I'm not editorializing, just trying to give you the facts as I see them.

Miss Hisler told me I would have to give everyone's money back. I did so with no argument, even to those kids (and there were quite a few, I'm happy to say) who insisted on keeping their copies of V.I.B. #1. I ended up losing money on the deal after all, but when summer vacation came I printed four dozen copies of a new story, an original called *The Invasion of the Star-Creatures,* and sold all but four or five. I guess that means I won in the end, at least in a financial sense. But in my heart I stayed ashamed. I kept hearing Miss Hisler asking why I wanted to waste my talent, why I wanted to waste my time, why I wanted to write junk.

– 19 –

Doing a serial story for *Dave's Rag* was fun, but my other journalistic duties bored me. Still, I had worked for a newspaper of sorts, word got around, and during my sophomore year at Lisbon High I became editor of our school newspaper, *The Drum.* I don't recall being given any choice in this matter; I think I was simply appointed. My second-in-command, Danny Emond, had even less interest in the paper than I did. Danny just liked the idea that Room 4, where we did our work, was near the girls' bathroom. "Someday I'll just go crazy and hack my way in there, Steve," he told me on more than one occasion. "Hack, hack, hack." Once he added, perhaps in an effort to justify himself: "The prettiest girls in school pull up their skirts in there." This struck me as so fundamentally stupid it might actually be wise, like a Zen koan or an early story by John Updike.

The Drum did not prosper under my editorship. Then as now, I tend to go through periods of idleness followed by periods of workaholic frenzy. In the schoolyear 1963–1964, *The Drum* published just one issue, but that one was a monster thicker than the Lisbon Falls telephone book. One night—sick to death of Class Reports, Cheerleading Updates, and some lamebrain's efforts to write a school poem—I created a satiric high school newspaper of my own when I should have been captioning photographs for *The Drum.* What resulted was a four-sheet which I called *The Village Vomit.* The boxed motto in the upper lefthand corner was not "All the News That's Fit to Print" but "All the Shit That Will Stick." That piece of dimwit humor got me into the only real trouble of my high school career. It also led me to the most useful writing lesson I ever got.

In typical *Mad* magazine style ("What, me worry?"), I filled the *Vomit* with fictional tidbits about the LHS faculty, using teacher nicknames the student body would immediately recognize. Thus Miss Raypach, the study-hall monitor, became Miss Rat

Pack; Mr. Ricker, the college-track English teacher (and the school's most urbane faculty member—he looked quite a bit like Craig Stevens in *Peter Gunn*), became Cow Man because his family owned Ricker Dairy; Mr. Diehl, the earth-science teacher, became Old Raw Diehl.

As all sophomoric humorists must be, I was totally blown away by my own wit. What a funny fellow I was! A regular mill-town H. L. Mencken! I simply must take the *Vomit* to school and show all my friends! They would bust a collective gut!

As a matter of fact, they *did* bust a collective gut; I had some good ideas about what tickled the funnybones of high school kids, and most of them were showcased in *The Village Vomit*. In one article, Cow Man's prize Jersey won a livestock farting contest at Topsham Fair; in another, Old Raw Diehl was fired for sticking the eyeballs of specimen fetal pigs up his nostrils. Humor in the grand Swiftian manner, you see. Pretty sophisticated, eh?

During period four, three of my friends were laughing so hard in the back of study-hall that Miss Raypach (Rat Pack to you, chum) crept up on them to see what was so funny. She confiscated *The Village Vomit,* on which I had, either out of overweening pride or almost unbelievable naiveté, put my name as Editor in Chief & Grand High Poobah, and at the close of school I was for the second time in my student career summoned to the office on account of something I had written.

This time the trouble was a good deal more serious. Most of the teachers were inclined to be good sports about my teasing—even Old Raw Diehl was willing to let bygones be bygones concerning the pigs' eyeballs—but one was not. This was Miss Margitan, who taught shorthand and typing to the girls in the business courses. She commanded both respect and fear; in the tradition of teachers from an earlier era, Miss Margitan did not want to be your pal, your psychologist, or your inspiration. She was there to teach business skills, and she wanted all learning to be done by the rules. *Her* rules. Girls in Miss Margitan's classes were sometimes asked to kneel on the floor, and if the hems of their skirts didn't touch the linoleum, they were sent home to change. No amount of tearful begging could soften her, no reasoning could modify her view of the world. Her detention lists were the longest of any teacher in the school, but her girls were routinely selected as valedictorians or salutatorians and usually went on to good jobs. Many came to love her. Others loathed her then and likely still do now, all these years later. These latter girls called her "Maggot" Margitan, as their mothers had no doubt before them. And in *The Village Vomit* I had an item which began, "Miss Margitan, known affectionately to Lisbonians everywhere as Maggot . . ."

Mr. Higgins, our bald principal (breezily referred to in the *Vomit* as Old Cue-Ball), told me that Miss Margitan had been very hurt and very upset by what I had written. She was apparently not too hurt to remember that old scriptural admonition which goes "Vengeance is mine, saith the shorthand teacher," however; Mr. Higgins said she wanted me suspended from school.

In my character, a kind of wildness and a deep conservatism are ound together like hair in a braid. It was the crazy part of me that had first written *The Village Vomit* and then carried it to school; now that troublesome Mr. Hyde had dubbed up and slunk out the back door. Dr. Jekyll was left to consider how my mom would look at me if she found out I had been suspended—her hurt eyes. I had to put thoughts of her out of my mind, and fast. I was a sophomore, I was a year older than most others in my class, and at six feet two I was one of the bigger boys in school. I desperately didn't want to cry in Mr. Higgins's office—not with kids surging through the halls and looking curiously in the window at us: Mr. Higgins behind his desk, me in the Bad Boy Seat.

In the end, Miss Margitan settled for a formal apology and two weeks of detention for the bad boy who had dared call her Maggot in print. It was bad, but what in high school is not? At the time we're stuck in it, like hostages locked in a Turkish bath, high school seems the most serious business in the world to just about all of us. It's not until the second or third class reunion that we start realizing how absurd the whole thing was.

A day or two later I was ushered into Mr. Higgins's office and made to stand in front of her. Miss Margitan sat ramrod-straight with her arthritic hands folded in her lap and her gray eyes fixed unflinchingly on my face, and I realized that something about her was different from any other adult I had ever met. I didn't pinpoint that difference at once, but I knew that there would be no charming this lady, no winning her over. Later, while I was flying paper planes with the other bad boys and bad girls in detention hall (detention turned out to be not so bad), I decided that it was pretty simple: Miss Margitan didn't like boys. She was the first woman I ever met in my life who didn't like boys, not even one little bit.

If it makes any difference, my apology was heartfelt. Miss Margitan really had been hurt by what I wrote, and that much I could understand. I doubt that she hated me—she was probably too busy—but she was the National Honor Society advisor at LHS, and when my name showed up on the candidate list two years later, she vetoed me. The Honor Society did not need boys "of his type," she said. I have come to believe she was right. A boy who once wiped his ass with poison ivy probably doesn't belong in a smart people's club.

I haven't trucked much with satire since then.

– 20 –

Hardly a week after being sprung from detention hall, I was once more invited to step down to the principal's office. I went with a sinking heart, wondering what new shit I'd stepped in.

It wasn't Mr. Higgins who wanted to see me, at least; this time the school guidance counsellor had issued the summons. There had been discussions about me, he said, and how to turn my "restless pen" into more constructive channels. He had enquired of John Gould, editor of Lisbon's weekly newspaper, and had discovered Gould had an opening for a sports reporter. While the school couldn't *insist* that I take this job, everyone in the front office felt it would be a good idea. *Do it or die,* the G.C.'s eyes suggested. Maybe that was just paranoia, but even now, almost forty years later, I don't think so.

I groaned inside. I was shut of *Dave's Rag,* almost shut of *The Drum,* and now here was the Lisbon *Weekly Enterprise.* Instead of being haunted by waters, like Norman Maclean in *A River Runs Through It,* I was as a teenager haunted by newspapers. Still, what could I do? I rechecked the look in the guidance counsellor's eyes and said I would be delighted to interview for the job.

Gould—not the well-known New England humorist or the novelist who wrote *The Greenleaf Fires* but a relation of both, I think—greeted me warily but with some interest. We would try each other out, he said, if that suited me.

Now that I was away from the administrative offices of Lisbon High, I felt able to muster a little honesty. I told Mr. Gould that I didn't know much about sports. Gould said, "These are games people understand when they're watching them drunk in bars. You'll learn if you try."

He gave me a huge roll of yellow paper on which to type my copy—I think I still have it somewhere—and promised me a wage of half a cent a word. It was the first time someone had promised me wages for writing.

The first two pieces I turned in had to do with a basketball game in which an LHS player broke the school scoring record. One was a straight piece of reporting. The other was a sidebar about Robert Ransom's record-breaking performance. I brought both to Gould the day after the game so he'd have them for Friday, which was when the paper came out. He read the game piece, made two minor corrections, and spiked it. Then he started in on the feature piece with a large black pen.

I took my fair share of English Lit classes in my two remaining years at Lisbon, and my fair share of composition, fiction, and poetry classes in college, but John Gould taught me more than any of them, and in no more than ten minutes. I wish I still had the piece—it deserves to be framed, editorial corrections and all—but I can remember pretty well how it went and how it looked after Gould had combed through it with that black pen of his. Here's an example:

> Last night, in the ~~well-loved~~ gymnasium of Lisbon High School, partisans and Jay Hills fans alike were stunned by an athletic performance unequalled in school history. Bob Ransom, ~~known as "Bullet" Bob for both his size and accuracy,~~ scored thirty-seven points. Yes, you heard me right. ~~B~~He did it with grace, speed . . . and with an odd courtesy as well, committing only two personal fouls in his ~~knight-like~~ quest for a record which has eluded Lisbon ~~thinclads~~ players since ~~the years of Korea~~ 1953 . . .

Gould stopped at "the years of Korea" and looked up at me. "What year was the last record made?" he asked.

Luckily, I had my notes. "1953," I said. Gould grunted and went back to work. When he finished marking my copy in the manner indicated above, he looked up and saw something on my face. I think he must have mistaken it for horror. It wasn't; it was pure revelation. Why, I wondered, didn't English teachers ever do this? It was like the Visible Man Old Raw Diehl had on his desk in the biology room.

"I only took out the bad parts, you know," Gould said. "Most of it's pretty good."

"I know," I said, meaning both things: yes, most of it was good—okay anyway, serviceable—and yes, he had only taken out the bad parts. "I won't do it again."

He laughed. "If that's true, you'll never have to work for a living. You can do *this* instead. Do I have to explain any of these marks?"

"No," I said.

"When you write a story, you're telling yourself the story," he said. "When you rewrite, your main job is taking out all the things that are *not* the story."

Gould said something else that was interesting on the day I turned in my first two pieces: write with the door closed, rewrite with the door open. Your stuff starts out being just for you, in other words, but then it goes out. Once you know what the story is and get it right—as right as you can, anyway—it belongs to anyone who wants to read it. Or criticize it. If you're very lucky (this is my idea, not John Gould's, but I believe he would have subscribed to the notion), more will want to do the former than the latter.

– 21 –

Just after the senior class trip to Washington, D.C., I got a job at Worumbo Mills and Weaving, in Lisbon Falls. I didn't want it—the work was hard and boring, the mill itself a dingy fuckhole overhanging the polluted

Androscoggin River like a workhouse in a Charles Dickens novel—but I needed the paycheck. My mother was making lousy wages as a housekeeper at a facility for the mentally ill in New Gloucester, but she was determined I was going to college like my brother David (University of Maine, class of '66, *cum laude*). In her mind, the education had become almost secondary. Durham and Lisbon Falls and the University of Maine at Orono were part of a small world where folks neighbored and still minded each other's business on the four- and six-party lines which then served the Sticksville townships. In the big world, boys who didn't go to college were being sent overseas to fight in Mr. Johnson's undeclared war, and many of them were coming home in boxes. My mother liked Lyndon's War on Poverty ("That's the war *I'm* in," she sometimes said), but not what he was up to in Southeast Asia. Once I told her that enlisting and going over there might be good for me—surely there would be a book in it, I said.

"Don't be an idiot, Stephen," she said. "With your eyes, you'd be the first one to get shot. You can't write if you're dead."

She meant it; her head was set and so was her heart. Consequently, I applied for scholarships, I applied for loans, and I went to work in the mill. I certainly wouldn't get far on the five and six dollars a week I could make writing about bowling tournaments and Soap Box Derby races for the *Enterprise*.

During my final weeks at Lisbon High, my schedule looked like this: up at seven, off to school at seven-thirty, last bell at two o'clock, punch in on the third floor of Worumbo at 2:58, bag loose fabric for eight hours, punch out at 11:02, get home around quarter of twelve, eat a bowl of cereal, fall into bed, get up the next morning, do it all again. On a few occasions I worked double shifts, slept in my '60 Ford Galaxie (Dave's old car) for an hour or so before school, then slept through periods five and six in the nurse's cubicle after lunch.

Once summer vacation came, things got easier. I was moved down to the dyehouse in the basement, for one thing, where it was thirty degrees cooler. My job was dyeing swatches of melton cloth purple or navy blue. I imagine there are still folks in New England with jackets in their closets dyed by yours truly. It wasn't the best summer I ever spent, but I managed to avoid being sucked into the machinery or stitching my fingers together with one of the heavy-duty sewing machines we used to belt the undyed cloth.

During Fourth of July week, the mill closed. Employees with five years or more at Worumbo got the week off with pay. Those with fewer than five years were offered work on a crew that was going to clean the mill from top to bottom, including the basement, which hadn't been touched in forty or fifty years. I probably would have agreed to work on this crew—it was time and a half—but all the positions were filled long before the foreman got down to the high school kids, who'd be gone in September. When I got back to work the following week, one of the dyehouse guys told me I should have been there, it was wild. "The rats down in that basement were big as cats," he said. "Some of them, goddam if they weren't as big as *dogs*."

Rats as big as dogs! Yow!

One day late in my final semester at college, finals

over and at loose ends, I recalled the dyehouse guy's story about the rats under the mill—big as cats, goddam, some as big as *dogs*—and started writing a story called "Graveyard Shift." I was only passing the time on a late spring afternoon, but two months later *Cavalier* magazine bought the story for two hundred dollars. I had sold two other stories previous to this, but they had brought in a total of just sixty-five dollars. This was three times that, and at a single stroke. It took my breath away, it did. I was rich.

– 22 –

During the summer of 1969 I got a work-study job in the University of Maine library. That was a season both fair and foul. In Vietnam, Nixon was executing his plan to end the war, which seemed to consist of bombing most of Southeast Asia into Kibbles 'n Bits. "Meet the new boss," The Who sang, "same as the old boss." Eugene McCarthy was concentrating on his poetry, and happy hippies wore bell-bottom pants and tee-shirts that said things like KILLING FOR PEACE IS LIKE FUCKING FOR CHASTITY. I had a great set of muttonchop sideburns. Creedence Clearwater Revival was singing "Green River"—barefoot girls, dancing in the moonlight—and Kenny Rogers was still with The First Edition. Martin Luther King and Robert Kennedy were dead, but Janis Joplin, Jim Morrison, Bob "The Bear" Hite, Jimi Hendrix, Cass Elliot, John Lennon, and Elvis Presley were still alive and making music. I was staying just off campus in Ed Price's Rooms (seven bucks a week, one change of sheets included). Men had landed on the moon, and I had landed on the Dean's List. Miracles and wonders abounded.

One day in late June of that summer, a bunch of us library guys had lunch on the grass behind the university bookstore. Sitting between Paolo Silva and Eddie Marsh was a trim girl with a raucous laugh, red-tinted hair, and the prettiest legs I had ever seen, well-displayed beneath a short yellow skirt. She was carrying a copy of *Soul on Ice,* by Eldridge Cleaver. I hadn't run across her in the library, and I didn't believe a college student could utter such a wonderful, unafraid laugh. Also, heavy reading or no heavy reading, she swore like a millworker instead of a coed. (Having been a millworker, I was qualified to judge.) Her name was Tabitha Spruce. We got married a year and a half later. We're still married, and she has never let me forget that the first time I met her I thought she was Eddie Marsh's townie girlfriend. Maybe a book-reading waitress from the local pizza joint on her afternoon off.

– 23 –

It's worked. Our marriage has outlasted all of the world's leaders except for Castro, and if we keep talking, arguing, making love, and dancing to the Ramones— gabba-gabba-hey—it'll probably keep working. We came from different religions, but as a feminist Tabby has never been crazy about the Catholics, where the men make the rules (including the God-given directive to always go in bareback) and the women wash the underwear. And while I believe in God I have no use for organized religion. We came from similar working-class backgrounds, we both ate meat, we were both political Democrats with typical Yankee suspicions of life outside New England. We were sexually compatible and monogamous by nature. Yet what ties us most strongly are the words, the language, and the work of our lives.

We met when we were working in a library, and I fell in love with her during a poetry workshop in the fall of 1969, when I was a senior and Tabby was a junior. I fell in love with her partly because I understood what she was doing with her work. I fell because *she* understood what she was doing with it. I also fell because she was wearing a sexy black dress and silk stockings, the kind that hook with garters.

I don't want to speak too disparagingly of my generation (actually I do, we had a chance to change the world and opted for the Home Shopping Network instead), but there was a view among the student writers I knew at that time that good writing came spontaneously, in an uprush of feeling that had to be caught at once; when you were building that all-important stairway to heaven, you couldn't just stand around with your hammer in your hand. *Ars poetica* in 1969 was perhaps best expressed by a Donovan Leitch song that went, "First there is a mountain / Then there is no mountain / Then there is." Would-be poets were living in a dewy Tolkien-tinged world, catching poems out of the ether. It was pretty much unanimous: serious art came from . . . *out there!* Writers were blessed stenographers taking divine dictation. I don't want to embarrass any of my old mates from that period, so here is a

fictionalized version of what I'm talking about, created
from bits of many actual poems:

> i close my eyes
> in th dark i see
> Rodan   Rimbaud
> in th dark
> i swallow th cloth
> of loneliness
> crow i am here
> raven i am here

If you were to ask the poet what this poem *meant,*
you'd likely get a look of contempt. A slightly uncomfortable silence was apt to emanate from the rest.
Certainly the fact that the poet would likely have been
unable to tell you anything about the mechanics of creation would not have been considered important. If
pressed, he or she might have said that there *were* no
mechanics, only that seminal spurt of feeling: first
there is a mountain, then there is no mountain, then
there is. And if the resulting poem is sloppy, based on
the assumption that such general words as "loneliness"
mean the same thing to all of us—hey man, so what,
let go of that outdated bullshit and just dig the heavi-
ness. I didn't cop to much of this attitude (although I
didn't dare say so out loud, at least not in so many
words), and was overjoyed to find that the pretty girl
in the black dress and the silk stockings didn't cop to
much of it, either. She didn't come right out and say
so, but she didn't need to. Her work spoke for her.

The workshop group met once or twice a week in the
living room of instructor Jim Bishop's house, perhaps a

dozen undergrads and three or four faculty members working in a marvellous atmosphere of equality. Poems were typed up and mimeographed in the English Department office on the day of each workshop. Poets read while the rest of us followed along on our copies. Here is one of Tabby's poems from that fall:

A GRADUAL CANTICLE FOR AUGUSTINE

The thinnest bear is awakened in the winter
by the sleep-laughter of locusts,
by the dream-blustering of bees,
by the honeyed scent of desert sands
that the wind carries in her womb
into the distant hills, into the houses of Cedar.

The bear has heard a sure promise.
Certain words are edible; they nourish
more than snow heaped upon silver plates
or ice overflowing golden bowls. Chips of ice
from the mouth of a lover are not always better,
Nor a desert dreaming always a mirage.
The rising bear sings a gradual canticle
woven of sand that conquers cities
by a slow cycle. His praise seduces
a passing wind, traveling to the sea
wherein a fish, caught in a careful net,
hears a bear's song in the cool-scented snow.

There was silence when Tabby finished reading. No one knew exactly how to react. Cables seemed to run through the poem, tightening the lines until they almost hummed. I found the combination of crafty diction and delirious imagery exciting and illuminating. Her poem also made me feel that I wasn't alone in my belief that good writing can be simultaneously intoxicating and idea-driven. If stone-sober people can fuck like they're out of their minds—can actually be out of their minds while caught in that throe—why shouldn't writers be able to go bonkers and still stay sane?

There was also a work-ethic in the poem that I liked, something that suggested writing poems (or stories, or essays) had as much in common with sweeping the floor as with mythy moments of revelation. There's a place in *A Raisin in the Sun* where a character cries out: "I want to fly! I want to touch the sun!" to which his wife replies, "First eat your eggs."

In the discussion that followed Tab's reading, it became clear to me that she understood her own poem. She knew exactly what she had meant to say, and had said most of it. Saint Augustine (A.D. 354–430) she knew both as a Catholic and as a history major. Augustine's mother (a saint herself) was a Christian, his father a pagan. Before his conversion, Augustine pursued both money and women. Following it he continued to struggle with his sexual impulses, and is known for the Libertine's Prayer, which goes: "O Lord, make me chaste . . . but not yet." In his writing he focused on man's struggle to give up belief in self in favor of belief in God. And he sometimes likened himself to a bear. Tabby has a way of tilting her chin down when she smiles—it makes her look both wise and severely cute. She did that then, I remember, and said, "Besides, I like bears."

The canticle is gradual perhaps because the bear's

awakening is gradual. The bear is powerful and sensual, although thin because he is out of his time. In a way, Tabby said when called upon to explicate, the bear can be seen as a symbol of mankind's troubling and wonderful habit of dreaming the right dreams at the wrong time. Such dreams are difficult because they're inappropriate, but also wonderful in their promise. The poem also suggests that dreams are powerful—the bear's is strong enough to seduce the wind into bringing his song to a fish caught in a net.

I won't try to argue that "A Gradual Canticle" is a great poem (although I think it's a pretty good one). The point is that it was a reasonable poem in a hysterical time, one sprung from a writing ethic that resonated all through my heart and soul.

Tabby was in one of Jim Bishop's rocking chairs that night. I was sitting on the floor beside her. I put my hand on her calf as she spoke, cupping the curve of warm flesh through her stocking. She smiled at me. I smiled back. Sometimes these things are not accidents. I'm almost sure of it.

– 24 –

We had two kids by the time we'd been married three years. They were neither planned nor unplanned; they came when they came, and we were glad to have them. Naomi was prone to ear infections. Joe was healthy enough but never seemed to sleep. When Tabby went into labor with him, I was at a drive-in movie in Brewer with a friend—it was a Memorial Day triple feature, three horror films. We were on the third movie *(The Corpse Grinders)* and the second sixpack when the guy in the office broke in with an announcement. There were still pole-speakers in those days; when you parked your car you lifted one off and hung it over your window. The manager's announcement thus rang across the entire parking lot: *"STEVE KING, PLEASE GO HOME! YOUR WIFE IS IN LABOR! STEVE KING, PLEASE GO HOME! YOUR WIFE IS GOING TO HAVE THE BABY!"*

As I drove our old Plymouth toward the exit, a couple of hundred horns blared a satiric salute. Many people flicked their headlights on and off, bathing me in a stuttery glow. My friend Jimmy Smith laughed so hard he slid into the footwell on the passenger side of the front seat. There he remained for most of the trip back to Bangor, chortling among the beercans. When I got home, Tabby was calm and packed. She gave birth to Joe less than three hours later. He entered the world easily. For the next five years or so, nothing else about Joe was easy. But he was a treat. Both of them were, really. Even when Naomi was tearing off the wallpaper above her crib (maybe she thought she was housekeeping) and Joe was shitting in the wicker seat of the rocker we kept on the porch of our apartment on Sanford Street, they were a treat.

– 25 –

My mother knew I wanted to be a writer (with all those rejection slips hanging from the spike on my bedroom wall, how could she not?), but she encouraged me to get a teacher's credential "so you'll have something to fall back on."

"You may want to get married, Stephen, and a garret by the Seine is only romantic if you're a bachelor," she'd said once. "It's no place to raise a family."

I did as she suggested, entering the College of Education at UMO and emerging four years later with a teacher's certificate . . . sort of like a golden retriever emerging from a pond with a dead duck in its jaws. It was dead, all right. I couldn't find a teaching job and so went to work at New Franklin Laundry for wages not much higher than those I had been making at Worumbo Mills and Weaving four years before. I was keeping my family in a series of garrets which overlooked not the Seine but some of Bangor's less appetizing streets, the ones where the police cruisers always seemed to show up at two o'clock on Saturday morning.

I never saw personal laundry at New Franklin unless it was a "fire order" being paid for by an insurance company (most fire orders consisted of clothes that *looked* okay but smelled like barbecued monkeymeat). The greater part of what I loaded and pulled were motel sheets from Maine's coastal towns and table linen from Maine's coastal restaurants. The table linen was desperately nasty. When tourists go out to dinner in Maine, they usually want clams and lobster. Mostly lobster. By the time the tablecloths upon which these delicacies had been served reached me, they stank to high heaven and were often boiling with maggots. The maggots would try to crawl up your arms as you loaded the washers; it was as if the little fuckers knew you were planning to cook them. I thought I'd get used to them in time but I never did. The maggots were bad; the smell of decomposing clams and lobster-meat was even worse. *Why are people such slobs?* I would wonder, loading feverish linens from Testa's of Bar Harbor into my machines. *Why are people such fucking slobs?*

Hospital sheets and linens were even worse. These also crawled with maggots in the summertime, but it was blood they were feeding on instead of lobster-meat and clam-jelly. Clothes, sheets, and pillowslips deemed to be infected were stuffed inside what we called "plague-bags" which dissolved when the hot water hit them, but blood was not, in those times, considered to be especially dangerous. There were often little extras in the hospital laundry; those loads were like nasty boxes of Cracker Jacks with weird prizes in them. I found a steel bedpan in one load and a pair of surgical shears in another (the bedpan was of no practical use, but the shears were a damned handy kitchen implement). Ernest "Rocky" Rockwell, the guy I worked with, found twenty dollars in a load from Eastern Maine Medical Center and punched out at noon to start drinking. (Rocky referred to quitting time as "Slitz o'clock.")

On one occasion I heard a strange clicking from inside one of the Washex three-pockets which were my responsibility. I hit the Emergency Stop button, thinking the goddam thing was stripping its gears or something. I opened the doors and hauled out a huge wad of dripping surgical tunics and green caps, soaking myself in the process. Below them, lying scattered across the colander-like inner sleeve of the middle pocket, was what looked like a complete set of human teeth. It crossed my mind that they would make an interesting necklace, then I scooped them out and tossed them in the trash. My wife has put up with a lot from me over the years, but her sense of humor stretches only so far.

– 26 –

From a financial point of view, two kids were probably two too many for college grads working in a laundry and the second shift at Dunkin' Donuts. The only edge we had came courtesy of magazines like *Dude, Cavalier, Adam,* and *Swank*—what my Uncle Oren used to call "the titty books." By 1972 they were showing quite a lot more than bare breasts and fiction was on its way out, but I was lucky enough to ride the last wave. I wrote after work; when we lived on Grove Street, which was close to the New Franklin, I would sometimes write a little on my lunch hour, too. I suppose that sounds almost impossibly Abe Lincoln, but it was no big deal— I was having fun. Those stories, grim as some of them were, served as brief escapes from the boss, Mr. Brooks, and Harry the floor-man.

Harry had hooks instead of hands as a result of a tumble into the sheet-mangler during World War II (he was dusting the beams above the machine and fell off). A comedian at heart, he would sometimes duck into the bathroom and run water from the cold tap over one hook and water from the hot tap over the other. Then he'd sneak up behind you while you were loading laundry and lay the steel hooks on the back of your neck. Rocky and I spent a fair amount of time speculating on how Harry accomplished certain bathroom cleanup activities. "Well," Rocky said one day while we were drinking our lunch in his car, "at least he don't need to wash his hands."

There were times—especially in summer, while swallowing my afternoon salt-pill—when it occurred to me that I was simply repeating my mother's life. Usually this thought struck me as funny. But if I happened to be tired, or if there were extra bills to pay and no money to pay them with, it seemed awful. I'd think *This isn't the way our lives are supposed to be going.* Then I'd think *Half the world has the same idea.*

The stories I sold to the men's magazines between August of 1970, when I got my two-hundred-dollar check for "Graveyard Shift," and the winter of 1973–1974 were just enough to create a rough sliding margin between us and the welfare office (my mother, a Republican all her life, had communicated her deep horror of "going on the county" to me; Tabby had some of that same horror).

My clearest memory of those days is of our coming back to the Grove Street apartment one Sunday afternoon after spending the weekend at my mother's house in Durham—this would have been right around the time the symptoms of the cancer which killed her started to show themselves. I have a picture from that day—Mom, looking both tired and amused, is sitting in a chair in her dooryard, holding Joe in her lap while Naomi stands sturdily beside her. Naomi wasn't so sturdy by Sunday afternoon, however; she had come down with an ear infection, and was burning with fever.

Trudging from the car to our apartment building on that summer afternoon was a low point. I was carrying

Naomi and a tote-bag full of baby survival equipment (bottles, lotions, diapers, sleep suits, undershirts, socks) while Tabby carried Joe, who had spit up on her. She was dragging a sack of dirty diapers behind her. We both knew Naomi needed THE PINK STUFF, which was what we called liquid amoxicillin. THE PINK STUFF was expensive, and we were broke. I mean stony.

I managed to get the downstairs door open without dropping my daughter and was easing her inside (she was so feverish she glowed against my chest like a banked coal) when I saw there was an envelope sticking out of our mailbox—a rare Saturday delivery. Young marrieds don't get much mail; everyone but the gas and electric companies seems to forget they are alive. I snagged it, praying it wouldn't turn out to be another bill. It wasn't. My friends at the Dugent Publishing Corporation, purveyors of *Cavalier* and many other fine adult publications, had sent me a check for "Sometimes They Come Back," a long story I hadn't believed would sell anywhere. The check was for five hundred dollars, easily the largest sum I'd ever received. Suddenly we were able to afford not only a doctor's visit and a bottle of THE PINK STUFF, but also a nice Sunday-night meal. And I imagine that once the kids were asleep, Tabby and I got friendly.

I think we had a lot of happiness in those days, but we were scared a lot, too. We weren't much more than kids ourselves (as the saying goes), and being friendly helped keep the mean reds away. We took care of ourselves and the kids and each other as best we could. Tabby wore her pink uniform out to Dunkin' Donuts and called the cops when the drunks who came in for coffee got obstreperous. I washed motel sheets and kept writing one-reel horror movies.

– 27 –

By the time I started *Carrie,* I had landed a job teaching English in the nearby town of Hampden. I would be paid sixty-four hundred dollars a year, which seemed an unthinkable sum after earning a dollar-sixty an hour at the laundry. If I'd done the math, being careful to add in all the time spent in after-school conferences and correcting papers at home, I might have seen it was a very thinkable sum indeed, and that our situation was worse than ever. By the late winter of 1973 we were living in a doublewide trailer in Hermon, a little town west of Bangor. (Much later, when asked to do the *Playboy* Interview, I called Hermon "The asshole of the world." Hermonites were infuriated by that, and I hereby apologize. Hermon is really no more than the armpit of the world.) I was driving a Buick with transmission problems we couldn't afford to fix, Tabby was still working at Dunkin' Donuts, and we had no telephone. We simply couldn't afford the monthly charge. Tabby tried her hand at confession stories during that period ("Too Pretty to Be a Virgin"—stuff like that), and got personal responses of the this-isn't-quite-right-for-us-but-try-again type immediately. She would have broken through if given an extra hour or two in every day, but she was stuck with the usual twenty-four. Besides, any amusement value the confession-mag formula (it's called the Three R's—Rebellion, Ruin, and Redemption) might have had for her at the start wore off in a hurry.

I wasn't having much success with my own writing, either. Horror, science fiction, and crime stories in the men's magazines were being replaced by increasingly graphic tales of sex. That was part of the trouble, but not all of it. The bigger deal was that, for the first time in my life, writing was *hard.* The problem was the teaching. I liked my coworkers and loved the kids—even the Beavis and Butt-Head types in Living with English could be interesting—but by most Friday afternoons I felt as if I'd spent the week with jumper cables clamped to my brain. If I ever came close to despairing about my future as a writer, it was then. I could see myself thirty years on, wearing the same shabby tweed coats with patches on the elbows, potbelly rolling over my Gap khakis from too much beer. I'd have a cigarette cough from too many packs of Pall Malls, thicker glasses, more dandruff, and in my desk drawer, six or seven unfinished manuscripts which I would take out and tinker with from time to time, usually when drunk. If asked what I did in my spare time, I'd tell people I was writing a book—what else does *any* self-respecting creative-writing teacher do with his or her spare time? And of course I'd lie to myself, telling myself there was still time, it wasn't too late, there were novelists who didn't get started until they were fifty, hell, even sixty. Probably plenty of them.

My wife made a crucial difference during those two years I spent teaching at Hampden (and washing sheets at New Franklin Laundry during the summer vacation). If she had suggested that the time I spent writing stories

on the front porch of our rented house on Pond Street or
in the laundry room of our rented trailer on Klatt Road
in Hermon was wasted time, I think a lot of the heart
would have gone out of me. Tabby never voiced a single
doubt, however. Her support was a constant, one of
the few good things I could take as a given. And whenever I see a first novel dedicated to a wife (or a husband),
I smile and think, *There's someone who knows.* Writing is a
lonely job. Having someone who believes in you makes
a lot of difference. They don't have to make speeches.
Just believing is usually enough.

– 28 –

While he was going to college my brother Dave worked
summers as a janitor at Brunswick High, his old alma
mater. For part of one summer I worked there, too. I
can't remember which year, only that it was before I
met Tabby but after I started to smoke. That would
have made me nineteen or twenty, I suppose. I got
paired with a guy named Harry, who wore green
fatigues, a big keychain, and walked with a limp. (He
did have hands instead of hooks, however.) One lunch
hour Harry told me what it had been like to face a
Japanese *banzai* charge on the island of Tarawa, all the
Japanese officers waving swords made out of Maxwell
House coffee cans, all the screaming enlisted men
behind them stoned out of their gourds and smelling of
burned poppies. Quite a raconteur was my pal Harry.

   One day he and I were supposed to scrub the rust-
stains off the walls in the girls' shower. I looked around

the locker room with the interest of a Muslim youth who for some reason finds himself deep within the women's quarters. It was the same as the boys' locker room, and yet completely different. There were no urinals, of course, and there were two extra metal boxes on the tile walls—unmarked, and the wrong size for paper towels. I asked what was in them. "Pussy-plugs," Harry said. "For them certain days of the month."

I also noticed that the showers, unlike those in the boys' locker room, had chrome U-rings with pink plastic curtains attached. You could actually shower in privacy. I mentioned this to Harry, and he shrugged. "I guess young girls are a bit more shy about being undressed."

This memory came back to me one day while I was working at the laundry, and I started seeing the opening scene of a story: girls showering in a locker room where there were no U-rings, pink plastic curtains, or privacy. And this one girl starts to have her period. Only she doesn't know what it is, and the other girls—grossed out, horrified, amused—start pelting her with sanitary napkins. Or with tampons, which Harry had called pussy-plugs. The girl begins to scream. All that blood! She thinks she's dying, that the other girls are making fun of her even while she's bleeding to death . . . she reacts . . . fights back . . . but how?

I'd read an article in *Life* magazine some years before, suggesting that at least some reported poltergeist activity might actually be telekinetic phenomena—telekinesis being the ability to move objects just by thinking about them. There was some evidence to suggest that young people might have such powers, the article said, especially girls in early adolescence, right around the time of their first—

Pow! Two unrelated ideas, adolescent cruelty and telekinesis, came together, and I had an idea. I didn't leave my post at Washex #2, didn't go running around the laundry waving my arms and shouting "Eureka!," however. I'd had many other ideas as good and some that were better. Still, I thought I might have the basis for a good *Cavalier* yarn, with the possibility of *Playboy* lurking in the back of my mind. *Playboy* paid up to two thousand dollars for short fiction. Two thousand bucks would buy a new transmission for the Buick with plenty left over for groceries. The story remained on the back burner for awhile, simmering away in that place that's not quite the conscious but not quite the subconscious, either. I had started my teaching career before I sat down one night to give it a shot. I did three single-spaced pages of a first draft, then crumpled them up in disgust and threw them away.

I had four problems with what I'd written. First and least important was the fact that the story didn't move me emotionally. Second and slightly more important was the fact that I didn't much like the lead character. Carrie White seemed thick and passive, a ready-made victim. The other girls were chucking tampons and sanitary napkins at her, chanting "Plug it up! Plug it up!" and I just didn't care. Third and more important still was not feeling at home with either the surroundings or my all-girl cast of supporting characters. I had landed on Planet Female, and one sortie into the girls' locker room at Brunswick High School years before wasn't much help in navigating there.

For me writing has always been best when it's intimate, as sexy as skin on skin. With *Carrie* I felt as if I were wearing a rubber wet-suit I couldn't pull off. Fourth and most important of all was the realization that the story wouldn't pay off unless it was pretty long, probably even longer than "Sometimes They Come Back," which had been at the absolute outer limit of what the men's magazine market could accept in terms of word-count. You had to save plenty of room for those pictures of cheerleaders who had somehow forgotten to put on their underpants—they were what guys really bought the magazines for. I couldn't see wasting two weeks, maybe even a month, creating a novella I didn't like and wouldn't be able to sell. So I threw it away.

The next night, when I came home from school, Tabby had the pages. She'd spied them while emptying my wastebasket, had shaken the cigarette ashes off the crumpled balls of paper, smoothed them out, and sat down to read them. She wanted me to go on with it, she said. She wanted to know the rest of the story. I told her I didn't know jack-shit about high school girls. She said she'd help me with that part. She had her chin tilted down and was smiling in that severely cute way of hers. "You've got something here," she said. "I really think you do."

– 29 –

I never got to like Carrie White and I never trusted Sue Snell's motives in sending her boyfriend to the prom with her, but I *did* have something there. Like a whole career. Tabby somehow knew it, and by the time I had piled up fifty single-spaced pages, I knew it, too. For one thing, I didn't think any of the characters who went to Carrie White's prom would ever forget it. Those few who lived through it, that was.

I had written three other novels before *Carrie*—*Rage, The Long Walk,* and *The Running Man* were later published. *Rage* is the most troubling of them. *The Long Walk* may be the best of them. But none of them taught me the things I learned from Carrie White. The most important is that the writer's original perception of a character or characters may be as erroneous as the reader's. Running a close second was the realization that stopping a piece of work just because it's hard, either emotionally or imaginatively, is a bad idea. Sometimes you have to go on when you don't feel like it, and sometimes you're doing good work when it feels like all you're managing is to shovel shit from a sitting position.

Tabby helped me, beginning with the information that the sanitary-napkin dispensers in high schools were usually not coin-op—faculty and administration didn't like the idea of girls' walking around with blood all over their skirts just because they happened to come to school short a quarter, my wife said. And I also helped myself, digging back to my memories of high school (my job teaching English didn't help; I was twenty-six by then, and on the wrong side of the desk), remembering what I knew about the two loneliest, most reviled girls in my class—how they looked, how they acted, how they were treated. Very rarely in my career have I explored more distasteful territory.

I'll call one of these girls Sondra. She and her mother lived in a trailer home not too far from me, with their dog, Cheddar Cheese. Sondra had a burbly, uneven voice, as if she were always speaking through a throatful of tightly packed phlegm. She wasn't fat, but her flesh had a loose, pale look, like the undersides of some mushrooms. Her hair clung to her pimply cheeks in tight Little Orphan Annie curls. She had no friends (except for Cheddar Cheese, I guess). One day her mother hired me to move some furniture. Dominating the trailer's living room was a nearly life-sized crucified Jesus, eyes turned up, mouth turned down, blood dribbling from beneath the crown of thorns on his head. He was naked except for a rag twisted around his hips and loins. Above this bit of breechclout were the hollowed belly and the jutting ribs of a concentration-camp inmate. It occurred to me that Sondra had grown up beneath the agonal gaze of this dying god, and doing so had undoubtedly played a part in making her what she was when I knew her: a timid and homely outcast who went scuttling through the halls of Lisbon High like a frightened mouse.

"That's Jesus Christ, my Lord and Savior," Sondra's mother said, following my gaze. "Have *you* been saved, Steve?"

I hastened to tell her I was saved as saved could be, although I didn't think you could ever be good enough to have *that* version of Jesus intervene on your behalf. The pain had driven him out of his mind. You could see it on his face. If *that* guy came back, he probably wouldn't be in a saving mood.

The other girl I'll call Dodie Franklin, only the other girls called her Dodo or Doodoo. Her parents were interested in only one thing, and that was entering contests. They were good at them, too; they had won all sorts of odd stuff, including a year's supply of Three Diamonds Brand Fancy Tuna and Jack Benny's Maxwell automobile. The Maxwell sat off to the left of their house in that part of Durham known as Southwest Bend, gradually sinking into the landscape. Every year or two, one of the local papers—the Portland *Press-Herald,* the Lewiston *Sun,* the Lisbon *Weekly Enterprise*—would do a piece on all the weird shit Dodie's folks had won in raffles and sweepstakes and giant prize drawings. Usually there would be a photo of the Maxwell, or Jack Benny with his violin, or both.

Whatever the Franklins might have won, a supply of clothes for growing teenagers wasn't part of the haul. Dodie and her brother Bill wore the same stuff every day for the first year and a half of high school: black pants and a short-sleeved checked sport shirt for him, a long black skirt, gray knee-socks, and a sleeveless white blouse for her. Some of my readers may not believe I am being literal when I say *every day,* but those who grew up in country towns during the fifties and sixties will know that I am. In the Durham of my childhood, life wore little or any makeup. I went to school with kids who wore the same neckdirt for months, kids whose skin festered with sores and rashes, kids with the eerie dried-apple-doll faces that result from untreated burns, kids who were sent to school with stones in their dinnerbuckets and nothing but air in their Thermoses. It wasn't Arcadia; for the most part it was Dogpatch with no sense of humor.

Dodie and Bill Franklin got on all right at Durham

Elementary, but high school meant a much bigger town, and for children like Dodie and Bill, Lisbon Falls meant ridicule and ruin. We watched in amusement and horror as Bill's sport shirt faded and began to unravel from the short sleeves up. He replaced a missing button with a paperclip. Tape, carefully colored black with a crayon to match his pants, appeared over a rip behind one knee. Dodie's sleeveless white blouse began to grow yellow with wear, age, and accumulated sweat-stains. As it grew thinner, the straps of her bra showed through more and more clearly. The other girls made fun of her, at first behind her back and then to her face. Teasing became taunting. The boys weren't a part of it; we had Bill to take care of (yes, I helped—not a whole lot, but I was there). Dodie had it worse, I think. The girls didn't just laugh at Dodie; they hated her, too. Dodie was everything they were afraid of.

After Christmas vacation of our sophomore year, Dodie came back to school resplendent. The dowdy old black skirt had been replaced by a cranberry-colored one that stopped at her knees instead of halfway down her shins. The tatty knee-socks had been replaced by nylon stockings, which looked pretty good because she had finally shaved the luxuriant mat of black hair off her legs. The ancient sleeveless blouse had given way to a soft wool sweater. She'd even had a permanent. Dodie was a girl transformed, and you could see by her face that she knew it. I have no idea if she saved for those new clothes, if they were given to her for Christmas by her parents, or if she went through a hell of begging that finally bore dividends. It doesn't matter, because mere clothes changed nothing. The teasing that day was worse than ever. Her peers had no intention of letting her out of the box they'd put her in; she was punished for even trying to break free. I had several classes with her, and was able to observe Dodie's ruination at first hand. I saw her smile fade, saw the light in her eyes first dim and then go out. By the end of the day she was the girl she'd been before Christmas vacation—a dough-faced and freckle-cheeked wraith, scurrying through the halls with her eyes down and her books clasped to her chest.

She wore the new skirt and sweater the next day. And the next. And the next. When the school year ended she was still wearing them, although by then the weather was much too hot for wool and there were always beads of sweat at her temples and on her upper lip. The home permanent wasn't repeated and the new clothes took on a matted, dispirited look, but the teasing had dropped back to its pre-Christmas levels and the taunting stopped entirely. Someone made a break for the fence and had to be knocked down, that was all. Once the escape was foiled and the entire company of prisoners was once more accounted for, life could go back to normal.

Both Sondra and Dodie were dead by the time I started writing *Carrie*. Sondra moved out of the trailer in Durham, out from beneath the agonal gaze of the dying savior, and into an apartment in Lisbon Falls. She must have worked somewhere close by, probably in one of the mills or shoe factories. She was epileptic and died during a seizure. She lived alone, so there was no one to help her when she went down with her head bent the wrong way. Dodie married a TV weatherman who gained something of a reputation in New England for his drawling downeast delivery. Following the birth of a child—I think it was their second—Dodie went into the cellar and put a .22 bullet in her abdomen. It was a lucky shot (or unlucky, depending on your point of view, I guess), hitting the portal vein and killing her. In town they said it was postpartum depression, how sad. Myself, I suspected high school hangover might have had something to do with it.

I never liked Carrie, that female version of Eric Harris and Dylan Klebold, but through Sondra and Dodie I came at last to understand her a little. I pitied her and I pitied her classmates as well, because I had been one of them once upon a time.

– 30 –

The manuscript of *Carrie* went off to Doubleday, where I had made a friend named William Thompson. I pretty much forgot about it and moved on with my life, which at that time consisted of teaching school, raising kids, loving my wife, getting drunk on Friday afternoons, and writing stories.

My free period that semester was five, right after lunch. I usually spent it in the teachers' room, grading papers and wishing I could stretch out on the couch and take a nap—in the early afternoon I have all the energy of a boa constrictor that's just swallowed a goat. The intercom came on and Colleen Sites in the office asked if I was there. I said I was, and she asked me to come to the office. I had a phone call. My wife.

The walk from the teachers' room in the lower wing to the main office seemed long even with classes in session and the halls mostly empty. I hurried, not quite running, my heart beating hard. Tabby would have had to dress the kids in their boots and jackets to use the neighbors' phone, and I could think of only two reasons she might have done so. Either Joe or Naomi had fallen off the stoop and broken a leg, or I had sold *Carrie.*

My wife, sounding out of breath but deliriously happy, read me a telegram. Bill Thompson (who would later go on to discover a Mississippi scribbler named John Grisham) had sent it after trying to call and discovering the Kings no longer had a phone. CONGRATULATIONS, it read. CARRIE OFFICIALLY A DOUBLEDAY BOOK. IS $2500 ADVANCE OKAY? THE FUTURE LIES AHEAD. LOVE, BILL.

Twenty-five hundred dollars was a very small advance, even for the early seventies, but I didn't know that and had no literary agent to know it for me. Before it occurred to me that I might actually need an agent, I had generated well over three million dollars' worth of income, a good deal of it for the publisher. (The standard Doubleday contract in those days was better than indentured servitude, but not much.) And my little high school horror novel marched toward publication with excruciating slowness. Although it was accepted in late March or early April of 1973, publication wasn't slated until the spring of 1974. This wasn't unusual. In those days Doubleday was an enormous fiction-mill churning out mysteries, romances, science fiction yarns, and Double D westerns at a rate of fifty or more a month, all of this in addition to a robust frontlist including books by heavy hitters like Leon Uris and Allen Drury. I was only one small fish in a very busy river.

Tabby asked if I could quit teaching. I told her no, not based on a twenty-five-hundred-dollar advance and only nebulous possibilities beyond that. If I'd been on my own, maybe (hell, *probably*). But with a wife and two kids? Not happening. I remember the two of us lying in bed that night, eating toast and talking until the small hours of the morning. Tabby asked me how much we'd make if Doubleday was able to sell paperback reprint rights to *Carrie,* and I said I didn't know. I'd read that Mario Puzo had just scored a huge advance for paperback rights to *The Godfather*—four hundred thousand dollars according to the newspaper—but I didn't believe *Carrie* would fetch anything near that, assuming it sold to paperback at all.

Tabby asked—rather timidly for my normally outspoken wife—if *I* thought the book would find a paperback publisher. I told her I thought the chances were pretty good, maybe seven or eight in ten. She asked how much it might bring. I said my best guess would be somewhere between ten and sixty thousand dollars.

"Sixty thousand dollars?" She sounded almost shocked. "Is that much even possible?"

I said it was—not *likely,* perhaps, but *possible.* I also reminded her that my contract specified a fifty-fifty paperback split, which meant that if Ballantine or Dell *did* pay sixty grand, we'd only get thirty. Tabby didn't dignify this with a reply—she didn't have to. Thirty thousand dollars was what I could expect to make in four years of teaching, even with annual salary increases thrown in. It was a lot of money. Probably just pie in the sky, but it was a night for dreaming.

— 31 —

Carrie inched along toward publication. We spent the advance on a new car (a standard shift which Tabby hated and reviled in her most colorful millworker's language) and I signed a teaching contract for the 1973–1974 academic year. I was writing a new novel, a peculiar combination of *Peyton Place* and *Dracula* which I called *Second Coming*. We had moved to a ground-floor apartment back in Bangor, a real pit, but we were in town again, we had a car covered by an actual warranty, and we had a telephone.

To tell you the truth, *Carrie* had fallen off my radar screen almost completely. The kids were a handful, both the ones at school and the ones at home, and I had begun to worry about my mother. She was sixty-one, still working at Pineland Training Center and as funny as ever, but Dave said she didn't feel very well a lot of the time. Her bedside table was covered with prescription painkillers, and he was afraid there might be something seriously wrong with her. "She's always smoked like a chimney, you know," Dave said. He was a great one to talk, since he smoked like a chimney himself (so did I, and how my wife hated the expense and the constant ashy dirt of it), but I knew what he meant. And although I didn't live as close to her as Dave and didn't see her as often, the last time I *had* seen her I could tell she had lost weight.

"What can we do?" I asked. Behind the question was all we knew of our mother, who "kept herself to herself," as she liked to say. The result of that philosophy was a vast gray space where other families have histories; Dave and I knew almost nothing about our father or his family, and little enough about our own mother's past, which included an incredible (to me, at least) eight dead brothers and sisters and her own failed ambition to become a concert pianist (she did play the organ on some of the NBC radio soaps and Sunday church shows during the war, she claimed).

"We can't do anything," Dave replied, "until she asks."

One Sunday not long after that call, I got another one from Bill Thompson at Doubleday. I was alone in the apartment; Tabby had packed the kids off to her mother's for a visit, and I was working on the new book, which I thought of as *Vampires in Our Town*.

"Are you sitting down?" Bill asked.

"No," I said. Our phone hung on the kitchen wall, and I was standing in the doorway between the kitchen and the living room. "Do I need to?"

"You might," he said. "The paperback rights to *Carrie* went to Signet Books for four hundred thousand dollars."

When I was a little kid, Daddy Guy had once said to my mother: "Why don't you shut that kid up, Ruth? When Stephen opens his mouth, all his guts fall out." It was true then, has been true all my life, but on that Mother's Day in May of 1973 I was completely speechless. I stood there in the doorway, casting the same shadow as always, but I couldn't talk. Bill asked if I was still there, kind of laughing as he said it. He knew I was.

I hadn't heard him right. Couldn't have. The idea allowed me to find my voice again, at least. "Did you say it went for forty thousand dollars?"

"Four *hundred thousand* dollars," he said. "Under the rules of the road"—meaning the contract I'd signed— "two hundred K of it's yours. Congratulations, Steve."

I was still standing in the doorway, looking across the living room toward our bedroom and the crib where Joe slept. Our place on Sanford Street rented for ninety dollars a month and this man I'd only met once face-to-face was telling me I'd just won the lottery. The strength ran out of my legs. I didn't fall, exactly, but I kind of whooshed down to a sitting position there in the doorway.

"Are you sure?" I asked Bill.

He said he was. I asked him to say the number again, very slowly and very clearly, so I could be sure I hadn't misunderstood. He said the number was a four followed by five zeros. "After that a decimal point and two more zeros," he added.

We talked for another half an hour, but I don't remember a single word of what we said. When the conversation was over, I tried to call Tabby at her mother's. Her youngest sister, Marcella, said Tab had already left. I walked back and forth through the apartment in my stocking feet, exploding with good news and without an ear to hear it. I was shaking all over. At last I pulled on my shoes and walked downtown. The only store that was open on Bangor's Main Street was LaVerdiere's Drug. I suddenly felt that I had to buy Tabby a Mother's Day present, something wild and extravagant. I tried, but here's one of life's true facts: there's nothing really wild and extravagant for sale at LaVerdiere's. I did the best I could. I got her a hair-dryer.

When I got back home she was in the kitchen, unpacking the baby bags and singing along with the radio. I gave her the hair-dryer. She looked at it as if she'd never seen one before. "What's this for?" she asked.

I took her by the shoulders. I told her about the paperback sale. She didn't appear to understand. I told her again. Tabby looked over my shoulder at our shitty little four-room apartment, just as I had, and began to cry.

– 32 –

I got drunk for the first time in 1966. This was on the senior class trip to Washington. We went on a bus, about forty kids and three chaperones (one of them was Old Cue-Ball, as a matter of fact), and spent the first night in New York, where the drinking age was then eighteen. Thanks to my bad ears and shitty tonsils, I was almost nineteen. Room to spare.

A bunch of us more adventurous boys found a package store around the corner from the hotel. I cast an eye over the shelves, aware that my spending money was far from a fortune. There was too much—too many bottles, too many brands, too many prices over ten dollars. Finally I gave up and asked the guy behind the counter (the same bald, bored-looking, gray-coated guy who has, I'm convinced, sold alcohol virgins their first bottle since the dawn of commerce) what was cheap. Without a word, he put a pint of Old Log Cabin whiskey down on the Winston mat beside the cash register. The sticker on the label said $1.95. The price was right.

I have a memory of being led onto the elevator later that night—or maybe it was early the next morning—by Peter Higgins (Old Cue-Ball's son), Butch Michaud, Lenny Partridge, and John Chizmar. This memory is more like a scene from a TV show than a real memory. I seem to be outside of myself, watching the whole thing. There's just enough of me left inside to know that I am globally, perhaps even galactically, fucked up.

The camera watches as we go up to the girls' floor. The camera watches as I am propelled up and down the hall, a kind of rolling exhibit. An amusing one, it seems. The girls are in nighties, robes, curlers, cold cream. They are all laughing at me, but their laughter seems good-natured enough. The sound is muted, as if I am hearing them through cotton. I am trying to tell Carole Lemke that I love the way she wears her hair, and that she has the most beautiful blue eyes in the world. What comes out is something like "Uggin-wuggin-blue eyes, wuggin-ruggin-whole world." Carole laughs and nods as if she understands completely. I am very happy. The world is seeing an asshole, no doubt, but he is a *happy* asshole, and everyone loves him. I spend several minutes trying to tell Gloria Moore that I've discovered The Secret Life of Dean Martin.

At some point after that I am in my bed. The bed holds still but the room starts to spin around it, faster and faster. It occurs to me that it's spinning like the turntable of my Webcor phonograph, on which I used to play Fats Domino and now play Dylan and the

Dave Clark Five. The room is the turntable, I am the spindle, and pretty soon the spindle is going to start tossing its platters.

I go away for a little bit. When I wake up, I'm on my knees in the bathroom of the double room I'm sharing with my friend Louis Purington. I have no idea how I got in there, but it's good that I did because the toilet is full of bright yellow puke. *Looks like Niblets,* I think, and that's all it takes to get me going again. Nothing comes up but whiskey-flavored strings of spit, but my head feels like it's going to explode. I can't walk. I crawl back to bed with my sweaty hair hanging in my eyes. *I'll feel better tomorrow,* I think, and then I go away again.

In the morning my stomach has settled a little but my diaphragm is sore from vomiting and my head is throbbing like a mouthful of infected teeth. My eyes have turned into magnifying glasses; the hideously bright morning light coming in through the hotel windows is being concentrated by them and will soon set my brains on fire.

Participating in that day's scheduled activities—a walk to Times Square, a boat ride to the Statue of Liberty, a climb to the top of the Empire State Building—is out of the question. Walking? Urk. Boats? Double urk. Elevators? Urk to the fourth power. Christ, I can hardly move. I make some sort of feeble excuse and spend most of the day in bed. By late afternoon I'm feeling a little better. I dress, creep down the hall to the elevator, and descend to the first floor. Eating is still impossible, but I believe I'm ready for a ginger ale, a cigarette, and a magazine. And who should I see in the lobby, sitting in a chair and reading a newspaper, but

Mr. Earl Higgins, alias Old Cue-Ball. I pass him as silently as I can, but it's no good. When I come back from the gift shop he's sitting with his newspaper in his lap, looking at me. I feel my stomach drop. Here is more trouble with the principal, probably even worse than the trouble I got into over *The Village Vomit*. He calls me over and I discover something interesting: Mr. Higgins is actually an okay guy. He bounced me pretty hard over my joke newspaper, but perhaps Miss Margitan had insisted on that. And I'd just been sixteen, after all. On the day of my first hangover I'm going on nineteen, I've been accepted at the state university, and I have a mill job waiting for me when the class trip is over.

"I understand you were too sick to tour New York with the rest of the boys and girls," Old Cue-Ball says. He eyes me up and down.

I say that's right, I'd been sick.

"A shame for you to miss the fun," Old Cue-Ball says. "Feeling better now?"

Yes, I was feeling better. Probably stomach flu, one of those twenty-four-hour bugs.

"I hope you won't get that bug again," he says. "At least not on this trip." He looks at me for a moment longer, his eyes asking if we understand each other.

"I'm sure I won't," I say, meaning it. I know what drunk is like, now—a vague sense of roaring goodwill, a clearer sense that most of your consciousness is out of your body, hovering like a camera in a science fiction movie and filming everything, and then the sickness, the puking, the aching head. No, I won't get that bug again, I tell myself, not on this trip, not ever. Once is enough, just to find out what it's like. Only an idiot would make a second experiment, and only a lunatic— a *masochistic* lunatic—would make booze a regular part of his life.

The next day we go on to Washington, making one stop in Amish country on the way. There's a liquor store near where the bus parks. I go in and look around. Although the drinking age in Pennsylvania is twenty-one, I must look easily that in my one good suit and Fazza's old black overcoat—in fact, I probably look like a freshly released young convict, tall and hungry and very likely not bolted together right. The clerk sells me a fifth of Four Roses without asking to see any ID, and by the time we stop for the night I'm drunk again.

Ten years or so later I'm in an Irish saloon with Bill Thompson. We have lots to celebrate, not the least of which is the completion of my third book, *The Shining*. That's the one which just happens to be about an alcoholic writer and ex-schoolteacher. It's July, the night of the All-Star baseball game. Our plan is to eat a good old-fashioned meal from the dishes set out on the steam table, then get shitfaced. We begin with a couple at the bar, and I start reading all the signs. HAVE A MANHATTAN IN MANHATTAN, says one. TUESDAYS ARE TWOFORS, says another. WORK IS THE CURSE OF THE DRINKING CLASS, says a third. And there, right in front of me, is one which reads: EARLY BIRD SPECIAL! SCREWDRIVERS A BUCK MONDAY—FRIDAY 8–10 A.M.

I motion to the bartender. He comes over. He's bald, he's wearing a gray jacket, he could be the guy who sold me my first pint back in 1966. Probably he is. I point to the sign and ask, "Who comes in at eight-fifteen in the morning and orders a screwdriver?"

I'm smiling but he doesn't smile back. "College boys," he replies. "Just like you."

— 33 —

In 1971 or '72, Mom's sister Carolyn Weimer died of breast cancer. My mother and my Aunt Ethelyn (Carolyn's twin) flew out to Aunt Cal's funeral in Minnesota. It was the first time my mother had flown in twenty years. On the plane trip back, she began to bleed profusely from what she would have called "her privates." Although long past her change of life by that point, she told herself it was simply one final menstrual period. Locked in the tiny bathroom of a bouncing TWA jet, she stanched the bleeding with tampons (*plug it up, plug it up,* as Sue Snell and her friends might have cried), then returned to her seat. She said nothing to Ethelyn and nothing to David and me. She didn't go to see Joe Mendes in Lisbon Falls, her physician since time out of mind. Instead of any of those things, she did what she always did in times of trouble: kept herself to herself. For awhile, things seemed to be all right. She enjoyed her job, she enjoyed her friends, and she enjoyed her four grandchildren, two from Dave's family and two from mine. Then things stopped being all right. In August of 1973, during a checkup following an operation to "strip" some of her outrageously varicose veins, my mother was diagnosed with uterine cancer. I think Nellie Ruth Pillsbury King, who once dumped a bowl of Jell-O on the floor and then danced in it while her two boys lay collapsed in the corner, screaming with laughter, actually died of embarrassment.

The end came in February of 1974. By then a little of the money from *Carrie* had begun to flow and I was able to help with some of the medical expenses—there was that much to be glad about. And I was there for the last of it, staying in the back bedroom of Dave and Linda's place. I'd been drunk the night before but was only moderately hungover, which was good. One wouldn't want to be too hungover at the deathbed of one's mother.

Dave woke me at 6:15 in the morning, calling softly through the door that he thought she was going. When I got into the master bedroom he was sitting beside her on the bed and holding a Kool for her to smoke. This she did between harsh gasps for breath. She was only semiconscious, her eyes going from Dave to me and then back to Dave again. I sat next to Dave, took the cigarette, and held it to her mouth. Her lips stretched out to clamp on the filter. Beside her bed, reflected over and over again in a cluster of glasses, was an early bound galley of *Carrie.* Aunt Ethelyn had read it to her aloud a month or so before she died.

Mom's eyes went from Dave to me, Dave to me, Dave to me. She had gone from one hundred and sixty pounds to about ninety. Her skin was yellow and so tightly stretched that she looked like one of those mummies they parade through the streets of Mexico on the Day of the Dead. We took turns holding the cigarette for her, and when it was down to the filter, I put it out.

"My boys," she said, then lapsed into what might have been sleep or unconsciousness. My head ached. I took a couple of aspirin from one of the many bottles of medicine on her table. Dave held one of her hands and I held the other. Under the sheet was not the body of our mother but that of a starved and deformed child. Dave and I smoked and talked a little. I don't remember what we said. It had rained the night before, then the temperature had dropped and the morning streets were filled with ice. We could hear the pause after each rasping breath she drew growing longer and longer. Finally there were no more breaths and it was all pause.

– 34 –

My mother was buried out of the Congregational Church at Southwest Bend; the church she'd attended in Methodist Corners, where my brother and I grew up, was closed because of the cold. I gave the eulogy. I think I did a pretty good job, considering how drunk I was.

– 35 –

Alcoholics build defenses like the Dutch build dikes. I spent the first twelve years or so of my married life assuring myself that I "just liked to drink." I also employed the world-famous Hemingway Defense. Although never clearly articulated (it would not be manly to do so), the Hemingway Defense goes something like this: as a writer, I am a very sensitive fellow, but I am also a man, and real men don't give in to their sensitivities. Only *sissy*-men do that. Therefore I drink. How else can I face the existential horror of it all and continue to work? Besides, come on, I can handle it. A real man always can.

Then, in the early eighties, Maine's legislature enacted a returnable-bottle and -can law. Instead of going into the trash, my sixteen-ounce cans of Miller Lite started going into a plastic container in the garage. One Thursday night I went out there to toss in a few dead soldiers and saw that this container, which had been empty on Monday night, was now almost full. And since I was the only one in the house who drank Miller Lite—

Holy shit, I'm an alcoholic, I thought, and there was no dissenting opinion from inside my head—I was, after all, the guy who had written *The Shining* without even realizing (at least until that night) that I was writing about myself. My reaction to this idea wasn't denial or disagreement; it was what I'd call frightened determination. *You have to be careful, then,* I clearly remember thinking. *Because if you fuck up—*

If I fucked up, rolled my car over on a back road some night or blew an interview on live TV, someone would tell me I ought to get control of my drinking, and telling an alcoholic to control his drinking is like telling a guy suffering the world's most cataclysmic case of diarrhea to control his shitting. A friend of mine who has been through this tells an amusing story about his first tentative effort to get a grip on his increasingly slippery life. He went to a counsellor and said his wife was worried that he was drinking too much.

"How much do you drink?" the counsellor asked.

My friend looked at the counsellor with disbelief. "All of it," he said, as if that should have been self-evident.

I know how he felt. It's been almost twelve years since I took a drink, and I'm still struck by disbelief when I see someone in a restaurant with a half-finished glass of wine near at hand. I want to get up, go over, and yell "Finish that! Why don't you finish that?" into his or her face. I found the idea of social drinking ludicrous—if you didn't want to get drunk, why not just have a Coke?

My nights during the last five years of my drinking always ended with the same ritual: I'd pour any beers left in the refrigerator down the sink. If I didn't, they'd talk to me as I lay in bed until I got up and had another. And another. And one more.

– 36 –

By 1985 I had added drug addiction to my alcohol problem, yet I continued to function, as a good many substance abusers do, on a marginally competent level. I was terrified not to; by then I had no idea of how to live any other life. I hid the drugs I was taking as well as I could, both out of terror—what would happen to me without dope? I had forgotten the trick of being straight—and out of shame. I was wiping my ass with poison ivy again, this time on a daily basis, but I couldn't ask for help. That's not the way you did things in my family. In my family what you did was smoke your cigarettes and dance in the Jell-O and keep yourself to yourself.

Yet the part of me that writes the stories, the deep part that knew I was an alcoholic as early as 1975, when I wrote *The Shining,* wouldn't accept that. Silence isn't what that part is about. It began to scream for help in the only way it knew how, through my fiction and through my monsters. In late 1985 and early 1986 I wrote *Misery* (the title quite aptly described my state of mind), in which a writer is held prisoner and tortured by a psychotic nurse. In the spring and summer of 1986 I wrote *The Tommyknockers,* often working until midnight with my heart running at a hundred and thirty beats a minute and cotton swabs stuck up my nose to stem the coke-induced bleeding.

Tommyknockers is a forties-style science fiction tale in which the writer-heroine discovers an alien spacecraft buried in the ground. The crew is still on board, not dead but only hibernating. These alien creatures got into your head and just started . . . well, tommyknocking around in there. What you got was energy and a kind of superficial intelligence (the writer, Bobbi Anderson, creates a telepathic typewriter and an atomic hot-water heater, among other things). What you gave up in exchange was your soul. It was the best metaphor for drugs and alcohol my tired, overstressed mind could come up with.

Not long after that my wife, finally convinced that I wasn't going to pull out of this ugly downward spiral on my own, stepped in. It couldn't have been easy—by then I was no longer within shouting distance of my right mind—but she did it. She organized an intervention group formed of family and friends, and I was treated to a kind of *This Is Your Life* in hell. Tabby began by dumping a trashbag full of stuff from my office out on the rug: beercans, cigarette butts, cocaine in gram bottles and cocaine in plastic Baggies, coke spoons caked with snot and blood, Valium, Xanax, bottles of Robitussin cough syrup and NyQuil cold medicine, even bottles of mouthwash. A year or so before, observing the rapidity with which huge bottles of Listerine were disappearing from the bathroom, Tabby asked me if I drank the stuff. I responded with self-righteous hauteur that I most certainly did not. Nor did I. I drank the Scope instead. It was tastier, had that hint of mint.

The point of this intervention, which was certainly as unpleasant for my wife and kids and friends as it was for me, was that I was dying in front of them. Tabby said I had my choice: I could get help at a rehab or I could get the hell out of the house. She said that she and the kids loved me, and for that very reason none of them wanted to witness my suicide.

I bargained, because that's what addicts do. I was charming, because that's what addicts are. In the end I got two weeks to think about it. In retrospect, this seems to summarize all the insanity of that time. Guy is standing on top of a burning building. Helicopter arrives, hovers, drops a rope ladder. *Climb up!* the man leaning out of the helicopter's door shouts. Guy on top of the burning building responds, *Give me two weeks to think about it.*

I did think, though—as well as I could in my addled state—and what finally decided me was Annie Wilkes, the psycho nurse in *Misery*. Annie was coke, Annie was booze, and I decided I was tired of being Annie's pet writer. I was afraid that I wouldn't be able to work anymore if I quit drinking and drugging, but I decided (again, so far as I was able to decide anything in my distraught and depressed state of mind) that I would trade writing for staying married and watching the kids grow up. If it came to that.

It didn't, of course. The idea that creative endeavor

and mind-altering substances are entwined is one of the great pop-intellectual myths of our time. The four twentieth-century writers whose work is most responsible for it are probably Hemingway, Fitzgerald, Sherwood Anderson, and the poet Dylan Thomas. They are the writers who largely formed our vision of an existential English-speaking wasteland where people have been cut off from one another and live in an atmosphere of emotional strangulation and despair. These concepts are very familiar to most alcoholics; the common reaction to them is amusement. Substance-abusing writers are just substance abusers—common garden-variety drunks and druggies, in other words. Any claims that the drugs and alcohol are necessary to dull a finer sensibility are just the usual self-serving bullshit. I've heard alcoholic snowplow drivers make the same claim, that they drink to still the demons. It doesn't matter if you're James Jones, John Cheever, or a stewbum snoozing in Penn Station; for an addict, the right to the drink or drug of choice must be preserved at all costs. Hemingway and Fitzgerald didn't drink because they were creative, alienated, or morally weak. They drank because it's what alkies are wired up to do. Creative people probably *do* run a greater risk of alcoholism and addiction than those in some other jobs, but so what? We all look pretty much the same when we're puking in the gutter.

– 37 –

At the end of my adventures I was drinking a case of sixteen-ounce tallboys a night, and there's one novel, *Cujo,* that I barely remember writing at all. I don't say that with pride or shame, only with a vague sense of sorrow and loss. I like that book. I wish I could remember enjoying the good parts as I put them down on the page.

At the worst of it I no longer wanted to drink and no longer wanted to be sober, either. I felt evicted from life. At the start of the road back I just tried to believe the people who said that things would get better if I gave them time to do so. And I never stopped writing. Some of the stuff that came out was tentative and flat, but at least it was there. I buried those unhappy, lackluster pages in the bottom drawer of my desk and got on to the next project. Little by little I found the beat again, and after that I found the joy again. I came back to my family with gratitude, and back to my work with relief—I came back to it the way folks come back to a summer cottage after a long winter, checking first to make sure nothing has been stolen or broken during the cold season. Nothing had been. It was still all there, still all whole. Once the pipes were thawed out and the electricity was turned back on, everything worked fine.

– 38 –

The last thing I want to tell you in this part is about my desk. For years I dreamed of having the sort of massive oak slab that would dominate a room—no more child's desk in a trailer laundry-closet, no more cramped kneehole in a rented house. In 1981 I got the one I wanted and placed it in the middle of a spacious, skylighted study (it's a converted stable loft at the rear of the house). For six years I sat behind that desk either drunk or wrecked out of my mind, like a ship's captain in charge of a voyage to nowhere.

A year or two after I sobered up, I got rid of that monstrosity and put in a living-room suite where it had been, picking out the pieces and a nice Turkish rug with my wife's help. In the early nineties, before they moved on to their own lives, my kids sometimes came up in the evening to watch a basketball game or a movie and eat pizza. They usually left a boxful of crusts behind when they moved on, but I didn't care. They came, they seemed to enjoy being with me, and I know I enjoyed being with them. I got another desk—it's hand-made, beautiful, and half the size of the *T. rex* desk. I put it at the far west end of the office, in a corner under the eave. That eave is very like the one I slept under in Durham, but there are no rats in the walls and no senile grandmother downstairs yelling for someone to feed Dick the horse. I'm sitting under it now, a fifty-three-year-old man with bad eyes, a gimp leg, and no hang-over. I'm doing what I know how to do, and as well as I know how to do it. I came through all the stuff I told you about (and plenty more that I didn't), and now I'm going to tell you as much as I can about the job. As promised, it won't take long.

It starts with this: put your desk in the corner, and every time you sit down there to write, remind yourself why it isn't in the middle of the room. Life isn't a sup-port-system for art. It's the other way around.

What Writing Is

Telepathy, of course. It's amusing when you stop to think about it—for years people have argued about whether or not such a thing exists, folks like J. B. Rhine have busted their brains trying to create a valid testing process to isolate it, and all the time it's been right there, lying out in the open like Mr. Poe's Purloined Letter. All the arts depend upon telepathy to some degree, but I believe that writing offers the purest distillation. Perhaps I'm prejudiced, but even if I am we may as well stick with writing, since it's what we came here to think and talk about.

My name is Stephen King. I'm writing the first draft of this part at my desk (the one under the eave) on a snowy morning in December of 1997. There are things on my mind. Some are worries (bad eyes, Christmas shopping not even started, wife under the weather with a virus), some are good things (our younger son made a surprise visit home from college, I got to play Vince Taylor's "Brand New Cadillac" with The Wallflowers at a concert), but right now all that stuff is up top. I'm in another place, a basement place where there are lots of bright lights and clear images. This is a place I've built for myself over the years. It's a far-seeing place. I know it's a little strange, a little bit of a contradiction, that a far-seeing place should also be a basement place, but that's how it is with me. If you construct your own far-seeing place, you might put it in a treetop or on the roof of the Empire State Building or on the edge of the Grand Canyon. That's your little red wagon, as Robert McCammon says in one of his novels.

This book is scheduled to be published in the late summer or early fall of 2000. If that's how things work out, then you are somewhere downstream on the time-line from me . . . but you're quite likely in your own far-seeing place, the one where you go to receive telepathic messages. Not that you *have* to be there; books are a uniquely portable magic. I usually listen to one in the car (always unabridged; I think abridged audiobooks are the pits), and carry another wherever I go. You just never know when you'll want an escape hatch: mile-long lines at tollbooth plazas, the fifteen minutes you have to spend in the hall of some boring college building wait-ing for your advisor (who's got some yank-off in there threatening to commit suicide because he/she is flunking Custom Kurmfurling 101) to come out so you can get his signature on a drop-card, airport boarding lounges, laundromats on rainy afternoons, and the absolute worst, which is the doctor's office when the guy is run-ning late and you have to wait half an hour in order to have something sensitive mauled. At such times I find a book vital. If I have to spend time in purgatory before going to one place or the other, I guess I'll be all right as long as there's a lending library (if there is it's probably stocked with nothing but novels by Danielle Steel and *Chicken Soup* books, ha-ha, joke's on you, Steve).

So I read where I can, but I have a favorite place and

probably you do, too—a place where the light is good and the vibe is usually strong. For me it's the blue chair in my study. For you it might be the couch on the sunporch, the rocker in the kitchen, or maybe it's propped up in your bed—reading in bed can be heaven, assuming you can get just the right amount of light on the page and aren't prone to spilling your coffee or cognac on the sheets.

So let's assume that you're in your favorite receiving place just as I am in the place where I do my best transmitting. We'll have to perform our mentalist routine not just over distance but over time as well, yet that presents no real problem; if we can still read Dickens, Shakespeare, and (with the help of a footnote or two) Herodotus, I think we can manage the gap between 1997 and 2000. And here we go—actual telepathy in action. You'll notice I have nothing up my sleeves and that my lips never move. Neither, most likely, do yours.

Look—here's a table covered with a red cloth. On it is a cage the size of a small fish aquarium. In the cage is a white rabbit with a pink nose and pink-rimmed eyes. In its front paws is a carrot-stub upon which it is contentedly munching. On its back, clearly marked in blue ink, is the numeral 8.

Do we see the same thing? We'd have to get together and compare notes to make absolutely sure, but I think we do. There will be necessary variations, of course: some receivers will see a cloth which is turkey red, some will see one that's scarlet, while others may see still other shades. (To color-blind receivers, the red tablecloth is the dark gray of cigar ashes.) Some may see scalloped edges, some may see straight ones.

Decorative souls may add a little lace, and welcome—my tablecloth is your tablecloth, knock yourself out.

Likewise, the matter of the cage leaves quite a lot of room for individual interpretation. For one thing, it is described in terms of *rough comparison,* which is useful only if you and I see the world and measure the things in it with similar eyes. It's easy to become careless when making rough comparisons, but the alternative is a prissy attention to detail that takes all the fun out of writing. What am I going to say, "on the table is a cage three feet, six inches in length, two feet in width, and fourteen inches high"? That's not prose, that's an instruction manual. The paragraph also doesn't tell us what sort of material the cage is made of—wire mesh? steel rods? glass?—but does it really matter? We all understand the cage is a see-through medium; beyond that, we don't care. The most interesting thing here isn't even the carrot-munching rabbit in the cage, but the number on its back. Not a six, not a four, not nineteen-point-five. It's an eight. This is what we're looking at, and we all see it. I didn't tell you. You didn't ask me. I never opened my mouth and you never opened yours. We're not even in the same *year* together, let alone the same room . . . except we *are* together. We're close.

We're having a meeting of the minds.

I sent you a table with a red cloth on it, a cage, a rabbit, and the number eight in blue ink. You got them all, especially that blue eight. We've engaged in an act of telepathy. No mythy-mountain shit; real telepathy. I'm not going to belabor the point, but before we go any further you have to understand that I'm not trying to be cute; there *is* a point to be made.

You can approach the act of writing with nervousness, excitement, hopefulness, or even despair—the sense that you can never completely put on the page what's in your mind and heart. You can come to the act with your fists clenched and your eyes narrowed, ready to kick ass and take down names. You can come to it because you want a girl to marry you or because you want to change the world. Come to it any way but lightly. Let me say it again: *you must not come lightly to the blank page.*

I'm not asking you to come reverently or unquestioningly; I'm not asking you to be politically correct or cast aside your sense of humor (please God you have one). This isn't a popularity contest, it's not the moral Olympics, and it's not church. But it's *writing,* damn it, not washing the car or putting on eyeliner. If you can take it seriously, we can do business. If you can't or won't, it's time for you to close the book and do something else.

Wash the car, maybe.

TOOLBOX

> *Grandpa was a carpenter,*
> *he built houses, stores and banks,*
> *he chain-smoked Camel cigarettes*
> *and hammered nails in planks.*
> *He was level-on-the-level,*
> *shaved even every door,*
> *and voted for Eisenhower*
> *'cause Lincoln won the war.*

That's one of my favorite John Prine lyrics, probably because my grandpa was also a carpenter. I don't know about stores and banks, but Guy Pillsbury built his share of houses and spent a good many years making sure the Atlantic Ocean and the harsh seacoast winters didn't wash away the Winslow Homer estate in Prout's Neck. Fazza smoked cigars, though, not Camels. It was my Uncle Oren, also a carpenter, who smoked the Camels. And when Fazza retired, it was Uncle Oren who inherited the old fellow's toolbox. I don't remember its being there in the garage on the day I dropped the cinderblock on my foot, but it probably was sitting in its accustomed place just outside the nook where my cousin Donald kept his hockey sticks, ice skates, and baseball glove.

The toolbox was what we called a big 'un. It had three levels, the top two removable, all three containing little drawers as cunning as Chinese boxes. It was handmade, of course. Dark wooden slats were bound together by tiny nails and strips of brass. The lid was held down by big latches; to my child's eye they looked like the latches on a giant's lunchbox. Inside the top was a silk lining, rather odd in such a context and made more striking still by the pattern, which was pinkish-red cabbage roses fading into a smog of grease and dirt. On the sides were great big grabhandles. You never saw a toolbox like this one for sale at Wal-Mart or Western Auto, believe me. When my uncle first got it, he found a brass etching of a famous Homer painting—I believe it was *The Undertow*—lying in the bottom. Some years later Uncle Oren had it authenticated by a Homer expert in New York, and a few years after that I believe he sold it for a good piece of money. Exactly how or why Fazza came by the engraving in the first place is a mystery, but there was no mystery about the origins of the toolbox—he made it himself.

One summer day I helped Uncle Oren replace a broken screen on the far side of the house. I might have been eight or nine at the time. I remember following him with the replacement screen balanced on my head, like a native bearer in a Tarzan movie. He had the toolbox by the grabhandles, horsing it along at thigh level. As always, Uncle Oren was wearing khaki pants and a clean white tee-shirt. Sweat gleamed in his graying Army crewcut. A Camel hung from his lower lip. (When I came in years later with a pack of Chesterfields in my breast pocket, Uncle Oren sneered at them and called them "stockade cigarettes.")

We finally reached the window with the broken screen and he set the toolbox down with an audible sigh of relief. When Dave and I tried to lift it from its place on the garage floor, each of us holding one of the handles, we could barely budge it. Of course we were just little kids back then, but even so I'd guess that Fazza's fully loaded toolbox weighed between eighty and a hundred and twenty pounds.

Uncle Oren let me undo the big latches. The common tools were all on the top layer of the box. There was a hammer, a saw, the pliers, a couple of sized wrenches and an adjustable; there was a level with that mystic yellow window in the middle, a drill (the various bits were neatly drawered farther down in the depths), and two screwdrivers. Uncle Oren asked me for a screwdriver.

"Which one?" I asked.

"Either-or," he replied.

The broken screen was held on by loophead screws, and it really didn't matter whether he used a regular screwdriver or the Phillips on them; with loopheads you just stuck the screwdriver's barrel through the hole at the top of the screw and then spun it the way you spin a tire iron once you've got the lugnuts loose.

Uncle Oren took the screws out—there were eight, which he handed to me for safekeeping—and then removed the old screen. He set it against the house and held up the new one. The holes in the screen's frame mated up neatly with the holes in the window-frame. Uncle Oren grunted with approval when he saw this.

He took the loophead screws back from me, one after the other, got them started with his fingers, then tightened them down just as he'd loosened them, by inserting the screwdriver's barrel through the loops and turning them.

When the screen was secure, Uncle Oren gave me the screwdriver and told me to put it back in the toolbox and "latch her up." I did, but I was puzzled. I asked him why he'd lugged Fazza's toolbox all the way around the house, if all he'd needed was that one screwdriver. He could have carried a screwdriver in the back pocket of his khakis.

"Yeah, but Stevie," he said, bending to grasp the handles, "I didn't know what else I might find to do once I got out here, did I? It's best to have your tools with you. If you don't, you're apt to find something you didn't expect and get discouraged."

I want to suggest that to write to your best abilities, it behooves you to construct your own toolbox and then build up enough muscle so you can carry it with you. Then, instead of looking at a hard job and getting discouraged, you will perhaps seize the correct tool and get immediately to work.

Fazza's toolbox had three levels. I think that yours should have at least four. You could have five or six, I suppose, but there comes a point where a toolbox becomes too large to be portable and thus loses its chief virtue. You'll also want all those little drawers for your screws and nuts and bolts, but where you put those drawers and what you put in them . . . well, that's your little red wagon, isn't it? You'll find you have most of the tools you need already, but I advise you to look at each one again as you load it into your box. Try to see each one new, remind yourself of its function, and if some are rusty (as they may be if you haven't done this seriously in awhile), clean them off.

Common tools go on top. The commonest of all, the bread of writing, is vocabulary. In this case, you can happily pack what you have without the slightest bit of guilt and inferiority. As the whore said to the bashful sailor, "It ain't how much you've got, honey, it's how you use it."

Some writers have enormous vocabularies; these are folks who'd know if there really *is* such a thing as an insalubrious dithyramb or a cozening raconteur, people who haven't missed a multiple-choice answer in Wilfred Funk's *It Pays to Increase Your Word Power* in oh, thirty years or so. For example:

> The leathery, undeteriorative, and almost inde-
> structible quality was an inherent attribute of
> the thing's form of organization, and pertained
> to some paleogean cycle of invertebrate evolu-
> tion utterly beyond our powers of speculation.
> —H. P. Lovecraft, *At the Mountains of Madness*

Like it? Here's another:

> In some [of the cups] there was no evidence
> whatever that anything had been planted; in
> others, wilted brown stalks gave testimony to
> some inscrutable depredation.
> —T. Coraghessan Boyle, *Budding Prospects*

And yet a third—this is a good one, you'll like it:

Someone snatched the old woman's blindfold from her and she and the juggler were clouted away and when the company turned in to sleep and the low fire was roaring in the blast like a thing alive these four yet crouched at the edge of the firelight among their strange chattels and watched how the ragged flames fled down the wind as if sucked by some maelstrom out there in the void, some vortex in that waste apposite to which man's transit and his reckonings alike lay abrogate.

—Cormac McCarthy, *Blood Meridian*

Other writers use smaller, simpler vocabularies. Examples of this hardly seem necessary, but I'll offer a couple of my favorites, just the same:

He came to the river. The river was there.
—Ernest Hemingway, "Big Two-Hearted River"

They caught the kid doing something nasty under the bleachers.
—Theodore Sturgeon, *Some of Your Blood*

This is what happened.
—Douglas Fairbairn, *Shoot*

Some of the owner men were kind because they hated what they had to do, and some of them were angry because they hated to be cruel, and some of them were cold because they had long ago found that one could not be an owner unless one were cold.

—John Steinbeck, *The Grapes of Wrath*

The Steinbeck sentence is especially interesting. It's fifty words long. Of those fifty words, thirty-nine have but one syllable. That leaves eleven, but even that number is deceptive; Steinbeck uses **because** three times, **owner** twice, and **hated** twice. There is no word longer than two syllables in the entire sentence. The structure is complex; the vocabulary is not far removed from the old Dick and Jane primers. *The Grapes of Wrath* is, of course, a fine novel. I believe that *Blood Meridian* is another, although there are great whacks of it that I don't fully understand. What of that? I can't decipher the words to many of the popular songs I love, either.

There's also stuff you'll never find in the dictionary, but it's still vocabulary. Check out the following:

"Egggh, whaddaya? Whaddaya want from me?"
"Here come Hymie!"
"Unnh! Unnnh! Unnnhh!"
"Chew my willie, Yo' Honor."
"Yeggghhh, fuck you, too, man!"

—Tom Wolfe, *Bonfire of the Vanities*

This last is phonetically rendered street vocabulary. Few writers have Wolfe's ability to translate such stuff to the page. (Elmore Leonard is another writer who can do it.) Some street-rap gets into the dictionary eventually, but not until it's safely dead. And I don't think you'll ever find **Yeggghhh** in Webster's Unabridged.

Put your vocabulary on the top shelf of your tool-box, and don't make any conscious effort to improve it. (You'll be doing that as you read, of course . . . but that comes later.) One of the really bad things you can do to your writing is to dress up the vocabulary, looking for long words because you're maybe a little bit ashamed of your short ones. This is like dressing up a household pet in evening clothes. The pet is embarrassed and the person who committed this act of premeditated cuteness should be even more embarrassed. Make yourself a solemn promise right now that you'll never use "emolument" when you mean "tip" and you'll never say **John stopped long enough to perform an act of excretion** when you mean **John stopped long enough to take a shit.** If you believe "take a shit" would be considered offensive or inappropriate by your audience, feel free to say **John stopped long enough to move his bowels** (or perhaps **John stopped long enough to "push"**). I'm not trying to get you to talk dirty, only plain and direct. Remember that the basic rule of vocabulary is *use the first word that comes to your mind, if it is appropriate and colorful.* If you hesitate and cogitate, you will come up with another word—of course you will, there's always another word—but it probably won't be as good as your first one, or as close to what you really mean.

This business of meaning is a very big deal. If you doubt it, think of all the times you've heard someone say "I just can't describe it" or "That isn't what I mean."

Think of all the times you've said those things yourself, usually in a tone of mild or serious frustration. The word is only a representation of the meaning; even at its best, writing almost always falls short of full meaning. Given that, why in God's name would you want to make things worse by choosing a word which is only cousin to the one you really wanted to use?

And *do* feel free to take appropriateness into account; as George Carlin once observed, in some company it's perfectly all right to prick your finger, but very bad form to finger your prick.

— 2 —

You'll also want grammar on the top shelf of your toolbox, and don't annoy me with your moans of exasperation or your cries that you *don't understand* grammar, you *never did understand* grammar, you flunked that *whole semester* in Sophomore English, writing is fun but grammar sucks the big one.

Relax. Chill. We won't spend much time here because we don't need to. One either absorbs the grammatical principles of one's native language in conversation and in reading or one does not. What Sophomore English does (or tries to do) is little more than the naming of parts.

And this isn't high school. Now that you're not worried that (a) your skirt is too short or too long and the other kids will laugh at you, (b) you're not going to make the varsity swimming team, (c) you're still going to be a pimple-studded virgin when you graduate (probably when you die, for that matter), (d) the physics teacher won't grade the final on a curve, or (e) nobody really likes you anyway AND THEY NEVER DID . . . now that all that extraneous shit is out of the way, you can study certain academic matters with a degree of concentration you could never manage while attending the local textbook loonybin. And once you start, you'll find you know almost all of the stuff anyway—it is, as I said, mostly a matter of cleaning the rust off the drillbits and sharpening the blade of your saw.

Plus . . . oh, to hell with it. If you can remember all the accessories that go with your best outfit, the contents of your purse, the starting lineup of the New York Yankees or the Houston Oilers, or what label "Hang On Sloopy" by The McCoys was on, you are capable of remembering the difference between a gerund (verb form used as a noun) and a participle (verb form used as an adjective).

I thought long and hard about whether or not to include a detailed section on grammar in this little book. Part of me would actually like to; I taught it successfully at high school (where it hid under the name Business English), and I enjoyed it as a student. American grammar doesn't have the sturdiness of British grammar (a British advertising man with a proper education can make magazine copy for ribbed condoms sound like the Magna goddam Carta), but it has its own scruffy charm.

In the end I decided against it, probably for the same reason William Strunk decided not to recap the basics when he wrote the first edition of *The Elements of Style:* if you don't know, it's too late. And those really incapable of grasping grammar—as I am incapable of playing certain guitar riffs and progressions—will have little or no use for a book like this, anyway. In that sense I am preaching to the converted. Yet allow me to go on just a little bit further—will you indulge me?

Vocabulary used in speech or writing organizes itself in seven parts of speech (eight, if you count interjections such as **Oh!** and **Gosh!** and **Fuhgeddaboudit!**). Communication composed of these parts of speech must be organized by rules of grammar upon which we agree. When these rules break down, confusion and misunderstanding result. Bad grammar produces bad sentences. My favorite example from Strunk and White is this one: **"As a mother of five, with another one on the way, my ironing board is always up."**

Nouns and verbs are the two indispensable parts of writing. Without one of each, no group of words can be a sentence, since a sentence is, by definition, a group of words containing a subject (noun) and a predicate (verb); these strings of words begin with a capital letter, end with a period, and combine to make a complete thought which starts in the writer's head and then leaps to the reader's.

Must you write complete sentences each time, every time? Perish the thought. If your work consists only of fragments and floating clauses, the Grammar Police aren't going to come and take you away. Even William Strunk, that Mussolini of rhetoric, recognized the delicious pliability of language. "It is an old observation," he writes, "that the best writers sometimes disregard the rules of rhetoric." Yet he goes on to add this thought, which I urge you to consider: "Unless he is certain of doing well, [the writer] will probably do best to follow the rules."

The telling clause here is *Unless he is certain of doing well.* If you don't have a rudimentary grasp of how the parts of speech translate into coherent sentences, how can you be certain that you *are* doing well? How will you know if you're doing ill, for that matter? The answer, of course, is that you can't, you won't. One who does grasp the rudiments of grammar finds a comforting simplicity at its heart, where there need be only nouns, the words that name, and verbs, the words that act.

Take any noun, put it with any verb, and you have a sentence. It never fails. **Rocks explode. Jane transmits. Mountains float.** These are all perfect sentences. Many such thoughts make little rational sense, but even the stranger ones (**Plums deify!**) have a kind of poetic weight that's nice. The simplicity of noun-verb construction is useful—at the very least it can provide a safety net for your writing. Strunk and White caution against too many simple sentences in a row, but simple sentences provide a path you can follow when you fear getting lost in the tangles of rhetoric—all those restrictive and nonrestrictive clauses, those modifying phrases, those appositives and compound-complex sentences. If you start to freak out at the sight of such unmapped territory (unmapped by you, at least), just remind yourself that rocks explode, Jane transmits, mountains float, and plums deify. Grammar is not just a pain in the ass; it's the pole you grab to get your thoughts up on their feet and walking. Besides, all those simple sentences worked for Hemingway, didn't they? Even when he was drunk on his ass, he was a fucking genius.

If you want to refurbish your grammar, go to your local used-book store and find a copy of *Warriner's English Grammar and Composition*—the same book most of us took home and dutifully covered with brown paper shopping-bags when we were sophomores and juniors in high school. You'll be relieved and delighted, I think, to find that almost all you need is summarized on the front and back endpapers of the book.

– 3 –

Despite the brevity of his style manual, William Strunk found room to discuss his own dislikes in matters of grammar and usage. He hated the phrase "student body," for instance, insisting that "studentry" was both clearer and without the ghoulish connotations he saw in the former term. He thought "personalize" a pretentious word. (Strunk suggests "Get up a letterhead" to replace "Personalize your stationery.") He hated phrases such as "the fact that" and "along these lines."

I have my own dislikes—I believe that anyone using the phrase "That's so cool" should have to stand in the corner and that those using the far more odious phrases "at this point in time" and "at the end of the day" should be sent to bed without supper (or writing-paper, for that matter). Two of my other pet peeves have to do with this most basic level of writing, and I want to get them off my chest before we move along.

Verbs come in two types, active and passive. With an active verb, the subject of the sentence is doing something. With a passive verb, something is being done *to* the subject of the sentence. The subject is just letting it happen. *You should avoid the passive tense.* I'm not the only one who says so; you can find the same advice in *The Elements of Style.*

Messrs. Strunk and White don't speculate as to why so many writers are attracted to passive verbs, but I'm willing to; I think timid writers like them for the same reason timid lovers like passive partners. The passive voice is safe. There is no troublesome action to contend with; the subject just has to close its eyes and think of England, to paraphrase Queen Victoria. I think unsure writers also feel the passive voice somehow lends their work authority, perhaps even a quality of majesty. If you find instruction manuals and lawyers' torts majestic, I guess it does.

The timid fellow writes **The meeting will be held at seven o'clock** because that somehow says to him, "Put it this way and people will believe *you really know.*" Purge this quisling thought! Don't be a muggle! Throw back your shoulders, stick out your chin, and put that meeting in charge! Write **The meeting's at seven.** There, by God! Don't you feel better?

I won't say there's no place for the passive tense. Suppose, for instance, a fellow dies in the kitchen but ends up somewhere else. **The body was carried from the kitchen and placed on the parlor sofa** is a fair way to put this, although "was carried" and "was placed" still irk the shit out of me. I accept them but I don't embrace them. What I would embrace is **Freddy and Myra carried the body out of the kitchen and laid it on the parlor sofa.** Why does the body have to be the subject of the sentence, anyway? It's dead, for Christ's sake! Fuhgeddaboudit!

Two pages of the passive voice—just about any business document ever written, in other words, not to mention reams of bad fiction—make me want to scream. It's weak, it's circuitous, and it's frequently tortuous, as well. How about this: **My first kiss will always be recalled by me as how my romance with Shayna was begun.** Oh, man—who farted, right? A simpler way to express this idea—sweeter and more forceful, as well—might be this: **My romance with Shayna began with our first kiss. I'll never forget it.** I'm not in love with this because it uses *with* twice in four words, but at least we're out of that awful passive voice.

You might also notice how much simpler the thought is to understand when it's broken up into *two* thoughts. This makes matters easier for the reader, and the reader must always be your main concern; without Constant Reader, you are just a voice quacking in the void. And it's no walk in the park being the guy on the receiving end. "[Will Strunk] felt the reader was in serious trouble most of the time," E. B. White writes in his introduction to *The Elements of Style,* "a man floundering in a swamp, and that it was the duty of anyone trying to write English to drain this swamp quickly and get his man up on dry ground, or at least throw him a rope." And remember: **The writer threw the rope,** not **The rope was thrown by the writer.** Please oh please.

The other piece of advice I want to give you before moving on to the next level of the toolbox is this: *The adverb is not your friend.*

Adverbs, you will remember from your own version of Business English, are words that modify verbs, adjectives, or other adverbs. They're the ones that usually end in -ly. Adverbs, like the passive voice, seem to have been created with the timid writer in mind. With the passive voice, the writer usually expresses fear of not being taken seriously; it is the voice of little boys wearing shoepolish mustaches and little girls clumping around in Mommy's high heels. With adverbs, the writer usually tells us he or she is afraid he/she isn't expressing himself/herself clearly, that he or she is not getting the point or the picture across.

Consider the sentence **He closed the door firmly.** It's by no means a terrible sentence (at least it's got an active verb going for it), but ask yourself if **firmly** really has to be there. You can argue that it expresses a degree of difference between **He closed the door** and **He slammed the door,** and you'll get no argument from me . . . but what about context? What about all the enlightening (not to say emotionally moving) prose which came *before* **He closed the door firmly?** Shouldn't this tell us how he closed the door? And if the foregoing prose *does* tell us, isn't **firmly** an extra word? Isn't it redundant?

Someone out there is now accusing me of being tiresome and anal-retentive. I deny it. I believe the road to hell is paved with adverbs, and I will shout it from the rooftops. To put it another way, they're like dandelions. If you have one on your lawn, it looks pretty and unique. If you fail to root it out, however, you find five the next day . . . fifty the day after that . . . and then, my brothers and sisters, your lawn is **totally, completely,** and **profligately** covered with dandelions. By then you see them for the weeds they really are, but by then it's—*GASP!!*—too late.

I can be a good sport about adverbs, though. Yes I can. With one exception: dialogue attribution. I insist that you use the adverb in dialogue attribution only in the rarest and most special of occasions . . . and not even then, if you can avoid it. Just to make sure we all know what we're talking about, examine these three sentences:

"Put it down!" she shouted.
"Give it back," he pleaded, "it's mine."
"Don't be such a fool, Jekyll," Utterson said.

In these sentences, shouted, pleaded, and said are verbs of dialogue attribution. Now look at these dubious revisions:

"Put it down!" she shouted menacingly.
"Give it back," he pleaded abjectly, "it's mine."
"Don't be such a fool, Jekyll," Utterson said contemptuously.

The three latter sentences are all weaker than the three former ones, and most readers will see why immediately. **"Don't be such a fool, Jekyll," Utterson said contemptuously** is the best of the lot; it is only a cliché, while the other two are actively ludicrous. Such dialogue attributions are sometimes known as "Swifties," after Tom Swift, the brave inventor-hero in a series of boys' adventure novels written by Victor Appleton II. Appleton was fond of such sentences as "Do your worst!" Tom cried bravely and "My father helped with the equations," Tom said modestly. When I was a teenager there was a party-game based on one's ability to create witty (or half-witty) Swifties. **"You got a nice butt, lady," he said cheekily** is one I remember; another is **"I'm the plumber," he said, with a flush.** (In this case the modifier is an adverbial phrase.) When debating whether or not to make some pernicious dandelion of an adverb part of your dialogue attribution, I suggest you ask yourself if you really want to write the sort of prose that might wind up in a party-game.

Some writers try to evade the no-adverb rule by shooting the attribution verb full of steroids. The result is familiar to any reader of pulp fiction or paperback originals:

> **"Put down the gun, Utterson!" Jekyll grated.**
> **"Never stop kissing me!" Shayna gasped.**
> **"You damned tease!" Bill jerked out.**

Don't do these things. Please oh please.

The best form of dialogue attribution is **said**, as in **he said, she said, Bill said, Monica said.** If you want to see this put stringently into practice, I urge you to read or reread a novel by Larry McMurtry, the Shane of dialogue attribution. That looks damned snide on the page, but I'm speaking with complete sincerity. McMurtry has allowed few adverbial dandelions to grow on his lawn. He believes in he-said/she-said even in moments of emotional crisis (and in Larry McMurtry novels there are a lot of those). Go and do thou likewise.

Is this a case of "Do as I say, not as I do?" The reader has a perfect right to ask the question, and I have a duty to provide an honest answer. Yes. It is. You need only look back through some of my own fiction to know that I'm just another ordinary sinner. I've been pretty good about avoiding the passive tense, but I've spilled out my share of adverbs in my time, including some (it shames me to say it) in dialogue attribution. (I have never fallen so low as "he grated" or "Bill jerked out," though.) When I do it, it's usually for the same reason any writer does it: because I am afraid the reader won't understand me if I don't.

I'm convinced that fear is at the root of most bad writing. If one is writing for one's own pleasure, that fear may be mild—*timidity* is the word I've used here. If, however, one is working under deadline—a school paper, a newspaper article, the SAT writing sample—that fear may be intense. Dumbo got airborne with the help of a magic feather; you may feel the urge to grasp a passive verb or one of those nasty adverbs for the same reason. Just remember before you do that Dumbo didn't need the feather; the magic was in him.

You probably *do* know what you're talking about, and can safely energize your prose with active verbs. And you probably *have* told your story well enough to believe that when you use **he said**, the reader will know how he said it—fast or slowly, happily or sadly. Your man may be floundering in a swamp, and by all means throw him a rope if he is . . . but there's no need to knock him unconscious with ninety feet of steel cable.

Good writing is often about letting go of fear and affectation. Affectation itself, beginning with the need to define some sorts of writing as "good" and other sorts as "bad," is fearful behavior. Good writing is also about making good choices when it comes to picking the tools you plan to work with.

No writer is entirely without sin in these matters. Although William Strunk got E. B. White in his clutches when White was but a naive undergraduate at Cornell (give them to me when they're young and they're mine forever, heh-heh-heh), and although White both understood and shared Strunk's prejudice against loose writing and the loose thinking which prompts it, he admits, "I suppose I have written *the fact that* a thousand times in the heat of composition, revised it out maybe five hundred times in the cool aftermath. To be batting only .500 this late in the season, to fail half the time to connect with this fat pitch, saddens me . . ." Yet E. B. White went on to write for a good many years following his initial revisions of Strunk's "little book" in 1957. I will go on writing in spite of such stupid lapses as **"You can't be serious," Bill said unbelievingly.** I expect you to do the same thing. There is a core simplicity to the English language and its American variant, but it's a slippery core. All I ask is that you do as well as you can, and remember that, while to write adverbs is human, to write **he said** or **she said** is divine.

– 4 –

Lift out the top layer of your toolbox—your vocabulary and all the grammar stuff. On the layer beneath go those elements of style upon which I've already touched. Strunk and White offer the best tools (and the best rules) you could hope for, describing them simply and clearly.

(They are offered with a refreshing strictness, beginning with the rule on how to form possessives: you always add 's, even when the word you're modifying ends in *s*— always write **Thomas's** bike and never **Thomas'** bike— and ending with ideas about where it's best to place the most important parts of a sentence. They say at the end, and everyone's entitled to his/her opinion, but I don't believe **With a hammer he killed Frank** will ever replace **He killed Frank with a hammer.**)

Before leaving the basic elements of form and style, we ought to think for a moment about the paragraph, the form of organization which comes after the sentence. To that end, grab a novel—preferably one you haven't yet read—down from your shelf (the stuff I'm telling you applies to most prose, but since I'm a fiction writer, it's fiction I usually think about when I think about writing). Open the book in the middle and look at any two pages. Observe the pattern—the lines of type, the margins, and most particularly the blocks of white space where paragraphs begin or leave off.

You can tell *without even reading* if the book you've chosen is apt to be easy or hard, right? Easy books contain lots of short paragraphs—including dialogue paragraphs which may only be a word or two long— and lots of white space. They're as airy as Dairy Queen ice cream cones. Hard books, ones full of ideas, narration, or description, have a stouter look. A *packed* look. Paragraphs are almost as important for how they look as for what they say; they are maps of intent.

In expository prose, paragraphs can (and should) be neat and utilitarian. The ideal expository graf contains a topic sentence followed by others which explain or amplify the first. Here are two paragraphs from the ever-popular "informal essay" which illustrate this simple but powerful form of writing:

When I was ten, I feared my sister Megan. It was impossible for her to come into my room without breaking at least one of my favorite toys, usually the favorite of favorites. Her gaze had some magical tape-destroying quality; any poster she looked at seemed to fall off the wall only seconds later. Well-loved articles of clothing disappeared from the closet. She didn't take them (at least I don't think so), only made them vanish. I'd usually find that treasured tee-shirt or my favorite Nikes deep under the bed months later, looking sad and abandoned among the dust kitties. When Megan was in my room, stereo speakers blew, window-shades flew up with a bang, and the lamp on my desk usually went dead.

She could be consciously cruel, too. On one occasion, Megan poured orange juice into my cereal. On another, she squirted toothpaste into the toes of my socks while I was taking a shower. And although she never admitted it, I am positive that whenever I fell asleep on the couch during half-time of the Sunday afternoon pro football games on TV, she rubbed boogers in my hair.

Informal essays are, by and large, silly and insubstantial things; unless you get a job as a columnist at your local newspaper, writing such fluffery is a skill you'll never use in the actual mall-and-filling-station world. Teachers assign them when they can't think of any other way to waste your time. The most notorious subject, of course, is "How I Spent My Summer Vacation." I taught writing for a year at the University of Maine in Orono and had one class loaded with athletes and cheerleaders. They liked informal essays, greeting them like the old high school friends they were. I spent one whole semester fighting the urge to ask them to write two pages of well-turned prose on the subject of "If Jesus Were My Teammate." What held me back was the sure and terrible knowledge that most of them would take to the task with enthusiasm. Some might actually weep while in the throes of composition.

Even in the informal essay, however, it's possible to see how strong the basic paragraph form can be. Topic-sentence-followed-by-support-and-description insists that the writer organize his/her thoughts, and it also provides good insurance against wandering away from the topic. Wandering isn't a big deal in an informal essay, is practically *de rigueur,* as a matter of fact—but it's a very bad habit to get into when working on more serious subjects in a more formal manner. Writing is refined thinking. If your master's thesis is no more organized than a high school essay titled "Why Shania Twain Turns Me On," you're in big trouble.

In fiction, the paragraph is less structured—it's the beat instead of the actual melody. The more fiction you read and write, the more you'll find your paragraphs forming on their own. And that's what you want. When composing it's best not to think too much about where paragraphs begin and end; the trick is to let

nature take its course. If you don't like it later on, fix it
then. That's what rewrite is all about. Now check out
the following:

> Big Tony's room wasn't what Dale had
> expected. The light had an odd yellowish cast
> that reminded him of cheap motels he'd stayed
> in, the ones where he always seemed to end up
> with a scenic view of the parking lot. The only
> picture was Miss May hanging askew on a push-
> pin. One shiny black shoe stuck out from
> under the bed.
>
> "I dunno why you keep askin me about
> O'Leary," Big Tony said. "You think my story's
> gonna change?"
>
> "Is it?" Dale asked.
>
> "When your story's true it don't change. The
> truth is always the same boring shit, day in and
> day out."
>
> Big Tony sat down, lit a cigarette, ran a hand
> through his hair.
>
> "I ain't seen that fuckin mick since last sum-
> mer. I let him hang around because he made
> me laugh, once showed me this thing he wrote
> about what it woulda been like if Jesus was on
> his high school football team, had a picture of
> Christ in a helmet and kneepads and everythin,
> but what a troublesome little fuck he turned
> out to be! I wish I'd never seen him!"

We could have a fifty-minute writing class on just this
brief passage. It would encompass dialogue attribution

(not necessary if we know who's speaking; Rule 17, omit needless words, in action), phonetically rendered language (**dunno, gonna**), the use of the comma (there is none in the line **When your story's true it don't change** because I want you to hear it coming out all in one breath, without a pause), the decision not to use the apostrophe where the speaker has dropped a *g* . . . and all that stuff is just from the top level of the toolbox.

Let's stick with the paragraphs, though. Notice how easily they flow, with the turns and rhythms of the story dictating where each one begins and ends. The opening graf is of the classic type, beginning with a topic sentence that is supported by the sentences which follow. Others, however, exist solely to differentiate between Dale's dialogue and Big Tony's.

The most interesting paragraph is the fifth one: **Big Tony sat down, lit a cigarette, ran a hand through his hair.** It's only a single sentence long, and expository paragraphs almost never consist of a single sentence. It's not even a very *good* sentence, technically speaking; to make it perfect in the *Warriner's* sense, there should be a conjunction (**and**). Also, what exactly is the purpose of this paragraph?

First, the sentence may be flawed in a technical sense, but it's a good one in terms of the entire passage. Its brevity and telegraphic style vary the pace and keep the writing fresh. Suspense novelist Jonathan Kellerman uses this technique very successfully. In *Survival of the Fittest,* he writes: **The boat was thirty feet of sleek white fiberglass with gray trim. Tall masts, the sails tied. *Satori* painted on the hull in black script edged with gold.**

It is possible to overuse the well-turned fragment (and Kellerman sometimes does), but frags can also work beautifully to streamline narration, create clear images, and create tension as well as to vary the prose-line. A series of grammatically proper sentences can stiffen that line, make it less pliable. Purists hate to hear that and will deny it to their dying breath, but it's true. Language does not always have to wear a tie and lace-up shoes. The object of fiction isn't grammatical correctness but to make the reader welcome and then tell a story . . . to make him/her forget, whenever possible, that he/she is reading a story at all. The single-sentence paragraph more closely resembles talk than writing, and that's good. Writing is seduction. Good talk is part of seduction. If not so, why do so many couples who start the evening at dinner wind up in bed?

The other uses of this paragraph include stage direction, minor but useful enhancement of character and setting, and a vital moment of transition. From protesting that his story is true, Big Tony moves on to his memories of O'Leary. Since the source of dialogue doesn't change, Tony's sitting down and lighting up could take place in the same paragraph, with the dialogue picking up again afterward, but the writer doesn't elect to do it that way. Because Big Tony takes a new tack, the writer breaks the dialogue into two paragraphs. It's a decision made instantaneously in the course of writing, one based entirely on the beat the writer hears in his/her own head. That beat is part of the genetic hardwiring (Kellerman writes a lot of frags because he *hears* a lot of frags), but it's also the result of the thousands of hours that writer has spent composing, and the *tens* of thousands of hours he/she may have spent reading the compositions of others.

I would argue that the paragraph, not the sentence, is the basic unit of writing—the place where coherence begins and words stand a chance of becoming more than mere words. If the moment of quickening is to come, it comes at the level of the paragraph. It is a marvellous and flexible instrument that can be a single word long or run on for pages (one paragraph in Don Robertson's historical novel *Paradise Falls* is sixteen pages long; there are paragraphs in Ross Lockridge's *Raintree County* which are nearly that). You must learn to use it well if you are to write well. What this means is lots of practice; you have to learn the beat.

– 5 –

Grab that book you were looking at off the shelf again, would you? The weight of it in your hands tells you other stuff that you can take in without reading a single word. The book's length, naturally, but more: the commitment the writer shouldered in order to create the work, the commitment Constant Reader must make to digest it. Not that length and weight alone indicate excellence; many epic tales are pretty much epic crap—just ask my critics, who will moan about entire Canadian forests massacred in order to print my drivel. Conversely, short doesn't always mean sweet. In some cases (*The Bridges of Madison County,* for instance), short means far *too* sweet. But there is that matter of commitment, whether a book is good or bad, a failure or a success.

Words have weight. Ask anyone who works in the shipping department of a book company warehouse, or in the storage room of a large bookstore.

Words create sentences; sentences create paragraphs; sometimes paragraphs quicken and begin to breathe. Imagine, if you like, Frankenstein's monster on its slab. Here comes lightning, not from the sky but from a humble paragraph of English words. Maybe it's the first really good paragraph you ever wrote, something so fragile and yet full of possibility that you are frightened. You feel as Victor Frankenstein must have when the dead conglomeration of sewn-together spare parts suddenly opened its watery yellow eyes. *Oh my God, it's breathing,* you realize. *Maybe it's even thinking. What in hell's name do I do next?*

You go on to the third level, of course, and begin to write real fiction. Why shouldn't you? Why should you fear? Carpenters don't build monsters, after all; they build houses, stores, and banks. They build some of wood a plank at a time and some of brick a brick at a time. You will build a paragraph at a time, constructing these of your vocabulary and your knowledge of grammar and basic style. As long as you stay level-on-the-level and shave even every door, you can build whatever you like—whole mansions, if you have the energy.

Is there any rationale for building entire mansions of words? I think there is, and that the readers of Margaret Mitchell's *Gone with the Wind* and Charles Dickens's *Bleak House* understand it: sometimes even a monster is no monster. Sometimes it's beautiful and we fall in love with all that story, more than any film or TV program could ever hope to provide. Even after a thousand pages we don't want to leave the world the writer has made for us, or the make-believe people who live there. You wouldn't leave after two thousand pages, if there were two thousand. The *Rings* trilogy of J. R. R. Tolkien is a perfect example of this. A thousand pages of hobbits hasn't been enough for three generations of post–World War II fantasy fans; even when you add in that clumsy, galumphing dirigible of an epilogue, *The Silmarillion,* it hasn't been enough. Hence Terry Brooks, Piers Anthony, Robert Jordan, the questing rabbits of *Watership Down,* and half a hundred others. The writers of these books are creating the hobbits they still love and pine for; they are trying to bring Frodo and Sam back from the Grey Havens because Tolkien is no longer around to do it for them.

At its most basic we are only discussing a learned skill, but do we not agree that sometimes the most basic skills can create things far beyond our expectations? We are talking about tools and carpentry, about words and style . . . but as we move along, you'd do well to remember that we are also talking about magic.

ON WRITING

There are no bad dogs, according to the title of a popular training manual, but don't tell that to the parent of a child mauled by a pit bull or a rottweiler; he or she is apt to bust your beak for you. And no matter how much I want to encourage the man or woman trying for the first time to write seriously, I can't lie and say there are no bad writers. Sorry, but there are *lots* of bad writers. Some are on-staff at your local newspaper, usually reviewing little-theater productions or pontificating about the local sports teams. Some have scribbled their way to homes in the Caribbean, leaving a trail of pulsing adverbs, wooden characters, and vile passive-voice constructions behind them. Others hold forth at open-mike poetry slams, wearing black turtlenecks and wrinkled khaki pants; they spout doggerel about "my angry lesbian breasts" and "the tilted alley where I cried my mother's name."

Writers form themselves into the pyramid we see in all areas of human talent and human creativity. At the bottom are the bad ones. Above them is a group which is slightly smaller but still large and welcoming; these are the competent writers. They may also be found on the staff of your local newspaper, on the racks at your local bookstore, and at poetry readings on Open Mike Night. These are folks who somehow understand that although a lesbian may be angry, her breasts will remain breasts.

The next level is much smaller. These are the really good writers. Above them—above almost all of us—are the Shakespeares, the Faulkners, the Yeatses, Shaws, and Eudora Weltys. They are geniuses, divine accidents, gifted in a way which is beyond our ability to understand, let alone attain. Shit, most geniuses aren't able to understand themselves, and many of them lead miserable lives, realizing (at least on some level) that they are nothing but fortunate freaks, the intellectual version of runway models who just happen to be born with the right cheekbones and with breasts which fit the image of an age.

I am approaching the heart of this book with two theses, both simple. The first is that good writing consists of mastering the fundamentals (vocabulary, grammar, the elements of style) and then filling the third level of your toolbox with the right instruments. The second is that while it is impossible to make a competent writer out of a bad writer, and while it is equally impossible to make a great writer out of a good one, it *is* possible, with lots of hard work, dedication, and timely help, to make a good writer out of a merely competent one.

I'm afraid this idea is rejected by lots of critics and plenty of writing teachers, as well. Many of these are liberals in their politics but crustaceans in their chosen fields. Men and women who would take to the streets to protest the exclusion of African-Americans or Native

Americans (I can imagine what Mr. Strunk would have made of these politically correct but clunky terms) from the local country club are often the same men and women who tell their classes that writing ability is fixed and immutable; once a hack, always a hack. Even if a writer rises in the estimation of an influential critic or two, he/she always carries his/her early reputation along, like a respectable married woman who was a wild child as a teenager. Some people never forget, that's all, and a good deal of literary criticism serves only to re-inforce a caste system which is as old as the intellectual snobbery which nurtured it. Raymond Chandler may be recognized now as an important figure in twentieth-century American literature, an early voice describing the anomie of urban life in the years after World War II, but there are plenty of critics who will reject such a judgment out of hand. He's a hack! they cry indignantly. A hack with pretensions! The worst kind! The kind who thinks he can pass for one of *us!*

Critics who try to rise above this intellectual hardening of the arteries usually meet with limited success. Their colleagues may accept Chandler into the company of the great, but are apt to seat him at the foot of the table. And there are always those whispers: *Came out of the pulp tradition, you know . . . carries himself well for one of those, doesn't he? . . . did you know he wrote for* Black Mask *in the thirties . . . yes, regrettable . . .*

Even Charles Dickens, the Shakespeare of the novel, has faced a constant critical attack as a result of his often sensational subject matter, his cheerful fecundity (when he wasn't creating novels, he and his wife were creating children), and, of course, his success with the book-reading groundlings of his time and ours. Critics and scholars have always been suspicious of popular success. Often their suspicions are justified. In other cases, these suspicions are used as an excuse not to think. No one can be as intellectually slothful as a really smart person; give smart people half a chance and they will ship their oars and drift . . . dozing to Byzantium, you might say.

So yes—I expect to be accused by some of promoting a brainless and happy Horatio Alger philosophy, defending my own less-than-spotless reputation while I'm at it, and of encouraging people who are "just not our sort, old chap" to apply for membership at the country club. I guess I can live with that. But before we go on, let me repeat my basic premise: if you're a bad writer, no one can help you become a good one, or even a competent one. If you're good and want to be great . . . fuhgeddaboudit.

What follows is everything I know about how to write good fiction. I'll be as brief as possible, because your time is valuable and so is mine, and we both understand that the hours we spend talking about writing is time we don't spend actually *doing* it. I'll be as encouraging as possible, because it's my nature and because I love this job. I want you to love it, too. But if you don't want to work your ass off, you have no business trying to write well—settle back into competency and be grateful you have even that much to fall back on. There is a muse,* but he's not going to come flut-

---

*Traditionally, the muses were women, but mine's a guy; I'm afraid we'll just have to live with that.

tering down into your writing room and scatter creative fairy-dust all over your typewriter or computer station. He lives in the ground. He's a basement guy. You have to descend to his level, and once you get down there you have to furnish an apartment for him to live in. You have to do all the grunt labor, in other words, while the muse sits and smokes cigars and admires his bowling trophies and pretends to ignore you. Do you think this is fair? *I* think it's fair. He may not be much to look at, that muse-guy, and he may not be much of a conversationalist (what I get out of mine is mostly surly grunts, unless he's on duty), but he's got the inspiration. It's right that you should do all the work and burn all the midnight oil, because the guy with the cigar and the little wings has got a bag of magic. There's stuff in there that can change your life.

Believe me, I know.

– 1 –

If you want to be a writer, you must do two things above all others: read a lot and write a lot. There's no way around these two things that I'm aware of, no shortcut.

I'm a slow reader, but I usually get through seventy or eighty books a year, mostly fiction. I don't read in order to study the craft; I read because I like to read. It's what I do at night, kicked back in my blue chair. Similarly, I don't read fiction to study the art of fiction, but simply because I like stories. Yet there is a learning process going on. Every book you pick up has its own lesson or lessons, and quite often the bad books have more to teach than the good ones.

When I was in the eighth grade, I happened upon a paperback novel by Murray Leinster, a science fiction pulp writer who did most of his work during the forties and fifties, when magazines like *Amazing Stories* paid a penny a word. I had read other books by Mr. Leinster, enough to know that the quality of his writing was uneven. This particular tale, which was about mining in the asteroid belt, was one of his less successful efforts. Only that's too kind. It was terrible, actually, a story populated by paper-thin characters and driven by outlandish plot developments. Worst of all (or so it seemed to me at the time), Leinster had fallen in love with the word *zestful*. Characters watched the approach of ore-bearing asteroids with *zestful smiles*. Characters sat down to supper aboard their mining ship with *zestful anticipation*. Near the end of the book, the hero swept the large-breasted, blonde heroine into a *zestful embrace*. For me, it was the literary equivalent of a smallpox vaccination: I have never, so far as I know, used the word *zestful* in a novel or a story. God willing, I never will.

Asteroid Miners (which wasn't the title, but that's close enough) was an important book in my life as a reader. Almost everyone can remember losing his or her virginity, and most writers can remember the first book he/she put down thinking: *I can do better than this. Hell, I am doing better than this!* What could be more encouraging to the struggling writer than to realize his/her work is unquestionably better than that of someone who actually got paid for his/her stuff?

One learns most clearly what not to do by reading

bad prose—one novel like *Asteroid Miners* (or *Valley of the Dolls, Flowers in the Attic,* and *The Bridges of Madison County,* to name just a few) is worth a semester at a good writing school, even with the superstar guest lecturers thrown in.

Good writing, on the other hand, teaches the learning writer about style, graceful narration, plot development, the creation of believable characters, and truth-telling. A novel like *The Grapes of Wrath* may fill a new writer with feelings of despair and good old-fashioned jealousy— "I'll never be able to write anything that good, not if I live to be a thousand"—but such feelings can also serve as a spur, goading the writer to work harder and aim higher. Being swept away by a combination of great story and great writing—of being flattened, in fact—is part of every writer's necessary formation. You cannot hope to sweep someone else away by the force of your writing until it has been done to you.

So we read to experience the mediocre and the out-right rotten; such experience helps us to recognize those things when they begin to creep into our own work, and to steer clear of them. We also read in order to measure ourselves against the good and the great, to get a sense of all that can be done. And we read in order to experience different styles.

You may find yourself adopting a style you find particularly exciting, and there's nothing wrong with that. When I read Ray Bradbury as a kid, I wrote like Ray Bradbury—everything green and wondrous and seen through a lens smeared with the grease of nostalgia. When I read James M. Cain, everything I wrote came out clipped and stripped and hard-boiled. When I read

Lovecraft, my prose became luxurious and Byzantine. I wrote stories in my teenage years where all these styles merged, creating a kind of hilarious stew. This sort of stylistic blending is a necessary part of developing one's own style, but it doesn't occur in a vacuum. You have to read widely, constantly refining (and redefining) your own work as you do so. It's hard for me to believe that people who read very little (or not at all in some cases) should presume to write and expect people to like what they have written, but I know it's true. If I had a nickel for every person who ever told me he/she wanted to become a writer but "didn't have time to read," I could buy myself a pretty good steak dinner. Can I be blunt on this subject? If you don't have time to read, you don't have the time (or the tools) to write. Simple as that.

Reading is the creative center of a writer's life. I take a book with me everywhere I go, and find there are all sorts of opportunities to dip in. The trick is to teach yourself to read in small sips as well as in long swallows. Waiting rooms were made for books—of course! But so are theater lobbies before the show, long and boring checkout lines, and everyone's favorite, the john. You can even read while you're driving, thanks to the audiobook revolution. Of the books I read each year, anywhere from six to a dozen are on tape. As for all the wonderful radio you will be missing, come on— how many times can you listen to Deep Purple sing "Highway Star"?

Reading at meals is considered rude in polite society, but if you expect to succeed as a writer, rudeness should be the second-to-least of your concerns. The least of all should be polite society and what it expects. If you intend to write as truthfully as you can, your days as a member of polite society are numbered, anyway.

Where else can you read? There's always the treadmill, or whatever you use down at the local health club to get aerobic. I try to spend an hour doing that every day, and I think I'd go mad without a good novel to keep me company. Most exercise facilities (at home as well as outside it) are now equipped with TVs, but TV—while working out or anywhere else—really is about the last thing an aspiring writer needs. If you feel you must have the news analyst blowhards on CNN while you exercise, or the stock market blowhards on MSNBC, or the sports blowhards on ESPN, it's time for you to question how serious you really are about becoming a writer. You must be prepared to do some serious turning inward toward the life of the imagination, and that means, I'm afraid, that Geraldo, Keith Obermann, and Jay Leno must go. Reading takes time, and the glass teat takes too much of it.

Once weaned from the ephemeral craving for TV, most people will find they enjoy the time they spend reading. I'd like to suggest that turning off that endlessly quacking box is apt to improve the quality of your life as well as the quality of your writing. And how much of a sacrifice are we talking about here? How many *Frasier* and *ER* reruns does it take to make one American life complete? How many Richard Simmons infomercials? How many whiteboy/fatboy Beltway insiders on CNN? Oh man, don't get me started. Jerry-Springer-Dr.-Dre-Judge-Judy-Jerry-Falwell-Donny-and-Marie, I rest my case.

When my son Owen was seven or so, he fell in love with Bruce Springsteen's E Street Band, particularly with Clarence Clemons, the band's burly sax player.

Owen decided he wanted to learn to play like Clarence. My wife and I were amused and delighted by this ambition. We were also hopeful, as any parent would be, that our kid would turn out to be talented, perhaps even some sort of prodigy. We got Owen a tenor saxophone for Christmas and lessons with Gordon Bowie, one of the local music men. Then we crossed our fingers and hoped for the best.

Seven months later I suggested to my wife that it was time to discontinue the sax lessons, if Owen concurred. Owen did, and with palpable relief—he hadn't wanted to say it himself, especially not after asking for the sax in the first place, but seven months had been long enough for him to realize that, while he might love Clarence Clemons's big sound, the saxophone was simply not for him—God had not given him that particular talent.

I knew, not because Owen stopped practicing, but because he was practicing only during the periods Mr. Bowie had set for him: half an hour after school four days a week, plus an hour on the weekends. Owen mastered the scales and the notes—nothing wrong with his memory, his lungs, or his eye-hand coordination—but we never heard him taking off, surprising himself with something new, blissing himself out. And as soon as his practice time was over, it was back into the case with the horn, and there it stayed until the next lesson or practice-time. What this suggested to me was that when it came to the sax and my son, there was never going to be any real play-time; it was all going to be rehearsal. That's no good. If there's no joy in it, it's just no good. It's best to go on to some other area, where the deposits of talent may be richer and the fun quotient higher.

Talent renders the whole idea of rehearsal meaningless; when you find something at which you are talented, you do it (whatever *it* is) until your fingers bleed or your eyes are ready to fall out of your head. Even when no one is listening (or reading, or watching), every outing is a bravura performance, because you as the creator are happy. Perhaps even ecstatic. That goes for reading and writing as well as for playing a musical instrument, hitting a baseball, or running the four-forty. The sort of strenuous reading and writing program I advocate—four to six hours a day, every day—will not seem strenuous if you really enjoy doing these things and have an aptitude for them; in fact, you may be following such a program already. If you feel you need permission to do all the reading and writing your little heart desires, however, consider it hereby granted by yours truly.

The real importance of reading is that it creates an ease and intimacy with the process of writing; one comes to the country of the writer with one's papers and identification pretty much in order. Constant reading will pull you into a place (a mind-set, if you like the phrase) where you can write eagerly and without self-consciousness. It also offers you a constantly growing knowledge of what has been done and what hasn't, what is trite and what is fresh, what works and what just lies there dying (or dead) on the page. The more you read, the less apt you are to make a fool of yourself with your pen or word processor.

– 2 –

If "read a lot, write a lot" is the Great Commandment—and I assure you that it is—how much writing constitutes a lot? That varies, of course, from writer to writer. One of my favorite stories on the subject—probably more myth than truth—concerns James Joyce.* According to the story, a friend came to visit him one day and found the great man sprawled across his writing desk in a posture of utter despair.

"James, what's wrong?" the friend asked. "Is it the work?"

Joyce indicated assent without even raising his head to look at the friend. Of course it was the work; isn't it always?

"How many words did you get today?" the friend pursued.

Joyce (still in despair, still sprawled facedown on his desk): "Seven."

"Seven? But James . . . that's *good,* at least for you!"

"Yes," Joyce said, finally looking up. "I suppose it is . . . but I don't know what *order* they go in!"

At the other end of the spectrum, there are writers like Anthony Trollope. He wrote humongous novels (*Can You Forgive Her?* is a fair enough example; for modern audiences it might be retitled *Can You Possibly Finish It?*), and he pumped them out with amazing regularity.

---

*There are some great stories about Joyce. My absolute favorite is that, as his vision failed, he took to wearing a milkman's uniform while writing. Supposedly he believed it caught the sunlight and reflected it down on his page.

His day job was as a clerk in the British Postal Department (the red public mailboxes all over Britain were Anthony Trollope's invention); he wrote for two and a half hours each morning before leaving for work. This schedule was ironclad. If he was in mid-sentence when the two and a half hours expired, he left that sentence unfinished until the next morning. And if he happened to finish one of his six-hundred-page heavyweights with fifteen minutes of the session remaining, he wrote **The End,** set the manuscript aside, and began work on the next book.

John Creasey, a British mystery novelist, wrote five hundred (yes, you read it correctly) novels under ten different names. I've written thirty-five or so—some of Trollopian length—and am considered prolific, but I look positively blocked next to Creasey. Several other contemporary novelists (they include Ruth Rendell/Barbara Vine, Evan Hunter/Ed McBain, Dean Koontz, and Joyce Carol Oates) have written easily as much as I have; some have written a good deal more.

On the other hand—the James Joyce hand—there is Harper Lee, who wrote only one book (the brilliant *To Kill a Mockingbird*). Any number of others, including James Agee, Malcolm Lowry, and Thomas Harris (so far), wrote under five. Which is okay, but I always wonder two things about these folks: how long did it take them to write the books they *did* write, and what did they do the rest of their time? Knit afghans? Organize church bazaars? Deify plums? I'm probably being snotty here, but I am also, believe me, honestly curious. If God gives you something you can do, why in God's name wouldn't you do it?

My own schedule is pretty clear-cut. Mornings belong to whatever is new—the current composition. Afternoons are for naps and letters. Evenings are for reading, family, Red Sox games on TV, and any revisions that just cannot wait. Basically, mornings are my prime writing time.

Once I start work on a project, I don't stop and I don't slow down unless I absolutely have to. If I don't write every day, the characters begin to stale off in my mind—they begin to *seem* like characters instead of real people. The tale's narrative cutting edge starts to rust and I begin to lose my hold on the story's plot and pace. Worst of all, the excitement of spinning something new begins to fade. The work starts to *feel* like work, and for most writers that is the smooch of death. Writing is at its best—always, always, always—when it is a kind of inspired play for the writer. I can write in cold blood if I have to, but I like it best when it's fresh and almost too hot to handle.

I used to tell interviewers that I wrote every day except for Christmas, the Fourth of July, and my birthday. That was a lie. I told them that because if you agree to an interview you have to say *something,* and it plays better if it's something at least half-clever. Also, I didn't want to sound like a workaholic dweeb (just a workaholic, I guess). The truth is that when I'm writing, I write every day, workaholic dweeb or not. That *includes* Christmas, the Fourth, and my birthday (at my age you try to ignore your goddam birthday anyway). And when I'm not working, I'm not working at all, although during those periods of full stop I usually feel at loose ends with myself and have trouble sleeping. For me, not working is the real work. When I'm writing, it's all the playground, and the worst three hours I ever spent there were still pretty damned good.

I used to be faster than I am now; one of my books *(The Running Man)* was written in a single week, an accomplishment John Creasey would perhaps have appreciated (although I have read that Creasey wrote several of his mysteries in *two days*). I think it was quitting smoking that slowed me down; nicotine is a great synapse enhancer. The problem, of course, is that it's killing you at the same time it's helping you compose. Still, I believe the first draft of a book—even a long one—should take no more than three months, the length of a season. Any longer and—for me, at least—the story begins to take on an odd foreign feel, like a dispatch from the Romanian Department of Public Affairs, or something broadcast on high-band shortwave during a period of severe sunspot activity.

I like to get ten pages a day, which amounts to 2,000 words. That's 180,000 words over a three-month span, a goodish length for a book—something in which the reader can get happily lost, if the tale is done well and stays fresh. On some days those ten pages come easily; I'm up and out and doing errands by eleven-thirty in the morning, perky as a rat in liverwurst. More frequently, as I grow older, I find myself eating lunch at my desk and finishing the day's work around one-thirty in the afternoon. Sometimes, when the words come hard, I'm still fiddling around at teatime. Either way is fine with me, but only under dire circumstances do I allow myself to shut down before I get my 2,000 words.

The biggest aid to regular (Trollopian?) production is working in a serene atmosphere. It's difficult for even the most naturally productive writer to work in an environment where alarms and excursions are the rule rather than the exception. When I'm asked for "the secret of my success" (an absurd idea, that, but impossible to get away from), I sometimes say there are two: I stayed physically healthy (at least until a van knocked me down by the side of the road in the summer of 1999), and I stayed married. It's a good answer because it makes the question go away, and because there is an element of truth in it. The combination of a healthy body and a stable relationship with a self-reliant woman who takes zero shit from me or anyone else has made the continuity of my working life possible. And I believe the converse is also true: that my writing and the pleasure I take in it has contributed to the stability of my health and my home life.

– 3 –

You can read anywhere, almost, but when it comes to writing, library carrels, park benches, and rented flats should be courts of last resort—Truman Capote said he did his best work in motel rooms, but he is an exception; most of us do our best in a place of our own. Until you get one, you'll find your new resolution to write a lot hard to take seriously.

Your writing room doesn't have to sport a Playboy Philosophy decor, and you don't need an Early American rolltop desk in which to house your writing implements. I wrote my first two published novels, *Carrie* and *'Salem's Lot,* in the laundry room of a doublewide trailer, pounding away on my wife's portable Olivetti typewriter and balancing a child's desk on my thighs; John Cheever reputedly wrote in the basement of his Park Avenue apartment building, near the furnace. The space can be humble (probably *should* be, as I think I have already suggested), and it really needs only one thing: a door which you are willing to shut. The closed door is your way of telling the world and yourself that you mean business; you have made a serious commitment to write and intend to walk the walk as well as talk the talk.

By the time you step into your new writing space and close the door, you should have settled on a daily writing goal. As with physical exercise, it would be best to set this goal low at first, to avoid discouragement. I suggest a thousand words a day, and because I'm feeling magnanimous, I'll also suggest that you can take one day a week off, at least to begin with. No more; you'll lose the urgency and immediacy of your story if you do. With that goal set, resolve to yourself that the door stays closed until that goal is met. Get busy putting those thousand words on paper or on a floppy disk. In an early interview (this was to promote *Carrie,* I think), a radio talk-show host asked me how I wrote. My reply—"One word at a time"—seemingly left him without a reply. I think he was trying to decide whether or not I was joking. I wasn't. In the end, it's always that simple. Whether it's a vignette of a single page or an epic trilogy like *The Lord of the Rings,* the work is always accomplished one word at a time. The door closes the rest of the world out; it also serves to close you in and keep you focused on the job at hand.

If possible, there should be no telephone in your writing room, certainly no TV or videogames for you to fool around with. If there's a window, draw the curtains or pull down the shades unless it looks out at a blank wall. For any writer, but for the beginning writer in particular, it's wise to eliminate every possible distraction. If you continue to write, you will begin to filter out these distractions naturally, but at the start it's best to try and take care of them before you write. I work to loud music—hard-rock stuff like AC/DC, Guns 'n Roses, and Metallica have always been particular favorites—but for me the music is just another way of shutting the door. It surrounds me, keeps the mundane world out. When you write, you want to get rid of the world, do you not? Of course you do. When you're writing, you're creating your own worlds.

I think we're actually talking about creative sleep. Like your bedroom, your writing room should be private, a place where you go to dream. Your schedule—in at about the same time every day, out when your thousand words are on paper or disk—exists in order to habituate yourself, to make yourself ready to dream just as you make yourself ready to sleep by going to bed at roughly the same time each night and following the same ritual as you go. In both writing and sleeping, we learn to be physically still at the same time we are encouraging our minds to unlock from the humdrum rational thinking of our daytime lives. And as your mind and body grow accustomed to a certain amount of sleep each night—six hours, seven, maybe the recommended eight—so can you train your waking mind to sleep creatively and work out the vividly imagined waking dreams which are successful works of fiction.

But you need the room, you need the door, and you need the determination to shut the door. You need a concrete goal, as well. The longer you keep to these basics, the easier the act of writing will become. Don't wait for the muse. As I've said, he's a hardheaded guy who's not susceptible to a lot of creative fluttering. This isn't the Ouija board or the spirit-world we're talking about here, but just another job like laying pipe or driving long-haul trucks. Your job is to make sure the muse knows where you're going to be every day from nine 'til noon or seven 'til three. If he does know, I assure you that sooner or later he'll start showing up, chomping his cigar and making his magic.

– 4 –

So okay—there you are in your room with the shade down and the door shut and the plug pulled out of the base of the telephone. You've blown up your TV and committed yourself to a thousand words a day, come hell or high water. Now comes the big question: What are you going to write about? And the equally big answer: Anything you damn well want. Anything at all . . . *as long as you tell the truth.*

The dictum in writing classes used to be "write what you know." Which sounds good, but what if you want to write about starships exploring other planets or a man who murders his wife and then tries to dispose of her body with a wood-chipper? How does the writer square either of these, or a thousand other fanciful ideas, with the "write-what-you-know" directive?

I think you begin by interpreting "write what you know" as broadly and inclusively as possible. If you're a plumber, you know plumbing, but that is far from the extent of your knowledge; the heart also knows things, and so does the imagination. Thank God. If not for heart and imagination, the world of fiction would be a pretty seedy place. It might not even exist at all.

In terms of genre, it's probably fair to assume that you will begin by writing what you love to read—certainly I have recounted my early love affair with the EC horror comics until the tale has gone stale. But I *did* love them, ditto horror movies like *I Married a Monster from Outer Space,* and the result was stories like "I Was a Teenage Graverobber." Even today I'm not above writing slightly more sophisticated versions of that tale; I was built with a love of the night and the unquiet coffin, that's all. If you disapprove, I can only shrug my shoulders. It's what I have.

If you happen to be a science fiction fan, it's natural that you should want to write science fiction (and the more sf you've read, the less likely it is that you'll simply revisit the field's well-mined conventions, such as space opera and dystopian satire). If you're a mystery fan, you'll want to write mysteries, and if you enjoy romances, it's natural for you to want to write romances of your own. There's nothing wrong with writing any of these things. What would be very wrong, I think, is to turn away from what you know and like (or love, the way I loved those old ECs and black-and-white horror flicks) in favor of things you believe will impress your friends, relatives, and writing-circle colleagues. What's equally wrong is the deliberate turning toward some genre or type of fiction in order to make money. It's morally wonky, for one thing—the job of fiction is to find the truth inside the story's web of lies, not to commit intellectual dishonesty in the hunt for the buck. Also, brothers and sisters, it doesn't work.

When I'm asked why I decided to write the sort of thing I do write, I always think the question is more revealing than any answer I could possibly give. Wrapped within it, like the chewy stuff in the center of a Tootsie Pop, is the assumption that the writer controls the material instead of the other way around.* The writer who is serious and committed is incapable of sizing up story material the way an investor might size up various stock offerings, picking out the ones which seem likely to provide a good return. If it could indeed be done that way, every novel published would be a best-seller and the huge advances paid to a dozen or so "big-name writers" would not exist (publishers would like that).

Grisham, Clancy, Crichton, and myself—among others—are paid these large sums of money because we are selling uncommonly large numbers of books to uncommonly large audiences. A critical assumption is sometimes made that we have access to some mystical

---

*Kirby McCauley, my first real agent, used to quote science fiction writer Alfred Bester (*The Stars My Destination, The Demolished Man*) on this subject. "The book is the boss," Alfie used to say in tones indicating that that closed the subject.

vulgate that other (and often better) writers either cannot find or will not deign to use. I doubt if this is true. Nor do I believe the contention of some popular novelists (although she was not the only one, I am thinking of the late Jacqueline Susann) that their success is based on literary merit—that the public understands true greatness in ways the tight-assed, consumed-by-jealousy literary establishment cannot. This idea is ridiculous, a product of vanity and insecurity.

Book-buyers aren't attracted, by and large, by the literary merits of a novel; book-buyers want a good story to take with them on the airplane, something that will first fascinate them, then pull them in and keep them turning the pages. This happens, I think, when readers recognize the people in a book, their behaviors, their surroundings, and their talk. When the reader hears strong echoes of his or her own life and beliefs, he or she is apt to become more invested in the story. I'd argue that it's impossible to make this sort of connection in a premeditated way, gauging the market like a racetrack tout with a hot tip.

Stylistic imitation is one thing, a perfectly honorable way to get started as a writer (and impossible to avoid, really; some sort of imitation marks each new stage of a writer's development), but one cannot imitate a writer's approach to a particular genre, no matter how simple what that writer is doing may seem. You can't aim a book like a cruise missile, in other words. People who decide to make a fortune writing like John Grisham or Tom Clancy produce nothing but pale imitations, by and large, because vocabulary is not the same thing as feeling and plot is light-years from the truth as it is understood by the mind and the heart. When you see a novel with **"In the tradition of** (John Grisham/Patricia Cornwell/Mary Higgins Clark/Dean Koontz)" on the cover, you know you are looking at one of these overcalculated (and likely boring) imitations.

Write what you like, then imbue it with life and make it unique by blending in your own personal knowledge of life, friendship, relationships, sex, and work. Especially work. People love to read about work. God knows why, but they do. If you're a plumber who enjoys science fiction, you might well consider a novel about a plumber aboard a starship or on an alien planet. Sound ludicrous? The late Clifford D. Simak wrote a novel called *Cosmic Engineers* which is close to just that. And it's a terrific read. What you need to remember is that there's a difference between lecturing about what you know and using it to enrich the story. The latter is good. The former is not.

Consider John Grisham's breakout novel, *The Firm*. In this story, a young lawyer discovers that his first job, which seemed too good to be true, really is—he's working for the Mafia. Suspenseful, involving, and paced at breakneck speed, *The Firm* sold roughly nine gazillion copies. What seemed to fascinate its audience was the moral dilemma in which the young lawyer finds himself: working for the mob is bad, no argument there, but the frocking pay is *great!* You can drive a Beemer, and that's just for openers!

Audiences also enjoyed the lawyer's resourceful efforts to extricate himself from his dilemma. It might not be the way most people would behave, and the *deus ex machina* clanks pretty steadily in the last fifty pages, but it *is* the way most of us would *like* to behave. And wouldn't we also like to have a *deus ex machina* in our lives?

Although I don't know for sure, I'd bet my dog and lot that John Grisham never worked for the mob. All of that is total fabrication (and total fabrication is the fiction-writer's purest delight). He *was* once a young lawyer, though, and he has clearly forgotten none of the struggle. Nor has he forgotten the location of the various financial pitfalls and honeytraps that make the field of corporate law so difficult. Using plainspun humor as a brilliant counterpoint and never substituting cant for story, he sketches a world of Darwinian struggle where all the savages wear three-piece suits. And—here's the good part—*this is a world impossible not to believe.* Grisham has been there, spied out the land and the enemy positions, and brought back a full report. He told the truth of what he knew, and for that if nothing else, he deserves every buck *The Firm* made.

Critics who dismissed *The Firm* and Grisham's later books as poorly written and who profess themselves to be mystified by his success are either missing the point because it's so big and obvious or because they are being deliberately obtuse. Grisham's make-believe tale is solidly based in a reality he knows, has personally experienced, and which he wrote about with total (almost naive) honesty. The result is a book which is—cardboard characters or no, we could argue about that—both brave and uniquely satisfying. You as a beginning writer would do well not to imitate the lawyers-in-trouble genre Grisham seems to have created but to emulate Grisham's openness and inability to do anything other than get right to the point.

John Grisham, of course, knows lawyers. What *you* know makes you unique in some other way. Be brave. Map the enemy's positions, come back, tell us all you know. And remember that plumbers in space is not such a bad setup for a story.

– 5 –

In my view, stories and novels consist of three parts: narration, which moves the story from point A to point B and finally to point Z; description, which creates a sensory reality for the reader; and dialogue, which brings characters to life through their speech.

You may wonder where plot is in all this. The answer—my answer, anyway—is nowhere. I won't try to convince you that I've never plotted any more than I'd try to convince you that I've never told a lie, but I do both as infrequently as possible. I distrust plot for two reasons: first, because our *lives* are largely plotless, even when you add in all our reasonable precautions and careful planning; and second, because I believe plotting and the spontaneity of real creation aren't compatible. It's best that I be as clear about this as I can—I want you to understand that my basic belief about the making of stories is that they pretty much make themselves. The job of the writer is to give them a place to grow (and to transcribe them, of course). If you can see things this way (or at least try to), we can work together comfortably. If, on the other hand, you decide I'm crazy, that's fine. You won't be the first.

When, during the course of an interview for *The New*

Yorker, I told the interviewer (Mark Singer) that I believed stories are found things, like fossils in the ground, he said that he didn't believe me. I replied that that was fine, as long as he believed that *I* believe it. And I do. Stories aren't souvenir tee-shirts or Game-Boys. Stories are relics, part of an undiscovered pre-existing world. The writer's job is to use the tools in his or her toolbox to get as much of each one out of the ground intact as possible. Sometimes the fossil you uncover is small; a seashell. Sometimes it's enormous, a *Tyrannosaurus Rex* with all those gigantic ribs and grinning teeth. Either way, short story or thousand-page whopper of a novel, the techniques of excavation remain basically the same.

No matter how good you are, no matter how much experience you have, it's probably impossible to get the entire fossil out of the ground without a few breaks and losses. To get even *most* of it, the shovel must give way to more delicate tools: airhose, palm-pick, perhaps even a toothbrush. Plot is a far bigger tool, the writer's jackhammer. You can liberate a fossil from hard ground with a jackhammer, no argument there, but you know as well as I do that the jackhammer is going to break almost as much stuff as it liberates. It's clumsy, mechanical, anticreative. Plot is, I think, the good writer's last resort and the dullard's first choice. The story which results from it is apt to feel artificial and labored.

I lean more heavily on intuition, and have been able to do that because my books tend to be based on situation rather than story. Some of the ideas which have produced those books are more complex than others, but the majority start out with the stark simplicity of a department store window display or a waxwork tableau. I want to put a group of characters (perhaps a pair; perhaps even just one) in some sort of predicament and then watch them try to work themselves free. My job isn't to *help* them work their way free, or manipulate them to safety—those are jobs which require the noisy jackhammer of plot—but to watch what happens and then write it down.

The situation comes first. The characters—always flat and unfeatured, to begin with—come next. Once these things are fixed in my mind, I begin to narrate. I often have an idea of what the outcome may be, but I have never demanded of a set of characters that they do things my way. On the contrary, I want them to do things *their* way. In some instances, the outcome is what I visualized. In most, however, it's something I never expected. For a suspense novelist, this is a great thing. I am, after all, not just the novel's creator but its first reader. And if *I'm* not able to guess with any accuracy how the damned thing is going to turn out, even with my inside knowledge of coming events, I can be pretty sure of keeping the reader in a state of page-turning anxiety. And why worry about the ending anyway? Why be such a control freak? Sooner or later every story comes out *somewhere*.

In the early 1980s, my wife and I went to London on a combined business/pleasure trip. I fell asleep on the plane and had a dream about a popular writer (it may or may not have been me, but it sure to God wasn't James Caan) who fell into the clutches of a psychotic fan living on a farm somewhere out in the back of the beyond. The fan was a woman isolated by her growing paranoia. She kept some livestock in the barn, including her pet pig, Misery. The pig was named after the continuing main character in the writer's best-selling bodice-rippers. My clearest memory of this dream upon waking was something the woman said to the writer, who had a broken leg and was being kept prisoner in the back bedroom. I wrote it on an American Airlines cocktail napkin so I wouldn't forget it, then put it in my pocket. I lost it somewhere, but can remember most of what I wrote down:

She speaks earnestly but never quite makes eye contact. A big woman and solid all through; she is an absence of hiatus. (Whatever *that* means; remember, I'd just woken up.) *"I wasn't trying to be funny in a mean way when I named my pig Misery, no sir. Please don't think that. No, I named her in the spirit of fan love, which is the purest love there is. You should be flattered."*

Tabby and I stayed at Brown's Hotel in London, and on our first night there I was unable to sleep. Some of it was what sounded like a trio of little-girl gymnasts in the room directly above ours, some of it was undoubtedly jet lag, but a lot of it was that airline cocktail napkin. Jotted on it was the seed of what I thought could be a really excellent story, one that might turn out funny and satiric as well as scary. I thought it was just too rich not to write.

I got up, went downstairs, and asked the concierge if there was a quiet place where I could work longhand for a bit. He led me to a gorgeous desk on the second-floor stair landing. It had been Rudyard Kipling's desk, he told me with perhaps justifiable pride. I was a little intimidated by this intelligence, but the spot was quiet and the desk seemed hospitable enough; it featured about an acre of cherrywood working surface, for one thing. Stoked on cup after cup of tea (I drank it by the gallon when I wrote . . . unless I was drinking beer, that is), I filled sixteen pages of a steno notebook. I like to work longhand, actually; the only problem is that, once I get jazzed, I can't keep up with the lines forming in my head and I get frazzled.

When I called it quits, I stopped in the lobby to thank the concierge again for letting me use Mr. Kipling's beautiful desk. "I'm so glad you enjoyed it," he replied. He was wearing a misty, reminiscent little smile, as if he had known the writer himself. "Kipling died there, actually. Of a stroke. While he was writing."

I went back upstairs to catch a few hours' sleep, thinking of how often we are given information we really could have done without.

The working title of my story, which I thought would be a novella of about 30,000 words, was "The Annie Wilkes Edition." When I sat down at Mr. Kipling's beautiful desk I had the basic situation—crippled writer, psycho fan—firmly fixed in my mind. The actual *story* did not as then exist (well, it did, but as a relic buried—except for sixteen handwritten pages, that is—in the earth), but knowing the story wasn't necessary for me to begin work. I had located the fossil; the rest, I knew, would consist of careful excavation.

I'd suggest that what works for me may work equally well for you. If you are enslaved to (or intimidated by) the tiresome tyranny of the outline and the notebook filled with "Character Notes," it may liberate you. At the very least, it will turn your mind to something more interesting than Developing the Plot.

(An amusing sidelight: the century's greatest supporter of Developing the Plot may have been Edgar Wallace, a best-selling potboiler novelist of the 1920s. Wallace invented—and patented—a device called the Edgar Wallace Plot Wheel. When you got stuck for the next Plot Development or needed an Amazing Turn of Events in a hurry, you simply spun the Plot Wheel and read what came up in the window: **a fortuitous arrival**, perhaps, or **Heroine declares her love**. These gadgets apparently sold like hotcakes.)

By the time I had finished that first Brown's Hotel session, in which Paul Sheldon wakes up to find himself Annie Wilkes's prisoner, I thought I knew what was going to happen. Annie would demand that Paul write another novel about his plucky continuing character, Misery Chastain, one just for her. After first demurring, Paul would of course agree (a psychotic nurse, I thought, could be very persuasive). Annie would tell him she intended to sacrifice her beloved pig, Misery, to this project. *Misery's Return* would, she'd say, consist of but one copy: a holographic manuscript bound in pigskin!

Here we'd fade out, I thought, and return to Annie's remote Colorado retreat six or eight months later for the surprise ending.

Paul is gone, his sickroom turned into a shrine to Misery Chastain, but Misery the pig is still very much in evidence, grunting serenely away in her sty beside the barn. On the walls of the "Misery Room" are book covers, stills from the Misery movies, pictures of Paul Sheldon, perhaps a newspaper headline reading FAMED ROMANCE NOVELIST STILL MISSING. In the center of the room, carefully spotlighted, is a single book on a small table (a cherrywood table, of course, in honor of Mr. Kipling). It is the Annie Wilkes Edition of *Misery's Return.* The binding is beautiful, and it should be; it is the skin of Paul Sheldon. And Paul himself? His bones might be buried behind the barn, but I thought it likely that the pig would have eaten the tasty parts.

Not bad, and it would have made a pretty good story (not such a good novel, however; no one likes to root for a guy over the course of three hundred pages only to discover that between chapters sixteen and seventeen the pig ate him), but that wasn't the way things eventually went. Paul Sheldon turned out to be a good deal more resourceful than I initially thought, and his efforts to play Scheherazade and save his life gave me a chance to say some things about the redemptive power of writing that I had long felt but never articulated. Annie also turned out to be more complex than I'd first imagined her, and she was great fun to write about— here was a woman pretty much stuck with "cockadoo-die brat" when it came to profanity, but who felt absolutely no qualms about chopping off her favorite writer's foot when he tried to get away from her. In the end, I felt that Annie was almost as much to be pitied as to be feared. And none of the story's details and incidents proceeded from plot; they were organic, each arising naturally from the initial situation, each an uncovered part of the fossil. And I'm writing all this with a smile. As sick with drugs and alcohol as I was much of the time, I had such fun with that one.

Gerald's Game and *The Girl Who Loved Tom Gordon* are two other purely situational novels. If *Misery* is "two characters in a house," then *Gerald* is "one woman in a bed-

room" and *The Girl Who* is "one kid lost in the woods."
As I told you, I *have* written plotted novels, but the
results, in books like *Insomnia* and *Rose Madder,* have
not been particularly inspiring. These are (much as I hate
to admit it) stiff, trying-too-hard novels. The only plot-
driven novel of mine which I really like is *The Dead
Zone* (and in all fairness, I must say I like that one a great
deal). One book which *seems* plotted—*Bag of Bones*—is
actually another situation: "widowed writer in a haunted
house." The back story of *Bag of Bones* is satisfyingly
gothic (at least I think so) and very complex, but none of
the details were premeditated. The history of TR-90
and the story of what widowed writer Mike Noonan's
wife was really up to during the last summer of her life
arose spontaneously—all those details were parts of the
fossil, in other words.

A strong enough situation renders the whole question of plot moot, which is fine with me. The most
interesting situations can usually be expressed as a
What-if question:

What if vampires invaded a small New England village? *('Salem's Lot)*

What if a policeman in a remote Nevada town went
berserk and started killing everyone in sight?
(Desperation)

What if a cleaning woman suspected of a murder she
got away with (her husband) fell under suspicion for a
murder she did not commit (her employer)? *(Dolores
Claiborne)*

What if a young mother and her son became trapped
in their stalled car by a rabid dog? *(Cujo)*

These were all situations which occurred to me—

while showering, while driving, while taking my daily walk—and which I eventually turned into books. In no case were they plotted, not even to the extent of a single note jotted on a single piece of scrap paper, although some of the stories (*Dolores Claiborne,* for instance) are almost as complex as those you find in murder mysteries. Please remember, however, that there is a huge difference between story and plot. Story is honorable and trustworthy; plot is shifty, and best kept under house arrest.

Each of the novels summarized above was smoothed out and detailed by the editorial process, of course, but most of the elements existed to begin with. "A movie should be there in rough cut," the film editor Paul Hirsch once told me. The same is true of books. I think it's rare that incoherence or dull storytelling can be solved by something so minor as a second draft.

This isn't a textbook, and so there aren't a lot of exercises, but I want to offer you one now, in case you feel that all this talk about situation replacing plot is so much woolly-headed bullshit. I am going to show you the location of a fossil. Your job is to write five or six pages of unplotted narration concerning this fossil. Put another way, I want you to dig for the bones and see what they look like. I think you may be quite surprised and delighted with the results. Ready? Here we go.

Everyone is familiar with the basic details of the following story; with small variations, it seems to pop up in the Police Beat section of metropolitan daily papers every other week or so. A woman—call her Jane—marries a man who is bright, witty, and pulsing with sexual magnetism. We'll call the guy Dick; it's the world's most Freudian name. Unfortunately, Dick has a dark side. He's short-tempered, a control freak, perhaps even (you'll find this out as he speaks and acts) a paranoid. Jane tries mightily to overlook Dick's faults and make the marriage work (why she tries so hard is something you will also find out; she will come onstage and tell you). They have a child, and for awhile things seem better. Then, when the little girl is three or so, the abuse and the jealous tirades begin again. The abuse is verbal at first, then physical. Dick is convinced that Jane is sleeping with someone, perhaps someone from her job. Is it someone specific? I don't know and don't care. Eventually Dick may tell you who he suspects. If he does, we'll both know, won't we?

At last poor Jane can't take it anymore. She divorces the schmuck and gets custody of their daughter, Little Nell. Dick begins to stalk her. Jane responds by getting a restraining order, a document about as useful as a parasol in a hurricane, as many abused women will tell you. Finally, after an incident which you will write in vivid and scary detail—a public beating, perhaps— Richard the Schmuck is arrested and jailed. All of this is back story. How you work it in—and *how much* of it you work in—is up to you. In any case, it's not the situation. What follows is the situation.

One day shortly after Dick's incarceration in the city jail, Jane picks up Little Nell at the daycare center and ferries her to a friend's house for a birthday party. Jane then takes herself home, looking forward to two or three hours' unaccustomed peace and quiet. Perhaps, she thinks, I'll take a nap. It's a house she's going to, even though she's a young working woman—the situation sort of demands it. How she came by this house and why she has the afternoon off are things the story will tell you and which will look neatly plotted if you come up with good reasons (perhaps the house belongs to her parents; perhaps she's house-sitting; perhaps another thing entirely).

Something pings at her, just below the level of consciousness, as she lets herself in, something that makes her uneasy. She can't isolate it and tells herself it's just nerves, a little fallout from her five years of hell with Mr. Congeniality. What else *could* it be? Dick is under lock and key, after all.

Before taking her nap, Jane decides to have a cup of herbal tea and watch the news. (Can you use that pot of boiling water on the stove later on? Perhaps, perhaps.) The lead item on *Action News at Three* is a shocker: that morning, three men escaped from the city jail, killing a guard in the process. Two of the three bad guys were recaptured almost at once, but the third is still at large. None of the prisoners are identified by name (not in *this* newscast, at least), but Jane, sitting in her empty house (which you will now have plausibly explained), knows beyond a shadow of a doubt that one of them was Dick. She knows because she has finally identified that ping of unease she felt in the foyer. It was the smell, faint and fading, of Vitalis hair-tonic. *Dick's* hair-tonic. Jane sits in her chair, her muscles lax with fright, unable to get up. And as she hears Dick's footfalls begin to descend the stairs, she thinks: *Only Dick would make sure he had hair-tonic, even in jail.* She must get up, must run, but she can't move . . .

It's a pretty good story, yes? I think so, but not exactly unique. As I've already pointed out, ESTRANGED HUBBY

BEATS UP (or MURDERS) EX-WIFE makes the paper every other week, sad but true. What I want you to do in this exercise is *change the sexes of the antagonist and protagonist* before beginning to work out the situation in your narrative—make the ex-wife the stalker, in other words (perhaps it's a mental institution she's escaped from instead of the city jail), the husband the victim. Narrate this without plotting—let the situation and that one unexpected inversion carry you along. I predict you will succeed swimmingly . . . if, that is, you are honest about how your characters speak and behave. Honesty in storytelling makes up for a great many stylistic faults, as the work of wooden-prose writers like Theodore Dreiser and Ayn Rand shows, but lying is the great unrepairable fault. Liars prosper, no question about it, but only in the grand sweep of things, never down in the jungles of actual composition, where you must take your objective one bloody word at a time. If you begin to lie about what you know and feel while you're down there, everything falls down.

When you finish your exercise, drop me a line at www.stephenking.com and tell me how it worked for you. I can't promise to vet every reply, but I *can* promise to read at least some of your adventures with great interest. I'm curious to know what kind of fossil you dig up, and how much of it you are able to retrieve from the ground intact.

– 6 –

Description is what makes the reader a sensory participant in the story. Good description is a learned skill, one of the prime reasons why you cannot succeed unless you read a lot and write a lot. It's not just a question of *how-to,* you see; it's also a question of *how much to.* Reading will help you answer how much, and only reams of writing will help you with the how. You can learn only by doing.

Description begins with visualization of what it is you want the reader to experience. It ends with your translating what you see in your mind into words on the page. It's far from easy. As I've said, we've all heard someone say, "Man, it was so great (or so horrible/strange/funny) . . . I just can't describe it!" If you want to be a successful writer, you *must* be able to describe it, and in a way that will cause your reader to prickle with recognition. If you can do this, you will be paid for your labors, and deservedly so. If you can't, you're going to collect a lot of rejection slips and perhaps explore a career in the fascinating world of telemarketing.

Thin description leaves the reader feeling bewildered and nearsighted. Overdescription buries him or her in details and images. The trick is to find a happy medium. It's also important to know *what* to describe and what can be left alone while you get on with your main job, which is telling a story.

I'm not particularly keen on writing which exhaustively describes the physical characteristics of the people in the story and what they're wearing (I find wardrobe inventory particularly irritating; if I want to read descriptions of clothes, I can always get a J. Crew catalogue). I can't remember many cases where I felt I had to describe what the people in a story of mine looked like—I'd rather let the reader supply the faces, the builds, and the clothing as well. If I tell you that Carrie White is a high school outcast with a bad complexion and a fashion-victim wardrobe, I think you can do the rest, can't you? I don't need to give you a pimple-by-pimple, skirt-by-skirt rundown. We all remember one or more high school losers, after all; if I describe mine, it freezes out yours, and I lose a little bit of the bond of understanding I want to forge between us. Description begins in the writer's imagination, but should finish in the reader's. When it comes to actually pulling this off, the writer is much more fortunate than the filmmaker, who is almost always doomed to show too much . . . including, in nine cases out of ten, the zipper running up the monster's back.

I think locale and texture are much more important to the reader's sense of actually being *in* the story than any physical description of the players. Nor do I think that physical description should be a shortcut to character. So spare me, if you please, the hero's **sharply intelligent blue eyes** and **outthrust determined chin;** likewise the heroine's **arrogant cheekbones.** This sort of thing is bad technique and lazy writing, the equivalent of all those tiresome adverbs.

For me, good description usually consists of a few well-chosen details that will stand for everything else. In most cases, these details will be the first ones that come to mind. Certainly they will do for a start. If you decide later on that you'd like to change, add, or delete, you can do so—it's what rewrite was invented for. But I think you will find that, in most cases, your first visualized details will be the truest and best. You should remember (and your reading will prove it over and over again should you begin to doubt) that it's as easy to overdescribe as to underdescribe. Probably easier.

One of my favorite restaurants in New York is the steakhouse Palm Too on Second Avenue. If I decide to set a scene in Palm Too, I'll certainly be writing about what I know, as I've been there on a number of occasions. Before beginning to write, I'll take a moment to call up an image of the place, drawing from my memory and filling my mind's eye, an eye whose vision grows sharper the more it is used. I call it a mental eye because that's the phrase with which we're all familiar, but what I actually want to do is open *all* my senses. This memory search will be brief but intense, a kind of hypnotic recall. And, as with actual hypnosis, you'll find it easier to accomplish the more you attempt it.

The first four things which come to my mind when I think of Palm Too are: (a) the darkness of the bar and the contrasting brightness of the backbar mirror, which catches and reflects light from the street; (b) the sawdust on the floor; (c) the funky cartoon caricatures on the walls; (d) the smells of cooking steak and fish.

If I think longer I can come up with more stuff (what I don't remember I'll make up—during the visualization process, fact and fiction become entwined), but there's no need for more. This isn't the Taj Mahal we're visiting, after all, and I don't want to sell you the place. It's also important to remember it's not about the setting, anyway—it's about the story, and it's *always* about the story. It will not behoove me (or you) to wander off into thickets of description just because it would be easy to do. We have other fish (and steak) to fry.

Bearing that in mind, here's a sample bit of narration which takes a character into Palm Too:

> The cab pulled up in front of Palm Too at quarter to four on a bright summer afternoon. Billy paid the driver, stepped out onto the sidewalk, and took a quick look around for Martin. Not in sight. Satisfied, Billy went inside.
>
> After the hot clarity of Second Avenue, Palm Too was as dark as a cave. The backbar mirror picked up some of the street-glare and glimmered in the gloom like a mirage. For a moment it was all Billy could see, and then his eyes began to adjust. There were a few solitary drinkers at the bar. Beyond them, the maître d', his tie undone and his shirt cuffs rolled back to show his hairy wrists, was talking with the bartender. There was still sawdust sprinkled on the floor, Billy noted, as if this were a twenties speakeasy instead of a millennium eatery where you couldn't smoke, let alone spit a gob of tobacco between your feet. And the cartoons dancing across the walls—gossip-column caricatures of downtown political hustlers, newsmen who had long since retired or drunk themselves to death, celebrities you couldn't quite recognize—still gambolled all the way to the ceiling. The air was redolent of steak and fried onions. All of it the same as it ever was.
>
> The maître d' stepped forward. "Can I help

you, sir? We don't open for dinner until six, but the bar—"

"I'm looking for Richie Martin," Billy said.

Billy's arrival in the cab is narration—action, if you like that word better. What follows after he steps through the door of the restaurant is pretty much straight description. I got in almost all of the details which first came to mind when I accessed my memories of the real Palm Too, and I added a few other things, as well—the maître d' between shifts is pretty good, I think; I love the undone tie and the cuffs rolled up to expose the hairy wrists. It's like a photograph. The smell of fish is the only thing not here, and that's because the smell of the onions was stronger.

We come back to actual storytelling with a bit of narration (the maître d' steps forward to center stage) and then the dialogue. By now we see our location clearly. There are plenty of details I could have added—the narrowness of the room, Tony Bennett on the sound system, the Yankees bumper-sticker on the cash register— but what would be the point? When it comes to scene-setting and all sorts of description, a meal is as good as a feast. We want to know if Billy has located Richie Martin—that's the story we paid our twenty-four bucks to read. More about the restaurant would slow the pace of that story, perhaps annoying us enough to break the spell good fiction can weave. In many cases when a reader puts a story aside because it "got boring," the boredom arose because the writer grew enchanted with his powers of description and lost sight of his priority, which is to keep the ball rolling. If the reader wants to know more about Palm Too than can be found above, he or she can either visit the next time he or she is in New York, or send for a brochure. I've already spilled enough ink here for me to indicate Palm Too will be a major setting for my story. If it turns out not to be, I'd do well to revise the descriptive stuff down by a few lines in the next draft. Certainly I couldn't keep it in on the grounds that it's good; it *should* be good, if I'm being paid to do it. What I'm not being paid to do is be self-indulgent.

There is straight description ("a few solitary drinkers at the bar") and a bit of rather more poetic description ("The backbar mirror . . . glimmered in the gloom like a mirage") in my central descriptive paragraph about Palm Too. Both are okay, but I like the figurative stuff. The use of simile and other figurative language is one of the chief delights of fiction—reading it and writing it, as well. When it's on target, a simile delights us in much the same way meeting an old friend in a crowd of strangers does. By comparing two seemingly unrelated objects—a restaurant bar and a cave, a mirror and a mirage—we are sometimes able to see an old thing in a new and vivid way.* Even if the result is mere clarity instead of beauty, I think writer and reader are participating together in a kind of miracle. Maybe that's drawing it a little strong, but yeah—it's what I believe.

When a simile or metaphor *doesn't* work, the results are sometimes funny and sometimes embarrassing. Recently I read this sentence in a forthcoming novel I

---

*Although "dark as a cave" isn't all that riveting; certainly we've heard it before. It is, truth to tell, a bit lazy, not quite a cliché but certainly in the neighborhood.

prefer not to name: "He sat stolidly beside the corpse, waiting for the medical examiner as patiently as a man waiting for a turkey sandwich." If there is a clarifying connection here, I wasn't able to make it. I consequently closed the book without reading further. If a writer knows what he or she is doing, I'll go along for the ride. If he or she doesn't . . . well, I'm in my fifties now, and there are a lot of books out there. I don't have time to waste with the poorly written ones.

The Zen simile is only one potential pitfall of figurative language. The most common—and again, landing in this trap can usually be traced back to not enough reading—is the use of clichéd similes, metaphors, and images. He ran **like a madman**, she was pretty **as a summer day**, the guy was **a hot ticket**, Bob fought **like a tiger** . . . don't waste my time (or anyone's) with such chestnuts. It makes you look either lazy or ignorant. Neither description will do your reputation as a writer much good.

My all-time favorite similes, by the way, come from the hardboiled-detective fiction of the forties and fifties, and the literary descendants of the dime-dreadful writers. These favorites include "It was darker than a carload of assholes" (George V. Higgins) and "I lit a cigarette [that] tasted like a plumber's handkerchief" (Raymond Chandler).

The key to good description begins with clear seeing and ends with clear writing, the kind of writing that employs fresh images and simple vocabulary. I began learning my lessons in this regard by reading Chandler, Hammett, and Ross MacDonald; I gained perhaps even more respect for the power of compact, descriptive language from reading T. S. Eliot (those ragged claws scuttling across the ocean floor; those coffee spoons), and William Carlos Williams (white chickens, red wheelbarrow, the plums that were in the ice box, so sweet and so cold).

As with all other aspects of the narrative art, you will improve with practice, but practice will never make you perfect. Why should it? What fun would that be? And the harder you try to be clear and simple, the more you will learn about the complexity of our American dialect. It be slippery, precious; aye, it be very slippery, indeed. Practice the art, always reminding yourself that your job is to say what you see, and then to get on with your story.

– 7 –

Let us now talk a little bit about dialogue, the audio portion of our programme. It's dialogue that gives your cast their voices, and is crucial in defining their characters—only what people do tells us more about what they're like, and talk is sneaky: what people say often conveys their character to others in ways of which they—the speakers—are completely unaware.

You can tell me via straight narration that your main character, Mistuh Butts, never did well in school, never even *went* much to school, but you can convey the same thing, and much more vividly, by his speech . . . and one of the cardinal rules of good fiction is never tell us a thing if you can show us, instead:

"What you reckon?" the boy asked. He doodled a stick in the dirt without looking up. What he drew could have been a ball, or a planet, or nothing but a circle. "You reckon the earth goes around the sun like they say?"

"I don't know what they say," Mistuh Butts replied. "I ain't never studied what thisun or thatun says, because eachun says a different thing until your head is finally achin and you lose your aminite."

"What's aminite?" the boy asked.

"You don't never shut up the questions!" Mistuh Butts cried. He seized the boy's stick and snapped it. "Aminite is in your belly when it's time to eat! Less you sick! And folks say *I'm* ignorant!"

"Oh, *appetite*," the boy said placidly, and began drawing again, this time with his finger.

Well-crafted dialogue will indicate if a character is smart or dumb (Mistuh Butts isn't necessarily a moron just because he can't say *appetite;* we must listen to him awhile longer before making up our minds on that score), honest or dishonest, amusing or an old sobersides. Good dialogue, such as that written by George V. Higgins, Peter Straub, or Graham Greene, is a delight to read; bad dialogue is deadly.

Writers have different skill levels when it comes to dialogue. Your skills in this area can be improved, but, as a great man once said (actually it was Clint Eastwood), "A man's got to know his limitations." H. P. Lovecraft was a genius when it came to tales of the macabre, but a terrible dialogue writer. He seems to have known it, too, because in the millions of words of fiction he wrote, fewer than *five thousand* are dialogue. The following passage from "The Colour Out of Space," in which a dying farmer describes the alien presence which has invaded his well, showcases Lovecraft's dialogue problems. Folks, people just don't talk like this, even on their deathbeds:

> "Nothin' . . . nothin' . . . the colour . . . it burns . . . cold an' wet . . . but it burns . . . it lived in the well . . . I seen it . . . a kind o' smoke . . . jest like the flowers last spring . . . the well shone at night . . . everything alive . . . sucked the life out of everything . . . in the stone . . . it must a'come in that stone . . . pizened the whole place . . . dun't know what it wants . . . that round thing the men from the college dug out'n the stone . . . it was that same colour . . . jest the same, like the flowers an' plants . . . seeds . . . I seen it the fust time this week . . . it beats down your mind an' then gets ye . . . burns ye up . . . It come from some place whar things ain't as they is here . . . one o' them professors said so . . ."

And so on and so forth, in carefully constructed elliptical bursts of information. It's hard to say exactly what's wrong with Lovecraft's dialogue, other than the obvious: it's stilted and lifeless, brimming with country cornpone ("some place whar things ain't as they is here"). When dialogue is right, we know. When it's wrong we also know—it jags on the ear like a badly tuned musical instrument.

Lovecraft was, by all accounts, both snobbish and painfully shy (a galloping racist as well, his stories full of sinister Africans and the sort of scheming Jews my Uncle Oren always worried about after four or five beers), the kind of writer who maintains a voluminous correspondence but gets along poorly with others in person—were he alive today, he'd likely exist most vibrantly in various Internet chat-rooms. Dialogue is a skill best learned by people who enjoy talking and listening to others—particularly listening, picking up the accents, rhythms, dialect, and slang of various groups. Loners such as Lovecraft often write it badly, or with the care of someone who is composing in a language other than his or her native tongue.

I don't know if contemporary novelist John Katzenbach is a loner or not, but his novel *Hart's War* contains some memorably bad dialogue. Katzenbach is the sort of novelist who drives creative-writing teachers mad, a wonderful storyteller whose art is marred by self-repetition (a fault which is curable) and an ear for talk that is pure tin (a fault which probably isn't). *Hart's War* is a murder mystery set in a World War II POW camp—a neat idea, but problematic in Katzenbach's hands once he really gets the pot boiling. Here is Wing Commander Phillip Pryce talking to his friends just before the Germans in charge of Stalag Luft 13 take him away, not to be repatriated as they claim, but probably to be shot in the woods.

Pryce grabbed at Tommy once again. "Tommy," he whispered, "this is not a coincidence! Nothing is what it seems! Dig deeper! Save him, lad, save him! For more than ever, now, I believe Scott is innocent! . . . You're on your own now, boys. And remember, I'm counting on you to live through this! Survive! Whatever happens!"

He turned back to the Germans. "All right, *Hauptmann,*" he said with a sudden, exceedingly calm determination. "I'm ready now. Do with me what you will."

Either Katzenbach does not realize that every line of the Wing Commander's dialogue is a cliché from a late-forties war movie or he's trying to use that similarity deliberately to awaken feelings of pity, sadness, and perhaps nostalgia in his audience. Either way, it doesn't work. The only feeling the passage evokes is a kind of impatient incredulity. You wonder if any editor ever saw it, and if so, what stayed his or her blue pencil. Given Katzenbach's considerable talents in other areas, his failure here tends to reinforce my idea that writing good dialogue is art as well as craft.

Many good dialogue writers simply seem to have been born with a well-tuned ear, just as some musicians and singers have perfect or near-perfect pitch. Here's a passage from Elmore Leonard's novel *Be Cool.* You might compare it to the Lovecraft and Katzenbach passages above, noting first of all that here we've got an honest-to-God exchange going on, and not a stilted soliloquy:

Chili . . . looked up again as Tommy said, "You doing okay?"

"You want to know if I'm making out?"

"I mean in your business. How's it going? I know you did okay with *Get Leo,* a terrific picture, terrific. And you know what else? It was good. But the sequel—what was it called?"

"Get Lost."

"Yeah, well that's what happened before I got a chance to see it, it disappeared."

"It didn't open big so the studio walked away. I was against doing a sequel to begin with. But the guy running production at Tower says they're making the picture, with me or without me. I thought, well, if I can come up with a good story . . ."

Two guys at lunch in Beverly Hills, and right away we know they're both players. They may be phonies (and maybe they're not), but they're an instant buy within the context of Leonard's story; in fact, we welcome them with open arms. Their talk is so real that part of what we feel is the guilty pleasure of anyone first tuning in and then eavesdropping on an interesting conversation. We're getting a sense of character, as well, although only in faint strokes. This is early on in the novel (page two, actually), and Leonard is an old pro. He knows he doesn't have to do it all at once. Still, don't we learn something about Tommy's character when he assures Chili that *Get Leo* is not only terrific, but also good?

We could ask ourselves if such dialogue is true to life or only to a certain *idea* of life, a certain stereotyped image of Hollywood players, Hollywood lunches, Hollywood deals. This is a fair enough question, and the answer is, perhaps not. Yet the dialogue *does* ring true to our ear; at his best (and although *Be Cool* is quite entertaining, it is far from Leonard's best), Elmore Leonard is capable of a kind of street poetry. The skill necessary to write such dialogue comes from years of practice; the art comes from a creative imagination which is working hard and having fun.

As with all other aspects of fiction, the key to writing good dialogue is honesty. And if you *are* honest about the words coming out of your characters' mouths, you'll find that you've let yourself in for a fair amount of criticism. Not a week goes by that I don't receive at least one pissed-off letter (most weeks there are more) accusing me of being foul-mouthed, bigoted, homophobic, murderous, frivolous, or downright psychopathic. In the majority of cases what my correspondents are hot under the collar about relates to something in the dialogue: "Let's get the fuck out of Dodge" or "We don't cotton much to niggers around here" or "What do you think you're doing, you fucking faggot?"

My mother, God rest her, didn't approve of profanity or any such talk; she called it "the language of the ignorant." This did not, however, keep her from yelling "Oh shit!" if she burned the roast or nailed her thumb a good one while hammering a picture-hook in the wall. Nor does it preclude most people, Christian as well as heathen, from saying something similar (or even stronger) when the dog barfs on the shag carpet or the car slips off the jack. It's important to tell the truth; so much depends upon it, as William Carlos Williams almost said when he was writing about that red wheelbarrow. The Legion of Decency might not like the word *shit,* and you might not like it much, either, but sometimes you're just stuck with it—no kid ever ran to his mother and said that his little sister just *defecated* in the tub. I suppose he might say *pushed* or *went woowoo,* but *took a shit* is, I fear, very much in the ballpark (little pitchers have big ears, after all).

You *must* tell the truth if your dialogue is to have the resonance and realism that *Hart's War,* good story though it is, so sadly lacks—and that holds true all the way down to what folks say when they hit their thumb with the hammer. If you substitute "Oh sugar!" for "Oh shit!" because you're thinking about the Legion of Decency, you are breaking the unspoken contract that exists between writer and reader—your promise to express the truth of how people act and talk through the medium of a made-up story.

On the other hand, one of your characters (the protagonist's old maid aunt, for instance) really *might* say *Oh sugar* instead of *Oh shit* after pounding her thumb with the hammer. You'll know which to use if you know your character, and we'll learn something about the speaker that will make him or her more vivid and interesting. The point is to let each character speak freely, without regard to what the Legion of Decency or the Christian Ladies' Reading Circle may approve of. To do otherwise would be cowardly as well as dishonest, and believe me, writing fiction in America as we enter the twenty-first century is no job for intellectual cowards. There are lots of would-be censors out there, and although they may have different agendas, they all want basically the same thing: for you to see the world they see . . . or to at least shut up about what you *do* see that's different. They are agents of the status quo. Not necessarily bad guys, but dangerous guys if you happen to believe in intellectual freedom.

As it happens, I agree with my mother: profanity and vulgarity *is* the language of the ignorant and the verbally challenged. *Mostly,* that is; there are exceptions, including profane aphorisms of great color and vitality. *They always fuck you at the drive-thru; I'm busier than a one-legged man in an ass-kicking contest; wish in one hand, shit in the other, see which one fills up first*—these phrases and others like them aren't for the drawing-room, but they *are* striking and pungent. Or consider this passage from *Brain Storm*, by Richard Dooling, where vulgarity becomes poetry:

> "Exhibit A: One loutish, headstrong penis, a barbarous cuntivore without a flyspeck of decency in him. The capscallion of all rapscallions. A scurvy, vermiform scug with a serpentine twinkle in his solitary eye. An orgulous Turk who strikes in the dark vaults of flesh like a penile thunderbolt. A greedy cur seeking shadows, slick crevices, tuna fish ecstasy, and sleep . . ."

Although not offered as dialogue, I want to reproduce another passage from Dooling here, because it speaks to the converse: that one can be quite admirably graphic without resorting to vulgarity or profanity at all:

> She straddled him and prepared to make the necessary port connections, male and female adapters ready, I/O enabled, server/client, master/slave. Just a couple of high-end biological

machines preparing to hot-dock with cable modems and access each other's front-end processors.

If I were a Henry James or Jane Austen sort of guy, writing only about toffs or smart college folks, I'd hardly ever have to use a dirty word or a profane phrase; I might never have had a book banned from America's school libraries or gotten a letter from some helpful fundamentalist fellow who wants me to know that I'm going to burn in hell, where all my millions of dollars won't buy me so much as a single drink of water. I did not, however, grow up among folks of that sort. I grew up as a part of America's lower middle class, and they're the people I can write about with the most honesty and knowledge. It means that they say shit more often than sugar when they bang their thumbs, but I've made my peace with that. Was never much at war with it in the first place, as a matter of fact.

When I get one of Those Letters, or face another review that accuses me of being a vulgar lowbrow— which to some extent I am—I take comfort from the words of turn-of-the-century social realist Frank Norris, whose novels include *The Octopus, The Pit,* and *McTeague,* an authentically great book. Norris wrote about working-class guys on ranches, in city laboring jobs, in factories. McTeague, the main character of Norris's finest work, is an unschooled dentist. Norris's books provoked a good deal of public outrage, to which Norris responded coolly and disdainfully: "What do I care for their opinions? I never truckled. I told them the truth."

Some people don't want to hear the truth, of course, but that's not your problem. What would be is wanting to be a writer without wanting to shoot straight. Talk, whether ugly or beautiful, is an index of character; it can also be a breath of cool, refreshing air in a room some people would prefer to keep shut up. In the end, the important question has nothing to do with whether the talk in your story is sacred or profane; the only question is how it rings on the page and in the ear. If you expect it to ring true, then you must talk yourself. Even more important, you must shut up and listen to others talk.

– 8 –

Everything I've said about dialogue applies to building characters in fiction. The job boils down to two things: paying attention to how the real people around you behave and then telling the truth about what you see. You may notice that your next-door neighbor picks his nose when he thinks no one is looking. This is a great detail, but noting it does you no good as a writer unless you're willing to dump it into a story at some point.

Are fictional characters drawn directly from life? Obviously not, at least on a one-to-one basis—you'd *better* not, unless you want to get sued or shot on your way to the mailbox some fine morning. In many cases, such as *roman à clef* novels like *Valley of the Dolls,* characters are drawn *mostly* from life, but after readers get done playing the inevitable guessing game about who's who, these stories tend to be unsatisfying, stuffed with shadowbox celebrities who bonk each other and then fade quickly from the reader's mind. I read *Valley of the Dolls* shortly after it came out (I was a cook's boy at a western Maine resort that summer), gobbling it up as eagerly as everyone else who bought it, I suppose, but I can't remember much of what it was about. On the whole, I think I prefer the weekly codswallop served up by *The National Enquirer,* where I can get recipes and cheesecake photographs as well as scandal.

For me, what happens to characters as a story progresses depends solely on what I discover about them as I go along—how they grow, in other words. Sometimes they grow a little. If they grow a lot, they begin to influence the course of the story instead of the other way around. I almost always start with something that's situational. I don't say that's right, only that it's the way I've always worked. If a story ends up that same way, however, I count it something of a failure no matter how interesting it may be to me or to others. I think the best stories always end up being about the people rather than the event, which is to say character-driven. Once you get beyond the short story, though (two to four thousand words, let's say), I'm not much of a believer in the so-called character study; I think that in the end, the story should always be the boss. Hey, if you want a character study, buy a biography or get season tickets to your local college's theater-lab productions. You'll get all the character you can stand.

It's also important to remember that no one is "the bad guy" or "the best friend" or "the whore with a heart of gold" in real life; in real life we each of us regard ourselves as the main character, the protagonist, the big cheese; the camera is on *us,* baby. If you can bring this attitude into your fiction, you may not find it easier to create *brilliant* characters, but it will be harder for you to create the sort of one-dimensional dopes that populate so much pop fiction.

Annie Wilkes, the nurse who holds Paul Sheldon prisoner in *Misery,* may seem psychopathic to us, but it's important to remember that she seems perfectly sane and reasonable to herself—heroic, in fact, a beleaguered woman trying to survive in a hostile world filled with cockadoodie brats. We see her go through dangerous moodswings, but I tried never to come right out and say "Annie was depressed and possibly suicidal that day" or "Annie seemed particularly happy that day." If I have to tell you, I lose. If, on the other hand, I can show you a silent, dirty-haired woman who compulsively gobbles cake and candy, then have you draw the conclusion that Annie is in the depressive part of a manic-depressive cycle, I win. And if I am able, even briefly, to give you a Wilkes'-eye-view of the world—if I can make you understand her madness— then perhaps I can make her someone you sympathize with or even identify with. The result? She's more frightening than ever, because she's close to real. If, on the other hand, I turn her into a cackling old crone, she's just another pop-up bogeylady. In that case I lose bigtime, and so does the reader. Who would want to visit with such a stale shrew? That version of Annie was old when *The Wizard of Oz* was in its first run.

It would be fair enough to ask, I suppose, if Paul Sheldon in *Misery* is me. Certainly *parts* of him are . . . but I think you will find that, if you continue to write fiction, every character you create is partly you. When you ask yourself what a certain character will do given a certain set of circumstances, you're making the decision based on what you yourself would (or, in the case of a bad guy, wouldn't) do. Added to these versions of your-self are the character traits, both lovely and unlovely, which you observe in others (a guy who picks his nose when he thinks no one is looking, for instance). There is also a wonderful third element: pure blue-sky imagina-tion. This is the part which allowed me to be a psychotic nurse for a little while when I was writing *Misery*. And being Annie was not, by and large, hard at all. In fact, it was sort of fun. I think being Paul was harder. He was sane, I'm sane, no four days at Disneyland there.

My novel *The Dead Zone* arose from two questions: Can a political assassin ever be right? And if he is, could you make him the protagonist of a novel? The good guy? These ideas called for a dangerously unstable politi-cian, it seemed to me—a fellow who could climb the political ladder by showing the world a jolly, jes'-folks face and charming the voters by refusing to play the game in the usual way. (Greg Stillson's campaign tactics as I imagined them twenty years ago were very similar to the ones Jesse Ventura used in his successful campaign for the governor's seat in Minnesota. Thank goodness Ventura doesn't seem like Stillson in any other ways.)

The Dead Zone's protagonist, Johnny Smith, is also an everyday, jes'-folks sort of guy, only with Johnny it's no act. The one thing that sets him apart is a limited abil-ity to see the future, gained as the result of a childhood accident. When Johnny shakes Greg Stillson's hand at a political rally, he has a vision of Stillson becoming the President of the United States and subsequently starting World War III. Johnny comes to the conclusion that the only way he can keep this from happening—the only way he can save the world, in other words—is by putting a bullet in Stillson's head. Johnny is different from other violent, paranoid mystics in only one way: he really *can* see the future. Only don't they all say that?

The situation had an edgy, outlaw feel to it that appealed to me. I thought the story would work if I could make Johnny a genuinely decent guy without turning him into a plaster saint. Same thing with Stillson, only backwards: I wanted him to be authentically nasty and really scare the reader, not just because Stillson is always boiling with potential violence but because he is so goddam *persuasive.* I wanted the reader to constantly be thinking: "This guy is out of control—how come somebody can't see through him?" The fact that Johnny *does* see through him would, I thought, put the reader even more firmly in Johnny's corner.

When we first meet the potential assassin, he's taking his girl to the county fair, riding the rides and playing the games. What could be more normal or likable? The fact that he's on the verge of proposing to Sarah makes us like him even more. Later, when Sarah suggests they cap a perfect date by sleeping together for the first time, Johnny tells her he wants to wait until they're married. I felt I was walking a fine line on that one—I wanted readers to see Johnny as sincere and sincerely in love, a straight shooter but not a tight-assed prude. I was able to cut his principled behavior a bit by giving him a childish sense of humor; he greets Sarah wearing a glow-in-the-dark Halloween mask (the mask hopefully works in a symbolic way, too; certainly Johnny is perceived as a monster when he points a gun at candidate Stillson). "Same old Johnny,"

Sarah says, laughing, and by the time the two of them are headed back from the fair in Johnny's old Volkswagen Bug, I think Johnny Smith has become our friend, just an average American guy who's hoping to live happily ever after. The sort of guy who'd return your wallet with the money still in it if he found it on the street or stop and help you change your flat tire if he came upon you broke down by the side of the road. Ever since John F. Kennedy was shot in Dallas, the great American bogeyman has been the guy with the rifle in a high place. I wanted to make this guy into the reader's friend.

Johnny was hard. Taking an average guy and making him vivid and interesting always is. Greg Stillson (like most villains) was easier and a lot more fun. I wanted to nail his dangerous, divided character in the first scene of the book. Here, several years before he runs for the U.S. House of Representatives in New Hampshire, Stillson is a young travelling salesman hawking Bibles to midwest country folk. When he stops at one farm, he is menaced by a snarling dog. Stillson remains friendly and smiling—Mr. Jes' Folks—until he's positive no one's home at the farm. Then he sprays teargas into the dog's eyes and kicks it to death.

If one is to measure success by reader response, the opening scene of *The Dead Zone* (my first number-one hardcover best-seller) was one of my most successful ever. Certainly it struck a raw nerve; I was deluged with letters, most of them protesting my outrageous cruelty to animals. I wrote back to these folks, pointing out the usual things: (a) Greg Stillson wasn't real; (b) the *dog* wasn't real; (c) I myself had never in my life put the boot to one of my pets, or anyone else's. I also pointed out what might have been a little less obvious—it was important to establish, right up front, that Gregory Ammas Stillson was an extremely dangerous man, and very good at camouflage.

I continued to build the characters of Johnny and Greg in alternating scenes until the confrontation at the end of the book, when things resolve themselves in what I hoped would be an unexpected way. The characters of my protagonist and antagonist were determined by the story I had to tell—by the fossil, the found object, in other words. My job (and yours, if you decide this is a viable approach to storytelling) is to make sure these fictional folks behave in ways that will both help the story and seem reasonable to us, given what we know about them (and what we know about real life, of course). Sometimes villains feel self-doubt (as Greg Stillson does); sometimes they feel pity (as Annie Wilkes does). And sometimes the good guy tries to turn away from doing the right thing, as Johnny Smith does . . . as Jesus Christ himself did, if you think about that prayer ("take this cup from my lips") in the Garden of Gethsemane. And if you do your job, your characters will come to life and start doing stuff on their own. I know that sounds a little creepy if you haven't actually experienced it, but it's terrific fun when it happens. And it will solve a lot of your problems, believe me.

– 9 –

We've covered some basic aspects of good storytelling, all of which return to the same core ideas: that practice is invaluable (and should feel good, really not like practice at all) and that honesty is indispensable. Skills in description, dialogue, and character development all boil down to seeing or hearing clearly and then transcribing what you see or hear with equal clarity (and without using a lot of tiresome, unnecessary adverbs).

There are lots of bells and whistles, too—onomatopoeia, incremental repetition, stream of consciousness, interior dialogue, changes of verbal tense (it has become quite fashionable to tell stories, especially shorter ones, in the present tense), the sticky question of back story (how do you get it in and how much of it belongs), theme, pacing (we'll touch on these last two), and a dozen other topics, all of which are covered—sometimes at exhausting length—in writing courses and standard writing texts.

My take on all these things is pretty simple. It's all on the table, every bit of it, and you should use anything that improves the quality of your writing and doesn't get in the way of your story. If you like an alliterative phrase—the knights of nowhere battling the nabobs of nullity—by all means throw it in and see how it looks on paper. If it seems to work, it can stay. If it doesn't (and to me this one sounds pretty bad, like Spiro Agnew crossed with Robert Jordan), well, that DELETE key is on your machine for a good reason.

There is absolutely no need to be hidebound and conservative in your work, just as you are under no obligation to write experimental, nonlinear prose because *The Village Voice* or *The New York Review of Books* says the novel is dead. Both the traditional and the modern are available to you. Shit, write upside down if you want to, or do it in Crayola pictographs. But no matter how you do it, there comes a point when you must judge what you've written and how well you wrote it. I don't believe a story or a novel should be allowed outside the door of your study or writing room unless you feel confident that it's reasonably reader-friendly. You can't please all of the readers all of the time; you can't please even *some* of the readers all of the time, but you really ought to try to please at least some of the readers some of the time. I think William Shakespeare said that. And now that I've waved that caution flag, duly satisfying all OSHA, MENSA, NASA, and Writers' Guild guidelines, let me reiterate that it's all on the table, all up for grabs. Isn't that an intoxicating thought? I think it is. Try any goddam thing you like, no matter how boringly normal or outrageous. If it works, fine. If it doesn't, toss it. Toss it even if you love it. Sir Arthur Quiller-Couch once said, "Murder your darlings," and he was right.

I most often see chances to add the grace-notes and ornamental touches after my basic storytelling job is done. Once in awhile it comes earlier; not long after I began *The Green Mile* and realized my main character was an innocent man likely to be executed for the crime of another, I decided to give him the initials J.C., after the most famous innocent man of all time. I first saw this done in *Light in August* (still my favorite Faulkner novel), where the sacrificial lamb is named Joe Christmas. Thus death-row inmate John Bowes became John Coffey. I wasn't sure, right up to the end of the book, if my J.C. would live or die. I *wanted* him to live because I liked and pitied him, but I figured those initials couldn't hurt, one way or the other.*

Mostly I don't see stuff like that until the story's done. Once it is, I'm able to kick back, read over what I've written, and look for underlying patterns. If I see some (and I almost always do), I can work at bringing them out in a second, more fully realized, draft of the story. Two examples of the sort of work second drafts were made for are symbolism and theme.

If in school you ever studied the symbolism of the color white in *Moby-Dick* or Hawthorne's symbolic use of the forest in such stories as "Young Goodman Brown" and came away from those classes feeling like a stupidnik, you may even now be backing off with your hands raised protectively in front of you, shaking your head and saying *gee, no thanks, I gave at the office.*

But wait. Symbolism doesn't have to be difficult and relentlessly brainy. Nor does it have to be consciously crafted as a kind of ornamental Turkish rug upon which the furniture of the story stands. If you can go along with the concept of the story as a pre-existing thing, a fossil in the ground, then symbolism must also be pre-existing, right? Just another bone (or set of them) in your new discovery. That's if it's there. If it isn't, so what? You've still got the story itself, don't you?

If it *is* there and if you notice it, I think you should bring it out as well as you can, polishing it until it

---

*A few critics accused me of being symbolically simplistic in the matter of John Coffey's initials. And I'm like, "What is this, rocket science?" I mean, come *on*, guys.

shines and then cutting it the way a jeweler would cut a precious or semiprecious stone.

Carrie, as I've already noted, is a short novel about a picked-on girl who discovers a telekinetic ability within herself—she can move objects by thinking about them. To atone for a vicious shower-room prank in which she has participated, Carrie's classmate Susan Snell persuades her boyfriend to invite Carrie to the Senior Prom. They are elected King and Queen. During the celebration, another of Carrie's classmates, the unpleasant Christine Hargensen, pulls a second prank on Carrie, this one deadly. Carrie takes her revenge by using her telekinetic power to kill most of her classmates (and her atrocious mother) before dying herself. That's the whole deal, really; it's as simple as a fairy-tale. There was no need to mess it up with bells and whistles, although I *did* add a number of epistolary interludes (passages from fictional books, a diary entry, letters, teletype bulletins) between narrative segments. This was partly to inject a greater sense of realism (I was thinking of Orson Welles's radio adaptation of *War of the Worlds*) but mostly because the first draft of the book was so damned short it barely seemed like a novel.

When I read *Carrie* over prior to starting the second draft, I noticed there was blood at all three crucial points of the story: beginning (Carrie's paranormal ability is apparently brought on by her first menstrual period), climax (the prank which sets Carrie off at the prom involves a bucket of pig's blood—"pig's blood for a pig," Chris Hargensen tells her boyfriend), and end (Sue Snell, the girl who tries to help Carrie, discovers she is not pregnant as she had half-hoped and half-feared when she gets her own period).

There's plenty of blood in most horror stories, of course—it is our stock-in-trade, you might say. Still, the blood in *Carrie* seemed more than just splatter to me. It seemed to *mean* something. That meaning wasn't consciously created, however. While writing *Carrie* I never once stopped to think: "Ah, all this blood symbolism will win me Brownie Points with the critics" or "Boy oh boy, *this* should certainly get me in a college bookstore or two!" For one thing, a writer would have to be a lot crazier than I am to think of *Carrie* as anyone's intellectual treat.

Intellectual treat or not, the significance of all that blood was hard to miss once I started reading over my beer- and tea-splattered first-draft manuscript. So I started to play with the idea, image, and emotional connotations of blood, trying to think of as many associations as I could. There were lots, most of them pretty heavy. Blood is strongly linked to the idea of sacrifice; for young women it's associated with reaching physical maturity and the ability to bear children; in the Christian religion (plenty of others, as well), it's symbolic of both sin and salvation. Finally, it is associated with the handing down of family traits and talents. We are said to look like this or behave like that because "it's in our blood." We know this isn't very scientific, that those things are really in our genes and DNA patterns, but we use the one to summarize the other.

It is that ability to summarize and encapsulate that makes symbolism so interesting, useful, and—when used well—arresting. You could argue that it's really just another kind of figurative language.

Does that make it necessary to the success of your

story or novel? Indeed not, and it can actually hurt, especially if you get carried away. Symbolism exists to adorn and enrich, not to create a sense of artificial profundity. *None* of the bells and whistles are about story, all right? Only *story* is about story. (Are you tired of hearing that yet? I hope not, 'cause I'm not even *close* to getting tired of saying it.)

Symbolism (and the other adornments, too) *does* serve a useful purpose, though—it's more than just chrome on the grille. It can serve as a focusing device for both you and your reader, helping to create a more unified and pleasing work. I think that, when you read your manuscript over (and when you *talk* it over), you'll see if symbolism, or the potential for it, exists. If it doesn't, leave well enough alone. If it does, however—if it's clearly a part of the fossil you're working to unearth—go for it. Enhance it. You're a monkey if you don't.

– 10 –

The same things are true of theme. Writing and literature classes can be annoyingly preoccupied by (and pretentious about) theme, approaching it as the most sacred of sacred cows, but (don't be shocked) it's really no big deal. If you write a novel, spend weeks and then months catching it word by word, you owe it both to the book and to yourself to lean back (or take a long walk) when you've finished and ask yourself why you bothered—why you spent all that time, why it seemed so important. In other words, what's it all about, Alfie?

When you write a book, you spend day after day

scanning and identifying the trees. When you're done, you have to step back and look at the forest. Not every book has to be loaded with symbolism, irony, or musical language (they call it prose for a reason, y'know), but it seems to me that every book—at least every one worth reading—is about *something*. Your job during or just after the first draft is to decide what something or something yours is about. Your job in the second draft—one of them, anyway—is to make that something even more clear. This may necessitate some big changes and revisions. The benefits to you and your reader will be clearer focus and a more unified story. It hardly ever fails.

The book that took me the longest to write was *The Stand*. This is also the one my longtime readers still seem to like the best (there's something a little depressing about such a united opinion that you did your best work twenty years ago, but we won't go into that just now, thanks). I finished the first draft about sixteen months after I started it. *The Stand* took an especially long time because it nearly died going into the third turn and heading for home.

I'd wanted to write a sprawling, multi-character sort of novel—a fantasy epic, if I could manage it—and to that end I employed a shifting-perspective narrative, adding a major character in each chapter of the long first section. Thus Chapter One concerned itself with Stuart Redman, a blue-collar factory worker from Texas; Chapter Two first concerned itself with Fran Goldsmith, a pregnant college girl from Maine, and then returned to Stu; Chapter Three began with Larry Underwood, a rock-and-roll singer in New York, before going back first to Fran, then to Stu Redman again.

My plan was to link all these characters, the good, the bad, and the ugly, in two places: Boulder and Las Vegas. I thought they'd probably end up going to war against one another. The first half of the book also told the story of a man-made virus which sweeps America and the world, wiping out ninety-nine per cent of the human race and utterly destroying our technology-based culture.

I was writing this story near the end of the so-called Energy Crisis in the 1970s, and I had an absolutely marvellous time envisioning a world that went smash during the course of one horrified, infected summer (really not much more than a month). The view was panoramic, detailed, nationwide, and (to me, at least) breathtaking. Rarely have I seen so clearly with the eye of my imagination, from the traffic jam plugging the dead tube of New York's Lincoln Tunnel to the sinister, Nazi-ish rebirth of Las Vegas under the watchful (and often amused) red eye of Randall Flagg. All this sounds terrible, *is* terrible, but to me the vision was also strangely optimistic. No more energy crisis, for one thing, no more famine, no more massacres in Uganda, no more acid rain or hole in the ozone layer. *Finito* as well to saber-rattling nuclear superpowers, and certainly no more overpopulation. Instead, there was a chance for humanity's remaining shred to start over again in a God-centered world to which miracles, magic, and prophecy had returned. I liked my story. I liked my characters. And still there came a point when I couldn't write any longer because I didn't know what to write. Like Pilgrim in John Bunyan's epic, I had come to a place where the straight way was lost. I wasn't the first writer to discover this awful place, and I'm a long way from being the last; this is the land of writer's block.

If I'd had two or even three hundred pages of single-spaced manuscript instead of more than five hundred, I think I would have abandoned *The Stand* and gone on to something else—God knows I had done it before. But five hundred pages was too great an investment, both in time and in creative energy; I found it impossible to let go. Also, there was this little voice whispering to me that the book was really good, and if I didn't finish I would regret it forever. So instead of moving on to another project, I started taking long walks (a habit which would, two decades later, get me in a lot of trouble). I took a book or magazine on these walks but rarely opened it, no matter how bored I felt looking at the same old trees and the same old chattering, ill-natured jays and squirrels. Boredom can be a very good thing for someone in a creative jam. I spent those walks being bored and thinking about my gigantic boondoggle of a manuscript.

For weeks I got exactly nowhere in my thinking—it all just seemed too hard, too fucking complex. I had run out too many plotlines, and they were in danger of becoming snarled. I circled the problem again and again, beat my fists on it, knocked my head against it . . . and then one day when I was thinking of nothing much at all, the answer came to me. It arrived whole and complete—gift-wrapped, you could say—in a single bright flash. I ran home and jotted it down on paper, the only time I've done such a thing, because I was terrified of forgetting.

What I saw was that the America in which *The*

Stand took place might have been depopulated by the plague, but the world of my story had become dangerously overcrowded—a veritable Calcutta. The solution to where I was stuck, I saw, could be pretty much the same as the situation that got me going—an explosion instead of a plague, but still one quick, hard slash of the Gordian knot. I would send the survivors west from Boulder to Las Vegas on a redemptive quest— they would go at once, with no supplies and no plan, like Biblical characters seeking a vision or to know the will of God. In Vegas they would meet Randall Flagg, and good guys and bad guys alike would be forced to make their stand.

At one moment I had none of this; at the next I had all of it. If there is any one thing I love about writing more than the rest, it's that sudden flash of insight when you see how everything connects. I have heard it called "thinking above the curve," and it's that; I've heard it called "the over-logic," and it's that, too. Whatever you call it, I wrote my page or two of notes in a frenzy of excitement and spent the next two or three days turning my solution over in my mind, looking for flaws and holes (also working out the actual narrative flow, which involved two supporting characters placing a bomb in a major character's closet), but that was mostly out of a sense of this-is-too-good-to-be-true unbelief. Too good or not, I knew it *was* true at the moment of revelation: that bomb in Nick Andros's closet was going to solve all my narrative problems. It did, too. The rest of the book ran itself off in nine weeks.

Later, when my first draft of *The Stand* was done, I was able to get a better fix on what had stopped me so completely in mid-course; it was a lot easier to think without that voice in the middle of my head constantly yammering *"I'm losing my book! Ah shit, five hundred pages and I'm losing my book! Condition red! CONDITION RED!!"* I was also able to analyze what got me going again and appreciate the irony of it: I saved my book by blowing approximately half its major characters to smithereens (there actually ended up being *two* explosions, the one in Boulder balanced by a similar act of sabotage in Las Vegas).

The real source of my malaise, I decided, had been that in the wake of the plague, my Boulder characters—the good guys—were starting up the same old technological deathtrip. The first hesitant CB broadcasts, beckoning people to Boulder, would soon lead to TV; infomercials and 900 numbers would be back in no time. Same deal with the power plants. It certainly didn't take my Boulder folks long to decide that seeking the will of the God who spared them was a lot less important than getting the refrigerators and air conditioners up and running again. In Vegas, Randall Flagg and his friends were learning how to fly jets and bombers as well as getting the lights back on, but that was okay—to be expected—because they were the bad guys. What had stopped me was realizing, on some level of my mind, that the good guys and bad guys were starting to look perilously alike, and what got me going again was realizing the good guys were worshipping an electronic golden calf and needed a wake-up call. A bomb in the closet would do just fine.

All this suggested to me that violence as a solution is woven through human nature like a damning red thread. That became the theme of *The Stand,* and I wrote the second draft with it fixed firmly in my mind. Again and again characters (the bad ones like Lloyd Henreid as well as the good ones like Stu Redman and Larry Underwood) mention the fact that "all that stuff [i.e., weapons of mass destruction] is just lying around, waiting to be picked up." When the Boulderites propose—innocently, meaning only the best—to rebuild the same old neon Tower of Babel, they are wiped out by more violence. The folks who plant the bomb are doing what Randall Flagg told them to, but Mother Abagail, Flagg's opposite number, says again and again that "all things serve God." If this is true—and within the context of *The Stand* it certainly is—then the bomb is actually a stern message from the guy upstairs, a way of saying "I didn't bring you all this way just so you could start up the same old shit."

Near the end of the novel (it *was* the end of the first, shorter version of the story), Fran asks Stuart Redman if there's any hope at all, if people ever learn from their mistakes. Stu replies, "I don't know," and then pauses. In story-time, that pause lasts only as long as it takes the reader to flick his or her eye to the last line. In the writer's study, it went on a lot longer. I searched my mind and heart for something else Stu could say, some clarifying statement. I wanted to find it because at that moment if at no other, Stu was speaking for me. In the end, however, Stu simply repeats what he has already said: *I don't know.* It was the best I could do. Sometimes the book gives you answers, but not always, and I didn't want to leave the readers who had followed me through hundreds of pages with nothing but some empty platitude I didn't believe myself. There is no *moral* to *The Stand,* no "We'd *better* learn or we'll probably destroy the

whole damned planet next time"——but if the theme
stands out clearly enough, those discussing it may offer
their own morals and conclusions. Nothing wrong with
that; such discussions are one of the great pleasures of the
reading life.

Although I'd used symbolism, imagery, and literary
homage before getting to my novel about the big plague
(without *Dracula,* for instance, I think there is no *'Salem's
Lot*), I'm quite sure that I never thought much about
theme before getting roadblocked on *The Stand.* I suppose
I thought such things were for Better Minds and Bigger
Thinkers. I'm not sure I would have gotten to it as soon as
I did, had I not been desperate to save my story.

I was astounded at how really useful "thematic
thinking" turned out to be. It wasn't just a vaporous
idea that English professors made you write about on
midterm essay exams ("Discuss the thematic concerns
of *Wise Blood* in three well-reasoned paragraphs——30
pts"), but another handy gadget to keep in the toolbox, this one something like a magnifying glass.

Since my revelation on the road concerning the
bomb in the closet, I have never hesitated to ask
myself, either before starting the second draft of a book
or while stuck for an idea in the first draft, just what it
is I'm writing about, why I'm spending the time when
I could be playing my guitar or riding my motorcycle,
what got my nose down to the grindstone in the first
place and then kept it there. The answer doesn't
always come right away, but there usually is one, and
it's usually not too hard to find, either.

I don't believe any novelist, even one who's written
forty-plus books, has too many thematic concerns; I

have many interests, but only a few that are deep enough to power novels. These deep interests (I won't quite call them obsessions) include how difficult it is—perhaps impossible!—to close Pandora's technobox once it's open (*The Stand, The Tommyknockers, Firestarter*); the question of why, if there is a God, such terrible things happen (*The Stand, Desperation, The Green Mile*); the thin line between reality and fantasy (*The Dark Half, Bag of Bones, The Drawing of the Three*); and most of all, the terrible attraction violence sometimes has for fundamentally good people (*The Shining, The Dark Half*). I've also written again and again about the fundamental differences between children and adults, and about the healing power of the human imagination.

And I repeat: *no big deal*. These are just interests which have grown out of my life and thought, out of my experiences as a boy and a man, out of my roles as a husband, a father, a writer, and a lover. They are questions that occupy my mind when I turn out the lights for the night and I'm alone with myself, looking up into the darkness with one hand tucked beneath the pillow.

You undoubtedly have your own thoughts, interests, and concerns, and they have arisen, as mine have, from your experiences and adventures as a human being. Some are likely similar to those I've mentioned above and some are likely very different, but you have them, and you should use them in your work. That's not all those ideas are there for, perhaps, but surely it's one of the things they are good for.

I should close this little sermonette with a word of warning—starting with the questions and thematic concerns is a recipe for bad fiction. Good fiction always begins with story and progresses to theme; it almost never begins with theme and progresses to story. The only possible exceptions to this rule that I can think of are allegories like George Orwell's *Animal Farm* (and I have a sneaking suspicion that with *Animal Farm* the story idea may indeed have come first; if I see Orwell in the afterlife, I mean to ask him).

But once your basic story is on paper, you need to think about what it means and enrich your following drafts with your conclusions. To do less is to rob your work (and eventually your readers) of the vision that makes each tale you write uniquely your own.

— 11 —

So far, so good. Now let's talk about revising the work—how much and how many drafts? For me the answer has always been two drafts and a polish (with the advent of word-processing technology, my polishes have become closer to a third draft).

You should realize that I'm only talking about my own personal mode of writing here; in actual practice, rewriting varies greatly from writer to writer. Kurt Vonnegut, for example, rewrote each page of his novels until he got them exactly the way he wanted them. The result was days when he might only manage a page or two of finished copy (and the wastebasket would be full of crumpled, rejected page seventy-ones and seventy-twos), but when the manuscript was finished, the *book* was finished, by gum. You could set it in type. Yet I think certain things hold true for most writers, and those are the ones I want to talk about now. If you've been writing awhile, you won't need me to help you much with this part; you'll have your own established routine. If you're a beginner, though, let me urge that you take your story through at least two drafts; the one you do with the study door closed and the one you do with it open.

With the door shut, downloading what's in my head directly to the page, I write as fast as I can and still remain comfortable. Writing fiction, especially a long work of fiction, can be a difficult, lonely job; it's like crossing the Atlantic Ocean in a bathtub. There's plenty of opportunity for self-doubt. If I write rapidly, putting down my story exactly as it comes into my mind, only looking back to check the names of my characters and the relevant parts of their back stories, I find that I can keep up with my original enthusiasm and at the same time outrun the self-doubt that's always waiting to settle in.

This first draft—the All-Story Draft—should be written with no help (or interference) from anyone else. There may come a point when you want to show what you're doing to a close friend (very often the close friend you think of first is the one who shares your bed), either because you're proud of what you're doing or because you're doubtful about it. My best advice is to resist this impulse. Keep the pressure on; don't lower it by exposing what you've written to the doubt, the praise, or even the well-meaning questions of someone from the Outside World. Let your hope of success (and your fear of failure) carry you on, difficult as that can be. There'll be time to show off what you've done when you finish . . . but even after finishing I think you must be cautious and give yourself a chance to think while the story is still like a field of freshly fallen snow, absent of any tracks save your own.

The great thing about writing with the door shut is that you find yourself forced to concentrate on story to the exclusion of practically everything else. No one can ask you "What were you trying to express with Garfield's dying words?" or "What's the significance of the green dress?" You may not have been trying to express *anything* with Garfield's dying words, and Maura could be wearing green only because that's what you saw when she came into sight in your mind's eye. On the other hand, perhaps those things *do* mean something (or will, when you get a chance to look at the forest instead of the trees). Either way, the first draft is the wrong place to think about it.

Here's something else—if no one says to you, "Oh Sam (or Amy)! This is *wonderful!*," you are a lot less apt to slack off or to start concentrating on the wrong thing . . . *being wonderful,* for instance, instead of *telling the goddam story.*

Now let's say you've finished your first draft. Congratulations! Good job! Have a glass of champagne, send out for pizza, do whatever it is you do when you've got something to celebrate. If you have someone who has been impatiently waiting to read your novel—a spouse, let's say, someone who has perhaps been working nine to five and helping to pay the bills while you chase your dream—then this is the time to give up the goods . . . if, that is, your first reader or readers will promise not to talk to you about the book until *you* are ready to talk to *them* about it.

This may sound a little high-handed, but it's really not. You've done a lot of work and you need a period of time (how much or how little depends on the individual writer) to rest. Your mind and imagination—two things which are related, but not really the same—have to recycle themselves, at least in regard to this one particular work. My advice is that you take a couple of days off—go fishing, go kayaking, do a jigsaw puzzle—and then go to work on something else. Something shorter, preferably, and something that's a complete change of direction and pace from your newly finished book. (I wrote some pretty good novellas, "The Body" and "Apt Pupil" among them, between drafts of longer works like *The Dead Zone* and *The Dark Half.*)

How long you let your book rest—sort of like bread dough between kneadings—is entirely up to you, but I think it should be a minimum of six weeks. During this time your manuscript will be safely shut away in a desk drawer, aging and (one hopes) mellowing. Your thoughts will turn to it frequently, and you'll likely be tempted a dozen times or more to take it out, if only to re-read some passage that seems particularly fine in your memory, something you'd like to go back to so you can re-experience what a really excellent writer you are.

Resist temptation. If you don't, you'll very likely decide you didn't do as well on that passage as you thought and you'd better retool it on the spot. This is bad. The only thing worse would be for you to decide the passage is even *better* than you remembered—why not drop everything and read the whole book over right then? Get back to work on it! Hell, you're ready! You're fuckin Shakespeare!

You're not, though, and you're not ready to go back to the old project until you've gotten so involved in a new one (or re-involved in your day-to-day life) that you've almost forgotten the unreal estate that took up three hours of your every morning or afternoon for a period of three or five or seven months.

When you come to the correct evening (which you well may have marked on your office calendar), take your manuscript out of the drawer. If it looks like an alien relic bought at a junk-shop or yard sale where you can hardly remember stopping, you're ready. Sit down with your door shut (you'll be opening it to the world soon enough), a pencil in your hand, and a legal pad by your side. Then read your manuscript over.

Do it all in one sitting, if that's possible (it won't be, of course, if your book is a four- or five-hundred-pager). Make all the notes you want, but concentrate on the mundane housekeeping jobs, like fixing misspellings and picking up inconsistencies. There'll be plenty; only God gets it right the first time and only a slob says, "Oh well, let it go, that's what copyeditors are for."

If you've never done it before, you'll find reading your book over after a six-week layoff to be a strange, often exhilarating experience. It's yours, you'll recognize it as yours, even be able to remember what tune was on the stereo when you wrote certain lines, and yet it will also be like reading the work of someone else, a soul-twin, perhaps. This is the way it should be, the reason you waited. It's always easier to kill someone else's darlings than it is to kill your own.

With six weeks' worth of recuperation time, you'll also be able to see any glaring holes in the plot or character development. I'm talking about holes big enough to drive a truck through. It's amazing how some of these things can elude the writer while he or she is occupied with the daily work of composition. And listen—if you spot a few of these big holes, you are *forbidden* to feel depressed about them or to beat up on yourself. Screw-ups happen to the best of us. There's a story that the architect of the Flatiron Building committed suicide when he realized, just before the ribbon-cutting ceremony, that he had neglected to put any men's rooms in his prototypical skyscraper. Probably not true, but remember this: someone *really did* design the *Titanic* and then label it unsinkable.

For me, the most glaring errors I find on the re-read have to do with character motivation (related to character development but not quite the same). I'll smack myself upside the head with the heel of my palm, then grab my legal pad and write something like p. 91: **Sandy Hunter filches a buck from Shirley's stash in the dispatch office. Why? God's sake, Sandy would NEVER do anything like this!** I also mark the page in the manuscript with a big ✂ symbol, meaning that cuts and/or changes are needed on this page, and reminding myself to check my notes for the exact details if I don't remember them.

I love this part of the process (well, I love *all* the parts of the process, but this one is especially nice) because I'm rediscovering my own book, and usually liking it. That changes. By the time a book is actually in print, I've been over it a dozen times or more, can quote whole passages, and only wish the damned old smelly thing would go away. That's later, though; the first read-through is usually pretty fine.

During that reading, the top part of my mind is concentrating on story and toolbox concerns: knocking out pronouns with unclear antecedents (I hate and mistrust pronouns, every one of them as slippery as a fly-by-night personal-injury lawyer), adding clarifying phrases where they seem necessary, and of course, deleting all the adverbs I can bear to part with (never all of them; never enough).

Underneath, however, I'm asking myself the Big Questions. The biggest: Is this story coherent? And if it is, what will turn coherence into a song? What are the recurring elements? Do they entwine and make a theme? I'm asking myself What's it all about, Stevie, in other words, and what I can do to make those underlying concerns even clearer. What I want most of all is *resonance,* something that will linger for a little while in Constant Reader's mind (and heart) after he or she has closed the book and put it up on the shelf. I'm looking for ways to do that without spoon-feeding the reader or selling my birthright for a plot of message. Take all those messages and those morals and stick em where the sun don't shine, all right? I want resonance. Most of all, *I'm looking for what I meant,* because in the second draft I'll want to add scenes and incidents that reinforce that meaning. I'll also want to delete stuff that goes in other directions. There's apt to be a lot of that stuff, especially near the beginning of a story, when I have a tendency to flail. All that thrashing around has to go if

I am to achieve anything like a unified effect. When I've finished reading and making all my little anal-retentive revisions, it's time to open the door and show what I've written to four or five close friends who have indicated a willingness to look.

Someone—I can't remember who, for the life of me—once wrote that all novels are really letters aimed at one person. As it happens, I believe this. I think that every novelist has a single ideal reader; that at various points during the composition of a story, the writer is thinking, "I wonder what he/she will think when he/she reads *this* part?" For me that first reader is my wife, Tabitha.

She has always been an extremely sympathetic and supportive first reader. Her positive reaction to difficult books like *Bag of Bones* (my first novel with a new publisher after twenty good years with Viking that came to an end in a stupid squabble about money) and relatively controversial ones like *Gerald's Game* meant the world to me. But she's also unflinching when she sees something she thinks is wrong. When she does, she lets me know loud and clear.

In her role as critic and first reader, Tabby often makes me think of a story I read about Alfred Hitchcock's wife, Alma Reville. Ms. Reville was the equivalent of Hitch's first reader, a sharp-eyed critic who was totally unimpressed with the suspense-master's growing reputation as an *auteur*. Lucky for him. Hitch say he want to fly, Alma say, "First eat your eggs."

Not long after finishing *Psycho,* Hitchcock screened it for a few friends. They raved about it, declaring it to be a suspense masterpiece. Alma was quiet until they'd all had their say, then spoke very firmly: "You can't send it out like that."

There was a thunderstruck silence, except for Hitchcock himself, who only asked why not. "Because," his wife responded, "Janet Leigh swallows when she's supposed to be dead." It was true. Hitchcock didn't argue any more than I do when Tabby points out one of my lapses. She and I may argue about many aspects of a book, and there have been times when I've gone against her judgment on subjective matters, but when she catches me in a goof, I know it, and thank God I've got someone around who'll tell me my fly's unzipped before I go out in public that way.

In addition to Tabby's first read, I usually send manuscripts to between four and eight other people who have critiqued my stories over the years. Many writing texts caution against asking friends to read your stuff, suggesting you're not apt to get a very unbiased opinion from folks who've eaten dinner at your house and sent their kids over to play with your kids in your backyard. It's unfair, according to this view, to put a pal in such a position. What happens if he/she feels he/she has to say, "I'm sorry, good buddy, you've written some great yarns in the past but this one sucks like a vacuum cleaner"?

The idea has some validity, but I don't think an unbiased opinion is exactly what I'm looking for. And I believe that most people smart enough to read a novel are also tactful enough to find a gentler mode of expression than "This sucks." (Although most of us know that "I think this has a few problems" actually means "This sucks," don't we?) Besides, if you really did write a stinker—it happens; as the author of *Maximum Overdrive*

I'm qualified to say so—wouldn't you rather hear the news from a friend while the entire edition consists of a half-dozen Xerox copies?

When you give out six or eight copies of a book, you get back six or eight highly subjective opinions about what's good and what's bad in it. If all your readers think you did a pretty good job, you probably did. This sort of unanimity does happen, but it's rare, even with friends. More likely, they'll think that some parts are good and some parts are . . . well, not so good. Some will feel Character A works but Character B is far-fetched. If others feel that Character B is believable but Character A is overdrawn, it's a wash. You can safely relax and leave things the way they are (in baseball, tie goes to the runner; for novelists, it goes to the writer). If some people love your ending and others hate it, same deal—it's a wash, and tie goes to the writer.

Some first readers specialize in pointing out factual errors, which are the easiest to deal with. One of my first-reader smart guys, the late Mac McCutcheon, a wonderful high school English teacher, knew a lot about guns. If I had a character toting a Winchester .330, Mac might jot in the margin that Winchester didn't make that caliber but Remington did. In such cases you've got two for the price of one—the error and the fix. It's a good deal, because you come off looking like you're an expert and your first reader will feel flattered to have been of help. And the best catch Mac ever made for me had nothing to do with guns. One day while reading a piece of a manuscript in the teachers' room, he burst out laughing—laughed so hard, in fact, that tears went rolling down his bearded cheeks. Because the story in question, *'Salem's Lot,* had not been intended as a laff riot, I asked him what he had found. I had written a line that went something like this: **Although deer season doesn't start until November in Maine, the fields of October are often alive with gunshots; the locals are shooting as many peasants as they think their families will eat.** A copy-editor would no doubt have picked up the mistake, but Mac spared me that embarrassment.

Subjective evaluations are, as I say, a little harder to deal with, but listen: if everyone who reads your book says you have a problem (Connie comes back to her husband too easily, Hal's cheating on the big exam seems unrealistic given what we know about him, the novel's conclusion seems abrupt and arbitrary), you've got a problem and you better do something about it.

Plenty of writers resist this idea. They feel that revising a story according to the likes and dislikes of an audience is somehow akin to prostitution. If you really feel that way, I won't try to change your mind. You'll save on charges at Copy Cop, too, because you won't have to show anyone your story in the first place. In fact (he said snottily), if you *really* feel that way, why bother to publish at all? Just finish your books and then pop them in a safe-deposit box, as J. D. Salinger is reputed to have been doing in his later years.

And yes, I can relate, at least a bit, to that sort of resentment. In the film business, where I have had a quasi-professional life, first-draft showings are called "test screenings." These have become standard practice in the industry, and they drive most filmmakers absolutely bugshit. Maybe they should. The studio shells out somewhere between fifteen and a hundred million dollars to make a film, then asks the director to recut it based on the opinions of a Santa Barbara multiplex audience composed of hairdressers, meter maids, shoe-store clerks, and out-of-work pizza-delivery guys. And the worst, most maddening thing about it? If you get the demographic right, test screenings seem to work.

I'd hate to see novels revised on the basis of test audiences—a lot of good books would never see the light of day if it was done that way—but come on, we're talking about half a dozen people you know and respect. If you ask the right ones (and if they agree to read your book), they can tell you a lot.

Do all opinions weigh the same? Not for me. In the end I listen most closely to Tabby, because she's the one I write for, the one I want to wow. If you're writing primarily for one person besides yourself, I'd advise you to pay very close attention to that person's opinion (I know one fellow who says he writes mostly for someone who's been dead fifteen years, but the majority of us aren't in that position). And if what you hear makes sense, then make the changes. You can't let the whole world into your story, but you can let in the ones that matter the most. And you should.

Call that one person you write for Ideal Reader. He or she is going to be in your writing room all the time: in the flesh once you open the door and let the world back in to shine on the bubble of your dream, in spirit during the sometimes troubling and often exhilarating days of the first draft, when the door is closed. And you know what? You'll find yourself bending the story even before Ideal Reader glimpses so much as the first sentence. I.R. will help you get outside yourself a little, to actually read your work in progress as an audience would while you're still working. This is perhaps the best way of all to make sure you stick to story, a way of playing to the audience even while there's no audience there and you're totally in charge.

When I write a scene that strikes me as funny (like the pie-eating contest in "The Body" or the execution rehearsal in *The Green Mile*), I am also imagining my I.R. finding it funny. I love it when Tabby laughs out of control—she puts her hands up as if to say *I surrender* and these big tears go rolling down her cheeks. I love it, that's all, fucking adore it, and when I get hold of something with that potential, I twist it as hard as I can. During the actual writing of such a scene (door closed), the thought of making her laugh—or cry—is in the back of my mind. During the rewrite (door open), the question—*is it funny enough yet? scary enough?*—is right up front. I try to watch her when she gets to a particular scene, hoping for at least a smile or—jackpot, baby!—that big belly-laugh with the hands up, waving in the air.

This isn't always easy on her. I gave her the manuscript of my novella *Hearts in Atlantis* while we were in North Carolina, where we'd gone to see a Cleveland Rockers–Charlotte Sting WNBA game. We drove north to Virginia the following day, and it was during this drive that Tabby read my story. There are some funny parts in it—at least *I* thought so—and I kept peeking over at her to see if she was chuckling (or at least smiling). I didn't think she'd notice, but of course she did. On my eighth or ninth peek (I guess it *could* have been my fifteenth), she looked up and snapped: "Pay attention to your driving before you crack us up, will you? Stop being so goddam *needy!*"

I paid attention to my driving and stopped sneaking peeks (well . . . almost). About five minutes later, I heard a snort of laughter from my right. Just a little one, but it was enough for me. The truth is that most writers *are* needy. Especially between the first draft and the second, when the study door swings open and the light of the world shines in.

– 12 –

Ideal Reader is also the best way for you to gauge whether or not your story is paced correctly and if you've handled the back story in satisfactory fashion.

Pace is the speed at which your narrative unfolds. There is a kind of unspoken (hence undefended and unexamined) belief in publishing circles that the most commercially successful stories and novels are fast-paced. I guess the underlying thought is that people have so many things to do today, and are so easily distracted from the printed word, that you'll lose them unless you become a kind of short-order cook, serving up sizzling burgers, fries, and eggs over easy just as fast as you can.

Like so many unexamined beliefs in the publishing business, this idea is largely bullshit . . . which is why, when books like Umberto Eco's *The Name of the Rose* or Charles Frazier's *Cold Mountain* suddenly break out of the pack and climb the best-seller lists, publishers and editors are astonished. I suspect that most of them ascribe these books' unexpected success to unpredictable and deplorable lapses into good taste on the part of the reading public.

Not that there's anything wrong with rapidly paced novels. Some pretty good writers—Nelson DeMille, Wilbur Smith, and Sue Grafton, to name just three—have made millions writing them. But you can overdo the speed thing. Move too fast and you risk leaving the reader behind, either by confusing or by wearing him/her out. And for myself, I *like* a slower pace and a bigger, higher build. The leisurely luxury-liner experience of a long, absorbing novel like *The Far Pavilions* or *A Suitable Boy* has been one of the form's chief attractions since the first examples—endless, multipart epistolary tales like *Clarissa*. I believe each story should be allowed to unfold at its own pace, and that pace is not always double time. Nevertheless, you need to beware—if you slow the pace down too much, even the most patient reader is apt to grow restive.

The best way to find the happy medium? Ideal Reader, of course. Try to imagine whether he or she will be bored by a certain scene—if you know the tastes of your I.R. even half as well as I know the tastes of mine, that shouldn't be too hard. Is I.R. going to feel there's too much pointless talk in this place or that? That you've underexplained a certain situation . . . or overexplained it, which is one of my chronic failings? That you forgot to resolve some important plot point? Forgot an entire *character,* as Raymond Chandler once did? (When asked about the murdered chauffeur in *The Big Sleep,* Chandler—who liked his tipple—replied, "Oh, him. You know, I forgot all about him.") These questions should be in your mind even with the door closed. And once it's open—once your Ideal Reader has actually read your manuscript—you should ask your questions out loud. Also, needy or not, you might want to watch and see when your I.R. puts your manuscript down to do something else. What scene was he or she reading? What was so easy to put down?

Mostly when I think of pacing, I go back to Elmore Leonard, who explained it so perfectly by saying he just left out the boring parts. This suggests cutting to speed the pace, and that's what most of us end up having to do (kill your darlings, kill your darlings, even when it breaks your egocentric little scribbler's heart, kill your darlings).

As a teenager, sending out stories to magazines like *Fantasy and Science Fiction* and *Ellery Queen's Mystery Magazine,* I got used to the sort of rejection note that starts *Dear Contributor* (might as well start off *Dear Chump*), and so came to relish any little personal dash on these printed pink-slips. They were few and far between, but when they came they never failed to lighten my day and put a smile on my face.

In the spring of my senior year at Lisbon High— 1966, this would've been—I got a scribbled comment that changed the way I rewrote my fiction once and forever. Jotted below the machine-generated signature of the editor was this *mot:* "Not bad, but PUFFY. You need to revise for length. Formula: 2nd Draft = 1st Draft − 10%. Good luck."

I wish I could remember who wrote that note— Algis Budrys, perhaps. Whoever it was did me a hell of a favor. I copied the formula out on a piece of shirt-cardboard and taped it to the wall beside my typewriter. Good things started to happen for me shortly after. There was no sudden golden flood of magazine sales, but the number of personal notes on the rejection slips went up fast. I even got one from Durant Imboden, the fiction editor at *Playboy*. That communiqué almost stopped my heart. *Playboy* paid two thousand dollars and up for short stories, and two grand was a quarter of what my mother made each year in her housekeeping job at Pineland Training Center.

The Rewrite Formula probably wasn't the only reason I started to get some results; I suspect another was that it was just my time, coming around at last (sort of like Yeats's rough beast). Still, the Formula was surely part of it. Before the Formula, if I produced a story that was four thousand words or so in first draft, it was apt to be five thousand in second (some writers are taker-outers; I'm afraid I've always been a natural putter-inner). After the Formula, that changed. Even today I will aim for a second-draft length of thirty-six hundred words if the first draft of a story ran four thousand . . . and if the first draft of a novel runs three hundred and fifty thousand words, I'll try my damndest to produce a second draft of no more than three hundred and fifteen thousand . . . three hundred, if possible. Usually it is possible. What the Formula taught me is that every story and novel is collapsible to some degree. If you can't get out ten per cent of it while retaining the basic story and flavor, you're not trying very hard. The effect of judicious cutting is immediate and often amazing—literary Viagra. You'll feel it and your I.R. will, too.

Back story is all the stuff that happened before your tale began but which has an impact on the front story.

Back story helps define character and establish motivation. I think it's important to get the back story in as quickly as possible, but it's also important to do it with some grace. As an example of what's not graceful, consider this line of dialogue:

"Hello, ex-wife," Tom said to Doris as she entered the room.

Now, it may be important to the story that Tom and Doris are divorced, but there *has* to be a better way to do it than the above, which is about as graceful as an axe-murder. Here is one suggestion:

"Hi, Doris," Tom said. His voice sounded natural enough—to his own ears, at least—but the fingers of his right hand crept to the place where his wedding ring had been until six months ago.

Still no Pulitzer winner, and quite a bit longer than *Hello, ex-wife,* but it's not all about speed, as I've already tried to point out. And if you think it's all about information, you ought to give up fiction and get a job writing instruction manuals—Dilbert's cubicle awaits.

You've probably heard the phrase *in medias res,* which means "into the midst of things." This technique is an ancient and honorable one, but I don't like it. *In medias res* necessitates flashbacks, which strike me as boring and sort of corny. They always make me think of those movies from the forties and fifties where the picture gets all swimmy, the voices get all echoey, and suddenly it's sixteen months ago and the mud-splashed convict we just saw trying to outrun the bloodhounds is an up-and-coming young lawyer who hasn't yet been framed for the murder of the crooked police chief.

As a reader, I'm a lot more interested in what's *going* to happen than what already *did*. Yes, there are brilliant novels that run counter to this preference (or maybe it's a prejudice)—*Rebecca,* by Daphne du Maurier, for one; *A Dark-Adapted Eye,* by Barbara Vine, for another—but I like to start at square one, dead even with the writer. I'm an A-to-Z man; serve me the appetizer first and give me dessert if I eat my veggies.

Even when you tell your story in this straightforward manner, you'll discover you can't escape at least *some* back story. In a very real sense, every life is *in medias res.* If you introduce a forty-year-old man as your main character on page one of your novel, and if the action begins as the result of some brand-new person or situation's exploding onto the stage of this fellow's life—a road accident, let's say, or doing a favor for a beautiful woman who keeps looking sexily back over her shoulder (did you note the awful adverb in this sentence which I could not bring myself to kill?)—you'll *still* have to deal with the first forty years of the guy's life at some point. How much and how well you deal with those years will have a lot to do with the level of success your story achieves, with whether readers think of it as "a good read" or "a big fat bore." Probably J. K. Rowling, author of the Harry Potter stories, is the current champ when it comes to back story. You could do worse than read these, noting how effortlessly each new book recaps what has gone before. (Also, the Harry Potter novels are just *fun,* pure story from beginning to end.)

Your Ideal Reader can be of tremendous help when it comes to figuring out how well you did with the back story and how much you should add or subtract on your next draft. You need to listen very carefully to the things I.R. didn't understand, and then ask yourself if *you* understand them. If you do and just didn't put those parts across, your job on the second draft is to clarify. If you don't—if the parts of the back story your Ideal Reader queried are hazy to you, as well—then you need to think a lot more carefully about the past events that cast a light on your characters' present behavior.

You also need to pay close attention to those things in the back story that bored your Ideal Reader. In *Bag of Bones,* for instance, main character Mike Noonan is a fortyish writer who, as the book opens, has just lost his wife to a brain aneurysm. We start on the day of her death, but there's still a hell of a lot of back story here, much more than I usually have in my fiction. This includes Mike's first job (as a newspaper reporter), the sale of his first novel, his relations with his late wife's sprawling family, his publishing history, and especially the matter of their summer home in western Maine— how they came to buy it and some of its pre–Mike-and-Johanna history. Tabitha, my I.R., read all this with apparent enjoyment, but there was also a two- or three-page section about Mike's community-service work in the year after his wife dies, a year in which his grief is magnified by a severe case of writer's block. Tabby didn't like the community-service stuff.

"Who cares?" she asked me. "I want to know more about his bad dreams, not how he ran for city council in order to help get the homeless alcoholics off the street."

"Yeah, but he's got *writer's block*," I said. (When a novelist is challenged on something he likes—one of his darlings—the first two words out of his mouth are almost always *Yeah but*.) "This block goes on for a year, maybe more. He has to do *something* in all that time, doesn't he?"

"I guess so," Tabby said, "but you don't have to bore me with it, do you?"

Ouch. Game, set, and match. Like most good I.R.s, Tabby can be ruthless when she's right.

I cut down Mike's charitable contributions and community functions from two pages to two paragraphs. It turned out that Tabby was right—as soon as I saw it in print, I knew. Three million people or so have read *Bag of Bones,* I've gotten at least four thousand letters concerning it, and so far not a single one has said, "Hey, turkey! What was Mike doing for community-service work during the year he couldn't write?"

The most important things to remember about back story are that (a) everyone has a history and (b) most of it isn't very interesting. Stick to the parts that are, and don't get carried away with the rest. Long life stories are best received in bars, and only then an hour or so before closing time, and if you are buying.

– 13 –

We need to talk a bit about research, which is a specialized kind of back story. And please, if you *do* need to do research because parts of your story deal with things about which you know little or nothing, remember that word *back*. That's where research belongs: as far in the background and the back story as you can get it. *You* may be entranced with what you're learning about flesh-eating bacteria, the sewer system of New York, or the I.Q. potential of collie pups, but your readers are probably going to care a lot more about your characters and your story.

Exceptions to the rule? Sure, aren't there always? There have been very successful writers—Arthur Hailey and James Michener are the first ones that come to my mind—whose novels rely heavily on fact and research. Hailey's are barely disguised manuals about how things work (banks, airports, hotels), and Michener's are combination travelogues, geography lessons, and history texts. Other popular writers, like Tom Clancy and Patricia Cornwell, are more story-oriented but still deliver large (and sometimes hard to digest) dollops of factual information along with the melodrama. I sometimes think that these writers appeal to a large segment of the reading population who feel that fiction is somehow immoral, a low taste which can only be justified by saying, "Well, ahem, yes, I *do* read [Fill in author's name here], but only on airplanes and in hotel rooms that don't have CNN; also, I learned a great deal about [Fill in appropriate subject here]."

For every successful writer of the factoid type, however, there are a hundred (perhaps even a thousand) wannabes, some published, most not. On the whole, I think story belongs in front, but some research is inevitable; you shirk it at your peril.

In the spring of 1999 I drove from Florida, where my wife and I had wintered, back to Maine. My second day on the road, I stopped for gas at a little station just off the Pennsylvania Turnpike, one of those amusingly antique places where a fellow still comes out, pumps your gas, and asks how you're doing and who you like in the NCAA tournament.

I told this one I was doing fine and liked Duke in the tournament. Then I went around back to use the men's room. There was a brawling stream full of snowmelt beyond the station, and when I came out of the men's, I walked a little way down the slope, which was littered with cast-off tire-rims and engine parts, for a closer look at the water. There were still patches of snow on the ground. I slipped on one and started to slide down the embankment. I grabbed a piece of someone's old engine block and stopped myself before I got fairly started, but I realized as I got up that if I'd fallen just right, I could have slid all the way down into that stream and been swept away. I found myself wondering, had that happened, how long it would have taken the gas station attendant to call the State Police if my car, a brand-new Lincoln Navigator, just continued to stand there in front of the pumps. By the time I got back on the turnpike again, I had two things: a wet ass from my fall behind the Mobil station, and a great idea for a story.

In it, a mysterious man in a black coat—likely not a human being at all but some creature inexpertly disguised to look like one—abandons his vehicle in front of a small gas station in rural Pennsylvania. The vehicle looks like an old Buick Special from the late fifties, but it's no more a Buick than the guy in the black coat was a human being. The vehicle falls into the hands of some State Police officers working out of a fictional barracks in western Pennsylvania. Twenty years or so later, these cops tell the story of the Buick to the grief-stricken son of a State Policeman who has been killed in the line of duty.

It was a grand idea and has developed into a strong novel about how we hand down our knowledge and our secrets; it's also a grim and frightening story about an alien piece of machinery that sometimes reaches out and swallows people whole. Of course there *were* a few minor problems—the fact that I knew absolutely zilch about the Pennsylvania State Police, for one thing—but I didn't let any of that bother me. I simply made up all the stuff I didn't know.

I could do that because I was writing with the door shut—writing only for myself and the Ideal Reader in my mind (my mental version of Tabby is rarely as prickly as my real-life wife can be; in my daydreams she usually applauds and urges me ever onward with shining eyes). One of my most memorable sessions took place in a fourth-floor room of Boston's Eliot Hotel—me sitting at the desk by the window, writing about an autopsy on an alien bat-creature while the Boston Marathon flowed exuberantly by just below me and rooftop boomboxes blasted out "Dirty Water," by The Standells. There were a thousand people down there below me in the streets, but not a single one in my room to be a party-pooper and tell me I got this detail wrong or the cops don't do things that way in western Pennsylvania, so nyah-nyah-nyah.

The novel—it's called *From a Buick Eight*—has been set aside in a desk drawer since late May of 1999, when the first draft was finished. Work on it has been delayed by circumstances beyond my control, but eventually I hope and expect to spend a couple of weeks in western Pennsylvania, where I've been given conditional permission to do some ride-alongs with the State Police (the condition—which seems eminently reasonable to me—was that I not make them look like meanies, maniacs, or idiots). Once I've done that, I should be able to correct the worst of my howlers and add some really nice detail-work.

Not much, though; research is back story, and the key word in back story is *back*. The tale I have to tell in *Buick Eight* has to do with monsters and secrets. It is *not* a story about police procedure in western Pennsylvania. What I'm looking for is nothing but a touch of verisimilitude, like the handful of spices you chuck into a good spaghetti sauce to really finish her off. That sense of reality is important in any work of fiction, but I think it is particularly important in a story dealing with the abnormal or paranormal. Also, enough details— always assuming they are the correct ones—can stem the tide of letters from picky-ass readers who apparently live to tell writers that they messed up (the tone of these letters is unvaryingly gleeful). When you step away from the "write what you know" rule, research becomes inevitable, and it can add a lot to your story. Just don't end up with the tail wagging the dog; remember that you are writing a novel, not a research paper. The story always comes first. I think that even James Michener and Arthur Hailey would have agreed with that.

– 14 –

I'm often asked if I think the beginning writer of fiction can benefit from writing classes or seminars. The people who ask are, all too often, looking for a magic bullet or a secret ingredient or possibly Dumbo's magic feather, none of which can be found in classrooms or at writing retreats, no matter how enticing the brochures may be. As for myself, I'm doubtful about writing classes, but not entirely against them.

In T. Coraghessan Boyle's wonderful tragicomic novel *East Is East,* there is a description of a writer's colony in the woods that struck me as fairy-tale perfect. Each attendee has his or her own little cabin where he or she supposedly spends the day writing. At noon, a waiter from the main lodge brings these fledgling Hemingways and Cathers a box lunch and puts it on the front stoop of the cottage. Very *quietly* puts it on the stoop, so as not to disturb the creative trance of the cabin's occupant. One room of each cabin is the writing room. In the other is a cot for that all-important afternoon nap . . . or, perhaps, for a revivifying bounce with one of the other attendees.

In the evening, all members of the colony gather in the lodge for dinner and intoxicating conversation with the writers in residence. Later, before a roaring fire in the parlor, marshmallows are toasted, popcorn is popped, wine is drunk, and the stories of the colony attendees are read aloud and then critiqued.

To me, this sounded like an absolutely enchanted writing environment. I especially liked the part about having your lunch left at the front door, deposited there as quietly as the tooth fairy deposits a quarter under a kid's pillow. I imagine it appealed because it's so far from my own experience, where the creative flow is apt to be stopped at any moment by a message from my wife that the toilet is plugged up and would I try to fix it, or a call from the office telling me that I'm in imminent danger of blowing yet another dental appointment. At times like that I'm sure all writers feel pretty much the same, no matter what their skill and success level: *God, if only I were in the right writing environment, with the right understanding people, I just KNOW I could be penning my masterpiece.*

In truth, I've found that any day's routine interruptions and distractions don't much hurt a work in progress and may actually help it in some ways. It is, after all, the dab of grit that seeps into an oyster's shell that makes the pearl, not pearl-making seminars with other oysters. And the larger the work looms in my day—the more it seems like an *I hafta* instead of just an *I wanna*—the more problematic it can become. One serious problem with writers' workshops is that *I hafta* becomes the rule. You didn't come, after all, to wander lonely as a cloud, experiencing the beauty of the woods or the grandeur of the mountains. You're supposed to be *writing,* dammit, if only so that your colleagues will have something to critique as they toast their goddam marshmallows there in the main lodge. When, on the other hand, making sure the kid gets to his basketball camp on time is every bit as important as your work in progress, there's a lot less pressure to produce.

And what *about* those critiques, by the way? How valuable are they? Not very, in my experience, sorry. A lot of them are maddeningly vague. *I love the feeling of Peter's story,* someone may say. *It had something . . . a sense of I don't know . . . there's a loving kind of you know . . . I can't exactly describe it . . .*

Other writing-seminar gemmies include *I felt like the tone thing was just kind of you know; The character of Polly seemed pretty much stereotypical; I loved the imagery because I could see what he was talking about more or less perfectly.*

And, instead of pelting these babbling idiots with their own freshly toasted marshmallows, everyone else sitting around the fire is often *nodding* and *smiling* and looking *solemnly thoughtful.* In too many cases the teachers and writers in residence are nodding, smiling, and looking solemnly thoughtful right along with them. It seems to occur to few of the attendees that if you have a feeling you just can't describe, you might just be, I don't know, kind of like, my sense of it is, maybe in the wrong fucking class.

Non-specific critiques won't help when you sit down to your second draft, and may hurt. Certainly none of the comments above touch on the language of your piece, or its narrative sense; these comments are just wind, offering no factual input at all.

Also, daily critiques force you to write with the door constantly open, and in my mind that sort of defeats the purpose. What good does it do you to have the waiter tiptoe soundlessly up to the stoop of your cabin with your lunch and then tiptoe away with equal solicitous soundlessness, if you are reading your current work aloud every night (or handing it out on Xeroxed sheets) to a group of would-be writers who are telling you they like the way you handle tone and mood but want to know if Dolly's cap, the one with the bells on it, is symbolic? The pressure to explain is always on, and a lot of your creative energy, it seems to me, is therefore going in the wrong direction. You find yourself constantly questioning your prose and your purpose when what you should probably be doing is writing as fast as the Gingerbread Man runs, getting that first draft down on paper while the shape of the fossil is still bright and clear in your mind. Too many writing classes make *Wait a minute, explain what you meant by that* a kind of bylaw.

In all fairness, I must admit to a certain prejudice here: one of the few times I suffered a full-fledged case of writer's block was during my senior year at the University of Maine, when I was taking not one but two creative-writing courses (one was the seminar in which I met my future wife, so it can hardly be counted as a dead loss). Most of my fellow students that semester were writing poems about sexual yearning or stories in which moody young men whose parents did not understand them were preparing to go off to Vietnam. One young woman wrote a good deal about the moon and her menstrual cycle; in these poems *the moon* always appeared as *th m'n*. She could not explain just why this had to be, but we all kind of felt it: th m'n, yeah, dig it, sister.

I brought poems of my own to class, but back in my dorm room was my dirty little secret: the half-completed manuscript of a novel about a teenage gang's plan to start a race-riot. They would use this for cover while ripping off two dozen loan-sharking operations and illegal drug-rings in the city of Harding, my fictional version of Detroit (I had never been within six hundred miles of Detroit, but I didn't let that stop or even slow me down). This novel, *Sword in the Darkness*, seemed very tawdry to me when compared to what my fellow students were trying to achieve; which is why, I suppose, I never brought any of it to class for a critique. The fact that it was also better and somehow truer than all my poems about sexual yearning and post-adolescent angst only made things worse. The result was a four-month period in which I could write almost nothing at all. What I did instead was drink beer, smoke Pall Malls, read John D. MacDonald paperbacks, and watch afternoon soap operas.

Writing courses and seminars do offer at least one undeniable benefit: in them, the desire to write fiction or poetry is taken seriously. For aspiring writers who have been looked upon with pitying condescension by their friends and relatives ("You better not quit your day job just yet!" is a popular line, usually delivered with a hideous Bob's-yer-uncle grin), this is a wonderful thing. In writing classes, if nowhere else, it is entirely permissible to spend large chunks of your time off in your own little dreamworld. Still—do you really need permission and a hall-pass to go there? Do you need someone to make you a paper badge with the word WRITER on it before you can believe you *are* one? God, I hope not.

Another argument in favor of writing courses has to do with the men and women who teach them. There are thousands of talented writers at work in America, and only a few of them (I think the number might be as low as five per cent) can support their families and themselves with their work. There's always some grant money available, but it's never enough to go around. As for government subsidies for creative writers, perish the thought. Tobacco subsidies, sure. Research grants to study the motility of unpreserved bull sperm, of course. Creative-writing subsidies, never. Most voters would agree, I think. With the exception of Norman Rockwell and Robert Frost, America has never much revered her creative people; as a whole, we're more interested in commemorative plates from the Franklin Mint and Internet greeting-cards. And if you don't like it, it's a case of tough titty said the kitty, 'cause that's just the way things are. Americans are a lot more interested in TV quiz shows than in the short fiction of Raymond Carver.

The solution for a good many underpaid creative writers is to teach what they know to others. This can be a nice thing, and it's nice when beginning writers have a chance to meet with and listen to veteran writers they may have long admired. It's also great when writing classes lead to business contacts. I got my first agent, Maurice Crain, courtesy of my sophomore comp teacher, the noted regional short story writer Edwin M. Holmes. After reading a couple of my stories in Eh-77 (a comp class emphasizing fiction), Professor Holmes asked Crain if he would look at a selection of my work. Crain agreed, but we never had much of an association—he was in his eighties, unwell, and died shortly after our first correspondence. I can only hope it wasn't my initial batch of stories that killed him.

You don't *need* writing classes or seminars any more than you need this or any other book on writing. Faulkner learned his trade while working in the Oxford, Mississippi, post office. Other writers have learned the basics while serving in the Navy, working in steel mills, or doing time in America's finer crossbar hotels. I learned the most valuable (and commercial) part of my life's work while washing motel sheets and restaurant tablecloths at the New Franklin Laundry in Bangor. You learn best by reading a lot and writing a lot, and the most valuable lessons of all are the ones you teach yourself. These lessons almost always occur with the study door closed. Writing-class discussions can often be intellectually stimulating and great fun, but they also often stray far afield from the actual nuts-and-bolts business of writing.

Still, I suppose you might end up in a version of that sylvan writer's colony in *East Is East:* your own little cottage in the pines, complete with word processor, fresh disks (what is so delicately exciting to the imagination as a box of fresh computer disks or a ream of blank paper?), the cot in the other room for that afternoon nap, and the lady who tiptoes to your stoop, leaves your lunch, and then tiptoes away again. That would be okay, I guess. If you got a chance to participate in a deal like that, I'd say go right ahead. You might not learn The Magic Secrets of Writing (there aren't any—bummer, huh?), but it would certainly be a grand time, and grand times are something I'm *always* in favor of.

– 15 –

Other than *Where do you get your ideas?*, the questions any publishing writer hears most frequently from those who want to publish are *How do you get an agent?* and *How do you make contact with people in the world of publishing?*

The tone in which these questions are asked is often bewildered, sometimes chagrined, and frequently angry. There is a commonly held suspicion that most newcomers who actually succeed in getting their books published broke through because they had an in, a contact, a rabbi in the business. The underlying assumption is that publishing is just one big, happy, incestuously closed family.

It's not true. Neither is it true that agents are a snooty, superior bunch that would die before allowing their ungloved fingers to touch an unsolicited manuscript. (Well okay, yeah, there are a *few* like that.) The fact is that agents, publishers, and editors are all looking for the next hot writer who can sell a lot of books and make lots of money . . . and not just the next hot *young* writer, either; Helen Santmyer was in a retirement home when she published . . . *And Ladies of the Club.* Frank McCourt was quite a bit younger when he published *Angela's Ashes,* but he's still no spring chicken.

As a young man just beginning to publish some short fiction in the t&a magazines, I was fairly optimistic about my chances of getting published; I knew that I had some game, as the basketball players say these days, and I also felt that time was on my side; sooner or later the best-selling writers of the sixties and seventies would either die or go senile, making room for newcomers like me.

Still, I was aware that I had worlds to conquer beyond the pages of *Cavalier, Gent,* and *Juggs.* I wanted my stories to find the right markets, and that meant finding a way around the troubling fact that a good many of the best-paying ones (*Cosmopolitan,* for instance, which at that time published lots of short stories) wouldn't look at unsolicited fiction. The answer, it seemed to me, was to have an agent. If my fiction was good, I thought in my unsophisticated but not entirely illogical way, an agent would solve all my problems.

I didn't discover until much later that not all agents are good agents, and that a good agent is useful in many other ways than getting the fiction editor at *Cosmo* to look at your short stories. But as a young man I did not yet realize that there are people in the publishing world—more than a few, actually—who would steal the pennies off a dead man's eyes. For me, that didn't really matter, because before my first couple of novels actually succeeded in finding an audience, I had little to steal.

You *should* have an agent, and if your work is salable, you will have only a moderate amount of trouble finding one. You'll probably be able to find one even if your work *isn't* salable, as long as it shows promise. Sports agents represent minor leaguers who are basically playing for meal-money, in hopes that their young clients will make it to the bigs; for the same reason, literary agents are often willing to handle writers with only a few publishing credits. You'll very likely find someone to handle your work even if your publishing credits are limited strictly to the "little magazines," which pay only in copies—these magazines are often regarded by agents and book publishers as proving-grounds for new talent.

You must begin as your own advocate, which means reading the magazines publishing the kind of stuff you write. You should also pick up the writers' journals and buy a copy of *Writer's Market,* the most valuable of tools for the writer new to the marketplace. If you're really poor, ask someone to give it to you for Christmas. Both the mags and *WM* (it's a whopper of a volume, but reasonably priced) list book and magazine publishers, and include thumbnail descriptions of the sort of stories each market uses. You'll also find the most salable lengths and the names of editorial staffs.

As a beginning writer, you'll be most interested in the "little magazines," if you're writing short stories. If you're writing or have written a novel, you'll want to note the lists of literary agents in the writing magazines and in *Writer's Market.* You may also want to add a copy of the *LMP (Literary Market Place)* to your reference shelf. You need to be canny, careful, and assiduous in your search for an agent or a publisher, but—this bears repeating—the most important thing you can do for yourself is *read the market.* Looking at the thumbnail rundowns in *Writer's Digest* may help (". . . publishes mostly mainstream fiction, 2,000–4,000 words, steer clear of stereotyped characters and hackneyed romance situations"), but a thumbnail is, leave us face it, just a thumbnail. Submitting stories without first reading the market is like playing darts in a dark room—you might hit the target every now and then, but you don't deserve to.

Here is the story of an aspiring writer I'll call Frank. Frank is actually a composite of three young writers I know, two men and one woman. All have enjoyed some success in their twenties as writers; none, as of this writing, are driving Rolls-Royces. All three will probably break through, which is to say that by the age of forty, I believe, all three will be publishing regularly (and probably one will have a drinking problem).

The three faces of Frank all have different interests and write in different styles and voices, but their approaches to the hurdles between them and becoming published writers are similar enough for me to feel comfortable about putting them together. I also feel that other beginning writers—you, for instance, dear Reader—could do worse than follow in Frank's footsteps.

Frank was an English major (you don't *have* to be an English major to become a writer, but it sure doesn't hurt) who began submitting his stories to magazines as a college student. He took several creative-writing courses, and many of the magazines to which he made submissions were recommended to him by his creative-writing teachers. Recommended or not, Frank carefully read the stories in each magazine, and submitted his own stories according to his sense of where each would fit best. "For three years I read every story *Story* magazine published," he says, then laughs. "I may be the only person in America who can make that statement."

Careful reading or not, Frank didn't publish any stories in those markets while attending college, although he *did* publish half a dozen or so in the campus literary magazine (we'll call it *The Quarterly Pretension*). He received personal notes of rejection from readers at several of the magazines to which he submitted, including *Story* (the female version of Frank said, "They *owed* me a note!") and *The Georgia Review.* During this time Frank subscribed to *Writer's Digest* and *The Writer,* reading them carefully and paying attention to articles about agents and the accompanying agency lists. He circled the names of several who mentioned literary interests he felt he shared. Frank took particular note of agents who talked about liking stories of "high conflict," an arty way of saying suspense stories. Frank is attracted to suspense stories, also to stories of crime and the supernatural.

A year out of college, Frank gets his first acceptance letter—oh happy day. It is from a little magazine available at a few newsstands but mostly by subscription; let's call it *Kingsnake.* The editor offers to buy Frank's twelve-hundred-word vignette, "The Lady in the Trunk," for twenty-five dollars plus a dozen cc's—contributor's copies. Frank is, of course, delirious; way past Cloud Nine. All the relatives get a call, even the ones he doesn't like (*especially* the ones he doesn't like, is my guess). Twenty-five bucks won't pay the rent, won't even buy a week's worth of groceries for Frank and his wife, but it's a validation of his ambition, and that—any newly published writer would agree, I think—is priceless: *Someone wants something I did! Yippee!* Nor is that the only benefit. It is a *credit,* a small snowball which Frank will now begin rolling downhill, hoping to turn it into a snow-boulder by the time it gets to the bottom.

Six months later, Frank sells another story to a magazine called *Lodgepine Review* (like *Kingsnake, Lodgepine* is a composite). Only "sell" is probably too strong a word; proposed payment for Frank's "Two Kinds of

Men" is twenty-five contributor's copies. Still, it's another credit. Frank signs the acceptance form (loving that line beneath the blank for his signature almost to death—PROPRIETOR OF THE WORK, by God!) and sends it back the following day.

Tragedy strikes a month later. It comes in the form of a form letter, the salutation of which reads *Dear Lodgepine Review Contributor*. Frank reads it with a sinking heart. A grant was not renewed, and *Lodgepine Review* has gone to that great writer's workshop in the sky. The forthcoming summer issue will be the last. Frank's story, unfortunately, was slated for fall. The letter closes by wishing Frank good luck in placing his story elsewhere. In the lower lefthand corner, someone has scribbled four words: *AWFULLY SORRY about this*.

Frank is AWFULLY SORRY, too (after getting loaded on cheap wine and waking up with cheap wine hangovers, he and his wife are SORRIER STILL), but his disappointment doesn't prevent him from getting his almost-published short story right back into circulation. At this point he has half a dozen of them making the rounds. He keeps a careful record of where they have been and what sort of response they got during their visit at each stop. He also keeps track of magazines where he has established some sort of personal contact, even if that contact consists of nothing but two scribbled lines and a coffee-stain.

A month after the bad news about *Lodgepine Review*, Frank gets some very good news; it arrives in a letter from a man he's never heard of. This fellow is the editor of a brand-new little magazine called *Jackdaw*. He is now soliciting stories for the first issue, and an old school friend of his—editor of the recently defunct *Lodgepine Review*, as a matter of fact—mentioned Frank's cancelled story. If Frank hasn't placed it, the *Jackdaw* editor would certainly like a look. No promises, but . . .

Frank doesn't *need* promises; like most beginning writers, all he needs is a little encouragement and an unlimited supply of take-out pizza. He mails the story off with a letter of thanks (and a letter of thanks to the ex–*Lodgepine* editor, of course). Six months later "Two Kinds of Men" appears in the premiere issue of *Jackdaw*. The Old Boy Network, which plays as large a part in publishing as it does in many other white-collar/pink-collar businesses, has triumphed again. Frank's pay for this story is fifteen dollars, ten contributor's copies, and another all-important credit.

In the next year, Frank lands a job teaching high school English. Although he finds it extremely difficult to teach literature and correct student themes in the daytime and then work on his own stuff at night, he continues to do so, writing new short stories and getting them into circulation, collecting rejection slips and occasionally "retiring" stories he's sent to all the places he can think of. "They'll look good in my collection when it finally comes out," he tells his wife. Our hero has also picked up a second job, writing book and film reviews for a newspaper in a nearby city. He's a busy, busy boy. Nevertheless, in the back of his mind, he has begun to think about writing a novel.

When asked what is the most important thing for a young writer who's just beginning to submit his or her fiction to remember, Frank pauses only a few seconds before replying, "Good presentation."

Say what?

He nods. "Good presentation, absolutely. When you send your story out, there ought to be a very brief cover-letter on top of the script, telling the editor where you've published other stories and just a line or two on what this one's about. And you should close by thanking him for the reading. That's especially important.

"You should submit on a good grade of white bond paper—none of that slippery erasable stuff. Your copy should be double-spaced, and on the first page you should put your address in the upper lefthand corner—it doesn't hurt to include your telephone number, too. In the righthand corner, put an approximate word-count." Frank pauses, laughs, and says: "Don't cheat, either. Most magazine editors can tell how long a story is just by looking at the print and riffling the pages."

I'm still a bit surprised at Frank's answer; I expected something that was a little less nuts-and-bolts.

"Nah," he says. "You get practical in a hurry once you're out of school and trying to find a place for yourself in the business. The very first thing I learned was that you don't get any kind of hearing at all unless you go in looking like a professional." Something in his tone makes me think he believes I've forgotten a lot about how tough things are at the entry-level, and perhaps he's right. It's been almost forty years since I had a stack of rejection-slips pinned to a spike in my bedroom, after all. "You can't make them like your story," Frank finishes, "but you can at least make it easy for them to try to like it."

As I write this, Frank's own story is still a work in

progress, but his future looks bright. He has published a total of six shorts now, and won a fairly prestigious prize for one of them—we'll call it the Minnesota Young Writers' Award, although no part of my Frank composite actually lives in Minnesota. The cash prize was five hundred dollars, by far his biggest paycheck for a story. He has begun work on his novel, and when it's finished—in the early spring of 2001, he estimates—a reputable young agent named Richard Chams (also a pseudonym) has agreed to handle it for him.

Frank got serious about finding an agent at about the same time he got serious about his novel. "I didn't want to put in all that work and then be faced with not knowing how to sell the damn thing when I was done," he told me.

Based on his explorations of the *LMP* and the lists of agents in *Writer's Market,* Frank wrote an even dozen letters, each exactly the same except for the salutation. Here is the template:

                                        June 19, 1999

Dear   :

    I am a young writer, twenty-eight years old, in search of an agent. I got your name in a *Writer's Digest* article titled "Agents of the New Wave," and thought we might fit each other. I have published six stories since getting serious about my craft. They are:

    "The Lady in the Trunk," *Kingsnake,* Winter 1996 ($25 plus copies)

    "Two Kinds of Men," *Jackdaw,* Summer 1997 ($15 plus copies)

"Christmas Smoke," *Mystery Quarterly*, Fall 1997 ($35)

"Big Thumps, Charlie Takes His Lumps," *Cemetery Dance*, January–February 1998 ($50 plus copies)

"Sixty Sneakers," *Puckerbrush Review*, April–May 1998 (copies)

"A Long Walk in These 'Yere Woods," *Minnesota Review*, Winter 1998–1999 ($70 plus copies)

I would be happy to send any of these stories (or any of the half dozen or so I'm currently flogging around) for you to look at, if you'd like. I'm particularly proud of "A Long Walk in These 'Yere Woods," which won the Minnesota Young Writers' Award. The plaque looks good on our living room wall, and the prize money— $500—looked excellent for the week or so it was actually in our bank account (I have been married for four years; my wife, Marjorie, and I teach school).

The reason I'm seeking representation now is that I'm at work on a novel. It's a suspense story about a man who gets arrested for a series of murders which occurred in his little town twenty years before. The first eighty pages or so are in pretty good shape, and I'd also be delighted to show you these.

Please be in touch and tell me if you'd like to

see some of my material. In the meantime, thank you for taking the time to read my letter.

Sincerely yours,

Frank included his telephone number as well as his address, and one of his target agents (not Richard Chams) actually called to chat. Three wrote back asking to look at the prize-winning story about the hunter lost in the woods. Half a dozen asked to see the first eighty pages of his novel. The response was big, in other words—only one agent to whom he wrote expressed no interest in Frank's work, citing a full roster of clients. Yet outside of his slight acquaintances in the world of the "little magazines," Frank knows absolutely nobody in the publishing business—has not a single personal contact.

"It was amazing," he says, "absolutely amazing. I expected to take whoever wanted to take *me*—if anybody did—and count myself lucky. Instead, I got to pick and choose." He puts down his bumper crop of possible agents to several things. First, the letter he sent around was literate and well-spoken ("It took four drafts and two arguments with my wife to get that casual tone just right," Frank says). Second, he could supply an actual list of published short stories, and a fairly substantial one. No big money, but the magazines were reputable. Third, there was the prize-winner. Frank thinks that may have been key. I don't know if it was or not, but it certainly didn't hurt.

Frank was also intelligent enough to ask Richard Chams and all the other agents he queried for a list of *their* bona fides—not a list of clients (I don't know if an agent who gave out the names of his clients would even be ethical), but a list of the publishers to whom the agent had sold books and the magazines to which he had sold short stories. It's easy to con a writer who's desperate for representation. Beginning writers need to remember that anyone with a few hundred dollars to invest can place an ad in *Writer's Digest,* calling himself or herself a literary agent—it isn't as if you have to pass a bar exam, or anything.

You should be especially wary of agents who promise to read your work for a fee. A few such agents are reputable (the Scott Meredith Agency used to read for fees; I don't know if they still do or not), but all too many are unscrupulous fucks. I'd suggest that if you're that anxious to get published, you skip agent-hunting or query-letters to publishers and go directly to a vanity press. There you will at least get a semblance of your money's worth.

– 16 –

We're nearly finished. I doubt if I've covered everything you need to know to become a better writer, and I'm sure I haven't answered all your questions, but I *have* talked about those aspects of the writing life which I can discuss with at least some confidence. I must tell you, though, that confidence during the actual writing of this book was a commodity in remarkably short supply. What I was long on was physical pain and self-doubt.

When I proposed the idea of a book on writing to my

publisher at Scribner, I felt that I knew a great deal about the subject; my head all but burst with the different things I wanted to say. And perhaps I *do* know a lot, but some of it turned out to be dull and most of the rest, I've discovered, has more to do with instinct than with anything resembling "higher thought." I found the act of articulating those instinctive truths painfully difficult. Also, something happened halfway through the writing of *On Writing*—a life-changer, as they say. I'll tell you about it presently. For now, just please know that I did the best I could.

One more matter needs to be discussed, a matter that bears directly on that life-changer and one that I've touched on already, but indirectly. Now I'd like to face it head-on. It's a question that people ask in different ways—sometimes it comes out polite and sometimes it comes out rough, but it always amounts to the same: *Do you do it for the money, honey?*

The answer is no. Don't now and never did. Yes, I've made a great deal of dough from my fiction, but I never set a single word down on paper with the thought of being paid for it. I have done some work as favors for friends—logrolling is the slang term for it— but at the very worst, you'd have to call that a crude kind of barter. I have written because it fulfilled me. Maybe it paid off the mortgage on the house and got the kids through college, but those things were on the side—I did it for the buzz. I did it for the pure joy of the thing. And if you can do it for joy, you can do it forever.

There have been times when for me the act of writing has been a little act of faith, a spit in the eye of despair. The second half of this book was written in that spirit. I gutted it out, as we used to say when we were kids. Writing is not life, but I think that sometimes it can be a way back to life. That was something I found out in the summer of 1999, when a man driving a blue van almost killed me.

ON LIVING:
A POSTSCRIPT

When we're at our summer house in western Maine—a house very much like the one Mike Noonan comes back to in *Bag of Bones*—I walk four miles every day, unless it's pouring down rain. Three miles of this walk are on dirt roads which wind through the woods; a mile of it is on Route 5, a two-lane blacktop highway which runs between Bethel and Fryeburg.

The third week in June of 1999 was an extraordinarily happy one for my wife and me; our kids, now grown and scattered across the country, were all home. It was the first time in nearly six months that we'd all been under the same roof. As an extra bonus, our first grandchild was in the house, three months old and happily jerking at a helium balloon tied to his foot.

On the nineteenth of June, I drove our younger son to the Portland Jetport, where he caught a flight back to New York City. I drove home, had a brief nap, and then set out on my usual walk. We were planning to go *en famille* to see *The General's Daughter* in nearby North Conway, New Hampshire, that evening, and I thought I just had time to get my walk in before packing everybody up for the trip.

I set out on that walk around four o'clock in the afternoon, as well as I can remember. Just before reaching the main road (in western Maine, any road with a white line running down the middle of it is a main road), I stepped into the woods and urinated. It was two months before I was able to take another leak standing up.

When I reached the highway I turned north, walking on the gravel shoulder, against traffic. One car passed me, also headed north. About three-quarters of a mile farther along, the woman driving the car observed a light blue Dodge van heading south. The van was looping from one side of the road to the other, barely under the driver's control. The woman in the car turned to her passenger when they were safely past the wandering van and said, "That was Stephen King walking back there. I sure hope that guy in the van doesn't hit him."

Most of the sightlines along the mile of Route 5 which I walk are good, but there is one stretch, a short steep hill, where a pedestrian walking north can see very little of what might be coming his way. I was three-quarters of the way up this hill when Bryan Smith, the owner and operator of the Dodge van, came over the crest. He wasn't on the road; he was on the shoulder. *My* shoulder. I had perhaps three-quarters of a second to register this. It was just time enough to think, *My God, I'm going to be hit by a schoolbus.* I started to turn to my left. There is a break in my memory here. On the other side of it I'm on the ground, looking at the back of the van, which is now pulled off the road and tilted to one side. This recollection is very clear and sharp, more like a snapshot than a memory. There is dust around the van's taillights. The license plate and the back windows are dirty. I register these things with no thought that I have been in an accident, or of anything else. It's a snapshot, that's all. I'm not thinking; my head has been swopped clean.

There's another little break in my memory here, and then I am very carefully wiping palmfuls of blood out of my eyes with my left hand. When my eyes are reasonably clear, I look around and see a man sitting on a nearby rock. He has a cane drawn across his lap. This is Bryan Smith, forty-two years of age, the man who hit me with his van. Smith has got quite the driving record; he has racked up nearly a dozen vehicle-related offenses.

Smith wasn't looking at the road on the afternoon our lives came together because his rottweiler had jumped from the very rear of his van into the back-seat area, where there was an Igloo cooler with some meat stored inside. The rottweiler's name is Bullet (Smith has another rottweiler at home; that one is named Pistol). Bullet started to nose at the lid of the cooler. Smith turned around and tried to push Bullet away. He was still looking at Bullet and pushing his head away from the cooler when he came over the top of the knoll; still looking and pushing when he struck me. Smith told friends later that he thought he'd hit "a small deer" until he noticed my bloody spectacles lying on the front seat of his van. They were knocked from my face when I tried to get out of Smith's way. The frames were bent and twisted, but the lenses were unbroken. They are the lenses I'm wearing now, as I write this.

– 2 –

Smith sees I'm awake and tells me help is on the way. He speaks calmly, even cheerily. His look, as he sits on his rock with his cane drawn across his lap, is one of pleasant commiseration: *Ain't the two of us just had the shittiest luck?* it says. He and Bullet left the campground where they were staying, he later tells an investigator, because he wanted "some of those Marzes-bars they have up to the store." When I hear this little detail some weeks later, it occurs to me that I have nearly been killed by a character right out of one of my own novels. It's almost funny.

Help is on the way, I think, and that's probably good because I've been in a hell of an accident. I'm lying in the ditch and there's blood all over my face and my right leg hurts. I look down and see something I don't like: my lap now appears to be on sideways, as if my whole lower body had been wrenched half a turn to the right. I look back up at the man with the cane and say, "Please tell me it's just dislocated."

"Nah," he says. Like his face, his voice is cheery, only mildly interested. He could be watching all this on TV while he noshes on one of those Marzes-bars. "It's broken in five I'd say maybe six places."

"I'm sorry," I tell him—God knows why—and then I'm gone again for a little while. It isn't like blacking out; it's more as if the film of memory has been spliced here and there.

When I come back this time, an orange-and-white van is idling at the side of the road with its flashers going. An emergency medical technician—Paul

Fillebrown is his name—is kneeling beside me. He's doing something. Cutting off my jeans, I think, although that might have come later.

I ask him if I can have a cigarette. He laughs and says not hardly. I ask him if I'm going to die. He tells me no, I'm not going to die, but I need to go to the hospital, and fast. Which one would I prefer, the one in Norway–South Paris or the one in Bridgton? I tell him I want to go to Northern Cumberland Hospital in Bridgton, because my youngest child—the one I just took to the airport—was born there twenty-two years before. I ask Fillebrown again if I'm going to die, and he tells me again that I'm not. Then he asks me if I can wiggle the toes on my right foot. I wiggle them, thinking of an old rhyme my mother used to recite sometimes: *This little piggy went to market, this little piggy stayed home.* I should have stayed home, I think; going for a walk today was a really bad idea. Then I remember that sometimes when people are paralyzed, they think they're moving but really aren't.

"My toes, did they move?" I ask Paul Fillebrown. He says they did, a good healthy wiggle. "Do you swear to God?" I ask him, and I think he does. I'm starting to pass out again. Fillebrown asks me, very slowly and loudly, bending down into my face, if my wife is at the big house on the lake. I can't remember. I can't remember where any of my family is, but I'm able to give him the telephone numbers of both our big house and the cottage on the far side of the lake where my daughter sometimes stays. Hell, I could give him my Social Security number, if he asked. I've got all my numbers. It's just everything else that's gone.

Other people are arriving now. Somewhere a radio is

crackling out police calls. I'm put on a stretcher. It hurts, and I scream. I'm lifted into the back of the EMT truck, and the police calls are closer. The doors shut and someone up front says, "You want to really hammer it." Then we're rolling.

Paul Fillebrown sits down beside me. He has a pair of clippers and tells me he's going to have to cut the ring off the third finger of my right hand—it's a wedding ring Tabby gave me in 1983, twelve years after we were actually married. I try to tell Fillebrown that I wear it on my right hand because the real wedding ring is still on the third finger of my left—the original two-ring set cost me $15.95 at Day's Jewelers in Bangor. That first ring only cost eight bucks, in other words, but it seems to have worked.

Some garbled version of this comes out, probably nothing Paul Fillebrown can actually understand, but he keeps nodding and smiling as he cuts that second, more expensive, wedding ring off my swollen right hand. Two months or so later, I call Fillebrown to thank him; by then I understand that he probably saved my life by administering the correct on-scene medical aid and then getting me to the hospital at a speed of roughly one hundred and ten miles an hour, over patched and bumpy back roads.

Fillebrown assures me that I'm more than welcome, then suggests that perhaps someone was watching out for me. "I've been doing this for twenty years," he tells me over the phone, "and when I saw the way you were lying in the ditch, plus the extent of the impact injuries, I didn't think you'd make it to the hospital. You're a lucky camper to still be with the program."

The extent of the impact injuries is such that the doctors at Northern Cumberland Hospital decide they cannot treat me there; someone summons a LifeFlight helicopter to take me to Central Maine Medical Center in Lewiston. At this point my wife, older son, and daughter arrive. The kids are allowed a brief visit; my wife is allowed to stay longer. The doctors have assured her that I'm banged up, but I'll make it. The lower half of my body has been covered. She isn't allowed to look at the interesting way my lap has shifted around to the right, but she is allowed to wash the blood off my face and pick some of the glass out of my hair.

There's a long gash in my scalp, the result of my collision with Bryan Smith's windshield. This impact came at a point less than two inches from the steel driver's-side support post. Had I struck that, I likely would have been killed or rendered permanently comatose, a vegetable with legs. Had I struck the rocks jutting out of the ground beyond the shoulder of Route 5, I likely also would have been killed or permanently paralyzed. I didn't hit them; I was thrown over the van and fourteen feet in the air, but landed just shy of the rocks.

"You must have pivoted to the left just a little at the last second," Dr. David Brown tells me later. "If you hadn't, we wouldn't be having this conversation."

The LifeFlight helicopter lands in the parking lot of Northern Cumberland Hospital, and I am wheeled out to it. The sky is very bright, very blue. The clatter of the helicopter's rotors is very loud. Someone shouts into my ear, "Ever been in a helicopter before, Stephen?" The speaker sounds jolly, all excited for me. I try to answer yes, I've been in a helicopter before—twice, in fact—but I can't. All at once it's very tough to breathe.

They load me into the helicopter. I can see one brilliant wedge of blue sky as we lift off; not a cloud in it. Beautiful. There are more radio voices. This is my afternoon for hearing voices, it seems. Meanwhile, it's getting even harder to breathe. I gesture at someone, or try to, and a face bends upside down into my field of vision.

"Feel like I'm drowning," I whisper.

Somebody checks something, and someone else says, "His lung has collapsed."

There's a rattle of paper as something is unwrapped, and then the someone else speaks into my ear, loudly so as to be heard over the rotors. "We're going to put a chest tube in you, Stephen. You'll feel some pain, a little pinch. Hold on."

It's been my experience (learned when I was just a wee lad with infected ears) that if a medical person tells you you're going to feel a little pinch, they're going to hurt you really bad. This time it isn't as bad as I expected, perhaps because I'm full of painkiller, perhaps because I'm on the verge of passing out again. It's like being thumped very high up on the right side of the chest by someone holding a short sharp object. Then there's an alarming whistle in my chest, as if I've sprung a leak. In fact, I suppose I have. A moment later the soft in-out of normal respiration, which I've listened to my whole life (mostly without being aware of it, thank God), has been replaced by an unpleasant *shloop-shloop-shloop* sound. The air I'm taking in is very cold, but it's air, at least, *air,* and I keep breathing it. I don't want to die. I love my wife, my kids, my afternoon walks by the lake. I also love to write; I have a book on writing that's sitting back home on my desk, half-finished. I don't want to die, and as I lie in the helicopter looking out at the bright blue summer sky, I realize that I am actually lying in death's doorway. Someone is going to pull me one way or the other pretty soon; it's mostly out of my hands. All I can do is lie there, look at the sky, and listen to my thin, leaky breathing: *shloop-shloop-shloop*.

Ten minutes later we set down on the concrete landing pad at CMMC. To me, it seems to be at the bottom of a concrete well. The blue sky is blotted out and the *whap-whap-whap* of the helicopter rotors becomes magnified and echoey, like the clapping of giant hands.

Still breathing in great leaky gulps, I am lifted out of the helicopter. Someone bumps the stretcher and I scream. "Sorry, sorry, you're okay, Stephen," someone says—when you're badly hurt, everyone calls you by your first name, everyone is your pal.

"Tell Tabby I love her very much," I say as I am first lifted and then wheeled, very fast, down some sort of descending concrete walkway. All at once I feel like crying.

"You can tell her that yourself," the someone says. We go through a door; there is air-conditioning and lights flowing past overhead. Speakers issue pages. It occurs to me, in a muddled sort of way, that an hour before I was taking a walk and planning to pick some berries in a field that overlooks Lake Kezar. I wouldn't pick for long, though; I'd have to be home by five-thirty because we were all going to the movies. *The General's Daughter,* starring John Travolta. Travolta was in the movie made out of *Carrie,* my first novel.

He played the bad guy. That was a long time ago.

"When?" I ask. "When can I tell her?"

"Soon," the voice says, and then I pass out again. This time it's no splice but a great big whack taken out of the memory-film; there are a few flashes, confused glimpses of faces and operating rooms and looming X-ray machinery; there are delusions and hallucinations fed by the morphine and Dilaudid being dripped into me; there are echoing voices and hands that reach down to paint my dry lips with swabs that taste of peppermint. Mostly, though, there is darkness.

– 3 –

Bryan Smith's estimate of my injuries turned out to be conservative. My lower leg was broken in at least nine places—the orthopedic surgeon who put me together again, the formidable David Brown, said that the region below my right knee had been reduced to "so many marbles in a sock." The extent of those lower-leg injuries necessitated two deep incisions—they're called medial and lateral fasciotomies—to release the pressure caused by the exploded tibia and also to allow blood to flow back into the lower leg. Without the fasciotomies (or if the fasciotomies had been delayed), it probably would have been necessary to amputate the leg. My right knee itself was split almost directly down the middle; the technical term for the injury is "comminuted intra-articular tibial fracture." I also suffered an acetabular fracture of the right hip—a serious derailment, in other words—and an open femoral intertrochanteric fracture in the same area. My spine was chipped in eight places. Four ribs were broken. My right collarbone held, but the flesh above it was stripped raw. The laceration in my scalp took twenty or thirty stitches.

Yeah, on the whole I'd say Bryan Smith was a tad conservative.

– 4 –

Mr. Smith's driving behavior in this case was eventually examined by a grand jury, who indicted him on two counts: driving to endanger (pretty serious) and aggravated assault (very serious, the kind of thing that means jail time). After due consideration, the District Attorney responsible for prosecuting such cases in my little corner of the world allowed Smith to plead out to the lesser charge of driving to endanger. He received six months of county jail time (sentence suspended) and a year's suspension of his privilege to drive. He was also put on probation for a year with restrictions on other motor vehicles, such as snowmobiles and ATVs. It is conceivable that Bryan Smith could be legally back on the road in the fall or winter of 2001.*

---

*Shortly before the hardcover edition of this book was published, Bryan Smith's driving skills became a moot point. In September of 2000, he was discovered dead in his small trailer home in western Maine. Smith was 43. As of this writing, the cause of his death remains undetermined.

– 5 –

David Brown put my leg back together in five marathon surgical procedures that left me thin, weak, and nearly at the end of my endurance. They also left me with at least a fighting chance to walk again. A large steel and carbon-fiber apparatus called an external fixator was clamped to my leg. Eight large steel pegs called Schanz pins run through the fixator and into the bones above and below my knee. Five smaller steel rods radiate out from the knee. These look sort of like a child's drawing of sunrays. The knee itself was locked in place. Three times a day, nurses would unwrap the smaller pins and the much larger Schanz pins and swab the holes out with hydrogen peroxide. I've never had my leg dipped in kerosene and then lit on fire, but if that ever happens, I'm sure it will feel quite a bit like daily pin-care.

I entered the hospital on June nineteenth. Around the twenty-fifth I got up for the first time, staggering three steps to a commode, where I sat with my hospital johnny in my lap and my head down, trying not to weep and failing. You try to tell yourself that you've been lucky, most incredibly lucky, and usually that works because it's true. Sometimes it doesn't work, that's all. Then you cry.

A day or two after those initial steps, I started physical therapy. During my first session I managed ten steps in a downstairs corridor, lurching along with the help of a walker. One other patient was learning to walk again at the same time, a wispy eighty-year-old woman named Alice who was recovering from a stroke. We cheered each other on when we had enough breath to do so. On our third day in the downstairs hall, I told Alice that her slip was showing.

"Your *ass* is showing, sonnyboy," she wheezed, and kept going.

By the Fourth of July I was able to sit up in a wheelchair long enough to go out to the loading dock behind the hospital and watch some of the fireworks. It was a fiercely hot night, the streets filled with people eating snacks, drinking beer and soda, watching the sky. Tabby stood next to me, holding my hand, as the sky lit up red and green, blue and yellow. She was staying in a condo apartment across the street from the hospital, and each morning she brought me poached eggs and tea. I could use the nourishment, it seemed. In 1997, after returning from a motorcycle trip across the Australian desert, I weighed two hundred and sixteen pounds. On the day I was released from Central Maine Medical Center, I weighed a hundred and sixty-five.

I came home to Bangor on July ninth, after a hospital stay of three weeks. I began a daily rehab program which includes stretching, bending, and crutch-walking. I tried to keep my courage and my spirits up. On August fourth I went back to CMMC for another operation. Inserting an IV into my arm, the anesthesiologist said, "Okay, Stephen—you're going to feel a little like you just had a couple of cocktails." I opened my mouth to tell him that would be interesting, since I hadn't had a cocktail in eleven years, but before I could get anything out, I was gone again. When I woke up this time, the Schanz pins in my upper thigh were gone. I could bend my knee again. Dr. Brown pronounced my recovery "on course" and sent me home for more rehab and physical therapy (those of us undergoing P.T. know that the letters actually stand for Pain and Torture). And in the midst of all this, something else happened. On July twenty-fourth, five weeks after Bryan Smith hit me with his Dodge van, I began to write again.

– 6 –

I actually began *On Writing* in November or December of 1997, and although it usually takes me only three months to finish the first draft of a book, this one was still only half-completed eighteen months later. That was because I'd put it aside in February or March of 1998, not sure how to continue, or if I should continue at all. Writing fiction was almost as much fun as it had ever been, but every word of the nonfiction book was a kind of torture. It was the first book I had put aside uncompleted since *The Stand,* and *On Writing* spent a lot longer in the desk drawer.

In June of 1999, I decided to spend the summer finishing the damn writing book—let Susan Moldow and Nan Graham at Scribner decide if it was good or bad, I thought. I read the manuscript over, prepared for the worst, and discovered I actually sort of liked what I had. The road to finishing it seemed clear-cut, too. I had finished the memoir ("C.V."), which attempted to show some of the incidents and life-situations which made me into the sort of writer I turned out to be, and I had covered the mechanics—those that seemed most important to me, at least. What remained to be done was the key section, "On Writing," where I'd try to answer some of the questions I'd been asked in seminars and at speaking engagements, plus all those I *wish* I'd been asked . . . those questions about the language.

On the night of June seventeenth, blissfully unaware that I was now less than forty-eight hours from my little date with Bryan Smith (not to mention Bullet the rottweiler), I sat down at our dining room table and listed all the questions I wanted to answer, all the points I wanted to address. On the eighteenth, I wrote the first four pages of the "On Writing" section. That was where the work still stood in late July, when I decided I'd better get back to work . . . or at least try.

I didn't *want* to go back to work. I was in a lot of pain, unable to bend my right knee, and restricted to a walker. I couldn't imagine sitting behind a desk for long, even in my wheelchair. Because of my cataclysmically smashed hip, sitting was torture after forty minutes or so, impossible after an hour and a quarter. Added to this was the book itself, which seemed more daunting than ever—how was I supposed to write about dialogue, character, and getting an agent when the most pressing thing in my world was how long until the next dose of Percocet?

Yet at the same time I felt I'd reached one of those crossroads moments when you're all out of choices. And I had been in terrible situations before which the writing had helped me get over—had helped me forget myself for at least a little while. Perhaps it would help me again. It seemed ridiculous to think it might be so, given the level of my pain and physical incapacitation, but there was that voice in the back of my mind, both patient and implacable, telling me that, in the words of the Chambers Brothers, Time Has Come Today. It's possible for me to disobey that voice, but very difficult to disbelieve it.

In the end it was Tabby who cast the deciding vote, as she so often has at crucial moments in my life. I'd like to think I've done the same for her from time to time, because it seems to me that one of the things marriage is about is casting the tiebreaking vote when you just can't decide what you should do next.

My wife is the person in my life who's most likely to say I'm working too hard, it's time to slow down, stay away from that damn PowerBook for a little while, Steve, give it a rest. When I told her on that July morning that I thought I'd better go back to work, I expected a lecture. Instead, she asked me where I wanted to set up. I told her I didn't know, hadn't even thought about it.

She thought about it, then said: "I can rig a table for you in the back hall, outside the pantry. There are plenty of plug-ins—you can have your Mac, the little printer, and a fan." The fan was certainly a must—it had been a terrifically hot summer, and on the day I went back to work, the temperature outside was ninety-five. It wasn't much cooler in the back hall.

Tabby spent a couple of hours putting things together, and that afternoon at four o'clock she rolled me out through the kitchen and down the newly installed wheelchair ramp into the back hall. She had made me a wonderful little nest there: laptop and printer connected side by side, table lamp, manuscript (with my notes from the month before placed neatly on top), pens, reference materials. Standing on the corner of the desk was a framed picture of our younger son, which she had taken earlier that summer.

"Is it all right?" she asked.

"It's gorgeous," I said, and hugged her. It *was* gorgeous. So is she.

The former Tabitha Spruce of Oldtown, Maine, knows when I'm working too hard, but she also knows that sometimes it's the work that bails me out. She got me positioned at the table, kissed me on the temple, and then left me there to find out if I had anything left to say. It turned out I did, a little, but without her intuitive understanding that yes, it *was* time, I'm not sure either of us would ever have found that out for sure.

That first writing session lasted an hour and forty minutes, by far the longest period I'd spent sitting upright since being struck by Smith's van. When it was over, I was dripping with sweat and almost too exhausted to sit up straight in my wheelchair. The pain in my hip was just short of apocalyptic. And the first five hundred words were uniquely terrifying—it was as if I'd never written anything before them in my life. All my old tricks seemed to have deserted me. I stepped from one word to the next like a very old man finding his way across a stream on a zigzag line of wet stones. There was no inspiration that first afternoon, only a kind of stubborn determination and the hope that things would get better if I kept at it.

Tabby brought me a Pepsi—cold and sweet and good—and as I drank it I looked around and had to laugh despite the pain. I'd written *Carrie* and *'Salem's Lot* in the laundry room of a rented trailer. The back hall of our house in Bangor resembled it enough to make me feel almost as if I'd come full circle.

There was no miraculous breakthrough that afternoon, unless it was the ordinary miracle that comes with any attempt to create something. All I know is that the words started coming a little faster after awhile, then a little faster still. My hip still hurt, my back still hurt, my leg, too, but those hurts began to seem a little farther away. I started to get on top of them. There was no sense of exhilaration, no buzz—not that day—but there was a sense of accomplishment that was almost as good. I'd gotten going, there was that much. The scariest moment is always just before you start.

After that, things can only get better.

– 7 –

For me, things have continued to get better. I've had two more operations on my leg since that first sweltering afternoon in the back hall, I've had a fairly serious bout of infection, and I continue to take roughly a hundred pills a day, but the external fixator is now gone and I continue to write. On some days that writing is a pretty grim slog. On others—more and more of them as my leg begins to heal and my mind reaccustoms itself to its old routine—I feel that buzz of happiness, that sense of having found the right words and put them in a line. It's like lifting off in an airplane: you're on the ground, on the ground, on the ground . . . and then you're up, riding on a magical cushion of air and prince of all you survey. That makes me happy, because it's what I was made to do. I still don't have much strength—I can do a little less than half of what I used to be able to do in a day—but I've had enough to get me to the end of this book, and for that I'm grateful. Writing did not save my life—Dr. David Brown's skill and my wife's loving care did that—but it has continued to do what it always has done: it makes my life a brighter and more pleasant place.

Writing isn't about making money, getting famous, getting dates, getting laid, or making friends. In the end, it's about enriching the lives of those who will read your work, and enriching your own life, as well. It's about getting up, getting well, and getting over. Getting happy, okay? Getting happy. Some of this book—perhaps too much—has been about how I learned to do it. Much of it has been about how you can do it better. The rest of it—and perhaps the best of it—is a permission slip: you can, you should, and if you're brave enough to start, *you will*. Writing is magic, as much the water of life as any other creative art. The water is free. So drink.

Drink and be filled up.

And Furthermore, Part I: Door Shut, Door Open

Earlier in this book, when writing about my brief career as a sports reporter for the Lisbon *Weekly Enterprise* (I was, in fact, the entire sports department; a small-town Howard Cosell), I offered an example of how the editing process works. That example was necessarily brief, and dealt with nonfiction. The passage that follows is fiction. It is completely raw, the sort of thing I feel free to do with the door shut—it's the story undressed, standing up in nothing but its socks and undershorts. I suggest that you look at it closely before going on to the edited version.

The Hotel Story

Mike Enslin was still in the revolving door when he saw Ostermeyer, the manager of the Hotel Dolphin, sitting in one of the overstuffed lobby chairs. Mike's heart sank a little. *Maybe should have brought the damned lawyer along again, after all,* he thought. Well, too late now. And even if Ostermeyer had decided to throw up another roadblock or two between Mike and room 1408, that wasn't all bad; it would simply add to the story when he finally told it.

Ostermeyer saw him, got up, and was crossing the room with one pudgy hand held out as Mike left the revolving door. The Dolphin was on Sixty-first Street, around the corner from Fifth Avenue; small but smart. A man and woman dressed in evening clothes passed Mike as he reached out and took Ostermeyer's hand, switching his small overnight case to his left hand in order to do it. The woman was blonde, dressed in black, of course, and the light, flowery smell of her perfume seemed to summarize New York. On the mezzanine level, someone was playing "Night and Day" in the bar, as if to underline the summary.

"Mr. Enslin. Good evening."

"Mr. Ostermeyer. Is there a problem?"

Ostermeyer looked pained. For a moment he glanced around the small, smart lobby, as if for help. At the concierge's stand, a man was discussing theater tickets with his wife while the concierge himself watched them with a small, patient smile. At the front desk, a man with the rumpled look one only got after long hours in Business Class was discussing his reservation with a woman in a smart black suit that could itself have doubled for evening wear. It was business as usual at the Hotel Dolphin. There was help for everyone except poor Mr. Ostermeyer, who had fallen into the writer's clutches.

"Mr. Ostermeyer?" Mike repeated, feeling a little sorry for the man.

"No," Ostermeyer said at last. "No problem. But, Mr. Enslin . . . could I speak to you for a moment in my office?"

So, Mike thought. *He wants to try one more time.*

Under other circumstances he might have been impatient. Now he was not. It would help the section on room 1408, offer the proper ominous tone the readers of his books seemed to crave—it was to be One Final Warning—but that wasn't all. Mike Enslin hadn't been sure until now, in spite of all the backing and filling; now he was. Ostermeyer wasn't playing a part. Ostermeyer was really afraid of room 1408, and what might happen to Mike there tonight.

"Of course, Mr. Ostermeyer. Should I leave my bag at the desk, or bring it?"

"Oh, we'll bring it along, shall we?" Ostermeyer, the good host, reached for it. Yes, he still held out some hope of persuading Mike not to stay in the room. Otherwise, he would have directed Mike to the desk . . . or taken it there himself. "Allow me."

"I'm fine with it," Mike said. "Nothing but a change of clothes and a toothbrush."

"Are you sure?"

"Yes," Mike said, holding his eyes. "I'm afraid I am."

For a moment Mike thought Ostermeyer was going to give up. He sighed, a little round man in a dark cutaway coat and a neatly knotted tie, and then he squared his shoulders again. "Very good, Mr. Enslin. Follow me."

The hotel manager had seemed tentative in the lobby, depressed, almost beaten. In his oak-paneled office, with the pictures of the hotel on the walls (the Dolphin had opened in October of 1910—Mike might publish without the benefit of reviews in the journals or the big-city papers, but he did his research), Ostermeyer seemed to gain assurance again. There was a Persian carpet on the floor. Two standing lamps cast a mild yellow light. A desk-lamp with a green lozenge-shaped shade stood on the desk, next to a humidor. And next to the humidor were Mike Enslin's last three books. Paperback editions, of course; there had been no hardbacks. Yet he did quite well. *Mine host has been doing a little research of his own,* Mike thought.

Mike sat down in one of the chairs in front of the desk. He expected Ostermeyer to sit behind the desk, where he could draw authority from it, but Ostermeyer surprised him. He sat in the other chair on what he probably thought of as the employees' side of the desk, crossed his legs, then leaned forward over his tidy little belly to touch the humidor.

"Cigar, Mr. Enslin? They're not Cuban, but they're quite good."

"No, thank you. I don't smoke."

Ostermeyer's eyes shifted to the cigarette behind Mike's right ear—parked there on a jaunty jut the way an oldtime wisecracking New York reporter might have parked his next smoke just below his fedora with the PRESS tag stuck in the band. The cigarette had become so much a part of him that for a moment Mike honestly didn't know what Ostermeyer was looking at. Then he remembered, laughed, took it down, looked at it himself, then looked back at Ostermeyer.

"Haven't had a cigarette in nine years," he said. "I had an older brother who died of lung cancer. I quit shortly after he died. The cigarette behind the ear . . ." He shrugged. "Part affectation, part superstition, I guess. Kind of like the ones you sometimes see on people's desks or walls, mounted in a little box with a sign saying BREAK GLASS IN CASE OF EMERGENCY. I sometimes tell people I'll light up in case of nuclear war. Is 1408 a smoking room, Mr. Ostermeyer? Just in case nuclear war breaks out?"

"As a matter of fact, it is."

"Well," Mike said heartily, "that's one less worry in the watches of the night."

Mr. Ostermeyer sighed again, unamused, but this one didn't have the disconsolate quality of his lobby-sigh. Yes, it was the room, Mike reckoned. *His* room. Even this afternoon, when Mike had come accompanied by Robertson, the lawyer, Ostermeyer had seemed less flustered once they were in here. At the time Mike had thought it was partly because they were no longer drawing stares from the passing public, partly because Ostermeyer had given up. Now he knew better. It was the room. And why not? It was a room with good pictures on the walls, a good rug on the floor, and good cigars—although not Cuban—in the humidor. A lot of managers had no doubt conducted a lot of business in here since October of 1910; in its own way it was as New York as the blonde woman in her black off-the-shoulder dress, her smell of perfume and her unarticulated promise of sleek sex in the small hours of the morning—New York sex. Mike himself was from Omaha, although he hadn't been back there in a lot of years.

"You still don't think I can talk you out of this idea of yours, do you?" Ostermeyer asked.

"I know you can't," Mike said, replacing the cigarette behind his ear.

What follows is revised copy of this same opening passage—it's the story putting on its clothes, combing its hair, maybe adding just a small dash of cologne. Once these changes are incorporated into my document, I'm ready to open the door and face the world.

~~The Hotel Story~~   **1408** ①

By Stephen King

② Mike Enslin was still in the revolving door when he
saw ~~Ostermeyer,~~ ^{Olin} the manager of the Hotel Dolphin,
sitting in one of the overstuffed lobby chairs. Mike's
heart sank ~~a little.~~ *Maybe should have brought the
damned lawyer along again, after all,* he thought.
Well, too late now. And even if ~~Ostermeyer~~ ^{Olin} had
decided to throw up another roadblock or two
between Mike and room 1408, that wasn't all bad; it ~~—
would simply add to the story when he finally told it.~~ **there were compensations.**
~~Ostermeyer saw him, got up, and~~ ^{Olin} was crossing
the room with one pudgy hand held out as Mike left
the revolving door. The Dolphin was on Sixty-first
Street, around the corner from Fifth Avenue, small
but smart. A man and woman dressed in evening
clothes passed Mike as he reached out and took
~~Ostermeyer's~~ ^{Olin's} hand, switching his small overnight

case to his left hand in order to do it. The woman was blonde, dressed in black, of course, and the light, flowery smell of her perfume seemed to summarize New York. On the mezzanine level, someone was playing "Night and Day" in the bar, as if to underline the summary.

"Mr. Enslin. Good evening."

"Mr. ~~Ostermeyer~~ Olin. Is there a problem?"

~~Ostermeyer~~ Olin looked pained. For a moment he glanced around the small, smart lobby, as if for help. At the concierge's stand, a man was discussing theater tickets with his wife while the concierge himself watched ~~them~~ with a small, patient smile. At the front desk, a man with the rumpled look one only got after long hours in Business Class was discussing his reservation with a woman in a smart black suit that could itself have doubled for evening wear. It was business as usual at the Hotel Dolphin. There was help for everyone except poor Mr. ~~Ostermeyer~~ Olin, who had fallen into the writer's clutches.

"Mr. ~~Ostermeyer~~ Olin?" Mike repeated, ~~feeling a little sorry for the man.~~

"No," Ostermeyer said at last. "~~No problem.~~ But, Mr. Enslin . . . could I speak to you for a moment in my office?"

So, Mike thought. ~~He wants to try one more time~~ *Well, and why not?*
~~Under other circumstances he might have been impatient. Now he was not~~ It would help the section on room 1408, ~~offer~~ add to the proper ominous tone the readers of his books seemed to crave, and that wasn't all. ~~it was to be One Final Warning—but that wasn't all,~~ Mike Enslin hadn't been sure until now, in spite of all the backing and filling; now he was. ~~Ostermeyer~~ Olin wasn't playing a part. ~~Ostermeyer~~ Olin was really afraid of room 1408, and what might happen to Mike there tonight.

"Of course, Mr. ~~Ostermeyer~~ Olin. ~~Should I leave my bag at the desk, or bring it?~~"

"Oh, Olin, we'll bring it along, shall we?" ~~Ostermeyer,~~ the good host, reached for ~~it. Yes, he still held out~~ Mike's bag. ~~some hope of persuading Mike not to stay in the room. Otherwise, he would have directed Mike to the desk . . . or taken it there himself.~~ "Allow me."

"I'm fine with it," Mike said. "Nothing but a change of clothes and a toothbrush."

"Are you sure?"

⑤ "Yes," Mike said, holding his eyes. "I'm afraid I'm already wearing my lucky Hawaiian shirt." He smiled. "It's the one with the ghost repellent."

~~For a moment Mike thought Ostermeyer was going to give up.~~ [Olin] He sighed, a little round man in a dark cutaway coat and a neatly knotted tie, ~~and then he squared his shoulders again.~~ "Very good, Mr. Enslin. Follow me."

The hotel manager had seemed tentative in the lobby, ~~depressed,~~ almost beaten. In his oak-paneled office, with the pictures of the hotel on the walls (the Dolphin had opened in October of 1910—Mike might publish without the benefit of reviews in the journals or the big-city papers, but he did his research), ~~Ostermeyer~~ [Olin] seemed to gain assurance again. There was a Persian carpet on the floor. Two standing lamps cast a mild yellow light. A desk-lamp with a green lozenge-shaped shade stood on the desk, next to a humidor. And next to the humidor were Mike Enslin's last three books. Paperback editions, of course; there had been no hardbacks. ~~Yet he did quite well.~~ *Mine host has been doing a little research of his own,* Mike thought.

⑥   Mike sat down ~~in one of the chairs~~ in front of the desk. He expected ~~Ostermeyer~~ Olin to sit behind the desk, ~~where he could draw authority from it,~~ but ~~Ostermeyer~~ Olin surprised him. He sat ~~in the other chair~~ took the chair ~~on what he probably thought of as the employees' side of the desk,~~ ^beside Mike, crossed his legs, then leaned forward over his tidy little belly to touch the humidor.

    "Cigar, Mr. Enslin? ~~They're not Cuban, but they're quite good.~~"

    "No, thank you. I don't smoke."

    ~~Ostermeyer~~ Olin's eyes shifted to the cigarette behind Mike's right ear—parked ~~there~~ on a jaunty jut the way an oldtime wisecracking New York reporter might have parked his next smoke just below ~~his fedora with~~ of his fedora. the PRESS tag stuck in the band. The cigarette had become so much a part of him that for a moment Mike honestly didn't know what ~~Ostermeyer~~ Olin was looking at. Then he ~~remembered,~~ laughed, took it down, looked at it himself, then looked back at ~~Ostermeyer~~ Olin.

    "Haven't had a ~~cigarette~~ one in nine years," he said.
⑦ "I had an older brother who died of lung cancer. I quit ~~shortly~~ after he died. The cigarette behind the

ear . . ." He shrugged. "Part affectation, part super- ~~Like the Hawaiian shirt. Or the cigarettes~~ stition, I guess. ~~Kind of like the ones~~ you some- times see on people's desks or walls, mounted in a little box with a sign saying BREAK GLASS IN CASE OF EMERGENCY. ~~I sometimes tell people I'll light up in case of nuclear war.~~ Is 1408 a smoking room, Mr. ~~Ostermeyer~~ *Olin*? Just in case nuclear war breaks out?"

"As a matter of fact, it is."

"Well," Mike said heartily, "that's one less worry in the watches of the night."

Mr. ~~Ostermeyer~~ *Olin* sighed again, ~~unamused~~ but this ~~one~~ *sigh* didn't have the disconsolate quality of his lobby-sigh. Yes, it was the ~~room~~ *office,* Mike reckoned. *His* ~~room~~ *office*. Even this afternoon, when Mike had come accompanied by Robertson, the lawyer, ~~Ostermeyer~~ *Olin* had seemed less flustered once they were in here. ~~At the time Mike had thought it was partly because they were no longer drawing stares from the passing public, partly because Oster- meyer had given up. Now he knew better. It was~~ the room. And why not? ~~It was a room with good~~ *Where else could you feel in charge, if not in your special place? Olin's office* pictures on the walls, a good rug on the floor, and good cigars—~~although not Cuban~~—in the humidor. A lot of managers had no doubt conducted a lot of business in here since ~~October of~~ 1910; in its own way it was as New York as the blonde ~~woman~~ in her black off-the-shoulder dress, her smell of perfume and her unarticulated promise of sleek New York sex in the small hours of the morning ~~New York sex~~. Mike himself was from Omaha, although he hadn't been back there in ~~a lot of~~ years.

"You still don't think I can talk you out of this idea of yours, do you?" ~~Ostermoyer~~ Olin asked.

"I know you can't," Mike said, replacing the cigarette behind his ear.

The reasons for the majority of the changes are self-evident; if you flip back and forth between the two versions, I'm confident that you'll understand almost all of them, and I'm hopeful that you'll see how raw the first-draft work of even a so-called "professional writer" is once you really examine it.

Most of the changes are cuts, intended to speed the story. I have cut with Strunk in mind—"Omit needless words"—and also to satisfy the formula stated earlier: 2nd Draft = 1st Draft – 10%.

I have keyed a few changes for brief explanation:

1. Obviously, "The Hotel Story" is never going to replace "Killdozer!" or *Norma Jean, the Termite Queen* as a title. I simply slotted it into the first draft, knowing a bet-

ter one would occur as I went along. (If a better title doesn't occur, an editor will usually supply his or her idea of a better one, and the results are usually ugly.) I like "1408" because this is a "thirteenth floor" story, and the numbers add up to thirteen.

2. Ostermeyer is a long and gallumphing name. By changing it to Olin via global replace, I was able to shorten my story by about fifteen lines at a single stroke. Also, by the time I finished "1408," I had realized it was probably going to be part of an audio collection. I would read the stories myself, and didn't want to sit there in the little recording booth, saying Ostermeyer, Ostermeyer, Ostermeyer all day long. So I changed it.

3. I'm doing a lot of the reader's thinking for him here. Since most readers can think for themselves, I felt free to cut this from five lines to just two.

4. Too much stage direction, too much belaboring of the obvious, and too much clumsy back story. Out it goes.

5. Ah, here is the lucky Hawaiian shirt. It shows up in the first draft, but not until about page thirty. That's too late for an important prop, so I stuck it up front. There's an old rule of theater that goes, "If there's a gun on the mantel in Act I, it must go off in Act III." The reverse is also true; if the main character's lucky Hawaiian shirt plays a part at the end of a story, it must be introduced early. Otherwise it looks like a *deus ex machina* (which of course it is).

6. The first-draft copy reads "Mike sat down in one of the chairs in front of the desk." Well, duh—where else is he going to sit? On the floor? I don't think so, and out it goes. Also out is the business of the Cuban cigars. This is

not only trite, it's the sort of thing bad guys are always saying in bad movies. "Have a cigar! They're Cuban!" Fuhgeddaboudit!

7. The first- and second-draft ideas and basic information are the same, but in the second draft, things have been cut to the bone. And look! See that wretched adverb, that "shortly"? Stomped it, didn't I? No mercy!

8. And here's one I didn't cut . . . not just an adverb but a Swiftie: **"Well," Mike said heartily** . . . But I stand behind my choice not to cut in this case, would argue that it's the exception which proves the rule. "Heartily" has been allowed to stand because I want the reader to understand that Mike is making fun of poor Mr. Olin. Just a little, but yes, he's making fun.

9. This passage not only belabors the obvious but repeats it. Out it goes. The concept of a person's feeling comfortable in one's own special place, however, seemed to clarify Olin's character, and so I added it.

I toyed with the idea of including the entire finished text of "1408" in this book, but the idea ran counter to my determination to be brief, for once in my life. If you would like to listen to the entire thing, it's available as part of a three-story audio collection, *Blood and Smoke*. You may access a sample on the Simon and Schuster Web site, http://www.SimonSays.com. And remember, for our purposes here, you don't need to finish the story. This is about engine maintenance, not joyriding.

And Furthermore, Part II:
A Booklist

When I talk about writing, I usually offer my audiences an abbreviated version of the "On Writing" section which forms the second half of this book. That includes the Prime Rule, of course: Write a lot and read a lot. In the Q-and-A period which follows, someone invariably asks: "What do *you* read?"

I've never given a very satisfactory answer to that question, because it causes a kind of circuit overload in my brain. The easy answer—"Everything I can get my hands on"—is true enough, but not helpful. The list that follows provides a more specific answer to that question. These are the best books I've read over the last three or four years, the period during which I wrote *The Girl Who Loved Tom Gordon, Hearts in Atlantis, On Writing,* and the as-yet-unpublished *From a Buick Eight.* In some way or other, I suspect each book in the list had an influence on the books I wrote.

As you scan this list, please remember that I'm not Oprah and this isn't my book club. These are the ones that worked for me, that's all. But you could do worse, and a good many of these might show you some new ways of doing your work. Even if they don't, they're apt to entertain you. They certainly entertained me.

Abrahams, Peter: *A Perfect Crime*
Abrahams, Peter: *Lights Out*
Abrahams, Peter: *Pressure Drop*
Abrahams, Peter: *Revolution #9*
Agee, James: *A Death in the Family*
Bakis, Kirsten: *Lives of the Monster Dogs*
Barker, Pat: *Regeneration*
Barker, Pat: *The Eye in the Door*
Barker, Pat: *The Ghost Road*
Bausch, Richard: *In the Night Season*
Blauner, Peter: *The Intruder*
Bowles, Paul: *The Sheltering Sky*
Boyle, T. Coraghessan: *The Tortilla Curtain*
Bryson, Bill: *A Walk in the Woods*
Buckley, Christopher: *Thank You for Smoking*
Carver, Raymond: *Where I'm Calling From*
Chabon, Michael: *Werewolves in Their Youth*
Chorlton, Windsor: *Latitude Zero*
Connelly, Michael: *The Poet*
Conrad, Joseph: *Heart of Darkness*
Constantine, K. C.: *Family Values*
DeLillo, Don: *Underworld*
DeMille, Nelson: *Cathedral*
DeMille, Nelson: *The Gold Coast*
Dickens, Charles: *Oliver Twist*
Dobyns, Stephen: *Common Carnage*
Dobyns, Stephen: *The Church of Dead Girls*
Doyle, Roddy: *The Woman Who Walked into Doors*

Elkin, Stanley: *The Dick Gibson Show*
Faulkner, William: *As I Lay Dying*
Garland, Alex: *The Beach*
George, Elizabeth: *Deception on His Mind*
Gerritsen, Tess: *Gravity*
Golding, William: *Lord of the Flies*
Gray, Muriel: *Furnace*
Greene, Graham: *A Gun for Sale* (aka *This Gun for Hire*)
Greene, Graham: *Our Man in Havana*
Halberstam, David: *The Fifties*
Hamill, Pete: *Why Sinatra Matters*
Harris, Thomas: *Hannibal*
Haruf, Kent: *Plainsong*
Hoeg, Peter: *Smilla's Sense of Snow*
Hunter, Stephen: *Dirty White Boys*
Ignatius, David: *A Firing Offense*
Irving, John: *A Widow for One Year*
Joyce, Graham: *The Tooth Fairy*
Judd, Alan: *The Devil's Own Work*
Kahn, Roger: *Good Enough to Dream*
Karr, Mary: *The Liars' Club*
Ketchum, Jack: *Right to Life*
King, Tabitha: *Survivor*
King, Tabitha: *The Sky in the Water* (unpublished)
Kingsolver, Barbara: *The Poisonwood Bible*
Krakauer, Jon: *Into Thin Air*
Lee, Harper: *To Kill a Mockingbird*
Lefkowitz, Bernard: *Our Guys*
Little, Bentley: *The Ignored*
Maclean, Norman: *A River Runs Through It and Other Stories*
Maugham, W. Somerset: *The Moon and Sixpence*

McCarthy, Cormac: *Cities of the Plain*
McCarthy, Cormac: *The Crossing*
McCourt, Frank: *Angela's Ashes*
McDermott, Alice: *Charming Billy*
McDevitt, Jack: *Ancient Shores*
McEwan, Ian: *Enduring Love*
McEwan, Ian: *The Cement Garden*
McMurtry, Larry: *Dead Man's Walk*
McMurtry, Larry, and Diana Ossana: *Zeke and Ned*
Miller, Walter M.: *A Canticle for Leibowitz*
Oates, Joyce Carol: *Zombie*
O'Brien, Tim: *In the Lake of the Woods*
O'Nan, Stewart: *The Speed Queen*
Ondaatje, Michael: *The English Patient*
Patterson, Richard North: *No Safe Place*
Price, Richard: *Freedomland*
Proulx, Annie: *Close Range: Wyoming Stories*
Proulx, Annie: *The Shipping News*
Quindlen, Anna: *One True Thing*
Rendell, Ruth: *A Sight for Sore Eyes*
Robinson, Frank M.: *Waiting*
Rowling, J. K.: *Harry Potter and the Chamber of Secrets*
Rowling, J. K.: *Harry Potter and the Prisoner of Azakaban*
Rowling, J. K.: *Harry Potter and the Sorcerer's Stone*
Russo, Richard: *Mohawk*
Schwartz, John Burnham: *Reservation Road*
Seth, Vikram: *A Suitable Boy*
Shaw, Irwin: *The Young Lions*
Slotkin, Richard: *The Crater*
Smith, Dinitia: *The Illusionist*
Spencer, Scott: *Men in Black*
Stegner, Wallace: *Joe Hill*

Tartt, Donna: *The Secret History*
Tyler, Anne: *A Patchwork Planet*
Vonnegut, Kurt: *Hocus Pocus*
Waugh, Evelyn: *Brideshead Revisited*
Westlake, Donald E.: *The Ax*

**"A WRITER OF TRUE VIRTUOSITY
AND TALENT."**
—*Fort Worth Star-Telegram*

**From the #1 *New York Times* bestselling
authors comes the second in the gripping
Clandestine Operations series featuring
Captain James Cronley.**

James Cronley's first successful Cold War mission for
the about-to-be-official new Directorate of Central
Intelligence has drawn all kinds of attention. He's now
a captain and in charge of a top secret spy operation.

A lot of people would like to know about the operation—not just the Soviets but also the Pentagon and
a seething J. Edgar Hoover. Cronley knows that if
anything goes wrong, he's finished. But he's already
caught up in more than one conspiracy . . .

Cronley has just uncovered a bizarre alliance between
a former German intelligence chief and the Mossad. A
German family whom Cronley never knew he had has
suddenly and suspiciously emerged. And he has a rendezvous with an undercover agent against the Soviets
known only as Seven-K.

And when he meets Seven-K, that's when he gets
a real surprise . . .

"It's a testament to the authors' skill and wide experience
that the pages seem to turn themselves."
—*Publishers Weekly*

"Pages cry out to be turned for the next thrilling chapter."
—BookReporter.com

continued . . .

continued . . .

TITLES BY W.E.B. GRIFFIN

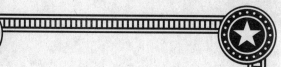

THE
ASSASSINATION
OPTION

A CLANDESTINE OPERATIONS NOVEL

W.E.B.
GRIFFIN

AND WILLIAM E. BUTTERWORTH IV

J

JOVE BOOKS
NEW YORK

JOVE

**An imprint of Penguin Random House LLC
375 Hudson Street, New York, New York 10014**

THE ASSASSINATION OPTION

A Jove Book / published by arrangement with the author

Copyright © 2014 by W.E.B. Griffin.
Penguin supports copyright. Copyright fuels creativity, encourages diverse voices,
promotes free speech, and creates a vibrant culture. Thank you for buying an authorized
edition of this book and for complying with copyright laws by not reproducing, scanning, or
distributing any part of it in any form without permission. You are supporting writers and
allowing Penguin to continue to publish books for every reader.

JOVE® is a registered trademark of Penguin Random House LLC.
The "J" design is a trademark of Penguin Random House LLC.
For more information, visit penguin.com.

ISBN: 978-0-515-15569-3

PUBLISHING HISTORY
G. P. Putnam's Sons hardcover edition / December 2014
Jove premium edition / December 2015

PRINTED IN THE UNITED STATES OF AMERICA

10   9   8   7   6   5   4   3   2   1

Cover photograph of eagle © niknikon / Getty Images.
Cover design by Eric Fuentecilla.

Penguin
Random
House

26 July 1777

The necessity of procuring good intelligence is apparent and need not be further urged.

George Washington
General and Commander in Chief
The Continental Army

FOR THE LATE

William E. Colby
An OSS Jedburgh First Lieutenant
who became director of the Central Intelligence
Agency.

Aaron Bank
An OSS Jedburgh First Lieutenant
who became a colonel and the father of
Special Forces.

William R. Corson
A legendary Marine intelligence officer
whom the KGB hated more than any other U.S.
intelligence officer—and not only because
he wrote the definitive work on them.

René J. Défourneaux
A U.S. Army OSS Second Lieutenant attached to
the British SOE who jumped into Occupied France
alone and later became a legendary U.S. Army
intelligence officer.

FOR THE LIVING

Billy Waugh
A legendary Special Forces Command Sergeant Major
who retired and then went on to hunt down the
infamous Carlos the Jackal. Billy could have
terminated Osama bin Laden in the early 1990s but
could not get permission to do so.
After fifty years in the business, Billy is still going
after the bad guys.

JOHNNY REITZEL
An Army Special Operations officer
who could have terminated the head terrorist
of the seized cruise ship *Achille Lauro* but could not
get permission to do so.

RALPH PETERS
An Army intelligence officer
who has written the best analysis of our war against
terrorists and of our enemy that I have ever seen.

AND FOR THE NEW BREED

MARC L
A senior intelligence officer, despite his youth, who
reminds me of Bill Colby more and more each day.

FRANK L
A legendary Defense Intelligence Agency officer
who retired and now follows in Billy Waugh's
footsteps.

AND
In Loving Memory of
Colonel José Manuel Menéndez
Cavalry, Argentine Army, Retired
He spent his life fighting Communism and
Juan Domingo Perón

OUR NATION OWES THESE PATRIOTS
A DEBT BEYOND REPAYMENT.

THE
ASSASSINATION
OPTION

PROLOGUE

Early in 1943, at a time when victory was by no means certain, Great Britain, the Union of Soviet Socialist Republics, and the United States of America—"the Allies"—signed what became known as "the Moscow Declaration." It stated that the leaders of Germany, Italy, and Japan—"the Axis Powers"—would be held responsible for atrocities committed during the war.

In December of that year, the Allied leaders—Prime Minister Winston Churchill of England, General Secretary Joseph V. Stalin of the Soviet Union, and President Franklin D. Roosevelt of the United States—met secretly in Tehran, Iran, under the code name Project Eureka. The meeting later came to be known as the Tehran Conference.

At a dinner in Tehran on December 29, 1943, while discussing the Moscow Declaration, Stalin proposed the summary execution of fifty thousand to one hundred thousand German staff officers immediately following the defeat of the Thousand-Year Reich. Roosevelt thought he was joking, and asked if he would be satisfied with "the summary execution of a lesser number, say, forty-nine thousand."

Churchill took the Communist leader at his word, and angrily announced he would have nothing to do with "the cold-blooded execution of soldiers who fought for their country," adding that he'd "rather be taken out in the courtyard and shot myself" than partake in any such action.

The war in Europe ended on May 8, 1945, with the unconditional surrender of Germany.

In London, on August 8, 1945, the four Allied powers—France, after its liberation, had by then become sort of a junior member—signed "the Agreement for the Prosecution and Punishment of the Major War Criminals of the European Axis Powers."

"The London Agreement" proclaimed that the senior Nazi leaders would be tried on behalf of the newly formed United Nations at Nuremberg, and that lesser officials would be tried at trials to be held in each of the four zones of occupation into which Germany was to be divided.

The Soviet Union wanted the trials to be held in Berlin, but the other three Allies insisted they be held in Nuremberg, in Bavaria, in the American Zone of Occupation. Their public argument was that not only was Nuremberg the ceremonial birthplace of Nazism, but also that the Palace of Justice compound, which included a large prison, had come through the war relatively untouched and was an ideal site for the trials.

What the Western Allies—aware of the Soviet rape of Berlin and that to get the Russians out of the American Sector of Berlin, U.S. General I.D. White had to quite seriously threaten to shoot on sight any armed Russian soldiers he found in the American Sector—were not saying publicly was that they had no intention of letting the Soviet Union dominate the trials.

They threw a face-saving bone to the Russians by agreeing that Berlin would be the "official home" of the tribunal.

The London Agreement provided that the International Military Tribunal (IMT) would, on behalf of the newly formed United Nations, try the accused war criminals. It would consist of eight judges, two named by each of the four Allied powers.

One judge from each country would preside at the trials. The others would sit as alternates.

Interpreters would translate the proceedings into French, German, Russian, and English, and written evidence submitted by the prosecution would be translated into the native language of each defendant. The IMT would not be bound by Anglo-American rules of evidence, and it would accept hearsay and other forms of evidence normally considered unreliable in the United States and Great Britain.

The IMT was given authority to hear four counts of criminal complaints: conspiracy, crimes against peace, war crimes, and crimes against humanity.

It has been argued that the Russians obliged the Western Allies by agreeing to hold the actual trials in Nuremberg in a spirit of cooperation. It has also been argued that there was a tit-for-tat arrangement. If the Russians agreed to Nuremberg, the Americans and the English would not bring up the Katyn Massacre.

What is known—provable beyond doubt—is that in 1943 the Germans took a number of captured American officers from their POW camp to the Katyn Forest, about twelve miles west of Smolensk, Russia.

The American officer prisoners were a mixed bag of Medical Corps officers, Judge Advocate General's Corps officers, and officers of the combat arms. In the latter group was Lieutenant Colonel John K. Waters, an Armor officer who had been captured in Tunisia. He was married to the former Beatrice Patton. His father-in-law was General George S. Patton. Waters later became a four-star general.

At Katyn, there were several recently reopened mass graves. As the Americans watched, other mass graves were reopened.

They contained the bodies of thousands of Polish officers who had surrendered in 1940 to the Red Army when the Russians invaded Poland from the East and Germany from the West.

The Germans told the Americans that the Polish officers had been taken from the Kozelsk prisoner-of-war camp to the forest in 1940—shortly after the surrender—by the Soviet NKVD. There, after their hands had been wired behind them, they were executed by pistol shots into the back of their heads.

The Germans permitted the American doctors to examine the corpses and to remove from their brains the bullets that had killed them. It was the opinion of the American doctors that the bodies had in fact been so murdered and had been decomposing since 1940.

The Americans were then returned to their POW camp. The bullets removed from the brains of the murdered Polish officers were distributed among them.

It is now known that there was some communication, in both directions, between the Allies and American prisoners of war in Germany. It is credible to assume that the prisoners who had been taken to Hammelburg managed to tell Eisenhower's headquarters in London what they had seen in the Katyn Forest, and possible, if by no means certain, that they managed to get the bullets to London, as well.

Very late in the war, in March 1945, General Patton gave a very unusual assignment to one of his very best tank officers, Lieutenant Colonel Creighton W. Abrams, who then commanded Combat Command B of the 4th Armored Division. Abrams had broken through the German lines to rescue the surrounded 101st Airborne Division at Bastogne, and was later to become chief of staff of the U.S. Army. The U.S. Army's main battle tank today is the Abrams.

The official story was that Patton told Abrams he feared the Germans would execute the American POWs being held in Oflag XIII-B, in Hammelburg, Germany, then fifty miles behind the German lines, when it appeared they would be liberated by the Red Army.

Abrams was ordered to mount an immediate mission to get to Hammelburg before the Russians did and to liberate the Americans. In the late evening of March 26, 1945, Task Force Baum—a company of medium tanks, a platoon of light tanks, and a company of armored infantry, under Captain Abraham Baum—set out to do so.

The mission was not successful. It was mauled by the Germans. When word of it got out, Patton was severely criticized for staging a dangerous raid to rescue his son-in-law. He denied knowing Colonel Waters was in Oflag XIII-B. When, shortly afterward, Oflag XIII-B was liberated by the Red Army, Waters was not there.

It later came out that Waters and 101st Airborne Division Second Lieutenant Lory L. McCullough (an interesting character, who learned that he had been awarded a battlefield commission only after he had been captured during Operation Marketgarden) had escaped from captivity while the Germans had been marching the prisoners on foot toward Hammelburg and had made their escape to North Africa through the Russian port of Odessa on the Black Sea.

When this came out, there was some knowledgeable speculation that Patton had known Waters was in Oflag XIII-B, and had been worried, because of Waters's knowledge of the Katyn Forest Massacre, that if the Red Army reached Hammelburg before the Americans, Waters would have been killed by the Red Army to keep his mouth shut.

Why else, this speculation asked, would Waters have elected his incredibly dangerous escape with McCullough rather than just stay where he was and wait in safety to be liberated?

The Katyn Forest Massacre was not unknown in the West. The Polish government in exile had proof of it as early as 1942. When it requested an investigation by the International Red Cross, Russia broke diplomatic relations with the Poles. Churchill had not wanted to annoy his Russian ally, and Roosevelt believed it was Nazi propaganda. The Russians wouldn't do anything like that.

And then, at the very end of the war, Major General Reinhard Gehlen, who had been chief of Abwehr Ost, the German military intelligence agency dealing with the Soviet Union, added some further light on the subject.

Gehlen had made a deal with Allen W. Dulles, who had been the Office of Strategic Services station chief in Berne, Switzerland, to turn over all of his assets—including agents in place in the Kremlin—to the OSS in return for the OSS protection of his officers and men, and their families, from the Red Army.

Among the documents turned over were some that Gehlen's agents had stolen from the Kremlin itself. They included photographic copies of NKVD chief Lavrentiy Beria's proposal, dated March 5, 1940, to execute all captured Polish officers. Gehlen also provided photographic copies of Stalin's personal approval of the proposal, signed by him on behalf of the Soviet Politburo, and reports from functionaries of the NKVD reporting in detail their execution of their orders. At least 21,768, and as many as 22,002, Poles had been murdered. Approximately 8,000 were military officers, approximately 6,000 were police officers, and the rest were members of the intelligentsia, landowners, factory owners, lawyers, officials, and priests.

The Americans could not raise this in the face of the Soviet Union, however, as they would have had to say where they got their information, and when the Nuremberg trials began, the Americans were denying any knowledge of the whereabouts of former Major General Reinhard Gehlen.

I

The MP at the gate did not attempt to stop the Packard Clipper when it approached. He had seen enough cars from the White House pool to know one when he saw one, and this one was also displaying a blue plate with two silver stars, indicating that it was carrying a rear admiral (upper half).

The MP waved the car through, saluted crisply, and then went quickly into the guard shack—which was actually a neat little tile-roofed brick structure, not a shack—and got on the phone.

"White House car with an admiral," he announced.

This caused activity at the main entrance. A Medical Corps lieutenant colonel, who was the Medical Officer of the Day—MOD—and a Rubenesque major of the Army Nurse Corps, who was the NOD—Nurse Officer of the Day—rushed to the lobby to greet the VIP admiral from the White House.

No Packard Clipper appeared.

"Where the hell did he go?" the MOD inquired finally.

"If it's who I think it is," the NOD said, "he's done this

before. He went in the side door to 233. The auto accident major they flew in from South America."

The MOD and the NOD hurried to the stairwell and quickly climbed it in hopes of greeting the VIP admiral from the White House to offer him any assistance he might require.

They succeeded in doing so. They caught up with Rear Admiral Sidney W. Souers and his aide-de-camp, Lieutenant James L. Allred, USN, as the latter reached to push open the door to room 233.

"Good morning, Admiral," the MOD said. "I'm Colonel Thrush, the Medical Officer of the Day. May I be of service?"

"Just calling on a friend, Colonel," the admiral replied. "But thank you, nonetheless."

He nodded to his aide to open the door.

The NOD beat him to it, and went into the room.

There was no one in the hospital bed, whose back had been cranked nearly vertical. A bed tray to one side held a coffee thermos, a cup, and an ashtray, in which rested a partially smoked thick, dark brown cigar. The room was redolent of cigar smoke.

"He must be in the toilet," the nurse announced, adding righteously, "He's not supposed to do that unassisted."

Lieutenant Allred went to the toilet door, knocked, and asked, "You okay, Major?"

"I was until you knocked at the door," a muffled voice replied.

"Thank you for your interest, Colonel, Miss," Admiral Souers said.

They understood they were being dismissed, said, "Yes, sir," in chorus, and left the room.

"Who is he?" the MOD asked.

"You mean the admiral, or the major?"

"Both."

"All I know about the admiral is that the word is that he's a pal of President Truman. And all I know about the major is that he was medically evac'd from someplace in South America, maybe Argentina, someplace like that, and brought here. Broken leg, broken arm, broken ribs. And no papers. No Army papers. He told one of the nurses he was in a car accident."

"I wonder why here?" the MOD asked. "There are very good hospitals in the Canal Zone, and that's a lot closer to Argentina than Washington."

The NOD shrugged.

"And that admiral showed up an hour after he did," she said. "And shortly after that, the major's family started coming. He has a large family. I think they're Puerto Ricans. They were all speaking Spanish."

"Interesting," the MOD said.

Major Maxwell Ashton III, Cavalry, detail Military Intelligence, a tall, swarthy-skinned, six-foot-three twenty-six-year-old, tried to rise from the water closet in his toilet by using a chromed support mounted to the wall. The support was on the left wall. Major Ashton's left arm was in a cast and the cast was in a sling. Using his right arm, he managed to rise about eighteen inches from the toilet seat before his hand slipped and he dropped back down.

He cursed. Loudly, colorfully, obscenely, and profanely, in Spanish, and for perhaps thirty seconds.

He then attempted to rise using the crutch he had rested against the toilet wall. On the third try, he made it. With great difficulty, he managed to get his pajama trousers up from the floor and over his right leg, which was encased in plaster of paris, and to his waist.

"Oh, you clever fucking devil, you!" he proclaimed, in English.

He unlocked the door, held it open with his forehead, and then managed to get the crutch into his armpit, which permitted him to escape the small room.

He was halfway to the bed when Lieutenant Allred attempted to come to his aid.

Ashton impatiently waved him off, made it to the bed, and, with difficulty, got in.

"You should have asked a nurse to help you," Allred said.

"I'm sure it's different in the Navy, but in the Cavalry, we consider it unbecoming an officer and a gentleman to ask women with whom we are not intimately acquainted to assist us in moving our bowels," Ashton said.

Admiral Souers laughed.

"I'm delighted to find you in a good mood, Max," he said. "How's it going?"

"Sir, do you really want to know?"

"I really do."

"I am torn between that proverbial rock and that hard place. On one hand, I really want to get the hell out of here. I am told that when I can successfully stagger to the end of the hall and back on my crutches, I will be considered 'ambulatory.' I can do that. But if I do it officially, that will mean I will pass into the hands of my Aunt Florence, who is camped out in the Hay-Adams extolling my many virtues to the parents of every unmarried Cuban female in her child-bearing years—of the proper bloodline, of course—between New York and Miami."

"That doesn't sound so awful to me," Allred said.

"What you don't understand, Jim—although I've told you this before—is that unmarried Cuban females of the proper bloodline do not fool around before marriage. And I am still in my fooling-around years."

"Or might be, anyway, when you get out of that cast," Admiral Souers said.

"Thank you, sir, for pointing that out to me," Ashton said.

Souers chuckled, and then asked, "What do you want first, the good news or the bad?"

"Let's start with the bad, sir. Then I will have something to look forward to."

"Okay. There's a long list of the former. Where do I start? Okay. General Patton died yesterday in Germany."

"I'm sorry to hear that. He always said he wanted to go out with the last bullet fired in the last battle."

"And a car wreck isn't the last battle, is it?" Souers replied.

"Unless it was an opening shot in the first of a series of new battles," Ashton said.

"We looked into that," Souers said. "General Greene— the European Command CIC chief? . . ."

Ashton nodded his understanding.

". . . was all over the accident. And he told me that's what it was, an accident. A truck pulled in front of Patton's limousine. His driver braked hard, but ran into the truck anyway. Patton slid off the seat and it got his neck, or his spine. He was paralyzed. Greene told me when he saw Patton in the hospital, they had him stretched out with weights.

Greene said it looked like something from the Spanish Inquisition."

"And what does General Gehlen have to say about it?" Ashton asked.

"I think if he had anything to say, Cronley would have passed it on. Why do you think it could be something other than an accident?"

Before Ashton could reply, Admiral Souers added, "Dumb question. Sorry."

Ashton answered it anyway.

"Well, sir, there are automobile accidents and then there are automobile accidents."

"Accidents happen, Max," Souers said.

"Sir, what happened to me was no accident," Ashton said.

"No, I don't think it was. And Frade agrees. But accidents do happen."

Ashton's face showed, Souers decided, that he thought he was being patronized.

"For example, sort of close to home, do you know who Lieutenant Colonel Schumann is? Or was?"

Ashton shook his head.

"He was Greene's inspector general. I met him when I was over there. Good man."

Ashton said nothing, waiting for the admiral to continue.

"More than a very good IG," Souers continued, "a good intelligence officer. He was so curious about Kloster Grünau that Cronley had to blow the engine out of his staff car with a machine gun to keep him out."

"That's a story no one chose to share with me," Ashton said drily.

"Well, we didn't issue a press release. The only reason I'm

telling you is to make my point about accidents happening. The day Patton died, Colonel Schumann went to his quarters to lunch with his wife. There was apparently a faulty gas water heater. It apparently leaked gas. Schumann got home just in time for the gas to blow up. It demolished the building."

"Jesus!"

"Literally blowing both of them away, to leave their two kids, a boy and a girl, as orphans."

"Jesus Christ!" Ashton said.

"Quickly changing the subject to the good news," Souers said. "Let's have the box, Jim."

"Yes, sir," Lieutenant Allred said, and handed the admiral a small blue box.

Souers snapped it open and extended it to Ashton.

"Would you like me to pin these to your jammies, Colonel, or would you rather do that yourself?"

"These are for real?" Ashton asked.

"Yes, Lieutenant Colonel Ashton, those are for real."

"In lieu of a Purple Heart?" Ashton asked.

"Prefacing this by saying I think you well deserve the promotion, the reason you have it is because I told the adjutant general I desperately needed you, and that the only way you would even consider staying in the Army would be if your services had been rewarded with a promotion."

Ashton didn't reply.

"Operative words, Colonel, 'would even *consider* staying.'"

Again, Ashton didn't reply.

"If nothing else, you can now, for the rest of your life, legitimately refer to yourself as 'colonel' when telling tales of your valiant service in World War Two to Cuban señoritas whom you wish to despoil before marriage."

"Sometimes it was really rough," Ashton said. "Either the steak would be overcooked, or the wine improperly chilled. Once, I even fell off my polo pony."

"Modesty becomes you, but we both know what you did in Argentina."

"And once I was struck by a hit-and-run driver while getting out of a taxi."

"That, too."

"I really wish, Admiral, that you meant what you said to the adjutant general."

"Excuse me?"

"That you desperately need me."

"They say, and I believe, that no man is indispensable. But that said, I really wish you weren't—what?—'champing at the bit' to hang up your uniform. With you and Frade both getting out—and Cletus wouldn't stay on active duty if they made him a major general—finding someone to run Operation Ost down there is going to be one hell of a problem."

Ashton raised his hand over his head.

When Souers looked at him in curiosity, he said, nodding toward the toilet, "No, sir. I am not asking permission to go back in there."

"This is what they call an 'unforeseen happpenstance,'" Admiral Souers said after a moment. "You're really willing to stay on active duty?"

Ashton nodded.

"Yes, sir."

"I have to ask why, Max."

"When I thought about it, I realized I really don't want to spend the rest of my life making rum, or growing sugarcane," Ashton said. "And I really would like to get the bastards who did this to me."

He raised both the en-casted arm resting on his chest and his en-casted broken leg.

"I was hoping you would say because you see it as your duty, or that you realize how important Operation Ost is, something along those lines."

"Who was it who said 'patriotism is the last refuge of the scoundrel'?"

"Samuel Johnson said it. I'm not sure I agree with it. And I won't insult you, Max, by suggesting you are unaware of the importance of Operation Ost. But I have to point out Romans 12:19." When he saw the confusion on Ashton's face, the admiral went on: "'Vengeance is mine, saith the Lord.' Or words to that effect."

"The Lord can have his after I have mine," Ashton said. "When do you become our nation's spymaster?"

"That title belongs to General Donovan, and always will," Souers said. "If you're asking when the President will issue his Executive Order establishing the United States Directorate of Central Intelligence, January first."

"Let me ask the rude question, sir," Ashton said. "And how does General Donovan feel about that?"

"Well, the Directorate will be pretty much what he recommended. Starting, of course, with that it will be a separate intelligence agency answering only to the President."

"I meant to ask, sir, how he feels about not being named director?"

Souers considered his reply before giving it.

"Not to go outside this room, I suspect he's deeply

disappointed and probably regrets taking on J. Edgar Hoover. My personal feeling is that the President would have given General Donovan the Directorate if it wasn't for Hoover."

"The President is afraid of Hoover?"

"The President is a very smart, arguably brilliant, politician who has learned that it's almost always better to avoid a bitter confrontation. I think he may have decided that his establishing the Directorate of Central Intelligence over Hoover's objections was all the bitter confrontation he could handle."

"How does Hoover feel about you?"

"He would have preferred—would *really* have preferred—to have one of his own appointed director. Once the President told him that there would be a Directorate of Central Intelligence despite his objections to it, Hoover seriously proposed Clyde Tolson, his deputy, for the job. But even J. Edgar doesn't get everything he wants."

"That wasn't my question, sir."

"He's hoping he will be able to control me."

"What's General Donovan going to do now?"

"You know he's a lawyer? A very good one?"

"Yes, sir."

"Well, the President, citing that, asked him to go to Nuremberg as Number Two to Supreme Court Justice Robert Jackson, who's going to be the chief American prosecutor."

"He threw him a bone, in other words?"

"Now that you're a lieutenant colonel, Colonel, you're going to have to learn to control your tendency to ask out loud questions that should not be asked out loud."

"Admiral, you have a meeting with the President at ten forty-five," Allred said.

Souers walked to the bed, extending his hand.

"I'll be in touch, Max," he said. "Get yourself declared ambulatory. The sooner I can get you back to Argentina, the better."

"I was thinking, sir, that I would go to Germany first, to have a look at the Pullach compound, and get with Colonel Mattingly and Lieutenant Cronley, before I go back to Buenos Aires."

"I think that's a very good idea, if you think you're up to all that travel," he said.

"I'm up to it, sir."

"I hadn't planned to get into this with you. That was before you agreed to stay on. But now . . ."

"Yes, sir?"

"Now that you're going to have to have a commander-subordinate relationship with Captain . . . *Captain* . . . Cronley . . ."

"Sorry, sir. I knew that the President had promoted Cronley for grabbing the uranium oxide in Argentina."

"And for his behavior—all right, his 'valor above and beyond the call of duty.'"

"Yes, sir."

"Prefacing this by saying I think he fully deserved the promotion, and the Distinguished Service Medal that went with it, and that I personally happen to like him very much, I have to tell you what happened after he returned to Germany."

"Yes, sir?"

"Admiral," Lieutenant Allred said, as he tapped his wristwatch, "the President . . ."

"The world won't end if I'm ten minutes late," Admiral Souers said. "And if it looks as if we'll be late, get on the radio to the White House and tell them we're stuck in traffic."

"Yes, sir."

"You know about those Negro troops who have been guarding Kloster Grünau? Under that enormous first sergeant they call 'Tiny'? First Sergeant Dunwiddie?"

"Cronley talked about him. He said he comes from an Army family that goes way back. That they were Indian fighters, that two of his grandfathers beat Teddy Roosevelt up San Juan Hill in Cuba during the Spanish American War."

"Did he mention that he almost graduated from Norwich? That his father was a Norwich classmate of Major General I.D. White, who commanded the Second Armored Division?"

"No, sir."

"Well, when Cronley returned to Germany, to Kloster Grünau, he learned that those black soldiers—the ones he calls 'Tiny's Troopers'—had grabbed a man as he attempted to pass through—going outward—the barbed wire around Kloster Grünau. He had documents on him identifying him as Major Konstantin Orlovsky of the Soviet Liaison Mission. They have authority to be in the American Zone.

"On his person were three rosters. One of them was a complete roster of all of General Gehlen's men then inside Kloster Grünau. The second was a complete roster of all of Gehlen's men whom we have transported to Argentina, and the third was a listing of where in East Germany, Poland, Hungary, et cetera, that Gehlen believed his men who had not managed to get out were.

"It was clear that Orlovsky was an NKGB agent. It was equally clear there was at least one of Gehlen's men—and very likely more than one—whom the NKGB had turned and who had provided Orlovsky with the rosters.

"When he was told of this man, Colonel Mattingly did what I would have done. He ordered Dunwiddie to turn the man over to Gehlen. Gehlen—or one or more of his officers—would interrogate Orlovsky to see if he'd give them the names of Gehlen's traitors.

"Do I have to tell you what would happen to them if the interrogation was successful?"

"They would 'go missing.'"

"As would Major Orlovsky. As cold blooded as that sounds, it was the only solution that Mattingly could see, and he ordered it carried out. And, to repeat, I would have given the same order had I been in his shoes.

"Enter James D. Cronley Junior, who had by then been a captain for seventy-two hours. When Dunwiddie told him what had happened, he went to see the Russian. He disapproved of the psychological techniques Gehlen's interrogator was using. Admittedly, they were nasty. They had confined him naked in a windowless cell under the Kloster Grünau chapel, no lights, suffering time disorientation and forced to smell the contents of a never-emptied canvas bucket that he was forced to use as a toilet.

"Cronley announced he was taking over the interrogation, and ordered Tiny's Troopers to clean the cell, empty the canvas bucket, and keep any of Gehlen's men from having any contact whatsoever with Orlovsky."

"What did Gehlen do about that? Mattingly?"

Souers did not answer the question.

"Cronley and Dunwiddie then began their own interrogation of Major Orlovsky. As Colonel Mattingly pointed out to me later, Orlovsky was the first Russian that either Dunwiddie or Cronley had ever seen."

"Sir, when did Colonel Mattingly learn about this? Did General Gehlen go to him?"

After a just perceptible hesitation, Souers answered the question.

"Colonel Mattingly didn't learn what Captain Cronley was up to until after Orlovsky was in Argentina."

"What?" Ashton asked, shocked.

"Cronley got on the SIGABA and convinced Colonel Frade that if he got Orlovsky to Argentina, he was convinced he would be a very valuable intelligence asset in the future."

"And Cletus agreed with this wild hair?"

"Colonel Frade sent Father Welner, at Cronley's request, to Germany to try to convince Orlovsky that Cronley was telling the truth when he said they would not only set him up in a new life in Argentina, but that General Gehlen would make every effort to get Orlovsky's family out of the Soviet Union and to Argentina."

"Gehlen went along with this?"

"The officer whom many of his peers believe is a better intelligence officer than his former boss, Admiral Canaris, ever was, was in agreement with our Captain Cronley from the moment Cronley told him what he was thinking."

"So this Russian is now in Argentina?"

"Where he will become your responsibility once you get there. At the moment, he's in the Argerich military hospital in Buenos Aires, under the protection of the Argentine Bureau of Internal Security, recovering from injuries he received shortly after he arrived in Argentina."

"Injuries?"

"The car in which he was riding was attacked shortly

after it left the airport by parties unknown. They used machine guns and Panzerfausts—"

"What?"

"German rocket-propelled grenades."

"Then they were Germans?"

"The BIS—and Cletus Frade—believes they were Paraguayan criminals hired by the Russians. So does Colonel Sergei Likharev of the NKGB."

"Who?"

"When Major Orlovsky realized that the NKGB was trying to kill him, and probably would do something very unpleasant to his wife and kids if General Gehlen could not get them out of the Soviet Union, he fessed up that his name is really Likharev and that he is—or was—an NKGB colonel. And gave up the names of Gehlen's traitors."

"What happened to them?"

"You don't want to know, Colonel Ashton."

"So Cronley did the right thing."

"I don't think that Colonel Mattingly would agree that the ends justify the means."

"But you do?"

"On one hand, it is inexcusable that Cronley went around Mattingly. On the other hand, we now have Colonel Likharev singing like that proverbial canary. And on the same side of that scale, General Gehlen has gone out of his way to let me know in what high regard he holds Cronley and Dunwiddie. But let me finish this."

"Yes, sir."

"After Frade informed me that he believed Likharev had truly seen the benefits of turning, and that he believed he would be of enormous value to us in the future, I was willing to overlook Cronley's unorthodoxy. Then Cronley got on the SIGABA and sent me a long message stating that he considered it absolutely essential that when he is transferred to the DCI that he have another commissioned officer to back him up, and that he wanted First Sergeant Dunwiddie commissioned as a captain—he said no one pays any attention to lieutenants—to fill that role.

"My first reaction to the message, frankly, was 'Just who the hell does he think he is?' I decided that it probably would be unwise to leave him in command of the Pullach compound. I then telephoned General Gehlen, to ask how he would feel about Major Harold Wallace—do you know who I mean?"

Shaking his head, Ashton said, "No, sir."

"He was Mattingly's deputy in OSS Forward . . ."

"Now I do, sir."

"And is now commanding the Twenty-seventh CIC, which is the cover for the Twenty-third CIC, to which Cronley and Dunwiddie are assigned. You are familiar with all this?"

"Yes, sir."

"I asked General Gehlen how he would feel if I arranged for Major Wallace to take over command of the Pullach compound. He replied by asking if he could speak freely. I told him he could. He said that in the best of all possible worlds, he would prefer that Colonel Mattingly and Major Wallace have as little to do with Pullach as possible. When I asked why, he said that he regarded the greatest threat to the Pullach compound operation—in other words, to Operation Ost—not the Russians but the U.S. Army bureaucracy.

"In case you don't know, the Pentagon—the deputy chief of staff for intelligence—has assigned two officers, a lieu-

tenant colonel named Parsons and a major named Ashley—
to liaise with Operation Ost at Pullach."

"Frade told me that, but not the names."

"DCS-G2 thinks they should be running Operation Ost.
Both Parsons and Ashley outrank Captain Cronley. See the
problem?"

"Yes, sir."

"I thought it could be dealt with, since Mattingly, in the
Farben Building, is a full colonel and could handle Parsons,
and further that Wallace could better stand up to Parsons
and Ashley than Cronley could."

Ashton nodded his understanding.

"General Gehlen disagreed. He told me something I didn't
know, that First Sergeant Dunwiddie's godfather is General
White, and that in private Dunwiddie refers to General White
as 'Uncle Isaac.' And he reminded me of something I already
knew: The President of the United States looks fondly upon
Captain Cronley."

"How did Gehlen know that?"

"I don't know, but I have already learned not to underestimate General Reinhard Gehlen. Gehlen put it to me that
he felt Parsons was under orders to somehow take control
of Pullach, that Mattingly, who is interested in being taken
into the Regular Army, is not going to defy the general staff
of the U.S. Army.

"Gehlen put it to me that DCS-G2 taking over Operation
Ost would be a disaster—reaching as far up as the President—
inevitably about to happen. And I knew he was right."

"Jesus!"

"And he said he felt that because both Dunwiddie and
Cronley had friends in high places, they would be the best

people to defend Operation Ost from being swallowed by DCS-G2. And I realized Gehlen was right about that, too.

"General White is about to return to Germany from Fort Riley to assume command of the Army of Occupation police force, the U.S. Constabulary. I flew out to Fort Riley on Tuesday and talked this situation over with him. He's on board.

"On January second, the day after the Directorate of Central Intelligence is activated, certain military officers—you, for example, and Captains Cronley and Dunwiddie—"

"*Captain* Dunwiddie, sir?" Ashton interrupted.

"Sometime this week, First Sergeant Dunwiddie will be discharged for the convenience of the government for the purpose of accepting a commission as Captain, Cavalry, detail to Military Intelligence.

"As I was saying, Cronley and Dunwiddie—and now you—will be transferred to the Directorate. Colonel Mattingly and Major Wallace will remain assigned to Counterintelligence Corps duties. I told General Greene that Colonel Frade suggested that for the time being they would be of greater use in the CIC and that I agreed with him."

When it looked as if Ashton was going to reply, Admiral Souers said, "Were you listening, Colonel, when I told you you're going to have to learn to control your tendency to ask questions out loud that should not be asked out loud?"

"Yes, sir. But may I ask a question?"

Souers nodded.

"It looks to me as if the effect of all this is that in addition to all the problems Cronley's going to have with Operation Ost, he's going to have to deal with Colonel Parsons—the Pentagon G2—and Colonel Mattingly, and maybe this CIC general, Greene, all of whom are going to try to cut him off at the knees."

Souers did not reply either directly or immediately, but finally he said, "I hope what you have learned in our conversation will be useful both when you go to Germany and later in Buenos Aires."

"Yes, sir. It will be."

Souers met Ashton's eye for a long moment, then smiled and turned and started to walk out of the room.

[TWO]
Kloster Grünau
Schollbrunn, Bavaria
American Zone of Occupation, Germany
0330 22 December 1945

Senior Watch Chief Maksymilian Ostrowski, a tall, blond twenty-seven-year-old, who was chief supervisor of Detachment One, Company "A," 7002nd Provisional Security Organization, woke instantly when his wristwatch vibrated.

He had been sleeping, fully clothed in dyed-black U.S. Army "fatigues" and combat boots, atop Army olive-drab woolen blankets on his bed in his room in what had once been the priory of a medieval monastery and was now a . . . what?

Ostrowski wasn't sure exactly what Kloster Grünau should be called now. It was no longer a monastery and was now occupied by Americans. He had learned that the Americans were guarding—both at Kloster Grünau and in a village, Pullach, near Munich—nearly three hundred former Wehrmacht officers and enlisted men and their families. Both the monastery and the village were under the protection of a company of heavily armed American soldiers. All of them were Negroes, and they wore the shoulder insignia of the 2nd Armored Division.

Ostrowski was no stranger to military life, and he strongly suspected that it had to do with intelligence. Just what, he didn't know. What was important to him was his belief that if he did well what he was told to do, he wouldn't be rounded up and forced to return to what he was sure was at best imprisonment and most likely an unmarked mass grave in his native Poland.

He sometimes thought he had lived two previous lives and was on the cusp of a third. The first had been growing up in Poland as the son of a cavalry officer. He had graduated from the Szkola Rycerska military academy in 1939. He just had time to earn his pilot's wings in the Polish Air Force when Germany and Russia attacked Poland. That life had ended when his father died leading a heroically stupid cavalry charge against German tanks, and he and some other young pilots for whom there were no airplanes to fly had been flown to first France and then England.

Life Two had been World War II. By the time that ended, he was Kapitan Maksymilian Ostrowski, 404th Fighter Squadron, Free Polish Air Force. The watch that had woken him by vibrating on his wrist was a souvenir of that life. Fairly late in the war, he had been at a fighter base in France, waiting for the weather to clear so they could fly in support of the beleaguered 101st Airborne Division in Bastogne.

There had been a spectacular poker game with a mixed bag—Poles, Brits, and Americans—of fellow fighter pilots. He liked Americans, and not only because he could remind them that he wasn't the first Pole to come to the Americans' aid in a war. He'd tell them Casimir Pulaski was the first. He'd tell them Pulaski had been recruited by Benjamin Franklin in Paris, went to America, saved George Washington's life, and became a general in the Continental Army before dying of wounds suffered in battle.

This tale of Polish-American cooperation had not been of much consolation to one of the American pilots, who, convinced the cards he held were better than proved to be the case, had thrown a spectacular watch into the pot. It was a gold-cased civilian—not Air Corps–issued—Hamilton chronograph. It had an easily settable alarm function that caused it to vibrate at the selected time.

Ostrowski's four jacks and a king had taken the pot.

On the flight line at daybreak the next morning, just before they took off, the American had come to him and asked, if he could come up with three hundred dollars, would Ostrowski sell him the watch?

Ostrowski was already in love with the chronograph, so he knew why the American pilot wanted it back. Reluctantly, he agreed to sell it. The pilot said he'd have the cash for him when they came back.

He didn't come back. The American had gone in—either shot down or pilot error—just outside Bastogne.

In Life Two, Ostrowski had worn an RAF uniform with the insignia of a captain and a "Poland" patch sewn to the shoulder. As what he thought of as Life Three began, he was wearing dyed-black U.S. Army "fatigues" with shoulder patches reading *Wachmann* sewn to each shoulder. There was no insignia of rank, as the U.S. Army had not so far come up with rank insignia for the Provisional Security Organization.

The Provisional Security Organization was new. It had

been created by the European Command for several reasons, primary among them that EUCOM had a pressing need for manpower to guard its installations—especially supply depots—against theft by the German people, and the millions of displaced persons—"DPs"—who were on the edge of starvation.

There were not enough American soldiers available for such duties. Germans could not be used, as this would have meant putting weapons in the hands of the just defeated enemy. Neither, with one significant exception, could guards be recruited from the DPs.

That exception was former members of the Free Polish Army and Air Force. When they were hastily discharged after the war, so they could be returned to Poland, many—most—of them refused to go. The officers, especially, were familiar with what had happened to the Polish officer corps in the Katyn Forest. They had no intention of placing themselves at the mercy of the Red Army. So they joined the hordes of displaced persons.

When, at the demand of the Soviets, several hundred of them had been rounded up for forcible repatriation, some broke out of the transfer compounds and more than two hundred of them committed suicide. This enraged General Eisenhower, who decreed there would be no more forcible repatriations, and ordered that former Free Polish soldiers and airmen being held be released.

Then someone in the Farben Building realized that the thousands of former Free Polish military men who refused to be repatriated were the solution to the problem of providing guards for EUCOM's supply depots.

Over the bitter objections of the State Department, which

Eisenhower ignored, the Provisional Security Organization was quickly formed. Although nothing was promised but U.S. Army rations and quarters, the dyed-black fatigues and U.S. Army "combat boots," and a small salary—paid in reichsmarks, which were all but worthless—there were so many applicants for the PSO that the recruiters could be choosy.

Training of the first batch of guards—in whose ranks was former Kapitan Maksymilian Ostrowski—was conducted by the 508th Parachute Infantry Regiment in a former Wehrmacht *kaserne* in Griesheim, near Frankfurt am Main.

It consisted primarily in instruction in the use of the U.S. Carbine, Cal. .30, and the Model 1911A1 pistol, caliber .45 ACP, with which the PSO would be armed. There were lectures concerning the limits of their authority, the wearing of the uniform, and that sort of thing. The instruction syllabus called for seventy-four hours of classes. The classes took two weeks. There were 238 students in Class One-45.

Officers and non-coms were obviously going to be required for the PSO, and ranks were established, and then filled from the ranks of the students in the first class. Ostrowski was appointed a "watch chief"—which roughly corresponded to second lieutenant—more, he thought, because he spoke English well than because he had been a captain in the Free Polish Air Force.

Company "A," 7002nd Provisional Security Organization, had then been loaded onto U.S. Army six-by-six trucks and driven down the autobahn to Munich, and then along winding country roads to the village of Pullach.

There Ostrowski learned that the entire village had been commandeered by the U.S. Army for unspecified purposes. Army Engineers were installing a triple fence, topped by concertina barbed wire. The fence and the guard towers made the village look like a prison camp.

It was there that he had first seen the Negro troops assigned to guard whatever it was that needed guarding. They all seemed to be enormous. That they were really guarding something was evident. They constantly circled the village in jeeps that carried ready-to-fire .50-caliber machine guns, and there were similar weapons in the guard towers.

The initial mission of Company "A" had nothing to do with the security of the village—which the Americans called "the compound"—but rather the protection of the Engineers' supplies—of which there were mountains—and equipment.

Company "A" was provided with U.S. Army twelve-man squad tents and a mobile mess, and went to work.

Ostrowski was not happy with his new duties—he saw himself as sergeant of the guard, which was quite a comedown from being a captain flying Spitfires and Hurricanes—but he had food to eat, clean sheets, and he thought it highly unlikely he would be rounded up for forcible repatriation.

Then, a week after they had moved to Pullach—the day he saw a GI sign painter preparing a sign that read GENERAL-BÜROS SÜD-DEUTSCHE INDUSTRIELLE ENTWICKLUNGSOR-GANISATION and wondered what the South German Industrial Development Organization might be—it was announced that Company "A" had been given the additional duty of guarding a monastery in Schollbrunn, in the Bavarian Alps. Promoted to senior watch chief, Ostrowski was put in charge of a sixty-man detachment, which was then trucked to Kloster Grünau.

There, he reported to the American in charge, a Mr. Cronley, who appeared to be in his early twenties, and his staff.

These were two enormous black men wearing 2nd Armored Division shoulder patches. One wore the sleeve insignia of a first sergeant and the other that of a technical sergeant. There was also a plump little man who was introduced as Mr. Hessinger.

Ostrowski had thought he had solved the mystery of what was going on. Both Mr. Cronley and Mr. Hessinger were in civilian attire. That is, they were wearing U.S. Army uniforms—Cronley the standard olive-drab Ike jacket and trousers, and Hessinger the more elegant officer's green tunic and pink trousers—but carrying no insignia of rank or branch of service. Instead, sewn to their lapels were small embroidered triangles around the letters *US*.

They were military policemen, Ostrowski quickly decided. More specifically, they were CID, which stood for Criminal Investigation Division, and who were, so to speak, the plain-clothes detectives of the Military Police Force. What was being constructed at Pullach was to be a military prison. It all fit. The three lines of fences, the guard towers, the floodlights, and as absolute proof, all those enormous Negro troops. They practically had "Prison Guard" tattooed on their foreheads.

"If you don't speak English," Mr. Cronley had begun the meeting, "I'm going to have a problem telling you what's going on here."

"I speak English, sir," Ostrowski said.

"And German, maybe?" the chubby little man asked in German.

He was, Ostrowski guessed, a German Jew who had some-how avoided the death camps and somehow become an American.

"Yes. And Russian. And, of course, Polish."

"That problem out of the way, what do we call you?" Mr. Cronley asked.

"My name is Maksymilian Ostrowski, sir."

"That's an unworkable mouthful," Cronley said. "It says here you're a senior watch chief. What the hell is that?"

"I believe it is equivalent to U.S. Army first lieutenant, sir."

Cronley had raised his right hand, as a priest giving a blessing does, and announced, "Since I can pronounce this, I christen thee Lieutenant Max. Go and sin no more."

"Jesus, Jim!" the enormous black first sergeant protested. But he was smiling.

"Any objections?" Cronley asked.

"No, sir."

"Any other officers in your organization?"

"Yes, sir. There is one who served as a tank lieutenant with the Free French."

"Okay. Then you and he will bunk and mess with us," Cronley said. "Sergeant Tedworth"—Cronley pointed to the technical sergeant—"who is Number Two to First Sergeant Dunwiddie"—Cronley pointed to the first sergeant—"who is my Number Two, will show you where your men will be quartered. I hope you brought somebody who can cook with you?"

"Yes, sir."

"You will answer to Sergeant Tedworth," Cronley went on. "You have any problems with that?"

Does he mean because I'm an officer?

"No, sir."

"Okay. Freddy, you go with Tedworth and Lieutenant Max and show them where they'll be. Then send Lieutenant

Max back here. If you find someone who can translate for Tedworth . . . Abraham Lincoln speaks German, Max, but not Polish . . ."

"Abraham Lincoln"? Oh, he means Sergeant Tedworth.

". . . Hessinger speaks Russian and tells me that's close to Polish. If there are no translation problems, Freddy, you come back. If there are, stay and translate. But send Lieutenant Max back. I need to bring him up to speed on what's going on around here ten minutes ago."

Mr. Hessinger nodded.

Twenty minutes later, Hessinger and Ostrowski had come back into what Ostrowski was to learn was called the "officers' mess." Cronley and Dunwiddie were sitting at a bar drinking beer.

"No translation problems?" Cronley asked.

"Between the Poles who speak German and Tedworth's guys who do likewise, no problem," Hessinger reported.

"Do you drink beer, Max?" Cronley asked.

"Yes, sir."

"Then you better have one before I tell you how close you'll be to getting shot working here."

What did he say?

Cronley gestured to Hessinger, who went behind the bar, found bottles of Löwenbräu and mugs, and handed one of each to Ostrowski.

"Tell me, Max, how you came to speak the King's English?"

"I spent the war years in England."

"Doing what?"

"I was in the Free Polish Air Force."

"Doing what?"

"Flying. Mostly Spitfires and Hurricanes."

"And then they wanted you to go back to Poland and you didn't want to go, and so became a DP. Is that about it?"

"Yes, sir."

"How do you feel about Germans, Max? Straight answer, please."

"I fought a war against them, Mr. Cronley."

"In other words, you don't like them very much?"

"Yes, sir."

"And the Russians? How do you feel about them?"

"I like them even less than the Germans."

"You ever hear of the Katyn Forest?"

"That's one of the reasons I didn't think it was wise for me to go home."

"What we're running here is a classified—a highly classified—operation. I'm not supposed to tell someone like yourself anything at all about it. But I don't see how you can do your job at all, much less well, until I tell you something about it."

"Yes, sir."

"So I'm going to tell you some things about it. Prefacing what I'm going to tell you by saying we're authorized to protect the security of this operation by any means, including the taking of life. Do you understand what I'm saying? And if you do, should I continue, or would you prefer to be sent back to Pullach? There would be no shame, or whatever, if you don't want to stay. I personally guarantee that you won't be forcibly repatriated if you choose to go back to Pullach. Think it over carefully."

My God, he's serious! What the hell is going on here? What am I letting myself in for?

After a long moment, Ostrowski came to attention and said, "I am at your orders, sir."

"Anybody got anything to say before I start this?" Cronley asked.

No one did.

"What we're doing here is protecting a substantial number of former German officers and enlisted men from the Russians, and from those Germans and others sympathetic to the Soviet Union," Cronley said.

When there was no reply, he went on: "Eventually, just about all of them will be moved to the Pullach compound. That process is already under way. Any questions so far?"

"May I ask why you're protecting them from the Russians?"

"No. And don't ask again. And make sure your men understand that asking that sort of question is something they just are not allowed to do. If they do, that will ensure immediate and drastic punishment. You can consider that your first order. Get that done as soon as possible."

"Tedworth's probably already done that," Hessinger said.

"Even if Sergeant Tedworth has already gotten into the subject, I want the warning to come from Lieutenant Max."

"Yes, sir."

"I think I should tell you, Lieutenant," Dunwiddie said, "without getting into details, that there already have been a number of deaths—"

"Two yesterday," Hessinger chimed in.

Dunwiddie gave him a withering look and went on: "—directly related to security breaches, attempted and successful, of this operation," Dunwiddie finished.

"The Russians have a very good idea of what's going on

in here," Cronley said. "We already have caught an NKGB colonel as he tried to sneak out of here with information given to him by German traitors. Your mission will be to augment the American soldiers—we call them 'Tiny's Troopers'—who have been guarding Kloster Grünau and are in the process of establishing security at the Pullach compound."

"Sir, may I ask a question?"

"Ask away, but don't be surprised if I reply you don't have the need to know."

"Sir, I understand. My question—questions, actually— are can we expect further attempts by the Reds to gain entrance to either place?"

"I think you can bet your ass they will," Cronley said.

"You said 'questions,' plural, Lieutenant?" Hessinger asked.

"Are there still the traitors inside you mentioned?"

Cronley answered carefully. "The NKGB colonel and the traitors he was dealing with are no longer a problem . . ."

My God, he means they have been "dealt with."

Which means killed.

". . . but we have to presume (a) there are more of them, and (b) that the NKGB will continue to attempt to contact them."

"I understand," Ostrowski said.

"I hope so," Cronley said.

Even as he spoke the word "understand," Ostrowski had thought that he not only understood what Cronley was telling him, but that his Third Life had really begun.

I've stumbled onto something important.

What I will be guarding here and at Pullach is not going to be what I expected—mountains of canned tomatoes and hundred-pound bags of rice in a Quartermaster Depot—but something of great importance to the U.S. Army and, by inference, the United States itself.

And, whatever it is, it's just getting started.

And if I play my cards right, I can get my foot on the first step of that ladder of opportunity everybody's always talking about.

And the way to start playing my cards right is to become the best lieutenant of the guard not only in Detachment One, Company "A," 7002nd Provisional Security Organization, but in the entire goddamned Provisional Security Organization.

Each night, Senior Watch Chief Ostrowski set his Hamilton chronograph to vibrate at a different time between midnight and six in the morning. He selected the hour by throwing a die on his bedside table. The first roll last night had come up three. That meant three o'clock. The second roll had come up three again. That meant, since three-sixths of sixty minutes is thirty, that he should set the Hamilton to vibrate at three thirty.

Next came the question of whether to get undressed, and then dress when the watch vibrated, or to nap clothed on top of the blankets. He opted in favor of not getting undressed.

When he was wakened, he did not turn on the bedside lamp. He was absolutely sure that at least one, and probably three, of his guards were watching his window so they could alert the others that Maksymilian the Terrible was awake and about to inspect the guard posts.

Instead, he made his way into the bath he shared with First Sergeant Dunwiddie—they were now on a "Tiny and Max" basis—and dressed there. First he put on a dyed-black U.S. Army field jacket, around which he put on a web belt that supported a holstered Model 1911A1 pistol. Then, since it had been snowing earlier in the evening and the ground was white, he put on a white poncho.

Then, without turning on any lights, using a red-filtered U.S. Army flashlight, he made his way downstairs and out of the building.

The Poles were guarding the outer perimeter, and sharing the guarding of the area between it and the second line of fences with Tiny's Troopers. The inner perimeter was guarded by the Americans only.

Twenty yards from the building, he saw the faint glow of another red-filtered flashlight, and quickly turned his own flashlight off. Fifty yards farther toward the inner fence, he saw that Technical Sergeant Tedworth, dressed as he was, was holding the other flashlight.

He wasn't surprised, as he knew Tedworth habitually checked the guards in the middle of the night. He also knew that Tedworth usually went to the outer perimeter to check the Poles first. It looked as if that's what he was up to now, so Ostrowski followed him.

If Tedworth found nothing wrong—one of the Poles, for example, hiding beside or inside something to get out of the icy winds—Ostrowski planned to do nothing. Tedworth would know the Poles were doing what they were supposed to do and that was enough.

If, however, Tedworth found a Pole seeking shelter from the cold—or worse, asleep—Ostrowski would then appear to take the proper disciplinary action himself. Tedworth would see not only that Ostrowski was on the job, but also that Maksymilian the Terrible could "eat ass" just about as well as Technical Sergeant Tedworth.

He had been following Tedworth for about ten minutes when the red glow of Tedworth's flashlight suddenly turned white. There was now a beam of white light pointed inward from the outer perimeter fence toward the second.

Ostrowski hurried to catch up.

He heard Tedworth bellow, "Halt! *Hände nach oben!*"

Ostrowski started running toward him, fumbling as he did to unholster his pistol.

Another figure appeared, dressed in dark clothing, approaching Tedworth in a crouch. Before Ostrowski could shout a warning, the man was on Tedworth. Tedworth's flashlight went flying as the man pulled him back.

Ostrowski remembered, cursing, that he had not chambered a round in the .45, and stopped running just long enough to work the action.

He could now see three men: Tedworth, now flailing around on the ground, the man who had knocked him over . . .

He looped something around Tedworth's throat. Probably a wire garrote.

. . . and another man in dark clothing who had come from the second line of wire.

Ostrowski was now ten meters from them, and was sure they hadn't seen him. He dropped to a kneeling position and, holding the .45 with both hands, fired first at the man wrestling with Tedworth, hitting him, and then as the second man looked at him, let off a shot at his head, which missed, and then a second shot at his torso, which connected.

Then he ran the rest of the way to the three men on the ground.

The man who had been wrestling with Tedworth was now reaching for something in his clothing. Ostrowski shot him twice. The man he had shot in the torso looked up at him with surprise on his face. His eyes were open but they were no longer seeing anything.

Blood was spurting from Tedworth's neck, and as Ostrowski watched, Tedworth finally got his fingers under the wire that had been choking him and jerked it off his body.

Tedworth looked at Ostrowski.

"Jesus H. Christ!" he said, spewing blood from his mouth.

"You're bleeding. We've got to get a compress on your neck," Ostrowski said.

Tedworth reached for his neck again and again jerked something loose. It was a cavalry-yellow scarf.

"Use this," he said. "It probably kept me alive."

Then he added, disgust oozing from his voice, "If you hadn't showed up, these cocksuckers would have got me!"

"Just lie there," Ostrowski ordered. "Hold the scarf against your neck. I'll go for help."

That didn't prove to be necessary. As he stood up, he saw first the light from three flashlights heading toward him, and then the headlights of a jeep.

II

[ONE]
The South German Industrial Development
Organization Compound
Pullach, Bavaria
The American Zone of Occupied Germany
1605 28 December 1945

A neat sign on the small snow-covered lawn of the small house identified it as the Military Government Liaison Office.

There were four rooms on the ground floor of the building and a large, single room on the second. The military government liaison officer—which was one of the cover titles Captain Cronley was going to use—lived there. A bathroom had been added to the second floor when the U.S. Army Corps of Engineers had hastily converted the village of Pullach into the South German Industrial Development Organization Compound.

The original bathroom on the ground floor and the kitchen had been upgraded to American standards at the same time. The main room on the ground floor held office furnishings. A smaller room provided a private office for the military government liaison officer. There was a small dining room next to the kitchen, and a smaller room with a sign reading LIBRARY held a substantial safe and a desk holding a SIGABA system. This was a communications device, the very existence of which was classified Secret. It provided secure, encrypted communication between Pullach, Kloster Grünau, Berlin, Washington, D.C., and Mendoza and Buenos Aires, Argentina.

There were five men in the downstairs office: Major Harold Wallace, a trim thirty-two-year-old wearing "pinks and greens"; James D. Cronley Jr.; First Sergeant Chauncey L. Dunwiddie, who like Cronley was wearing an olive-drab Ike jacket and trousers; Sergeant Friedrich Hessinger, in pinks and greens whose lapels bore small embroidered triangles with the letters *US* in their centers; and finally, a civilian, a slight, pale-faced forty-three-year-old with a prominent thin nose, piercing eyes, and a receding hairline. His name was Reinhard Gehlen, and he was wearing an ill-fitting, on-the-edge-of-ragged suit. As a generalmajor of the Oberkommando of the Wehrmacht, Gehlen had been chief of Abwehr Ost, the German intelligence agency dealing with the "Ost," which meant the East, and in turn the Union of Soviet Socialist Republics.

Gehlen and Cronley were sitting in upholstered chairs, drinking coffee. Major Wallace and First Sergeant Dunwiddie were seated at one of the desks as Hessinger hovered over them, like a schoolteacher tutoring backward students, as they signed sheafs of forms.

Finally, Hessinger proclaimed, "That's it. You are now a civilian and can no longer say cruel and unkind things to me."

He spoke with a thick, somewhat comical German accent. A German Jew, he had escaped Nazi Germany and gone to the United States in 1938. Shortly after his graduation, summa cum laude, from Harvard College, he had been drafted. Physically unable to qualify for an officer's commission, he had been assigned to the Counterintelligence Corps and sent to Germany, where it was believed he would be very useful in running down Nazis and bringing them to trial.

He was now doing something quite different.

"Aw, come on, Fat Freddy, my little dumpling," Dunwiddie said, skillfully mocking Hessinger's thick accent, "when have I ever said anything cruel or unkind to you?"

Cronley laughed out loud. Major Wallace and General Gehlen tried, and failed, not to smile.

"Whenever have you not?" Hessinger said. "Now can I trust you to deliver these documents to General Greene's sergeant? Or am I going to have to send them by courier?"

"Freddy," Cronley asked, "why couldn't we have done what you just did tomorrow in the Farben Building? For that matter, why does this civilian have to go to Frankfurt to have Greene pin on his bars?"

"Because you can't be commissioned the day you get discharged as an enlisted man. That's what the regulations say. General Greene's sergeant was very specific about that, and when I checked, he was right. And he said General Greene thought it would be a nice thing for him to do."

And it will also serve to remind everybody that he's a general and I'm a brand-new captain.

"Maybe Colonel Mattingly will be there," Cronley said. "Maybe we can ask him to pin on your bars. I'd love to see that."

"Let that go, Jim," Dunwiddie said. "If it doesn't bother me, why are you bothered?"

"Because I am a champion of the underdog, and in particular of the retarded underdog."

"You guys better get down to the *bahnhof* if you're going to catch the Blue Danube," Major Wallace said.

The Blue Danube was the military train that ran daily in each direction between Vienna and Berlin.

"We're not taking the Blue Danube," Cronley said.

"Why not?"

"Two reasons. One, I can't afford to take two days off just so this fat civilian can get his bars pinned on by General Greene."

"And two?"

"General Gehlen cannot ride the Blue Danube. Americans only."

"You're taking General Gehlen?"

"We're going to drive to Kloster Grünau, where I have some things to do. In the morning, we're going to fly to Eschborn. There, if I can trust Freddy, we will be met by a vehicle assigned to the 711th Quartermaster Mess Kit Repair Company, which will transport us to the Farben Building. That is set in concrete, right, Freddy?"

"The ambulance will be at Eschborn," Hessinger confirmed.

"You're asking for trouble with those mess kit repair bumper markings on those ambulances, Jim," Major Wallace said.

"The bumpers read MKRC. It's not spelled out."

"And if some MP gets first curious and then nasty?"

"Then I will dazzle him with my CIC credentials," Cronley said. "Which is another reason I'm going to Frankfurt. I want to ask General Greene about not only keeping the credentials after January second but getting more, so I can give them to half a dozen of Tiny's guys."

"Does Colonel Mattingly know you're bringing the general with you?"

"No, he doesn't," Cronley said simply. And then went on, "After Tiny becomes an officer, we will all get back in the ambulance, go back to Eschborn, get back in the Storch, and come back here. God willing, and if the creek don't rise, we should be back before it gets dark."

When Cronley, Gehlen, and Dunwiddie were in the car—an Opel Kapitän, now painted olive drab and bearing Army markings—Dunwiddie said, "You didn't tell Major Wallace about what happened at Kloster Grünau."

"You noticed, huh?"

"You going to tell me why not?"

"First of all, nothing happened at Kloster Grünau. Write that down."

"You mean two guys we strongly suspect were NKGB agents penetrated Kloster Grünau, tried to kill Tedworth, were killed by Ostrowski, and then buried in unmarked graves, that 'nothing'?"

"If I had told Wallace about that incident that never happened, he would have felt duty bound to tell Mattingly. Mattingly, to cover his ass, would have brought this to the attention of at least Greene, and maybe the EUCOM G2. A platoon of EUCOM brass, all with Top Secret clearances, all of whom are curious as hell about Kloster Grünau, would descend on our monastery to investigate the incident. It would be both a waste of time and would compromise Operation Ost. As Captain Cronley of the Twenty-third CIC, I can't tell them to butt out. So I didn't tell Wallace. Okay?"

"Okay. Incident closed."

"Not quite. I haven't figured out what to do with Ostrowski."

"Meaning?"

"That I haven't figured out what to do about . . . or with him."

"For example?"

"You do hang on like a starving dog does to a bone, don't you, Mr. Dunwiddie?"

"What are you thinking?"

"Among other things, he could fly one of our Storchs. He used to fly Spitfires."

"That would mean we would have an ex-Luftwaffe pilot and a Polish DP flying airplanes we're not supposed to have in the first place. And among what other things?"

"The OSS used to have civilian employees. Maybe the Directorate of Central Intelligence can."

"Interesting thought," General Gehlen said. "Ostrowski is an interesting man."

"With all respect, sir," Dunwiddie said, "whenever you and Captain Cronley agree on something, I worry."

[TWO]
Office of the Chief, Counterintelligence Corps
Headquarters, European Command
The I.G. Farben Building
Frankfurt am Main
American Zone of Occupation, Germany
1145 29 December 1945

Major Thomas G. Derwin, who was thirty-four, five feet ten, weighed 165 pounds, and to whose green tunic lapels were pinned the crossed rifles of Infantry and whose shoulder bore the embroidered insignia of Army Ground Forces, pushed open the door under the sign identifying the suite of offices of the chief, Counterintelligence Corps, European Command.

Derwin was carrying two canvas suitcases, called Valv-Paks. He set them down just inside the door and looked around the office. There were four people in it. One of them, sitting behind a desk, was a Women's Army Corps—WAC—chief warrant officer, an attractive woman in her late twenties. She was wearing the female version of pinks and greens—a green tunic over a pink skirt.

The three men were wearing OD Ike jackets and trousers. One of them was a stocky, nearly bald master sergeant. He was sitting behind a desk next to the WAC's desk. Sitting slumped in chairs before the master sergeant's desk were a captain—a good-looking young guy—and an enormous black man whose uniform was bare of any insignia of rank.

As they rose to their feet, Derwin realized he knew the captain.

Cronley, he thought. *James D. Cronley Jr. I had him in a*

Techniques of Surveillance class at Holabird. They were so short of officers in Germany that they pulled him out of school and sent him over here before he finished. Then I saw him again at the officers' club at Holabird a couple of months ago. He said he was in the States as an escort officer for some classified material.

And then, immediately, Derwin knew he was wrong.

What the hell. I've just spent twenty-six hours flying over here. Brain-wise, I'm not functioning on all six cylinders. Which is not going to help me when I meet my new boss. First impressions do matter. That captain is not Cronley. Cronley's a second lieutenant. Amazing physical resemblance.

"May I help you, sir?" the master sergeant asked.

"I'm Major Derwin, Sergeant. Reporting for duty."

"Yes, sir, we've been expecting you," the WAC said. "I'll let the general know you're here."

She went to an interior door and pushed it open.

"General, Major Derwin is here."

"Captain," Derwin asked, "has anyone ever told you that you bear a striking resemblance to a second lieutenant named Cronley?"

"Yes, sir," the captain said, smiling. "I've heard that."

A stocky, forty-three-year-old officer with a crew cut appeared in the inner office door. His olive-drab uniform had the single star of a brigadier general on its epaulets.

That has to be my new boss, Brigadier General H. Paul Greene, chief, Counterintelligence, European Command.

And he looks like the tough sonofabitch everybody says he is.

General Greene looked at the WAC.

"Why didn't you tell me these two were here?"

The captain answered for her.

"We're waiting for General Gehlen, sir. He said he'd like to be present, and I thought it was a nice gesture on his part, so I brought him along."

Did he say "General Gehlen"? Not, certainly, General-major Reinhard Gehlen?

"And where is General Gehlen?"

"As we tried to sneak in the back door, General Smith's convoy rolled up," Captain Cronley replied. "He asked the general if he had a few minutes for him, and of course General Gehlen did."

General Smith? General Walter Bedell Smith, chief of staff to General of the Army Dwight D. Eisenhower, commander in chief, European Command?

"And that surprised you?" General Greene said, chuckling.

"No, sir, it did not."

"You're Derwin?"

"Yes, sir, I'm Major Derwin."

The general's face showed he was thinking.

"Okay, everybody come in," he said finally. "They call that 'killing two birds with one stone.'"

He turned and they followed him into the office.

There was an elegantly turned out, handsome colonel of Armor slouched on a couch before a coffee table. He wore a green Ike jacket over pink trousers. His trousers were pulled up high enough to reveal highly polished Tanker boots.

The general went behind his desk.

Derwin marched up to it, came to attention, and saluted.

"Sir, Major Thomas G. Derwin reporting for duty."

The general returned the salute, said, "You may stand at

ease," then extended his hand. "Welcome to EUCOM CIC, Major. How was the flight?"

The general gestured for the captain to sit, and he did so, in an armchair at one end of the coffee table.

"Long and noisy, sir."

"I am having symptoms of caffeine deficiency," the general said, raising his voice.

"Antidote on the way, General," a female voice called.

A moment later, the WAC chief warrant officer pushed a wheeled tray holding a silver coffee service into the room.

"We can pour our own coffee, Alice—or get Cronley to pour it . . ."

Did he say Cronley?

". . . and then no calls except from the Command Group. When General Gehlen appears, show him in."

"Yes, sir," the WAC officer said.

"Cronley, what's Gehlen doing here?" the Armor colonel asked, somewhat unpleasantly.

"He said that he'd like to be present, so I brought him along."

"Was that necessary?" the colonel asked.

"I thought it was appropriate," Cronley replied.

The colonel doesn't like Captain Cronley. And Cronley— twice—didn't append "sir" when replying to the colonel's questions.

But he—and Greene—let him get away with it.

"Bob, this is Major Derwin. Major, this is Colonel Robert Mattingly, my deputy," the general said.

"Welcome to EUCOM, Major," Mattingly said, and offered his hand.

"Coffee, Cronley, coffee," General Greene said.

"Yes, sir," Cronley said. He stood up and started pouring coffee for everybody.

When he got to Derwin, Derwin asked, "Have we met, Captain?"

"Yes, sir," Cronley said.

"At Holabird?"

"Yes, sir."

The sonofabitch is smiling. What's so funny?

The master sergeant appeared at the door.

"Sir," he announced, "Generals Smith and Gehlen."

General Smith, a tall, trim, erect officer who was in ODs, and General Gehlen walked into the office. Everyone rose and stood to attention.

I'll be damned, Derwin thought. *That is him, General-major Reinhard Gehlen, former chief of Abwehr Ost, the intelligence agency of the German high command, dealing with the Ost . . . which meant the Russians.*

What the hell is he doing here?

With General Walter Bedell Smith, Ike's Number Two?

What's going on here?

"Rest, gentlemen, please," Smith said. "General Gehlen just told me what he was doing in Frankfurt, and I invited myself to the ceremony. I hope that's all right."

"Yes, sir, of course," General Greene said, not quite succeeding in concealing his surprise.

General Smith turned to Captain Cronley.

"Cronley, right?"

"Yes, sir."

"I had no idea who you were, Captain, just now at the rear entrance. Until General Eisenhower corrected me a few minutes ago, I thought the Captain Cronley who is to be chief, DCI-Europe, was going to be a barnacle-encrusted naval officer formerly on Admiral Souers's staff."

General Greene and Colonel Mattingly dutifully chuckled at General Smith's wit.

Major Derwin wondered, *What the hell is DCI-Europe? And who the hell is Admiral Souers?*

"No, sir. I'm just a simple, and junior, cavalryman."

"Well, you may be junior, Captain, but you're not simple. General Eisenhower also told me the circumstances of your recent promotion. I'm pleased to make your acquaintance."

He offered Cronley his hand.

"Yes, sir," Cronley said.

General Smith turned to the enormous black man.

"Now to the second case of mistaken identity," he said, and then asked, "Son, are you still a first sergeant?"

"Sir, at the moment I'm sort of in limbo. I was discharged yesterday."

He spoke softly in a very deep voice.

"Then I will call you what I used to call your father," General Smith said, "when, in the age of the dinosaurs, I was his company commander and your dad was one of my second lieutenants: Tiny."

"That's fine with me, sir."

"Tiny, I had no idea until just now, when General Gehlen told me, that you were even in the Army, much less what you've done and what you're about to do. Just as soon as things slow down a little, you're going to have to come to dinner. My wife remembers you as a tiny—well, maybe not tiny—infant."

"That's very kind of you, sir."

"Homer, where the hell is the photographer?"

A full colonel, wearing the insignia of an aide-de-camp to a four-star general, stepped into the office.

"Anytime you're ready for him, General," he said.

The general waved the photographer, a plump corporal carrying a Speed Graphic press camera, into the room.

"What's the protocol for this, Homer?" General Smith asked.

"First, the insignia is pinned to his epaulets, sir . . ."

"General Greene can do the left and I'll do the right," General Smith said.

"And then he takes the oath with his hand on a Bible."

"So then we need a Bible and a copy of the oath," General Smith said.

"I know the oath, sir," Dunwiddie said.

"And here's the Bible," the WAC officer said, "and the bars."

"And your role in this, Corporal," General Smith said, "is to take pictures. You ready?"

"Yes, sir."

"Which we will send to your parents, Tiny."

"Thank you, sir."

"And—I'm glad I thought of this—to General Isaac Davis White, your father's classmate at Norwich."

"That's a marvelous idea, General," Cronley said.

"Excuse me?"

"I understand, sir, that General White thought Tiny should have been commissioned a long time ago."

As he spoke, Cronley looked at Colonel Mattingly. Mattingly glared icily at him. Major Derwin picked up on it.

What the hell is that all about?

Flashbulbs exploded as Smith and Greene pinned the twin silver bars of a captain—known as "railroad tracks"—to Dunwiddie's epaulets.

"Who holds the Bible?" General Smith inquired. "What about that, Homer?"

"That's not prescribed, sir. Sometimes a wife, or a mother, or even somebody else."

"Sir," Dunwiddie asked, "what about Captain Cronley?"

"That'd work."

CWO Alice McGrory handed the Bible to Captain Cronley. He stood between Generals Smith and Greene and held the Bible up to him.

"Anytime you're ready, Tiny," General Smith said.

Dunwiddie laid his left hand on the Bible and raised his right.

"I, Chauncey Luther Dunwiddie," he boomed in a basso profundo voice, "having been appointed captain . . ."

He paused just perceptibly, and then continued slowly, pronouncing each syllable, ". . . in the United States Army, do solemnly swear that I will support and defend the Constitution of the United States against all enemies, foreign and domestic; that I will bear true faith and allegiance to the same; that I take this obligation freely, without any mental reservation or purpose of evasion; and that I will well and faithfully discharge the office upon which I am about to enter." He paused a final time, and then proclaimed, "So help me God!"

There was a moment's silence.

"I must have heard people take that oath a thousand times," General Smith said. "But never quite like that. Very impressive, Tiny. Moving." He paused. "Permit me to be first,

Captain Dunwiddie, to welcome you into the officer corps of the United States Army."

He extended his hand, and Dunwiddie took it, said, "Thank you, sir." Then he asked, "Permission to speak, sir?"

Smith nodded and said, "Granted."

"Sir, as the general will understand, this moment is of great personal importance to the captain. The captain would very much like to have a memento of General Gehlen being here."

Smith's face tensed, and it was a long moment before he replied.

"Frankly, Captain, my initial reaction was to deny that request. But on reflection I realized that a photograph of us with General Gehlen among us ranks pretty low on the list of highly classified material with which you are already entrusted.

"General Gehlen, if you would, please stand here with us," General Smith went on. Then he turned to the photographer. "Corporal, the photograph you are about to take, the negatives and prints thereof, will be classified Top Secret–Presidential. You will personally develop the negative. You will then make four eight-by-ten-inch prints from the negative. You will then burn the negative. You will see that I get two of those prints, one of which I will send to Admiral Souers, and the other to General White. You will also give two prints to General Greene, who will get them to Captain Dunwiddie. You understand all that, son, or should I go over it again?"

Who the hell, Major Derwin again wondered, *is Admiral Souers?*

"I understand, sir."

"And I don't want you telling the boys in the photo lab anything about this. Clear?"

"Yes, sir."

"All right, gentlemen," General Smith said, "stand tall and say 'Cheese.'"

Ninety seconds later, General Smith and his entourage were gone.

"Let me add my 'welcome to the officer corps of the United States Army' to General Smith's, Captain Dunwiddie," General Greene said.

"Thank you, sir."

"And mine," Colonel Mattingly said, without much enthusiasm.

"Thank you, sir," Dunwiddie repeated.

"What I'm going to do now is bring Major Derwin up to speed on what's going on around here. You're welcome to stay for that, of course."

"I think we can pass on that, sir," Captain Cronley said.

"It's always a pleasure to see you, General," Greene said.

"Thank you," Gehlen said.

Cronley stood to attention.

"Permission to withdraw, sir?"

"Post," Greene said.

Cronley saluted, did an about-face movement, and started for the door. He waved General Gehlen and Captain Dunwiddie ahead of him and then followed them out of the office.

Colonel Mattingly stood up.

"If you don't need me, sir?"

"I think it would be best if you stuck around for this, Bob," Greene said.

"Yes, sir. Of course," Colonel Mattingly said, and sat down.

"I suppose the best place to start, Major, is to tell you that what just transpired in here is classified. Twice. Maybe three times. First as Top Secret–Presidential. And as Top Secret–Lindbergh. And of course as simple Top Secret. You got that?"

"Yes, sir."

"All of that also applies to what I'm going to tell you now. And the best place to start that is at the beginning.

"On December twenty-first, Lieutenant Colonel Anthony Schumann, who was the inspector general of European Command CIC, and also of the Army Security Agency, Europe—which reports to the ASA in Washington through me, I think I should tell you—went home for lunch. Moments after he arrived, as well as we can put things together, there was an explosion. Apparently, the gas water heater had leaked, filled the house with gas, and something set it off. Maybe Mrs. Schumann lit the stove. We just don't know. There was a considerable explosion, which totally destroyed his quarters and severely damaged the houses on either side and across the street."

"My God!" Derwin said.

"And killed Colonel and Mrs. Schumann. Phrased as delicately as possible, there will have to be a closed-casket funeral. Tony Schumann was a fine officer and a close friend. A true tragedy.

"Obviously a replacement was necessary. There were several reasons why I had to go outside EUCOM CIC for a replacement. One is that, as I'm sure you know, we are very short of officers. We are even shorter of officers with the proper security clearances. A Top Secret clearance, dealing with what we're dealing with here, is as common as a Confidential clearance elsewhere.

"So I appointed Major James B. McClung, the ASA Europe Chief . . . you know who I mean?"

"Is that 'Iron Lung' McClung, sir?"

Greene nodded and went on.

". . . to temporarily add the duties of IG to all the other things on his plate. He was—is—the only officer available to me with the Top Secret–Lindbergh and Top Secret–Presidential clearances. Then I called Admiral Souers—"

"Excuse me, sir. Who?"

"Rear Admiral Sidney W. Souers," Greene answered, paused, and then said, "Well, let's deal with that. Have you heard the rumors that there will be a successor organization to the Office of Strategic Services?"

"Yes, sir."

"Well, let me give you the facts. Shortly after the President put the OSS out of business, he reconsidered the wisdom of that decision. There were certain operations of the OSS that had to be kept running, for one thing, and for another, Admiral Souers told me, he came to recognize the nation needed an intelligence organization, with covert and clandestine capabilities, that could not be tied down by putting it under either the Pentagon or the FBI. It had to report directly to him. More precisely, to the President.

"On January first, the President will sign an Executive Order establishing the Directorate of Central Intelligence, and name Admiral Souers as its director. Admiral Souers has been assigned to the Office of Naval Intelligence. But, he's been more than that. When the President realized that certain clandestine operations started by the OSS and which could not be turned off like a lightbulb needed someone to run them until he decided what to do about them, he turned to Admiral Souers. It is germane to note that the President and the admiral are close personal friends.

"Further, when the President realized there had to be a successor organization to the OSS, and that there were, for him, insurmountable problems in naming General Donovan to be its director, and that he did not want the Pentagon to have its man in that position, or someone who owed his allegiance to FBI Director J. Edgar Hoover, he again turned to Admiral Souers.

"Colonel Mattingly, would you like to add to, or comment upon, what I just told Major Derwin?"

"No, sir. I think you covered everything."

"Feel free to interrupt me at any time, Bob."

"Thank you, sir."

"As I was saying, when Colonel Schumann . . . was taken from us, I needed someone who could be given Presidential and Lindbergh clearances, and I needed him right away, so I called Admiral Souers and explained the problem. He said he would take the matter up personally with the G2 of the Army. He called back the next day, told me the G2 had proposed three officers and given him access to their dossiers, and he felt you best met our requirements. He proposed sending you over here immediately to see if Colonel Mattingly and I agreed.

"Which brings us to Colonel Mattingly. Mattingly was OSS. In the last months of the war, he was chief, OSS Forward. When the OSS was put out of business, he was assigned to me, to EUCOM CIC, as my deputy."

"And now the colonel will be in this reconstituted OSS, the Directorate of Central Intelligence?"

"No. And please permit me to do the talking, Major," Greene said. "But since we have started down that road: At Admiral Souers's request—when he speaks, he speaks with the authority of the President—Headquarters, War Department, has tasked EUCOM CIC with providing the Directorate of Central Intelligence-Europe with whatever support, logistical and other, the chief, DCI-Europe, feels it needs. With me so far, Major?"

"I think so, sir. May I ask a question, sir?"

"Please do."

"Who will be the chief, DCI-Europe?"

"Captain James D. Cronley Junior. You just met him." Major Derwin's face showed his surprise, or shock.

"There are reasons for this—"

"A couple of months ago he was a second lieutenant at Holabird!" Derwin blurted. "I had him in Techniques of Surveillance."

"I strongly suspect that as soon as Admiral Souers can find a more senior officer, say a colonel, or perhaps even a senior civilian, to appoint as chief, DCI-Europe, he will do so. But for the moment, it will be Captain Cronley."

"General, may I suggest we get into Operation Ost?" Mattingly said.

"This is the time, isn't it?" Greene said, and began to tell Major Derwin about Operation Ost.

Five minutes or so later, General Greene concluded the telling by saying, "I'm sure that you can understand, Major, since compromise of Operation Ost would not only be detrimental to the interests of the United States but would embarrass the highest officials of our government, why it behooves all of us to exert our maximum efforts to make sure it is not compromised."

"Yes, sir, I certainly can," Major Derwin said.

"And why any officer who does anything, even inadvertently, that causes any such compromise might as well put his head between his knees and kiss his ass goodbye? Because, even if his court-martial doesn't sentence him to spend twenty years polishing the linoleum in the solitary confinement wing of the Leavenworth Disciplinary Barracks, his military career is over."

"I understand, sir," Major Derwin said.

"I really hope you do," General Greene said. "We will now get into your duties with regard to the Pullach compound and Operation Ost. They can be summed up succinctly. They are invisible to you, unless it comes to your attention that someone is showing an unusual interest in them. If that happens, you will bring this immediately to the attention of Colonel Mattingly or myself. Or, of course, and preferably, to Captain Cronley or Captain Dunwiddie. You understand that?"

"Yes, sir."

"Any questions, Major?"

"Just one, sir."

"It is?"

"May I ask about Captain Cronley, sir?"

"What about Captain Cronley?"

"Sir, as I mentioned, two months ago, less, I saw him at Holabird as a second lieutenant—"

"If you are asking how he became a captain so quickly, Major, I can tell you it was a reward for something he did."

"May I ask what, sir?"

"No," General Greene said. "But I can tell you—although his promotion order is classified Secret—that the promotion authority was 'Verbal Order of the President.'"

"Yes, sir."

"Unless you have something for Major Derwin, Colonel Mattingly?"

"No, sir."

"Then what I am going to do now, Major Derwin, is have the sergeant major put you in a car and send you over to see Major McClung. He will get you settled in quarters and then show you where you should begin your duties as inspector general."

"Yes, sir."

"That will be all, Major. You are dismissed."

[THREE]
The I.G. Farben Building
Frankfurt am Main
American Zone of Occupation, Germany
1225 29 December 1945

It took Captains Cronley and Dunwiddie and General Gehlen five minutes to get from General Greene's office to the "back door" of the huge building, which until the completion of the Pentagon in January 1943 had been the largest office building in the world.

The office of the chief, Counterintelligence Corps, European Command, was in the front of the extreme left wing (of six wings) in the curved five-story structure. The "back door" was in Sub-Level One between Wing Three and Wing Four.

First they had to walk down a long corridor to the connecting passageway between the wings.

There, Cronley and Dunwiddie had to "sign out" at a desk manned by two natty sergeants of the 508th Parachute Infantry Regiment, which was charged with both the internal and the external security of the building. The paratroopers wore white pistol belts, holsters, and spare magazine holders, and the white lacings in their glistening boots had once been parachute shroud lines.

The senior of the paratroop sergeants remembered that when the shabby Kraut civilian had passed in through their portal with General Walter Bedell Smith's entourage, he had wisely not demanded that any of them sign in, or that he be permitted to examine the contents of the briefcases the Kraut and General Smith's aide-de-camp were carrying.

As a consequence, the sergeant not only passed General Gehlen out without examining the contents of his ancient and battered briefcase, but also gave him a pink slip, as he had given one to Cronley and Dunwiddie, which would permit them to exit the building.

Then the trio walked down the long corridor that connected the wings to the center, where they got on what most inhabitants of the Farben Building called the "dumbwaiter." Technically it was known as a "paternoster lift." It was a chain of open compartments, each large enough for two people, that moved slowly and continuously in a circle from Sub-Level Two to Floor Five. Passengers stepped into one of the compartments and rode it until they reached the desired floor, and then stepped off.

Cronley, Dunwiddie, and Gehlen got on the dumbwaiter and were carried down to Sub-Level One, where they got off.

Here there was another paratroop-manned checkpoint. The sergeant in charge here accepted the pink slips they had been given, but signaled to General Gehlen that he wanted to inspect his briefcase.

"Herr Schultz is with me, Sergeant," Cronley said, showing the sergeant the leather folder holding the ID card and badge that identified him as a special agent of the Counterintelligence Corps. "That won't be necessary."

The sergeant considered that a moment, and then said, "Yes, sir," and motioned that Gehlen could leave the building. He did so, and Cronley followed him.

They were now in a narrow, below-ground-level, open-to-the-sky passageway.

There were three Packard Clippers parked against the wall. The "back door" to the Farben Building was also, so to speak, the VIP entrance. The Packards were the staff cars of Generals Eisenhower, Smith, and Lucius D. Clay, the military governor of the U.S. Occupied Zones. The Packards were, not surprisingly, highly polished.

There was also what had begun its military service as an ambulance, a three-quarter-ton 4×4. It was not polished, and the red crosses that had once been painted on the sides and roof had been painted over. Stenciled in white paint on the left of its bumpers was the legend 711 MKRC—which indicated that the vehicle was assigned to the—nonexistent—711th Quartermaster Mess Kit Repair Company—and on the right, the numeral 7, which signified that it was the seventh vehicle of its kind assigned to the 711th.

There were three paratroopers, one of them a sergeant, standing by the right front fender of the former ambulance, arguing with an enormous Negro soldier, a sergeant, who was leaning against the fender, his arms crossed over his chest. Even leaning against the fender, the sergeant towered over the paratroopers.

When the sergeant saw Cronley and the others approaching, he came to attention and saluted. Cronley returned the salute and asked, "Is there some problem?"

"You know about this vehicle, Captain?" the paratroop sergeant asked.

"Didn't they teach you it is customary for sergeants to salute officers before addressing them, Sergeant?"

"Yes, sir. Sorry, sir," the paratroop sergeant said, and saluted. Cronley returned it.

"Herr Schultz, if you'll get in the back with Captain Dunwiddie?" Cronley said, and then turned to the paratroop sergeant. "Is there a problem with this vehicle?"

"Sir, only the general's cars are allowed to park here."

"There are exceptions to every rule, Sergeant," Cronley said, and produced his CIC credentials. "In this case—it's an intelligence matter—I ordered the sergeant to wait here for me until I could bring Herr Schultz out. We didn't want him standing around where he could be seen. Weren't you here when General Smith passed him into the building?"

"Yes, sir."

"You did the right thing to question the vehicle, Sergeant."

"Thank you, sir."

"Carry on, Sergeant," Cronley ordered crisply. Then he turned to the black sergeant. "Well, Sergeant Phillips, what do you say we get out of here?"

"Yes, sir," Sergeant Phillips said. He got behind the wheel and Cronley got in the front seat beside him.

When they were rolling, Cronley said, "Those CIC credentials do come in handy, don't they?"

"Enjoy them while you can," Dunwiddie said. "I think we're about to lose them."

"I will bring up the subject of keeping them—and getting some more for some of your guys—to General Greene when there's an opportunity. I didn't want to do that when Mattingly was there—he can probably come up with a dozen reasons to take them away from us."

"I don't suppose it's occurred to you that making nice to Colonel Mattingly would be a good idea."

"I thought about that."

"And?"

"Mattingly is never going to forgive me for me, not him, being named chief, DCI-Europe," Cronley replied, "even though I had nothing to do with it. Or forgive you, Captain Dunwiddie, for those new bars on your epaulets."

"Speaking of which," Sergeant Phillips said, "they look real good on you, Tiny. Congratulations."

"Thanks, Tom," Dunwiddie said.

"Who's going to be the new Top Kick? Tedworth?" Phillips asked.

"Who else?" Dunwiddie said.

"General, can you tell me what General Smith wanted with you?"

"Of course," Gehlen said. "Two things. Once it was determined he had the right Captain Cronley—the Army one, not a naval officer—he asked if I 'was comfortable' with you being named chief, DCI-Europe. I assured him I was. And then he handed me this to give to you."

He handed Cronley a business-sized envelope. Cronley's name and the legend "By Officer Courier" was on it. When he opened it, he saw that it contained a second envelope. This one was addressed:

```
CAPTAIN JAMES D. CRONLEY JR.
CHIEF, DCI-EUROPE
C/O GENERAL WALTER B. SMITH
SUPREME HEADQUARTERS, EUROPEAN COMMAND
BY OFFICER COURIER
```

He tore the second envelope open and read the letter it contained.

```
        TOP SECRET PRESIDENTIAL NUCLEAR

              The White House
               Washington, D.C.

Rear Admiral Sidney W. Souers, USN
Special Assistant to the President


December 24, 1945


Duplication Forbidden
Copy 1 of 2
Page 1 of 8

        TOP SECRET PRESIDENTIAL NUCLEAR
```

TOP SECRET PRESIDENTIAL NUCLEAR

RAdm Souers/Capt Cronley 24 Dec 1945
Copy 1 of 2
Page 2 of 8
Duplication Forbidden

Captain James D. Cronley Jr.
Chief, DCI-Europe
C/O General Walter B. Smith
Supreme Headquarters, European Command
By Officer Courier

Dear Jim:

  The information herein, with which
Lieutenant Colonel Ashton is familiar,
is to be shared only with General Gehlen,
General White, and Dunwiddie. It is to be
hoped he will be Captain Dunwiddie by the
time you get this. If his commission has
not come through, let me know immediately.

  This concerns the establishment of the
Directorate of Central Intelligence and its
operations in the near future.

  Until the OSS's arrangement with General
Gehlen provided the names of Soviet

TOP SECRET PRESIDENTIAL NUCLEAR

TOP SECRET PRESIDENTIAL NUCLEAR

RAdm Souers/Capt Cronley 24 Dec 1945

Copy 1 of 2

Page 3 of 8

Duplication Forbidden

intelligence officers seeking to breach the
secrecy of the Manhattan Project, and the
names of Manhattan Project personnel who
were in fact engaged in treasonous
espionage on behalf of the USSR, it was
J. Edgar Hoover's often announced position
that the FBI had been completely
successful in maintaining the secrets of
the Manhattan Project.

Hoover maintained this position, even
after being given the aforementioned
intelligence, up and until President
Truman informed Marshal Stalin in Potsdam
on July 18, 1945, that we possessed the
atomic bomb, and from Stalin's reaction
concluded he was telling Stalin something
Stalin already knew.

Faced with the undeniable proof that the
USSR had penetrated the Manhattan Project,
Director Hoover said that what he had

TOP SECRET PRESIDENTIAL NUCLEAR

TOP SECRET PRESIDENTIAL NUCLEAR

RAdm Souers/Capt Cronley 24 Dec 1945
Copy 1 of 2
Page 4 of 8
Duplication Forbidden

really meant to say was that of course the FBI had known all along of Soviet spies in the Manhattan Project, but that so far he had been unable to develop sufficient evidence that would stand up in court to arrest and indict the spies and traitors. He assured the President at that time that he would order the FBI to redouble its efforts to obtain such evidence.

The President had taken me into his confidence about this even before Potsdam, and when he asked what I thought should be done, I recommended that he turn the investigation of Soviet espionage in the Manhattan Project over to General Donovan and the OSS. He replied that to do so would be tantamount to authorizing an "SS-like" secret police force in the United States, and he was absolutely unwilling to do anything like that. Furthermore, the

TOP SECRET PRESIDENTIAL NUCLEAR

TOP SECRET PRESIDENTIAL NUCLEAR

RAdm Souers/Capt Cronley 24 Dec 1945
Copy 1 of 2
Page 5 of 8
Duplication Forbidden

President said, he had already decided to
abolish the OSS.

There the situation lay dormant, until
the President decided he had been too
hasty in shutting down the OSS and had
come to the conclusion that there was a
great need for an organization with both
covert and clandestine capabilities and
answerable only to the chief executive.

In late November, the President told
me that he had decided to establish by
Executive Order the Directorate of Central
Intelligence (DCI) as of January 1, 1946,
and intended to name me as director. He
told me one of the reasons for his
decision was that he knew I found the
notion of an American SS as repugnant as
he did.

I told the President that unless the DCI
was given authority to deal with

TOP SECRET PRESIDENTIAL NUCLEAR

TOP SECRET PRESIDENTIAL NUCLEAR

RAdm Souers/Capt Cronley 24 Dec 1945
Copy 1 of 2
Page <u>6</u> of <u>8</u>
Duplication Forbidden

significant Soviet intelligence efforts
in the United States, such as
the Manhattan Project, I would reluctantly
have to decline the honor of becoming
director, DCI.

The President said it was politically
impossible for him to publicly or
privately take any responsibility for
counterintelligence activities within the
United States from Mr. Hoover and the FBI
and give it to the DCI. He then pointed
out in the draft of the Executive Order
establishing the DCI the phrase "and
perform such other activities as the
President may order."

He said that if I were DDCI, he would
order me to "investigate and deter any
efforts by any foreign power to penetrate
the Manhattan Project, or any such activity,
and to report any findings and any actions
taken, directly and only to him."

TOP SECRET PRESIDENTIAL NUCLEAR

TOP SECRET PRESIDENTIAL NUCLEAR

RAdm Souers/Capt Cronley 24 Dec 1945

Copy 1 of 2

Page 7 of 8

Duplication Forbidden

The President said that he did not feel
that Mr. Hoover would have any need to
know of these orders. The President also
said that in none of his conversations
with Director Hoover had the subject of
"Operation OST" come up, either by name,
or as a general subject such as the
rumor that we have been sending Germans
to Argentina. The President said he
found this odd, as I had told him FBI
agents were in Europe attempting to
question you, and others, on the subject.
The President said he did not understand
Mr. Hoover's particular interest in
Operation OST, as it is none of the FBI's
business.

At this point in our conversation the
President again offered me the directorship
of the DCI. I informed the President that
if I could name Lieutenant Colonel Ashton
as deputy director, DCI-Western Hemisphere,

TOP SECRET PRESIDENTIAL NUCLEAR

TOP SECRET PRESIDENTIAL NUCLEAR

RAdm Souers/Capt Cronley 24 Dec 1945

Copy 1 of 2

Page 8 of 8

Duplication Forbidden

with overall responsibility for Operation
OST, and you as DDDCI-Europe, with
responsibility for Operation Ost in Europe,
I would accept the honor he offered.

The President told me to tell you and
Colonel Ashton that he feels confident you
both can establish an amicable, cooperative
relationship between the DCI and the FBI
while at the same time keeping secret
those matters which do not fall within the
FBI's areas of responsibility or interest.

He also said to send you his best
wishes.

With best personal regards,

Sidney W. Souers

Sidney W. Souers
Rear Admiral, USN
Director, DCI

TOP SECRET PRESIDENTIAL NUCLEAR

Cronley handed the letter to Gehlen.

"Please give it to Captain Dunwiddie when you've read it, General," he said.

When Tiny had read the letter, Cronley said, "My take on that letter is that Truman is afraid of Hoover. Otherwise, he would just tell Hoover to butt out."

When no one replied, he asked, "Can I interpret the silence to mean you agree with me?"

"You can interpret my silence to mean I am obviously not in a position where I can presume to comment on anything the President of the United States does or does not do," Gehlen said. "I would, however, suggest that both President Truman and Admiral Souers seem to feel confident that both you and Colonel Ashton can deal with a very difficult situation."

"Shit," Cronley said, and looked at Dunwiddie. "And you?"

After a moment, Dunwiddie avoided the question, instead asking, "Lieutenant Colonel Ashton? I thought he was a major, and in Walter Reed with a broken leg?"

"In other words, no comment, right?" Cronley asked.

Dunwiddie said nothing.

"As to your question," Cronley said. "Applying my Sherlock Holmesian logic to it, I deduce Ashton (a) has been promoted, and (b) that he will shortly appear here, broken leg or not. Obviously, if he was in Walter Reed, we could not share this letter with him."

"Wiseass," Dunwiddie said.

Gehlen chuckled.

"I further deduce," Cronley went on, "that Lieutenant

Colonel Ashton is coming over here to familiarize himself with his new underlings."

"Other than that Otto Niedermeyer speaks highly of him, I don't know much about Colonel Ashton," Gehlen said.

"All I really know about him is that he's a Cuban—an American whose family grows sugarcane and makes rum in Cuba—and that Clete likes him. The little I saw of him when I was in Argentina, I liked," Cronley said. "He's really . . . what's the word? 'Polished.' Or maybe 'suave.' He can charm the balls off a brass monkey."

"Now that's an interesting phrase," Gehlen said, chuckling.

"I have no idea what it means," Cronley confessed.

"Would you be surprised to hear it has nothing to do with the testicles of our simian cousins?" Dunwiddie asked.

Tiny has found a way to change the subject.

Well, what did I expect him to say? "I agree it looks like Truman is throwing us off the bus"?

"Pay attention, General," Cronley said. "Professor Dunwiddie's lecture is about to start."

"Until breech-loading rifled-barrel naval cannon came along," Dunwiddie began, "men-of-war, as warships were then called, fired round iron balls from their smooth-barreled cannon. These balls often contained a black powder charge, with a fuse that was lit just before the ball was rammed down the cannon muzzle. Is this too technical for you, Captain Cronley, sir, or should I continue?"

Gehlen chuckled.

"Carry on, Captain Dunwiddie," Cronley ordered.

"As you are aware, balls tend to roll around on flat surfaces," Dunwiddie continued. "They tend to roll around even more on flat surfaces which are themselves moving, as the deck of ships on the high seas tend to do. Since the balls the Navy was using weighed up to one hundred pounds, you can see where this was a problem. The problem was compounded by the explosive shells to which I previously referred.

"Phrased simply, if some of the black powder in the explosive shells came out of the touch hole—that's where they put the fuse—while it was rolling around on the deck, it made for a highly combustible environment. Even worse was the possibility that glowing embers—debris from previous firing of the cannon—would find the touch hole of the explosive ball as it rolled around the deck crushing feet and breaking ankles. Bang. Big bang.

"A solution had to be found, and one was. A clever sailor, one I like to think claimed my beloved Norwich as his alma mater, although I can't prove this—"

"General," Cronley asked, "has Captain Dunwiddie mentioned in passing that he went to Norwich University?"

"Not as often as Sergeant Hessinger has mentioned he went to Harvard, but yes, he has. No more than thirty or forty times," Gehlen replied.

"As I was saying," Dunwiddie went on, "a clever nautical person came up with a solution for the problem of cannonballs rolling and sometimes exploding on the deck. The balls, he concluded, had to be in some manner restrained from rolling around, and the method of restraint had to permit getting the iron cannonballs from where they would be restrained into the mouth of the cannon quickly when that was required. And without causing the sparks which occur when steel and/or iron collide. Said sparks would tend to set off both the barrels of black powder and the explosive cannonballs.

"What he came up with were plates, into which he hammered depressions so that the cannonballs wouldn't roll around. He made the plates from brass so they wouldn't spark and set off the black powder. For reasons lost in the fog of history, he called these indented brass plates 'monkeys.' When they were getting ready to fight, they put the shells, the balls, on these monkeys until they were needed. Moving the balls, which weighed up to one hundred pounds, off the brass monkey was recognized to be very difficult. Any further questions?"

"Interesting," Gehlen said. "Now that you've brought it up, I remember seeing cannonballs stacked that way, forming sort of a pyramid, on your "Old Ironsides" in Boston Harbor." He paused, and corrected himself: "The USS *Constitution*."

"You've been on the *Constitution*?" Cronley blurted, in surprise.

"As a young officer," Gehlen said. "When it seemed that I was destined to serve as an intelligence officer, I was treated to a tour of the United States."

Sergeant Phillips announced, "We're here."

Cronley looked out the window and saw they were approaching the gate to the Eschborn Airfield.

"Great," Cronley said. "And now that Professor Dunwiddie's history lesson is over, we can return to our noble duties stemming the Red Tide. Maintaining as we do so an amicable relationship with the FBI."

He expected a chuckle from General Gehlen, but when he looked at him, he saw a look of concern.

Jesus, what did my automatic mouth blurt out now?

"Sir, if I said something . . ."

Gehlen shook his head. "No, Jim, you didn't say anything out of place. What popped back into my mind—I have a tendency to find a black lining in every silver cloud—when you said 'stemming the Red Tide' was something I thought when I was with General Smith earlier. You said it mockingly, but in fact—don't misunderstand me, please, I know you take it as seriously as I do—that's what we're trying to do. But there are so very few of us who really understand the problem. And so many clever Russians."

Cronley's mouth went on automatic again. He regretted what he was saying as the words came out of his mouth: "Not to worry, General. One of us went to Norwich."

There was no expression on Gehlen's face for a long moment, but just as Cronley was trying to frame an appropriate apology, Gehlen smiled and said, "That somehow slipped my mind, but now that you've brought it up, it certainly does wonders dispelling my clouds of impending disaster."

III

When he took the Storch off from Eschborn, Cronley had been worried about the flight, although he said nothing to either General Gehlen or Tiny.

For one thing, the weather was iffy, and it gets dark early in Germany in December. If the weather got worse, he'd have to land somewhere short of Munich, which meant at an infantry regiment or artillery battalion airstrip somewhere. As far as the officers there would be concerned, in addition to wondering what he was doing flying a Kraut around in a former Luftwaffe airplane, they would be reluctant to house overnight or, for that matter, feed said seedy-looking Kraut.

Flashing the CIC credentials would overcome those problems, of course, but it would provide those officers with a great barroom story to share with the world.

You won't believe what flew into the strip yesterday. An ex-Luftwaffe Storch, with Army markings, and carrying two CIC captains and a Kraut. Wouldn't say what they were doing, of course. Makes you wonder.

And even if he could make it through the weather to

Bavaria, by the time they got there, it might be too dark to land on the strip at the Pullach compound. That would mean he would have to go into Schleissheim—the Munich military post airfield—which had runway lights.

But there would be problems at Schleissheim, too. The Storch would attract unwanted attention, and so would General Gehlen. And they would have to ask the Schleissheim duty officer for a car to take them to the Vier Jahreszeiten, as the Kapitän was at Kloster Grünau, and Major Wallace was sure to be off somewhere in their only other car, the Opel Admiral.

An hour out of Munich, the answer came: *Don't go to Munich. Go to Kloster Grünau. Have a couple of drinks and a steak. Go to bed. And in the morning, get in the Kapitän and drive to Pullach.*

He picked up the intercom microphone.

"General, would you have any problems if we spent the night at the monastery?"

"As far as I know, there's absolutely nothing waiting for me in Munich."

"Next stop, Kloster Grünau."

Technical Sergeant Tedworth, his cavalry-yellow scarf not quite concealing the bandages on his neck, was waiting for them in the ambulance. Cronley was not surprised to see Ostrowski was behind the wheel.

Cronley had something to tell him, and this was as good a time as any.

"Tedworth, Sergeant Hessinger—"

"Sir, he wants you to call him as soon as possible," Tedworth cut him off. "He says it's important."

"Sergeant, it's not polite to cut your commanding officer off in the middle of a sentence."

"Sorry, sir."

"Not only impolite but the wrong thing to do, since what I was going to say, had I not been rudely interrupted, was that Sergeant Hessinger has informed me that while I do not have promotion authority in normal circumstances, I do in extraordinary circumstances. I have decided that First Sergeant Dunwiddie, having created a vacant first sergeant position by becoming a commissioned officer, is such an extraordinary circumstance. I was about to tell you I am sure that Captain Dunwiddie will be happy to sell you the first sergeant chevrons he no longer needs at a reasonable price."

"I'll be damned," Tedworth said. "Thank you."

"You will of course be expected to pay for the intoxicants at your promotion party, which will commence just as soon as we get to the bar."

"First Sergeant Tedworth," Tedworth said wonderingly. "I will be damned!"

"You will be aware, I'm sure, First Sergeant Tedworth, that henceforth you will be marching in the footsteps of the superb non-commissioned officer who preceded you and will be expected to conduct yourself accordingly," Dunwiddie said solemnly.

"*Captain* Dunwiddie and *First Sergeant* Tedworth," Tedworth went on. "Who would have ever thought, Tiny, when we joined Company 'A'?"

And then he regained control.

"Captain, I think you better call Fat Freddy," he said. "He said it was really important."

"Immediately after I take a leak—my back teeth are

floating—and I have a stiff drink of Scotland's finest," Cronley said.

•

"Twenty-third CIC, Special Agent Hessinger."

"And how are you, Freddy, on this miserable December evening?"

"When are you coming here?"

"That's one of the reasons I called, Freddy, to tell you Captain Dunwiddie and myself—plus two others whose names I would prefer not to say on this line while some FBI numbnuts are listening—will be celebrating First Sergeant Tedworth's promotion in the country and will not be returning to Munich until tomorrow."

"I don't think Colonel Parsons is going to like that."

"What? What business is it of his?"

"He called here and said General Greene had suggested he and Major Ashley take you to dinner to get to know you. He said he made reservations here in the Vier Jahreszeiten for eight o'clock and he expects to see you there."

That's disappointing. I thought Greene was going to maintain complete neutrality. But what he's obviously doing—or trying to do—is help this bastard Parsons take over Operation Ost for the Pentagon.

Why should that surprise me? Greene, ultimately, is under the Pentagon G2. They don't like the Directorate of Central Intelligence and they really don't want Operation Ost being run by a very junior captain. Greene knows on which side of the piece of toast the butter goes.

Wait a minute!

Do I detect the subtle hand of Colonel Robert Mattingly? Oh, do I!

Mattingly thinks—and with good reason—that he should be chief, DCI-Europe. Instead, I am. But there's nothing he can do about it. Unless, of course, as a result of my youth and inexperience I get into a scrap with Parsons. Then he can step in—Greene would suggest Mattingly step in—to save something from the wreckage. For the good of the service.

I can see that sonofabitch suggesting to General Greene that Parsons take me to dinner "to get to know me." I can also see Parsons reasoning that Greene is on his side—otherwise why the "get to know him" suggestion—and interpreting "get to know him" to mean making it clear to the junior captain that this is still the Army, and in the Army, lieutenant colonels tell junior captains what to do, and junior captains say, "Yes, sir."

But I can't take orders from a lieutenant colonel whose mission it is to take over Operation Ost.

So what do I do?

"Would you be shocked to hear that I am not thrilled with the prospect of Colonel Parsons buying me dinner?"

"You not being thrilled doesn't matter. Colonel Mattingly called and said Colonel Parsons would probably call and invite you to dinner, and you had better go. Alone."

Well, there's the proof. I can hear Mattingly saying, "Parsons went out of his way, Admiral, to get along with Cronley. He even invited him to a private dinner. Cronley refused to go."

Making nice to Parsons tonight would be just delaying the inevitable confrontation. Mattingly—or maybe Parsons himself, he's clever—would make sure there was a confrontation.

Back to what do I do?

What I do is get this over with.

But as the soon-to-be chief, DCI-Europe, not as Junior Captain Cronley.

Which means I take off this Ike jacket with its brand-new captain's bars and put on the one with the civilian U.S. triangles.

"You know how to get Parsons on the phone, Freddy?"

"He's here in the hotel."

"Please call him back and tell him you've heard from Mister, repeat, Mister Cronley and he, General Gehlen, and Captain Dunwiddie, who had already planned to dine at the Vier Jahreszeiten at eight, would be delighted if he and Major Whatsisname could join us."

"You heard what I said about Colonel Mattingly saying you should go to dinner alone?"

"Anything else for me, Freddy?"

"Oberst Mannberg asked me when General Gehlen will be back. He says he has something to report."

"Whatever that might be, I don't think we want to share it with the FBI, do we?"

"So what do I tell Mannberg?"

"Tell him the general will be in your office just before we go to dinner with Colonel Parsons and Major Whatsis-name."

[TWO]
Suite 507
Hotel Vier Jahreszeiten
Maximilianstrasse 178
Munich, American Zone of Occupation, Germany
1935 29 December 1945

Former Colonel Ludwig Mannberg was sitting with Sergeant Friedrich Hessinger at the latter's desk, both of them bent over a chessboard. They both stood when Cronley, followed by Gehlen and Dunwiddie, came into the room.

Mannberg was wearing a well-tailored suit and tie. Fat Freddy was in pinks and greens.

Cronley thought, more objectively than unkindly, *Looking at the two of them, you'd think Gehlen was a black marketeer caught dealing in cigarettes and Hershey bars and Mannberg was his lawyer. His English lawyer. I'm going to have to do something about getting the general some decent clothes.*

How am I going to do that? "Excuse me, General, but in that ratty suit, you look like an unsuccessful black marketeer."

"I just had one of my famous inspirations," Cronley announced. "Freddy, call the dining room and tell them there will be two more at dinner."

"Who?" Hessinger asked.

"You and Oberst Mannberg."

"Is that wise, Jim?" Dunwiddie asked. "Mattingly said you were to go alone."

"I know," Cronley said. "Do it, Freddy."

"General," Mannberg said, "we have heard from Seven-K."

Who the hell is "Seven-K"?

"And?" Gehlen asked.

"She reports Natalia Likharev and her sons, Sergei and Pavel, do in fact occupy a flat at Nevsky Prospekt 114 in Leningrad. It's a luxury apartment building reserved for senior officers of the NKGB."

Seven-K, you soaking-wet-behind-the-ears amateur intelligence officer, is obviously Gehlen's agent in Russia. If they said his name out loud, someone might hear. She?

"Which means," Gehlen said, "especially since the NKGB knows Colonel Likharev is now in Argentina, that they are watching them very carefully, and that it's just a matter of time before she is arrested. *Pour encourager les autres.*"

To encourage other NKGB officers not to change sides because the penalty is having your wife and kids sent to Siberia. Or shot. Or tortured. Or all of the above.

"Yes, sir," Mannberg agreed. "She also reports the Underground Railroad is in disarray."

"She"? That's twice Mannberg said "she." Seven-K is a woman?

Jesus, stupid! You should know the Russians have women spies. One of them made a horse's ass out of you. So why should Gehlen having female agents be such a surprise?

"Underground Railroad"? As in the States? Getting slaves out of the South? Mannberg is obviously talking about this woman's setup to get the Likharevs out of Russia. Interesting that the Russians use a term from American history.

Gehlen said, "Send her 'Act at your discretion.'"

"Signed?" Mannberg asked.

Gehlen pointed his index finger at his chest.

I wonder what your code name is?

"Jawohl, Herr General," Mannberg said.

"Why don't we all go down to the bar and have a drink before we feed the nice men from the Pentagon?" Cronley asked.

"Once again," Dunwiddie said, "are you sure that's what you want to do, have us all there?"

"I don't want to face them all by my lonesome," Cronley replied.

But that's not the only reason I want everybody there.

In three days I will become chief, Directorate of Central Intelligence-Europe, which means essentially Operation Ost. I have zero, zilch, qualifications to be given such an enormous responsibility. But I will have it, and I am about to compound the problem of the Pentagon's determination to take over control of Operation Ost from what they correctly believe to be a wholly unqualified—and very junior—officer by shifting into what Colonel Robert Mattingly has often referred to as my "loose-cannon" mode.

Specifically, I am going to apply what I was taught at my alma mater, Texas A&M: The best defense is a good offense.

If I told Tiny and Fat Freddy what I plan to do, they would conclude that I was once again going to do something monumentally stupid—and God knows I have quite a history of doing that. They would possibly, even probably, go along with me out of loyalty, but that's a two-way street.

If, as is likely, even probable, this blows up in my face, I want both Tiny and Freddy to be able to truthfully tell Mattingly, and/ or General Greene—for that matter, Admiral Souers—that they had no idea how I planned to deal with Lieutenant Colonel Parsons and Major Ashley. So, I can't tell them.

The same applies to General Gehlen. While my monumental

ego suggests he would probably think it might be a good idea, I don't know that. So I can't tell him. If I did, and he suggested ever so politely that I was wrong, I would stop. And I can't stop, because it's the only way I can think of to deal with Parsons and Ashley.

[THREE]
The Main Dining Room
Hotel Vier Jahreszeiten
Maximilianstrasse 178
Munich, American Zone of Occupation, Germany
2000 29 December 1945

Lieutenant Colonel George H. Parsons and Major Warren W. Ashley were not in the dining room when Cronley, Gehlen, Mannberg, Dunwiddie, and Hessinger arrived, but the table was set with places for everyone.

Important people arrive last, right? Screw you, Parsons!

Cronley took the chair at the head of the table.

"General, why don't you sit here?" Cronley said, pointing to the first side chair. "So that when Colonel Parsons arrives, he can sit across from you."

Gehlen, his face expressionless, sat where Cronley suggested.

Cronley then pointed to people and chairs, and everyone sat where he pointed.

Twenty minutes later, Colonel Parsons—a tall, trim forty-five-year-old—and Major Ashley—a shorter thirty-six-year-old version of Parsons—walked into the dining room. Both were in pinks and greens, and both of them wore the lapel insignia of the General Staff Corps and the shoulder insignia of the Military District of Washington.

Parsons marched on Cronley, who stood up but didn't put down his whisky glass.

"Glad to see you again, Cronley," Parsons said. "Sorry to be late. Tied up. Couldn't be helped."

"Good evening, Colonel," Cronley replied. "I was about to introduce you to General Gehlen, but he just told me he thinks you met when he was in Washington."

"No," Parsons said.

"My mistake," Gehlen said. "There was a Colonel Parsons at Fort Hunt, and I thought it might be you. But—"

"I don't have the pleasure of Herr Gehlen's acquaintance," Parsons said, and put out his hand.

"Herr Gehlen"? Okay, Colonel, if you want to go down that route, fine.

"And this is Oberst—Colonel—Mannberg, General Gehlen's deputy," Cronley said. "And Mr. Hessinger, who is my chief of staff, and Captain Dunwiddie, my deputy." He paused and then said, "And you're Major Ashburg, right?"

"Ashley, Captain Cronley, Ashley," Ashley corrected him.

"Right," Cronley said. "I'm bad with names. Well, gentlemen, I'm really glad you were free to join us. We're celebrating Captain Dunwiddie's commissioning."

"General Greene mentioned that you had been . . ." Parsons began.

Cronley interrupted him by calling for a waiter.

". . . in Frankfurt," Parsons went on, "for the promotion ceremony."

"Yes, we flew up when General Smith let it be known

that (a) he would like to participate, and (b) that he wanted a word with General Gehlen."

"General Smith wanted to participate?" Major Ashley asked, either dubiously or in surprise.

Thank you for that question, Major Ashley.

"It turned out—Dunwiddie never told us—that when he was born—what did General Smith say, Tiny? 'In the age of the dinosaurs'?—his father's company commander was Captain Smith."

"Oh, so you're from an Army family, Captain?" Parsons asked.

"Yes, sir."

"And you, Captain Cronley?"

The waiter appeared, saving Cronley from having to answer. When the waiter had taken their orders, Parsons had a fresh question.

"Let me go off on a tangent," he said. "You said you flew up to Frankfurt, and presumably flew back. Is there reliable air service between here and Frankfurt? The reason I ask is that it's a long ride on the train, and I expect that I'll have to—myself and Major Ashley will have to—go up there often."

"You're asking about MATS? The Air Force Military Air Transport Service?"

"Yes, of course."

"I really have no idea."

"But you just said you flew back and forth to Frankfurt today. How did you do that?"

"I loaded the general and Dunwiddie into a Storch, wound up the rubber bands, and took off."

"What's a Storch?"

"It's a German airplane. Sort of a super Piper Cub. We have two of them."

"You're a pilot? An aviator?"

Cronley nodded.

"I don't remember seeing pilot's wings when I saw you in uniform at the Schlosshotel Kronberg," Parsons said. "And that raises another question in my mind. If you don't mind my asking."

"Ask away. Isn't that what this is all about? Finding out about each other?"

"Why is it you're not wearing your uniform now? I mean, isn't that civilian attire?"

"As a special agent of the CIC, I'm allowed to wear 'civilian attire' when I think it's necessary."

"But you're not a CIC special agent, are you?"

"Until January second, I am a special agent of the CIC, assigned to the Twenty-third CIC Detachment," Cronley said, and then indicated Dunwiddie and Hessinger. "We all are."

"And on January second?"

"Then we will all be transferred to DCI-Europe. I would have thought General Greene or Colonel Mattingly would have explained that."

"It's not clear in my mind," Parsons said.

"And after that, you and the sergeant here will have to wear your uniforms?" Major Ashley asked. His tone of voice made it a challenge.

"Who told you Special Agent Hessinger is a sergeant?"

"You don't use the term 'sir' often, do you, Captain?" Ashley snapped.

"I guess I don't. Sorry. Blame it on the OSS."

"'Blame it on the OSS'?" Ashley parroted sarcastically.

"The OSS was—and I suppose the DCI will be—a little lax about the finer points of military courtesy," Cronley said. "My question to you, Major, was who told you Special Agent Hessinger is a sergeant?"

"As a matter of fact, it was Colonel Mattingly."

"I'm surprised. He knows better."

"My question to you, Captain," Ashley snapped, "is whether after Two January you will wear the prescribed uniform."

"After Two January the chief, DCI-Europe, will prescribe what DCI-Europe personnel will wear," Cronley said. "Right now, I don't think that will often be a uniform revealing our ranks to the world."

Ashley opened his mouth to reply. Cronley saw Parsons just perceptibly shake his head, which silenced Ashley.

Two waiters appeared and handed out menus.

They ordered.

"You understand, of course, Mr. Cronley," Colonel Parsons said, "that Major Ashley was understandably curious."

"Mister Cronley"? Was that a slip of the tongue?

Or is he being nice?

If he's being nice, why is he being nice?

"Absolutely," Cronley said. "Curiosity's a common affliction of intelligence officers, isn't it?"

"Absolutely," Parsons agreed with a smile. "My wife says, aside from my drinking, it's my worst character flaw."

Everyone laughed dutifully.

"Truth to tell, I'm a little curious about what you're going to do after Two January."

"Do about what, Colonel?"

"Identifying yourself, yourselves."

"To whom?"

"Hypothetical situation?"

"Why not?"

"You and Mr. Hessinger and Captain Dunwiddie—in civilian attire—are riding down the super highway here—what's it called?"

"The autobahn."

"The *autobahn*, in that magnificent German automobile Major Wallace drives . . ."

"The Opel Admiral," Dunwiddie furnished.

"Thank you. And, deep in conversation about how to repel the Red Threat to all we hold dear, you let the Admiral get a little over the speed limit. The ever-vigilant military police pull you over."

"Don't let it get around, Colonel, but your hypothetical situation actually happened several times to Colonel Mattingly."

"Really?"

"He was driving me from Kloster Grünau to Rhine-Main to catch the plane to Buenos Aires. In his magnificent German automobile, his Horch. Have you ever seen his Horch? That's a really magnificent car."

"I don't think I'd recognize a Horch if one ran over me."

"Between the monastery and Rhine-Main, the MPs pulled him over three times for speeding. The last citation was for going three times the speed limit."

"You're pulling my leg."

"No, I am not. Three times the speed limit is a hundred and seventy KPH, or a little over a hundred miles an hour—"

"Cronley," Major Ashley interrupted him, "why don't you let the colonel continue with his hypothetical?"

"Sorry," Cronley said. "Go ahead, Colonel."

"So there you are, by the side of the road, and the MP says, 'Sir, let me see your identification, please.' What are you going to do?"

"Follow the example shown me by Colonel Mattingly," Cronley replied. "Dazzle him with my CIC special agent credentials. Telling him I am rushing somewhere in the line of duty."

"But you won't have CIC credentials after One January," Ashley said.

"Oh, but I will."

"No, you won't," Ashley snapped. "You'll then be in the Directorate of Central Intelligence, not the CIC."

"I'm sure Colonel Parsons has his reasons for not telling you about that," Cronley said.

"Not telling him what about that?" Parsons asked.

"Now I'm in a spot," Cronley said. "Maybe this hypothetical wasn't such a good idea after all."

"What are you talking about, Cronley?" Parsons asked.

Not only am I no longer "Mister Cronley," but he's using the tone of voice lieutenant colonels use when dealing with junior captains who have done something to annoy them.

"Colonel, I'm just surprised that General Greene—and especially Colonel Mattingly; after all, he did tell you Hessinger is a sergeant—didn't tell you about this. But they obviously had their reasons. But what the hell, they didn't ask me not to tell you, so I will."

Colonel Parsons gave Major Ashley another don't-say-anything shake of the head, but it was too late.

"*Ask* you not to tell us what?" Ashley snapped sarcastically.

Three waiters marched up to the table carrying their dinner.

Serving it was an elaborate ceremony, but finally everything was served and the waiters left.

I am now going to pretend I think the hypothetical is closed.

"Do you know the officers' clubs import this beef from Denmark?" Cronley asked. "It seems they're leaning over backwards to avoid any suggestion that the clubs are taking the best beef from the Quartermaster—"

"You were saying something, Mr. Cronley," Colonel Parsons interrupted him, "about General Greene not telling me something?"

"Right," Cronley said.

He paused before going on: "Oh, what the hell. I don't want to be stuffy about this—God knows there's a hell of a lot classified Secret and Top Secret that shouldn't be classified at all—but this is justifiably classified . . ."

"Meaning you're not going to tell us?" Ashley asked, rather nastily.

"No, Major, I've decided you have the need to know about this, so I'm going to tell you. But I also have to tell you this is classified Top Secret–Presidential."

"You are aware, Cronley, are you not, that both Colonel Parsons and myself hold Top Secret–Presidential clearances?" Ashley said, angrily sarcastic. "We're entitled to know."

Well, I finally got you to blow up, didn't I?

And I ain't through.

"What you and Colonel Parsons are entitled to know about the DCI, about Operation Ost, Major, is what I decide you have the need to know."

If that doesn't set Parsons off, nothing will.

Greatly surprising Cronley, it didn't.

"Warren, Mr. Cronley is right," Parsons said. "Why don't we let him tell us what he thinks we should know?"

I'll be damned.

But why is it that I don't think I've won?

"I'll tell you what I can, sir, about the DCI and the CIC," Cronley said. "The basic idea is, as you're fully aware, to hide Operation Ost from just about everybody who does not have a genuine need to know. Everybody, in this sense, includes the FBI and that part of the CIC engaged in looking for Nazis. As well, of course, as just about everybody else."

"Admiral Souers explained that to me in some detail," Parsons said.

"Yes, sir, he told me that he had. But what he didn't tell you, and what General Greene apparently hasn't told you—and I really wish he had—and what I'm going to tell you now, is how the admiral decided the concealment could best be accomplished."

"And how is that?" Ashley demanded.

"Warren," Colonel Parsons said warningly.

Now Parsons's on my side?

What the hell is going on?

"When Admiral Souers told me that, at his request, and with the President's approval, the Army was going to task EUCOM-CIC with the logistical support of DCI-Europe, I suggested to him that I'd like to use EUCOM-CIC for more than that."

"*You* suggested that *you'd* like?" Ashley demanded sarcastically.

"Warren, shut up!" Parsons ordered curtly.

Well, if nothing else, I really have Parsons's attention.

"I suggested to the admiral that we could conceal a great deal of DCI-Europe within the CIC," Cronley went on. "For example, if we let people think that the Pullach compound is a CIC installation, and that General Gehlen's people were being employed by the CIC to track down Nazis . . ."

"But you're calling it the South German Industrial Development Organization Compound," Parsons said.

"Admiral Souers raised the same objection, sir. I suggested that if the Pullach compound was actually being used by the CIC as a Nazi-hunting center, they wouldn't put that on the sign. The sign would say something like the General-Büros Süd-Deutsche Industrielle Entwicklungsorganisation."

"Clever," Colonel Parsons said thoughtfully. "And, I gather, Admiral Souers and General Greene went along with your ideas?"

"Admiral Souers did. I don't think General Greene was unhappy with them."

"And, in any case," Parsons said, "what General Greene might think is moot, isn't it?"

"Colonel, I don't know this, but I think that if General Greene didn't like any of this, he would have told Admiral Souers, and I know the admiral would have listened. What I'm guessing is that General Greene didn't have any major objections."

Parsons considered that for a moment, and then said, "You're probably right. And now that I think about it, why should he have had problems with what the admiral asked him to do? Your suggestions make a lot of sense."

Yeah, I immodestly believe they do. But since your basic interest here is to get Operation Ost put under the deputy chief of staff for intelligence, and the only way you're going to be able to do that is to get me to fuck up royally, I don't think you're as pleased with my good suggestions as you're letting on.

"I find all of this fascinating," Parsons said. "And I suspect Warren does, too."

"Sir?"

"Warren and I have spent most of our careers in intelligence, Mr. Cronley, but just about all of it on the analytical side. Isn't that so, Warren?"

"Yes, sir."

"As opposed to the operational side is what I mean. What I suppose could be called the nitty-gritty side. So I find all these little operational details fascinating. I never would have thought of hiding a secret operation the way you're going to do it. A secret operation having absolutely nothing to do with the secret organization in which you're hiding it. Absolutely fascinating. Brilliant, even!"

Where the hell is he going with this?

"So I'd like to ask a favor of you, Mr. Cronley."

"Anything I can do for you, Colonel, of course."

"Cut me a little slack when we start working together."

"I don't think I follow you, Colonel."

"When I said, before, that my wife regards my curiosity as my worst character flaw, she was right on the money. And I know myself well enough to know that when we are working together I'll come across things that I know are none of my business, but which will cause my curiosity to shift into high gear.

"When that happens, and I ask you—or any of your people—questions that are out of bounds, I want you to feel perfectly free—and tell your people to feel absolutely free—to cut me off at the knees. Just say, 'That's none of your business,' and that will be the end of it. I won't take offense, and I'll stop asking questions. How does that sound, Mr. Cronley?"

Actually, you smooth sonofabitch, that's what I already decided to do if you and ol' Warren here got too curious. Cut you off at the knees.

"That's very gracious of you, Colonel," Cronley said. "Thank you. And I appreciate your understanding that there will be things going on around the Pullach compound that the fewer people know about, the better."

And I will now wait for the other shoe to drop.

Where's he going to go from here?

"Well, enough of this," Parsons said. "Why don't we change the subject?"

Cronley was so surprised at the other shoe that he blurted, "To what?"

"Women and politics are supposed to be forbidden subjects," Parsons said. "Either topic is fine with me."

He got the dutiful laughter he expected.

Then he grew serious.

"General Greene told me that he went to see General Patton shortly before he died. He said the scene was pretty grim."

Well, that's changing the subject, all right.

Where's he going with this?

"It just goes to show, doesn't it, that you never know what tomorrow will bring?" Parsons asked.

"Sir?"

"Losing your life, painfully, as a result of what General Greene said was really nothing but a fender-bender. And then your IG . . . or the CIC's . . . IG?"

Cronley felt his stomach tighten.

Jesus Christ, what does he know, what has he heard, about that?

"Sir?"

"The poor chap goes home for lunch, and his hot water heater blows up. Blows him and his wife up."

"I see what you mean," Cronley said.

And now where are you going to go?

"Let's get off those depressing subjects," Parsons said. "To what? Back to my curiosity, I suppose. I got the feeling, Mr. Cronley, from the way you rattled off 'General-Büros Süd-Deutsche,' et cetera, so smoothly that you're comfortable speaking German?"

"I speak German, Colonel."

"Fluently?"

"Yes, sir. My mother is a Strasbourgerin. A war bride from the First World War. I got my German from her. Colonel Mannberg tells me I could pass myself off as a Strasbourger."

"I'm jealous," Parsons said. "I got what little German I have from West Point, and I was not what you could call a brilliant student of languages. What about you, Captain Dunwiddie? How's your German?"

"I can get by, sir."

"You said before you're from an Army family. Do you also march in the Long Gray Line?"

"No, sir. I'm Norwich."

"Fine school. Did you know that General White, I.D. White, who commanded the 'Hell on Wheels'—the Second Armored Division—went to Norwich?"

"Yes, sir," Dunwiddie said. "I did."

"Warren, like General George Catlett Marshall, went to

VMI," Parsons said. "That leaves only you, Mr. Hessinger. I'm not sure if I can ask General Gehlen or Colonel Mannberg, or whether that would be none of my business."

"I never had the privilege of a university education, Colonel," Gehlen said.

Cronley was surprised, both at that, and also that Gehlen had chosen to reply, to furnish information, however harmless it was, about himself.

"I wasn't bright enough to earn a scholarship," Gehlen went on. "My father, who owned a bookstore, couldn't afford to send me to school. Germany was impoverished after the First World War. So I got what education I could from the books in my father's store. And then, the day after I turned eighteen, I joined the Reichswehr as a recruit. My father hated the military, but he was glad to see me go. One less mouth to feed."

What the hell is Gehlen up to? He didn't deliver that personal history lesson just to be polite.

"The what? You joined the what?" Ashley asked.

"The Reichswehr, Major," Hessinger furnished, "was the armed forces of the Weimar Republic. It was limited by the Versailles treaty to eighty-five thousand soldiers and fifteen thousand sailors. No aircraft of any kind. It existed from 1919 to 1935, when Hitler absorbed it into the newly founded Wehrmacht."

Fat Freddy delivered that little lecture because Gehlen delivered his history lesson. Which means he's figured out why Gehlen suddenly decided to chime in.

Why can't I?

Because I'm not as smart as either of them, that's why.

"You seem very familiar with German history, Mr. Hessinger," Parsons said.

"It is the subject of my—interrupted by the draft—doctoral thesis, Colonel."

"And you were where when you were drafted?"

"Harvard, sir."

"But you're German, right?"

"I am an American citizen, sir, who was born in Germany."

"And that leaves you, Colonel Mannberg," Parsons said.

"My university is Philipps-Universität in Marburg an der Lahn, Colonel," Mannberg said.

"Well, truth being stranger than fiction," Parsons said, "I know something about your university, Colonel. Are you aware that your school has been training American intelligence officers since our Civil War? Maybe even before our Civil War? And that we plan to resume that just as soon as we can?"

"I didn't know that you were going to resume that program, Colonel, but I knew about it. When we were at Philipps, your General Seidel and I were in the same *Brüderschaft*—fraternity."

Is that what Gehlen's been up to? Setting the stage for letting Parsons know that Mannberg and Seidel, the EUCOM G2, are old college fraternity buddies?

And how come Mannberg didn't tell me that?

"How interesting!" Parsons said. "And have you been in touch with General Seidel since the war ended?"

"Yes, I have," Mannberg said. "Actually, he tasked the CIC to find me. And, of course, they did."

And now I will sit here with bated breath waiting to see where all this goes.

It went nowhere.

As they talked, they had been eating.

When they had finished eating, they were through talking.

Parsons said something to the effect that while he hated to leave good company, he "and Warren have a lot on our plates for tomorrow" and that they were "reluctantly going to have to call it a night."

Hands were shaken all around, and thirty seconds later Colonel Parsons and Major Ashley had left.

When they were out of earshot, Gehlen asked, "Jim, would you think that talking this over while it's still fresh in our minds might be a good idea?"

Cronley nodded.

Gehlen, with his usual courtesy, is going to hand me my ass on a platter.

"Why don't we go upstairs to my room?" he said.

[FOUR]
Suite 527
Hotel Vier Jahreszeiten
Maximilianstrasse 178
Munich, American Zone of Occupation, Germany
2155 29 December 1945

Suite 527—an elegantly furnished bedroom, sitting room, bath, and small office—was Cronley's, although he rarely spent the night in it or, for that matter, used it at all.

He had inherited it, so to speak, from the OSS. When

Colonel Robert Mattingly had commanded OSS Forward, he had requisitioned all of the fifth floor's right wing for the OSS when it had been decided to put—hide—General Gehlen's people at least temporarily in Kloster Grünau.

Mattingly had no intention of spending his nights on a GI cot in a cold, former, and until very recently long-deserted former monastery in the middle of nowhere when the five-star Vier Jahreszeiten was available to him.

When the OSS was disbanded, and Mattingly became deputy chief, CIC-Europe, he had put Kloster Grünau under then Second Lieutenant Cronley. And turned Suite 527 over to him. At the time Cronley had thought it was a nice, if misguided, gesture. The very things that made the Vier Jahreszeiten appealing to Mattingly—it was a playground for senior officers and their wives and enforced a strict code of dress and decorum—made it unappealing to a young second lieutenant.

Cronley now believed that it was far less benevolence on Mattingly's part that gave him access to "the fifth floor" than Mattingly's desire to distance himself as far as possible from Kloster Grünau and what was going on there. There was a very good chance that Operation Ost was going to blow up in everyone's face, and Mattingly wanted to be far away when that happened.

"I don't know what's going on at Kloster Grünau. I turned the whole operation over to Cronley. I never went down there. Why, I even gave him my suite in the Vier Jahreszeiten because I never used it.

"Now, as far as FILL IN THE BLANK going so wildly wrong down there under his watch, I certainly don't want to belittle what Cronley did in Argentina, but the cold fact is that

he was made a captain before he even had enough time in grade to be promoted to first lieutenant, and he really didn't have the qualifications and experience to properly handle something like Kloster Grünau."

Everyone filed into suite 527, and everyone but Cronley, who leaned against an inner wall, found seats.

The Louis XIV chair under Dunwiddie disappeared under his bulk.

If that collapses, it will add a bit of sorely needed levity to this gathering.

"Gentlemen," Cronley said in a serious tone, "if Captain Dunwiddie will forgo delivering the speech about the havoc a loose cannon can cause rolling about on a dinner table that he's been mentally rehearsing for the past hour, we can go directly to seeing if anything at all can be salvaged from that disastrous dinner."

Dunwiddie and Hessinger shook their heads. Mannberg and Gehlen smiled.

"I will admit, Jim," Gehlen said, "that if you had told us beforehand how you were going to confront Colonel Parsons, it might have gone a little better than it did. But it wasn't a disaster, by any means."

"As you may have noticed, General, I'm a little slow. You don't think that was a total disaster?"

Gehlen shook his head.

"'Know thine enemy,'" Hessinger quoted. "Sun Tzu, *The Art of War.*"

"Precisely," Gehlen said.

"It looked to me like we gave him a lot of information about us. But what did we learn about him?" Cronley asked.

"We confirmed much of what we presumed about him," Gehlen said. "Most important, I suggest, we confirmed what I said a few days ago about the greatest danger posed to Operation Ost—that it will come from the Pentagon, not the Russians. And Colonel Parsons is going to be a formidable adversary."

"You think he's that smart, that dangerous?" Cronley asked.

"For several reasons, yes, I do. I presumed the Pentagon was going to send a highly intelligent officer as their liaison officer, since his purpose would go beyond a liaison function. His primary mission is to clip the just-born bud of the Directorate of Central Intelligence before it has a chance to blossom, and return it and its functions to where it belongs, under the assistant chief of staff for intelligence in the Pentagon.

"We saw that Parsons is highly intelligent—and I think Ashley, too, is not quite what he would wish us to believe. In other words, I judge him to be far more intelligent and competent—and thus more dangerous—than a well-meaning, if not too bright, subordinate who has to be reined in when his enthusiasm gets the better of him."

"You think that 'Shut up, Warren' business was theater, rehearsed theater, sir?" Dunwiddie asked.

"Theater? Yes. Rehearsed? Not necessarily. I would judge the two of them have worked together before. They didn't, they thought, have to rehearse much to deal with a junior captain whom they thought would be facing them alone. That didn't happen. And then the junior captain proved a far more able adversary than they anticipated he would be."

Does he mean that? Or is he being nice? Or charming, for his own purposes?

"What makes Colonel Parsons and Major Ashley especially dangerous is that they believe passionately in their mission," Gehlen said. "Almost Mossad-like."

"Excuse me?" Cronley asked.

"The Zionist intelligence apparatus," Hessinger said.

"And once again, apparently, Hessinger knows all about something I never heard of," Cronley said. "Lecture on, professor."

Gehlen smiled and gestured to Hessinger to continue.

"The Zionists, the Jews," Hessinger explained, "want their own homeland, their own country, in what is now Palestine. Until they get it, they've got sort of a shadow government, *à la* the British. Including an intelligence service. It has many names, but most commonly, the Mossad."

"And are you planning to move to Palestine?" Cronley challenged.

"Not me. I'm an American," Hessinger replied. "I'll do what I can to help the Zionists, of course, but my plan for the future is to become a professor at Harvard."

"I'm glad you brought that up, Friedrich," Gehlen said.

"Sir?"

"'I'll do what I can to help, of course,'" Gehlen parroted. "There are two things that make the Mossad so good, Jim. And they are really good. Even better than the Vatican. One is that they really believe in their cause. The second is what Friedrich just said. Jews all over the world are willing to help them, even eager. Even when helping them violates the law.

"The same, I think, is true of Colonel Parsons and Major

Ashley. Not only do they really believe Operation Ost, and the entire DCI, should be under the Pentagon, but as Jews all over, like our friend Friedrich here, are willing to help the Mossad, so will just about everybody in the Army support Parsons and Ashley."

"I got the feeling earlier today that General Smith is on our side," Cronley said.

"I'm sure he is. But I am not sure about every member of his staff who is in a position to help Colonel Parsons and hurt the DCI."

"For the good of the service," Dunwiddie said, drily sarcastic.

"Jesus Christ!" Cronley said. "So what it boils down to is that it's us against just about everybody."

"President Truman seems to be on our side. Or vice versa," Gehlen said.

"Even though we're the good guys," Cronley went on, "maybe what we should do is connect somehow with this Mossad. Maybe they could show us where we can get some help. Right now, I feel like Custer at the Little Big Horn. Where did all these Indians come from?"

He expected a chuckle, or at least a smile, from Gehlen and the others. Dunwiddie and Hessinger did in fact smile. But Gehlen's face was expressionless.

"You're a Jew, Freddy," Cronley went on. "How's chances you can get your co-religionists, the super spies of Mossad, to come galloping to our rescue before we're scalped?"

Hessinger, smiling, gave him the finger.

"Actually, in a sense, that's already happening," Gehlen said.

"Sir?"

What the hell is he talking about?

"Seven-K in Leningrad is a double agent. She's an NKGB officer and a Mossad agent," Gehlen said.

"My God!" Cronley said.

Gehlen smiled and nodded, and then went on: "One of the things Mossad is very good at is getting Jews out of Russia. When I realized getting Mrs. Likharev and her children out of Russia was really important, I asked her to help."

This is surreal. His agent—which means our agent— in Leningrad is an agent—a female agent—of this super Jewish intelligence organization—Mossad—that I never heard of?

"Why would she do that?" Hessinger asked before Cronley could open his mouth to ask the identical question.

"Over the years, we have been helpful to one another," Gehlen said. "I thought of that when Colonel Parsons told us he has had little experience with the 'nitty-gritty' side of intelligence. This is the nitty-gritty side."

"I'm lost," Cronley confessed.

"You're aware that middle- to high-level swine in the Schutzstaffel grew rich by allowing foreign Jews—so-called *Ausländer Juden*—particularly those in the United States— to buy their relatives and friends out of the death camps and to safety in Argentina or Paraguay?"

"Cletus Frade told me," Cronley said.

"I hadn't heard about that," Dunwiddie said.

"Once the ransom money had been paid, Tiny," Gehlen explained, "SS officers would go to Dachau or Auschwitz or wherever and remove the prisoners 'for interrogation.' They were not questioned, because the camps were run by the SS. Nor were they questioned when they reported the prisoners had died during interrogation. That happened often during SS interrogation.

"What actually happened to the prisoners was that they were taken first to Spain, and then to Portugal, where they boarded vessels of neutral powers for transportation to South America.

"When this came to my attention, I knew I couldn't stop it. The corruption went right to the top of the Nazi hierarchy. If not to Heinrich Himmler himself, then to those very close to him. But the idea of getting people out of prison camps had a certain fascination for me. I didn't understand the fascination, but it was there. I told Ludwig here, and Oberst Niedermeyer—you met Otto in Argentina, right, Jim?"

"Yes, sir."

"I told them to think about it, and Otto came up with Mossad. We knew they had been active in the Soviet Union for a long time. The question then became what did we have that they wanted? And the corollary, what did they have that we wanted?"

"What was the Mossad doing in Russia?" Cronley asked.

"Zion's business," Mannberg said. "Somehow that had gone right over my head—and if I may say so, the general's."

"I don't know what that means," Cronley said.

"What they were interested in was this homeland they want in Palestine. It didn't really matter to them whether the Soviets won the war or we did," Mannberg said, and then clarified, "*the Germans* did. What they wanted to do was get as many Zionist leaders out of Russia as they could. The Soviets, who didn't trust them, had jailed many of them, sent them to Siberia, or had them locked up in concentration camps."

"When Germany moved into Russia," Gehlen picked up

Mannberg's narrative, "and took over the NKGB prison camps, the SS either killed all the Jews they found in them on the spot, or marched them off to become laborers. And among the people the SS marched off were many of the Zionist leaders Mossad wanted to get out of Russia and to Palestine.

"So, more than a little belatedly, I realized there was common cause between Abwehr Ost and Mossad. They had penetrated the highest levels of the Kremlin, far more successfully than we had. On the other hand, my people, especially those who were in the SS, could get into the SS prison and slave labor systems. And get people out of them with the same ease—actually far more ease—than the SS could take prisoners from the death camps.

"So I arranged to meet with the lady who was to become Seven-K."

"How did you know with whom to meet?"

"We knew who she was. Her given name is Rahil, by the way."

"What?"

"Rahil—Russian for Rachel," Gehlen said.

"Jesus!"

"I thought you would find that interesting," Gehlen said.

"Interesting?" Dunwiddie asked. "Fascinating! Two spies named Rachel."

"Fuck you, Tiny!" Cronley flared.

"Temper, temper, Captain, sir," Dunwiddie said.

"You're never going to forget that, are you?"

"Probably not, and I'm not going to let you forget Rachel, either."

"Now I don't know what anybody's talking about,"

Hessinger said. "Who the hell is Rachel? You're not talking about Colonel Schumann's wife . . . Or are—"

"Private joke, Freddy," Dunwiddie said. "Sorry."

"As I was saying," Gehlen said, "I arranged, with some difficulty, to meet with Seven-K in Vienna. In the Hotel Sacher. Before she met me, I had to turn Ludwig over to some of her people, to guarantee her safe return. But finally we met, and over Sachertorte and coffee—"

"Over what?" Cronley asked.

"A chocolate layer cake for which the Hotel Sacher is famous," Hessinger furnished. "I had my first when I was eight or nine, and still remember how delicious it was."

"Ours, unfortunately, was not," Gehlen said. "It was made with powdered eggs and ersatz sugar, and the coffee was made from acorns, but nevertheless, we struck our first deal.

"If she would get me certain information, I would try to get two people, two Zionists, out of the hands of the SS. She gave me the names, and Ludwig got them out of an SS-run factory in Hungary. I don't think they were Zionists, but she got me the information I asked for."

"How could you know it was the right information?"

"The general knew the answers before he posed the question," Mannberg said.

"You may have noticed, Ludwig, my tendency to ask stupid questions," Cronley said.

"Now that you mention it, Captain, sir . . ." Dunwiddie said.

Mannberg chuckled.

"I would suggest to the both of you," Gehlen said, on the edge of unpleasantness, "that Captain Cronley's ability to get his mind around all aspects of a statement, to question everything about a situation, not only is useful, but is far greater than your own. Jim, I hope you always ask whatever questions occur to you."

He let that sink in a moment, and then went on.

"I was impressed with her from the first. Her ability to get from Moscow, where she was then stationed, to Vienna proved that she was high ranking. It required false identity documents, et cetera, and carried the real risk that it was an Abwehr Ost plan to seize her.

"I don't know this, but I suspect she told Nikolayevich Merkulov, the commissar of state security, or his deputy, Ivan Serov, that I had made overtures. They had to give her permission to go to Vienna. Why did they do so? For much the same reasons that I authorized Ludwig to meet with Mr. Dulles in Bern, when he first made overtures to me, to see what the head of OSS Europe had in mind.

"But what to keep in mind here is that what Rahil wanted to learn was what she might get from Abwehr Ost that would benefit Mossad, and only secondarily the NKGB.

"What is that phrase, Jim, you so often use? 'Cutting to the chase'? Cutting to the chase here, very slowly, very carefully, Rahil and I developed mutual trust. I was useful to her, and she was useful to me. Much of what I learned about the plans of the NKGB for Abwehr Ost personnel when they won the war, I learned from Rahil."

He paused for a moment and then went on.

"And much of what the NKGB initially learned about Mr. Dulles's postwar plans for Abwehr Ost, they learned from me. It was what you call a 'tough call,' but in the end I decided it was necessary to tell her. It further cemented both our relationship with her and hers with her superiors in the NKGB.

"But I was not in contact with her from the time I surrendered to Major Wallace until I decided the importance of getting Mrs. Likharev out of Russia justified the risk. I wasn't sure, when I told Ludwig to try to reestablish the link, that she was still alive, or more importantly would be willing to reestablish our relationship.

"Fortunately for us, she has apparently decided—and let me restate this—that the good the Süd-Deutsche Industrielle Entwicklungsorganisation can do *for the Mossad* justifies the risks entailed in getting the Likharevs out of Russia."

"What good can we do Mossad?" Cronley asked.

"Rahil will think of something," Gehlen said. "And if she manages to get the Likharevs out, we will be in her debt."

"Yes, we will," Cronley thought out loud.

"I don't think Colonel Parsons even suspects anything about the Likharev situation," Gehlen said. "And we have to keep it that way. It's just the sort of thing he's looking for."

"I don't see where that will be a problem," Cronley said.

"The problems that cause the most trouble are often the ones one doesn't suspect will happen," Gehlen said.

No one replied.

"If you don't have anything else for us, Jim," Gehlen went on, "may I suggest we're through here?"

"I'll drive you to Pullach, General," Hessinger said. "I'm going to need the Kapitän in the morning."

"I'll drive everybody to Pullach," Cronley said. "I have to go to Kloster Grünau. When do you need the car in the morning?"

"Nine. Nine thirty. No later than ten."

"I'll either have one of Tiny's guys bring it back tonight, or I'll bring it back in the morning."

"You want me to go with you, Jim?"

"No. Thank you, but no."

"What do you have to do tonight at Kloster Grünau?" Dunwiddie asked.

"There's a problem with one of the Storchs. I promised Schröder I'd have a look at it."

"Tonight?"

"I promised him yesterday."

That's all bullshit. Schröder didn't say anything about a problem with a Storch.

What I want to do is have a little time to think, and I won't have it if I stay in Pullach, and I don't want to spend the night in the Vier Jahreszeiten.

But I didn't have to think about coming up with an excuse to go to Kloster Grünau. The excuse—the story, the bullshit, the lie—leapt to my lips.

Why am I surprised?

Everybody in this surreal world I'm now living in lies so often about everything, and I'm so used to that it never even occurred to me to tell the simple truth that I need some time to think.

[FIVE]
Kloster Grünau
Schollbrunn, Bavaria
American Zone of Occupation, Germany
0015 30 December 1945

The conclusion Cronley reached after thinking all the way to Kloster Grünau was that not only would he be way over his head when he became chief, DCI-Europe, but that Admiral Souers damned well knew it.

So why isn't there some grizzled full-bird colonel available to do what I'm clearly unqualified to do?

The non-availability of such a grizzled full-bird colonel—and Lieutenant Colonel Maxwell T. "Polo" Ashton would not qualify as a grizzled lieutenant colonel even if he showed up here, which, considering his broken leg and other infirmities, I now think seems highly unlikely—was not a satisfactory answer to the question.

So what to do?

Face it that Gehlen has taken over Operation Ost.

Not for any political reasons, but because nature abhors a vacuum.

So how do I handle that?

Sit there with my ears open and my mouth shut?

It's already obvious that he and ol' Ludwig are only telling me what they think I can be trusted to know.

Not one word about Mata Hari, the super Mossad spy, until tonight.

Aka Rachel.

And didn't Fat Freddy pick up on that?

Does he suspect anything? Fat Freddy is pretty damned smart.

So what do I do about Gehlen not telling me what I should be told?

"See here, General, you and ol' Ludwig are going to have to tell me everything."

To which he would say, "Absolutely," and tell me not one goddamned thing he doesn't think I should know.

So what should I do?

Admit you don't have a fucking clue what to do, and place your faith in the truism that God takes care of fools and drunks, and you fully qualify as both.

When he drove the Kapitän past the second barrier fence, Cronley saw that floodlights were on in the tent hangar built for the Storchs.

Maybe something is wrong with one of them. Truth being stranger than fiction.

He drove to the hangar.

Kurt Schröder was working on the vertical stabilizer assembly of one of them. And apparently being assisted by Lieutenant Max—whose name Cronley was wholly unsure he could ever pronounce.

Schröder seemed surprised to see him. Maksymilian Ostrowski looked as if he had been caught with his hand in the candy jar.

"We've got a frayed cable, not serious, but I thought I'd replace it," Schröder said.

"And drafted Lieutenant Max to help you?"

"I hope that's all right, sir," Ostrowski said.

"Fine with me, if it's okay with Kurt."

Cronley's half-formed wild idea about the Pole popped back into his mind.

Where the hell did that come from?

And now that it's back and I'm entirely sober, I can see it's really off the wall.

Or is it?

Why the hell not?

Who's going to tell me no?

None of us are supposed to be flying the Storchs, so what's the difference?

"Tell me, Max," Cronley said, "what's the name of your guy who served with the Free French?"

"Jaworski, Pawell Jaworski, sir."

"Could *Pawell Jaworski* take over the guard detachment?"

Ostrowski thought it over for a long moment.

"Yes, sir. I'm sure he could."

"Okay. On your way to bed, wake him up and tell him that as of 0600 tomorrow, that's what he'll be doing."

"Yes, sir," Ostrowski said. "Captain, may I ask what this is about?"

"Oh, I guess I didn't get into that, did I?"

"No, sir, you did not."

"Presuming, of course, that Kurt can get that vertical stabilizer assembly back together and working, what he's going to do at 0600 is start checking you out on the Storch."

"Checking me out?"

"They didn't use that term in the Free Polish Air Force?"

"Yes, sir. I know what it means."

"Try not to bend my airplane, Max. I've grown rather fond of it."

Cronley turned and walked out of the tent hangar.

That was probably a stupid thing to do.

Colonel Mattingly would almost certainly think so.

But since I'll be running, as of January 2, DCI-Europe, I don't have to worry about what that bastard thinks.

That's my plan for the future.

Do whatever the hell I think will be good for Operation Ost, and keep doing it until somebody hands me my ass on a shovel.

Abraham Lincoln Tedworth, his sleeves now adorned with the first sergeant's chevrons to which he had been entitled since 1700 the previous day, was waiting for him when he walked into the bar.

"This came in about ten minutes ago, Captain."

He handed Cronley a SIGABA printout.

"Top, I just relieved Lieutenant Max as commander of the Polish Guard," Cronley announced.

"With all respect, sir, that was a dumb move."

That's what they call loyalty downward.

"I deeply appreciate your unfailing confidence in my command decisions, First Sergeant."

"Well, you better reconsider that one. Max is a damned good man."

"That's why I am transferring him to the Operation Ost Air Force. I told Schröder to check him out in a Storch."

Tedworth thought that over for a minute, and then announced, "Now that, sir, is a fine command decision."

"I'm glad you approve, First Sergeant," Cronley said, and then read the SIGABA printout:

```
PRIORITY

TOP SECRET LINDBERGH

DUPLICATION FORBIDDEN

FROM POLO

VIA VINT HILL TANGO NET

2210 GREENWICH 30 DECEMBER 1945

TO ALTARBOY

UNDERSIGNED WILL ARRIVE RHINE-MAIN MATS
FLIGHT 343 ETA 0900 2 JANUARY 1946. USUAL
HONORS WILL NOT BE REQUIRED. A SMALL BRASS
BAND WILL SUFFICE.

POLO

END

TOP SECRET LINDBERGH
```

IV

[ONE]
Arriving Passenger Terminal
Rhine-Main USAF Base
Frankfurt am Main
American Zone, Occupied Germany
0915 2 January 1946

Cronley watched through the windows of the terminal building as the passengers debarked from the Military Air Transport Service Douglas C-54 "Skymaster," which had just flown—via Gander, Newfoundland, and Prestwick, Scotland—from Washington.

The procession down the ladder and into the terminal building was led by a major general, two brigadier generals, some other brass. Then came four senior non-coms, and finally a long line of women and children. They were "dependents" joining their husbands, called "sponsors," in the Army of Occupation.

When the dependents came into the terminal, they were emotionally greeted by the sponsors in a touching display of connubial affection.

Cronley's mind filled with the memory of his explaining the system to the Squirt at Camp Holabird the day they were married. The day before the drunken sonofabitch in the eighteen-wheeler ran head-on into her on US-1 in Washington.

He forced his mind off the subject.

No one was coming down the stairway.

What did you do, Polo? Miss the goddamn plane?

And then Lieutenant Colonel Maxwell Ashton III appeared in the door of the aircraft. In pinks and greens. He was on crutches. His right leg and left arm were in casts.

He stared down the stairs. Then, apparently deciding the crutches would be useless, he threw them down the stairs.

Jesus, he's going to try to hop down the stairs!

"Go get him, Tiny," Cronley ordered. "Before he breaks his other leg."

"They won't let me out there," Dunwiddie protested.

"Show them the goddamn CIC badge and go get him!"

"Right."

"And you go with him, and get the crutches," Cronley ordered.

"Yes, sir," Maksymilian Ostrowski said, and headed for the door.

Ostrowski was wearing, as Cronley was, a U.S. Army woolen olive-drab Ike jacket and trousers with "civilian" triangles sewn to the lapels. Dunwiddie was in pinks and greens.

Cronley, after thinking about it overnight, had decided to have Ostrowski fly the second Storch from Kloster Grünau to Rhine-Main to meet Ashton. For one thing, Schröder had reported—not surprisingly, since Ostrowski had been flying Spitfires and Hurricanes—that it had taken less than an hour for him to be convinced the Pole could fly a Storch. For another, Ostrowski spoke "British English" fluently. When he called the Rhine-Main control tower, that would not cause suspicion, as Schröder's heavily German-accented English would.

But the real reason he had ordered Ostrowski to fly the second Storch was to test his theory that he could—DCI-Europe could—get away with not only flying the Storchs that were supposed to be grounded *but* having them flown by a German and a Pole, and hiding both behind CIC credentials to which they were not entitled.

It would either work or it wouldn't. If they suddenly found themselves being detained by outraged Air Force officers—or for that matter, outraged Army officers—calling for somebody's scalp, better to have that happen now, when Ashton was in Germany. A newly promoted lieutenant colonel might not be able to do much against the forces aligned against DCI-Europe, but he would have a lot more clout than a newly promoted captain.

Tiny, flashing his CIC wallet, and with Ostrowski on his heels, got past the Air Force sergeant keeping people from going onto the tarmac, and without trouble.

The young sergeant might have been dazzled by the CIC credentials, Cronley thought. But it was equally possible that he had been dazzled by an enormous, very black captain he knew he could not physically restrain from going anywhere he wanted to.

As Tiny started up the stairs, two at a time, another man appeared in the airplane door. A stocky, somewhat florid-faced man in his late forties, wearing the uniform of a U.S. Navy lieutenant.

He was somehow familiar.

Jesus Christ! That's El Jefe!

The last time Cronley had seen Lieutenant Oscar J. Schultz, USNR, he had been wearing the full regalia of an Argentine gaucho, a billowing white shirt over billowing black trousers; a gaily printed scarf; a wide-brimmed leather hat; knee-high black leather boots; a wide, silver-coin-adorned leather belt; and, tucked into the belt, the silver scabbard of a horn-handled knife the size of a cavalry saber.

El Jefe had once been Chief Radioman Oscar Schultz of the destroyer USS *Alfred Thomas*, DD-107, hence the reference *El Jefe*, the chief. Schultz had been drafted into the OSS by then-Captain Cletus Frade, USMCR, when the *Thomas* had sailed into Buenos Aires on a friendly visit to the neutral Argentine Republic. And also to surreptitiously put ashore a radar set and a SIGABA communications system for the OSS.

Frade thought he needed a highly skilled, Spanish-speaking (El Jefe had done two tours at the U.S. Navy base at Cavite in the Philippines) communications and radar expert more than the *Thomas* did, and General William Donovan, then head of the OSS, had not only agreed, but had had a word with the chief of naval operations.

Two days later, the *Thomas* had sailed from Buenos Aires without Chief Schultz. Schultz set up shop on Estancia San Pedro y San Pablo, Frade's enormous ranch, where Cronley had met him and where he had quickly acquired both the regalia of a gaucho and a Rubenesque lady friend, who became known as "the other Dorotea," the first being Señora Dorotea Frade.

More importantly, he had become an important member of "Team Turtle," the code name for Frade's OSS operation in Argentina. So important that he had been given a direct commission as an officer.

What the hell is El Jefe doing here?

Before the question had run through his mind, Cronley knew the answer.

Admiral Souers, knowing that Polo would refuse the assistance of a nurse, even a male nurse, although he really needed it, had ordered Schultz up from Argentina so that he could assist and protect Polo while he traveled to Germany and then back to Argentina.

That noble idea seemed to be destined to become a spectacular disaster.

As Tiny bounded up the stairway, El Jefe, seeing an enormous black man headed for his charge, started bounding down them to defend him.

Cronley recalled Cletus Frade telling him that El Jefe enjoyed the deep respect of the gauchos of the estancia, despite his refusal to get on a horse, because he had become both the undisputed bare-knuckles pugilist of the estancia and the undisputed hand-wrestling champion. Gauchos add spice, Cletus had told him, to their hand-wrestling fun by holding hands over their unsheathed razor-sharp knives.

Captain Dunwiddie and Lieutenant Schultz had a brief conversation near the top of the stairs. Then, suddenly, as if they had practiced the action for months, they had Polo in a "handbasket" between them and were carrying him—like the bridegroom at a Hebrew wedding—down the stairs, across the tarmac, and into the passenger terminal.

Cronley was surprised that no one seemed to pay much attention.

"Welcome to occupied Germany," Cronley said, as Schultz and Dunwiddie set Ashton on his feet and Ostrowski handed him his crutches. "Please keep in mind that VD walks the streets tonight, and penicillin fails once in seven times."

Ashton shook his head.

"Thanks," he said to Dunwiddie, Schultz, and Ostrowski. "Where's the colonel?"

"Which colonel would that be?"

"Mattingly."

"I don't know. I hope he's far from here."

"The admiral said I should see him as soon as I got here. I've got a letter for him. What do you mean you hope he's far from here?"

A letter? From Souers to Mattingly? Why does that scare me?

"We're going to have to have a little chat before you see him," Cronley said. He gestured toward the door. "Your ambulance awaits."

"I don't need an ambulance."

"You do unless you want to walk all the way across Rhine-Main airfield."

"What's all the way across the field?"

"The Storchs in which we are going to fly to Kloster Grünau—the monastery—to have our little chat."

"How they hanging, kid?" Schultz demanded of Captain Cronley.

"One beside the other. How about yours?"

"I don't have to tell you, do I, about how lousy I feel about what happened to the Squirt?"

"No. But thank you."

"I really liked that little broad," Schultz said. "Mean as a snake, but nice, you know?"

"Yeah," Cronley said.

"You know, Jim, that you have my condolences," Max Ashton said. "Tragic!"

Cronley saw the sympathy, the compassion, in their eyes.

[TWO]
Kloster Grünau
Schollbrunn, Bavaria
American Zone of Occupation, Germany
1340 2 January 1946

Lieutenant Colonel Maxwell Ashton III tapped the remnants of his steak on his plate with his knife and fork and then announced, "Not too bad. Not grass-fed on the pampas, of course, and—not to look the gift horse in the mouth—this red wine frankly does not have the *je ne sais quoi* of an Estancia Don Guillermo Cabernet Sauvignon. But one must expect to make certain sacrifices when one goes off to battle the Red Menace on foreign shores, mustn't one?"

He got the dutiful chuckles he expected.

"Colonel Frade came to see me shortly before El Jefe and I got on the airplane—" Ashton began to go on.

"In Washington?" Cronley interrupted. "Cletus is in Washington?"

"He was there briefly en route to Pensacola, Florida, where he will be released from active service in the United States Marine Corps. I appreciate your interest, but I would appreciate even more your permitting me to continue."

"Sorry."

"Colonel Frade was kind enough to offer a few suggestions vis-à-vis my trip here. He recommended that should Colonel Mattingly not be able to find time in his busy schedule to meet me at Frankfurt, so that I might give him Admiral Souers's letter—"

"Why did he think Mattingly was going to meet you at Rhine-Main?" Cronley interrupted again.

Ashton ignored the interruption and went on, "I should ask whoever met us to take us to the Schlosshotel Kronberg, where we could rest in luxurious accommodations overnight, to recuperate from our journey. Then, the following morning, I could go to the I.G. Farben Building to meet with Colonel Mattingly, deliver the admiral's letter to him, and perhaps meet with General Greene and possibly even General Smith.

"Following that meeting, or meetings, Colonel Frade suggested we then reserve a compartment on a railroad train charmingly titled 'the Blue Danube' and travel to Munich to meet with you, Captain Cronley, your staff, and General Gehlen, preferably at the Hotel Vier Jahreszeiten, which he assured me would provide El Jefe and myself luxury accommodations equal to those of the Schlosshotel Kronberg.

"Instead . . . as someone once said, 'the best-laid plans gang aft agley,' which I suspect means get royally fucked up . . . Captain Cronley meets us at the airport, tells me he has no idea where Colonel Mattingly is, but that he hopes wherever he is it is far away. He then stuffs me into the really uncomfortable backseat of a little airplane and flies me through every storm cloud he could find to a medieval monastery in the middle of fucking nowhere."

Cronley smiled, but he recalled seeing—a dozen times, more—Ashton wince with pain as the Storch had been tossed about by turbulence during the flight from Frankfurt.

"Now, one would suspect," Ashton went on, "that, in normal circumstances, this deviation from the plan would annoy, perhaps even anger, your new commanding officer. These are not normal circumstances, however.

"I was given the opportunity, first while lying in my bed of pain in Walter Reed, and then whilst flying across the Atlantic, and finally as I flew here from Frankfurt, to consider what the circumstances really are.

"To start, let me go back to the beginning. The admiral came to see me at Walter Reed. Bearing my new silver oak leaves. He told me they were intended more as an inducement for me to stay on active duty than a recognition of my superior leadership characteristics.

"I then told him I didn't need an inducement to stay on active duty, as I was determined to get the bastards who did this to me."

He raised his broken arm.

"He immediately accepted my offer, which I thought surprised him more than a little. Not immediately, but right after he left, I began to wonder why. The cold facts seemed to be that not only was I going to have to hobble around on crutches for the next several months but—more importantly—I was in fact no more qualified to take over Operation Ost from Colonel Frade than Jim was to handle Operation Ost in Germany.

"Certainly, I reasoned, although I had heard time and again that finding experienced people for the new DCI was going to be difficult, there had to be two or three or four experienced spooks—Colonel Mattingly–like senior spooks—who had joined the ranks of the unemployed when the OSS went out of business, who would be available. And Colonel Frade had made the point over and over that not all members, just an overwhelming majority of officers of the conventional intelligence operations, were unable to find their asses using both hands.

"I came up with a theory immediately, but dismissed it as really off the wall.

"And then I was given the letter—the carefully sealed letter in the double envelope—to deliver to Colonel Mattingly. 'What,' I wondered, 'does the admiral wish to tell Colonel Mattingly that he doesn't want me to know?'

"When I thought, at length, about this, my initial off-the-wall theory started coming back, and each time it did it made more sense.

"The conclusion I reached, after considering everything, is that Admiral Souers has decided that you and I, Jim—and of course Captain Dunwiddie—are expendable. I have also concluded that Colonel Frade—whatever his limitations are, no one has ever accused him of being slow—is, if not party to this, fully aware of it."

"How do you mean 'expendable,' Colonel?" Dunwiddie asked.

"Available for sacrifice for the greater good," Ashton said. "Consider this, please. To whom does Admiral Souers—with absolute justification—owe his primary loyalty?"

"The President," Cronley said softly. "Oh, Jesus!"

"Who must be protected whatever it takes," Ashton said.

"Why are you telling us this?" Dunwiddie asked.

"Well, after thinking it over, I decided that—as far as I'm concerned—it's all right. What we're doing is important. But I decided that it would be dishonest of me, now that I've figured it out, not to tell you. Before we go further, in other words, I wanted you to have the opportunity to opt out."

"'Before we go further'?" Dunwiddie parroted.

"What I've decided to do is live with the possibility, actually the probability, that Operation Ost is going to blow up in my face, and that when that happens, Souers, as he should, is going to throw me to the wolves to protect the President. And for that matter, Eisenhower and Smith. That's one of the things I've decided."

"And the others?" Cronley asked.

"That if Operation Ost blows up in my face, it's going to be because of a bad decision of mine. Not because Mattingly or General Greene 'suggest' something to me and I dutifully follow their suggestion to do—more importantly, not to do—something and it blows up."

"For instance?" Cronley asked softly.

"For instance, Colonel Frade suggested to me that I should act 'with great caution' in dealing with our traitor. I don't intend to heed that advice. My first priority is going to be finding out who the sonofabitch is, and then putting out his lights. I don't care if he spent three years holding Gehlen's hand on the Russian front and has Joe Stalin's girlfriend's phone number, he's a dead man."

"By traitor, you mean the man who let the NKGB know we were sending Colonel Likharev to Argentina?" Cronley asked.

"With all the details of when and how," Ashton confirmed. "Gehlen has to be taught that he's working for us, and that our deal with him is to protect his people from the Russians. The deal didn't include protecting his people from us. He has to be taught, right now, that we won't tolerate a loose cannon."

"There are people in Gehlen's organization who are working for the NKGB—"

"You already had figured that out, huh?"

"And we're working on finding out who they are."

"'We're' meaning you and Gehlen, right? Isn't that what's called sending the fox into the chicken coop to see what happened to the hens? Frankly, Jim, I thought you had more sense than that."

"You will be astonished, Colonel, when I tell you how little sense I have had."

"What the hell does that mean?"

"Shortly after I returned from Argentina, I met a woman. The wife of the CIC-Europe IG. Shortly after that—"

"Wait a minute! You're talking about this woman whose water heater blew up?"

Cronley nodded.

"There has to be a point to this narrative of your sexual exploits."

"I told her about Colonel Sergei Likharev, then known to us as Major Konstantin Orlovsky, about whom she had heard from her husband and was curious. And the night I put him on the plane to Buenos Aires, I told her about that."

"And she ran her mouth?"

"I don't think they call it running the mouth when an NKGB agent reports to her superiors the intelligence she was sent to get."

Ashton looked at Cronley for a long moment.

"You're saying the wife of the CIC IG was an NKGB agent?" he asked incredulously.

"We're saying that both of them, the IG, too, were NKGB agents," Dunwiddie said.

"And the water heater explosion?"

"My orders from Colonel Frade, about finding and dealing

with the leak, were to get out of General Gehlen's way when he was dealing with it. I complied with that order."

"And didn't tell Mattingly, or Greene—for that matter, Frade—about your suspicions?"

"They weren't suspicions. The only way the NKGB could have learned about our sending Likharev to Argentina, and when and how, was from my loving Rachel," Cronley said.

"And, as the general pointed out," Dunwiddie said, "a day or two after we caught Likharev sneaking out of here, Colonel Schumann showed up here and demanded to be let in. It took shooting his engine out with a .50-caliber Browning to keep him out. The general suggested Colonel Schumann's interest in Kloster Grünau was because he suspected we had Orlovsky/Likharev."

"My God!" Ashton said.

"Gehlen further suggested that how Jim planned to deal with the situation wasn't practical."

"He said it was childish," Cronley corrected him.

"And this impractical, childish situation was?" Ashton asked.

"I was going to shoot both of them and then go tell Mattingly why."

"General Gehlen said Jim going to the stockade—"

"Or the hangman's noose," Cronley interjected.

". . . made no sense."

"You didn't even consider going to Mattingly and telling him what you suspected? You just—"

"You're going to have to learn that when you tell Mattingly anything . . ." Cronley interrupted.

"I'm going to have to learn?" Ashton interrupted. "I don't think I like you telling me anything I *have* to do."

". . . Mattingly will look at it through the prism of what's good for Colonel Robert Mattingly," Cronley finished.

"Did you just hear what I said, Captain Cronley?"

"Yeah, Colonel Ashton, I heard. But you better get used to it. That won't be the last time I'll tell you what I think you have to do. Don't get blinded by those silver oak leaves. What the hell makes you think you can get off the plane and start telling us what to do? You don't know enough of what's going—"

"Enough," Tiny boomed. "Goddamn it! Both of you, stop right there!"

He sounded like the first sergeant he had so recently been, counseling two PFCs who were doing something really stupid.

And then, as if he had heard what he'd said, and was now cognizant that captains cannot talk to lieutenant colonels as if they are PFCs doing something really stupid, he went on jocularly, "In the immortal words of the great lover of our revolutionary era, the revered Benjamin Franklin, 'We must hang together, gentlemen, else, we shall most assuredly hang separately.'"

Ashton glowered at him for a long moment.

Finally he said, "Actually, Jim, I must admit the little fellow has a point."

"Every once in a great while, he's right about something," Cronley said, and then added, "I was out of line. I apologize."

"Apology rejected as absolutely unnecessary," Ashton said.

After a moment, he went on. "So what's next?"

"Before we get to what's next," El Jefe said, "I have a request."

"For what?"

"Is there a .45 around here that I can have?"

"Why do you want a .45?" Dunwiddie asked.

"Well, when people try to kill me, I like to have something to defend myself."

When there was no reply, El Jefe went on.

"This Colonel Mattingly of yours may think a gas leak took out this CIC colonel and his wife, but I don't think the NKGB is swallowing that line. I think they may want to come back here and play tit for tat."

"They already have," Cronley said. "A week ago, Ostrowski killed two of them. They already had a wire garrote around Sergeant Tedworth's neck."

"Correct me if I'm wrong," El Jefe said, "but following that, it was really heads-up around here, right? Double the guard, that sort of thing?"

Cronley and Dunwiddie nodded.

"So I think what these Communists will do is wait until you relax a little, and then try it again. At least that's what the Chinese Communists did."

"The Chinese?" Ashton and Cronley said on top of each other.

"When I was a young sailor, I did two hitches with the Yangtze River Patrol. The Chinese Communists were always trying to kill us. What they did was try. If that failed, they waited patiently until we relaxed a little and then tried again. And again. Most of the time, that worked. We used to say we got double time for retirement because the Navy knew most of us wouldn't live long enough to retire."

"Interesting," Dunwiddie said. "That's how the Apaches operated."

"Two things, Captain Cronley," Ashton said. "When you get Lieutenant Schultz a .45, would you get me one, too?"

"Yes, sir."

"And one last question. If you didn't want to go to Colonel Mattingly with it, why didn't you go to General Greene and tell him what you suspected—all right, knew—about Colonel Whatsisname and his wife?"

Dunwiddie answered for him: "General Gehlen said that the Schumanns were sure to have contingency plans—ranging from denial through disappearing—in case they were exposed. He said he didn't think we could afford to take the chance they were outwitting us. Jim and I agreed with him."

"So you went along with having Gehlen clip them," Ashton said.

"We don't *know* that Gehlen had them clipped," Cronley said.

"You don't know the sun will come up in the morning, either. But you would agree it's likely, right?"

When Cronley didn't reply, Ashton said, "I suggest, operative word, 'suggest,' that our next step is to meet with General Gehlen."

"I respectfully suggest our next step is getting the .45s," El Jefe said. "*Then* we can go talk to this general."

"Every once in a great while, the chief's right about something," Ashton said.

[THREE]
Kloster Grünau
Schollbrunn, Bavaria
American Zone of Occupation, Germany
1520 2 January 1946

CIC Special Agent Friedrich Hessinger and a very large, very black sergeant with a Thompson submachine gun cradled in his arms like a hunter's shotgun walked into the officers' mess.

Captain J. D. Cronley, Captain Chauncey L. Dunwiddie, First Sergeant Abraham Lincoln Tedworth, and a man in a naval officer's uniform were sitting at the bar drinking coffee. A lieutenant colonel sitting in a chair, with his en-casted leg resting on a small table, also held a coffee cup.

The sergeant smiled and, without disturbing the Thompson, saluted.

"Those captain's bars look good on you, Top," he said.

Dunwiddie returned the salute.

"Flattery will get you everywhere," he said. "Thanks, Eustis."

"And these stripes?" Tedworth asked, pointing to his chevrons. "How do they look on me?"

"Every once in a while, the Army makes a really big mistake," the sergeant said.

"That will cost you, Eustis. Sooner or later that will really cost you," Tedworth replied. "Now, get over to the motor pool and tell them to have an ambulance, with a couch, ready in ten minutes. We're going into Munich."

"And then come back here?"

"Wait there until I send for you."

"You got it, Top."

When he had gone, Cronley said, "Good man."

"Yes, he is," Dunwiddie agreed. "When he's told to do something, he does it. Not like some fat Kraut-Americans, like the one I'm looking at."

Hessinger held up both hands, a gesture that meant both that he didn't understand and that he surrendered.

"Captain Cronley, did you, or did you not, tell Fat Freddy to arm himself before driving out here?"

"I recall saying something along those lines to Special Agent Hessinger, yes," Cronley said.

"'Sorry, sir. No excuse, sir' will not be a satisfactory excuse, Sergeant Hessinger," Dunwiddie said.

Hessinger hoisted the skirt of his tunic. The butt of a Model 1911A1 .45 ACP pistol became visible above his hip.

"Say 'I apologize' to Freddy," Cronley said, laughing. And then he added, "Come here, Freddy, I want to see that holster."

Hessinger complied.

"Where the hell did you get that?"

"I had a shoemaker make half a dozen of them," Hessinger replied. "They call them 'Secret Service High Rise Cross Draw Holsters.' There was a schematic in one of the books on General Greene's sergeant major's shelf."

"Colonel Ashton, Lieutenant Schultz, meet Special Agent Hessinger, sometimes known as 'One Surprise After Another Hessinger,'" Cronley said.

They shook hands.

"Your funny accent," El Jefe said. "What are you, German?"

"I was. Now I am an American."

"Can I have a look at that holster?" Ashton asked.

Hessinger hoisted the skirt of his tunic again and said, "They also work under an Ike jacket, Colonel."

Schultz took a good look, and then asked, "Who would I have to kill to get one of them?"

Hessinger didn't say anything, but he looked at Dunwiddie.

Cronley laughed.

"I have enough for everybody," Hessinger said. "I thought we would need more than one, so I had the extras made for us."

Cronley laughed again and then asked, "Freddy, how long have you been carrying a .45 in that Secret Service holster?"

"Ever since Tedworth caught the Russian," Hessinger said. "The first Russian. I thought the NKGB might try to kidnap one of us, and then try to make a swap. You didn't think about that?"

No, goddammit, I didn't.

One more entry in the stupid column.

Cronley saw El Jefe scribble something on a piece of paper and hand it to Ashton.

What the hell is that?

"Freddy," Cronley asked, "you just said 'we' and 'for us.' How strongly do you feel about that?"

"When I was growing up, my father told me you couldn't choose your parents, but you should choose your associates. Then I was drafted and found out you can't choose either," Hessinger said. "Why do I think there is a question behind that question?"

"Because you're not nearly as dumb as you look?" Dunwiddie asked.

"Now that you're an officer, you're not supposed to insult junior enlisted men," Hessinger said. "Isn't that right, Captain Cronley?"

"Absolutely. That's two apologies you owe Fat Freddy, Captain Dunwiddie."

"And one, I would say, Captain Cronley, that you owe the sergeant," Ashton said.

"Excuse me, Colonel," Hessinger said. "We do this all the time. What it is is that they're jealous of my education."

"Did I mention that Hessinger is a Harvard graduate, Colonel?" Cronley asked.

"I'll try not to hold that against you, Sergeant Hessinger," Ashton said. "We all have a cross to bear, and your Harvard diploma must be a very heavy one."

There were chuckles all around. Even Hessinger smiled.

"Why did you ask me what you asked before?" he asked.

"Freddy, what if I told you Colonel Ashton believes, and so do Tiny and me, that if Operation Ost blows up in our face, everybody from Admiral Souers on down is going to throw us to the wolves?"

"That surprises you? In Russian literature there are many vignettes of the nobility throwing peasants out of troikas to save themselves from the wolves. Which is of course the etymological source of that expression."

"What's a troika?" El Jefe asked.

"A horse-drawn sleigh," Dunwiddie furnished.

"Three horses, side by side," Hessinger further amplified, using his hands to demonstrate.

"If we can turn from this fascinating lecture on Russian customs to the subject at hand, stemming the tide of the Red Menace?" Cronley asked. "Freddy, we've decided that if getting tossed from this three-horse buggy is the price that we have to pay for trying to protect Operation Ost and the President, okay, we'll take our lumps."

Hessinger was now paying close attention.

"And, further, we have decided that if we get tossed from the buggy, it will be because we fucked up somehow, not because we blindly followed the friendly suggestions of anybody—Mattingly, Greene, or even the admiral—on how to do the job.

"And, we have concluded that despite our best efforts, the odds are we're going to wind up over our asses in the snow with the wolves gnawing on our balls. Both the colonel and I have decided, with Captain Dunwiddie concurring, that we have to ask you whether or not you wish to join the lunatics or whether you should return to the bona fide CIC and chase Nazis."

"In other words, Tubby," El Jefe said, "there's no reason you should get your ass burned because these two nuts think they're Alan Ladd and Errol Flynn saving the world for Veronica Lake and Mom's apple pie. You want to take my advice, get as far away from this as soon as you can."

"Thank you just the same," Hessinger said, "but I don't want your advice. What I do want is for you, Jim, to tell me what I have done to make you think you had to ask me that question."

"What does that mean, Tubby?" El Jefe asked. "Are you in, or are you out?"

"Don't call me Tubby."

"Why not? It fits."

"They can call me 'Fat Freddy' or whatever they want. They're my friends. You're not. You can either call me 'Sergeant Hessinger' or 'Mr. Hessinger.' Got it, Popeye the Sailor Man?"

"Enlisted men aren't supposed to talk to officers like that, Freddy," Dunwiddie said.

"When I'm in my CIC suit," Hessinger said, pointing to the blue triangles on his lapels, "nobody's supposed to know I'm an enlisted man."

"Mr. Hessinger's got you, Captain Dunwiddie," Cronley said, and added, "Yet again."

"May I infer, Mr. Hessinger, that you wish to remain allied with us, despite the risks doing so entails?" Ashton asked.

"Yes, sir. He didn't have to ask me that."

"No offense intended, Freddy," Cronley said.

"Offense taken, thank you very much," Hessinger said.

"At this point, I would like to introduce an intelligence analysis I received a short time ago," Ashton said. "Would you read this aloud, Captain Dunwiddie?"

Ashton handed Dunwiddie a small sheet of paper.

That's what El Jefe handed him.

"'If Jim wants to let him go, overrule him. Trust me. We need this guy,'" Dunwiddie read.

Hessinger looked at El Jefe for a long moment, and then said, "Thank you, Lieutenant Schultz."

"Just the honest judgment of an old chief petty officer, Mr. Hessinger."

"You can call me Fat Freddy, if you like."

"Thank you. Fat Freddy, if you ever call me 'Popeye the Sailor Man' again, I will tear off one of your legs and shove it up your ass."

"Moving right along," Ashton said, "what I think we

should do now is go to Munich and meet with General Gehlen."

"Stopping along the way wherever Fred has stashed the other five .45 holsters he said he has," El Jefe said. "I want one."

"They're in the Kapitän," Hessinger said. "I thought you would need them, so I brought them out here with me."

[FOUR]
Quarters of the U.S. Military Government
Liaison Officer
The South German Industrial Development
Organization Compound
Pullach, Bavaria
The American Zone of Occupied Germany
1735 2 January 1946

Ashton had trouble getting off the couch, which had been bolted to the floor of the ambulance, and then had more trouble getting out of the ambulance and onto his crutches. The ground behind the ambulance's doors was covered with frozen snow ruts. Ashton looked to be in great danger of falling, but bluntly refused Schultz's and Dunwiddie's offer of "a ride": "When I need help, I'll ask for it."

So the others followed him very slowly as he hobbled on his crutches through the snow from the curb to the small, tile-roofed building.

"Who is this guy?" Schultz demanded of Cronley, "and what's he got to do with us?"

"What guy?"

"The military government liaison officer."

Cronley motioned for El Jefe to come close, and then whispered in his ear, "We really can't afford this getting out, Popeye, it's something we really don't want Joe Stalin to find out. It's me. One more brilliant move to deceive and confuse our enemy."

"Wiseass."

Hessinger plodded through the snow and opened the door for Ashton. Then he held it for Cronley, Schultz, and Dunwiddie.

Former Major General Gehlen and former Colonel Mann-berg were in the living room of the building, sitting in armchairs reading the *Stars and Stripes*. Both rose when they saw Ashton come in.

Ashton made his way to Mannberg and awkwardly held out his hand to him.

"General Gehlen, I am Lieutenant Colonel Ashton."

"I'm Reinhard Gehlen," Gehlen said. "This is Ludwig Mannberg, my deputy."

Cronley thought: *I would have made the same mistake. Good ol' Ludwig looks like what Hollywood movies have taught us senior German officers look like. And the general looks like a not-very-successful black marketeer.*

But that does it. Gehlen gets some decent clothes.

"Well, I hope that's not a harbinger of future confusion," Ashton said.

"Sometimes, Colonel, confusion in our profession is useful, wouldn't you agree?" Gehlen asked.

"Max," Cronley ordered, "sit down before you fall down."

"I'm sure you've noticed, General, that every once in a great while Captain Cronley does have a good idea."

He hobbled to an empty armchair and collapsed into it.

"This is Lieutenant Schultz," Cronley said.

"El Jefe?" Mannberg asked.

Schultz nodded.

"How did you know they call me that?" he asked, on the edge of unpleasantly.

"Otto Niedermeyer is one of your admirers," Mannberg said in Spanish. "He warned me not to arm-wrestle with you."

"Did he tell you I also cheat at chess?" El Jefe asked in Spanish.

"Not in so many words," Mannberg said in German.

"In English, Colonel," El Jefe said, in English, "we have a saying—'It takes one to know one.'"

Mannberg laughed.

Very clever, Cronley thought. *They haven't been together sixty seconds, and already they know how well the other speaks German, Spanish, and English. All of these guys are far more clever than I am.*

"Ludwig," Cronley said, "see if you can guess where Colonel Ashton got his Spanish. Say something in Spanish, Max."

"I have need of the bathroom. Where is it?" Ashton said in Spanish.

"Interesting accent," Mannberg said. "Not pure castellano, but close. Is that the Argentine version?"

El Jefe went to Ashton and pulled him out of the armchair.

"Through that door," Cronley said. "First door to the right."

"Actually, it's Cuban," Ashton said, and then switched to English. "If you will hand me my goddamn crutches, I can handle it from here. But while I'm communing with nature, see if Captain Cronley has any medicine."

"What kind of medicine?" Cronley asked, with concern in his voice.

"Almost anything that comes out of a bottle reading 'Distilled in Scotland' will do," Ashton said, as he began to lurch across the room.

When he was out of earshot, Gehlen said, "Interesting man. I like his sense of humor."

"Don't be too quick to judge him by that," Cronley said. "He's very good at what he does."

As the words came out of his mouth, Cronley thought, *What am I doing? Warning Gehlen about the man he's now working for? That's absolutely ass-backwards!*

"He would not have been selected as Cletus Frade's replacement if he was not very good at what he does," Gehlen said.

So what's the truth there?

Ashton is very good. That's true.

But it's also true that he was selected as an expendable who can be thrown to the wolves.

"That's true, of course," Cronley began. "But there is another, frankly unpleasant, possib—"

"Freddy," El Jefe interrupted him, "I'm not feeling too well myself, so while you're getting the colonel's medicine, how about making a dose for me?"

He looked at Cronley. "How about you? A little medicine for you?"

El Jefe didn't want me to get into that subject—for that matter, any subject—with Gehlen while Ashton is out of the room.

And he's right.

And Gehlen and ol' Ludwig certainly picked up on that.

And Tiny did.

And, of course, Fat Freddy.

I just had my wrist slapped in public.

And deserved it.

"A splendid idea," Cronley said. "I wonder why I didn't think of that myself?"

Because I'm stupid, that's why.

Ashton hobbled, far from nimbly, across the room and again collapsed into the armchair.

Hessinger handed him a glass of whisky, straight, and then offered a bowl of ice cubes. Ashton waved them away and took a healthy swallow of the scotch.

"Gentlemen," he said, "I had an idea just now. That sometimes happens to me when I am in that circumstance and have nothing to read while waiting for Mother Nature to turn her attention to me. And since I am drunk with the power with which Admiral Souers has invested me, we're going to try it. I ask your indulgence.

"There will be no briefing of Lieutenant Schultz and myself in the usual sense. Instead of each of you, junior first, taking turns telling El Jefe and me what has happened in the past—which of course the others already know—we are going to reverse the procedure . . ."

Where the hell is he going with this?

". . . specifically, General Gehlen is going to start by telling us of the most recent development in our noble crusade against the Red Menace—which not all of you, perhaps none of you, will know. Then, I will ask, and all of you may ask, questions to fill in the blanks in our knowledge. This is known as 'reverse engineering.' General Gehlen, please tell us all what you would have told Captain Cronley had he walked in here just now, and Lieutenant Schultz and myself were nowhere around."

Gehlen, a slight smile on his lips, looked at Cronley, who shrugged.

"Very well," Gehlen said. "I would have said, 'Jim, we've heard again from Seven-K.'"

"Aha!" Ashton said. "We've already turned up something I know nothing about. What is Seven-K?"

"It's a her," Cronley said. "Aka Rahil."

"And who is Seven-K, aka Rahil?"

"An old acquaintance of the general's and Ludwig's," Cronley said, smiling at Gehlen.

Ashton picked up on the smile and, literally visibly, began to suspect that his leg was being pulled.

"Tell me about the lady," Ashton said.

"Tell you what about her?"

"Why was she sending you a message?"

"She wants fifty thousand dollars," Gehlen said. "*Another* fifty thousand dollars." He paused, and then, anticipating Ashton's next question, added: "She'd probably say for expenses."

"You've already given this woman fifty thousand dollars? For what?"

"Expenses," Cronley said, smiling.

"What's so goddamn funny?"

"Funny?"

"You're smiling."

"With pleasure, because your idea seems to be working so well," Cronley said.

"I told you to tell me about this woman."

"Well, for one thing, she's Jewish," Cronley said.

"What's that got to do with anything?"

"You ever heard of the Mossad?"

"This woman is Mossad? A Mossad agent?"

"And also a *Podpolkóvnik* of the NKGB," Gehlen said.

"A what?" Ashton asked.

"More probably, General, by now a *Polkóvnik*," Mann-berg said. "That massive wave of promotions right after the war?"

"You're probably right, Ludwig," Gehlen said, and then, to Ashton, added: "The NKGB jokes that one either gets promoted or eliminated."

"What's that you said, General, 'Pod-pol' something?" Ashton asked.

"A *Podpolkóvnik* is a lieutenant colonel," Gehlen explained. "And a *Polkóvnik*, a colonel."

Ashton, visibly, thought something over and then made a decision.

"Okay," he said. "I find it hard to believe that you're pull-ing my leg. On the other hand, with Cronley anything is possible. If you have been pulling my chain, the joke's over. Enough."

"We have not been pulling either your chain or your leg, Colonel," Cronley said.

"You have just heard from a woman who is both a Mossad agent and an NKGB colonel. She wants fifty thousand dollars—in addition to the fifty thousand dollars you have already given her. Is that correct?"

Gehlen and Mannberg nodded. Cronley said, "Yes, sir."

"Where is this woman located?"

"The last we heard," Gehlen said, "in Leningrad. But there's a very good chance she's en route to Vienna."

"Why?" Ashton asked, and then interrupted himself. "First, tell me why you have given her fifty thousand dollars."

"Because she told us she would need at least that much money to get Polkóvnik Likharev's wife and sons out of Russia," Gehlen said.

"Jesus Christ!" Ashton exclaimed, and then asked, "You think she can?"

"We're hoping she can," Gehlen said.

"Where the hell did you get fifty thousand dollars to give to this woman?"

Gehlen didn't reply, but instead looked at Cronley.

"In Schultz's briefcase," Ashton said, "there is fifty thousand dollars. The admiral gave it to me just before we got on the plane. He called it 'start-up' money, and told me to tell you to use it sparingly because he didn't know how soon he could get you any more. That suggests to me that the admiral didn't think you had any money. Hence, my curiosity. Have you been concealing assets from the admiral? If not, where did this fifty thousand come from?"

"From me, Polo," Cronley said. "I came into some money when . . . my wife . . . passed on. A substantial amount of cash. Cletus pulled some strings with the judge of probate in Midland to settle the estate right away. I gave a power of attorney to Karl Boltitz—he's going to marry Beth, the Squirt's sister—and he got the cash, gave it to Clete, Clete took it to Buenos Aires, and then when he sent Father Welner over here, got him to carry it to me."

"Fifty thousand dollars?" Ashton asked incredulously.

"Just for the record, I'm loaning that fifty thousand, repeat, *loaning* it, to the DCI. I expect it back."

"Cletus didn't tell me anything about this."

"Maybe he thought you didn't have to know," Cronley replied.

"And now this woman wants another fifty thousand. What are you going to do about that?"

"Whatever General Gehlen thinks I should."

"You've got another fifty thousand?"

"Father Welner brought me something over two hundred twenty thousand."

"Does Mattingly . . . does anybody else . . . know about this?"

Cronley shook his head.

"Do you realize how deep you're in here?"

Cronley nodded.

"I asked before," Ashton said. "Do you think this woman can get Likharev's family out?"

"Nothing is ever sure in our profession," Gehlen replied.

Ashton made a *Come on* gesture.

Gehlen took a short moment to collect his thoughts.

"I've learned, over the years, when evaluating a situation like this," he said, "to temper my enthusiasm for a project by carefully considering the unpleasant possibilities. The worst of these here is the possibility that we are not dealing with Rahil at all. One of the reasons there was that wave of promotions to which Ludwig referred a moment ago was because there were a large number of vacancies. Fedotov purged the NKGB—"

"Who?" Ashton interrupted.

"Pyotr Vasileevich Fedotov, chief of counterintelligence. He purged the NKGB of everyone about whose loyalty he had the slightest doubt. Rahil certainly was someone at whom he looked carefully.

"Now, if she was purged, we have to presume that Fedotov learned of her relationship with me."

"Even if she was not purged, General," Mannberg said.

"Even if she was not purged," Gehlen agreed, "it is logical to presume that Fedotov knows of our past relationship."

"Which was?" Polo asked.

"We got Russian Zionists out of Schutzstaffel concentration camps for her, and in turn she performed certain services for Abwehr Ost. I doubt that Rahil told Fedotov the exact nature of our relationship, certainly not during the war, or even in any postwar interrogations, if she was purged. But we have to presume he knows there was a relationship.

"What I'm leading up to here is that even before the NKGB found us at Kloster Grünau, they suspected we were in American hands, under American protection, in other words . . ."

"I think they knew that was your intention, General," Mannberg said. "To place us under American protection. All they had to do was find out where we were. And I believe von Plat and Boss gave them both. We don't know when either von Plat or Boss were turned."

"Who are they?" Ashton asked.

"We're getting off the subject," Gehlen said.

"Who are you talking about?" Ashton pursued.

"Polo, are you sure you want to go there?" Cronley asked. Ashton nodded.

Cronley looked at Gehlen.

"Jim," Ashton said, "you don't need General Gehlen's permission to answer any question I put to you."

Cronley shrugged.

"Oberstleutnant Gunther von Plat and Major Kurt Boss of Abwehr Ost surrendered to the OSS when the general did," Cronley replied. "Boss was SS, a dedicated Nazi. Von Plat was Wehrmacht. We were just about to load Boss on a plane for Buenos Aires when Cletus and Father Welner turned Polkóvnik Likharev. Likharev told Cletus these were the guys who'd given him the rosters he had when Tedworth caught him sneaking out of Kloster Grünau. Clete told us."

"Where are these guys now?" Ashton asked.

"No one seems to know," Cronley said.

"You mean they got away? Or that you took them out?"

Cronley didn't reply.

"Polo, the next time Cronley asks you if you want to go somewhere, why don't you turn off your automatic mouth and think carefully before you say yes?" Schultz asked.

Well, that's interesting, Cronley thought. *El Jefe just told Polo to shut up.*

Told. Not politely suggested.

And Polo took it. He looked as if he was about to say something, but then changed his mind.

And that suggests that Cletus sent El Jefe here to do more than help Polo get on and off the airplane.

And that raises the question, what did El Jefe do for Clete in Argentina?

Once El Jefe got the SIGABA set up, it could have been maintained by some kid fresh from the ASA school. But El Jefe stayed in Argentina.

And was directly commissioned.

Just for running the SIGABA installation? That doesn't make sense.

If Clete had to take somebody out, or do something else really black, who would he ask to help?

A nice young Cuban American polo player who had never heard a shot fired in anger, much less fired one himself?

Or a grizzled old sailor who had served not only in the Philippines but also on the Yangtze River Patrol?

Why didn't Clete tell me what El Jefe's actual function was?

Because you don't talk about things like that to someone who doesn't have the need to know.

So what's El Jefe's mission here?

Whatever it is, it's not to keep his mouth shut when Polo does, or asks, something stupid.

He's here to keep Polo out of trouble.

No.

More than that. El Jefe is here to see—and probably to report to the admiral—what's going on here.

So what's he going to report?

That Captain James D. Cronley Jr. is indeed the loose cannon everyone says he is?

That I'm dealing with a Mossad/NKGB agent and haven't told the admiral anything about it?

"Returning to the worst possible scenario," Gehlen said, "there is a real possibility that what the NKGB decided when we contacted Seven-K was that it might give them a chance to get their hands on me."

"How would they do that?" El Jefe asked.

"In her—what we presume was her—last message, she

twice referred to a Herr Weitz, who was demanding more dollars."

"Who's he?" Ashton asked.

"I don't know anyone of that name, and neither does Oberst Mannberg. But in our previous relationship I met twice with Rahil in the Café Weitz in Vienna. That's why I suggested she may be headed for Vienna."

"Where Fedotov's people may be waiting for you at the Café Weitz when you go there to give her the fifty thousand dollars," Mannberg said.

"Where Fedotov's people may be waiting for me when I go there to give her the fifty thousand dollars," Gehlen parroted in confirmation.

"I'm just a simple sailor, General," El Jefe said. "You're going to have to explain that to me. Why couldn't you get her the money through an intermediary? How'd you get her the first fifty thousand?"

"Through an intermediary," Gehlen said. "But we can't do that again."

"Why not?"

"Because she wants to make sure, or at least that's what I'm expected to believe, that she is afraid this is a scheme to kidnap, or at least compromise, her. She said, to—in Jim's charming phrase—'cut to the chase'—"

"To hell with Jim's charming phrase," Schultz cut him off. "I just told you, I'm just a simple sailor. Take it slowly, step by step."

Has the general picked up that El Jefe is now giving the orders?

You can bet your ass, he has!

Gehlen nodded.

"As I'm sure you know, one of the great advantages the Allies had over us was that you had broken our Enigma code. We—and I include myself in 'we'—were simply unable to believe you could do that. I had only heard rumors of your SIGABA system, rumors I discounted until Jim showed me the one installed at Kloster Grünau. And now here."

He pointed to a closed door.

"The Soviet systems are by no means as sophisticated as either," he went on. "They have therefore to presume that whenever they send an encrypted message, someone else is going to read it. So they use what could probably be called a personal code within the encrypted message. Making reference to something only the addressee will understand. 'Herr Weitz,' for example, immediately translated to 'Café Weitz' in my mind. Sometimes it takes a half dozen messages back and forth to clarify the message, but it works."

"I'm with you," El Jefe said.

"Rahil—or whoever is using her name—expressed concern that we might be trying to entrap her, and that the only proof she would accept that we were not would be for me to personally deliver to Herr Weitz the additional fifty thousand dollars he was demanding.

"Subsequent clarifying messages seem to confirm this interpretation. She wants me to meet with her, to give her the money, in the Café Weitz in Vienna."

"No way," Cronley heard himself saying.

"Excuse me?" Gehlen said.

Ashton and Schultz looked at him in mingled surprise and annoyance.

Is that my automatic mouth running away on me again?

Or am I doing what I'm supposed to be doing, command-ing Operation Ost?

With overwhelming immodesty, the latter.

So I have to do this.

"The general is not going to meet with whoever's going to be waiting for him in the Café Weitz. I'm not going to take the chance that the Russians'll grab him."

"*You're* not?" Ashton asked, sarcastically incredulous. "Who the hell . . ."

El Jefe held up his hand, ordering Ashton to stop.

". . . do I think I am?" Cronley picked up. "Until you relieve me—and I'm not sure you have that authority—I'm chief, DCI-Europe . . ."

And probably out of my fucking mind!

". . . and as long as I am, I'm not going to take any chances of losing the general."

"So how, hotshot, are you going to get this Russian lady the fifty thousand she wants?" El Jefe asked.

"I'll take it to her," Cronley said.

And how the hell am I going to do that?

"How the hell are you going to do that?" Ashton de-manded. "Have you ever even been to Vienna?"

"No. But I know where the *bahnhof* is, and that a train called the Blue Danube goes from there to Vienna every day at 1640."

"Oh, shit!" Ashton said disgustedly.

"Let him finish," El Jefe said. "Let's hear how the chief, DCI-Europe, wants to handle this."

"Ludwig, do you know what this lady looks like?"

"I know what she looked like in 1943," Mannberg said.

"Okay, so Ludwig, Lieutenant Max, and I go to Vienna," Cronley said.

And do what?

"Who is Max . . . what you said?" El Jefe asked. "That Polish-Englishman who flew us to the monastery?"

"Right."

"And what's he going to do?"

"Guard Colonel Mannberg. I don't want him grabbed by the Russians, either."

"Can he do that?" El Jefe asked. "More important, will he want to?"

"He killed the two NKGB guys who had the wire around Tedworth's neck," Cronley said. "Yeah, he can do it. And he wants to do more than he's doing right now."

"You mean, more than flying the Storch?"

"Actually, he's not supposed to be flying the Storch. Officially, he's in charge of the Polish guards at Kloster Grünau."

"Just so I have things straight in my mind, Captain Cronley," Ashton said. "You have this guy who's not in the service—technically, he's a displaced person, employed as a quasi–military watchman, right?"

"Right."

"Flying an airplane you're not supposed to have?"

"Right."

"And now you want to involve him in a delicate, top secret DCI operation?" Ashton asked. And then he went on, "Why are you smiling, Schultz? You think this is funny? Cronley doing this, doing any of this, on his own—which means absolutely no . . . authority? You think that's funny?"

"I was thinking it reminded me of when we were starting up in Argentina," Schultz said. "When Clete realized we needed some shooters to protect us from the Nazis, what he did was ask Colonel Graham to send some Marines down from the States. Graham told him to write up a formal request and send it to General Donovan.

"Clete never wrote a formal request, of course. What he did do was put gauchos—most of them had been in the cavalry, I'll admit—from Estancia San Pedro y San Pablo on the job. Then he sent the OSS a bill. Nine dollars a day, plus three dollars for rations and quarters, per man. The OSS paid without asking him a question. By the time the war was over, we had three hundred some gauchos in 'Frade's Private Army' on the payroll. If the OSS was willing to pay for hiring necessary civilian employees in Argentina, more than three hundred of them, I don't think the admiral will much care if Jim hires a few here."

"Are you telling me you're in agreement with what he's proposing?"

"I haven't heard everything he's proposing, but so far he's making a lot of sense," Schultz said. Then he turned to Cronley: "Okay, you, the colonel here, and that Polish-Englishman are in Vienna. Where did he learn English like that, by the way?"

"He was in England with the Free Polish Air Force. They were sort of in the RAF."

"So that's where he learned to fly?" El Jefe said. "So what do you do in Vienna?"

I'm making this up as I go along. Doesn't he see that?

"We go to the Café Weitz. Colonel Mannberg by himself, Max and me together."

"Why?"

"Mannberg so he can see Rahil, or she him. Max to protect Mannberg in case it is the NKGB waiting for him. After that, we play it by ear."

"Wrong," El Jefe said with finality.

Uh-oh.

Well, I got pretty far for somebody who is making it up as he goes along.

"You can't go, because by now the NKGB knows what you look like," El Jefe said. "I don't want to have to tell the admiral that you're on your way to Siberia. Or send you home in a body bag. So I'll tell you what we'll do. I'll go with the Polish-Englishman. Or the English-Polack. Whatever he is. And then we'll play it by ear."

"Oscar, I was there when the admiral told you he didn't want you getting into anything you shouldn't," Ashton said.

"Then you must have been there when he said I was running things but not to tell anybody unless I decided we had to," Schultz said. "And when the admiral said you were not to even think about running the whole operation until you were off those crutches. I'm going to Vienna. Period. Okay?"

"You know the admiral'll be furious when he hears about this."

"Then let's make sure he doesn't hear about it until after we pull it off, and Mrs. Whatsername and the kids are in Argentina. Then we'll tell him, and maybe he won't be so furious."

"My God!" Ashton said.

"How do we get to Vienna?" Schultz asked.

"On the train," Cronley said.

"Is it too far to drive? I'd like to have wheels in Vienna."

"It's not far, Lieutenant Schultz," Gehlen said. "It's about a six-hour drive. The problem is—"

"Why don't you try calling me 'Chief,' General? I'm more comfortable with that."

"Certainly. Chief, the problem is crossing the borders. Austria has been divided among the Allies. The American Zone of Austria abuts the American Zone of Germany. Permission, even for Americans, is required to move across that border. And then, like Berlin, Vienna is an island within the Russian Zone of Austria. Permission is required to cross the Russian Zone."

"Permission from who?" El Jefe asked. "The Russians?"

"Freddy?" Cronley said.

"I don't know if this applies here," Hessinger said, "but if someone from the Twenty-third CIC wants to go to Vienna, I would cut travel orders. Major Wallace went there a couple of weeks ago. I cut travel orders for him, and then took them to Munich Military Post, who stamped them approved. You need that to get on the train. That would work for Captain Cronley, but Oberst Mannberg and Ostrowski?"

"Because they're not American, you mean?"

"Yes, sir."

"Not a problem," Schultz said.

"Not a problem?" Cronley parroted.

"I have goodies in my briefcase, in addition to the start-up money," Schultz said. He went into his briefcase and rummaged through it. He came up with a plastic-covered identity card and handed it to Cronley.

On one side was Schultz's photo. Above it were the

letters *DCI*. Below it was the number 77, printed in red. On the other side was the legend:

Office of the President of the United States
Directorate of Central Intelligence
Washington, D.C.

The Bearer of This Identity Document

Oscar J. Schultz

Is acting with the authority of the President of the United States as an officer of the Directorate of Central Intelligence. Any questions regarding him or his activities should be addressed to the undersigned only.

Sidney W. Souers

SIDNEY W. SOUERS, REAR ADMIRAL
DIRECTOR, U.S. DIRECTORATE OF CENTRAL
INTELLIGENCE

"After we put Colonel Mannberg's—and the English-Polack's—pictures on one of these, do you think this Munich Military Post is going to ask them if they're American?" El Jefe asked.

"Very impressive," Cronley said. "Do I get one of these?" He handed the card to Gehlen.

"I've got twenty-five of them," El Jefe said. "I can get more, but I thought that would be enough for now."

"If I may?" Gehlen said.

"Go ahead."

"I can make a small contribution. Seal the cards you brought in plastic."

"How are you going to do that?" Schultz asked.

"Abwehr Ost's special documents facility survived the war," Gehlen said. "Amazingly intact."

"Survived where?" Schultz asked.

"Here in Munich. In a sub-basement of the Paläontologisches Museum on Richard-Wagner Strasse."

"I thought that was pretty much destroyed," Hessinger said.

"Not the sub-basement," Mannberg said. "But just about everything else."

"We're back to getting something to drive in Vienna. What I'd like to have is a couple of cars—I'm too old to ride around in a jeep in this weather—and maybe a small truck—like that ambulance you had at the airport."

"That's no problem," Cronley said. "We have half a dozen of them. I don't know about cars. If we ask the Ordnance Depot for cars, they'll want to know why we want them."

"No, they won't," Schultz said. "I've got another letter from the admiral in my briefcase. This one directs all U.S. Army facilities to provide DCI-Europe with whatever support we ask for."

He produced the letter and passed it around.

"That'll do it," Hessinger pronounced. "I recommend you get Fords or Chevrolets, not German cars."

"Why would you recommend that?" Cronley asked.

"Because there's no spare parts for the German ones."

"So what's left to do?"

"Except for getting the cars, cutting the orders, and getting these ID cards filled out, I can't think of a thing," Hessinger said.

"Except wait to hear from Rahil," Gehlen said. "That would be useful."

"The one thing I didn't expect you to be, General, is a wiseass," Schultz said.

"Life is full of surprises, isn't it, Chief?" Gehlen said.

Cronley saw they were smiling at each other.

And that Mannberg and Ashton, seeing this, seemingly disapproved.

Screw the both of you!

V

[ONE]
Quarters of the U.S. Military Government
Liaison Officer
The South German Industrial Development
Organization Compound
Pullach, Bavaria
The American Zone of Occupied Germany
1305 4 January 1946

"How'd you do at the Ordnance Depot, Freddy?" Cronley asked, when Hessinger, trailed by First Sergeant Tedworth, came into what they were now calling "the sitting room."

"I got us four 1942 Fords, one with three hundred miles on the odometer, one with forty-five thousand, and the other two somewhere between the extremes."

"I was hoping for at least one Packard Clipper," Cronley said.

"Even if you could get one, that would be stupid," Hessinger said.

"Stupid? What have you got against Packards?"

"A Packard would draw unwanted attention. As will painting 'Mess Kit Repair Company' on the bumpers of the Fords. I came to talk to you about that."

"Painting what on them?" Oscar Shultz asked.

He was sitting with Maksymilian Ostrowski at the bar.

They were hunched over mugs of coffee and the *Stars and Stripes*. El Jefe had exchanged his naval uniform—and Ostrowski his dyed-black fatigues—for Army woolen OD Ike jackets and trousers. Civilian triangles were sewn to the lapels.

"You have to have your unit painted on the bumpers of your vehicles," Cronley explained. "Since I didn't want to paint 'CIC' on them, and certainly don't want to paint 'HQ DCI-Europe' on them, I told Freddy to have what we have on all the other vehicles—'711th MKRC'—painted on them."

"Which is?"

"It stands for the nonexistent 711th Mess Kit Repair Company," Cronley explained.

"Very funny, but one day some MP is going to get really curious," Hessinger said.

"What would you paint on them, Freddy?" El Jefe asked.

The question was unexpected, and it showed.

"Maybe some military government unit," he said after a moment.

"Freddy, when you don't like something, always be prepared to offer something better," Schultz said. "Write that on your forehead. It's up to Cronley, but I sort of like the sound of Seven-One-One-Em-Kay-Are-See."

"Yes, sir."

"And don't call me 'sir,' Freddy. I am trying to pass myself off as a civilian."

"I thought Captain Cronley would continue to be unreasonable," Hessinger said, "so I got him and Captain Dunwiddie these."

He handed each of them a small box.

"Oh, Freddy, you're sweet, but you shouldn't have!" Dunwiddie mocked.

"What the hell is this?" Cronley asked.

"Quartermaster Corps lapel insignia," Hessinger said. "It is possible that when you are stopped by the MPs, they will be less suspicious if they think you're in the Quartermaster Corps. Those swords you're wearing now . . ."

"Sabers, Freddy," Cronley corrected him. "Cavalry *sabers*."

". . . might make them curious."

"He's right," El Jefe said.

"Again. That's why I hate him. He's right too often," Cronley said. "Thanks, Freddy."

"I will be disowned if anybody in my family hears I'm trying to pass myself off as a Quartermaster Corps officer," Dunwiddie said.

"Say, 'Thank you, Freddy,'" Cronley ordered.

"Thank you, Freddy," Dunwiddie said.

One of the three telephones on the bar rang. The ring sound told them it was a leather-cased Signal Corps EE-8 field telephone connected to the guardhouse on the outer ring of fences.

Ostrowski picked it up, thumbed the TALK switch, answered it in Polish, listened, and then turned to Cronley.

"Captain, there are two CIC agents at the checkpoint. They have packages and letters for Lieutenant Cronley."

"What?"

Ostrowski repeated what he had announced.

"Pass them in," Dunwiddie ordered. "Have them report to me."

The two CIC agents came into the sitting room. Both were in their early thirties. He recognized both of them from his days at the XXIInd CIC Detachment in Marburg.

He knew they were enlisted men because they had not

been billeted with the officers. He also knew that they were "real" CIC agents, as opposed to Special Agent (2nd Lt) J. D. Cronley Jr., who had been sort of a joke CIC special agent, whose only qualification for the job was his fluent German.

What the hell is going on?

What are these two guys doing here?

With packages? And letters?

What kind of packages?

Letters from whom?

"How you been, Lieutenant?" the heavier of the two agents asked of Cronley.

Cronley now remembered—or thought he did—that the man's name was Hammersmith. And that he was a master sergeant.

"Okay," Cronley replied. "How's things in Marburg?"

"About the same. What is this place?"

"If there is no objection from anyone, I'll ask the questions," Dunwiddie said.

The CIC agent displayed his credentials.

"No offense, Captain," Special Agent Hammersmith said, "but this is a CIC matter. I'll handle it from here."

Dunwiddie pulled his own CIC credentials from his jacket and displayed them.

"As I was saying, I'll ask the questions," Dunwiddie said.

"Sorry, sir," Hammersmith said. "I didn't know."

"You've got packages for Cronley?" Dunwiddie asked. "And letters?"

"Yes, sir," Hammersmith said. He took two letter-sized envelopes from his Ike jacket and extended them to Dunwiddie.

"They're addressed to Special Agent Cronley, sir."

"Then give them to him," Dunwiddie ordered. "Packages?"

"Four, sir. They're in our car. They're addressed to Lieutenant Cronley."

"One of you go get the packages. Ostrowski, help him."

"Yes, sir," Hammersmith and Ostrowski said on top of each other. Then Hammersmith gestured to the other CIC agent to get the packages.

"Now, who sent you here?" Dunwiddie asked.

"Major Connell, who's the Twenty-second CIC's exec, sent us to General Greene's office in the Farben Building. Then Colonel Mattingly sent us here."

"Hessinger, did we get a heads-up about this?" Dunwiddie asked.

"No, sir."

Dunwiddie looked at Cronley, who had just finished reading one of the letters.

He extended it to Dunwiddie.

"When you're finished, give it to El Jefe," he said.

Robert M. Mattingly

Colonel, Armor

2 January 1946

Special Agent J. D. Cronley, Jr., CIC

c/o XXIIIrd CIC Detachment

Munich

BY HAND

CC: Rear Admiral Sidney W. Souers

Lt Col Maxwell Ashton III

Dear Jim:

Vis-à-vis the packages addressed to you at the XXIInd CIC Detachment, and which were opened and seized as contraband by agents of the Postal Section, Frankfurt Military Post Provost Marshal Criminal Investigation Division.

I have assured both Major John Connell, of the XXIInd CIC Detachment, and the FMP DCI that the cigarettes, coffee, Hershey Bars, and canned hams were being introduced into Occupied Germany in connection with your official duties. The four packages of same were released and will be delivered to you with this letter.

May I suggest that you notify General
Greene, or myself, the next time you feel
it necessary to directly import such
materials, so that we may inform the DCI
and avoid a recurrence of what happened
here?

With best personal regards, I am,

Sincerely,

Robert M. Mattingly
ROBERT M. MATTINGLY
COLONEL, ARMOR

When Dunwiddie had read the first letter, he passed it to
Schultz and then looked at Cronley. Cronley was not finished with what looked like a very long handwritten letter.

It was.

F-BAR-Z RANCH

BOX 21, RURAL ROUTE 3

MIDLAND, TEXAS

Christmas Eve 1945

Dear Jim,

*I really hate to burden you with this, but there is no other
option.*

*We have — your mother has — heard from her family in
Strasbourg. This came as a surprise to us, as the only time
we have ever heard from them was a few years before the
war when they notified us that your mother's mother —
your grandmother — had passed on.*

That obviously needs an explanation, so herewith.

*In early November of 1918, I was a very young (twenty-
six), just-promoted major. Colonel Bill Donovan sent me
to Strasbourg to get the facts concerning rumors that he
(and General Pershing) had heard about the Communists
wanting to establish a "Soviet Government" there.*

*After the abdication of the German Emperor, Wilhelm,
the Communists had done so in Munich, and were trying
to do so in Berlin and elsewhere.*

*Our little convoy (I had with me four officers and a half
dozen sergeants traveling in half a dozen Army Model T
Fords) arrived in Strasbourg on November sixth and
found very nice accommodations in the Maison Rouge
Hotel.*

*I immediately sent one of the officers and one of the
sergeants back to Col. Donovan's HQ with the news we
were in Strasbourg and prepared to carry out our orders
to report daily on the situation.*

*I was by then already convinced I had been given the best
assignment of my military career. It had nothing to do*

with the Communists, but rather with a member of the staff of the Maison Rouge, a strikingly beautiful blond young woman who had, blushing charmingly as she did so, told me her name was Wilhelmina.

Right. I had met your mother.

She had also told me that she could not possibly have dinner, or even a cup of coffee, with me, else her father would kill her.

Nothing would dissuade her from this, but over the next few days, I managed to spend enough time with her at the front desk to conclude that she was not immune to my charm and manly good looks, and it was only her father's hate of all things American that kept her from permitting our relationship to blossom.

The Communists solved the problem for us. On November 11, 1918 — Armistice Day — they started trying to take over the city. There was resistance, of course, and a good deal of bloodshed. Citizens were ordered by the French military government to stay off the streets, and to remain where they were.

The threat was real. Two of my officers and one of my sergeants were beaten nearly to death by the Communists.

Your mother's family lived on the outskirts of town and it would have been impossible for her to even try to get home. The Maison Rouge installed her (and other employees) in rooms in the hotel.

She was there for almost two weeks, during which time our relationship had the opportunity to bloom.

Finally, on November 22, General Henri Gouraud, the French military governor, had enough of the Communists. Troops, including Moroccan Goumiers, moved into the city and restored order. Brutally.

The next morning, I loaded your mother into a Model T and drove her home. I had the naïve hope that her father would be grateful that I had protected his daughter during the trouble and would be at least amenable to my taking her to dinner, if not becoming her suitor.

Instead, when he saw us pull up outside your mother's home, he erupted from the house and began to berate her for bringing shame on the family. I managed to keep my mouth shut during this, but when she indignantly denied — with every right to do so — that anything improper had happened between us, this served only to further enrage him.

I would say he slapped her, but the word is inadequate to describe the blow he delivered, which knocked her off her feet. At this point, I lost control and took him on. He wound up on the ground with a bloody nose and some lost teeth.

I loaded your mother, who was by then hysterical, back into the Model T and returned to the Maison Rouge.

When we got there, we found Colonel Donovan and a company of infantry. They had come to rescue us from the

Communists. The French had already done that, of course.

When I explained my personal problems to Donovan, he said there was one sure way to convince your mother's father that my intentions were honorable, and that was to marry her.

To my delight and surprise, your mother agreed. We drove that same morning to Paris, armed with two letters from Donovan: one to the American ambassador, the other to the manager of the Hotel Intercontinental on rue de Castiglione.

The ambassador married us late that afternoon, and issued your mother an American passport. We spent the night in the Intercontinental and then drove back to Strasbourg as man and wife.

There was a black wreath on the door of your mother's house when we got there. Her father had suffered a fatal heart attack during the night.

Your mother's mother and other relatives attributed this to the thrashing I'd given him. While obviously there was a connection, I have to point out that your mother told me he had had three previous heart attacks.

Your mother was told she would not be welcome at the funeral services.

I managed to get myself assigned to the Army of Occupation, and your mother and I moved to

Baden-Baden, where I served as liaison officer to the French authorities.

We were there nearly six months, during which she made numerous attempts to open a dialogue with her family, all of which they rejected.

Then, on a beautiful day in June, we boarded the _Mauretania_ at Le Havre. Eleven days later, we were in New York, a week after that I was relieved from active duty, and four days after that we got off the Texas & Pacific RR "Plains Flyer" in Midland.

There was no more communication between your mother and her family until May (June?) of 1938, when she received a letter (since they had our address, it was proof they had received your mother's letters) from a Frau Ingebord Stauffer, who identified herself as the wife of Luther Stauffer, and he (Luther) as the son of Hans-Karl Stauffer, your mother's brother.

That would make Luther your first cousin. In this letter, Frau Stauffer told your mother that her mother — your grandmother — had died of complications following surgery.

When your mother replied to this letter, there was no reply.

We next heard from Frau Stauffer the day of Marjie's funeral. That night, your mother told me that she had received a letter begging for help for her literally starving family. I asked to see it, and she replied, "I tore it up. We have enough of our own sad stories around here."

That was good enough for me, and I didn't press her.

A week or so later, however, she asked me if I had the address from the 1938 letter, that she had thought things over and decided she could not turn her back on your Cousin Luther, his wife and children.

I was surprised, until I thought it over, that she didn't remember the address, Hachelweg 675, as it was that of her home where I had the run-in with your grandfather. Your mother said she intended to send a "small package or two" to your Cousin Luther's family.

The next development came when the postmaster told her they could neither guarantee nor insure packages to Strasbourg, as they seemed to disappear in the French postal system.

Your mother then asked me if she "dared" to ask you to help. I told her you would be happy to do anything for her that was within your power.

Now, between us, man-to-man.

What this woman has asked for is cigarettes, coffee, chocolate, and canned ham. According to the <u>Dallas Morning News</u>, these things are the real currency in Germany these days, as they were after the First World War.

There are four large packages of same en route to you.

This woman also asked for dollars. I told your mother not to send money, as that would be illegal and certainly get you in trouble.

If you can deliver the packages to this woman without getting yourself in trouble, please do so.

Knowing these people as I do, however, I suspect that if this pull on the teat of your mother's incredible kindness is successful, it will not be their last attempt to get as much as they can from her.

Do whatever you think is necessary to keep them from starving, and let me know what that costs. But don't let them make a fool of you, me, or — most important — your mother.

As I wrote this, I realized that while I have always been proud of you, knowing that I could rely on your mature judgment to deal with this made me even more proud to be your father.

Love,
Dad

Cronley was still reading the long letter when Ostrowski and the CIC agent came back with two heavy packages and announced there were two more. Dunwiddie waited until they had returned with these before reaching for the letter Cronley, finally finished reading it, was now holding thoughtfully.

"It's personal," Cronley said. "From my father."

"Sorry," Dunwiddie said.

Cronley changed his mind. He handed Dunwiddie the letter, and then went to one of the boxes—all of which had white tape with "Evidence" printed on it stuck all over them—and, using a knife, opened it.

He pulled out an enormous canned ham.

"Anyone for a ham sandwich?" he asked.

"Does that about conclude your business here?" Dunwiddie asked Special Agent Hammersmith.

"Sir, could I get a receipt?" Hammersmith asked.

"Hessinger, type up a receipt for the special agent," Dunwiddie ordered. "Get his name. 'I acknowledge receipt from Special Agent . . .'"

"Hammersmith," Hammersmith furnished.

"'. . . of one official letter, one personal letter, and four cartons, contents unknown.' For Captain Cronley's signature."

"Yes, sir."

"*Captain* Cronley?" Hammersmith asked.

Dunwiddie did not respond to the question, instead saying, "Special Agent Hessinger can arrange rooms for the night for you, if you'd like, in the Vier Jahreszeiten hotel in Munich."

"I'd appreciate that," Hammersmith said, adding, "Captain, can I ask what's going on around here?"

"No, you can't," Dunwiddie said simply.

Hessinger came back into the sitting room with the announcement that the two CIC agents had gone.

"Jim, you knew those guys when you first came to Germany, right?" El Jefe asked.

Cronley nodded.

"In Marburg," he said. "And the first thing they're going to do when they get back there is tell Major Connell—"

"Who is he?" El Jefe asked.

"The Twenty-second's executive officer. But he really runs

the outfit. 'Major, you're not going to believe this, but that wet-behind-the-ears second lieutenant you put on the road block? He's now a captain, and . . .'"

"That can't be helped," Dunwiddie said. "You are now a captain. And if this Major Connell is curious enough to ask Mattingly, Mattingly will either tell him how you got promoted or that it's none of his business."

"Or tell him," Hessinger said, "just between them, that for reasons he doesn't understand, Jim was transferred to the DCI. Where . . . witness the black market goodies . . . he has already shown he's absolutely way over his head and a petty crook to boot."

"You don't like Colonel Mattingly much, do you, Freddy?" El Jefe asked.

"He is a man of low principle," Hessinger announced righteously.

Cronley laughed.

"Don't laugh," Hessinger said. "He's determined to get you out of chief, DCI-Europe, and himself in. You noticed he sent copies of that letter to the admiral and Ashton? Showing what a really nice guy he is and what an incompetent *dummkopf* black marketeer you are."

"Where is Ashton, by the way?" Cronley asked.

"He asked for a car to take him into the PX in Munich," Hessinger began.

"Christ, Freddy, we could have sent somebody shopping for him," Cronley said. "I don't want him breaking his other leg staggering around the PX on crutches."

"I offered that," Hessinger said. "He refused. But don't worry."

"Why the hell not?"

"Because he really went to the orthopedic ward of the 98th General Hospital in Schwabing. I told Sergeant Miller—"

"Who?"

"Taddeus Miller. Staff sergeant. One of my guys," Dunwiddie furnished.

". . . to (a) not let him out of his sight, and (b) to call me and let me know where he really was."

"You didn't think he was going to the PX?"

"He was lying when he told me that. I could see that."

"You could see that he was lying?"

"I could see that he was lying. I always know."

"You always know?"

"Just about all the time, I know. You and General Gehlen are the only ones I can't always tell."

"Thank you very much," Cronley said.

"I have to know why you think so," El Jefe said.

"You don't want to know. He knows," Hessinger said. "It's not a criticism, it's a statement of fact."

Which means he didn't suspect a thing about Rachel until I fessed up.

Which makes me wonder how low I've fallen in his estimation?

Or Tiny's?

How far is all the way down?

"Quickly changing the subject," Dunwiddie said. "What are you going to do with your black market goodies, Captain, sir?"

"I'm tempted to burn them, give them to the Red Cross . . ."

"But you can't, right, because of your mother?" Hessinger asked. "Your parents?"

Cronley gave him an icy look, but didn't immediately reply. Finally he said, "I don't have the time to just run off to Strasbourg to play the Good Samaritan, do I?"

"You might. You never know."

"Freddy, you are aware that we're waiting to hear from Seven-K?" Cronley asked.

"Of course I am. What I am suggesting is that I don't think she's going to say 'Meet me at the Café Weitz tomorrow at noon.' There will probably be four or five days between her message and the meeting. Perhaps there will be time then. Or perhaps our trip to Vienna can be tied in with your trip to Strasbourg."

"Got it all figured out, have you, Freddy?" El Jefe said.

"Not all figured out. I learned about Jim's family just now, when you did. But by the time we hear from Rahil, I will probably have a workable plan."

"The thing I like about him is his immodesty," El Jefe said.

"When one is a genius, one finds it hard to be modest," Hessinger said solemnly.

"Jesus Christ, Freddy!" Cronley said, laughing.

"My own modesty compels me to admit that I didn't make that up," Hessinger said. "Frank Lloyd Wright, the architect, said it to a *Chicago Tribune* reporter."

[TWO]
Quarters of the U.S. Military Government
Liaison Officer
The South German Industrial Development
Organization Compound
Pullach, Bavaria
The American Zone of Occupied Germany
1625 8 January 1946

When the door closed on Lieutenant Colonel George H. Parsons and Major Warren W. Ashley, Cronley looked around the table at General Gehlen, Mannberg, El Jefe, Hessinger, and Tiny and said, "Why does it worry me that they were so charming?"

Gehlen chuckled.

"I would say that it has something to do with a 'well done' message General Magruder sent Colonel Parsons," Hessinger said. "For the time being it is in their interest to be charming."

"What are you talking about?" Dunwiddie asked.

"What 'well done' message?" Cronley asked.

"The Pentagon sent a request for an update on Russian troop strength, especially tanks, in Silesia. You knew that, right?"

"And the general got it for us. Them."

"The general already had that intelligence on his Order of Battle. So the Pentagon asked for it one day, and the next day it was in Washington. Then General Magruder sent Colonel Parsons a 'well done' message. I am suggesting that if being charming to us produces 'well done' messages from General Magruder, Colonel Parsons is happy to polish our brass balls."

"I don't think you have that metaphor down perfectly, Freddy," Tiny said, chuckling, "but I take your point."

"How do you know Magruder sent the 'well done' message?" Cronley asked.

It took Hessinger a moment to frame his reply.

"I thought it would be in our interest to know what General Magruder and Colonel Parsons were saying to each other," he said finally. "So I established a sort of sub-rosa arrangement with Technical Sergeant Colbert of the ASA."

"This I have to hear," El Jefe said. "A sub-rosa arrangement to do what?"

"Give us copies of every message back and forth."

"In exchange for what?" El Jefe asked.

"You told me, when I told you we didn't have enough people to do what we're supposed to do, you said that I should keep my eyes open for people we could use, that you—we—now had the authority to recruit people from wherever for the DCI."

"So?"

"Sergeant Colbert has ambitions to be a professional intelligence officer. She thinks the next step for her would be to get out of the ASA and join the DCI."

"And you told him you could arrange that?" Cronley asked. "And then, 'she'? 'Her'?"

Hessinger nodded.

"I told her—her name is Claudette Colbert, like the movie actress—"

"Like the movie actress? Fascinating!" Cronley said. "Is there another one? Sergeant Betty Grable, maybe?"

"—that I would bring the subject up with you at the first opportunity. And I suggested to her that you would be favorably impressed if she could continue to get us all messages between the Pentagon and Colonel Parsons without getting caught."

"Jesus!" Cronley exclaimed. "Freddy, I'm sure that you considered that if we had this movie star sergeant transferred to us, she would no longer be in a position to read Parsons's messages."

"I did. She tells me that it will not pose a problem."

"Did *Claudette Colbert* tell you why not?" El Jefe asked.

"As a gentleman, I did not press her for details," Hessinger said. "But I suspect it has something to do with her blond hair, blue eyes, and magnificent bosom. Women so endowed generally get whatever they want from men."

"Is that so?"

"That is so. When Claudette looked at me with those blue eyes and asked me for help in getting into the DCI, I was tempted for a moment to shoot you and offer her the chief, DCI-Europe, job."

"Thinking with your dick again, were you?" Cronley asked.

"That was a joke," Hessinger said. "I don't do that. We all have seen what damage thinking with your dick can do."

As Cronley thought, *That was a shot at me for fucking Rachel Schumann*, he simultaneously felt anger sweep through him, and sensed Tiny's and General Gehlen's eyes on him.

I can't just take that. Friends or not, I'm still his commanding officer.

So what do I do?

Stand him at attention and demand an apology?

Royally eat his ass out?

His mouth went on automatic and he heard himself say,

"The damage that thinking with one's male appendage can cause is usually proportional to the size of the organ, wouldn't you agree, Professor Hessinger? In other words, it is three times more of a problem for me than it is for you?"

Dunwiddie chuckled nervously.

El Jefe smiled and shook his head.

Cronley realized that he was now standing up, legs spread, with his hands on his hips, glaring down at Hessinger, who was still in his chair.

"Okay, Sergeant Hessinger," Cronley snapped. "The amusing repartee is over. Let's hear exactly what I've done to so piss you off that you felt justified in going off half-cocked to enlist the services of a large-breasted ASA female non-com in a smart-ass scheme that could have caused—may still cause—enormous trouble for us without one goddamn word to me or Captain Dunwiddie?"

Hessinger got to his feet.

"I asked you a question, Sergeant!"

Hessinger's eyes showed he was frightened, even terrified.

"I was out of line, Captain. I'm sorry."

"Sorry's not good enough, fish!"

Where the hell did that come from? "Fish"?

College Station.

The last time I stood with my hands on my hips screaming at a terrified kid, a fish, scaring the shit out of him, I was an eighteen-year-old corporal in the Corps . . .

He saw the kid, the fish, standing at rigid attention, staring straight ahead as he was abusing him, reciting, "Sir, not being informed to the highest degree of accuracy, I hesitate to articulate for fear that I may deviate from the true course of rectitude. In short, sir, I am a very dumb fish, and do not know, sir."

I didn't like abusing a helpless guy then, and I don't like doing it here.

"Sit down, Freddy," Cronley said, putting his hand on Hessinger's shoulder. "Just kidding."

Hessinger sat—collapsed—back into his chair.

"But you will admit, I hope, that going off that way to corrupt the blue-eyed, nicely teated blond without telling either Tiny or me was pretty stupid."

"Yes, sir. I can see that now."

"So what were you pissed off about?"

Hessinger met his eyes for a moment, then averted them, then met them again.

"You really want me to tell you?"

"Yeah, Freddy, I really do."

And I really do. I didn't say that to Freddy to make nice.

"My skills are underutilized around here," Hessinger said.

"Freddy," Tiny said, "this place would collapse without you. And we all know it."

"You mean, I am very good at such things as making hotel reservations, getting vehicles and other things from supply depots, et cetera?"

"And getting us paid," Tiny said. "Don't forget that."

"Those are the things a company clerk does. So what you're saying is that I am a very good company clerk and supply sergeant."

"Actually, Freddy, I think of you as our adjutant, our administrative officer."

"Sergeants—and that's what I am, a pay grade E-4 sergeant—can't be adjutants or administrative officers."

"You're also a special agent of the CIC," Cronley argued.

"Nobody here is a bona fide CIC agent," Hessinger said. "You just kept the badges so you can get away with doing things you shouldn't be doing."

Jesus, he's pissed off because I promoted Tedworth to first sergeant!

Or, that's part of it.

"Sergeant Hessinger," Cronley said, "at your earliest convenience, cut a promotion order promoting you to master sergeant."

"You can't do that," Hessinger said.

"Why not? You told me I had the authority to promote Sergeant Tedworth."

"Sergeant Tedworth was a technical sergeant, pay grade E-6. You had the authority to promote him one grade, to first sergeant pay grade E-7. You can't skip grades when you promote people. People can be promoted not more than one pay grade at a time, and not more often than once a month."

"Okay. Problem solved," Tiny said. "Cut an order today, promoting you to staff sergeant. Then, a month from today, cut another one making you a technical sergeant. And a month after that . . . getting the picture?"

"That would work. Thank you."

"Happy now, Freddy?" Cronley asked.

"That I will get my overdue promotions, yes, but that does not deal with the basic problem of my being underutilized in the past, and will continue to be underutilized in the DCI."

"And how, Staff Sergeant Hessinger," Cronley asked, "would you suggest I deal with that?"

"If you would transfer Sergeant Miller to me—right now I am borrowing him from First Sergeant Tedworth—that would free me to spend more time doing more important things than making hotel reservations and stocking the bar here."

"Presumably, Captain Dunwiddie, you are aware that Sergeant Hessinger has been borrowing Sergeant Miller from Sergeant Tedworth?" Cronley asked.

Dunwiddie nodded.

"It's okay with Tedworth. He said we've been overworking Freddy. Miller's a good man."

"That raises the question in my mind whether Sergeant Miller is anxious to solve our personnel problem, or whether Abraham Lincoln Tedworth pointed his finger at him and said, 'Get your ass over to Hessinger's office and do what you're told.'"

"He came to me asking if I could use him," Hessinger said.

"I would like to hear that he's a volunteer from his lips," Cronley said. "And now that I think about it, I would like to hear from Claudette Colbert's ruby-red lips that she, too, is really a volunteer. But Sergeant Miller first. Where is he, Freddy?"

"Outside, in the ambulance."

"Outside, in the ambulance"? What the hell is that all about?

"Go get him."

When the door had closed on Hessinger, Dunwiddie

said, "Don't let this go to your head, Captain, sir, but I thought you handled that pretty well."

"Me, too," El Jefe said.

The door opened and one of Gehlen's men, a tall, gaunt blond man whose name Cronley couldn't recall but he remembered had been a major, came in.

He marched up to Mannberg, came to attention, clicked his heels, and handed him a sheet of paper. Mannberg read it, handed it to General Gehlen, and then ordered, "There will probably be a reply. Wait outside."

The former major bobbed his head, clicked his heels again, turned on his heels, and marched out of the room.

"We have heard from Seven-K," Gehlen said. "Quote, 'Herr Weitz expects his friend to pay him not later than the fourteenth.' End quote."

"Today's the eighth," Cronley said. "That gives us six days to get to Vienna."

"Vienna's not the other side of the world," Dunwiddie said. "That shouldn't be a problem."

The door opened again.

Hessinger and Staff Sergeant Miller came in.

Miller was as coal black as Tiny Dunwiddie, but where Dunwiddie was massive, Miller was thin, almost gaunt. He towered over Hessinger.

Christ, Tiny's six four and this guy is six, seven inches taller than that. He has to be close to seven feet tall.

Sergeant Miller marched up to Cronley, came to attention, and crisply saluted.

"Sir, Staff Sergeant Miller, Taddeus L., reporting to the captain as ordered, sir!"

Cronley returned the salute.

"At ease, Sergeant," Cronley ordered.

"Captain Cronley," Gehlen said. "Excuse me?"

"Sir?"

"Before we get into this, I think we should reply to Seven-K."

"Sure."

"And what should I say?"

"Say 'Ludwig always pays his debts on time,'" Hessinger said.

Gehlen looked at him in mingled disbelief and annoyance.

"Freddy," Cronley said, annoyance—even anger—in his tone, "shut up. No one asked you."

"I know. That's what I meant before when I said I was underutilized around here."

"Let's hear what he has to say," El Jefe said. "Starting with who's Ludwig?"

"Colonel Mannberg's Christian name is Ludwig. We can safely presume they know that. So they will not be surprised when he, and not the general, shows up at the Café Weitz."

"What makes you think I will not be going to the Café Weitz?" Gehlen asked.

He tried, but failed, to keep an icy tone out of his voice.

"I would be very surprised, General," Hessinger replied, "if Captain Cronley would expose you to that risk. I am extremely reluctant to expose Colonel Mannberg to that risk, but I can see no alternative."

"*You* are 'extremely reluctant,' are you, Freddy?" Cronley asked sarcastically. "You've given our little problem a great deal of thought, I gather? And come up with the solutions?"

"Our problems, plural. Yes, I have."

"'Problems, plural'?" Cronley parroted. "And the others are?"

"The other is you dealing with your family in Strasbourg."

"That's a personal problem that I will deal with myself, thank you just the same," Cronley said.

"No. The chief, DCI-Europe, doesn't have personal problems."

"What are you suggesting, Freddy?"

"That it is entirely possible that when you knock on your cousin Luther's door, bearing the black market Hershey bars and canned ham, he will smile gratefully at you and ask you in. Maybe he will even embrace you and kiss your cheek. And the next we will hear of you is when the new Rachel sends us a message saying we can have you back just as soon as we send Colonel Likharev into the Russian Zone of Berlin. Or maybe Vienna."

"My God!" Gehlen breathed. "That possibility never entered my mind."

After a very long moment, Cronley said, "Sergeant Miller, you never should have heard any of this."

"Mr. Hessinger has made me aware of the situation, sir."

"Okay. I'm not surprised. But I have to ask this. Are you a volunteer? Or did Tedworth, or for that matter Captain Dunwiddie, volunteer your services for you?"

"Sir, I went to Mr. Hessinger and told him I thought I could be more useful working for him, for DCI, than I could as just one more sergeant of the guard."

"Okay. With the caveat that I think you may—hell, certainly will—come to regret doing that, you're in."

"Thank you, sir."

"Okay, Freddy," Cronley ordered. "Let's hear your solutions to our problems, plural."

"Right now?"

"Right now."

"Taddeus, please get my briefcase from the ambulance," Hessinger said. "And while you're doing that, I will get started by talking about the death and resurrection of the 711th MKRC."

"Why don't you get started talking about something important?" Cronley challenged.

"A unit called the 711th Quartermaster Mess Kit Repair Company is a sophomoric joke . . ."

"So you have been saying," Cronley said.

"Shut up, Jim," El Jefe said. "Let's hear what he has to say."

Cronley recognized the tone of command in Schultz's voice and shut up.

". . . but within Captain Cronley's original idea, which was to provide a cover for our vehicles, there is a good deal that can be saved.

"For example," Hessinger began his lecture, "while there is obviously no such organization as a Quartermaster Mess Kit Repair Company, I don't think anyone would smile at, or question, a Quartermaster Mobile Kitchen Renovation Company.

"What does the 711th QM Mobile Kitchen Renovation Company do? It renovates the mobile kitchens of the European Command, each company-sized unit of which has a mobile kitchen. That means that no one would question our vehicles—our former ambulances—being anywhere in

Occupied Germany or Liberated Austria, where there might be an Army mobile kitchen in need of renovation.

"Personnel assigned to the 711th might be authorized a three-day pass from their labors, so that they might visit such cultural centers as Strasbourg . . ."

What later became known as "Hessinger's First Lecture" lasted an hour and fifteen minutes, and covered every detail of both problems facing the DCI. It recommended the reassignment of more of Tiny's Troopers to DCI duties, and replacing them with Ostrowski's Poles. And the designation of Kloster Grünau as home station for the 711th, with signs announcing that status being placed on the fence surrounding the monastery.

But finally it was over.

"All of this needs polishing," Hessinger concluded.

"Everything always needs polishing, as we say in the Navy," El Jefe said.

"We had a similar saying, oddly enough, in the Wehrmacht," General Gehlen said.

"So what do you want me to do now?" Hessinger asked.

"Get me an ambulance driver, and a road map to Strasbourg," Cronley said. "I want to go there either tomorrow or the day after and get that out of the way before I go to Vienna."

"I will drive, and I don't need a road map," Hessinger replied.

"You're going with me to Strasbourg?"

"Me and four of Tiny's Troopers. Them in an ambulance, you and me—Second Lieutenant Cronley and Sergeant Hessinger of the 711th Quartermaster Mobile Kitchen Renovation Company—in the Ford with the three hundred–odd miles on the odometer."

"Do I have any say in this?"

"I wouldn't think so, Second Lieutenant Cronley," El Jefe said. "It looks to me that Professor Hessinger has things well in hand."

"There is one little problem we haven't discussed," Cronley said.

"Which is?"

"How do we get Mannberg, Ostrowski, and that fifty thousand dollars to Vienna?"

"Yeah," Hessinger said thoughtfully.

"I'd like to send them on the Blue Danube, but we can't get them on the Blue Danube because they're not American."

"Yeah," Hessinger repeated thoughtfully.

"I have a brilliant idea," Cronley said. "Inasmuch as I am exhausted after dealing with Lieutenant Colonel Parsons, Major Ashley, and Staff Sergeant Hessinger, why don't we put off solving that until tomorrow morning?"

"Yeah," Hessinger said thoughtfully, for the third time.

VI

[ONE]
Quarters of the U.S. Military Government
Liaison Officer
The South German Industrial Development
Organization Compound
Pullach, Bavaria
The American Zone of Occupied Germany
0755 9 January 1946

"Sign this, please," Hessinger said, laying a sheet of paper on the table.

"What is it?" Cronley asked, and then read. "I'll be damned, 'Special Orders No. 1, Headquarters, Military Detachment, Directorate of Central Intelligence-Europe. Subject: Promotion of Enlisted Personnel.' What took you so long, Freddy? Or should I say 'Staff Sergeant Hessinger'?"

"I didn't know how to do it, so I called Sergeant Major Thorne."

"Who?"

"General Greene's sergeant major."

"And he told you how?"

"Correct."

"I was hoping that you had spent the night thinking about how we're going to get Mannberg, Ostrowski, and the fifty thousand to Vienna."

"I came up with several ideas, all of which are probably illegal," Hessinger said.

"Save them until the general and Mannberg get here."

General Gehlen, in another of his ill-fitting, ragged suits, and Colonel Mannberg, in his usual Wehrmacht uniform stripped of all insignia but a red stripe down the trouser legs, came in almost precisely at eight.

Cronley wasn't sure if he was impressed with their Teutonic punctuality or annoyed by it. He rose as Gehlen approached the table, as a gesture of courtesy, and Gehlen waved him back into his seat, shaking his head to suggest he didn't think the gesture was necessary.

By quarter after eight, the others—Dunwiddie, Schultz, Ostrowski, and Tedworth—had taken their places and begun their breakfast, and Cronley had finished his.

"What we left hanging last night," Cronley said, "was the question of getting Mannberg, Ostrowski, and the fifty thousand dollars to Vienna. The problem is that neither of them can get on the Blue Danube because they're not Americans. And the one solution I see for the problem is predictably illegal."

"What's your solution?"

"Give both of them DCI-Europe identity cards."

"You're right," Dunwiddie said. "That would be illegal. And it wouldn't be long before Colonel Mattingly heard about it. And he's just waiting for you to screw up."

"Your suggestion?"

"Put Colonel Mannberg in a Provisional Security Organization uniform and give him a PSO identity card. No one would question you having two Wachmann—Mannberg and Ostrowski—with you."

"That would work," Mannberg said.

No, mein lieber Oberst, it wouldn't.

"No, it would not," Cronley said. "I don't think this officers' hotel . . . what's it called?"

"The Bristol," Hessinger furnished. "And it's not just an officers' hotel. Majors and up."

". . . this majors-and-up officers' hotel is going to accommodate two DP watchmen," Cronley finished.

"So what's your solution?" Dunwiddie asked.

"I'm going to give both Mannberg and Ostrowski DCI identity cards."

"I don't think that would be smart," Schultz said.

"Well, then the choice is yours, Jefe," Cronley said. "Relieve me and you figure this out. Or let me do what I think is best. And giving Mannberg and Ostrowski DCI identity cards is what I think is best."

It took thirty seconds—which seemed much longer—for El Jefe to reply.

"When I think about it," he said finally, "I still think it's risky as hell, but I don't think it would be illegal. You're the chief, DCI-Europe. You can do just about anything you want."

"Until somebody catches him doing something we all know he shouldn't be doing, you mean," Dunwiddie said.

"Discussion over, Captain Dunwiddie," Cronley said. "How are you with a tape measure?"

"Excuse me?"

"While we're getting the DCI credentials filled out and sealed in plastic, we need somebody who knows how to determine sizes to take the colonel's and Ostrowski's measurements. Are you our man to do that?"

"What for?"

"So that you can go to the QM officers' clothing sales store and get Colonel Mannberg a couple of sets of ODs and a set of pinks and greens."

"I didn't think about that," Hessinger said.

"And get Ostrowski a set of pinks and greens while you're at it," Cronley said. "We don't want anyone to look out of place in this majors-and-up hotel in Vienna, do we?"

"I have one more thing to say, and then I'll shut up," Dunwiddie said.

"Say it."

"I can see the look—'I've got the sonofabitch now'—on Colonel Mattingly's face when he hears about this."

Cronley looked as if he was about to reply, but then changed his mind.

"I'd much prefer to put the colonel—and Max, too—in civilian clothing," he said. "Suits and ties. But that's out of the question, isn't it?" Cronley asked.

"I have civilian clothing," Mannberg said. "Or my sister does."

"Your sister?"

"And I think Max could wear some of it," Mannberg said.

"Your sister has your civilian clothing?" Cronley asked. Mannberg nodded.

"I sent it to her when the general and I went to the East," he said.

"And she still has it?" Cronley asked. "Where?"

"We have a farm near Hanover," Mannberg said. "In the British Zone."

"Pay attention," Cronley said. "The chief, DCI-Europe, is about to lay out our plans. While General Gehlen's documents people are doing their thing with the DCI credentials, and Captain Dunwiddie is measuring Mannberg and Ostrowski and then going shopping for them, First Sergeant Tedworth is going to get in one of our new Fords and drive to Hanover to reclaim Colonel Mannberg's wardrobe. Any questions?"

[TWO]
Hachelweg 675
Strasbourg, Département Bas-Rhin, France
1255 10 January 1946

The olive-drab 1943 Ford Deluxe pulled to the curb and stopped. The driver, yet another enormous black sergeant, this one Sergeant Albert Finney, got out from behind the wheel and ran around the back of the car to open the rear passenger door.

Cronley got out. He was wearing an OD woolen uniform. His shoulder insignia, a modification of the wartime insignia of Supreme Headquarters, Allied Expeditionary Force (SHAEF), identified him as being assigned to the European Command (EUCOM). The gold bars of a second lieutenant were pinned to his epaulets, and the insignia of the Quartermaster Corps to his lapels.

Hessinger got out of the front seat. He was also wearing an OD Ike jacket and trousers. The first time Cronley had ever seen him not wearing his pinks and greens was that morning. His uniform was now adorned with staff sergeant's chevrons, QMC lapel insignia, and the EUCOM shoulder patch.

Two other of Tiny's Troopers and the ambulance were parked down the street just within sight of Hachelweg 675.

The fourth had made his way to the back of Hachelweg 675, with orders from Sergeant Hessinger to "follow anyone who comes out the back door when we knock at the front."

Staff Sergeant Hessinger had orders for Second Lieutenant Cronley and Sergeant Finney, as well. "Remember," he said in German, "the only German either of you knows is *'Noch ein Bier, bitte'* and *'Wo ist die Toilette?'*"

"Jawohl, Herr Feldmarschall," Cronley had replied.

"You already told us that, Freddy," Sergeant Finney said in German.

He opened the trunk of the Ford and took out an open cardboard box. Four cartons of Chesterfield cigarettes, on their ends, were visible. So was an enormous canned ham.

Hessinger opened a gate in a stone wall and walked up to the house, with Cronley and Finney following him. The tile-roofed two-story building looked very much like Cronley's house in the Pullach compound, except that it desperately needed a paint job, several new windows, and roof repairs.

Cronley and Finney had been given a lecture by Professor Hessinger on the history of Strasbourg on the way from Pullach. He told them that over the years it had gone back and forth between being French and German so often that Strasbourgers never really knew to whom they owed their allegiance.

Cronley was surprised, even a little ashamed, that he had never given the subject much thought before. His mother spoke German; she had taught him to speak German from the time he was an infant. He had naturally presumed that she was a German. Or had been before his father had brought her to Midland, after which she was an American.

But when they had crossed the border today, it had been into France. Strasbourg was in France.

Hessinger told them it had been French until after the Franco-Prussian War, when, in 1871, the Treaty of Frankfurt had given it to the newly formed German Empire. The Germans had promptly "Germanified" the area, and surrounded it with a line of massive forts, named after distinguished Germans, such as von Moltke, Bismarck, and Crown Prince von Sachsen.

After World War I, Hessinger had lectured, the area was given back to the French by the Treaty of Versailles. The French, after renaming the forts—Fort Kronprinz von Sachsen, for example, became Fort Joffre, after the famous French general, and Fort Bismarck became Fort Kléber—held Strasbourg until June of 1940, when the Germans invaded France and promptly reclaimed Strasbourg for the Thousand-Year Reich.

Four years later, Hessinger said, the French 2nd Armored Division rolled into Strasbourg and hoisted the French tricolor on every flagpole they could find.

"Strasbourgers," Hessinger said, and Cronley couldn't tell if his leg was being pulled or not, "keep German and French flags in their closets, so they can hang the right one out of their windows depending on who they're being invaded by this week."

There was a large door knocker, a brass lion's head, on the door. Freddy banged it twice.

Jesus, this is my mother's house, Cronley thought. *She went through this door as a little girl.*

And where we got out of the car is where Dad punched her father's—my grandfather's—lights out.

The door was opened—just a crack.

Cronley could see a woman. She had blond hair, brushed tight against her skull. She looked to be in her thirties, and she didn't look as if she was close to starvation.

"We are looking for Herr Luther Stauffer," Hessinger announced in German.

The woman shook her head, but otherwise didn't reply.

"Then Frau Stauffer," Hessinger said. "Frau Ingebord Stauffer."

The woman tried to close the door. She couldn't. After a moment, Cronley saw why: Hessinger had his foot in the doorjamb.

He also saw the fear in the woman's face.

It grew worse when Hessinger snapped, like a movie Nazi in a third-rate film, *"Papiere, bitte!"*

The woman, her face now showing even more fear, stepped back from the door.

And then the door opened.

A man appeared. He was blond, needed a shave, appeared to be in his middle to late thirties, and looked strangely familiar.

Why do I think my cousin Luther has been hiding behind the door?

"Oh, you're American," the man said in German, and then turned and said, "It's all right, dear, they're Americans."

Then the man asked, "How can I help you, Sergeant?"

"We're looking for Herr Luther Stauffer," Freddy said.

"May I ask why?"

"It's a family matter, not official," Freddy said.

"A family matter?" the man asked, taking a close look at Cronley.

"A family matter," Freddy repeated.

"I am Luther Stauffer."

"Lieutenant," Freddy said in English, "I think we found your cousin."

Hessinger, Cronley, and Finney all decided, judging by the man's reaction to Freddy's question, that Luther Stauffer spoke—or at least understood—English.

"Tell him, Sergeant, please, that I have some things for him from his aunt, Wilhelmina Stauffer Cronley," Cronley said.

Freddy did so.

"Give him the box, Sergeant Finney," Cronley ordered.

As Finney extended the box, Stauffer pulled the door fully open and said, gesturing, "Please come in."

"What did he say?" Cronley asked.

Hessinger made the translation.

"Then go in," Cronley ordered.

"Yes, sir."

They found themselves in a small living room.

Finney extended the box to Stauffer again.

"This is for me?" Stauffer asked.

"From your aunt, Wilhelmina Stauffer Cronley," Hessinger said. "You are that Luther Stauffer, right? Frau Cronley is your aunt?"

"Yes," Stauffer said, as he put the box on the table.

"If that's so," Hessinger said, "then Lieutenant Cronley is your cousin."

Stauffer and Cronley looked at each other. Stauffer put out his hand, and Cronley took it.

Stauffer turned to his wife and quite unnecessarily announced, "The officer is my cousin." Then he turned to Cronley and said, "I'm sorry, I didn't get your name."

Cronley almost told him, but at the last second caught himself, and instead asked, "What's he asking?"

"He wants to know your name," Hessinger said.

"James. James D. Cronley Junior."

Stauffer took his hand again and said, "James. *Ich bin Luther.*"

Frau Stauffer took a look in the box.

"Oh, so much," she said.

"Tell her my mother got a letter from them, and then wrote me, and here we are," Cronley ordered.

Hessinger made the translation.

Frau Stauffer pulled out a drawer in a massive chest of drawers, came out with a photo album, laid it on the table and began to page through it. Finally, she found what she wanted, and motioned for Cronley to look.

It was an old photograph. Husband, wife, and two young children, a boy of maybe ten and a girl who looked to be several years younger.

"Luther's Papa," Frau Stauffer said, laying her finger on the boy, and then moving it to the girl. *"Dein mutter."*

"She says the girl in the picture is your mother," Hessinger translated.

"Ask him," Frau Stauffer asked, "if he has a picture of his mother now."

Hessinger translated.

As a matter of fact, I have two of her. Right here in my wallet.

Let me show you.

The first one was taken at College Park, the day I graduated from A&M. That's Mom, the lady in the mink coat with the two pounds of pearls hanging around her neck. The girl sitting on the fender of the custom-bodied Packard 280 is our neighbor's kid. Sort of my little sister. I called her "the Squirt."

In this picture, that's my mom standing next to President Truman. That's my dad, pinning on my captain's bars. This was taken the day after I married the Squirt, and the day she got herself killed.

"Tell her, 'Sorry. I have a couple, but I left them back at the Kloster.'"

Hessinger made the translation but, picking up on Cronley's slip, said, *"kaserne,"* not "Kloster."

Cronley saw on Luther's face that the translation was unnecessary.

Why is Cousin Luther pretending he doesn't speak English?

"Kloster?" Luther asked.

And he picked up on that, too.

"The lieutenant's little joke," Hessinger said. "Our *kaserne* is in the middle of nowhere, twenty miles outside Munich. The lieutenant jokes that we're all monks, kept in a *kloster* far from the sins of the city."

Luther smiled and then asked, "What exactly do you do in the Army?"

"Lieutenant, he wants to know exactly what you do in the Army."

"Tell him the 711th is responsible for making sure that the equipment in every mess hall in the European Command—and for that matter, in U.S. Forces in Austria— meets Army standards."

Hessinger made the translation. Luther confessed he didn't completely understand. Hessinger made that translation, too.

"You tell him what we do, Sergeant," Cronley ordered.

Hessinger rose to the challenge. He delivered a two-minute

lecture detailing the responsibility the 711th QM Mobile Kitchen Renovation Company had with regard to maintaining the stoves, ovens, refrigerators, dishwashers, and other electromechanical devices to be found in U.S. Army kitchens.

He explained that there were three teams who roamed Germany, Austria, and France inspecting and repairing such devices. Team 2 was commanded by Lieutenant Cronley. A dishwasher had broken down in Salzburg, and Team 2 had been dispatched to get it running.

Lieutenant Cronley had decided, Hessinger told Luther, that since Strasbourg was more or less on their way to the malfunctioning dishwasher, it was an opportunity for him to drop off the things his mother had sent to her family.

Cronley wasn't sure whether Hessinger had prepared this yarn before they got to Strasbourg or was making it up on the spot. But it sounded credible, and Cousin Luther seemed to be swallowing it whole.

"So you're going to Salzburg?" Luther asked.

Hessinger nodded.

"And from there?"

Why don't I think that's idle curiosity?

Before Hessinger could reply, Cronley said, "Ask him what he does."

"The lieutenant asks what your profession is," Hessinger said.

"I'm an automobile mechanic," Luther replied. "Or I was before the war. Now there are very few automobiles."

Hessinger translated.

"Ask him what he did in the war," Cronley ordered.

As Hessinger translated, Cronley saw that not only had Cousin Luther understood the question as he had asked it, but that he didn't like it, and was searching his mind for a proper response.

What the hell is this all about?

"Do you understand about Strasbourg?" Luther asked. "How over the years it has passed back and forth between French and German control?"

"Not really," said Hessinger, who had delivered a ten-minute lecture on the subject on the way to Strasbourg.

"Well . . ." Luther began.

Hessinger shut him off with a raised hand.

"Lieutenant, your cousin says Strasbourg has been under German and French control for years."

"Really?"

"Go on, Herr Stauffer," Hessinger ordered.

"Well, before the war, we were French," Luther explained. "And then when the Germans came, we were Germans again."

Hessinger translated.

"So what?"

"The lieutenant says he doesn't understand," Hessinger said to Luther.

"When the Germans came, they said I was now a German, and in 1941 I was conscripted into the German Army," Luther said.

There's something fishy about that.

When Hessinger had made the translation, Cronley said, "Ask him what he did in the German Army."

"The lieutenant wants to know what you did in the German Army."

"I was a common soldier, a grenadier, and then I escaped and hid out until the war was over."

Cousin Luther, that is not the truth, the whole truth, and nothing but.

What the hell are you up to?

Hessinger made the translation.

"Tell him I'm glad he made it through the war," Cronley said, and then asked, "How are we fixed for time, Sergeant?"

Hessinger looked at his watch.

"Sir, we're going to have to get on the road," Hessinger replied, and then told Luther the lieutenant was glad that he had made it through the war.

"Tell him we have to leave," Cronley ordered.

When Hessinger had done so, and Luther had replied, he made that unnecessary translation:

"He said he's sorry to hear that, but understands. He says he's very happy with your mother's gifts, and that he hopes this will not be the last time you come to Strasbourg."

"Tell him that if my mother sends some more things, I'll see that he gets them," Cronley said, and put out his hand to Luther.

"And where will you go from Salzburg?" Luther asked.

Hessinger looked to Cronley for permission to answer. Cronley nodded, hoping Luther didn't see him.

"Vienna," Hessinger said, and then, "He wanted to know where we're going from Salzburg. I told him. I hope that's all right."

"Sure. Why not?"

Frau Stauffer said *"Danke schön"* when she shook Cronley's hand, and looked as if she wanted to kiss him.

He smiled at her and walked to and out the door.

The Stauffers waved as they drove off.

[THREE]

When Sergeant Finney pulled the Ford up behind the ambulance, another of Tiny's Troopers—this one a corporal—got out of it and walked to the car.

Finney rolled the window down.

"We're through here. Go get Sergeant Graham," he ordered. "He's somewhere behind the house."

"You got it, Sarge," the corporal said, and took off at a trot.

"Tell me, Sergeant Finney," Cronley said, "now that you are a member of DCI-Europe, what is your professional assessment of Herr Stauffer?"

Finney thought it over for a moment, and then said, "That Kraut is one lying motherfucker."

Cronley didn't reply for a moment, then, coldly furious, said softly, "Sergeant, if you ever say that—or something like that—in my hearing again, you'll spend the rest of your time in Germany as a private walking around Kloster Grünau with a Garand on your shoulder."

"Yes, sir," Finney said, and then, "Captain, I'm sorry. I guess I just forgot he's your cousin."

"That's not what I'm talking about," Cronley said. "My lying Kraut kinsman doubtless has many faults, but I don't think we have any reason to suspect that he ever had incestuous relations with his mother."

"Sorry, Captain."

"You might want to pass the word around that that phrase is *strengstens verboten*. It turns my stomach."

"*Jawohl, Herr Kapitän.*"

"And your take on Luther Stauffer, Mr. Hessinger?"

"The question is not whether he was lying to us, but why," Hessinger said. "I think we should find out why."

"How are we going to do that?"

"I think the first thing to do is see if we can find the Strasbourg office of the DST."

"The what?"

"The Direction de la Surveillance du Territoire," Hessinger said. "It's sort of the French CIC, except that it's run by the French National Police, not the army. They may have something on Cousin Luther."

"Okay."

"And before we do that, I suggest we change out of our Quartermaster Corps uniforms," Hessinger said. "I think we'll get more cooperation from our French Allies as CIC agents than we would as dishwasher machine repairmen."

"Why don't we go whole hog and dazzle them with our DCI credentials?"

"Because (a) I would be surprised if word of the DCI's establishment has worked its way through the French bureaucracy, and (b) even if it has, we want to make discreet inquiries."

[FOUR]
Office of the Chief
Direction de la Surveillance du Territoire
Département Bas-Rhin
Strasbourg, France
1335 10 January 1946

When his sergeant showed Cronley, Hessinger, and Finney into his office, Commandant Jean-Paul Fortin of the Strasbourg office of the DST rose behind his desk.

He was a natty man in his early thirties with a trim mustache. He was wearing U.S. Army ODs with French insignia. There were shoulder boards with four gold stripes attached to the epaulets, and a brass representation of a flaming bomb pinned to his left breast pocket. On his desk, in what Cronley thought of as an in-basket, was his uniform cap.

Cronley thought the hat was called a "kepi." It had a flat circular top and what looked like a patent leather visor. The top was red. There were four gold stripes on a dark blue crown, and in the center of the top was another flaming bomb.

Cronley remembered what Luther had said about his being conscripted into the German grenadiers. A flaming bomb was a grenade.

"Thank you for seeing us, Commandant," Cronley said.

He offered his CIC credentials. Commandant Fortin examined them and then looked questioningly at Hessinger and Finney. They produced their credentials, and Fortin examined them carefully.

"*Bon,*" he said. "I regret that I have not much the English."

Oh, shit!

"It is to be hoped that you have the French?"

"Unfortunately, no," Hessinger said.

"Is possible German?"

"We all speak German, Major," Cronley said.

"Wunderbar!" Fortin said. "But of course, being in the CIC, you would. Now, how may the DST be of service to the CIC?"

"We're interested in a man named Luther Stauffer," Cronley said. "We've heard he was originally from Strasbourg, and we're wondering if the DST has anything on him."

"Herr Cronley, if you don't mind me saying so, you sound like a Strasbourger yourself."

"My mother, Commandant Fortin, was a Strasbourgerin. I learned my German from her."

"So was mine, a Strasbourgerin, I mean."

"Mine married an American right after the First World War," Cronley said. "And if you don't mind my asking, I've always been led to believe the DST was a police organization."

"It is. I've been seconded to it," Fortin said, and then bellowed, "Sergeant!"

When the sergeant appeared, Fortin said, "Check in the files for a man named . . ." He looked at Cronley.

"Stauffer," Hessinger furnished. "Luther Stauffer."

"Oui, mon Commandant."

"What is this Stauffer fellow wanted for?" Fortin asked.

"We didn't mean to give that impression," Hessinger said. "His name came up in an investigation of black market activities, that's all. We'd just like to know who he is."

"I thought your Criminal Investigation, DCI, did those sort of investigations."

"Most of the time, they do," Hessinger said.

Commandant Fortin is good. Is this going to blow up in our faces?

"To return to your earlier question," Fortin said, "there were . . . how do I say this delicately? . . . certain *awkward* problems here in Strasbourg. When the Germans came in 1940, there were some policemen, including senior officers, who were not too terribly unhappy."

"'Better Hitler than Blum'?" Hessinger said.

"Exactly," Fortin said. "I'm glad you understand."

"I don't," Cronley blurted, and immediately regretted it.

Fortin looked at Hessinger and signaled that Hessinger should make the explanation.

"He was premier of France for a while," Hessinger began. "A Jew, an anti-fascist, and a socialist, who thought the state should control the banks and industry. This enraged the bankers and businessmen in general, and they began to say, 'Better Hitler than Blum.' He was forced out of office before the war. After 1940, he was imprisoned by the Vichy government, and then by the Germans. We liberated him from a concentration camp, and he returned to France."

"I'm glad you understand," Fortin said. "The only thing I would add to that is that when he returned to France, Blum immediately redivided the Fourth Republic into those who love him, and those who think he should have been shot in 1939."

"May I ask where you stand on Monsieur Blum?" Hessinger asked.

"A career officer such as myself would never dream of saying that a senior French official should be shot. Or fed to the savage beasts."

"I appreciate your candor, Commandant," Cronley said. "And I apologize for my ignorance."

Fortin waved his hand, to signal *No apology necessary.*

"As I was saying, when the Germans came, many senior police officers were willing to collaborate with them. Many, perhaps most, of the junior policemen were not. The Germans hauled them off to Germany as slave laborers. Many of them died in Germany.

"When we—I had the honor of serving with General Philippe Leclerc's Free French Second Armored Division—tore down the swastika and raised the Tricolor over the Strasbourg Cathedral again, some of the senior police officers who had collaborated with the Boche were shot trying to escape, and the rest were imprisoned for later trial.

"That left Strasbourg without a police force worthy of the name. General Leclerc established an ad hoc force from the Second Armored and named me as its chief. He knew I was a Strasbourger. I have been here since, trying to establish a police force. That has proved difficult, as there are very few men in Strasbourg from whom to recruit. And policemen from elsewhere in France are reluctant to transfer here—"

He was interrupted when his sergeant came back into the office.

"I found two in the files, *mon Commandant*," he announced. "A Stauffer, Karl, and a Stauffer, Luther."

He laid the files on Fortin's desk, as Cronley wondered, *Do I have another cousin?*

Fortin examined the folders.

"I believe you said 'Stauffer, Luther'?"

"That's the name we have, Commandant," Hessinger said.

"I thought it rang a bell," Fortin said. "Very interesting man. You're not the only one, Herr Cronley, who'd like to talk to him."

"You want him?" Cronley asked.

"That's why he's interesting," Fortin said. "We've been looking for him, but so, I've come to believe, was the Schutz-staffel."

He offered the file to Cronley, who overcame his curiosity and handed it to Hessinger with the explanation, "Mr. Hessinger is my expert in reading dossiers."

"I mentioned before," Fortin went on, "that when the Germans came in 1940, some of our fellow Strasbourgers, Herr Cronley, were not unhappy to see them. Some of them, in fact, were so convinced that Hitler was the savior of Europe, and National Socialism the wave of the future, that they joined the Légion des Volontaires Français.

"Luther Stauffer was one of them. He joined the LVF as a *feldwebel*—sergeant—and went off to Germany for training."

"So he was a collaborator?"

"So it would appear," Fortin said. "The LVF, after training, was sent to what the Boche called 'the East,' as the Wehrmacht approached Moscow. They fought the Russians there, and whether through bravery or ineptitude, suffered severe losses and were returned to Germany."

"You seem to know quite a bit about this volunteer legion," Cronley said.

"Keeping up with them became sort of a hobby with me while we were in England. And as I had been assigned to military intelligence, it wasn't difficult."

"How'd you get to England?"

"I was with Général de Brigade de Gaulle at Montcornet, and I was one of the officers he selected to accompany him to England when he flew there on June seventeenth, 1940."

"I don't know what that means," Cronley confessed.

"There are those, including me," Hessinger chimed in, "who believe the only battle the Germans lost in France in 1940 was Montcornet."

"You know about it?"

"De Gaulle attacked with two hundred tanks and drove the Germans back to Caumont," Hessinger replied.

"Where most of our tanks were destroyed by Stukas," Fortin said. "Who attacked us at their leisure because our fighter aircraft were deployed elsewhere," Fortin said. "Anyway, to answer Herr Cronley's question, a month to the day after Montcornet, I flew to England with Général de Gaulle."

If de Gaulle flew you to England with him, and you were with Leclerc when he liberated Strasbourg, and then became the Strasbourg chief of police, how come you're still a major?

Answer: You're not. You just want people to think you're not as important as you really are.

Colonel Sergei Likharev of the NKGB didn't want people to think he was as important as he is, so he called himself Major Konstantin Orlovsky.

I wonder if your real name is Fortin, Commandant— probably Colonel—Fortin?

"What was left of the Légion des Volontaires Français," Fortin went on, "was assigned relatively unimportant duties in Germany—guarding supply depots, that sort of thing."

"And Stauffer was among them?" Cronley asked.

"Oh, yes. The Boche liked him. He'd been awarded the Iron Cross and promoted to *leutnant* for his service in the East. Then, in September 1944, a month after Général Leclerc and the French Second Armored Division liberated Paris, the Germans merged all French military collaborators into what they called the 'Waffen-Grenadier-Brigade der SS Charlemagne.'"

"'*All* French military collaborators'?" Cronley parroted.

"The Boche had also formed the Horst Wessel brigade of young Frenchmen. Other collaborators had had a quasi-military role in Organisation Todt, which built the defenses in Normandy and elsewhere—the defenses that had failed to stop the Allied invasion. Then there was the collaborationist version of the Secret State Police, the Geheime Staatspolizei, which was known as the Milice. And there were others who fled as the Allies marched across France.

"The Germans didn't trust many of them, but they apparently did trust Leutnant Stauffer. He was taken into the SS as a *sturmführer*—a captain—and put to work training the newcomers."

"And here is Sturmführer Stauffer," Hessinger said, as he handed Cronley the dossier.

Cronley looked at the photograph of a young man in uniform.

I'll be a sonofabitch, Cousin Luther was an SS officer.

Fortin extended his hand for the dossier, looked at it, and said, "Forgive me for saying this, Mr. Cronley, but he looks very much like you."

"I noticed," Cronley said.

"In February 1945," Fortin went on, "the brigade was renamed 'the Thirty-third Waffen-Grenadier-Division der

SS Charlemagne,' then loaded on a train and sent to fight the Red Army in Poland. On February twenty-fifth it was attacked by troops of the Soviet First Belorussian Front and scattered. What was left of them retreated to the Baltic coast, were evacuated by sea to Denmark, and later sent to Neustretlitz, in Germany, for refitting.

"The last time anyone saw Sturmführer Stauffer was when he went on a three-day leave immediately after getting off the ship in Germany," Fortin said matter-of-factly. "We think it reasonable to believe he deserted the SS at that time, even before his comrades reached Neustretlitz. It is possible, even likely, that he made his way here to Strasbourg and went into hiding."

"You think he deserted because he could see the war was lost?" Cronley asked.

"I'm sure he knew that, but I think it more likely that he heard somehow—he was an SS officer—what the Boche had in mind for them."

"Berlin?" Hessinger asked.

Fortin nodded.

"The remaining collaborators," Fortin amplified, "about seven hundred of them, went to Berlin in late April, just before the Red Army surrounded the city. A week later, when the Battle for Berlin was over, what few were left of them— thirty—surrendered to the Russians.

"According to the Russians, they fought bravely, literally until they had fired their last round of ammunition. I'd like to believe that. But on the other hand, what other option did they have?"

"Desertion?" Cronley asked.

"Desertion was more dangerous than fighting the Russians, as those thirty survivors learned. Of the seven hundred men who went to Berlin, seventy-two died at the hands of the SS for attempting to desert. They were hung from lamp poles *pour encourager les autres.*"

"You have no idea where Luther Stauffer is?" Cronley asked.

"I have not been entirely truthful with you, Mr. Cronley," Fortin said. "I wouldn't be surprised if at this moment he's at Hachelweg 675 here in Strasbourg."

They locked eyes for a moment.

"And I have not been entirely truthful with you, either, Commandant Fortin," Cronley said.

He took his Directorate of Central Intelligence identification from his Ike jacket and handed it to Fortin.

Fortin examined it carefully and then handed it back.

"I'm impressed," he said. "The DCI has only been in business since the first of January, and here you are—what? a week and two days later?—already hard at work."

"And I'm surprised that the Strasbourg chief of police has even heard about the DCI."

"I'm just a simple policeman," Fortin said, with a straight face, "but I try to stay abreast of what's going on in the world. Are you going to tell me what your real interest in Luther Stauffer is, Mr. Cronley?"

"He's my cousin. I should lead off with that. He—actually his wife—wrote my mother begging for help, saying they were starving. She sent food—canned hams, coffee, cigarettes, et cetera—to me and asked that I deliver them to him."

"And?"

"When we were in his house, all three of us sensed that he wasn't telling us the truth. He said he was conscripted into the German Army . . ."

"Where he served as a common soldier, a grenadier," Hessinger injected.

". . . which sounded fishy to us, so Mr. Hessinger suggested that the police might be able to tell us something about him."

"I'm disappointed," Fortin said. "Frankly, I was hoping the DCI was working on the Odessa Organization. I'm almost as interested in that as I am in dealing with our collaborators."

"I'm sorry, I don't know what you're talking about."

"It stands for the Organisation der ehemaligen SS-Angehörigen," Hessinger said. "Organization of Former German SS Officers."

"Sort of a VFW for Nazis?" Cronley asked.

"'VFW'?" Fortin parroted.

"Veterans of Foreign Wars," Cronley explained. "An American veterans organization. My father has been president of VFW Post 9900 in Midland as long as I can remember."

"Your father was in the First War?" Fortin asked.

"He was. And he was here in Strasbourg when the Communists tried to take over the city. That's where he met my mother."

"Which you said is why you speak German like a Strasbourger," Fortin said. "And your mother, I gather, maintained a close relationship with her family here?"

"No. Quite the opposite. Once she married my father, her family wanted nothing to do with her. The only contact she ever had with them was a letter before the war saying her mother had died. And then the letter asking for help."

"What would your reaction be if I told you that once I get what I want to know from Luther Stauffer about Odessa, I'm going to arrest him and charge him with collaboration?"

"Why is Odessa so important?"

"The purpose of Odessa is to help SS officers get out of Germany so they can't be tried for war crimes. I like SS officers only slightly more than I like collaborators."

"What I have heard of Odessa," Hessinger said, "is that it's more fancy than fact."

"Then, Herr Hessinger, you have heard wrong," Fortin said simply.

"I can ask General Greene what he knows about Odessa," Cronley said to Hessinger.

"And what is your relationship with the chief of CIC of the European Command?" Fortin asked.

So he knows who Greene is. Commandant Fortin does get around, doesn't he?

"He tells me what I want to know," Cronley said.

"I'm just a simple policeman," Fortin repeated. "So when I look at you, Mr. Cronley, I see a young man. Logic tells me you are either a junior civilian or a junior officer. And that makes me wonder why the chief of CIC, European Command, would tell you anything he didn't want to tell you."

When you can't think of anything else, tell the truth.

"Actually, I'm a captain seconded to DCI," Cronley said. "The reason General Greene will tell me everything I want to know is because he has been ordered to do so by Admiral Souers, who speaks with the authority of President Truman."

"And who do you work directly for, Captain Cronley?"

Army captains are rarely, if ever, directly subordinate to Navy admirals. And "Commandant" Fortin knows that. So the truth—that I work directly under Admiral Souers—won't work here.

"We have a phrase, Commandant, 'Need to Know.' With respect, I don't think you have the need to know that."

"I'm familiar with the phrase, Captain."

"If you don't mind, Commandant, I prefer 'Mr. Cronley.'"

"Of course," Fortin said. "I asked you before, Mr. Cronley, what your reaction would be if I told you I sooner or later intend to arrest your cousin Luther and see that he's tried as a collaborator?"

Cronley very carefully considered his reply before deciding again that when all else fails, tell the truth.

"I don't think I'd like the effect that would have on my mother."

"But you just told me she's had no contact with him since she married."

"He's her nephew. She's a woman. A kind, gentle, loving, Christian woman."

"And that would stop you from helping me put him in prison?"

"The way you were talking, I thought you meant you were going to put a blindfold on him and stand him against a wall."

"If I had caught him when we liberated Strasbourg, I would have. But Général de Gaulle says that we must reunite France, not exacerbate its wounds, and as an officer, I must obey that order. The best I can hope for is that when I finally go to arrest him, he will resist and I will be justified in shooting him. If he doesn't, he'll probably be sentenced to twenty years. Answer the question."

"I have no problem with your trying him as a collaborator," Cronley said. And then, he thought aloud: "I could tell my mother I knew nothing about him, or his arrest."

"But you would be reluctant to lie to your mother?" Fortin challenged.

Cronley didn't reply.

"Because she is, what did you say, 'a kind, gentle, loving, Christian woman'?"

Again Cronley didn't reply.

"Allow me to tell you about the kind, gentle, and loving Christian women in my life, Mr. Cronley. There have been two. One was my mother, and the second my wife. When the Mobilization came in March of 1939, I was stationed at Saumur, the cavalry school. I telephoned my mother and told her I had rented a house in Argenton, near Saint-Martin-de-Sanzay, near Saumur, and that I wanted her to come there and care for my wife, who was pregnant, and my son while I was on active service.

"She would hear nothing about it. She said that she had no intention of leaving her home to live in the country. She said what I should do is send my family to my home in Strasbourg.

"I reminded her that we seemed about to go to war, and if that happened, there was a chance—however slim—that the Germans would occupy Strasbourg as they had done before. Mother replied that it had happened before and she'd really had no trouble with the Germans.

"So my wife went to stay with my mother.

"About six months after I went to England with Général de Gaulle, the Milice and the SS appeared at her door and took my mother, my wife, and my children away for interrogation. They apparently believed that I hadn't gone to England, but was instead here, in Strasbourg, organizing the resistance.

"That was the last anyone saw of my mother, my wife, or my children. I heard what had happened from the resistance, so the first thing I did when I got back to Strasbourg with Général Leclerc was go to the headquarters of the Milice. The collaborators, my French countrymen, had done a very good job of destroying all their records.

"I have heard, but would rather not believe, that when the Milice, my countrymen, were through with their interrogation of my mother, my wife, and my children, their bodies were thrown into the Rhine."

"My God!" Cronley said.

"Your kids, too? Those miserable motherfuckers!" Sergeant Finney exclaimed bitterly in English.

Cronley saw on Fortin's face that he had heard the expression before.

Which means he speaks English far better than he wanted us to think.

Of course he speaks English, stupid! He spent almost four years in England.

Both Hessinger and Finney looked at Cronley, who had his tongue pushing against his lower lip, visibly deep in thought.

Finally he said, very softly, "My sentiments exactly, Sergeant Finney."

He turned to Fortin.

"Commandant, I really don't know what to say."

"I don't expect you to say anything, Mr. Cronley," Fortin said. "I just wanted you to understand my deep interest in your cousin, and in Odessa."

"Just as soon as we get back, I'll find out what General Greene knows about it, and get back to you with whatever he tells me."

I will also go to General Gehlen, who probably knows more about Odessa than anyone else.

But I can't tell you about Gehlen, can I, Commandant?

Even if Gehlen's never mentioned it to me.

And why hasn't he?

"I would be grateful to you if you did that."

"Is there anything else I can do for you?"

"Possibly."

"Anything."

"You didn't tell your cousin you're an intelligence officer?"

"Of course not."

"What did you tell him you do?"

"Repair dishwashing machines," Cronley said, chuckling.

"Excuse me?"

"Freddy, tell Commandant Fortin all about the 711th QM Mobile Kitchen Renovation Company."

Hessinger did so.

"I wondered," Fortin said, when Hessinger had finished his little lecture. "The European Command has no record of the 711th anything. When you parked your car in front of Hachelweg 675 and the ambulance with the red crosses painted over down the street, it piqued my curiosity, and I had Sergeant Deladier"—he pointed to the outer office—"call Frankfurt and ask about it."

"I hope Frankfurt . . . I presume you mean EUCOM . . . didn't have its curiosity piqued," Cronley said.

Fortin shook his head.

"Deladier's a professional. He's been with me a long time," Fortin said. "And you would say your cousin accepted this?"

"I think he did."

"You would think so. What about you, Sergeant? Do you think Herr Stauffer thinks you're dishwashing machine repairmen?"

"Yes, sir. We had our act pretty much together. I think Stauffer believed us."

"Your act pretty much together?"

"We were all . . . not just me . . . in uniform. Mr. Cronley as a Quartermaster Corps second lieutenant, Mr. Hessinger as a staff sergeant. Stauffer had no reason not to believe what we told him."

"In addition to you being dishwashing machine repairmen, what else did you tell him?"

"We told him our next stop was Salzburg," Hessinger answered for him. "He seemed to find that very interesting."

"Because it would take you across the border into U.S. Forces Austria from EUCOM," Fortin said. "Crossing borders is a major problem for Odessa. Tell me, Sergeant, how much talking did you do when you were in the house?"

Finney thought it over for a moment before replying, "Commandant, I don't think I opened my mouth when I was in the house. All I did was carry the black market stuff."

"In other words, all you were was the driver of the staff car?"

"Yes, sir."

"Let me offer a hypothetical," Fortin said. "Let us suppose you were too busy, Second Lieutenant Cronley, to yourself deliver more cigarettes, coffee, et cetera, to your cousin Luther and instead sent Sergeant Finney to do it for you.

"Do you think your cousin might either prevail upon Sergeant Finney to take something—maybe a few cartons of cigarettes, or a canned ham—to, say, Salzburg as either a goodwill gesture, or because he could make a little easy money doing so?"

"I see where you're going, Commandant," Hessinger said.

"Start out more or less innocently, and then as Sergeant Finney slid down the slippery slope of corruption, move him onto other things such as moving a couple of men—'going home, they don't have papers'—across the border. *Und so weiter.*"

"Yeah," Cronley said.

"These people routinely murder people who get in their way. With that in mind, would you be willing to have Sergeant Finney do something like this?"

"That's up to Sergeant Finney," Cronley said.

"Hell, yes, I'll do it. I'd like to burn as many of these moth— sonsofbitches as I can," Finney said.

"Thank you for cleaning up your language, Sergeant Finney," Cronley said. "I really would have hated to have had to order Mr. Hessinger to wash your mouth out with soap."

Finney smiled at him.

"I would suggest that in, say, a week Sergeant Finney deliver another package to Herr Stauffer," Fortin said. "How does that fit into your schedule?"

"Not a problem," Cronley said. "We have to be in Vienna on the fourteenth."

"Vienna?" Fortin asked.

"So we can be back at the monastery on the sixteenth. Finney could deliver a second package the next day, the seventeenth. That's a week from today."

"Why do I think you're not going to tell me what you're going to do in Vienna?"

"Because you understand that there are some things simple policemen just don't have the need to know," Cronley said.

"That's cruel," Fortin said, smiling, and put out his hand. "I'm perfectly willing to believe you're a second lieutenant of the Quartermaster Corps."

"It's been a pleasure meeting you, Simple Policeman," Cronley said. "I look forward to seeing you again soon."

[FIVE]
Suite 307
The Bristol Hotel
Kaerntner Ring 1
Vienna, Austria
1600 14 January 1946

It was time to go to what everybody hoped would be a meeting with Rahil, aka Seven-K, at the Café Weitz, and Cronley and Schultz had just finished putting the fifty thousand dollars intended for her in former Oberst Ludwig Mannberg's Glen plaid suit when there came a knock at the door.

Putting the money into Mannberg's suit had proved more difficult than anyone had thought it would be. It had come from the States packed in $5,000 packets, each containing one hundred fifty-dollar bills. There were ten such packets, each about a half-inch thick.

Mannberg's suit was sort of a souvenir of happier times, when young Major Mannberg had not only been an assistant military attaché at the German embassy in London but been in a position to pay for bespoke clothing from Anderson & Sheppard of Savile Row.

Cronley had not ever heard the term "bespoke" until today, but now he understood that it meant "custom-tailored" and that custom-tailored meant that it had been constructed about the wearer's body, and that meant room had been provided for a handkerchief, wallet, and maybe car keys, but not to accommodate twenty packets of fifty $50-dollar bills, each half an inch thick and eight inches long.

When they had finished, Mannberg literally had packs of money in every pocket in the suit jacket, and every pocket in his trousers. He also had a $2,500 packet in each sock. The vest that came with the suit was on the bed.

Ostrowski was larger than Mannberg and just barely fit into one of Mannberg's suits, providing he did not button the buttons of the double-breasted jacket. But to conceal the .45 pistol he was carrying in one of the holsters Hessinger had had made, he was going to have to keep his hand in the suit jacket pocket to make sure the pistol was covered.

"Who the hell is that?" Cronley asked, when the knock on the door came.

"There's one way to find out," El Jefe said, and went to the door and opened it. Ostrowski hurriedly shoved his pistol under one of the cushions of the couch he was sitting on.

There were three men at the door, all wearing ODs with U.S. triangles.

The elder of them politely asked, "Mr. Schultz?"

El Jefe nodded.

"If you don't mind, I'd like to ask you a few questions," the man said, and produced a set of CIC credentials. "May we come in?"

El Jefe backed away from the door and waved them in.

The three of them looked suspiciously around the room.

"What's the nature of your business in Vienna, Mr. Schultz, if you don't mind my asking?"

"What's this all about?" Schultz asked.

"Please, just answer the question."

"Why don't you have a look at this?" Schultz said, extending his DCI identification. "It will explain why I don't answer a lot of questions."

"Don't I know you?" one of them, the youngest one, asked of Cronley.

"You look familiar," Cronley said, and found, or thought he did, the name. "Surgeon, right?"

"Spurgeon," the man corrected him.

"I never saw one of these before," the CIC agent said, after examining El Jefe's DCI credentials.

"I'm not surprised," El Jefe said.

"Major, I knew this fellow at Holabird," the younger agent said.

"What?"

"We took Surveillance together," the younger agent said. "Right?"

"Under Major Derwin," Cronley confirmed.

"Terrible Tommy Derwin," Agent Spurgeon said. He put out his hand. "Cronley, right?"

"James D., Junior."

"Are you working?"

Cronley nodded.

"Doing what?"

"I'm sort of an aide-de-camp to Mr. Schultz."

"You're CIC?" the older agent asked.

Cronley produced his CIC credentials.

"I should have known it would be something like this," the older agent said.

"What would be something like this?" Schultz asked.

"Well, we encourage the people in the hotel to report suspicious activity, and one of the assistant managers did."

"Did he tell you what I did that was suspicious?" El Jefe asked.

"Well, he said he heard your men speaking Russian."

"Guilty as charged," Ostrowski said. "He must have overheard Ludwig and me."

He nodded toward Mannberg.

"You sound English," the older CIC agent said.

"Guilty as charged," Max repeated, and showed him his DCI credentials.

"Gentlemen, I'm sorry," the older agent said, "but you're in the business, and you know how these things happen."

"Not a problem," Schultz said. "You were just doing your job."

"You going to be in town for a while, Cronley?" Agent Spurgeon asked.

"We're leaving tomorrow," Schultz answered for him.

"Pity," Spurgeon said. "I was hoping we could have a drink and swap tales about Terrible Tommy Derwin and other strange members of the faculty of Holabird High."

"Sorry, we have to go," Schultz said.

"I guess you know that Derwin is here," Cronley said.

"He's here?"

"He's the new CIC/ASA inspector general for EUCOM," Cronley said.

"Oh, yeah," the senior agent said. "The old one, Colonel Schumann, blew himself up, didn't he?"

"Him and his wife," Cronley confirmed.

"Well, we'll get out of here," the senior agent said. "I'm really sorry about this, Mr. Schultz."

"You were just doing your job," El Jefe repeated.

"If there's ever anything we can do for you, just give us a yell."

"Can't think of a thing, but thanks."

Hands were shaken all around, and the Vienna CIC team left.

When they had, Cronley asked, "What the hell was that all about?"

El Jefe shrugged, then looked at his wristwatch and said, "We'd better get going."

[SIX]
Café Weitz
Gumpendorferstrasse 74
Vienna, Austria
1650 14 January 1946

When Cronley, El Jefe, and Finney walked into the Café Weitz, several of the waiters were drawing heavy curtains over the large windows looking out on the street. This would keep people on Gumpendorferstrasse, and on the trolley cars running down it, from looking into the café.

The curtains were drawn every night as darkness fell. During the day, the curtains were open, so Café Weitz patrons could look out onto Gumpendorferstrasse and the trolley cars.

But drawing the curtains did something else. During the day, looking out from the café gave the patrons a look at the empty windows of the bombed-out, roofless five-story apartment buildings across the street. With the curtains drawn, they were no longer visible.

And with the drawn curtains shutting out any light from the street, the only light in the café came from small bulbs in wall fixtures and in three chandeliers and small candles burning in tiny lamps on all the tables. This served to hide the shabbiness of the café's curtains and walls and everything else, and to offer at least a suggestion of its prewar elegance.

In one corner of the room, a string quartet (or quintet or sextet, it varied with the hour) of elderly musicians in formal clothing played continuously, mostly Strauss, but sometimes tunes from Hungarian light opera.

Cronley knew all this because he had come to the café three times before. So had everybody else. Cronley thought of it as reconnaissance, but Schultz called it "casing the joint."

After the first visit, they had gone back to the hotel, then, at Mannberg's suggestion, drawn maps of the café from memory. Very few of the first maps drawn agreed on any of the details except the location of the doors and the musicians, but the third, final maps drawn were pretty much identical.

It was decided that Cronley, El Jefe, and Sergeant Finney, who were all wearing OD Ike jackets with civilian insignia, would enter the café first and take the closest table they could find to the musicians. This would give them a pretty good view of most of the interior. Then Mannberg would enter, alone, and take a table that would be in clear view of anyone coming into the café. On his heels, but not with him, would be Maksymilian Ostrowski, who would take the closest table he could find to the door of the vestibule outside the restrooms, which, they were guessing, would be where, presuming she showed up, Seven-K/Rahil would take the money from Mannberg.

Or where agents of the NKGB would attempt to steal the fifty thousand dollars from Mannberg. Ostrowski's job was to see that that didn't happen.

Cronley pointed to a table near the musicians, and a waiter who looked like he was in his mid-eighties led them to it and pulled out chairs for them.

A dog yipped at Cronley and he turned to see a tiny hot dog, as they called dachshunds back in Midland, in the lap of an old lady. About half the old women in the place had dogs of all sizes with them.

Cronley barked back at the tiny dachshund, wondering if it was a puppy or whether there was such a thing as a miniature dachshund.

Then he ordered a pilsner, the same for Finney, and El Jefe said he would have a pilsner and a Slivovitz.

"What the hell is that?"

"Hungarian plum brandy. Got a kick like a mule."

Cronley was tempted, but resisted. If they were going to meet a top-level agent of both the NKGB and the Mossad, he obviously should not be drinking anything that had a kick like a mule.

"And ask him if they have any peanuts," El Jefe said.

"I brought some, when they didn't have any last night," Finney said, and produced a tin can of Planters peanuts, opened it, and put it on the table.

The tiny dachshund barked.

Cronley looked at him.

"Franz Josef," the old lady said in English, "likes peanuts."

Cronley offered Franz Josef a peanut, which he quickly devoured.

"Is that a full-sized dog, or is he a puppy?" Cronley asked in German.

He felt Finney's knee signal him under the table, and saw that Mannberg had come into the café.

"Franz Josef is four," she said, this time in German.

"He's so small," Cronley said, and fed the dog another peanut.

He took a closer look at the woman. She wasn't as old as he had originally thought, maybe fifty-something, or sixty-something, but not really old. She had rouged cheeks and wore surprisingly red lipstick.

"Good things come in small packages," the old lady said.

"So they say," Cronley said. "Would you like a peanut? A handful of peanuts?"

"You are very kind," the old lady said in English. "A *kavalier*."

Cronley offered her the can of peanuts.

"A what?" he asked.

"You know, a man in armor on a horse. Thank you for the peanuts."

"My pleasure," Cronley said, and fed Franz Josef another peanut.

Finney's knee signaled him again, and he saw Max Ostrowski walk across the room, take a table near the door to the restroom vestibule. Then he leaned a chair against the table to show it was taken and walked into the restroom vestibule.

Cronley saw an old woman wearing an absurd hat and two pounds of costume jewelry march regally across the room and enter the restroom vestibule.

Shit!

Whatever is going to happen in there is now going to have to be put on hold until the old lady finishes taking her leak.

"Let me taste that," Cronley said, pointing to Schultz's Slivovitz.

El Jefe handed him the glass, and Cronley took a small sip.

His throat immediately started burning, and he reached quickly for his beer.

"Don't say I didn't warn you," El Jefe said, chuckling.

Five long minutes later, Cronley asked rhetorically, "What the hell's taking that old woman so long?"

Three minutes after that, the old woman finally came out and marched regally back across the café to her table.

"How long have you been in Vienna?" the old lady with the dog asked.

"This is the fourth day. We leave tomorrow."

"You're in the Army?"

"I work for the Army. I work with kitchen equipment."

"You Americans do everything with a machine."

"Yes, ma'am. We try to."

Finney's knee signaled him again and he saw Mannberg stand up and walk into the restroom vestibule. A moment later, Ostrowski followed him.

The waiter delivered the beer and another Slivovitz.

Finney paid for it.

Ostrowski came out of the restroom vestibule and sat at his table.

A minute or so later, Mannberg came out of the vestibule, laid money on his table, and, standing, drank what was left of his pilsner.

Then he walked out of the Café Weitz.

Ostrowski got to his feet a minute later and did the same thing.

I don't know what the hell went on in the bathroom, but obviously Mannberg somehow found out Rahil/Seven-K wasn't coming.

Shit!

I wonder what spooked her?

El Jefe had obviously come to much the same conclusion.

"I don't know about you two, but I'm going to go back to the hotel," he said.

"Yeah," Cronley said. "So long, Franz Josef."

The dog yipped at him again.

Cronley gave the can of peanuts to the woman.

"It was nice talking to you," he said.

"Yes, it was," she said. "And I thank you, and Franz Josef thanks you for the peanuts."

"My pleasure. *Auf wiedersehen.*"

Cronley, Finney, and El Jefe had gone to the Café Weitz in the Ford staff car. Mannberg had taken the streetcar from Ringstrasse, and Ostrowski had walked.

They returned to the Hotel Bristol the same way.

When Ostrowski walked into the lobby of the hotel, Cronley, Finney, and Schultz were in the dining room.

When they saw him, Schultz asked, very concerned, "Where the hell is Ludwig? We should have brought everybody back here."

He stopped when he saw Mannberg come through the revolving doors into the lobby.

Mannberg walked to them and sat down.

"So what do we do now?" Cronley asked.

"Flag down the waiter so I can get one of those," Mannberg said, indicating Cronley's glass of whisky.

"That's not what I meant," Cronley said.

"Oh," Mannberg said, thinking he now understood the question. "We go back to Pullach. We're through here."

"Jesus Christ!" Cronley flared. "What do we do about getting the money to Seven-K?"

"By now, I'm sure she has it," Mannberg said. "I gave it to her man—actually her woman—in the restroom vestibule."

"Seven-K was there?"

"Yes, Jim, she was," Mannberg said, smiling broadly.

"She was in the café? Where?"

"Sitting next to you while you were feeding her and her dog peanuts."

VII

[ONE]
Quarters of the U.S. Military Government
Liaison Officer
The South German Industrial Development
Organization Compound
Pullach, Bavaria
The American Zone of Occupied Germany
1735 15 January 1946

It had taken Cronley, Hessinger, and Finney nine hours to drive the 270 miles from Vienna to Pullach in the Ford staff car. Schultz, Ostrowski, and Mannberg, who had left Vienna later on the Blue Danube, were already "home"—and sitting at the bar—when the three walked in. Captain Chauncey L. Dunwiddie, Major Maxwell Ashton III, and First Sergeant Abraham L. Tedworth were sitting at a table.

As Cronley headed for the toilet, Dunwiddie called, "My guys with you?"

He referred to the men who had gone to Strasbourg and then Vienna with Cronley in one of the ambulances and those in the two ambulances who had gone directly to Vienna.

"Very quickly, as my back teeth are floating," Cronley replied. "They left when we did, but since there is an MP checkpoint every other mile on the road, God only knows when they'll get here."

He then disappeared into the toilet, emerged a few minutes later, and went to the bar.

"Wait a minute before you get into that," Hessinger said, indicating the bottle of Haig & Haig Cronley had taken from behind the bar and was opening.

"With all due respect, Staff Sergeant Hessinger, I have earned this," Cronley said, and gave him the finger.

Hessinger appeared about to reply, and then went into the toilet. He came out two minutes later, and as Sergeant Finney went in, announced, "I have been thinking of something for the past two hours that will probably make me very unpopular when I bring it up."

"Then don't bring it up," Cronley said.

"We have to make a record, a report, of what we have been doing," Hessinger said. "And we have to do it before we start drinking."

When Cronley didn't immediately reply, Hessinger went on: "Sooner or later, somebody is going to want to know what we've been doing. Somebody is going to want to look at our records. And when that happens, saying 'We haven't been keeping any records' is not going to be an acceptable answer."

"Jesus!" Cronley said.

"He's right, Jim," El Jefe said. "We at least need to keep after-action reports."

"And who do we report to?" Cronley asked.

El Jefe didn't immediately reply, and Cronley saw on his face that he was giving the subject very serious consideration.

"I don't know why I didn't think of this," El Jefe said, after a long moment, and then answered his own question.

"Because Cletus didn't do after-action reports. But that was then and in Argentina. This is now and you're in Germany. Cletus didn't have two different groups of people looking over his shoulder to find something, anything, proving he was incompetent. You do, Jim."

"Two groups?"

"Colonel Mattingly. And the two from the Pentagon . . ."

"Lieutenant Colonel Parsons and Major Ashley," Hessinger furnished.

"And then there's the problem of how do we keep the wrong people from getting their hands on the after-action reports Freddy is right in saying we have to make," Schultz went on.

"Classify them Top Secret–Presidential and Top Secret–Lindbergh," Cronley suggested.

"How do we keep the wrong people who hold Top Secret–Presidential and Top Secret–Lindbergh clearances from seeing them? Like Mattingly? And Whatsisname? McClung, the ASA guy?"

"And Dick Tracy," Cronley said.

"Who?" Ashton asked.

"Major Thomas G. Derwin, the new CIC/ASA inspector general. He's got all the clearances."

"Why do you call him 'Dick Tracy'?"

"He was more or less affectionately so known when he was teaching Techniques of Surveillance at Holabird High."

"You mean the CIC Center at Camp Holabird?" Ashton asked.

"Yes, I do," Cronley said. "One of the spooks who came to El Jefe's room in the Bristol was a fellow alumnus."

"What spooks who came to your room in the hotel?"

Cronley told him.

Ashton thought about that for a moment, and then said, "I know what we can do. About keeping the wrong people from seeing the after-action reports, I mean. Send them to me."

"I thought we were talking about the spooks who came to my room," El Jefe said.

Ashton ignored him and went on, "And once I get them, as chief, Operation Ost, I can decide who else should see them. I will decide nobody else should see them. That way, they would be on file in case, for example, the admiral wants to."

"That'd work," El Jefe said.

"Problem solved," Cronley said sarcastically. "Now all we have to do is write the after-action report—"

"Reports," Hessinger interrupted. "Plural. Starting, I suggest, with Tedworth grabbing Colonel Likharev."

"We need an after-action report on that?" Cronley asked, and as the words came out of his mouth, realized they would.

"On everything," Schultz confirmed.

"As I was about to say, I don't know how to write an after-action report," Cronley said.

"I do," Hessinger said.

"Congratulations. You are now our official after-action-report writer," Cronley said. "Have at it."

"I don't have the time," Hessinger said. "Since I am no longer the company clerk. We need somebody else to do it."

"You're talking about Staff Sergeant Miller? Your new deputy?"

"He can help, but I'm talking about Claudette Colbert," Hessinger said.

"Who?" Ashton asked.

"There are apparently two," Cronley said. "The movie star and Hessinger's. Hessinger's Claudette Colbert is an ASA tech sergeant who wants to be an intelligence officer," Cronley said.

"What about her?" El Jefe asked.

"She takes shorthand, and she types sixty words a minute," Hessinger said. "We could really use her."

"Not to mention, she intercepts for us what Parsons and Ashley are saying to the Pentagon. And vice versa," Cronley said.

"Then get her, Jim," Schultz said. "The admiral gave you authority to recruit people. Call Major McClung and tell him you want her."

"There's two problems with that," Cronley said. "I've never laid eyes on Sergeant Colbert, and until I—"

"You're recruiting her to push a typewriter, Jim, right? So what do you care what she looks like?"

"That's not what I meant. Freddy says she's a good-looking female. But I want to make sure she understands what she's letting herself in for."

"So send for her and ask her."

"Before he does that, he better find out if Major McClung is going to let her go," Hessinger said.

"Right," El Jefe said. "Get on the secure line and call Major McClung."

"How did you know we have a secure line to the ASA?"

"Because when I asked Sergeant Tedworth to show me your SIGABA installation, I saw how amateurishly the

ASA—being Army—had set up your secure line and showed them the smart—Navy—way to do it," El Jefe said. "Sergeant Tedworth, would you please go in there and get the secure line phone for Mr. Cronley?"

"Yes, sir."

"Any questions, Mr. Cronley?"

Cronley shook his head.

"Not even about me calling you 'Mr. Cronley'?" El Jefe pursued.

"Okay. Why did you refer to me as 'Mr. Cronley'?"

"Because if when you call Major McClung you identify yourself as 'Captain Cronley,' he will be reminded that he outranks you. If you say you're 'Mr. Cronley,' that won't happen. 'Misters' don't have ranks, they have titles. For example, 'chief, DCI-Europe.'"

"But ol' Iron Lung knows I'm a captain. Also, I suspect he doesn't like me," Cronley argued. "Given those facts' bearing on the problem, my suggestion is that you call him."

"When I'm gone, Mr. Cronley, say tomorrow or the day after tomorrow, you're going to have to deal with ol' Iron Lung—and others in the Farben Building—"

"You'll be gone tomorrow? Or the day—"

"I hadn't planned to get into this yet," El Jefe said. "But why not? This is as good a time as any.

"Freddy was not the only one having profound thoughts on the way back from Vienna," Schultz went on. "Okay, where to start? With my orders from the admiral. The admiral thinks that we don't—you don't—fully understand how potentially valuable an intelligence asset Colonel Likharev is—"

"But we've already turned him," Cronley argued.

"He's turned *for the moment*, for two reasons: You did a very good job, Jim, of selling him on his duty as a Christian, as a man, to do whatever he can to save his family from the attentions of the NKGB. You told him you would try to get his family out of Russia. And then the NKGB tried to kill him."

"I don't understand where you're trying to go with this," Cronley said.

"You know Colonel Sergei Likharev as well as anybody, Jim. What do you think he's doing practically every waking moment?"

Cronley thought a moment.

"Wondering if we can get his family out?" he asked finally.

"How about him wondering if you just said you were going to get his family out? Wondering if you never had any intention to do that? Wondering if you could be expected to try to hand him a line like that? In reversed circumstances, it's something he would have tried himself."

"But I wasn't lying!"

"I don't think he's convinced about that. I think every day he grows a little more convinced that he's been lied to. That one day, he'll be told, 'Sorry, we tried to get them out and it just didn't work.' And, frankly, one day we might have to do just that."

"Jesus!"

"And getting his family out is all he has to live for. If he loses that, I wouldn't be surprised if he tried to take himself out."

"Jesus!"

"And even if we kept him from doing that, and we're

damned sure going to try to, he'll shut off the flow of intel. Either refuse to answer any more questions, or hand us some credible bullshit and send us on one wild-goose chase after another. And he'd be good at that.

"So what I thought on the way from Vienna is that Polo and I have to go to Argentina and look him in the eye and tell him everything that's happened and is happening. Everything. Including you loaning the DCI the hundred thousand of your own money, and meeting Rahil/Seven-K in the Café Weitz. Even you feeding her dog peanuts and not having a clue who she was."

"Why would he believe you? Or Polo?"

"Likharev, like many good intel officers, can look into somebody's eyes and intuit if they're lying. Or not. Freddy says he can do that. I believe him. I think Colonel Mannberg can do it. And I wouldn't be surprised if you could. Hell, I know you can. You wouldn't have been able to turn Likharev in the first place if you hadn't known in your gut when he was lying and when he was telling the truth."

"Okay," Cronley said. "I can do it. Let's say you're right and Likharev can do it. So he looked in my eyes and decided I wasn't lying about trying to get his family out. Doesn't that count?"

"That was then. Now he's had time to think his gut reaction was flawed."

"Okay. So now what?"

"I told you. Polo and I are on the next SAA flight to Buenos Aires. Leaving you here to deal with Major McClung and the others by your lonesome."

"Christ!"

"Hand Mr. Cronley the telephone, Sergeant Tedworth."

"My father could do that," Captain Dunwiddie said thoughtfully. "Look in my eyes and tell if I was lying."

"Thank you for sharing that with us, Captain Dunwiddie," Major Ashton said. "And now that I think about it, several young women I have known have had that ability."

The telephone was an ordinary handset and cradle mounted on an obviously "locally manufactured" wooden box about eight inches tall. There were three toggle switches on the top of the box, and a speaker was mounted on the side. A heavy, lead-shielded cable ran from it to the room in which the SIGABA system was installed.

"The left toggle switch turns the handset on," El Jefe said. "The one in the middle turns on the loudspeaker, and the one on the right turns on the microphone. I suggest you leave that one off."

"The line has been checked, and you're into the ASA control room in Frankfurt, Mr. Cronley," First Sergeant Tedworth said. "Just flick the left toggle."

"Is that the truth? Let me look into your eyes, First Sergeant," Cronley said, as he flipped the left toggle switch, and then the center one.

Almost immediately, there came a male voice.

"Control room, Sergeant Nesbit."

"J. D. Cronley for Major McClung."

"Hold one."

Thirty seconds later, the voice of Major "Iron Lung" boomed from the speaker.

"What can I do for you, Cronley?"

"I want to steal one of your people from you."

"I was afraid of that. General Greene showed me that *EUCOM will provide* letter."

"Actually, I want more than one of your people," Cronley said, and as the words came out he realized he was in "automatic mouth mode."

"I was afraid of that, too. Okay, who?"

"I've only got one name right now, somebody I know wants to come work for us."

"Okay, who?"

"One of your intercept operators, Tech Sergeant Colbert."

There was a just perceptible pause before McClung asked, "What do you want her for, besides intercepting messages between Colonel Parsons and the Pentagon?"

Christ, he knows!

Why am I surprised?

Because you forgot "to know your enemy," stupid.

So what do I do now?

I don't know, but lying to Major McClung isn't one of my options.

"That, too, but right now I want her because she can take shorthand and type sixty words a minute. Colonel Ashton has told me our record keeping, especially after-action reports, is unacceptably in arrears."

"Meaning nonexistent?"

"That's what the colonel alleges."

"Welcome to the world of command," McClung said, chuckling. "Okay, you can have her. Who do I transfer her to?"

I don't have a fucking clue!

"Hold on," Cronley said.

Hessinger scribbled furiously on his clipboard and then handed it to Cronley.

Cronley read aloud what Hessinger had written:

"Military Detachment, Directorate of Central Intelligence, Europe, APO 907."

After a moment, McClung said, "Okay, who else?"

"Let me get back to you after I talk to them and ask if they want to come with us."

"Okay. Makes sense. I don't know what I would do if I were an ASA non-com and was asked to join the DCI."

"Why would you not want to?"

"Your DCI is a dangerous place to be. People, powerful people, don't like you. You ever hear of guilt by association?"

"How do you know that powerful people don't like me? Us?"

"I'm chief of ASA Europe. I listen to everybody's telephone calls and read all their messages."

"Well, I'll ask them anyway."

"Do that. When you find out, let me know."

"Will do."

"That all, Cronley?"

"I guess so."

"McClung out," he said, and Cronley sensed that the line was no longer operating. He hung up the handset and then flipped the toggle switches off.

"Now, that wasn't so hard, was it, Jim?" El Jefe asked.

"When I called McClung, I had him in the Enemies column," Cronley said. "Now I don't think so."

"Why not? Something he said?"

"More the tone. Of the entire conversation, but especially in his voice."

"So, what we should do now is, while staring into the

eyes of people we're talking to to see if they're lying, listen to the tone of their voices to see if they like us, or not?"

"May I say something?" Ludwig Mannberg asked.

"You don't have to ask permission to speak around here, Colonel," Cronley said.

"I had the same feeling about this officer, listening to his tone," Mannberg said. "I think Jim is right. But I also feel obliged to say that, in my experience, it is very dangerous to rely on intuition. And very easy to do so. Intuition can be often, perhaps most often, relied upon. But when you *want to rely* on intuition, don't. That's when it will fail you."

"I think I'm going to write that down," El Jefe said. "And I'm not being a wiseass." He paused and then went on. "No, I won't write it down. I don't have to. I won't forget 'when you want to rely on intuition, don't.' Thanks, Ludwig."

"Yeah, me, too," Cronley said. "Thank you for that." He paused. "Now what do we do?"

"If you really can't think of anything else to do, why don't you get Sergeant Colbert in here?" Hessinger asked.

[TWO]
Office of the U.S. Military Government
Liaison Officer
The South German Industrial Development
Organization Compound
Pullach, Bavaria
The American Zone of Occupied Germany
1755 15 January 1946

Technical Sergeant Claudette Colbert knocked at the door, heard the command "Come," opened the door, marched into the office up to the desk of the liaison officer, came to attention, raised her hand in salute, and barked, "Technical Sergeant Colbert reporting to the commanding officer as ordered, sir."

In doing so, she shattered a belief Captain James D. Cronley Jr. had firmly held since his first days at Texas A&M, which was, *Unless you're some kind of a pervert, into kinky things like fetishes, a female in uniform is less sexually attractive than a spittoon.*

He would have thought this would be even more true if the uniform the female was wearing, as Sergeant Colbert was, was what the Army called "fatigues." Generously tailored to afford the wearer room to move while performing the hard labor causing the fatigue, "fatigues" conceal the delicate curvature of the female form at least as well as, say, a tarpaulin does when draped over a tank.

It was not true of Technical Sergeant Colbert now.

Cronley returned the salute in a Pavlovian reflex, and similarly ordered, "Stand at ease," and then, a moment later, added, "Have a seat, Sergeant," and pointed to the chair Hessinger had placed six feet from his desk.

Technical Sergeant Colbert sat down.

She found herself facing Captain Cronley, and on the left side of his desk, Lieutenant Colonel Ashton, Captain Dunwiddie, and Staff Sergeant Hessinger. Lieutenant Oscar Schultz, USN, Maksymilian Ostrowski, and former Colonel Ludwig Mannberg were seated to the right of Cronley's desk.

Only Colonel Ashton and Captain Dunwiddie were wearing the insignia of their ranks. Everyone else was wearing the blue triangles of civilian employees of the Army, including Ostrowski, whom Claudette knew to be a Pole and a DP guard. Ex-colonel Mannberg was wearing a very well-tailored suit.

Cronley, who was having thoughts he knew he should not be having about how Sergeant Colbert might look in the shower, forced them from his mind and asked himself,

How the hell do I handle this, now that she's here?

Shift into automatic mode and see what happens when I open my mouth?

In the absence of any better, or any other, idea . . .

"Sergeant, Sergeant Hessinger tells me that you would like to move to the DCI from the ASA. True?"

"Yes, sir."

"Why?"

"I've been on the fringes of the intelligence business, sir, since I came into the ASA. And the more I've learned about it, the more I realized I'd like to be in it. As more than an ASA intercept sergeant. As an intelligence officer."

"What would you like to do in what you call the intelligence business?"

"I don't know, sir. Once I get into the DCI, something will come up."

"What if I told you that what you would do if you came to DCI is typing and taking shorthand?"

"Sir, I would have my foot in the door. So long as you understood that I don't want to be a secretary, starting out taking shorthand and typing would be okay with me."

"DCI inherited from the OSS the notion that the best qualified person for the job gets the job and the authority that goes with it. You understand that? It means you would be working for Hessinger, although you outrank him. Would you be all right with that?"

"Yes, sir."

"Has anyone else got any questions for Sergeant Colbert?" Cronley asked.

There came shaken heads, a chorus of no's and uh-uhs.

"Okay, Sergeant Colbert, let's give it a try," Cronley said. "You can consider yourself a member of DCI from right now. What is that officially, Freddy?"

"Military Detachment, Directorate of Central Intelligence, Europe, APO 907," Hessinger furnished.

"Sir?" Sergeant Colbert said.

"Yes?"

"Sir, with respect, I have conditions. Before I'll agree to be transferred to DCI."

Now, what the hell?

"Conditions, Sergeant?" Cronley asked unpleasantly. "Before you 'agree to be transferred'? You don't have to agree to being transferred. I decide whether or not that will happen."

"Sir, with respect. Would you want me in DCI if I didn't want to be here?"

Turn off the automatic mouth or you really will say something stupid.

"What sort of conditions, Sergeant?" Lieutenant Colonel Ashton asked.

Cronley saw Schultz flash Ashton a withering look, and then he said, "She has a point, Jim."

"What sort of conditions, Sergeant?" Cronley asked.

"Just two things, sir. I'd like permission to wear civilian triangles. And if you're issuing what I guess could be called special IDs, I'd like one of those, too. I suppose what I'm saying—"

"That will not pose a problem," Cronley said. "We're all aware that it's easier to get things done if you're not wearing rank insignia. And that ties in with what I said before that in the DCI, authority is based on your job, not your rank."

"Yes, sir. Thank you, sir."

"You said 'two things,' Sergeant."

"Yes, sir. I'd like to bring three of my girls with me."

What?

Her girls?

Jesus Christ, she's a dyke!

"Excuse me, Sergeant?"

"They want to get out of the ASA house . . ."

That she was queer never entered my mind!

Until just now.

So much for that intuition bullshit we were just talking about!

". . . and not only will they be useful here, but they'll be able to keep an eye on anything going to or from Washington," Sergeant Colbert went on, and then stopped, and then went on again, "It's not what you're thinking, sir."

So what do I say now?

Ask her what she thinks I'm thinking?

Cronley was literally struck dumb.

"Sir, I'm no more interested in other women—that way—than you are in other men."

"Sergeant, I hope I didn't say anything to suggest—"

"May I continue, sir?" she interrupted.

How could I possibly say no?

"Certainly," Cronley said.

"I'm glad this came up," she began. "To clear the air. One of the reasons I want to get out of the WAC is because I'm really tired of being suspected of being a dyke. And I've learned that every man, officer or enlisted, who looks at me thinks there is no other explanation for an attractive, unmarried woman being in the WAC except that she's a lesbian."

Cronley thought: *That's true. It may not be fair, but it's true.*

But he remained struck dumb.

"I'm heterosexual," Sergeant Colbert said. "And so are the women I want to bring with me into DCI. Is that clear?"

Cronley found his voice.

"Perfectly clear," he said. "And I appreciate your candor, Sergeant Colbert. Hessinger, get the names of the women Sergeant Colbert wants to bring with her, and see that they're transferred."

"Yes, sir," Hessinger said.

Sergeant Colbert stood up, came to attention, and looked at Cronley.

What the hell is that all about?

"Permission to withdraw, sir?" she asked.

Oh!

"Granted," Cronley said.

Sergeant Colbert saluted. Cronley returned it. Sergeant Colbert executed a snappy "left turn" movement and marched toward the door.

Cronley's automatic mouth switched on.

"Colbert! Just a minute, please."

She stopped, did a snappy "about face" movement, and stood at attention.

"Sir?"

"First of all, at ease," Cronley said. "You can knock off just about all the military courtesy, Colbert. For one thing, this isn't the Farben Building. For another, I'm wearing triangles, not bars. Pass that word to your girls."

"Yes, sir."

"Welcome to DCI, Claudette. Freddy will see that you have everything you need."

"Thank you."

She smiled and left the room.

Hessinger started to follow her, but stopped halfway to the door and asked, "Where do I put them?"

"To live, you mean? I hadn't thought about that," Cronley admitted.

"I think it would be a good idea if you did," Hessinger said.

"And I'm sure you have already given the subject some thought and are going to share those thoughts with me."

"I think it would be a good idea to get the three women she's bringing with her out of the ASA building, where they are now. With half a dozen other women, who are probably very curious about what's going on over here."

"So?"

"So I suggest you take the 'Guesthouse' sign off the guesthouse and put up one that says 'Female Quarters, Off Limits to Male Personnel.'"

"Do it."

"And I suggest that as soon as I can get Sergeant Colbert into blue triangles, you put her in one of our rooms in the Vier Jahreszeiten. She'll be working there."

"And what is Major Wallace going to think about that?"

"You'll have to think of something to tell him, and I think you should count on Major McClung telling him by this time tomorrow that you stole her from him."

Shit, I didn't think about that. McClung will certainly tell Wallace . . .

Or will he?

Now that I think about it, I don't think he will.

But this is probably one of those times that Mannberg talked about, when you really want to trust your gut feeling, and therefore shouldn't.

"As soon as you get Sergeant Colbert into blue triangles, put her in the Vier Jahreszeiten," Cronley said. "What she's doing there is none of Major Wallace's business."

Hessinger nodded and left the room.

"Don't let it go to your head, Jim," El Jefe said, "but you handled the sergeant well. Finally. For a while, I thought she was going to eat you alive."

"'Formidable' describes her well, doesn't it?"

"So does 'well stacked.' Is that going to be a problem, now that she's made it so plain she's not a dyke?"

"Not for me. Ostrowski may have to watch himself."

That got the expected chuckles.

"So what do we do now?" Cronley asked.

"You get on the phone and get Polo and me seats on the next SAA flight to Buenos Aires. If they're sold out, tell them they're going to have to bump two people."

"What makes you think they'd do that?"

"Because, for the moment, at least until Juan Perón takes it away from us, South American Airways is a DCI asset and you're chief, DCI-Europe."

"But do they know that?"

"I told Cletus to make sure they know."

There he goes again.

"I told Cletus . . ."

El Jefe is a lot more—and probably was for a long time—than just Clete's communications expert.

And the admiral sent him here. And not to take care of Polo.

So how do I find out what he's really up to?

Ask him?

Why not?

The worst that could happen would be for him to pretend he doesn't know what I'm talking about.

So I'll ask him.

But not now. In private, when the moment is right.

Cronley reached for the telephone, dialed zero and told the Pullach compound operator to get him South American Airways at the Rhine-Main Air Force Base.

Five minutes later, he put the phone in its cradle and turned to Schultz.

"You're on SAA Flight 233, departing Rhine-Main at 1700 tomorrow."

"Which means we'll have to be there at 1600," Schultz replied.

"Which means we can have a late breakfast and leave here at ten, ten thirty. Or even eleven," Cronley said. "That'll give us plenty of time for Ostrowski and me to fly you up there."

"No," Schultz said. "What that means is that so I can make my manners to Generals Smith and Greene, and the admiral would be very disappointed if I didn't, we have to get up in the dark so that we can leave at first light. And that means, of course, that you don't get anything more to drink tonight. Nor does Ostrowski."

It makes sense that he has to see Greene, but General Walter Bedell Smith, Eisenhower's deputy? I'm supposed to believe he's only a Navy lieutenant, the same as an Army captain, and he's going in for a social chat with General Smith? Even if the admiral sent him, there's something going on nobody's telling me.

Like there's something nobody's telling me about the appointment of Captain James D. Cronley Jr. as chief, Directorate of Central Intelligence, Europe. There's something very fishy about that, too. There's at least a platoon of ex-OSS colonels and light birds, now unemployed, better qualified than I am who should be sitting here.

My gut tells me—and screw Ludwig's theory that when you really want to trust your intuition, don't—that El Jefe has the answers to all of this.

So how do I get him to tell me?

I don't have a fucking clue.

"Or I could stay here and drink my supper and have Kurt Schröder fly you to Frankfurt."

"No."

"He's a much better Storch pilot than I am, El Jefe,"

Cronley said. "He flew General Gehlen and Ludwig Mannberg all over Russia."

"You're going to fly me to Frankfurt. Period."

"Yes, sir."

[THREE]
Office of the Chief, Counterintelligence Corps
Headquarters, European Command
The I.G. Farben Building
Frankfurt am Main
American Zone of Occupation, Germany
1135 16 January 1946

"Well, Colonel Ashton," General Greene said, coming from
behind his desk as Cronley pushed Ashton's wheelchair into
his office, "I'm really glad to see you. I was getting a little
worried."

"Sir?"

Greene looked at his wristwatch.

"In twenty-five minutes, we're having lunch with General Smith. He is big on punctuality. You cut it pretty
short."

"I didn't know about the lunch," Ashton said.

"You must be Lieutenant Schultz," Greene said, offering
his hand. "Admiral Souers speaks very highly of you."

"That's very kind of the admiral," Schultz said.

Greene looked at Cronley, said, "Cronley," but did not
offer his hand.

"This is Colonel Mattingly, my deputy," Greene said.

Schultz, Ashton, and Mattingly shook hands. Mattingly
ignored Cronley.

"I understand that you met my CIC chief in Vienna," Greene said. "Colonel Stevens?"

Cronley thought, *Well, it didn't take Greene long to hear about that, did it?*

"We had a visit from the CIC in Vienna, but I didn't get his name," Schultz said.

"What was that about?"

"Apparently one of the hotel managers heard two of my people speaking Russian, and turned us in as suspicious characters."

"He didn't say what you were doing in Vienna."

"I didn't tell him," Schultz said.

"So he said. He also said that one of his agents knew Cronley."

"As I understand that," Schultz said, "they were apparently in CIC school together."

"Where they were students in Major Derwin's class on Techniques of Surveillance," General Greene said. "Which brings us, Cronley, to Major Derwin."

"Sir?"

"Major Derwin wants to talk to you."

What the hell for?

"Yes, sir?"

"He didn't tell me why, but he said he'd like to do so as soon as possible. What about today?"

"Not today, sir. As soon as I load these gentlemen onto the Buenos Aires flight, I have to get back to Munich."

"Well, when can I tell the major you will have time for him?"

"Sir, just about anytime after I get back to Munich. Anytime tomorrow."

"What's so important, Cronley," Colonel Mattingly demanded, "that you have to get back to Munich today? You don't actually expect Major Derwin to come to Munich to ask you what he wants to ask you, do you?"

"Colonel, if Major Derwin wants to ask me anything, I'll be in Munich," Cronley said.

General Greene, before Mattingly could reply to that, said, "Why don't we head for the generals' mess? It's always wiser to be earlier for an appointment with a general than late."

"Colonel Ashton," Cronley asked, "would it be all right if I waited for you and Lieutenant Schultz here after I get a sandwich in the snack bar?"

"Certainly."

"The guest list I got from General Smith's aide has you on it, Cronley," General Greene said. "You, Colonel Ashton, Lieutenant Schultz, and me."

Oh, so that's why Mattingly's pissed. He didn't get invited to break bread with Beetle Smith and I did.

That should delight me. But it doesn't.

I suppose I really am afraid of Colonel Robert Mattingly.

[FOUR]
The General Officers' Mess
The I.G. Farben Building
Frankfurt am Main
American Zone of Occupation, Germany
1159 16 January 1946

General Walter Bedell Smith, trailed by his aide-de-camp, a full colonel, marched into the general officers' mess, where General Greene, Ashton, Schultz, and Cronley were standing waiting for him just inside the door.

"Homer, why don't you check inside and see everything's set up, and then catch a sandwich or something while we eat? This is one of those top secret lunches behind a curtain one hears about, and you're not invited."

"Not a problem, General," the aide said, smiling, and went into the dining room.

"How are you, Paul?" Smith asked General Greene.

"Holding up under difficult circumstances, General."

"Welcome to the club, General."

Smith turned to Cronley.

"How are you, son? And how's our midget friend holding up?"

He means Tiny.

"Very well, sir. Tiny's holding the fort up in Munich."

"I'm Walter Smith, Colonel," Smith said to Ashton. "I guess you're the one I should have asked how he's holding up."

"I'm all right, sir. Thank you."

"And you," Smith said to Schultz, "by the process of elimination, must be 'the chief'?"

"Some people still call me that, General," Schultz said.

"Including Admiral Souers," Smith said. "He tells me you two are old shipmates?"

Cronley had never heard that before.

Why not?

"Yes, sir. That's true."

"Actually, when he told me he was sending you to Europe, I thought I heard an implication that there is more to your relationship than just being old shipmates."

Schultz seemed to be framing his reply when he saw he didn't have to. General Smith's aide was walking quickly back across the room to them.

"All set up, sir."

"Thanks, Homer. See you in forty-five minutes. Wait a minute. You're going to Buenos Aires today, right? How are you going to get out to Rhine-Main?"

From the look on General Greene's face, this was news—surprising news—to him, but he reacted quickly to it:

"I'll send them in one of my cars, General," he said.

"Homer, lay on a Packard for these gentlemen," General Smith said. "If there's no spare, use mine."

"Yes, sir."

"General, that's not necessary," Schultz said.

"I understand that chiefs feel free to argue with admirals, Chief, but please don't argue with a general. A wounded warrior and the executive assistant to the director of Central Intelligence deserve no less than one of our Packards. Do it, Homer."

"Yes, sir."

What did he call El Jefe? "The executive assistant to the director of Central Intelligence"?

And Greene's face showed he had never heard that before, either.

Smith took El Jefe's arm and led him across the dining room.

"We'll be in Ike's dining room," he said. "Ike's in Berlin."

Ike's dining room turned out to be an alcove off the main room, the windows of which provided a panoramic view of the bombed-out ruins of buildings as far as the eye could see.

There was a table, now set at one end for five, but capable, Cronley guessed, of seating ten, maybe a dozen people comfortably.

Smith stood behind the chair at the head of the table, and indicated where the others were to sit. El Jefe and General Greene were seated close to Smith, and Cronley found himself seated across from Ashton.

A waiter in a starched white jacket appeared. Cronley guessed he was a sergeant.

"There will be no menus today," General Smith announced. "I'm really pressed for time. Anybody who doesn't like a steak, medium rare, a baked potato, and green beans is out of luck. Charley, serve the food and then draw the curtain and make sure we're not interrupted."

"Yes, sir," the waiter said.

Serving the food and putting two silver coffee services on the table took very little time.

"Okay," General Smith said. "General Eisenhower really wanted to be here today, but our Russian friends in Berlin are being difficult. And the reason he wanted to be here— and the reason he asked Admiral Souers to send someone senior over here—is because he wanted to hear from someone who knows what's really going on with Operation Ost. More precisely, he's concerned about the level of threat of exposure. And since there is, I devoutly hope, no paper trail, that will have to be word of mouth. And I think we should start by hearing the opinion of the junior officer involved. Captain Cronley."

Shit!

Cronley stood up.

"Sir—"

"Sit down, please," General Smith said, "and tell me the first thing that comes to your mind vis-à-vis Operation Ost being compromised."

Oh, what the hell. When in doubt, tell the truth.

"Sir, the first thing that comes to my mind is that we just started to make a paper trail."

"That's very interesting," Smith said softly. "And whose idea was that?"

"My . . . I guess he could be called my administrative officer. Staff Sergeant Hessinger."

"And you thought this idea of your *staff sergeant* was a good idea?"

"Sir, Hessinger said something to the effect that eventually somebody is going to want to look at our records. And if that happens, and we say, 'We haven't been keeping any records,' that's not going to be an acceptable answer."

"And I agreed, General," Schultz said. "And told Cronley to start making after-action reports on everything of significance that's happened at Kloster Grünau—"

"Where?" Smith interrupted.

"The monastery," Schultz furnished.

General Smith nodded his understanding.

"And at the Pullach compound. And about everything else he's done of significance anywhere."

"And who gets these after-action reports?" Smith asked.

"Colonel Ashton," Cronley said. "As responsible officer for Operation Ost. And he sits on them, hoping that no one will ever want to see them."

General Smith considered that for a full thirty seconds.

"Your sergeant was right, Cronley," he said. "Napoleon said, 'An army travels on its stomach,' but the U.S. Army travels on its paper trails. If this thing blows up in our faces, and we didn't have any kind of a paper trail, (a) they wouldn't believe it, and (b) in the absence of a paper trail, we could be accused of anything. I think General Eisenhower would agree. I also think it would be a good idea if I had a look at them, in case they needed . . . what shall I say? . . . a little editing."

"Yes, sir," Cronley said.

"Not your decision to make," Smith said. "Chief, what about it?"

After a moment, Schultz said, "Hand-carry them to General Smith personally. Either you or Tiny."

"Yes, sir."

"Back to the basic question, Cronley: What is your assessment of the risk of exposure of Operation Ost? Increased, diminished, or no change?"

"Greatly diminished, sir."

"Why?"

"Sir, just about all of General Gehlen's Nazis are already in Argentina. There's a dozen, maybe twenty, still unaccounted for in Eastern Europe. If we can get them out, either to West Germany or Italy, we'll use the Vatican to get them to Argentina. I mean, we're no longer going to use SAA to transport them."

"If you're right, and I have no reason to doubt that you are, that's good news," General Smith said. "Colonel Ashton, what's your assessment of the same thing, this blowing up in our faces in Argentina?"

"Sir, I'll probably regret saying this, but I don't think it's much of a problem, and the chances diminish by the day."

"Why do you say that?"

Schultz answered for him: "General, the only people looking for Nazis in Argentina are the FBI. And since Juan Domingo Perón and the Catholic Church don't want any Nazis found, the FBI is going to have a very hard time finding any."

"You don't sound as if you're rooting for the FBI," Smith said. "Doesn't that make you uncomfortable?"

"No, sir, it doesn't. President Truman and General Eisenhower getting burned by J. Edgar Hoover over Operation Ost is what makes me, and Admiral Souers, uncomfortable."

"I'd forgotten that you have spent so much time in South America," General Smith said, but it was a question, and everybody at the table knew it.

When Schultz didn't reply immediately, Smith made a statement that was clearly another question: "Chief, in the lobby just now, I said that I thought, when he told me he was sending you to Europe, that Admiral Souers was implying there's more to your relationship than being old shipmates. Then Homer appeared before you could reply. Or saved you from having to reply."

"You sure you want me to get into that, General?"

"Only if you're comfortable telling me."

"Comfortable, no, but the admiral trusts you, which means I do, and I think you have the right to know," Schultz said. "So okay. The admiral and I were shipmates on battleship USS *Utah* in 1938. He was then a lieutenant commander and I had just made chief signalman. About the time he made commander, and went to work for the chief of Naval Intelligence, the Navy sent me to Fort Monmouth, in New Jersey, to see what the Army Signal Corps was up to. My contact in ONI was Commander Souers. I kept him up to speed about what the Army was developing—radar, for one thing—and, more important, what became the SIGABA system."

"It's an amazing system," General Smith said. "You were involved in its development?"

"Yes, sir, I was. In 1943, I installed a SIGABA system on a destroyer, the USS *Alfred Thomas*, DD-107, which then sailed to the South Atlantic to see what kind of range we could get out of it. To keep SIGABA secret, only her captain and two white hats I had with me knew what the real purpose of that voyage was.

"We called at Buenos Aires, official story 'courtesy visit' to Argentina, which was then neutral. Actual purpose, so that I could get some SIGABA parts from Collins Radio, which were flown down there in the embassy's diplomatic pouch.

"A Marine captain comes on board, in a crisp khaki uniform, wearing naval aviator's wings, the Navy Cross, the Distinguished Flying Cross, and the third award of the Purple Heart . . ."

"Cletus?" Cronley asked.

"Who else? Anyway, he tells the skipper he understands that he has a SIGABA expert on board and he wants to talk to him. Cletus Frade is a formidable guy. The skipper brings Captain Frade to the radio shack.

"He says he's heard I'm a SIGABA expert. I deny I ever heard of SIGABA. 'What is it?'

"He says, 'Chief, if you ever lie to me again, I'll have you shot. Now, are you a capable SIGABA repairman or not?'

"I tell him I am. He asks me if I know anything about the RCA 103 Radar—which was also classified Top Secret at the time—and I tell him yes. He says, 'Pack your sea bag, Chief, orders will soon come detaching you from this tin can and assigning you to me.'

"I don't know what the hell's going on, but I'm not worried. The skipper's not going to let anybody take me off the *Alfred Thomas*. Who the hell does this crazy Marine think he is? The chief of Naval Operations?

"At 0600 the next morning, so help me God, there is an Urgent message over the SIGABA. Very short message. Classified Top Secret–Tango, which security classification I'd never heard of until that morning. 'Chief Signalman Oscar J. Schultz detached USS *Alfred Thomas*, DD-107, assigned personal staff Captain Cletus Frade, USMCR, with immediate effect. Ernest J. King, Admiral, USN, Chief of Naval Operations.'

"At 0800, Cletus is waiting for me on the wharf. In civvies, driving his Horch convertible, with a good-looking blond sitting next to him. It's Dorotea, his Anglo-Argentine wife. He says we're going out to the ranch, and should be there in time for lunch.

"'Sir,' I say, 'what's going on here?'

"'Congratulations, Chief, you are now a member of Team Turtle of the Office of Strategic Services. The team's out at the ranch. What we do, among other things, is look for German submarines, supposedly neutral ships that supply German submarines, and then we sink them or blow them up or arrange for the Navy to do that for us. We use the RCA 103 Radar to find them, and the SIGABA to pass the word to the Navy. So we need you to keep those technological marvels up and running.'"

"That's quite a story," General Smith said.

"Yeah. But let me finish, General, it gets better."

"I wouldn't miss it for the world," General Smith said.

"So we go out to the ranch. I found out later that it's about as big as Manhattan Island. Really. Cletus owns it. He inherited it, and a hell of a lot else, from his father, who was murdered at the orders, so the OSS guys told me, of Heinrich Himmler himself when it looked like El Coronel Frade was going to become president of Argentina.

"And I met the team. All a bunch of civilians in uniform. Well, maybe not in uniform. But not professional military men, if you know what I mean. No offense, Polo."

"None taken, El Jefe. That's what we were, civilians in uniform. On those rare occasions when we wore uniforms."

"Admiral Souers—by then he was Rear Admiral, Lower Half—finally learned that I'd been shanghaied off the USS *Alfred Thomas*. He got a message to me saying that he couldn't get me out of Argentina, but I could still be of use to the Office of Naval Intelligence by reporting everything I could learn about what Frade and Team Turtle were up to. The admiral said that it was very important to ONI.

"By then, I'd already heard about the trouble Clete was having with the naval attaché of our embassy—a real asshole—and the FBI and some other people supposed to be on our side, and I'd gotten to know the OSS guys. So first I told Clete what the admiral wanted, told him I wasn't going to do it, and then I got on the SIGABA and told the admiral I wasn't going to report to ONI on Team Turtle and why.

"I got a short message in reply. 'Fully understand. Let me know if I can ever help with anything Frade needs.'"

"And then one thing led to another, General," Ashton said. "First, El Jefe became de facto chief of staff to Frade, and then de jure. Or more or less de jure. Without telling El Jefe that he was going to, Clete got on the horn—the SIGABA—to Admiral Souers and told him he was going to ask the Navy to commission El Jefe and was the admiral going to help or get in the way?"

"Two weeks later," El Jefe picked up the story, "the naval attaché was forced to swear me in as a lieutenant, USNR. The attaché couldn't say anything, of course, but that really ruined his day, which is why I asked Clete to have him ordered to do it."

General Smith chuckled.

"The reason I look so spiffy in my uniform is that it's practically brand new," El Jefe said. "I don't think it's got two weeks' wear on it."

"You didn't wear it because you were too cheap to buy more gold stripes when you were made a lieutenant commander," Ashton said. "Or when Clete got you promoted to commander so you'd outrank me and could take command of what was still the OSS, Southern Cone, when he took off his uniform."

Schultz gave him the finger.

"Clete thought—and he was right—that it looked better if people thought I was a chief, rather than an officer," Schultz said. "So we kept my change of status quiet."

"You're a full commander, Oscar?" Cronley asked.

"I retired a couple of weeks ago as a commander, U.S. Naval Reserve, Jim," Schultz said. "What I am now is a member of what they call the Senior Executive Service of the Directorate of Central Intelligence. My title is executive assistant to the director."

When Cronley didn't reply, Schultz said, "Why are you so surprised? You've been around the spook business long enough to know that nothing is ever what it looks like."

"Like the chief, DCI-Europe, isn't what he looks like?"

"Meaning what?"

"Meaning that I'm very young, wholly inexperienced in the spook business, and pretty slow, so it took me a long time to figure out that there's something very fishy about a very junior captain being chief, DCI-Europe, and that no one wants to tell him what's really going on."

"Well, Jim, now that you have figured that out, I guess we'll have to tell you. I will on the way to the airport."

"Why don't you tell him now?" General Smith said. "I think General Greene should be privy to this."

"Yes, sir," Schultz said. "Okay. Where to start? Okay. When President Truman was talked into disbanding the OSS—largely by J. Edgar Hoover, but with a large assist by the Army, no offense, General—"

"Tell it like it is, Chief," General Smith said.

"He first realized that he couldn't turn off everything the OSS was doing—especially Operation Ost, but some other operations, too—like a lightbulb. So he turned to his old friend Admiral Souers to run them until they could be turned over to somebody else.

"Admiral Souers convinced him—I think Truman had figured this out by himself, so I probably should have said, the admiral convinced the President that the President was right in maybe thinking he had made a mistake by shutting down the OSS.

"The admiral didn't know much about Operation Ost, except that it existed. Truman told him what it was. The admiral knew I was involved with it in Argentina, so he sent for me to see what I thought should be done with it.

"The President trusted his old friend the admiral, and the admiral trusted his old shipmate. Okay? The President was learning how few people he could trust, and learning how many people he could not trust, starting with J. Edgar Hoover.

"So Truman decided a new OSS was needed. Who to run it? The admiral.

"So what to do about Operation Ost, which was important for two reasons—for the intel it had about the Russians, and because if it came out we'd made the deal with Gehlen and were smuggling Nazis out of Germany, Truman would be impeached, Eisenhower would be court-martialed, and we'd lose the German intelligence about our pal Joe Stalin.

"So how do we hide Operation Ost from J. Edgar Hoover, the Army, the Navy, the State Department, the *Washington Post*, et cetera, et cetera? We try to make it look unimportant. How do we do that? We pick some obscure bird colonel to run it. Which bird colonel could we trust?

For that matter, which light bird, which major, could we trust?

"And if we found one, that would raise the question, which full colonel, which light bird, would General Gehlen trust? I mean really trust, so that he'd really keep up his end of the deal?

"The President says, 'What about Captain Cronley?'"

"You were there, Chief?" General Smith asked. "You heard him say that?"

"I was there. I heard him say that. The admiral said, 'Harry, that's ridiculous!' and the President said, 'Who would think anything important would be handed to a captain?'

"The admiral said, 'Who would think *anything* in the intelligence business would be handed over to a captain?'

"And the President said, 'There are captains and then there are captains. I know. I was one. This one, Cronley, has just been given the DSM and a promotion to captain by the commander in chief for unspecified services connected with intelligence. J. Edgar knows it was because Cronley found the submarine with the uranium oxide on it. J. Edgar would not think there was anything funny if Captain Cronley were given some unimportant job in intelligence that might get him promoted.'

"The admiral said something about giving Cronley Operation Ost because no one would think Operation Ost was important if a captain was running it, and the President said, 'For that reason, I think we should name Captain Cronley chief, DCI-Europe, and let that leak.'

"'Harry,' the admiral said, "'General Gehlen is an old-school Kraut officer. I don't think he'll stand still for taking orders from a captain.'

"And the President said, 'Why don't we ask him?'"

"So we asked General Gehlen. So there you sit, Mr. Chief, DCI-Europe. Okay? Any questions?"

"How soon can I expect to be relieved when you find some bird colonel you can trust, who's acceptable to General Gehlen and should have this job?"

"The job is yours until you screw up—or one of your people does—and Operation Ost is blown."

"Then I get thrown to the wolves?"

"Then you get thrown to the wolves. If that happens, try to take as few people down with you as you can. Any questions?"

"No, sir," Cronley said, and a moment later, "Thanks, Oscar."

[FIVE]
Suite 507
Hotel Vier Jahreszeiten
Maximilianstrasse 178
Munich, American Zone of Occupation, Germany
2010 16 January 1946

There had been a delay in the departure of SAA flight 233, so Cronley had told Max Ostrowski, "Head home. That way, if I have to go to Munich instead of Kloster Grünau, there will be only one Storch parked in the transient area to arouse curiosity, not two."

When Schultz and Ashton finally got off the ground, he knew there was no chance of his making it to the monastery strip before dark, so he went to the snack bar in the terminal and had a greasy hamburger, fries, and a Coke before leaving Rhine-Main.

He had another—much better—hamburger at Schleiss-heim, the Munich military post airfield, when he landed, and then got a ride to the hotel.

As he walked down the corridor to his room, he saw light under the door to 507, which was where Fat Freddy held court, and he pushed the huge door handle down and walked in.

I will tell Freddy everything Schultz said in the generals' mess and see what he has to say.

Hessinger was not behind the desk. Technical Sergeant Claudette Colbert was.

She rose from behind the desk at which she was typing when she saw him.

She was wearing a "pink" as in pinks-and-greens officer's skirt and a khaki shirt, and he saw an officer's green tunic on the coatrack.

Well, it didn't take much time for her to get in triangles, did it?

"Good evening, sir."

"Now that you're a civilian, you can drop the 'sir,' Claudette."

"Sorry, I forgot."

"Where's Freddy?"

"He said he was going to visit a friend."

"Yeah."

"He left a number, shall I call him for you?"

"I try not to call Freddy when he's visiting friends. He sulks."

She smiled.

"Is Mr. Ostrowski with you?"

"He's at Kloster Grünau. I had to wait until Schultz and Ashton took off, which meant it was too dark for me to land there. So I came here."

"Major Derwin called. He said he'd like to see you at ten hundred tomorrow."

What does that sonofabitch want?

"Wonderful!"

"Can I get you anything?"

"No, thank you. I'm going to go to my room, have a stiff drink, and go to bed."

"How did things go with General Greene?"

"It was interesting, Claudette, but not worthy of an after-action report."

Subject: Screw Up and Get Thrown to the Wolves.

"That's what I've been doing," she said, nodding at the typewriter. "After-action reports."

"Claudette—"

"My friends call me 'Dette,'" she said.

"Because if they shortened it the other way, it would be 'Claude'?"

"And I don't want to be called 'Claude.'"

"Well, Dette, as I was about to say, Freddy will push you around if you let him. Don't let him. It's quarter after eight. Knock off. The after actions aren't that important."

"Okay, I'll finish this one and knock off," she said. "Thank you."

"Good night, Dette."

"Good night . . . What should I call you?"

"Good question. When no one's around, call me Jim. Otherwise, Mr. Cronley."

"Got it. Good night, Jim."

"Good night," Cronley said, and walked out.

Cronley went to his room, which was actually a suite, found a bottle of scotch, poured himself a stiff drink, and then decided he would first have a shower and then have the drink, catch the 2100 news broadcast on the American Forces Network Munich radio station, and then go to bed.

Ten minutes later, as he pulled on the terrycloth bathrobe that came with the suite, he heard over AFN Munich that he was just in time for the news. It was always preceded by a solemn voice proclaiming, "Remember, soldier! VD walks the streets tonight! And penicillin fails once in seven times!"

And he wondered again, as he often did, how Daddy or Mommy explained the commercial to nine-year-old Jane or Bobby when they asked, "Daddy, what's that man talking about?"

When he came out of the bathroom, Technical Sergeant Colbert was sitting in an armchair.

"You almost got a look at something you don't want to see," he snapped. "What the hell are you doing in here?"

"Well, I finished the first after-action report, and thought you might want to see it. Wrong guess?"

"I don't think being in my room is smart," he said.

"Since Freddy gave me the master key, I thought coming in made more sense than waiting in the hall for you to finish your shower," she said. "Shall I leave?"

"Let me see the after action," he said.

She got out of the chair, walked to him, and handed him some typewritten sheets of paper. He glanced at the title: "Likharev, Sergei, Colonel NKGB, Capture Of."

He became aware that she was still standing close to him.

He looked at her.

"We cleared up one misunderstanding between us yesterday," she said. "Why don't we clear up this one?"

"Which one is that?"

"Officers, and you're a good one, don't fool around with enlisted women, right?"

"I'm glad you understand that."

"And everyone knows that a recently widowed officer would have absolutely no interest in becoming romantically involved with another woman, especially a subordinate enlisted woman seven years older than he is, right?"

She must have really gone through my personal files.

"Right again. Is there going to be a written test on this?"

"But you would agree that there is a great difference between a continuing romantic involvement and an every-once-in-a-while-as-needed purely physical relationship, if both parties (a) are aware of the difference, and (b) have been forced into the strangest perversion of them all?"

"What the hell would that be?"

"Oscar Wilde said it was celibacy," she said.

"I don't think I like this conversation, Sergeant Colbert."

She laughed deep in her throat, and then pointed at his midsection.

His erect penis had escaped his bathrobe.

Her right hand reached for it, and with her left she pulled his face down to hers.

She encountered little, virtually no, resistance.

VIII

[ONE]
Suite 507
Hotel Vier Jahreszeiten
Maximilianstrasse 178
Munich, American Zone of Occupation, Germany
0955 17 January 1946

Knowing that Major Thomas G. "Dick Tracy" Derwin was either already behind the door or would be there shortly triggered many thoughts in Cronley's mind as he put his hand on the enormous door lever and pushed down.

He remembered being with Derwin at the officers' club bar in Camp Holabird when the Squirt came in.

He remembered why his fellow spooks in training had called Derwin "Dick Tracy," and that it had not been rooted in admiration.

What the hell does he want from me?

He had dressed to meet him. That is, in triangled pinks and greens, not in his captain's tunic, as that would have established the captain/major relationship between them.

While he was putting on the triangled pinks and greens, he had thought about Ludwig Mannberg's elegant wardrobe, now shared with Max Ostrowski. He thought it would be a good idea to get some civvies for himself. There were a lot of bona fide U.S. civilians around wearing civvies, so why not?

The problem there was, where could he get some? He had two Brooks Brothers suits in Midland—two because his mother said he could be counted on to spill soup on the first one he put on—and he didn't think they would fit anyway.

And, of course, he was concerned, deeply concerned, about what was going to happen when he faced Sergeant Claudette Colbert after their most-of-the-night romp in the sheets, which was probably the dumbest thing he'd done since he started screwing Rachel Schumann. Or more accurately, had allowed Rachel Schumann to play him for the three-star naïve fool he could not deny being.

There were only two good things he could think of concerning his new relationship with Sergeant Colbert. He was willing to bet she wasn't an NKGB agent, and she sure knew how to romp.

And he wondered about not if, but how soon Fat Freddy would pick up on what was going on between him and good ol' Sergeant Colbert.

He pushed open the door and entered the room.

Fat Freddy was behind his desk and Dette behind hers, hammering furiously at her typewriter. The door to Major Harold Wallace's office was open. He was chatting with Major Thomas G. Derwin, who sat in front of his desk with a briefcase on his lap. Both looked out at him.

"Good morning, sir," Freddy said. "Major Derwin is here to see you. He's in with Major Wallace."

"Sir," Dette said, "General Gehlen said that he'd like to see you as soon as it's convenient."

When Cronley looked at Colbert, she met his eyes. She smiled warmly, but it was just that, nothing more or less.

"Did he say where he was?"

"At the compound, sir."

"Please call him back and tell him I'll come out there as soon as Major Derwin and I have finished talking about whatever he wants to talk about."

"Yes, sir. I'll make sure a car is available."

Cronley walked to Wallace's office door.

"Good morning, gentlemen."

"Major Derwin has been waiting to see you, Jim," Wallace said.

"Captain Cronley," Derwin said.

"I'm sorry to have kept you waiting, Major," Cronley said. "What's on your mind?"

"It would be better, I think, if we discussed that privately."

What the hell does he want?

"Sounds ominous. Did one of Tiny's Troopers complain I've been mean to him?"

Derwin didn't reply.

"Why don't we go in my office?" Cronley asked.

Derwin got to his feet and walked to the door. As they walked across the outer office, Dette asked, "Can I get you and the major coffee, sir?"

"That would be very nice, Dette, thank you," Cronley said. He turned to Major Derwin. "Should I ask Miss Colbert to bring her book?"

"No. That won't be necessary," Derwin said firmly.

The office, now that of the chief, DCI-Europe, had formerly been the office of Colonel Robert Mattingly and reflected both the colonel's good taste and his opinion of his own importance in the scheme of things. It therefore was larger and more elegantly furnished than Wallace's office, and he saw that Derwin had picked up on that.

"Have a seat, please, Major," Cronley said. "And when Miss Colbert has gotten us some coffee, you can tell me what's on your mind."

Derwin took a seat, holding his briefcase on his lap, but said nothing.

Dette came into the office, laid a coffee set on the table, poured, and then left.

"Okay, Major. Let's have it," Cronley said.

"Something has come to my attention, Cronley, that I thought, in the interest of fairness, I would ask you about before I go any further with my investigation."

There he goes again, playing Dick Tracy. "My investigation."
What the hell's going on?

"Which is?"

"What would you care to tell me about your relationship with my predecessor, the late Lieutenant Colonel Anthony Schumann?"

"Excuse me?"

"And with Colonel Schumann's wife, Mrs. Rachel Schumann?"

"Why are you asking?"

"Please, Captain Cronley, just answer the question."

"Okay. I knew both of them."

"How well?"

"Slightly."

"So you're telling me there's nothing to the story that you tried to kill Colonel Schumann?"

"Oh, for Christ's sake!"

"Once again, Cronley, please answer my question."

Cronley leaned forward and depressed the intercom lever.

"Dette, would you ask Major Wallace to come in here, please? Right now?"

"Yes, sir."

"At the moment, Cronley, I have nothing to say to Major Wallace," Derwin said.

Wallace put his head in the door sixty seconds later.

"What's up?"

"Come on in and close the door," Cronley said. "And then, when no one else can hear us, please tell Major Derwin what you know about my attempt to murder the late Colonel Schumann. He's investigating that."

"What?" Wallace asked incredulously, chuckling. "Seriously?"

"He sounds very serious to me."

"This is a serious matter," Derwin said.

"What should I tell him, Jim?" Wallace asked.

"Everything . . . well, maybe not *everything*. And make sure he understands that whatever you tell him is classified Top Secret–Presidential."

"What I am about to tell you, Major Derwin," Wallace said, with a smile, "is classified Top Secret–Presidential."

Derwin didn't reply.

"The penalty for divulging Top Secret–Presidential material to anyone not authorized access to same is castration with a dull bayonet, followed by the firing squad, as I'm sure you know."

"I have to tell you, Major, I don't find anything humorous in this," Derwin said.

"Stick around, it gets much funnier," Wallace said. "Well, one day Colonel Schumann—and a dozen associates—found himself on a back road not far from here—I've always wondered what he was doing out in the boonies . . ."

"Me, too," Cronley said.

Now I know, of course, what the sonofabitch was doing there. He was looking for it. He wanted to find out what was going on at Kloster Grünau so he could tell his handler in the NKGB.

". . . but anyway, there he was, and he comes up on a monastery, or what had been a monastery, Kloster Grünau, surrounded by fences and concertina barbed wire. On the fence were signs, 'Twenty-third CIC' and, in English and German, 'Absolutely No Admittance.'

"Colonel Schumann had never heard of the Twenty-third CIC, and he thought as IG for CIC Europe he should have heard of it."

"What was this place?" Derwin asked.

"You don't have the need to know that, Major," Cronley said.

"You're not in a position to tell me what I need to know, Cronley," Derwin snapped.

"Yeah, he is," Major Wallace said. "But anyway, Schumann, being the zealous inspector general he was . . . I shouldn't be making fun of him, the poor bastard got himself blown up. Sorry. Anyway, Schumann drives up the road and is immediately stopped by two jeeps, each of which has a pedestal-mounted .50-caliber Browning machine gun and four enormous soldiers, all black, in it.

"He tells them he wants in, and they tell him to wait.

"A second lieutenant wearing cowboy boots shows up.

He's the security officer for Kloster Grünau. His name is James D. Cronley Junior."

"A second lieutenant named Cronley?" Major Derwin asked.

"This was before he got promoted."

"I'd like to hear about that, too," Derwin said.

"That's also classified Top Secret–Presidential," Wallace said. "Anyway, Second Lieutenant Cronley politely tells Lieutenant Colonel Schumann that nobody gets into Kloster Grünau unless they have written permission from either General Greene or Colonel Robert Mattingly.

"Lieutenant Colonel Schumann, somewhat less politely, tells Second Lieutenant Cronley that second lieutenants don't get to tell lieutenant colonels, especially when he is the CIC IG, what he can't do. And tells his driver to 'drive on.'

"Second Lieutenant Cronley issues an order to stop the staff car.

"One of the .50s fires one round.

"Bang.

"Right into the engine block of Colonel Schumann's staff car. It stops.

"At that point, Colonel Schumann decides that since he's outgunned, the smart thing to do is make a retrograde movement and report the incident to General Greene. He does so just as soon as he can get back to Frankfurt, dragging the disabled staff car behind one of his remaining vehicles.

"General Greene tells him Second Lieutenant Cronley was just carrying out his orders, and for Colonel Schumann not only to not try again to get into Kloster Grünau but also to not ask questions about it, and finally to forget he was ever there.

"End of story," Wallace concluded. "Did I leave anything out, Jim?"

"No. That was fine. Thank you."

"Any questions, Major?"

"That story poses more questions than it answers," Derwin said. "What exactly is going on at this monastery?"

"I told you before, Major, you don't have the need to know that," Cronley said.

"And I'm more than a little curious, Cronley, how you became a captain so . . . suddenly."

"I'm sure you are," Cronley said, and then: "Oh, hell, let's shut this off once and for all."

He went to a door and opened it. Behind it was a safe. He worked the combination, opened the door, took out a manila envelope, and then took two 8×10-inch photographs from it.

"These are classified Top Secret–Presidential, Major," he said, as he handed them to Major Derwin.

"Do I get to look, Jim?" Major Wallace asked.

"Who's the fellow pinning on the bars?" Wallace asked a moment later. "I recognize the guy wearing the bow tie, of course."

"My father."

"Why is President Truman giving you a decoration?" Derwin asked. "What is that?"

Wallace answered for him: "It's the Distinguished Service Medal."

"What did Cronley do to earn the DSM?"

"The citation is also classified," Cronley said.

He took the photographs back, put them back in the envelope, put the envelope back in the safe, closed the door, spun the combination dial, and then closed the door that concealed the safe.

"Are we now through playing Twenty Questions, Major Derwin?" Cronley asked.

"For the moment."

"I want to play," Major Wallace said.

"Excuse me?" Major Derwin said.

"I want to play Twenty Questions, too. What the hell is this all about, Derwin? You're not a CIC special agent, you're the CIC IG—without any authority whatever over the DCI—so why are you asking Cronley all these questions?"

"That, as Cronley has said so often today, is something you don't have the need to know."

"I'm making it my business," Wallace said. "My first question is, who told you Cronley shot up Schumann's staff car? No, who told you he tried to murder the poor bastard?"

"I learned that from a confidential source."

"What confidential source?"

"You don't have the need to know, Major Wallace."

"Do you want me to get on the horn to General Greene, tell him what you've been doing, and have him order you to tell me all about your confidential source?"

"Why would you want to do that?"

"For a number of reasons, including Colonel Tony Schumann was a friend of mine, but primarily because the Army has handed me a CIC supervisory special agent's credentials and told me to look into things I think smell fishy."

"You're interfering with my investigation, Major," Derwin said.

Wallace reached for the telephone on Cronley's desk, dialed zero, and said, "Get me General Greene."

"That won't be necessary," Derwin said.

"Cancel that," Wallace said, and put the handset into its cradle.

Derwin went into his briefcase and pulled out a business envelope that he handed to Wallace.

"This was hand-delivered to me at my quarters in the Park Hotel," he said.

"Hand-delivered by whom?" Wallace asked, as he took a sheet of paper from the envelope.

"I mean, it was left at the desk of the Park, and put in my box there, not mailed."

"I never would have guessed," Wallace said sarcastically, "since there's no address on the envelope, only your name."

A moment later, he said, his voice dripping with disgust, "Jesus H. Christ!"

He handed the sheet of paper to Cronley.

DEAR MAJOR DERWIN:

THERE ARE THOSE WHO BELIEVE THE EXPLOSION
WHICH TOOK THE LIVES OF YOUR PREDECESSOR,
LIEUTENANT COLONEL ANTHONY SCHUMANN, AND
HIS WIFE WAS NOT ACCIDENTAL, AND FURTHER
THAT THE PROVOST MARSHAL'S INVESTIGATION
OF THE INCIDENT WAS SUSPICIOUSLY
SUPERFICIAL.

THERE ARE THOSE WHO WONDER WHY CAPTAIN
JAMES D. CRONLEY JR., OF THE XXIIIRD CIC
DETACHMENT, WAS NOT QUESTIONED BY THE

CRIMINAL INVESTIGATION DIVISION IN THE
MATTER, OR, FOR THAT MATTER, BY THE CIC, IN
VIEW OF THE SEVERAL RUMORS CIRCULATING
CONCERNING CRONLEY:

THAT HIS RELATIONSHIP WITH MRS. SCHUMANN
WAS FAR MORE INTIMATE THAN APPROPRIATE.

THAT COLONEL SCHUMANN NARROWLY AVOIDED
BEING MURDERED BY CRONLEY AT THE SECRET
INSTALLATION, A FORMER MONASTERY, CRONLEY
RUNS IN SCHOLLBRUNN.

THAT AMONG THE MANY SECRETS OF THIS
INSTALLATION, KLOSTER GRÜNAU, ARE A NUMBER
OF RECENTLY DUG UNMARKED GRAVES.

It took Cronley about fifteen seconds to decide the author of the letter had NKGB somewhere in his title, or—
considering the other Rahil—*her* title.

"I have determined both that this letter was typed on
an Underwood typewriter, and the paper on which this is
typed is government issue," Major Derwin said.

"You're a regular Dick Tracy, aren't you, Derwin?" Wallace said.

"Excuse me?"

"I mean, that really narrows it down, doesn't it? There
are probably twenty Underwood typewriters here in the Vier
Jahreszeiten and twenty reams of GI paper. I wonder how
many Underwoods there are in the Farben Building, but I'd

guess four, five hundred and three or four supply rooms full of GI typewriter paper."

"I was suggesting that it suggests this was written by an American."

"You're a regular Sherlock Holmes, aren't you, Derwin?"

"There's no call for sarcasm, Major Wallace," Derwin said.

"That's coming to me very naturally, Major Derwin," Wallace said. "Permit me to go through this letter one item at a time.

"Item one: The explosion which killed my friend Tony Schumann and his wife was thoroughly—not superficially—investigated, not only by the DCI but also by the Frankfurt military post engineer and by me. And I was there before the DCI was even called in. The gas line leading to his water heater developed a leak. The fucking thing blew up. Tony and his wife were in the wrong place at the wrong time. Period. End of that story.

"So far as Cronley's 'intimate' relationship is concerned, I was here when Cronley was ordered, *ordered*, to take Mrs. Schumann to dinner. He was as enthusiastic about doing so as he would have been . . . I don't know what . . . about going to the dentist for a tooth-yanking.

"I've already dealt with that nonsensical allegation that Cronley attempted to murder Colonel Schumann at Kloster Grünau. That brings us to the unmarked graves at the monastery. What about that, Cronley? Have you been burying people out there in unmarked graves?"

Truth to tell, which I obviously can't, there are three I know about, those of the three men, almost certainly NKGB agents,

*that Max Ostrowski killed when they damn near killed Ser-
geant Abraham Lincoln Tedworth.*

*And then I suspect, but don't know—and I don't want to
know—that former Oberstleutnant Gunther von Plat and
former Major Kurt Boss are looking up at the grass in the
cloister cemetery. They disappeared shortly after Clete turned
Colonel Sergei Likharev in Argentina, and he told Clete, and
Clete told me to tell General Gehlen, that they had been the bad
apples in Gehlen's basket who had given him the rosters of
Gehlen's people Tedworth found on Likharev.*

"Every Friday afternoon," Cronley said. "We call it 'the
Kloster Grünau Memorial Gardens Friday Afternoon Burial
Services and Chicken Fry.'"

Wallace laughed, then turned to Major Derwin.

"What have you done with this thing, Derwin? Have you
shown it to anybody else? The DCI, maybe? Anybody else?"

"I was not at that point in my investigation—"

"Your investigation?" Wallace asked, heavily sarcastic.
"Derwin, were you ever a CIC agent in the field?"

"Of course I was."

"Where?"

"What has that got to do with anything?"

"I can check your records."

"I was the special agent in charge of the Des Moines
office."

"That's all?"

"And then I was transferred to CIC Headquarters."

"You mean the CIC School?"

"The school is part of CIC Headquarters."

"And since I don't think there were many members of the

Japanese Kempei Tai, or of Abwehr Intelligence, running around Des Moines, Iowa, what you were doing was ringing doorbells, doing background investigations? 'Mrs. Jones, your neighbor Joe Glutz, now in the Army, is being considered for a position in which he will have access to classified information. We are checking to see if he can be trusted with it. Which of his sexual deviations would you like to tell me about?'"

"I don't have to put up with this . . . this being mocked and insulted."

"The first thing that comes to my mind is for me to go to General Greene and give him my take on you, which is that you saw when you were being sent to replace my good friend Tony Schumann, you decided it was going to give you a chance to be a real CIC agent. And then when whatever miserable sonofabitch in our ranks decided to stick it to Cronley sent you that letter, you saw it as your chance to be a hotshot.

"But if I did that, and he shipped your ass to the Aleutian Islands to count snowballs, which he would do, and which you would deserve for your Dick Tracy bullshit, the prick in our midst who tried to stab Cronley in the back would hear about it and crawl back into his hole.

"And I am determined to find that bastard and nail him to the wall.

"So what you are going to do, Major Derwin, is put that goddamn letter back in your briefcase and then drop your quote investigation unquote. And forget investigations, period. You will keep that letter so that you take it out from time to time to remind you how close you came to getting shipped to the Aleutians. If you get another letter, or if there is any other contact with Cronley's buddy the letter writer, I want to hear about it.

"Now, if this is satisfactory to you, get out of here and get in your car, and go to Frankfurt or anywhere else and do what an IG is supposed to do. If this is not satisfactory to you, I am going to get on the horn and call General Greene and tell him what a bad boy you have been. Which is it to be?"

"I really don't understand your attitude—"

"Which is it to be?" Wallace snapped.

"I don't seem to have much choice in the matter, do I?" Derwin said, mustering what little dignity he could. Then he turned to Cronley: "Captain Cronley, I assure you it wasn't my intention to accuse you of any wrongdoing. I was just . . ."

"If that's intended as an apology, Major Derwin. Accepted."

Christ, I actually feel sorry for him.

Derwin nodded at Wallace and walked out of the office.

"Jesus Christ, Jim," Wallace said. "Do you believe that?"

"I don't know what to think," Cronley said.

"Think about candidates for the letter writer," Wallace said. "I think we can safely remove Colonel Mattingly and myself from the list of suspects . . ."

I'll be goddamned. Maybe it wasn't the Russians. Maybe it was Mattingly. Wallace, no. Mattingly, maybe.

". . . but who else can you think of who is green with jealousy that you're now the chief, DCI-Europe?"

Cronley shook his head, and then his mouth went on automatic.

"Be glad they didn't give you the job," he said.

Wallace looked at him curiously.

What the hell, why not tell him?

Screw Ludwig, I'm going with my gut feeling about Wallace.

Wallace's one of the good guys.

"I had lunch with General Smith yesterday," Cronley said. "And General Greene. And Lieutenant Colonel Ashton. And Lieutenant Schultz, who is really not Lieutenant Schultz, by the way, or even Commander Schultz, which is what he really was when he was working for Cletus Frade, but executive assistant to the director, Directorate of Central Intelligence."

"Interesting."

"And I raised the subject of why was I named chief, DCI-Europe, when there were so many fully qualified people of appropriate rank and experience around. And Schultz told me."

"Like Bob Mattingly, you mean?"

"And you."

"And what did Schultz tell you?"

"Mattingly, first. Schultz didn't come right out and say this . . ."

"But?"

"I got the feeling the admiral thinks Mattingly is more interested in his Army career than the DCI."

"Explain that."

"That since he's thinking of his Army career, he'd be more chummy with the assistant chief of staff for intelligence—with the Pentagon generally, and ONI, and the FBI—than the admiral wants his people to be. He was in ONI, and he knows how unhappy they were when Truman started up the DCI to replace the OSS, which they thought they'd buried once and for all."

Wallace didn't reply to that immediately, but Cronley thought he saw him nod just perceptibly, as if accepting what Cronley had told him.

Then Wallace asked, "And that applies to me, too?"

"I was given the job, the title, because no one is going to think that something important like Operation Ost is going to be handed to a very junior captain. Or the corollary of that, DCI-Europe—and Operation Ost—can't be very important if they gave it to a very junior captain."

"That makes a perverse kind of sense, I suppose."

"Which brings us to you."

"Oh?"

"Nobody told me this either, but if—more than likely when—this blows up and I get thrown to the wolves—and they did tell me to expect getting thrown to the wolves— somebody's going to have to take over from me."

"You mean me?" Wallace asked dubiously.

"Think about it. You're only a major, not a full-bull colonel. You've got an unimportant job running a small— actually phony—CIC detachment close to DCI-Europe. It would seem natural to give you something unimportant like DCI-Europe when the young incompetent running it, as predicted, FUBAR . . ."

"'Fucked Up Beyond Any Repair.'" Wallace chuckled as he made the translation.

"The executive assistant to the director of the Directorate of Central Intelligence shows up here," Cronley said. "He says, 'I guess you heard how Cronley blew it.' You say, 'Yes, sir.' El Jefe says, 'Wallace, you're ex-OSS. I would be very surprised if while you were sitting here with your thumb in your ass running this phony CIC detachment, you didn't snoop around and learn a hell of a lot about what Cronley was doing.'

"Then he says, 'We were counting on this. So tell me what you know, or suspect, and I will fill in the blanks before I have you transferred to DCI, and you take over as chief, DCI-Europe.'"

"Jesus Christ!"

"Yeah. Anyway, that's my take."

"If you're right, why wouldn't Schultz have told you to keep me up to speed on what you're doing?"

"Because he's being careful. He knows you were Mattingly's Number Two in the OSS. He didn't tell me to tell you anything. This is my scenario."

"Schultz doesn't know we're having this little chat?"

"I thought about asking him if I could, and decided not to because he probably would have said, 'Hell, no!'"

"But you're going to tell me anyhow?"

"I'll tell you as much as I can, but there's a lot going on you neither have the need to know nor want to know."

"Like what?"

"Next question?"

"So what are you going to tell me? And for that matter, why?"

"Despite Ludwig Mannberg's theory that when you really want to trust a gut feeling, don't—my gut tells me I can trust you."

"I realize I'm expected to say, 'Of course you can.' But I'll say it anyway."

"There are two operations I think you should know about. One involves my cousin Luther . . ."

"Your *cousin* Luther?" Wallace asked incredulously.

"My cousin Luther and Odessa," Cronley confirmed, and proceeded to relate that story.

When he had finished, Wallace asked, "You realize that Odessa is the CIC's business, and none of yours?"

"I'm making it mine," Cronley said. "And the second operation I think you should know about is our getting Colonel Likharev's family out of Russia."

"Whose family out of Russia?"

"The NKGB major Sergeant Tedworth caught sneaking out of Kloster Grünau turned out to be an NKGB colonel by the name of Sergei Likharev. We shipped him to Argentina, where Clete and Schultz turned him . . ."

He went on to tell Wallace the details of that, finishing, "That's what we were doing in Vienna, giving a Russian female NKGB agent, who also works for Mossad, a hell of a lot of expense money.

"And just before our little chat with Dick Tracy Derwin, Claudette Colbert—"

"Hessinger's new and, I must say, very-well-put-together assistant? Is her first name really Claudette, like the movie star?"

"Yes, but she prefers to be called 'Dette.'"

"And is Freddy dallying with her?"

"No. Freddy sees her as his way out of being what he calls 'the company clerk,' and he's not going to screw that up by fooling around with her."

"She makes me really sorry there's that sacred rule

forbidding officers to fool around with enlisted women," Wallace said, and then quickly added, "Just kidding, just kidding."

"Anyway, Dette told me just before we had our chat with Derwin that General Gehlen wants to see me as soon as possible. I think that's because he's heard from Seven-K . . ."

"His Soviet asset?"

Cronley nodded. "Aka Rahil. And I've started to think of her as our asset. So far we've given her a hundred thousand dollars."

"One hundred thousand?" Wallace parroted incredulously.

Cronley nodded again. "And she'll be worth every dime if she can get Likharev's family out and he stays turned."

"You think he will stay turned?"

"Yeah," Cronley said thoughtfully after a moment.

"Gratitude?"

"A little of that, but primarily because . . . he's smart . . . He will realize that once we get his family to Argentina, that's not the end of it. The NKGB will know that he's alive and turned and has his family with him. And the NKGB can't just quit. Likharev knows they'll really be looking for him to make an example, *pour encourager les autres*, of what happens to senior NKGB officers who turn, and we're the only protection he has."

"Yeah," Wallace said.

"So, instead of going out to Schleissheim and removing the Storch from curious eyes, I'm going to have to go to Pullach."

"Can I ask about that?"

"Ask about what?"

"You and the Storchs. Now that EUCOM has been told to give DCI-Europe anything it wants, why don't you get a couple, or three or four, L-4s and get rid of the Storchs? And all the problems having them brings with it?"

"The Storch is a better airplane than the Piper Cub. And only Army aviators are allowed to fly Army airplanes, and I'm not an Army aviator . . ."

"I'd forgotten that."

". . . and I don't want two, three, or four Army aviators out here, or at the Pullach compound, seeing a lot of interesting things that are none of their business."

"Understood," Wallace said, then added, "You're good, Jim. You really try to think of everything, don't you?"

"Yes, I do. And one time in, say, fifty times I do think of everything. The other forty-nine times something I didn't think of bites me in the ass."

Wallace chuckled.

"Or something comes out of the woodwork, like Dick Tracy?"

"Like Dick Tracy," Cronley agreed. "Do you think you turned him off for good?"

"Yeah. I think the more he thinks about it, the more he will decide the best way to cover his ass is to stop playing Dick Tracy."

"Jesus, I hope so," Cronley said, and then stood up and walked out of his office.

[TWO]

"Where's the car?" Cronley asked Hessinger.

"Wait one, please," Hessinger said, and then, raising his voice, called, "Colbert, are you about finished in there?"

"Be right there," she called, and came out of the supply room.

"Claudette has finished four of the after-action reports," Hessinger said. "I need you to look at them as soon as possible."

"Not now, Freddy. I have to see General Gehlen. Maybe after that."

"I propose to have Claudette drive you out to Pullach. She drives, you read the after actions, and tell her what, if anything, needs to be fixed. Okay?"

Cronley didn't immediately reply.

"And then," Hessinger said, "she drives you wherever you have to go, Schleissheim, or back here, or even out to Kloster Grünau, when you're through with the general."

"Don't look so worried, Mr. Cronley," Claudette said. "I'm a pretty good driver, for a woman, if that's what's worrying you."

"Let's go. Where's the car?"

"By now it should be out front," she said. "Let me get my purse and a briefcase for the after actions."

"'Individuals in possession of documents classified Top Secret or above must be suitably armed when such documents are being transported outside a secure area,'" Hessinger said.

Obviously quoting verbatim whatever Army regulation that is from memory.

"I've got my snub-nosed .38 in my purse," Claudette announced.

"Where did you get a snub-nosed .38?" Cronley asked.

"I brought mine from the ASA," Claudette said. "I thought I'd need it here. 'The officer or non-commissioned officer in charge of an ASA communications facility where Top Secret or above material is being handled, or may be handled, shall be suitably armed.'"

And that, too, was quoted verbatim from memory.

Then she added, "Don't worry, Mr. Cronley, I know how to use it. Actually, I shot Expert with it the last time I was on the range."

"And where is your .45, Mr. Cronley?" Hessinger asked.

"In my room."

"You should go get it, and not only because of the classified documents, if you take my meaning, as I am sure you do."

"I stand chastised," Cronley said. "I'll go get my pistol and meet you out front, Dette."

"Yes, sir."

Five minutes later, when he walked through the revolving door onto Maximilianstrasse, the Opel Kapitän was at the curb, with the rear door open and Claudette at the wheel.

He looked at the door, then closed it and got in the front seat beside Claudette.

She didn't say anything at first, but when they were away from the curb, she said, "I was trying to make it easy for you. Opening the rear door, I mean."

"How so?"

"Officers ride in the backseat, when enlisted women are driving."

"But we are not an officer and an enlisted woman, Miss Colbert. We are dressed as two civilian employees of the Army are dressed, and hoping the people think we work for the PX."

She chuckled.

"And I wanted to be sure that you didn't think I was trying to get cozy when I shouldn't."

"Never entered my mind. What you should be worried about—what *we* should be worried about—is Freddy, who is twice as smart as he looks, and he looks like Albert Einstein. Do you think . . . ?"

"I don't think he thinks anything. Read the after actions. That's what's on his mind."

He opened her briefcase and took out the after-action reports. There were four:

```
LIKHAREV, SERGEI, COLONEL NKGB, CAPTURE OF

LIKHAREV, SERGEI, COLONEL NKGB, RESULTS OF
CAPTAIN CRONLEY'S INTERROGATION OF

LIKHAREV, SERGEI, COLONEL NKGB, TRANSPORT
TO ARGENTINA OF

TEDWORTH, ABRAHAM L., FIRST SERGEANT,
ATTEMPTED NKGB MURDER OF
```

Cronley read all of them carefully, decided they were better than he expected they would be, and then made a few minor changes to each so that Freddy would know he had read them.

"Very nice, Dette," Cronley said, putting them back in her briefcase.

"I got the details of Tedworth grabbing the Russian from Tedworth," she said. "And the details of Ostrowski saving him from getting garroted from him and Ostrowski. The interrogation and transport stuff I got from Freddy."

"These are first class," Cronley said. "I moved a couple of commas around so Freddy would see I'd really read them, but they were fine as done. You're really good at this sort of thing."

"I'm also very good at Gregg shorthand," she said. "Which is really causing me an awful problem right now."

What the hell is she talking about?

"The reason Freddy wanted you to come to us from the ASA is because you can take shorthand. How is that a problem?"

"You remember when you came out of your office, Freddy had to call me out of the supply closet?"

Cronley nodded.

"What I was doing in there was taking shorthand."

"Of what?"

"What was being said in your office. What went on between you and Major Derwin and Major Wallace."

"What?"

"As soon as I reported to Freddy, he told me about Colonel Mattingly, who he said absolutely could not be trusted, and that while he thought Major Wallace could be trusted, he wasn't sure."

Freddy really brought her on board, didn't he?

"He's right about Mattingly, but I can tell you Major Wallace is one of the good guys."

"So I learned when I was in the supply closet."

"I still don't understand what you being in the closet has

to do with you . . . ." He stopped. "Jesus, Freddy bugged Mattingly's office? My office?"

"Actually, that's how I met him," she said.

"Find someplace to pull off the road," Cronley said. "We're almost to Pullach, and I want to finish this conversation before we get there."

"Yes, sir."

"Sir"?

She turned onto a dirt road and drove far enough down it so the Kapitän could not be seen from the paved road.

"You're not supposed to sit with the engine idling in a Kapitän," she said, almost as if to herself. "But it's as cold as that witch's teat we hear so much about, so to hell with it. I'll leave it running."

"You were telling me how you met Freddy," Cronley said.

"Before you moved the ASA Munich station into the Pullach compound, Freddy started hanging out around it. Around me. I thought he wanted to get into my pants. I knew who he was—that he was in the mysterious, not-on-the-books CIC detachment—and I thought just maybe he could help me get out of the ASA, at least into his branch of the CIC, so I didn't run him off.

"Finally, when he thought it was safe, he took me to the movies. After the movie—it was *They Were Expendable.* You know, Robert Montgomery and John Wayne? About PT boats in the Philippines?"

"I remember the movie," Cronley said.

"So after the movie, when Freddy was driving me back to my *kaserne*—in this car, by the way—he pulls off onto a dark street, and I thought, here it comes, and started asking myself how much I really wanted out of the ASA and into the intelligence business.

"But what he whipped out was his CIC credentials. He said what he was going to say to me was classified. Then he said he had reason to want to bug two offices, and he didn't want anyone to know he was doing it."

"Why did he go to you for that?" Cronley asked.

"The ASA—Army Security Agency—started out making sure nobody was tapping Army telephones. It went from that to making sure nobody was bugging Army offices, and finally to intercepting radio signals. Freddy knew that. You didn't?"

"I must have slept through that lecture at the CIC School. Or chalk it up to my all-around naïveté, innocence, about things I ought to know."

"Oddly enough, some women find naïveté and innocence to be charming, even erotic, characteristics in younger men. But to fill in the blanks in your education, the ASA teaches ASAers courses in how to find bugs. It therefore follows if you know how to take them out, you know how to put them in. *Verstehen Sie?*"

Actually, she should have said du. Du *is the intimate form of* Sie. *And God knows we have been intimate.*

This is not the time for language lessons.

"Okay, so where did you get the bugs you put in for Freddy?"

"There's a rumor going around that the ASA sometimes installs bugs, too. Anyway, I got half a dozen bugs from the supply room. And installed them in what was then

Mattingly's office, now yours, and in Wallace's. And Freddy promised to see what he could do about getting me transferred out of ASA."

"When did you put these bugs in?"

"A long time ago. Or what seems like a long time ago. You were then a second lieutenant in charge of the guards at the mysterious Kloster Grünau."

"That does seem like a long time ago, doesn't it?" Cronley said. "Which means Freddy regularly bugged both Mattingly and Wallace."

"He did. You didn't know this?"

Cronley shook his head.

"And today he ordered you to . . . what's the word, transcribe? . . ."

Colbert nodded.

". . . my conversation with Major Derwin?"

"Right. Which is the original source of my loyalty dilemma. And it gets worse."

"Explain that to me, now that we've already established that I'm naïve and innocent."

"When Freddy said, 'Derwin worries me. Get in there and get a record of what's said, and don't let Cronley know,' that put me in a hell of a spot. Freddy lived up to his end of his deal with me—there I was in triangles—and I obviously owed my loyalty to him.

"On the other hand—and this has nothing, well, *almost* nothing, to do with you sweeping me off my feet with that innocence and naïveté I find so erotic—you got me out of the ASA, you're my boss and Freddy's boss . . . Getting the picture? So what do I do? Who gets my loyalty?"

"You did the right thing to tell me about this," he said.

"Even if that was betraying Freddy's trust in me? Even if that means you will no longer trust him?"

"Pay attention. Freddy didn't tell me about the bugs because if he got caught, he could pass a lie-detector test saying I knew nothing about the bugs. And he told you not to let me know you were listening to the bugs because he had a good idea, was worried about, Derwin's interest in me. And he really didn't want me to know you heard either what Derwin asked me or what my answers were."

"You mean you were fooling around with Colonel Schumann's wife?"

And here we are at decision time. Do I tell her everything, or not?

I don't have any choice.

She's either part of this team, or she's not.

And I can't send her back to the ASA because (a) she's already learned too much about Freddy, and now about me, and (b) I believe what they say about hell having no fury like a pissed-off female, and (c) she would have every right to be thoroughly pissed off because she's done nothing wrong.

So once again, it's fuck Ludwig Mannberg's firm belief that if you really want to trust your intuition, don't.

"Turn that around, Dette. Rachel Schumann was fooling around with me. More accurately, she was making a three-star fool of me."

"She was into the erotic attraction of your innocence and naïveté, is that what you're saying?"

"In hindsight, I don't think she liked me at all. I think she held me in great contempt . . . and, from her viewpoint, rightly so. She was playing me like a violin, to coin a phrase."

"Her viewpoint?"

"That of an NKGB operative. And for all I know, an NKGB officer. Probably an NKGB officer."

"You're telling me this colonel's wife was a Russian spy?"

"Him, too."

"My God!"

"Welcome to the wonderful world of intelligence."

"What information did she want from you?"

"Whatever she could get about Kloster Grünau and Operation Ost generally, and whatever she could get about Likharev specifically."

"You're implying she got it. From you."

"She got what she wanted to know about Likharev. From me."

"Like what?"

"Like the fact that he wasn't buried in an unmarked grave at Kloster Grünau, despite an elaborate burial we conducted for him in the middle of the night. That he was in fact on his way to Argentina. And because I gave her that information, people died and were seriously wounded—Americans and Argentines—in Argentina, and the NKGB damned near managed to take out Likharev."

"You're sure about all this?"

"I'm sure about all this."

"Then there was something fishy about the explosion that killed this woman? Her and her husband?"

"Listen carefully. The only thing I *know* is that there was an explosion. That said explosion was investigated by everybody and his brother, including Major Wallace, who thought, still thinks, which we had better not forget, that Schumann was a fine officer and a good friend—and nothing fishy was uncovered."

"But you have your suspicions, right?"

"Next question?"

"So what do I do with my Gregg notes?"

"Transcribe them accurately and in full, give them to Freddy, who already knows everything, and don't tell Freddy we had this little chat. Questions?"

"No, sir," she said, then, "Yes, one. A big one. Where the hell did I get the idea you're naïve and innocent?"

"Does that mean I've lost the erotic appeal that went along with that?"

"Perish the thought! I meant nothing of the kind!"

"Put the car in gear, please, Miss Colbert. Before we get in trouble, we better go see the general."

She did so, and then parroted, "'*We* better go see the general'?"

"Yeah. I think it's important that you get to know one another. And when we finish, you can bring Freddy up to speed on what he had to say. Thereby sparing me from having to do so."

[THREE]
Office of the U.S. Military Government
Liaison Officer
The South German Industrial Development
Organization Compound
Pullach, Bavaria
The American Zone of Occupied Germany
1205 17 January 1946

As they were passing through the final roadblock and into the inner compound, the massive sergeant manning it, when he was sure Colbert was concentrating on the striped barrier pole as it rose, winked at Cronley and gave him a thumbs-up in appreciation of her physical attributes. Cronley winked back.

When they went into the "Military Government" building, they found General Reinhard Gehlen, Colonel Ludwig Mannberg, Major Konrad Bischoff, and Captain Chauncey Dunwiddie sitting around a coffee table.

"Oh, I'm so glad you could finally find time for us in your busy schedule," Dunwiddie greeted Cronley sarcastically. "Where the hell were you?"

Cronley's mouth went on automatic: "'Where the hell were you, *sir*?' is the way you ask that question, Captain Dunwiddie," he snapped.

His anger dissipated as quickly as it had arisen. "What the hell's the matter with you, Tiny? You got out of the wrong side of the bed?" He turned to Gehlen and the others. "Sorry to be late. Couldn't be helped. I was being interrogated by Major Derwin."

"The CIC IG?" Tiny asked incredulously. "What was that about?"

"This is getting out of hand," Cronley said. "Time out." He made the *Time-out* signal with his hands.

"This meeting is called to order by the chief, DCI-Europe, who yields to himself the floor. First order of business: Gentlemen, this is Miss Claudette Colbert. She is now Mr. Hessinger's deputy for administration. She comes to us from the ASA, where she held all the proper security clearances. You already know Colonel Mannberg, Dette, and you may know Captain Dunwiddie. That's former Major Konrad Bischoff, of General Gehlen's staff, and this, of course, is General Gehlen."

"Mannberg has been telling me about you, Fraulein," Gehlen said, and bobbed his head. "Welcome!"

"Your call, General," Cronley said. "Do you want to start with why you wanted to see me, or why I was delayed getting out here?"

"Actually, I'm curious about the major," Gehlen said. "Derwin, you said?"

"Yes, sir. Major Thomas G. Derwin. When Colonel Schumann died, Major Derwin was sent from the CIC School to replace him as the CIC/ASA inspector general. When I was a student at the CIC School, I was in Major Derwin's classes on the Techniques of Surveillance. Major Derwin was known to me and my fellow students as 'Dick Tracy.'"

"I gather he is not one of your favorite people," Gehlen said drily. "What did he want?"

"He said he wanted to ask me about credible rumors he'd heard about (a) my having an 'inappropriate relationship' with the late Mrs. Schumann, and (b) that I had attempted to murder Colonel Schumann at Kloster Grünau."

"And what did you tell him, Jim?" Mannberg asked.

"I asked Major Wallace to join us. He explained to Major Derwin what had happened at Kloster Grünau when Colonel Schumann had insisted on going in, and told Major Derwin that the idea I had had an inappropriate relationship with Mrs. Schumann was absurd."

"Jim," Tiny said, "are you sure you want Sergeant Colbert to hear this?"

"She already has. And since she's wearing triangles, why don't you stop calling her 'Sergeant'?"

"And then?" General Gehlen asked.

"Major Wallace asked Major Derwin from whom he'd heard the rumors, and after some resistance, Derwin produced a typewritten letter he said had been put in his box at the Park Hotel, where he lives."

"Who was the letter from?" Gehlen asked.

Cronley held up his hand in a *Wait* gesture.

"It began by saying the water heater explosion was suspicious, and the investigation 'superficial.' That set Wallace off. He said that he personally investigated the explosion, that he got there before the CID did, and there was nothing suspicious about it.

"He really lost his temper. He said the only reason he wasn't getting on the telephone to General Greene, to tell him what an asshole Derwin was—"

"He used that word?"

"Did he, Dette?"

"Words to that effect, sir," Claudette said.

"How would she know?" Tiny challenged. "She was in there with you?"

"Let me finish, please, Tiny, then I'll get to that," Cronley said. "Wallace said the only reason he wasn't going to General Greene, who would almost certainly relieve Derwin, was because he was determined to find out who wrote the letter to Derwin, and if Derwin was relieved, whoever wrote it would crawl back in his hole, or words to that effect, and he'd never catch him. He also told Derwin to call off his 'investigation' of the allegations in the letter as of that moment."

"Did Major Wallace have any idea who wrote the letter?" Mannberg asked.

"He thinks it's someone, one of us, who doesn't think I should have been named chief, DCI-Europe."

"That's what it sounds like to me," Gehlen said. "And you think Major Derwin will cease his investigation?"

"Yes, sir. I don't think he wants to cross Major Wallace. You knew Wallace was a Jedburgh?"

"Yes, I did."

"Did I leave anything out, Dette?"

"Sir, you didn't get into the tail end of your conversation with Major Wallace."

"I asked before, was Serg— Miss Colbert in there with you?" Tiny said.

"Fat Freddy put bugs in what was Mattingly's office, and Wallace's. Or, actually, Miss Colbert did, when Freddy asked her to."

"You knew about that?" Tiny asked.

Cronley shook his head.

"I think, when Freddy thinks the moment is right, he'll tell me."

"Then how did you find out?" Tiny asked.

"With your permission, sir?" Claudette said, before Cronley could open his mouth. "When Mr. Hessinger ordered me to transcribe what would be said between Mr. Cronley and Major Derwin, I realized I could not do that without Mr. Cronley's knowledge, so I told him."

"Afterward?" Mannberg asked.

"Yes, sir."

"Why?"

"There is no question in my mind that I owe Mr. Cronley my primary loyalty, sir."

"What was 'the tail end' of your conversation with Wallace?" Tiny asked.

"I told him what I learned from El Jefe in the Farben Building. Why I'm chief, DCI-Europe. And I told him that Lieutenant Schultz hasn't been a lieutenant for some time, and that he retired a little while ago as a commander, and is now executive assistant to the director of the Directorate of Central Intelligence. A few little things like that."

"Why? He doesn't have the need to know about little things like that," Tiny said.

"Because I've come to understand that unless I want to be tossed to the wolves—did I mention El Jefe told me that was a distinct possibility?—I'm going to need all the friends I can get that I can trust. And after carefully considering Ludwig's theory that when you really want to trust your intuition, that's when you shouldn't, I decided, Fuck it . . . Sorry, Dette."

She gave a deprecating gesture with her left hand.

"I decided (a) Wallace can be trusted, and (b) I need him. And the more time I've had to think it over, the more I think I made the right decision."

"Even though Wallace was Mattingly's Number Two in the OSS?" Tiny challenged.

"Mattingly was a politician in the OSS. The only time he ever served behind the enemy lines, if you want to put it like that, is when he flew over Berlin in a Piper Cub to see what he could see for General White. Wallace jumped into France three times. And into Norway once with a lieutenant named Colby. My gut feeling is that he's one of us."

"One of us? I was never behind enemy lines, or jumped anywhere. Where do I fit into 'us'?"

"I'm tempted to say you get a pass because you're a re-tard," Cronley said. "But you're one of us because you got a Silver Star, two Purple Hearts, and promotion to first ser-geant in the Battle of the Bulge. You've heard more shots fired in anger than I ever heard. Mattingly never heard one. Not one. Do you take my point, Captain Dunwiddie?"

"I take your point, Captain Cronley," General Gehlen said, and then added, "Tiny, he's right, and you know it."

Dunwiddie threw up his hands in a gesture of surrender.

"Is this where someone tells me that we've heard from the lady with the dachshund?" Cronley asked innocently.

"It is," Mannberg said, chuckling. "Go ahead, Konrad."

"It is Seven-K's opinion," former Major Konrad Bischoff began, "that the exfiltration of Mrs. Likharev and her chil-dren from their present location—which I believe is in Poland, although I was not told that, and Seven-K's man in Berlin said he doesn't know—"

"Seven-K's man in Berlin?" Cronley interrupted.

A look of colossal annoyance flashed across Bischoff's face at the interruption.

Fuck you, I don't like you, either, you sadistic, arrogant sonofabitch!

"Answer the question, Konrad," Mannberg said softly, in German. The softness of his tone did not at all soften the tone of command.

"NKGB Major Anatole Loskutnikov," Bischoff said.

"We've worked with him before," Gehlen said. "We suspect he also has a Mossad connection."

"And you sent Bischoff to Berlin to meet with him?"

"Correct."

"And what did Loskutnikov tell you?" Cronley asked.

"That Seven-K believes it would be too dangerous to try to exfiltrate the Likharev woman and her children . . ."

Not "Mrs. Likharev"? She's a colonel's wife. You wouldn't refer to Mannberg's wife as "the Mannberg woman," would you? You really do think all Russians are the untermensch, *don't you?*

". . . through either Berlin or Vienna."

"So what does she suggest?"

Bischoff ignored the question.

"According to Loskutnikov, Seven-K says the exfiltration problem is exacerbated by the mental condition of the woman and the children—"

"Meaning what?" Cronley interrupted. "They're afraid? Or crazy?"

Bischoff ignored him again.

"—which is such that travel by train or bus is dangerous."

"I asked you two questions, Bischoff, and you answered neither."

"Sorry," he said, visibly insincere. "What were they?"

"Since Bischoff is having such difficulty telling you, Jim, what he told me," General Gehlen said, "let me tell you what he told me."

"Please," Cronley said.

"A lot of this, you will understand, is what I am inferring from what Bischoff told me and what I know of this, and other, situations."

"Yes, sir."

"Understandably, Mrs. Likharev is upset—perhaps terrified—by the situation in which she now finds herself. She has been taken from the security of her Nevsky Prospekt apartment in Leningrad and now is on the run. I agree with Bischoff that she and the children are probably in Poland. She knows what will happen if the NKGB finds them. Children sense when their mother is terrified, and it terrifies them.

"Seven-K knows that if they travel by train or bus, the odds are that a terrified woman will attract the attention of railroad or bus station police, who will start asking questions. Even with good spurious documents, which I'm sure Seven-K has provided, travel by bus or train is dangerous.

"So that means travel by car, or perhaps truck. By car, providing that they have credible identification documents, would be safer than travel by truck. What is an obviously upper-class Russian woman doing riding around in a truck in Poland with two children?"

"I get it."

"To use your charming phrase, Jim, 'cutting to the chase,'

what Seven-K proposes is that the Likharevs be transported to Thuringia . . ."

"My massive ignorance has just raised its head."

"The German state, the East German state, which borders on Hesse in the Kassel-Hersfeld area. Do you know that area?"

"I've been to both Hersfeld and Kassel. When I first came to Germany, I was assigned to the Twenty-second CIC Detachment in Marburg. But do I know the area? No."

Gehlen nodded.

"And then be turned over to us and then taken across the border."

"Turned over to us?"

"Preferably to Americans, but if that is not possible, to us. Seven-K says Mrs. Likharev cannot be trusted to have control of her emotions to the point that she could cross the border with her children alone."

"Turned over to whomever in East Germany?"

Gehlen nodded.

"I can see it now," Cronley said, "Fat Freddy, Tiny, and me sneaking across the border."

"Not to mention what the lady and her kids would do when they saw the Big Black Guy," Tiny said. "If Tedworth and I terrified Likharev, what would she do when she saw me?"

"We could use the Storchs to get them," Cronley said thoughtfully. "If we had someplace to land . . ."

"Could you do that?" Gehlen asked.

"I don't know, but I know where to get an expert opinion."

"From whom?" Tiny asked, and then he understood.

"If you ask Colonel Wilson about this, he'll get right on the horn to Mattingly."

"We don't know that," Cronley said. "We'll have to see how much I can dazzle him with my DCI credentials."

"It's a lousy idea, Jim," Tiny said.

"It's a better idea than you and me trying to sneak back and forth across the border with a woman on the edge of hysteria and two frightened kids. Saddle up, Dette, I need a ride to the airport. I'm off to see Hotshot Billy Wilson."

[FOUR]
En Route to Schleissheim Army Airfield
1255 17 January 1946

"Is there anything I should know about this Colonel Wilson you're going to see?" Claudette asked.

"Aside from the fact that he's twenty-five years old, you mean?"

"Twenty-five and a lieutenant colonel? You're pulling my leg."

"No, I'm not. Do you remember seeing that newsreel of General Mark Clark landing in a Piper Cub on the plaza by the Colosseum in the middle of Rome when he took the city?"

She nodded.

"Hotshot Billy was flying the Cub. And I guess you know that General Gehlen surrendered to the OSS on a back road here in Bavaria?"

"I heard that story."

"Wilson flew our own Major Harold Wallace, then Mattingly's deputy, there to accept the surrender. And Mattingly got Wilson to turn over his Storchs to me when the Air Force didn't like the Army having any. Wilson is the aviation officer of the Constabulary. As soon as he gets here, which may be very soon, any day, Major General I.D. White, whom Tiny refers to as 'Uncle Isaac,' because White is his godfather, will assume command of the Constabulary. And before he went into the OSS, Mattingly was sort of a fair-haired boy in White's Second Armored Division."

"That's a lot of disjointed facts."

"That occurred to me as I sat here thinking about it. So, thinking aloud: Presuming we can find someplace to land in Thuringia, someplace being defined as a small field—the Storch can land on about fifty feet of any kind of a runway, and get off the ground in about a hundred fifty feet—near a country road, getting Mrs. Likharev and her kids out in our Storchs makes a lot more sense than sending people into East Germany on foot to try to, first, find them, and then try to walk them back across the border."

"Storchs, plural? Who's going to fly them?"

"I'll fly one, and maybe Max Ostrowski the other one."

"Maybe?"

"I won't know if he'll be willing to take the chance until I ask him," Cronley said simply. "So the question is, where can I find, just over the Hesse/Thuringia border, a suitable field near a suitable country road? I don't have a clue, but I think Colonel Wilson will not only be able to get this information for me, but have other helpful suggestions to make.

"Or he may not. He may decide to pick up the phone and call Mattingly and say, 'You won't believe what Loose Cannon Cronley's up to.'

"You're going to take that risk?"

Cronley didn't reply directly, instead saying, "Mannberg has a saying, 'Whenever you really want to trust your intuition, don't.' In this case, I'm going to trust my intuition about Colonel Wilson. I don't see where I have any choice."

"Where is this Colonel Wilson? At Sonthofen?"

"Yeah. It's about a hundred miles, a hundred and fifty kilometers, from Munich. Take me about an hour to get there."

"And then you're coming back here?"

"If there's enough time, I'll go out to Kloster Grünau. I want to keep the Storch out of sight as much as possible."

"Well, if you need anything, you know where to find me."

Fifteen minutes later, as he began his climb-out from Schleissheim, he realized that as he climbed into the Storch, Miss Colbert had repeated the same words she had said to him in the Kapitän.

And he concluded that the repetition had not been either coincidental or innocent.

IX

Ground Control had ordered Army Seven-Oh-Seven—Cronley's Storch—to take Taxiway Three Left to the Transient parking area, but before he got there, a checkerboard-painted *Follow me* jeep pulled in front of him, and the driver frantically gestured for Cronley to follow him.

He did so and was led to a hangar, where a sergeant signaled him to cut his engine, and then half a dozen GIs pushed the Storch into the hangar and closed the doors once it was inside.

Lieutenant Colonel William W. Wilson appeared, and stood, hands on his hips, looking at the Storch.

Cronley climbed down from the airplane.

"Good afternoon, Colonel," he said.

"You're not going to salute?"

"I'm a civilian today," Cronley said, pointing to the triangles. "Civilians don't salute."

"They're not supposed to fly around in aircraft the Air Corps has grounded as unsafe, either," Wilson said.

"Are you going to turn me in?"

"No, but I am going to ask what the hell you're doing here."

"I need a large favor and some advice."

"You picked a lousy time."

"I saw all the frantic activity. What's up, an IG inspection?"

"Worse, much worse," Wilson said. "Well, let's go somewhere where no one will be able to see me talking to you."

He led Cronley to a small office he'd been to before, the day Wilson had turned the Storchs over to him, and then waved him into a chair.

"Okay. What sort of advice are you looking for?"

Cronley didn't reply, instead handing Wilson his DCI credentials.

"Okay," Wilson said, after examining them and handing them back. "Colonel Mattingly told me about this, but I am nevertheless touched that you're sharing this with me. And, of course, am suitably impressed with your new importance."

"I'm not important, but what I need your advice about is very important."

"And highly classified? I shouldn't tell anybody about this little chat?"

"Especially not Colonel Robert Mattingly."

"Sorry, Cronley. I can't permit you to tell me to whom I may or may not tell anything I want. And that especially includes Colonel Robert Mattingly, who is, you may recall, both a friend and the deputy chief of CIC-Europe. Is our conversation over?"

"No. I'll have to take a chance on your good judgment."

"*You'll* have to take a chance on *my* good judgment?" Wilson parroted softly.

"Right."

"I can't wait to hear this."

"I am in the process of getting the wife and children of NKGB Colonel Sergei Likharev out of Russia and to Argentina."

"That must be an interesting task. Who is Colonel Whatsisname and why are you being so nice to him?"

"One of Tiny's Troopers caught him sneaking out of Kloster Grünau . . ." Cronley began the story, and finished up, ". . . whom we have reason to believe are now in Poland."

"And how much of this does good ol' Bob Mattingly know?"

"More, I'm sure, than I like. But not everything."

"And Hank Wallace?"

"He knows just about everything."

"And you don't think he's going to share it with ol' Bob?"

"I don't think he will."

"Did you tell him not to? *Ask* him not to?"

"I did."

"And he agreed?"

"Yes, he did."

"Now how do you envision my role in this cloak-and-dagger enterprise?"

Cronley told him.

When he had finished, Wilson said, "Oddly enough, I was up there several days ago. What used to be the Fourteenth Armored Cavalry Regiment and is now the Fourteenth Constabulary Regiment is stationed in Fritzlar. While I was there, very carefully avoiding any intrusion into the air space of Thuringia, I flew the border. I wasn't looking for them, of course, but I saw a number of places into which I believe one could put an aircraft such as a Storch."

"Could you mark them on a map for me?"

"I'll do better than that," Wilson said. "At first light tomorrow, an L-4 aircraft attached to the Fourteenth Constab will fly the border and take pictures of fields in Thuringia which look suitable for what you propose."

"Thank you," Cronley said.

"Always willing to do what I can for a noble cause," Wilson said.

"And will you tell me, teach me, what you know about doing something like this?"

"That will depend on whether General White tells me whether I can or not."

"Isn't he in the States? At Fort Leavenworth?"

"He *was* in the States at Fort *Riley*, the Cavalry School. Right now, he's somewhere en route here—the route being Washington-Gander, Newfoundland-Prestwick, Scotland-Rhine-Main—where he is tentatively scheduled to land at ten tomorrow morning."

"I didn't know that."

"Not many people do. I didn't even tell good ol' Bob Mattingly when my spies told me. What is important is the moment General White sets foot in Germany, he becomes commanding general of the United States Constabulary. When that happens, I don't do anything without his specific permission. Especially something like this."

"When is he coming here?"

"First, he has to make his manners to General Eisenhower, or General Smith, or General Clay—or all three. When that's done, he can get on his train and come to Sonthofen."

"His train? He's coming here by train? When does he get here? Can you get me in to see him?"

"Tranquillity, reflection, and great patience, I am told, are the hallmarks of the successful intelligence officer," Wilson said. "Slow down."

"Yes, sir."

"Better."

"Yes, he's coming by train. When Generals Eisenhower, Smith, Clay, and other senior brass were assigned private trains, it looked like the rest of the private trains would be doled out to other deserving general officers before General White returned from Fort Riley to assume command of the Constab, and he wouldn't get one.

"That, of course, was an unacceptable situation for those of us who devotedly serve General White. So one of the as-yet-unassigned private trains was spirited away to Bad Nauheim and parked on the protected siding where Hitler used to park his private train. It was suitably decorated with Constabulary insignia, but kept out of sight until now. It is scheduled to leave Bad Nauheim at 0700 tomorrow for the Frankfurt Hauptbahnhof, where it will be ready for him when the aforementioned senior officers are through with him."

"Then he is coming here. Back to my question, when he gets here, can you get me in to see him?"

"Simple answer, no. In addition to his pals and cronies who will meet the plane at Rhine-Main, all of the senior officers of the Constabulary, and its most senior non-commissioned officers, will be lining the corridors here to make their manners to General White."

"I've got to get him to tell you you can help me."

"You are aware of the relationship between Captain Dunwiddie and the general?"

"I am."

"My suggestion: Load Captain Dunwiddie on a Storch and fly him to Rhine-Main first thing in the morning. General White will be delighted to see him, and the odds are he will invite Captain Dunwiddie to ride the train with him from Frankfurt here. Although it will be crowded by many of General White's legion of admirers, including me, I'm sure there would still be room for the pilot who had flown Tiny to meet his Uncle Isaac. And if you get lucky, maybe you could get the general's undivided attention for a half hour or so to make your pitch. How much of this does Tiny know?"

"Everything."

"Smart move."

"Thank you," Cronley said. "I don't mean for that, for everything."

"Mr. Cronley, Hotshot Billy Wilson is really not the unmitigated three-star sonofabitch most would have you believe he is."

[TWO]
Suite 507
Hotel Vier Jahreszeiten
Maximilianstrasse 178
Munich, American Zone of Occupation, Germany
1735 17 January 1946

"Twenty-third CIC, Miss Colbert speaking."

"Miss Colbert, this is Captain Cronley."

"Yes, sir?"

"Is Mr. Hessinger or Major Wallace there?"

"No, sir. They left about five minutes ago. There's a Tex-Mex dinner dance at the Munich Engineer Officers' Club. They won't be back until very late. Is there anything I can do for you?"

"It looks like you're going to have to, Miss Colbert. Get on the horn to Captain Dunwiddie and tell him (a) this is not a suggestion, then (b) he's to get out to Kloster Grünau right away. He is to tell Max Ostrowski to fly him and Kurt Schröder—"

"Excuse me, sir. I want to get this right. Kurt Schröder is the other Storch pilot, correct?"

"Correct. Tell him to fly here—I'm at Schleissheim, just landed here—at first light, and I will explain things when they're here."

"Yes, sir. I'll get right on it."

"Oh, almost forgot. Tell Captain Dunwiddie to wear pinks and greens and to bring a change of uniform."

"Yes, sir, pinks and greens. Is there anything else you need, sir?"

"I think you know what that is. Do you suppose you could bring it to my room? I'll be there in about twenty minutes."

"It will be waiting for you, sir."

[THREE]
Suite 527
Hotel Vier Jahreszeiten
Maximilianstrasse 178
Munich, American Zone of Occupation, Germany
1935 17 January 1946

"As much as I would like to continue this discussion of
office business with you, Miss Colbert," Cronley said, "I
haven't had anything to eat since breakfast and need sus-
tenance. Let's go downstairs and get some dinner."

"And while I can think of nothing I'd rather do than
continue to discuss office business with you like this, Captain Cronley . . ."

"You mean in a horizontal position, and unencumbered
by clothing?"

". . . and seem to have somehow worked up an appetite
myself, I keep hearing this small, still voice of reason crying
out, 'Not smart! Not smart!'"

"I infer that you would react negatively to my suggestion
that we get some dinner and then come back and resume
our discussion of office business?"

"Not smart! Not smart!"

"Oddly enough, I have given the subject some thought.
Actually, a good deal of thought."

"And?"

"It seems to me that the best way to deal with our problem
is for me to treat you like one of the boys. By that I mean
while I don't discuss office business with them as we do, if
I'm here at lunchtime, or dinnertime, and Freddy is here, or
Major Wallace, or for that matter, General Gehlen, I

sometimes have lunch or dinner with them. Not every time, but often. I'm suggesting that having an infrequent dinner— or even a frequent dinner—with you would be less suspicious than conspicuously not doing so. Take my point?"

"I don't know, Jim."

"Additionally, I think if we listen to your small, still voice of reason when it pipes up, as I suspect it frequently will, and do most of the things it suggests, we can maintain the secret of our forbidden passion."

"It will be a disaster for both of us if we can't."

"I know."

After a moment, she shrugged and said, "I am hungry. Put your clothes on."

"With great reluctance."

"Yeah."

Lieutenant Colonel George H. Parsons and Major Warren W. Ashley were at the headwaiter's table just inside the door to the dining room when Cronley and Colbert walked in.

"Oh, Cronley," Parsons said, "in for dinner, are you?"

Actually I'm here to steal some silverware and a couple of napkins.

"Right. Good evening, Colonel. Major."

The headwaiter appeared.

"Table for four, gentlemen?"

"Two," Cronley said quickly. "We're not together."

"But I think we should be," Parsons said. "I would much rather look at this charming young woman over my soup than at Major Ashley."

The headwaiter took that as an order.

"If you'll follow me, please?"

They followed him to a table.

"You are, I presume, going to introduce your charming companion?" Colonel Parsons said, as a waiter distributed menus.

"Miss Colbert, may I introduce Lieutenant Colonel Parsons and Major Ashley?"

"We've met," Claudette said. "At the Pullach compound."

"I thought you looked familiar," Ashley said. "You're the ASA sergeant, right?"

"She was," Cronley answered for her. "Now she's a special agent of the Twenty-third CIC, on indefinite temporary duty with DCI."

"I see," Parsons said.

"But, as I'm sure you'll understand, we don't like to talk much about that," Cronley said.

"Of course," Parsons said. "Well, let me say I'll miss seeing you at the Pullach compound." He turned to Cronley. "Sergeant . . . I suppose I should say 'Miss' . . . ?"

"Yes, I think you should," Cronley said.

"*Miss* Colbert handled our classified traffic with Washington," Parsons went on. "Which now causes me to wonder how secure they have been."

"I'm sure, Colonel, that they were, they are, as secure as the ASA can make them," Cronley said. "Or was that some sort of an accusation?"

"Certainly not," Parsons said.

Cronley chuckled.

"Did I miss something, Mr. Cronley?"

"What I was thinking, Colonel, was 'Eyes Only.'"

"Excuse me?"

"Way back from the time I was a second lieutenant, every time I saw that I wondered, 'Do they really believe that?' Actually, 'They can't really believe that.'"

"I don't think I follow you," Parsons said.

"I know I don't," Ashley said.

"Okay. Let's say General Eisenhower in Frankfurt wants to send a secret message to General Clay in Berlin. He doesn't want anybody else to see it, so he makes it 'Eyes Only, General Clay.'"

"Which means only General Clay gets to see it," Ashley said. "What's funny about that?"

"I'll tell you. Eisenhower doesn't write, or type, the message himself. He dictates it to his secretary or whatever. He or she thus gets to see the message. Then it goes to the message center, where the message center sergeant gets to read it. Then it goes to the ASA for encryption, and the encryption officer and encryption sergeant get to read it. Then it's transmitted to Berlin, where the ASA people get it and read it, and decrypt it, then it goes to the message center, where they read it, and finally it goes to General Clay's office, where his secretary or his aide reads it, and then says, 'General, sir, there is an Eyes Only for you from General Eisenhower. He wants to know . . .' So how many pairs of eyes is that, six, eight, ten?"

"You have a point, Cronley," Colonel Parsons said. "Frankly, I never thought about that. But that obviously can't be helped. The typists, cryptographers, et cetera, are an integral part of the message transmission process. All you can do is make sure that all of them have the appropriate security clearances."

"That's it. But why 'Eyes Only'?"

"I have no answer for that," Parsons said. "But how do

you feel about someone, say, the cryptographer, sharing what he—or she—has read in an Eyes Only, or any classified message, with someone not in the transmission process?"

"Do you remember, Colonel, what Secretary of State Henry Stimson said when he shut down the State Department's cryptanalytic office?"

"Yes, I do. 'Gentlemen don't read other gentlemen's mail.' I think that was a bit naïve."

"You know what I thought when I heard that?" Cronley asked rhetorically. "And I think it applies here."

"I don't know what you're talking about," Major Ashley said.

"I wondered, 'How can I be sure you're a gentleman whose mail I shouldn't read unless I read your mail?'"

"How does this apply here?" Ashley asked sarcastically.

"Hypothetically?"

"Hypothetically or any other way."

"Okay. Let's say, hypothetically, that when Miss Colbert here was in charge of encrypting one of your messages to the Pentagon, and had to read it in the proper discharge of her duties, she reads 'If things go well, the bomb I placed in the Pentagon PX will go off at 1330. Signature Ashley.'"

"This is ridiculous!" Ashley snapped.

"You asked how it applies," Cronley said. "Let me finish."

Ashley didn't reply.

"What is she supposed to do? Pretend she hasn't read it? Decide on her own that it's some sort of sick joke and can be safely ignored? Decide that it's real, but she can't say anything because she's not supposed to read what she's encrypting? In which case the bomb will go off as scheduled. Or go to a superior officer—one with all the proper security clearances—and tell him?"

"This is absurd," Ashley said.

"It's thought provoking," Colonel Parsons said, and then turned to Colbert.

"See anything you like on the menu, Miss Colbert?"

"My problem, Colonel, is that I don't see anything on the menu I don't like."

"Shall we have a little wine with our dinner?" Colonel Parsons asked. "Where's the wine list?"

[FOUR]
Suite 527
Hotel Vier Jahreszeiten
Maximilianstrasse 178
Munich, American Zone of Occupation, Germany
2105 17 January 1946

"Stop that," Claudette said. "I didn't come here for that."

"I thought you'd changed your mind."

"Are you crazy?"

"I don't know about crazy," Cronley said. "How about 'overcome with lust'?"

"You just about admitted to Colonel Parsons that I've been feeding you his messages to the Pentagon."

"The moment he saw you with me, he figured that out himself," Cronley said. "I never thought he was slow."

"And that doesn't bother you?"

"He would have heard sooner or later that you defected to DCI."

"Jimmy, please don't do that. You know what it does to me."

"That's why I'm doing it."

"So what's going to happen now?"

"Well, after I get your tunic off, I'll start working on your shirt."

"What's Parsons going to do now?"

"Spend an uncomfortable thirty minutes or so with Ashley, wondering what incriminating things they said in the messages you turned over to Hessinger and me."

"Jimmy, I told you to stop that."

"Yeah, but you didn't sound as if you really meant it."

"And then what's he going to do?"

"See about getting another communications route to the Pentagon. Which will probably be hard, as he would first have to explain what's wrong with the one he has, and then if he did that, said he had good reason to believe I was reading his correspondence, he would then have to explain to Greene, or ol' Iron Lung, what it was he wanted to tell the Pentagon he didn't want me to know.

"Oh, there they are! I knew they had to be in there somewhere!"

"Are you listening to me? What if Freddy comes back and comes in here? . . . Oh, God, Jimmy! . . . Jimmy, let me do that, before you tear something!"

[FIVE]
Schleissheim Army Airfield
Munich, American Zone of Occupation, Germany
0545 18 January 1946

Captain Chauncey L. Dunwiddie squeezed himself out of the Storch, and a moment later, Max Ostrowski followed him. Kurt Schröder started to follow Ostrowski.

"Stay in there, Kurt," Cronley called to him, "we're leaving right away." And then asked, "Have you enough fuel to make Eschborn?"

Schröder gave him a thumbs-up.

"Why are we going to Frankfurt?" Dunwiddie asked.

"Actually, we're going to Rhine-Main," Cronley said, directing his answer to Ostrowski.

"Rhine-Main or Eschborn?"

"Rhine-Main, and we have to be there by nine thirty."

"Got it," Ostrowski said, and headed back for the Storch.

"Why are we going to Frankfurt?" Tiny asked.

"Get in the airplane, I'll tell you on the way."

"I've got things to do in Pullach."

"Not as important as this. Get in the goddamn airplane."

"Yes, *sir*," Tiny replied sarcastically.

"Schleissheim departure control, Army Seven-Oh-Seven, a flight of two aircraft, request taxi and takeoff."

"Army Seven-Oh-Seven, take Taxiway Three to threshold of Two Seven."

"Schleissheim departure control, Army Seven-Oh-Seven, on the threshold of Two Seven. Direct, VFR to Rhine-Main. Request takeoff."

"Army Seven-Oh-Seven, you are number one on Two Seven."

"Schleissheim, Oh-Seven rolling."

"Why are we going to Frankfurt?"

"For Christ's sake, Tiny, put a fucking cork in it."

"Army Seven-Oh-Seven. Schleissheim. Say again?"

"You had something you wished to ask me, Captain Dunwiddie?"

"Why are we going to Frankfurt?"

"We are going to see your beloved Uncle Isaac."

"You're referring to General White?"

"Unless you have another godfather you call Uncle Isaac."

"You're saying General White is in Frankfurt?"

"ETA Rhine-Main ten hundred."

"How do you know that?"

"Hotshot Billy Wilson told me."

"You're referring to Lieutenant Colonel Wilson?"

"Who else, for Christ's sake, is known as 'Hotshot Billy'?"

"And why are you taking me to Frankfurt?"

"Because I need ten minutes, maybe a little more, of White's time, just as soon as I can get it, and you're going to arrange it."

"I'll do no such thing."

"What?"

"My personal relationship with General White is exactly that, personal. And if you don't mind, please refer to him as '*General* White.'"

"Are you constipated, or what?"

Dunwiddie did not reply.

"Just for the record, Captain Dunwiddie, I do not wish to intrude on your personal relationship with General White. I'm not going to ask him, for example, if he has any pictures of you as a bare-ass infant on a bearskin rug he'd be willing to share with me. This is business."

"Official?"

"Yes, official."

"Then I suggest that if you need to see General White that you contact his aide-de-camp and ask for an appointment."

"If I had the time, maybe I would. But I don't have the time."

"Would you care to explain that?"

"Hotshot Billy told me he can't do anything more for me to get Mrs. Likharev and the kids across the border than he already has, unless he gets permission from White."

"Can you tell me what Colonel Wilson has done for you so far?"

"He told me that when, a couple of days ago, he flew the East/West German border around Fritzlar, he thinks he saw places, fields, roads, right across the border in Thuringia where we could get the Storchs in and out.

"And as we speak, at least one and maybe more than one Piper Cub of the Fourteenth Constab—"

"The nomenclature is L-4," Dunwiddie interrupted.

"—which is stationed in Fritzlar, is flying the border taking aerial photographs of these possible landing sites. He has promised to give me what they bring back. But when I asked him to teach me and Ostrowski and Schröder what he knows about snatch operations—and Hotshot Billy knows a lot—he said he couldn't do anything more, now that White has returned to Germany, without White's permission."

"That's the way things are done in the Army."

"Fuck you, Tiny."

"You might as well turn the airplane around, Jim. Because I flatly refuse to be in any way involved with getting General White involved in one of your loose-cannon schemes."

"Before I respond to that, I think I should tell you the reason I know White will be in Frankfurt is because Wilson told me. And it was Wilson who suggested that the quickest way for me to get permission from White for him to help me was to get you to Frankfurt to meet your Uncle Isaac when he gets off the plane. Wilson says he's sure White will invite you to ride on his private train, and if you get on it, so will I. How could they do less for the man who flew Chauncey to meet his Uncle Isaac?"

"You're not listening, Jim. I refuse to become involved."

"You're not listening. I told you this was important. And a word to the wise: I've had about all of your West Point bullshit I can handle, Tiny."

"I went to Norwich, not West Point. So did General White."

"Well, pardon me all to hell. I forgot that Wilson's the West Pointer, not you and your Uncle Isaac. Same comment, I've had enough of this bullshit. Grow the fuck up, you're in the intelligence business, not on the parade ground of some college. That *I will not lie, cheat, or steal, or tolerate those who do* philosophy doesn't work here."

"I beg to disagree."

"You will get me on that fucking train, Tiny, because this isn't a suggestion, or a request, it's what you proper soldiers call a direct order. Once I'm in with the general, you can tell him you're there against your will, or even— shit, why not?—that I threatened to shoot you if you wouldn't go along."

"Now you're being sophomoric."

"Am I? You saw how little the assassination option upset me when it was necessary. I will do whatever is necessary to get Mrs. Likharev and her two kids out of the East. If I thought I had to shoot you because you were getting in the way of my getting them out, I would."

"You're crazy."

"Or dedicated. Now take off your headset. I have no further interest in hearing anything you might wish to say."

[SIX]
Rhine-Main USAF Air Base
Frankfurt am Main
American Zone of Occupation, Germany
0955 18 January 1946

As Cronley trailed a *Follow me* jeep down a taxiway to a remote area of the Rhine-Main airfield, he saw there was an unusual number of Piper Cubs parked on the grass beside the taxiway. And then he saw that just about all of them bore U.S. Constabulary markings.

There were a number of vehicles lined up beside a mobile stairway where the general's plane was expected to stop. Three buses, one of them bearing Constabulary insignia, three 6x6 trucks, a dozen staff cars, and two Packard Clippers.

He hand-signaled Tiny first to look where he was pointing, and then for him to put on his headset.

"There's a welcoming party," he said. "Jesus, there's even a band."

Dunwiddie did not reply.

"I don't know how long it's going to take for General White to get off his plane and into one of those Packards, but it won't take long, and I can't afford you giving me any trouble. Got it?"

Dunwiddie did not reply.

When the *Follow me* had led Cronley to where he wanted him to park the Storch on the grass—maybe a quarter mile from the cars and buses—an Air Force major wearing an Airfield Officer of the Day brassard drove up.

Oh, shit!

More trouble about the Storchs.

Cronley got out of the airplane as the major got out of his jeep.

"Interesting airplane, Captain," the major said.

Christ, I forgot I'm wearing my bars!

Belatedly, Cronley saluted.

"They're great airplanes," Cronley agreed. "Plural," he added, pointing to the Storch with Ostrowski and Schröder in it.

"I also understand the Air Force has grounded them."

Cronley took his DCI credentials from his pocket and handed them to the major.

"Not all of them. I hope I won't break your heart when

I tell you the Air Force really doesn't own the skies or everything that flies."

"Those are the first credentials like that I ever saw," the major said.

"There's not very many of them around," Cronley said.

"How can I be of service to the Directorate of Central Intelligence?"

"Don't say that out loud, for one thing," Cronley said, smiling.

"Okay," the major said, returning the smile. "And aside from that?"

"I need to get the Storchs fueled and on their way as soon as possible."

"On their way and out of sight?" the major asked.

"That, too."

"That I can do. I'll have a fuel truck come out here."

"And then I have to be in that crowd welcoming General White back to Germany."

"Quite a crowd," the major said, gesturing around the field at all the L-4s. "I would say that every other colonel and lieutenant colonel in the Constabulary is here to watch General White get off the plane."

"So I see. But the skies will fall and the world as we know it will end if we're not standing there when the general gets off the plane."

He pointed to Dunwiddie in the Storch.

"Well, I wouldn't want that on my conscience. I'll make you a deal. I've never been close to a Storch before. If you can arrange a tour for me of one of those airplanes, I'll take you over there in my jeep."

"Deal," Cronley said.

He waved at Max Ostrowski to get out of his Storch, and then called, "Captain Dunwiddie, you may deplane."

"Yes, sir?" Ostrowski asked.

"The major is going to take Captain Dunwiddie and me over there. He's also going to get a fuel truck sent here. When he comes back, show him around the Storch. Then as soon as you're fueled, you and Kurt head for home. I'll get word to you there what happens next."

"Yes, sir."

Cronley saw the major had picked up on Ostrowski's British accent. But he didn't say anything.

The major motioned for Cronley to get in the jeep. Cronley motioned for Dunwiddie to get in the jeep.

"After thinking it over," Dunwiddie said, "I've decided you're entitled to the benefit of the doubt."

Cronley nodded, but didn't say anything.

Almost as soon as the jeep started moving, the radio in the jeep went off:

"Attention, all concerned personnel. The VIP bird has landed."

"I'm not surprised," Cronley said. "I am famous for my ability to make the world follow my schedule."

The major laughed.

As they got close to where the VIP bird would apparently be, they were waved to a stop by a sergeant of the U.S. Constabulary. He was wearing a glossily painted helmet liner bearing the Constabulary "Circle C" insignia and glistening leather accoutrements, and a Sam Browne belt, to which was attached a glistening pistol holster and spare magazine holsters.

"End of the line," the major said.

"Thanks," Cronley said, offering his hand.

When he got out of the jeep, he remembered to salute.

A lieutenant and a sergeant marched up to them. They, too, wore the natty Constabulary dress uniform, and the sergeant held a clipboard.

The lieutenant saluted crisply.

"Good morning, gentlemen," he said. "May I have your names, please?"

"If that's a roster of some kind," Cronley said, "I don't think we're on it."

"Excuse me, sir," the lieutenant said. "I didn't see the patch."

What the hell is he talking about?

"'Hell on Wheels' comrades are in the rear rank of those greeting General White," the lieutenant said. "Senior officers and personal friends are in the first rank. If you'll follow the sergeant, please?"

Aha! He saw the 2nd Armored patch on Tiny's shoulder. That's what he's talking about!

They followed the sergeant with the clipboard toward the reception area.

There they were met by a Constabulary major.

They exchanged salutes.

"'Hell on Wheels' comrades in the rear rank, by rank," the major said, pointing to two ranks of people lined up.

"Yes, sir," Tiny said. "Thank you, sir."

I think I have this ceremony figured out.

Majors and up and personal friends are in the front row.

Anybody who served under General White in the 2nd "Hell on Wheels" Armored Division is a "comrade"—which, con-

*sidering our relationship with the Soviet Union, seems to be an
unfortunate choice of words—and is in the rear row.*

*Tiny belongs in the front row, and I don't belong here at
all, but this is not the time to bring that up.*

What I'll try to do is pass myself off as a comrade.

They found themselves about three-quarters of the way
down the rear rank, between a major wearing a 2nd Armored
Division patch and a first sergeant. Cronley guessed there
were forty-odd, maybe fifty-odd, people in each rank.

They had just taken their positions when a Douglas
C-54 transport with MILITARY AIR TRANSPORT SERVICE
lettered along its fuselage taxied up. In the side window of
the cockpit was a red plate with two silver stars on it.

The band started playing.

*That's "Garry Owen." The song of the 7th Cavalry
Regiment.*

*I know that because I was trained to be a cavalry officer
and they played it often enough at College Station to make
us aware of our cavalry heritage.*

*And where I learned that the 7th Cavalry, Brevet Briga-
dier General George Armstrong Custer commanding, got
wiped out to the last man at the Battle of the Little Big Horn.*

*I've never quite figured out how getting his regiment
wiped out to the last man made Custer a hero.*

The mobile stairs were rolled up to the rear door of
the C-54.

The door opened.

A woman with a babe in arms appeared in the doorway,
and then started down the stairs.

She was followed by fifteen more women, and about

that many officers and non-coms, who were quickly ushered into the buses waiting for them.

Clever intelligence officer that I am, I deduce that the airplane's primary purpose was to fly dependents over here. Dependents and officers and non-coms who were needed here as soon as possible. General White was just one more passenger.

Is there a first-class compartment on Air Force transports?

The procession came to an end.

The band stopped playing.

A stocky, muscular officer in woolen ODs appeared in the aircraft door. There were two stars pinned to his "overseas cap."

The band started playing "Garry Owen" again.

People in the ranks began to applaud.

Someone bellowed "Atten-hut!"

Cronley saw that it was a full colonel standing facing the two ranks of greeters.

When the applause died, the colonel did a crisp about-face movement and saluted.

The major general at the head of the stairs returned it crisply.

That is one tough sonofabitch.

The tough sonofabitch turned and then with great care helped a motherly looking woman down the stairs.

They then disappeared from sight.

Three minutes later, the general appeared, now shaking hands with the major standing ahead of Cronley in the comrades and personal friends rank. He was trailed by the woman and a handful of aides.

They disappeared again to reappear sixty seconds or so later, now in front of Captain Dunwiddie.

"Chauncey, I'm delighted to see you!" the general said. "Honey, look who's here! Chauncey!"

The woman stood on her toes and kissed Captain Dunwiddie.

Major General I.D. White looked at Captain Cronley.

"You are, Captain?"

"Cronley, sir. James D. Junior."

"You hear that, Paul?"

"Yes, sir."

"Bingo!"

"Yes, sir."

"Correct me if I'm wrong. What's next is that I go to make my manners to General Eisenhower . . ."

"To General Smith, sir. General Eisenhower is in Berlin."

"Okay. And Mrs. White goes to the *bahnhof* to get on my train?"

"Yes, sir."

"Put these two in the car with her," General White ordered.

"Yes, sir."

General White stepped in front of the first sergeant standing next to Cronley.

"How are you, Charley?" he asked. "Good to see you."

[SEVEN]
Dining Compartment, Car #1
Personal Train of the Commanding General,
U.S. Constabulary
Track 3, Hauptbahnhof
Frankfurt am Main
American Zone of Occupation, Germany
1305 18 January 1946

Captains Cronley and Dunwiddie rose when Major General White walked into the dining compartment trailed by two aides.

"Sit," he said.

He walked to his wife, bent and kissed her, and then sat down.

The train began, with a gentle jerking motion, to get under way.

"Tim!" General White called.

"Yes, sir?" a captain wearing the insignia of an aide-de-camp replied.

"Find the booze, and make me a stiff one."

"Bourbon or scotch, sir?"

"Scotch," he said. "Georgie always drank scotch."

"I.D.," Mrs. White said, "it's one o'clock in the afternoon."

"And make Mrs. White one," the general said. "She's going to need it. Hell, bring the bottle, ice, everything. We'll all have a drink to Georgie."

"I have no idea what you're talking about," Mrs. White said.

"General Smith was kind enough to fill me in on the

last days of General George Smith Patton Junior," White said. "He knew I would be interested."

"Oh," she said.

"Would you like Captain Cronley and myself to withdraw, sir?" Tiny asked.

White considered that a moment.

"No, Chauncey, you stay. You can write your dad and tell him what General Smith told me. Then I won't have to. So far as Captain Cronley is concerned, I would be surprised if he doesn't already know. Do you?"

"Yes, sir. I believe I've heard."

"Besides, I have business with Captain Cronley I'd like to get out of the way before we go into the dining car for our festive welcome-back-to-Germany luncheon."

"Sir?"

The aide appeared with whisky, ice, and glasses, and started pouring drinks.

"First of all, it was an accident. Georgie was not assassinated by the Russians. Or anyone else. To put all rumors about assassination to rest. It was a simple crash. Georgie's driver slammed on the brakes, Georgie slipped off the seat, and it got his spine.

"The car was hardly damaged. It's a 1939/40 Cadillac. General Smith asked me if I wanted it, and as I couldn't think of a polite way to say no, I said, 'Yes, thank you.'

"They knew from the moment they got him in the hospital—and Georgie knew, too—that he wasn't going to make it. But they decided no harm would be done if they tried 'desperate measures.' These were essentially stretching him out, with claws in his skin and muscles to relieve pressure on his injured spine, and administering sufficient morphine to deal with the pain the stretching caused.

"The Army then flew Beatrice over here. Little Georgie is at West Point. He was discouraged from coming with his mother.

"The morphine, or whatever the hell they were giving Georgie for the pain, pretty well knocked him out.

"So, after Beatrice arrived, Georgie stopped taking the morphine whenever Beatrice was with him. When she finally left his room to get some sleep, he got them to give him morphine. Then Beatrice ordered that a cot be brought into his room so she wouldn't have to leave him."

"Oh, my God!" Mrs. White said.

"So, he stopped taking the morphine. Period. And eventually, he died. Instead of getting killed by the last bullet fired in the last battle, Georgie went out in prolonged agony, stretched out like some heretic they were trying to get to confess in the Spanish Inquisition."

White's voice seemed to be on the cusp of breaking.

Mrs. White rose and went to him, and put her arms around him, and for a minute he rested his head against her bosom.

Then he straightened.

Cronley saw a tear run down his cheek.

Mrs. White leaned over and picked up a shot glass from the table.

"Gentlemen," she said, "if I may, I give you . . ."

Everyone scrambled for a glass and to get to their feet.

". . . the late General George Smith Patton Junior, distinguished officer and Christian gentleman," she finished.

And then she drained the shot glass.

The others followed suit. Somebody said, "Hear, hear."

"You may recall, Captain Cronley," White said, as he sat down, "that when you told me your name at Rhine-Main, I said, 'Bingo.'"

"Yes, sir."

"One of the first things I planned to do on arrival here was to send for you."

"Sir?"

"Got the briefcase, Paul?" General White asked.

Whatever this is about, the Patton business is apparently over.

Why was I on the edge of tears? The only time I ever saw him was in the newsreels. The last time, he was pissing in the Rhine.

"Sir, I've never let it out of my sight," White's senior aide-de-camp, a lieutenant colonel, said.

He then set a leather briefcase on the table, opened it, took out a sheet of paper, and handed it to Cronley.

"Please sign this, Captain," he said, and produced a fountain pen.

"What is that?" Dunwiddie asked.

"Although your curiosity seems to have overwhelmed your manners, Chauncey," General White said, "I'll tell you anyway. It's a briefcase full of money. One hundred thousand dollars, to be specific."

He turned to Cronley.

"Admiral Souers asked me to bring that to you, Captain," he said. "And to say 'thank you.'"

"What's that all about?" Mrs. White asked.

"You heard what I just said to Chauncey? About curiosity?"

"What's that all about?" she repeated.

"I won't tell her, Captain. You may if you wish."

"Ma'am, it's a replenishment of my—the DCI's—operating funds."

"In other words, you're not going to tell me?"

"He just did. Told you all he can," General White said. "And while we're on the subject of Admiral Souers, Captain Cronley, he told me of your role in getting done what Colonel Mattingly was unable to do—get Chauncey his commission. Thank you."

"No thanks necessary, sir."

"And on that subject, where is Bob Mattingly?"

No one replied.

White looked at Cronley.

"What is it about Colonel Mattingly that you're not telling me, Captain?"

"I don't know where he is, sir. I presume he's in his office in the Farben Building."

"But he wasn't at Rhine-Main, and he's not on the train. Is he, Paul?"

"Not so far as I know, General."

"Okay. Chauncey, who told you to be at Rhine-Main?"

"Captain Cronley."

"Captain Cronley—and you are warned, I'm already weary of playing Twenty Questions—who told you when we were arriving at Rhine-Main?"

"Colonel Wilson, sir."

"And why do you suppose he told you that?"

"Sir, I told Colonel Wilson I needed ten minutes of your time, and he suggested that if Tiny . . . Captain Dunwiddie and I met your plane, I might be able to get it."

"There's a protocol for getting ten minutes of my time. You get in touch with my aide-de-camp and ask for an appointment, whereupon he schedules one. Is there some reason you couldn't do that?"

Cronley didn't immediately respond.

"And Colonel Wilson is damned well aware of that protocol."

He looked at his watch.

"There's no time now. I'm due at my festive lunch. But as soon as that's over, get Hotshot Billy in here, and we'll get to the bottom of this."

"Yes, sir," his senior aide said.

"What this looks like to me, Captain Cronley, is that you tried to use my personal relationship with Captain Dunwiddie to get around established procedures. I find that despicable. And, so far as you're concerned, Chauncey . . ."

"Uncle Isaac, Cronley doesn't have time for your established procedures," Dunwiddie said.

"What did you say?" White demanded.

"I said, 'Uncle Isaac, Cronley doesn't have time—'"

White silenced him with a raised hand.

"My festive lunch will just have to wait," he said. "Tim, my compliments to Colonel Wilson. Please inform him I would be pleased if he could attend me at his earliest convenience."

The junior aide-de-camp said, "Yes, sir," and headed for the door.

He slid it open, went through it, and slid it closed.

Thirty seconds later, the door slid open again.

Lieutenant Colonel William W. Wilson came through

it, marched up to General White, saluted, and holding it, barked, "Sir, Lieutenant Colonel Wilson reporting to the commanding general as ordered, sir."

White returned the salute with a casual wave of his hand in the general direction of his forehead.

"Waiting for me in the vestibule, were you, Bill?"

"Yes, sir. I hoped to get a minute or two of the general's time."

"How modest of you! Captain Cronley hoped to get ten minutes."

Wilson didn't reply.

"Where to start?" General White asked rhetorically. "Bill, Captain Cronley tells me you suggested he bring Chauncey to Rhine-Main because he wanted the aforementioned ten minutes of my valuable time, and you thought his bringing Chauncey would help him achieve that goal. True?"

"Yes, sir."

"And you are going to tell me why this is so important, right?"

"Sir, I suggest that Captain Cronley could do that better than I can."

White looked at Cronley, and when Cronley didn't immediately open his mouth, said, "You heard the colonel, Captain. Cat got your tongue?"

"General, the subject is classified Top Secret–Presidential . . ." Cronley said uneasily.

"And these people, so far as you know, might be Russian spies?" General White said, waving his hand at his aides and his wife.

"Sir—"

"Actually, I'm not sure about her, so throughout our twenty-nine years of married bliss, I have never shared so much as a memorandum classified 'confidential' with her. As far as Colonel Davidson and Captain Wayne are concerned, if you say anything I think they should not have heard, I'll have them shot and have their bodies thrown off the train. You may proceed."

"Yes, sir. Sir, we have turned a Russian, NKGB Colonel Sergei Likharev—"

"Who is 'we'? Are you referring to Colonel Mattingly? Is that why he's among the missing?"

"No, sir. Colonel Mattingly had nothing to do with turning Colonel Likharev. Tiny and I turned him."

"You and Chauncey turned an NKGB colonel?" White asked incredulously.

"Uncle Isaac, please give Jim, and me, the benefit of the doubt," Tiny said.

"I.D.," Mrs. White ordered, "get off your high horse and hear the captain out."

"You may proceed, Captain Cronley," General White said.

"Yes, sir. Sir, one of the reasons Colonel Likharev turned was because we promised him—"

"'We' being you and Chauncey?"

"Yes, sir."

"Promised him what?"

"You'll never find out if you keep interrupting him," Mrs. White said. "Put a cork in it!"

"Sir, we, Tiny and me, promised Likharev we would try to get his family—his wife, Natalia, and their sons, Sergei and Pavel, out of Russia. This is important because Mr. Schultz believes, and he's right, that by now Likharev is starting to think that we lied to him about trying to get his family out—"

"Excuse me, Captain," Mrs. White interrupted. "Mr. Schultz? You mean Lieutenant Schultz? The old CPO?"

"Yes, ma'am."

"Now the admiral's Number Two," General White said. "You met him the first time Admiral Souers came to Fort Riley."

"Pardon the interruption. Please go on, Captain," Mrs. White said.

"Yes, ma'am. Well, we've gotten them—I should say, General Gehlen's agents in Russia have gotten them—out of Leningrad as far as Poland. That's what that hundred thousand is all about. It went to General Gehlen's agents. Now we have to get them . . .

". . . So when Colonel Wilson said he couldn't help us any more without your permission, I decided I had to get your permission. And here we are."

General White locked his fingers together and rocked his hands back and forth for a full thirty seconds.

Finally, he asked, "Bill, what are the odds Cronley could pull this off?"

"Sir, I would estimate the odds at just about fifty-fifty," Wilson said.

General and Mrs. White exchanged a long look, after which White resumed rocking his finger-locked hands together for about fifteen seconds.

"George Patton was always saying we're going to have to fight the Russians sooner or later," he said finally.

He looked at his wife again. She nodded.

"Try to not let this be the lighting of the fuse that does that," General White said.

"Sir, does that mean . . . ?" Colonel Wilson began.

"It means, Bill, that while you are providing Captain Cronley with whatever he needs, you will try very hard not to light the fuse that starts World War Three."

"Yes, sir."

X

[ONE]
Conference Compartment, Car #2
Personal Train of the Commanding General,
U.S. Constabulary
Approaching Hauptbahnhof
Munich, American Zone of Occupation, Germany
1615 18 January 1946

The sliding door from the corridor opened and Captain Chauncey L. Dunwiddie stepped inside.

The commanding general, United States Constabulary, was sitting at a twenty-foot-long highly polished wooden conference table around which were also seated more than a dozen officers, the junior of them a lieutenant colonel.

General I.D. White's eyebrows rose in disbelief.

"What?" General White asked.

Captain James D. Cronley Jr. slid into the room.

"Oh, I now understand," General White said. "You two decided the red Conference in Session light was actually advertising a brothel."

Mrs. White slipped into the room.

"I didn't hear that," she said.

"Hear what, my love?"

"I insisted they make their manners," she announced.

"So that I would not have to hear you complaining that they hadn't."

"Why are they making their manners? We're nowhere near Sonthofen."

"They're getting off in Munich."

"I've seen Chauncey a total of twenty minutes," he protested.

"Duty calls, apparently," she said.

Tiny came to attention.

"Permission to withdraw, sir?"

"Granted."

Tiny saluted, followed a half second later by Cronley.

The general returned them.

Cronley started to follow Mrs. White out of the conference compartment.

"Cronley!"

Captain Cronley froze in mid-step and then turned to face General White.

"Yes, sir?"

"The next time you want to talk to me, seek an appointment. I've told Colonel Davidson to put you ahead of everybody but my wife."

"Yes, sir. Thank you, sir."

[TWO]
The Hauptbahnhof
Munich, American Zone of Occupation, Germany
1635 18 January 1946

The private train of the commanding general, U.S. Constabulary, rolled into what little was left of the *bahnhof*—it had been nearly destroyed during the war, and the recently started reconstruction had taken down what little had remained after the bombing—and stopped.

The door to the first car of the train slid open.

Two Constabulary troopers stepped onto the platform. One of them came to attention to the left of the door and the other to the right.

As first Captain James D. Cronley Jr. and then Captain Chauncey L. Dunwiddie came through the door, the troopers saluted crisply.

Captains Cronley and Dunwiddie returned the salute.

One of the troopers put a glistening brass whistle—which had been hanging from his epaulet on a white cord—to his lips and blew twice.

The train immediately began to move. The troopers went quickly through the door and it slid closed.

Captain Cronley addressed those waiting on the platform, Mr. Friedrich Hessinger and Miss Claudette Colbert.

"How nice of you to meet us. And now that you have seen the evidence of the high regard in which Captain Dunwiddie and myself are held by the U.S. Constabulary, I am sure we will be treated with greater respect and deference than you have shown in the past."

"Well, I'm awed," Miss Colbert said.

"You got us to come down here to watch you get off the train?" Mr. Hessinger asked incredulously.

"What happened," Tiny said, "is that Colonel Wilson was showing us the communications on the train, and asked if there was anyone we wanted to call. Our leader said, 'Let's get Freddy on the phone, and have him pick us up at the *bahnhof.* Save the price of a taxicab.' So he did."

"A cab would have cost you fifty cents!" Hessinger complained.

"'A penny saved is a penny earned,'" Cronley quoted piously. "Isn't that true, Miss Colbert?"

"And 'A fool and his money are soon parted,'" she replied.

Their eyes met momentarily.

He forced the mental image this produced of Miss Colbert in her birthday suit from his mind.

Nose to the grindstone, Cronley!

"Is Major Wallace in the office?" he asked.

"Probably for the next five minutes," Freddy said. "He really hates missing Happy Hour at the Engineer O Club, and that starts at five o'clock."

"I may have to ruin his evening," Cronley said. "We've got a lot to do, and we're going to need him."

"For instance?" Freddy asked.

"I'll tell you at the office," Cronley said, "when I tell him."

"For instance," Tiny said, "we've got to get the Storchs to Sonthofen first thing in the morning, which means I'm going to have to go out to Kloster Grünau and set that, and some other things, up. Do I just take the Kapitän?"

"I can drive you out there," Claudette said.

"Do it. We'll need the Kapitän in the morning," Cronley ordered.

[THREE]
Hotel Vier Jahreszeiten
Maximilianstrasse 178
Munich, American Zone of Occupation, Germany
1705 18 January 1946

Major Harold Wallace was checking to ensure the door to Suite 507 was securely locked when Cronley and Hessinger came down the corridor.

"What would it take to get you to miss Happy Hour at the Engineer O Club?"

"Not much, as I have something to tell you," Wallace said. "I didn't know if you were coming back here today or not."

He unlocked the door and waved Cronley and Hessinger into the office.

As soon as Cronley was in the office, he said, "Maybe I can save us both time. What would you say if I told you I need your help with getting Mrs. Likharev and offspring over the border?"

"The first thing that pops into my mind is that you have FUBAR something somehow."

"Not yet. But that's probably inevitable."

"And the second thing is that you don't want me to mention this to Colonel Mattingly. True?"

"True."

"One of the things I thought you might be interested

in hearing is that Colonel Mattingly was on the horn a couple of hours ago—"

"You haven't answered my question. Can I tell you what problems I have without Mattingly hearing about any of them?"

"I thought that question had arisen and been disposed of," Wallace said, just a little sharply.

"Sorry," Cronley said, and a moment later, added: "I apologize."

Wallace nodded, then said, "The officer in question was on the horn a couple of hours ago. It has come to his attention that General White has returned to Germany, specifically, that he flew into Rhine-Main, where a large number of friends and others met him, and then, after making his manners to General Smith, set off for Sonthofen on his private train. He was curious as to why he was not (a) informed of this, and (b) was not invited to the arrival at Rhine-Main or to ride on the train."

"And he thought you might know?"

"That, and he wondered if Tiny, because of his relationship with the general, knew about this, and didn't think he would be interested."

"Tiny knew about it because I told him. I don't know if he would have told Mattingly or not . . . He probably would have, being the good soldier he is . . . but he didn't have the time."

"And who told you?"

"Hotshot Billy Wilson."

"The plot thickens. What the fuck is going on?"

Cronley told him all that had happened.

During the recitation, Cronley saw that Hessinger was

unable to keep his face from registering surprise, concern, alarm, and disbelief. Or various combinations of the foregoing.

"But, I just thought of this," Cronley concluded. "Mattingly not getting invited may be innocent. I mean, nobody consciously decided, 'Let's not tell Mattingly.'"

"Explain that."

"General Smith, who knew he was coming, either presumed Mattingly knew or, more than likely, didn't give a damn about who was going to be at Rhine-Main or on the train. Anyway, after he told Hotshot Billy—"

"Why would Smith tell Hotshot Billy?"

"They were coconspirators in the Let's Save a Train for General White business. Wilson told me Smith was disgusted with all the three stars fighting like ten-year-olds over who gets a train, and decided they would get the proper message if two-star White showed up with one.

"Try to follow my reasoning: Smith told Wilson, expecting that Wilson would . . . as he did . . . spread the word around in the Constabulary. He didn't tell Mattingly because he figured Mattingly was in the Farben Building and would know. Did Smith tell Greene? I don't know. Probably not. So if Greene didn't know, he couldn't tell Mattingly. And if he did know, he didn't tell him because he thought he would already have heard."

Wallace grunted.

"General White asked where Mattingly was."

"How do you know that?"

"Because he asked me where he was."

"You were on the train?"

"Tiny and I just got off it."

"As soon as Bob Mattingly hears that you and Tiny were on that train—and he will—you're the villains, you know that? The master politician will decide he's been out-politicked by two captains he doesn't much like anyway. And he's one ruthless sonofabitch. I've seen him in action. Christ, I actually wondered if he wrote that *Cronley's been fucking Mrs. Rachel Schumann* letter to Dick Tracy."

"If I'm putting you on the spot now, asking for help and don't tell Mattingly . . ."

"You are. But after our little chat the other day, I did some thinking of my own."

"About what?"

"About why I'm here running what you so accurately describe as a 'phony CIC detachment.'"

"I shouldn't have said that."

"Why not? It's true. So why am I here doing it? Two reasons, the most important probably being that ol' Bob can throw me to the wolves you mentioned. 'I'm really surprised that Major Wallace didn't learn that Cronley was doing black masses, running a brothel, making bootleg whisky, and burying people in unmarked graves at Kloster Grünau. Maybe being a Jedburgh doesn't really qualify someone to be an intelligence officer.'"

He looked at Cronley as if expecting a reply, and when none came, went on: "Reason two: If I was in the Farben Building doing what I should be doing . . ."

"Which is?"

"Intelligence. Advising Greene. Or maybe General Clay. This may come as a shock to you, but when I was not being a heroic Jedburgh, parachuting behind enemy lines à la Errol Flynn or Alan Ladd, I was a pretty good intelligence officer.

A better one than Bob Mattingly. And, while I was wallowing in self-pity, I wondered why I never got a silver leaf, or an eagle. And wondered if it was because good ol' Bob Mattingly liked me where I was, as a major. I did the work, and he got the credit."

Cronley's mouth went on automatic.

"If you were good in the OSS, you can bet your ass El Jefe knows it. Which is why—"

"I'm here running a phony CIC outfit, so that I can step in and replace you when you FUBAR everything?"

"Yeah."

"Well, I thought about that, too, and what I decided to do, Captain Cronley, is make goddamn sure you don't FUBAR anything. So tell me your problems vis-à-vis getting Mrs. Likharev and her children across a border. I have a little experience in that sort of thing."

"Thank you."

"Which brings us to Friend Freddy," Wallace said. "Who has been sitting there like a sponge, soaking all this in."

"Sir?"

"Are you willing to deceive Colonel Mattingly and anyone else who gets in our way? Or are you thinking of some way you can cover your ass?"

"You have no right to think that about me!" Freddy flared.

"Correct answer," Wallace said. "Fortunately for you. I always hate to use the assassination option, even when it's called for."

"So do Cronley and I," Hessinger said.

Wallace's eyebrows rose.

"One day we'll have to exchange secrets," he said. "But

not now. Before Brunhilde walks in from wherever she is . . ."

It took Cronley a moment to realize he was talking about Claudette Colbert.

"She's driving Tiny out to Kloster Grünau," he said.

". . . we have to decide about her. Do we bring her into this? Yes or no. If yes, how far? Only so far as needed? Or total immersion? Freddy, you first, you're junior. If I ask Jim first, you're liable to go along with whatever he says."

"What did you say, 'total immersion'?" Hessinger said. "Yes. All the way."

"May I ask why you have such confidence in the lady?"

"She has ambitions. We can help her achieve them."

"And you don't think she'd expose us?"

"No. But even if she did, we'd still have that option you mentioned."

"Jim?" Wallace asked.

"I agree with Freddy."

"Tiny, I presume, is a given?" Wallace asked.

"Captain Dunwiddie has one weakness for our line of work," Freddy said. "His family, his education at Norwich, has inculcated in him the officer's honor code."

"You're saying that's bad?"

"I'm saying that he might not be able to do some of the things we may have to do."

"I'd say we might have to explain to him the necessity of doing some of the things we may have to do," Cronley said.

"Well, what's your call?" Wallace said. "In or out?"

"In. With that caveat," Freddy said.

After a just perceptible hesitation, Cronley said, "In."

"That brings us to Ostrowski and Schröder," Wallace said. "What makes you think that both—or either—are going to volunteer to go along with this?"

"I think both will, but we need only one volunteer."

"You're not thinking you can carry this off, moving the woman and the two kids, using just one Storch, are you?"

"No. Two Storchs. One of which I will fly."

"And what does Billy Wilson think of that idea?"

"I think I overcame most of his objections. Most of which centered around both Max and Schröder being more experienced pilots than me."

"And?"

"Tomorrow, I go back to flight school at Sonthofen."

"Are you willing to listen to further argument, from other people with experience in this sort of thing?"

"Who do you have in mind?"

"Me, for one. And General Gehlen and Colonel Mannberg. I was about to suggest that we invite the general for dinner. By the time he could get here, Brunhilde should be back."

"Freddy," Cronley ordered, "get on the phone and ask General Gehlen if he and Colonel Mannberg will join us for dinner."

Hessinger picked up the secure telephone.

"This brings back many memories," Wallace said. "Most of them unpleasant, of planning operations like this in London. Specifically, one of the first lessons we learned. Painfully. And that is, unless everyone with a role in an operation knows everything about it, it will almost certainly go wrong."

[FOUR]
Office of the Chief, DCI-Europe
Hotel Vier Jahreszeiten
Maximilianstrasse 178
Munich, American Zone of Occupation, Germany
1745 18 January 1946

When Claudette Colbert returned from driving Dunwiddie to Kloster Grünau, Cronley greeted her the moment she closed the door. "Dette, we're going to have a meeting. I want it to be formal. Set it up in my office. I'll be at the head of the table. Put General Gehlen at the other end . . ."

"I get the idea."

"Major Wallace will be joining us."

"Got it."

"And, for the future, as soon as you can, arrange with your former buddies in the ASA to make absolutely sure it's not bugged, with emphasis on my office."

"Done," she said. "I mean, already done. I arranged for that when I came here. It was last swept just before we went to pick you up at the *bahnhof*, and they'll sweep it again at 0500 tomorrow."

"Great! You are a woman of amazing talents."

"Of all kinds," she said.

She looked around the room to make sure no one was looking at her, and then, smiling, stuck her tongue out at him in a manner which she intended to be, and which he interpreted to be, somewhere between naughty and lascivious.

When General Gehlen and Colonel Mannberg arrived ten minutes later, the conference table was already set. There was a lined pad, three pencils, and a water glass before each chair. There was a water pitcher in the center of the table, and a small canvas sack, which was stenciled all over, in bright yellow, "BURN." In front of Cronley's chair was a secure telephone.

Gehlen had brought former Major Konrad Bischoff with him.

Mannberg and Bischoff were in well-tailored suits and looked like successful businessmen. Cronley thought, for the umpteenth time, that Gehlen looked like an unsuccessful black marketeer.

I guess Bischoff saw Mannberg in his nice suit and figured, what the hell, if he can do it, why not me?

Claudette, who was sitting to Cronley's side with her shorthand notebook in front of her, looked at Cronley questioningly.

"Miss Colbert, will you set a place for Major Bischoff? Konrad, this is Miss Colbert, our new administrative officer."

Bischoff nodded at her curtly and sat down. Claudette got a lined pad, three pencils, and a water glass and set them before him.

"Before we get started, General," Cronley said, "I know you've met Major Wallace, but I don't know how much you know about him."

"Actually, Jim," Gehlen replied, "the three of us, Ludwig, Konrad, and I, were very much aware of the irony when Major Wallace flew into Elendsalm to accept our surrender. We'd been hoping to . . . have a chat . . . with him for years. We almost succeeded twice, once in Norway and again in Moravia. But failed. And now there he is, all smiles, coming to chat with us."

"You didn't mention that, General, either at Elendsalm or here," Wallace said, smiling.

"At the time, Major, it didn't seem to be the appropriate thing to do."

"And here?"

"Jim never shared with me what you're really doing here, and I thought it was best . . ."

"To let the sleeping dog lie?"

"Sleeping tiger, perhaps. We always thought you were far more dangerous than a dog."

"I'm flattered."

"And are you now going to tell us what you've been really doing here?"

"I don't expect you to believe this, General, but nothing. What I'm doing now is working for Jim. But we don't want that to get around."

"Understood."

"That out of the way," Cronley said, "let's get started. First things first. Major Wallace was telling me earlier that the OSS learned . . . painfully, he said . . . that if all parties to an operation are not involved in all aspects of its planning, the operation goes wrong."

Cronley saw Gehlen and Mannberg nod just perceptibly in agreement.

"So to make sure that doesn't happen here, how do we handle that?"

Hessinger raised his hand.

Resisting with effort the temptation to say, "Yes, Freddy, you may. But don't dawdle in the restroom, and remember to wash your hands," Cronley asked, simply, "Hessinger?"

Hessinger stood up.

"Since Major Wallace brought that up, I have given the matter some thought," he said. "What I suggest is the following: That we have a . . . how do I describe this? I will rephrase. I suggest that Miss Colbert take minutes of this meeting. Every member of this group . . . which brings us to that. What is the group? I suggest the group consists of those present, plus, of course, Captain Dunwiddie. And either or both Max Ostrowski and Kurt Schröder, presuming they volunteer for this operation."

"Tiny is in the process of finding that out," Cronley interrupted. "I think they both will."

"Very well," Hessinger said. "We define the group as those present, plus Captain Dunwiddie, and possibly, to be determined, Schröder and Ostrowski. When Miss Colbert types the minutes of this meeting—in one copy only—she will append at the end the names of the group . . . every member of the group, including those who were not present. Every member of the group will sign by his name, acknowledging that he is familiar with the contents.

"Then, tomorrow, when Captain Dunwiddie comes here, he will read the minutes—which will be, twenty-four hours a day, in the custody of Miss Colbert or myself—and sign them, acknowledging that he is familiar with everything.

"If he has something to add—hypothetically, that Ostrowski does not wish to participate—Miss Colbert or I will type this up as Annex 1 to the minutes, again appending the names of all members of the group, who, when then they read Annex 1, will sign again to acknowledge they are familiar with the added information. *Und so weiter* through what I suspect will be Annex 404."

Hessinger looked as if he had something else to say, but decided against saying it. He sat down.

After twenty seconds, Wallace said, "That'd work."

Gehlen said, chuckling, "Freddy—Feldmarschal von Moltke—where were you when I needed a really smart general staff officer to find a simple solution to answer a complex problem, and all I had was Ludwig?"

Mannberg smiled, then applauded, and a moment later, so did Bischoff, Wallace, and Cronley.

My God, Fat Freddy is actually blushing!

"Miss Colbert," Cronley said, "item one, in your transcript of these proceedings, will be the adoption of Mr. Hessinger's 'How to Keep Everybody Who Needs to Know Up to Speed' plan."

"Yes, sir," Claudette said.

"May I suggest, Jim," Gehlen said, "that item two be a report of your trip to Frankfurt?"

"Yes, sir. But I think I'd better begin that with a report of my meeting with Colonel Wilson. As I think everybody knows . . ."

"And when do you think you'll have these aerial photographs of places where the Storchs could touch down?" Major Wallace asked.

"I didn't ask, which was stupid of me," Cronley replied. "But I would guess that a Piper Cub with the film aboard—I told you at least two Constabulary Cubs from the Fourteenth would be used?—was at Sonthofen before the train got there. And I wouldn't be surprised if when Wilson picks me up at Schleissheim in the morning, he has prints with him."

"I'd like a look at them," Bischoff said. "Actually, what I'd like to do is get copies of them to Seven-K."

"And if they were intercepted some way, don't you think the Russians would thereafter wonder why the Americans were so interested in obscure Thuringian fields and back roads that they shot aerials of them?" Wallace asked sarcastically.

"Good point," Gehlen said.

"You have common maps, presumably?" Wallace asked.

What the hell is a common map?

Oh. Seven-K and Bischoff have identical maps.

"Yes, of course we do."

"Presumably with . . . imaginative . . . coordinates?"

Gehlen chuckled.

What the hell does that mean?

"Of course," Bischoff said tightly.

"Then I suggest that the thing to do is get the pilots who shot the aerials to match them to a standard map, and then we change those coordinates to the imaginative ones. Would that be the thing to do, General?"

"Presuming the imaginative coordinates have not been compromised."

"You think it's worth taking the chance?"

"I don't think we have much choice."

"Okay with you, Jim?"

He's asking my permission to do something, and I don't have a fucking clue what that something is.

"Absolutely."

Wallace reached for the secure telephone.

"Major Wallace," he said. "Authorization Baker Niner Three Seven. I say again, Baker Niner Three Seven. Get me

Lieutenant Colonel Wilson at Constab headquarters in Sonthofen.

"Colonel, this is the Bavarian office of the German-American Tourist Bureau. It has come to our attention that you have been taking pictures which might be suitable for our next 'Visit Beautiful Occupied Bavaria' brochure . . .

"Well, that would depend on who you might think it is . . .

"Congratulations, Hotshot! You have just won the cement bicycle and an all-expenses-paid tour of the beautiful Bavarian village of Pullach . . .

"No. I haven't, actually. I'm parched. But as soon as I get off the phone, in other words, after you answer, truthfully, a couple of questions, I intend to quickly remedy that situation . . .

"The first is, I need to know, presuming they came out and you have them, if you've thought of matching the photos taken this morning to a GI map? My boss has been wondering . . .

"Yes, as a matter of fact I am talking about him. But I thought you were the one everyone calls 'the Boy Wonder.'"

Wallace turned to Cronley.

"Colonel Wilson wishes me to remind you that he's done this sort of thing before, and knows what's required. He will bring what's required when he picks you up in the morning."

He turned back. "Final question, Bill. On a scale of one to ten, what's our chances of carrying this off . . . ?"

"That bad, huh? Well, it's been nice chatting with you. Green Valley out."

Cronley's mouth went on automatic. He parroted, "'Green Valley'? What the hell is that?"

"A code name from another time," Wallace said. "*My* code name."

"I had the feeling you knew one another," General Gehlen said. "You said 'that bad.' Colonel Wilson doesn't think much of our chances?"

"Colonel Wilson said I should know better than to try to estimate the chances of an operation being successful."

"What did he mean by that?" Cronley asked. "Why not?"

"The only pertinent question to be asked is, 'Is it necessary?' And you've already made that decision, haven't you?"

"Yeah, I have," Cronley said, as much to himself as in response to Wallace's question.

"Konrad," General Gehlen asked, "once we get them, how long is it going to take to get the coordinates of possible pickup sites to Seven-K?"

"That would depend, Herr General, on whether we send them by messenger—"

"Which would be slower in any event than by radio, even if we knew where Rahil is," Mannberg interrupted.

"But would present less of a risk of interception," Bischoff argued.

"It would take too much time," Gehlen said. "The time element here is critical. Rahil is greatly exposed moving around Poland or Bohemia, Moravia—"

"General," Wallace interrupted, smiling, "that's Czechoslovakia again. The Protectorate of Bohemia and Moravia is history. You lost the war."

"Indeed, we did. What I meant to say, Green Valley, was that Seven-K is greatly exposed moving around that *part of the world* with a Russian woman and two Russian children with the NKGB looking for them."

"Well, if you think they're in what used to be Moravia, people other people are looking for are sometimes very hard to find in Moravia. Even by . . ."

Gehlen shook his head, and smiled.

"Searchers directed by Major Konrad Bischoff of Abwehr Ost," he said.

"We heard you were personally directing the searchers," Wallace said.

"Perhaps if I had, we would have met sooner than we did," Gehlen said. "What happened was that my man normally in charge of important searches, Oberst Otto Niedermeyer, wasn't available, so Kon—"

"You're talking about the guy I met in Argentina?" Cronley blurted.

"I'm sure we are, Jim," Gehlen said.

Jesus, this intelligence business is really a small world, isn't it?

"So Konrad got the job of . . . trying to arrange a conversation with Green Valley," Gehlen concluded.

"And damned near succeeded," Wallace said. "There I was, all by my lonesome in a muddy field in picturesque Králický Sněžník. I could actually hear your motorcycles coming up the valley, and no sign of anything in the sky to get me the hell out of there. I was about to kiss my . . . rear end . . . goodbye, when there was Billy Wilson coming down the valley in his puddle jumper, about ten feet off the ground."

"We saw him," Bischoff said. "We were looking for a Lysander—"

"A what?" Cronley asked.

"A British ground cooperation aircraft, Jim," Gehlen

explained. "With short field capability. The OSS used them often in situations like Major Wallace's."

"Which we expected to land, and then get stuck in the muddy fields," Bischoff explained.

"But instead you got Hotshot Billy in an L-4, with oversized tires," Wallace said. "He touched down and I got in and away we went."

"We were amazed when you got off the ground," Bischoff said. "You flew right over us."

"Which brings us to that," Wallace said.

"Excuse me?" Gehlen said.

"Once Bill Wilson landed that Piper Cub, I was in it in about twenty seconds, tops, and we took off," Wallace said. "That's not going to happen with Mrs. Likharev and her two kids."

"Point well taken," Gehlen said.

And now these guys are sitting around, cheerfully remembering the day Wallace almost, but not quite, got caught behind enemy lines.

Almost like friends.

Almost, hell—really like friends.

Thank God that I got Wallace involved in this.

"It's entirely possible, even likely," Gehlen said, "that the Likharev children, and perhaps even Mrs. Likharev herself, have never been in an airplane before."

"And the children will see they are about to be separated from their mother and handed over to strangers," Mannberg added.

Cronley actually felt a chill as the epiphany began to form.

Oh, shit, it took me a long time even to start figuring this out.

I never even questioned how come an OSS veteran, a major, a Jedburgh, who had been Mattingly's Number Two, got himself demoted to commanding officer of a CIC detachment with no mission except to cover DCI.

Jesus, there were three majors in the XXIInd CIC in Marburg. It would have made much more sense to send any one of them to a bullshit job in Munich, and it makes no sense at all for them to have sent somebody like Wallace, who—what did he say that he should be doing, "advising Greene or maybe General Clay"?

Who is "them" who sent Wallace here?

"The obvious corollary of that is that Mrs. Likharev, already distressed by her situation," Gehlen said, "will be even more distressed at the prospect of her being separated from her children."

Mattingly?

Wallace knows (a) that what he was ordered to do here is a bullshit job, and (b) who ordered him here.

So why did he put up with it?

Because what he's really doing here is keeping an eye on me and Gehlen and company.

And Gehlen knows that. That's why he told El Jefe he'd rather not have either Mattingly or Wallace at DCI. He'd rather have me. So El Jefe had Wallace assigned to the bullshit job.

Why?

To keep Gehlen happy.

And to put Wallace in a place where he'd have plenty of time and opportunity to keep an eye on both Gehlen and me.

And since Wallace has to know this, that means he's working for Schultz, has been working for Schultz all along.

"They, the Likharev woman and the children, will have to be tranquilized," Bischoff said matter-of-factly.

"I can see that now," Wallace said sarcastically, "the Boy Wonder here, hypodermic needle in hand, chasing Russian kids all over some Thuringian field, while your agent tries to defend him from their mother."

So that's what you think of me, "the Boy Wonder"?

Why not?

You know what a fool I am.

"There are other ways to sedate people," Gehlen said, chuckling. "But getting the Likharevs onto, into, the airplanes is a matter of concern. I suggest we think about—not talk about—the problem while we have our dinner."

"I suggest," Wallace said, "that until we get the aerials, and their coordinates, from Bill Wilson tomorrow, there's nothing much to talk or think about. One step at a time, in other words."

"Concur," Gehlen said, and stood up.

"I should have my notes typed up by the time you get back," Claudette Colbert said.

"While I appreciate your devotion to duty, Claudette," Wallace said, "that'll wait until tomorrow, too. You stick your notes in the safe and come to dinner with us."

And what's your real role in this, Claudette?

Did my innocence and naïveté really cause you to throw your maidenly modesty to the winds?

Or did someone tell you that I tell females with whom I am cavorting sexually everything they want to know?

And if so, who told you that? Is Fat Freddy part of this?

Or have you been working for Wallace all along, and he told you to get to me through Hessinger?

[FIVE]
Suite 527
Hotel Vier Jahreszeiten
Maximilianstrasse 178
Munich, American Zone of Occupation, Germany
0310 19 January 1946

"Fuck it," Captain James D. Cronley Jr. announced and swung his legs out of bed.

He was in his underwear. He found the shirt he had discarded when he went to bed, and then his uniform trousers. He pulled on socks, made a decision between Shoes, Men's Low Quarter, Brown in Color, and Uribe Boots, San Antonio, Texas, choosing to jam his feet into the latter.

Then he walked to his door, unlocked it, and went down the corridor to Suite 522, where he both pushed the doorbell and knocked at the door.

A full ninety seconds later, Major Harold Wallace, attired in his underwear, opened the door.

"If you're looking for Brunhilde, Romeo, she's in 533," Major Wallace said.

"I'm looking for you, Colonel," Cronley said.

"Colonel? How much have you had to drink, Jim?"

"Not a drop. Not a goddamn drop."

"What's on your mind at this obscene hour?"

"I have some questions I need to have answered."

"Such as?"

"How long have you been working for Schultz?"

"How long have I what?"

"I think you heard me, Colonel."

"I think you better go back down the corridor and jump in your little bed."

"I'm not going to do that until I get some answers," Cronley said.

Cronley gestured with his hand around the room. "And to put your mind at rest, Colonel, about the wrong people hearing those answers, I told Brunhilde to have the ASA guys sweep your suite for bugs after dinner and again at midnight."

"And if I don't choose to answer your questions?"

"Then we're going to have trouble."

"You're threatening me?"

"I'm making a statement of fact."

"Your pal Cletus warned me not to underestimate you," Wallace said, and waved him into the room.

Wallace sat in an armchair, and motioned for Cronley to sit on a couch.

"Okay. What questions have you for me?"

"Let's start with how long you've been a colonel."

"What makes you think I am a colonel? Where the hell did you come up with that?"

"If you're going to play games with me, Colonel, we'll be here a long time."

Wallace looked at him for a long thirty seconds before replying.

"Why are you asking?"

"I figure if I get a straight answer to that, straight answers to my other questions will follow."

"And if I give you a straight answer, then what? You tell the world?"

"You know me better than that."

"I guess I knew this conversation was coming, but I didn't think it would be this soon. Been doing a lot of thinking, have you?"

"Since just before we went to dinner. I'm sorry I didn't start a lot earlier. So, what's your answer?"

"I was promoted to colonel the day after Bill Wilson pulled me out of Králický Sněžník. It was April Fools' Day, 1945. I guess that's why I remember the exact date. Is that what tipped you off?"

"Wilson's a starchy West Pointer. You called him 'Hotshot.' He doesn't like to be called 'Hotshot.' So how were you getting away with it? Maybe because you outrank him? And if that's true . . ."

"You figured that out, did you, you clever fellow?"

"It started me thinking about what else I didn't know."

"For example?"

"You brought up 'my pal Cletus.' Does he know what's going on here?"

"What do you think?" Wallace said sarcastically.

"You met him before—him and El Jefe—before the day you came to Marburg with him and Mattingly, to pick up Frau von Wachtstein?"

Wallace nodded.

"In—the middle of 1943, I forget exactly when—Wild Bill Donovan decided that David Bruce, the OSS station chief in London, should be brought up to speed on what was happening in Argentina. Things that could not be written down.

"Bruce couldn't leave London, so he sent me, as sort of

a walking notebook. I spent three weeks there with Cletus and El Jefe. Which is how, since we are laying all our secrets on the table, you got in the spook business."

"I don't understand."

"When we got back to OSS Forward—the Schlosshotel Kronberg in Taunus—that night, after picking up Frau von Wachtstein, we—Mattingly, Frade, and I—had a private dinner. Toward the end of it, Mattingly mentioned the trouble we were having finding an officer to command Tiny's Troopers, who were going to provide security not only for Kloster Grünau but for the Pullach compound when we got that up and running."

"Why didn't you just get Tiny a commission?"

"All I knew about Tiny at the time was that he was a first sergeant who'd got himself a Silver Star in the Battle of the Bulge. I didn't know he'd almost graduated from Norwich. And I certainly didn't know he called General White 'Uncle Isaac.' I'm now sure Mattingly did, and knew that Lieutenant Dunwiddie would ask questions First Sergeant Dunwiddie couldn't ask. Mattingly likes to be in control."

"You don't like him much, do you?"

"Mattingly is a very good politician. You need people like that. I was telling you how you got in the spook business."

"Sorry."

"So Cletus said, what about Jim Cronley? What they've got him doing is sitting at an unimportant roadblock in the boonies, or words to that effect, to which Mattingly replied, that wouldn't work. You'd need a Top Secret–OSS clearance to work at Kloster Grünau. You didn't have one, and he couldn't imagine anyone giving you one. Mattingly said he was surprised that you even had a Top Secret–CIC clearance, or words to that effect.

"This seemed to piss ol' Cletus off. I don't think he likes Mattingly much anyway. Cletus said, 'Well, I'll bet you his Uncle Bill would give him one.' And Mattingly bit. 'His Uncle Bill? Who the hell is his Uncle Bill?'

"He's not really his uncle. But Jimmy calls him that.

"And Mattingly bit again.

"What's Cronley's Uncle Bill got to do with Top Secret–OSS clearances?

"'Just about everything,' Cletus said. 'I'm talking about General Donovan. He and Jimmy's father won World War One together.'

"I was looking at Mattingly. I could see on his face that he was weighing the advantages of having Wild Bill's nephew under his thumb against the risks of having Wild Bill's nephew under his thumb, and as usual was having trouble making a major decision like that. So he looks at me for a decision, and since I had already decided—wrong decision, as it turned out—that you couldn't cause much trouble at Kloster Grünau, I nodded. And that is how you became a spook."

"Did Cletus know you were a colonel?"

"Sure."

"So why were you pretending to be a major?"

"When David Bruce set up OSS Forward, he knew it would be facing two enemies, the Germans and the U.S. Army. Colonel Mattingly is very good at dealing with U.S. Army bureaucrats, if properly supervised. I provided that supervision and dealt with the enemy. It was easier to do that if people thought I was a major."

"And then, when DCI came along . . ."

"The admiral thought that I was the guy who should keep an eye on Gehlen."

"And the chief, DCI-Europe?"

"And the chief, DCI-Europe, and Schultz thought I could do that better if everybody thought I was a major. It never entered anybody's mind that Little Jimmy Cronley would be the one to figure this out, and then Little Jimmy does. Or figures out most of it. And tells me, touching the cockles of my heart, that he has decided to trust me and needs my help. So I confess to him what I think needs to be confessed, and hope that's the end of it.

"And then you appear, in the middle of the goddamn night, and tell me you've been thinking. As I said, Clete warned me not to underestimate you, but I did. And, this taking place in the middle of the night, I told you more than I should have. Frankly, the assassination option occurred to me."

"You wouldn't tell me that if you planned to use it."

"At least not until after we get Mrs. Likharev and kiddies across the border," Wallace said. "Any more questions?"

"Where does Claudette fit in all this?"

"I haven't quite figured that out myself," Wallace said. "I'm tempted to take her and Freddy's version, that she wanted out of the ASA . . ."

"She's not working for you?"

Wallace shook his head.

". . . and was willing to let Freddy into her pants as the price to be paid to get out."

"Freddy's not fucking her," Cronley said.

"He said with a certainty I find fascinating."

Cronley didn't reply.

"One possibility that occurs to me is that you know Freddy has not been bedding Brunhilde because you are."

Again, Cronley didn't reply.

"Well, that went right over my head," Wallace said. "You're a regular fucking Casanova, aren't you, Boy Wonder? Fucking Brunhilde is pretty goddamn stupid for a number of reasons."

Then Wallace saw the look on Cronley's face.

"Okay. So what else is there that you don't want to tell me?"

Cronley remained silent.

"Goddammit, Jim. Answer the question. What else do you know that I should?"

Cronley exhaled audibly.

"You're not going to like this," he said.

"Understood. That's why I insist you tell me."

"I suspect—suspect, not know—that Gehlen was responsible for that gas water heater explosion."

"Gehlen had Tony Schumann and his wife killed, is that what you're saying?"

Cronley nodded.

"Why would he order that?"

"Because the Schumanns were NKGB agents."

"That's preposterous!"

"It's true."

"How could you possibly know that?"

"You know that the NKGB was waiting for Likharev when he went to Buenos Aires?"

"Yes. So what? The Soviet Trade Mission to the Republic

of Argentina knew we had him, they knew we were sending people to Argentina, so they started watching the airport. That's what Cletus thinks, and I agree with him."

"They knew exactly when he would arrive in Buenos Aires," Cronley said. "They probably had six, eight, maybe ten hours to set up that ambush. The ambush involved a lot of people, at least a dozen. They even used Panzerfausts. A lot of planning had to be involved. They weren't just keeping an eye on the airport on the off chance that Likharev would show up."

Wallace considered that a moment.

"How could they possibly know exactly when he would arrive?"

"Because I told Rachel Schumann and she told her—their—handler."

"What the hell are you talking about?"

"After we loaded him on the plane at Rhine-Main, I went to the Park Hotel . . . next to the *bahnhof*?"

"I know where it is."

"And Rachel came to see me there."

"Why would she do that?"

"Because the Boy Wonder called her. The Boy Wonder had just loaded an NKGB major—this was before Clete turned him, and we learned Likharev's really a colonel—on an airplane, and the Boy Wonder thought he was entitled to a little prize for all his good work. Like some good whisky and a piece of ass."

"You were fucking Rachel Schumann?" Wallace asked incredulously.

"In hindsight, in a nonsexual sense, Rachel was fucking me. At the time, I thought it was my masculine charm. And I thought all her questions about Kloster Grünau were simply feminine curiosity. So, when she showed up at the Park Hotel for fun and games, I proudly told her what I had just done. And thirty minutes later, she left. She had to go home, she said, to her husband.

"So when we heard what had happened in Buenos Aires, I put two and two together. The only way the Russians in Buenos Aires could have heard the precise details of when Likharev would get there was because they had gotten them from Rachel. And I'd given them to Rachel. The only other people who knew the details were Tiny and Hessinger, and I didn't think either one of them would have tipped the NKGB. So I finally gathered my courage and fessed up."

"To Gehlen?"

"Gehlen, Tiny, and Hessinger. Gehlen wasn't as surprised, or as contemptuous, as I thought he would be. He said that he'd always wondered what Colonel Schumann was doing on that obscure back road in Schollbrunn, the day I shot up his car, why he had been so determined to get inside Kloster Grünau right then."

"That's all?"

"Well, he talked me out of my solution to the problem."

"Which was?"

"I wanted to shoot both of them and then tell General Greene why I had. General Gehlen said the damage was done, and my going to the stockade, or the gallows, would accomplish nothing. And so, coward that I am, I accepted his advice."

After a long moment, Wallace said, "We joke about the assassination option, but sometimes . . ."

"So I've learned."

"You're sure . . . ?"

"The other thing I've learned is never to be sure about anything."

"And Tiny? And Hessinger? Are you sure they can be . . ."

"Trusted? As sure as I am of anything."

"What does Brunhilde know about this?"

"I don't *know* what she knows, but I'm presuming she knows everything."

"And do you think she might somehow try to use this knowledge to further her intelligence career?"

"I don't *know* she wouldn't, but how could I be sure?"

"You can't. Have you told her what you've been thinking?"

"No."

"You ever hear that the bedroom is usually where the most important secrets are compromised?"

"I guess I'm proof of that, aren't I?"

"That argument could be reasonably made," Wallace said drily.

"Colonel," Cronley began, and stopped.

"What, Cronley?"

"Sir, the only thing I can say in my defense is that I very seldom make the same mistake twice."

"I'm glad you said that," Wallace said. "Both things."

"Sir? Both things?"

"I'm glad you seldom make the same mistake twice, and I'm glad you said 'Colonel.'"

"Sir?"

"For one thing, you are hereby cautioned not to say it out loud again," Wallace said. "But don't forget it. Now that my secret—that I'm the senior officer of the DCI present for duty—is no longer a secret to you, remember that when you have the urge to go off half-cocked. Get my permission before you do just about anything. For example, like forming an alliance with Commandant Jean-Paul Fortin of the Strasbourg office of the DST to investigate Odessa. I have a gut feeling that somehow that's going to wind up biting you in the ass. And if your ass gets bitten, so does mine."

"You want me to try to get out of that?"

"To coin a phrase, that cow is already out of the barn. But I want to hear everything that comes your way about that operation."

"Yes, sir."

"So long as you don't FUBAR anything that would necessitate your being relieved; the longer, in other words, everybody but you—correction: you, Hessinger, and Dunwiddie—believes you to be the chief, DCI-Europe, the better. So conduct yourself accordingly, Captain Cronley."

"Yes, sir. Sir, you didn't mention Gehlen."

"An inadvertent omission. Gehlen knows. But let's keep him in the dark a little. He's smarter than both of us, but I don't think he should be the tail wagging our dog. And unless we're very careful, that's what'll happen. That which-tail-should-wag-whose-dog analogy, by the way, came from the admiral, via Schultz."

"Yes, sir."

"Anything else?"

"Can't think of anything, sir."

"Then go to bed, Captain Cronley."

XI

The olive-drab Stinson L-5, which had large "Circle C" Constabulary insignia painted on the engine nacelle, came in very low and very slow and touched down no more than fifty feet from the end of the runway. The pilot then quickly got the tail wheel on the ground and braked hard. The airplane stopped.

The pilot, Captain James D. Cronley Jr., looked over his shoulder at his instructor pilot, Lieutenant Colonel William W. Wilson, and inquired, "Again?"

"If you went around again, could you improve on that landing?"

"I don't think I could."

"Neither do I. Actually, that wasn't too bad for someone who isn't even an Army aviator."

Cronley didn't reply.

"How many tries is that?" Williams said.

"I've lost count."

"Well, whatever the number, I think I have put my life

at enormous risk sufficiently for one day. Call the tower and get taxi instructions to Hangar Three."

Cronley did so.

When he had finished talking to the tower, and they were approaching Hangar Three, Lieutenant Colonel Wilson said, "I didn't hear the proper response, which would have been, 'Yes, sir,' when I told you to call the tower."

"Sorry."

"And the proper response to my last observation should have been, 'Sorry, sir. No excuse, sir.'"

"With all possible respect, go fuck yourself, Colonel, sir."

Wilson laughed delightedly.

"I wondered how long it would take before you said something like that," he said. "Your patience with your IP during this phase of your training has been both commendable and unexpected."

Cronley, smiling, shook his head and said, "Jesus Christ!"

Wilson asked innocently, "Yes, my son?"

A sergeant wanded them to a parking space on the tarmac between another L-5 and a Piper L-4.

They got out of the Stinson. Wilson watched as Cronley put wheel chocks in place and tied it down.

"Now comes the hard part," Wilson said. "Making decisions. Deciding what to do is always harder than actually doing it."

He waved Cronley toward a small door in the left of Hanger Three's large sliding doors.

Inside, as Cronley expected them to be, were both of what he thought of as "his Storchs." They had been flown from

Kloster Grünau, with a stop in Munich, to Sonthofen that morning by Kurt Schröder and Max Ostrowski.

They were being painted. Perhaps more accurately, "unpainted." Wilson had told him what was planned for the aircraft: Since it might be decided—Wilson had emphasized "might"—to use the Storchs to pick up Likharev's family in East Germany, the planes would have to go in "black," which meant all markings that could connect the planes with the U.S. government would have to be removed.

That would have to be done now. There would not be time for the process if they waited for a decision about which airplanes would be used.

This meant the XXIIIrd CIC identification Cronley had painted on the vertical stabilizer after he'd gotten the planes from Wilson had to be removed—not painted over. Similarly, so did the Constabulary insignia Wilson had painted over when he gave the planes to Cronley. And the Star and Bar insignia of a U.S. military aircraft painted on the fuselage had to go, too. Removed, not overpainted. And when that was done, both would have to be painted non-glossy black.

When Cronley stepped into the hangar through the small door, Schröder and Ostrowski were sitting, Ostrowski backwards, on folding metal chairs watching soldier mechanics spray-painting the vertical stabilizer on one of the Storchs.

When Cronley started for them, Wilson touched his arm and pointed toward the hangar office.

"Our little chat first. You can chat with them later."

Cronley was surprised when he entered Wilson's office to see Major Harold Wallace and former Oberst Ludwig Mannberg. Wallace was standing next to a corkboard to which an aerial chart, a standard Corps of Engineers map, and a great many aerial photos were pinned. Mannberg was sitting at Wilson's desk.

Wilson was apparently as surprised to see them as Cronley was.

"To what do I owe this unexpected pleasure?" Wilson asked.

Wallace gestured at the corkboard.

"I decided the best place to do this was here."

"How'd you get here?"

"You see that C-45 parked on the tarmac?"

"Yes, I saw it."

"I wouldn't want this to get around, but I have friends in the Air Corps," Wallace said. "I borrowed that."

"The Air Corps loaned you a C-45?"

"I thought we might need one."

"Which means two Air Corps pilots get to know a lot more than I'm comfortable with?" Wilson said. "Or at the very least will ask questions we can't have them asking."

"Oddly enough, Colonel," Wallace said, "those thoughts occurred to me, too. So as soon as we landed here . . ."

He sounds like a colonel dealing with a lieutenant colonel who has annoyed him.

". . . I loaded the C-45 pilots into two of your puddle jumpers and had them flown back to Fürstenfeldbruck. You can fly C-45s, right?"

Wilson nodded.

"So can I," Cronley blurted.

Wallace looked at him.

"I find that very interesting. If true, it may solve one of our problems. But first things first. How did he do in flight school?"

"He's almost as good a pilot as he thinks he is."

"In other words, in your professional judgment, he could safely land an L-5—or an L-4 or one of those newly painted airplanes out there in the hangar—on some remote field or back road in Thuringia, load someone who probably won't want to go flying aboard, and take off again?"

"Yes, he could," Wilson said.

"I'm really sorry to hear that," Wallace said. "It would have been better if I could have told him, 'Sorry, you flunked flight school. I can't let you risk getting either Mrs. Likharev or the kiddies killed.'"

"If I didn't think I could do it, I wouldn't insist on flying one of the Storchs," Cronley said.

"You wouldn't *insist*, Captain Cronley?" Wallace asked sarcastically.

I am being put in my place.

In a normal situation, he would be right, and I would be wrong.

But whatever this situation is, it's not normal.

In this Through-the-Looking-Glass world, allowing myself to be put in my place—just do what you're told, Cronley—would be dereliction of duty.

"Yes, sir. Sir, while I really appreciate the assistance and expert advice you and Colonel Wilson are giving me, the last I heard, I was still chief, DCI-Europe, and the decisions to do, or not do, something are mine to make."

"You've considered, I'm sure, that you could be relieved as chief, DCI-Europe?" Wallace asked icily.

"I think of that all the time, sir. As I'm sure you do. But, until that happens . . ."

"I realize you don't have much time in the Army, Captain, but certainly somewhere along the way the term 'insubordinate' must have come to your attention."

"Yes, sir. I know what it means. Willful disobedience of a superior officer. My immediate superior officer is the director of the Directorate of Central Intelligence, Admiral Souers. Isn't that your understanding of my situation?"

Wallace glowered at him for a long fifteen seconds.

"We are now going to change the subject," he said finally. "Which is not, as I am sure both you and Colonel Wilson understand, the same thing as dropping the subject. We will return to it in due course."

Wallace looked at him expectantly.

He's waiting for me to say, "Yes, sir."

But since I have just challenged his authority to give me orders, I can't do that.

So what do I do?

His mouth went on automatic.

"Sure. Why not?" he said.

Cronley saw Wallace's face tighten, but he didn't respond directly.

But he will eventually.

"Why are you so determined to use the Storchs?" Wallace asked.

"Why don't you think it's a good idea?"

"Okay. Worst-case scenario. Assuming you are flying an L-4 or an L-5. You land but can't, for any one of a dozen reasons that pop into my mind, take off. There you are with a dozen Mongolians aiming their PPShs at you. Getting the picture?"

"What's a—what you said?"

"A Russian submachine gun. The Pistolet Pulyemet Shpagin. It comes with a seventy-five-round drum magazine."

"Okay. What was the question?"

"They are probably going to ask what you are doing on that back road. My theory is that it would be best to be naïve and innocent. I suggest you would look far more naïve and innocent if you were wearing ODs, with second lieutenant's gold bars on your epaulets and flying a Piper or a Stinson than you would wearing anything and flying a Storch with no markings.

"You could say you were a liaison pilot with the Fourteenth Constabulary Regiment in Fritzlar, flying from there to, say, Wetzlar, and got lost and then had engine trouble and had to land."

Cronley didn't reply.

After a moment, Wallace said, "Please feel free to comment on my worst-case scenario."

"You mean I can ask why it didn't mention Mrs. Likharev and the boys? I thought they were the sole reason for this exercise. Where are they in your scenario when the Russians are aiming their PP-whatevers at me?"

"You insolent sonofabitch, you!" Wallace flared, and immediately added: "Sorry. You pushed me over the edge."

Cronley didn't reply.

"Okay, smart-ass. Let's hear your scenario. Your best-case scenario," Wallace said.

"Okay. We—Ostrowski, Schröder, me, both Storchs, and a couple of ASA radio guys—are in a hangar in Fritzlar. If they don't have a hangar, we'll build one like the one we built at Kloster Grünau, out of tents. We're hiding the Storchs, is the idea.

"We hear from Seven-K, who tells us at which of the possible pickup points she and the Likharevs will be and when. We tell her, 'Okay.'

"Ostrowski and I get in one Storch, Schröder in the other. We fly across the border, pick up Mrs. Likharev and the boys, and bring them back to Fritzlar. I haven't quite figured out how to get them from Fritzlar to Rhine-Main yet. Maybe in that C-45 you borrowed from the Air Force."

"And where in your best-case scenario are the Russians with the PPShs in my worst-case scenario?" Wallace asked, softly but sarcastically.

"We are going to be in and out so fast that unless they're following Seven-K down those remote roads, the Russians probably won't even know we were there."

"Isn't that wishful thinking?" Wallace asked.

"What was it Patton said, 'Do not take counsel of your fears'?"

"He also said," Oberst Mannberg interjected, "'In war, nothing is impossible provided you use audacity.'"

"Now that we understand the military philosophy behind this operation," Wallace snapped, "let's talk specifics. Starting with why the Storchs?"

"It's a much better airplane than either the L-4 or the L-5."

"And you feel qualified to fly one of them onto what's almost sure to be a snow-covered and/or icy back road? Or onto a snow-covered field?"

"Well, Schröder has a lot of experience doing just that.

I think Colonel Mannberg will vouch for that. And I have a little experience doing that myself."

"The snow-covered pastures around Midland, Texas?" Wallace challenged.

"I never flew a Storch in the States," Cronley said. "But I did fly one off of and onto the ice around the mouth of the Magellan Strait in Patagonia. Trust me, there is more snow and ice there than there is anywhere in Texas or Germany."

"You flew a Storch down to the mouth of the Strait of Magellan?" Wallace asked dubiously.

"No. Actually I flew a Lockheed Lodestar down there. I flew Cletus's Storch *while* I was down there. I also flew a Piper Cub when I was down there." He paused and looked at Wallace. "Look, Colonel Wilson told you I'm competent to fly this mission. Isn't that enough?"

"I'll decide what's—"

"Jim," Mannberg interrupted, "you said, I think, that you and Ostrowski would fly in one Storch?"

It was a bona fide question, but everyone understood it served to prevent another angry exchange between Cronley and Wallace.

Cronley looked at Wallace.

"Answer the man," Wallace said.

"We land. Me first," Cronley said. "Ostrowski gets out and goes to Seven-K, or whoever is with Mrs. Likharev and the boys. He says, 'Mrs. Likharev, we'll have you over the border—'"

"Ostrowski speaks Russian?" Wallace challenged.

"He does, and better than Schröder," Cronley said. "Let me finish. Ostrowski says, 'Mrs. Likharev, we'll have you and the boys over the border in just a few minutes. And the way we're going to do that is put you and him'—he points to the smaller boy—'in that airplane'—pointing to the Storch Schröder has by now landed—'and I will take this one in that airplane'—he points to the Storch I'm flying.

"He leads Mrs. Likharev to Schröder's Storch . . ."

"What if she doesn't want to go? What if she's hysterical? What if Seven-K has already tranquilized her?" Wallace challenged.

". . . where Schröder says, in Russian, with a big smile, 'Hi! Let's go flying.' They get in Schröder's plane and he takes off. Ostrowski and the older boy get in my airplane, and I take off," Cronley finished.

"What if she doesn't want to go? What if she's hysterical? What if Seven-K has already tranquilized her?" Wallace repeated.

"I thought you wanted my *best*-case scenario?" Cronley replied, and then went on before Wallace could reply. "But, okay. Let's say she's been tranquilized—let's say they've all been tranquilized—then no problem getting them into the planes. If she's hysterical, then Ostrowski tranquilizes her, and the boys, too, if necessary."

"And how are you going to get all of them into the planes?"

"The boys are small."

"How do you know that?"

"Because when Tiny and I were working on Likharev, he told us his son was too young to get in the Young Pioneers. That makes him less than twelve."

"There are two boys . . ."

"If one of them was old enough to be a Young Pioneer, he would have said so. That makes both of the boys less than twelve." He paused, then added: "Feel free to shoot holes in my scenario."

Wallace looked as if he was about to reply, but before he could, Mannberg said, "Not a hole, but an observation: When we were doing this sort of thing in the East, whenever possible, we tried to arrange some sort of diversion."

Wallace looked at him for a moment, considered that, but did not respond. Instead he said, "Tell me about you being able to fly a C-45."

"My father has one," Cronley said. "I've never been in a C-45, but I'm told it's a Beech D-18. What they call a 'Twin Beech.'"

"And Daddy let you fly his airplane?"

"Daddy did."

"How often?"

"The last I looked, often enough to give me about three hundred hours in one."

"You are *licensed* to fly this type of aircraft?" Wallace asked dubiously.

Cronley felt anger well up within him, but controlled it.

"I've got a commercial ticket which allows me to fly Beech D-18 aircraft under instrument flight rules," Cronley said calmly.

"So why is it you're not an Army aviator?"

Cronley's anger flared, and his mouth went on automatic.

"I wanted to be an Army aviator, but my parents are married and that disqualified me."

As soon as the words were out of his mouth, he regretted them.

But the response he got from Army aviator Wilson was not what he expected.

Wilson smiled and shook his head, and said, "Harry, if his flying that C-45 is important, I can give him a quick check ride. To satisfy you. I'm willing to take his word. Actually, he has more time in the Twin Beech than I do."

"You're telling me, Cronley," Wallace said, "that if I told you to get in that C-45 and fly it to Fritzlar, you could do that?"

"I could, but I'd rather have the check ride Colonel Wilson offered first."

"Bill, how long would that take?"

"Thirty, forty minutes. No more than an hour."

"Do it," Wallace ordered. "I've got some phone calls to make."

"Now?"

"Now," Wallace said. "To coin a phrase, time is of the essence."

[TWO]
U.S. Air Force Base
Fritzlar, Hesse
American Zone of Occupation, Germany
1615 19 January 1946

"Fritzlar Army Airfield, Air Force Three Niner Niner, a C-45, at five thousand above Homberg, estimate ten miles south. Approach and landing, please," Cronley said into his microphone.

After a moment, there was a response.

"Air Force Three Niner Niner, this is Fritzlar U.S. Air Force Base. By any chance, are you calling me?"

"Shit," Cronley said, and then pressed the TALK button. "Fritzlar, Niner Niner, affirmative. Approach and landing, please."

When he had received and acknowledged approach and landing instructions, Cronley replaced the microphone in the clip holder on the yoke.

Captain C. L. Dunwiddie, who was sitting in the copilot's seat, asked, "Why do I suspect your best-laid plans have gone agley?"

"I thought this was going to be a Constabulary landing strip. It's an Air Force base, and I think the Air Force is going to wonder what two cavalry officers are doing with one of their airplanes."

"Fritzlar, Three Niner Niner on the ground at fifteen past the hour. Close me out, please."

"Niner Niner, you are closed out. Take Taxiway Three Left and hold in position. You will be met."

"Niner Niner, Roger," Cronley said, and then turned to Tiny and pointed out the window. "Not only an Air Force base, but a big one."

There were three very large hangars, a control tower atop a base operations building, and other buildings. Too many to count, but at least twenty P-47 "Thunderbolt" fighters were on the tarmac or in one of the hangars.

"And one that seems to have avoided the war," Dunwiddie said. "I don't see any signs of damage—bomb or any other kind—at all."

"Here comes the welcoming committee," Cronley said, pointing at a jeep headed toward them down the taxiway.

The jeep drove right up to the nose of the C-45.

An Air Force major, who was wearing pilot's wings and

had an AOD brassard on his arm, stood up in the jeep, pointed to the left engine, and then made a slashing motion across his throat, telling Cronley to shut down that engine. He then made gestures mimicking the opening of a door.

Cronley gave him a thumbs-up and started to shut down the left engine.

The jeep turned and drove around the left wing, obviously headed for the C-45's fuselage door.

"I don't suppose you know how to open the door?" Cronley asked Dunwiddie.

Dunwiddie got out of his seat and headed toward the door.

"Welcome to Fritzlar, Captain," the Air Force major said, as he stepped into the cockpit.

Well, if he's seen the railroad tracks, he's seen the cavalry sabers. And the blank spot on my tunic where pilot's wings are supposed to go.

Now what?

"Thank you," Cronley said.

"The word we got is to get you out of sight. And the way we're going to do that is have you taxi to the center one of those hangars"—he pointed to the row of three large hangars—"where we will push you inside, and where your people are waiting for you."

"Your people"? Who does he mean?

"Fine," Cronley said. "Actually, we don't care who sees the C-45. But very early tomorrow morning there will be two Storchs we really don't want anybody to see."

"We'll be ready for them," the Air Force major said.

Cronley advanced the throttle and began to taxi.

"I'm not supposed to ask questions . . ." the major said.

"But?"

"You just said 'Storchs,' didn't you?"

Cronley nodded.

"That funny-looking German light airplane?"

"There are those of us who love that funny-looking German light airplane."

"I've never actually seen one."

"Well, you'll have your chance in the morning. And I'll bet you could play I'll-show-you-mine-if-you-show-me-yours with the pilot of one of them. He used to fly Spitfires for the Free Polish Air Force, and I know he'd like a good look at one of those P-47s."

"Great!" the major said.

"Just don't talk about them being here to anybody, okay?"

"The word I got was 'Just give them what they ask for and don't ask questions.'"

"Major, I didn't hear you ask any questions."

"That's right. And I really wondered about the guys in the back."

"They're Special Service soldiers. We're going to put on a soldier show for the Constabulary troopers."

"The hell you are!"

"They sing gospel songs. You know, like 'What a Friend We Have in Jesus,' 'When the Roll Is Called Up Yonder,' songs like that."

"That's why they need those Thompson submachine guns, right? 'Repent, or else?'"

"No. They're for use on Air Force officers who can't resist the temptation to go in the O Club and say, 'Guys, you won't believe what just flew in here.'"

"My lips are sealed," the major said, and then added, "really."

"Good," Cronley said.

A dozen or so Air Force mechanics in coveralls were waiting in front of the hangar. One of them, a tough-looking master sergeant, signaled for Cronley to cut his engine.

Cronley did so, and as soon as the propellers stopped turning, the men started to push the C-45 tailfirst into the hangar.

"I'll need this thing fueled," Cronley said to the Air Force major.

"Consider it done. When are you leaving?"

"I'm usually the last person they tell things like that. But I was a Boy Scout and like to be prepared."

Once they were inside the hangar, it seemed even larger than it did from the tarmac. Cronley saw three jeeps and two three-quarter-ton trucks lined up, all bearing Constabulary insignia. He asked the two questions on his mind:

"How come this place is intact? What did the Germans use it for?"

"The story I heard is that the Krauts used it to train night fighters, and to convert airplanes to night fighters. They ran out of material to convert airplanes, and then they ran out of fuel for the night fighter trainer planes they had. How it avoided being bombed—or even strafed—I don't know. Maybe, when our guys flew over it, there were no planes on the ground, so they looked elsewhere for something to shoot up. That's what I would have done. What's the point in shooting up a hangar when you can shoot up planes on the ground? Or locomotives? When you shoot up a locomotive, that's something. You get a great big cloud of escaping steam."

"Sounds like fun."

"It was, except when they were shooting back. And sometimes they did."

"The Constabulary is here on the airfield?"

"Yeah. The airbase and the *kaserne* are one and the same thing."

They were now well inside the hangar. The left of the double doors closed, and the closing right door stopped, leaving a ten-foot opening.

So those Constabulary vehicles can get out, obviously.

The C-45 stopped moving.

The Air Force major rose from the copilot's seat and stood in the opening to the passenger section. Cronley remained seated until he saw the major stepping into the passenger section, and then he stood up.

When he looked down the aisle, he saw that Tiny and Tiny's Troopers and one of the two ASA sergeants had already gotten off the airplane. As soon as the second ASA sergeant had gone through the door, the Air Force major went through it.

Cronley looked out the door and saw there were maybe twenty Constabulary troopers in formation facing the aircraft. They wore glistening helmet liners, white parkas, and highly polished leather Sam Browne belts, and were carrying Thompson submachine guns slung over their shoulders.

He turned and went down the stair doors backwards.

Someone bellowed, "Ah-ten-hut!"

Oh, shit, some senior officer, maybe the Eleventh regimental commander, is here. That explains all the troopers lined up.

We're not the only people in this hangar.

Cronley turned from the stair doors for a look.

A massive Constabulary officer—almost as large as Tiny—marched up to Cronley, came to attention, and raised his hand crisply in salute. Cronley saw a second lieutenant's bar glistening on the front of his helmet liner.

"Sir," the second lieutenant barked, "welcome to the Eleventh Constabulary Regiment!"

Mutual recognition came simultaneously.

"Jimmy?" the second lieutenant inquired incredulously.

I'll be goddamned, Cronley thought, but did not say aloud, *that's Bonehead Moriarty!*

Second Lieutenant Bruce T. Moriarty and Captain James D. Cronley Jr. were not only close friends but alumni and 1945 classmates of the Agricultural and Mechanical College of Texas, more popularly known as Texas A&M.

At College Station, Moriarty had experienced difficulty in his first month having his hair cut to the satisfaction of upperclassmen. He had solved the problem by shaving his skull, hence the sobriquet "Bonehead."

Captain C. L. Dunwiddie, who would have been Norwich '45 had he not dropped out so as not to miss actively participating in World War II, and who was standing in front of the line of eight of his troopers, saw the interchange between the Constab Second John and Cronley and had a perhaps Pavlovian response.

"Lieutenant!" he boomed.

He caught Lieutenant Moriarty's attention. When he saw that the command had come from Captain Dunwiddie and that the captain was beckoning to him with his index finger, he performed a right turn movement and marched over to him, wondering as he did, *Who the hell is he? I'm six-three-and-a-half and 255, and he's a lot bigger than me.*

Bonehead came to attention before Tiny, saluted, and inquired, "Yes, sir?"

"Listen to me carefully, Lieutenant," Captain Dunwiddie said to Second Lieutenant Moriarty. "You do not know Captain Cronley. You have never seen him ever before in your life. Any questions?"

"No, sir."

"Carry on, Lieutenant."

"Yes, sir."

Lieutenant Moriarty saluted. Captain Dunwiddie returned it. Lieutenant Moriarty did a precise about-face movement, and then marched back to Captain Cronley, where he executed a precise left turn movement.

"Sir, Colonel Fishburn's compliments. The colonel would be pleased to receive you, sir, at your earliest convenience. I have a jeep for you, sir. And men to guard your aircraft."

"Captain Dunwiddie and I also have men to guard my airplane," Cronley said. "And two other non-coms who'll need a place to sleep. I suggest we leave that for later, while Captain Dunwiddie and I make our manners to Colonel Fishburn. I presume Captain Dunwiddie is included in the colonel's invitation?"

"Yes, sir, I'm sure he is."

"Well, then, I suggest you leave one of your sergeants in charge of your men, I'll leave one of my sergeants in charge of mine, and we'll go see Colonel Fishburn."

"Yes, sir."

"Captain, can I have a word?"

Cronley turned and saw that he was being addressed by Technical Sergeant Jerry Mitchell of the ASA.

Mitchell, a lanky Kansan, was the senior of the ASA non-coms Major "Iron Lung" McClung had loaned to DCI-Europe.

"Anytime, Jerry."

"Did you see that control tower, or whatever it is?"

He pointed upward and to the rear of the hangar.

There was a control-tower-like four-story structure attached to the rear of Hangar Two. There was a second, free-standing six-story structure, painted in a yellow-and-black checkerboard pattern and bristling with antennae, across the field.

"Yes, I did."

"It looks like they have two," Mitchell said.

"Yeah. And you would like to use this one, right?"

"Yes, sir."

"Bonehead, who would we have to see to use the building in the back of the hangar? We need it for our radios."

"You'd have to ask the post engineer."

"What about Colonel Fishburn? Could he give us permission to use it?"

"Of course, but you're supposed to go through channels."

"Mitch, the building is yours," Cronley said to Sergeant Mitchell. Then he turned to Lieutenant Moriarty. "Take me to your leader, Bonehead."

[THREE]
Office of the Regimental Commander
11th Constabulary Regiment
U.S. Air Force Base, Fritzlar, Hesse
American Zone of Occupation, Germany
1705 19 January 1946

"Sir, the officers Lieutenant Moriarty met at the airport are here," the sergeant major said.

"Send them in, Sergeant Major," a deep voice called.

The sergeant major gestured to Cronley and Dunwiddie to pass through the colonel's portal. Cronley gestured to Lieutenant Moriarty to come along.

Cronley and Dunwiddie marched through the door, stopped, and came to attention six feet from the colonel's desk. Moriarty stopped behind Dunwiddie.

Cronley raised his hand in salute.

"Sir, Captains Cronley, J. D., and Dunwiddie, C. L., at your orders."

Colonel Richard L. Fishburn, Cavalry, a tall, lean, sharp-featured man, returned the salute crisply.

"You may stand at ease, gentlemen," he said, then went on, "Very nice, but I don't think that courteous 'at your orders' statement is accurate." He paused, then went on again: "I saw you on the train when you made your manners to General White. Correct?"

"Yes, sir."

"I have received my orders vis-à-vis your visit from General White," Colonel Fishburn said. "Not directly. Via Lieutenant Colonel Wilson. Who, while not a cavalryman, is at least a West Pointer, and therefore most likely would not say he was speaking for the general, if that were not the case. Wouldn't you agree?"

Dunwiddie and Cronley said, "Yes, sir," in chorus.

"I have a number of questions, but the orders I have are to provide you whatever you need and not ask questions of you. Colonel Wilson told me he will explain everything to me personally when he honors the regiment with his presence first thing in the morning. So, gentleman, what can I do for you between now and then?"

"Sir, we brought ten men with us," Cronley said. "They will need quarters."

"Not a problem. Lieutenant Moriarty, take care of that."

"Yes, sir."

"And, sir, we need a secure place where our radiomen can set up their equipment and erect an antenna. There's a sort of second control tower attached to Hangar Two that I'd like to use."

"That, of course, makes me wonder why you brought your own communications, but of course I can't ask. Moriarty, is letting these people use that building going to pose a problem?"

"No, sir."

"And I presume you would be pleased to ensure these gentlemen are fed and are given someplace to rest their weary heads tonight?"

"Yes, sir."

"Well, that would seem to cover everything. Unless you have something?"

"No, sir," Cronley and Dunwiddie said in chorus.

Colonel Fishburn looked at Cronley as if he expected him to say something.

After a moment, Cronley realized what Colonel Fishburn expected.

He raised his hand in salute.

"Permission to withdraw, sir?"

"Granted," Colonel Fishburn said, returning the salute.

"Atten-hut," Cronley ordered. "About-face. Forward, march."

Captain Dunwiddie and Lieutenant Moriarty obeyed the orders and the three officers marched out of the regimental commander's office.

The jeeps that had carried them from the hangar were waiting at the curb outside the headquarters building. Their drivers came to attention when they saw Cronley, Dunwiddie, and Moriarty come out of the building.

Cronley put his hand on Moriarty's arm when they were halfway between the building and the jeeps.

"Hold it a minute, Bonehead," he said.

"Can I infer now you know me?" Moriarty said.

"How could I ever forget you?"

"Are you going to tell me what the hell's going on?"

"If you have a bottle of decent whisky in your BOQ, I'll tell you what I can. And if you don't have a bottle of decent whisky, why don't we stop at the Class VI store on our way to your BOQ?"

Moriarty, after an awkward pause, said, "I don't have a BOQ, Jim."

"So where do you sleep?"

"Ginger and I are in Dependent Quarters."

After another awkward pause, Cronley replied, "That's right. You married Ginger, didn't you?"

"You were there, Jimmy. All dressed up in your brand-new second lieutenant's uniform, holding a saber over us as we came out of the chapel."

And if I wasn't the world's champion dumb fuck, that's what I should have done, married the Squirt the day after I graduated.

The Squirt was one of Ginger's bridesmaids, but I didn't pay any attention to her. I wanted to—and did—jump the bones of another bridesmaid, a blond from Hobbs whose name I can't even remember now. Probably couldn't remember the next day.

And look where I am now!

"I don't think my seeing Ginger—or Ginger seeing me—right now is a good idea, Bonehead."

"She knows I went to the airport to meet some big shot," Moriarty said. "She'll ask me how that went. And I don't lie to Ginger."

"Can she keep her mouth shut?"

"Fuck you!"

"Bonehead, what we're doing here is classified Top Secret–Presidential," Cronley said.

Moriarty looked at him for a long five seconds.

"So what do I tell my wife, Captain Cronley, sir?"

"Jim, I suggest you go see Mrs. Moriarty and play that by ear," Dunwiddie said.

"You work for him, Captain? I thought it was the other way around," Moriarty said to Dunwiddie.

"I work for him, Lieutenant."

"Why don't we all go make our manners to Mrs. Moriarty?" Cronley asked.

[FOUR]
Officer Dependent Quarters O-112
11th Constabulary Regiment
U.S. Air Force Base, Fritzlar, Hesse
American Zone of Occupation, Germany
1725 19 January 1946

Mrs. Virginia "Ginger" Adams Moriarty was redheaded, freckled, twenty-two years old, and conspicuously pregnant.

"Well, I'll be!" she greeted Cronley. "Look what the cat dragged in! I guess you're with the big shot Bruce met. Hey! What's with the captain's bars?"

A moment later, having seen the look on Cronley's face, she said, "Why don't we all pretend I didn't say what I just said. Let me start all over." She then did so: "Jim, what a pleasant surprise."

"Hey, Ginger."

"I think you know how devastated Bruce and I were when we heard about Marjie."

"Thank you. Ginger, this is Chauncey Dunwiddie, who is both my executive officer and my best friend."

"My friends, for reasons I can't imagine, Mrs. Moriarty, call me 'Tiny.' I hope you will."

"Welcome to our humble abode, Captain Tiny."

"Thank you. Mrs. Moriarty, I'd like to show—"

"If you want me to call you 'Captain Tiny,' you're going to have to call me 'Ginger.'"

"Deal. Ginger, I'd like to show you something."

"Will that hold until I give you something to cut the dust of the trail?"

"I'm afraid not," Tiny said, and extended his DCI credentials to her.

She studied them carefully.

"Wow!" she said. "Have you got one of these, Jim?"

"He does," Dunwiddie said, and put out his hand for the credentials.

"Tiny," Cronley said, and when Dunwiddie looked at him, he pointed to Moriarty.

Dunwiddie handed the credentials to Moriarty.

"Jesus!" Bonehead said, after he had examined them.

"Don't blaspheme," Ginger said.

"Sorry," he said.

"Well, Marjie always said Jimmy was going to be somebody special," Ginger said, and then added, "I guess I can't ask what's going on."

"You want to tell them, Jim, or should I?" Tiny asked.

Cronley pointed at Dunwiddie, mostly because his mind was flooded with images of the Squirt and he didn't trust himself to speak.

"Ginger, Bonehead, what I'm about to tell you is classified Top Secret–Presidential. And even if we succeed in doing what we're here to try doing, you are to tell no one at any time anything about it. Understood?"

Both nodded.

"In the next couple of days, we're going to try to pick up a woman, a Russian woman, and her two sons in Thuringia and bring them back across the border."

"Can I ask why?" Moriarty asked.

"I'm sorry, I don't think you have the need to know that. But I will tell you that it's important. Not just a mercy mission."

"Got it," Bonehead said.

"I understand," Ginger said.

"The only reason I've told you this much is so you won't go around asking questions. Any questions you would ask would attract attention to us. And we don't want to attract any attention at all. Understand?"

"Got it," Bonehead said again.

"I understand," Ginger said. "The rumors are already starting."

"What rumors are those?" Cronley asked.

"That you're the advance party for a secret—or at least not yet announced—visit by General White."

"Where'd you hear that?"

"This afternoon—fifteen minutes ago. In the checkout line at the commissary."

Cronley made a *Give me more* gesture with his hands.

"Well, one of the girls—one of the officers' wives—said that she had heard from a friend of hers in Sonthofen . . . you know what I mean?"

"I was there earlier today," Cronley said.

"Constabulary Headquarters," Ginger went on. "Anyway, the girl in line said she had heard from a friend of hers, whose husband is also a Constab officer, that they were preparing General White's train . . . You know he has a private train?"

"Colonel Fishburn said he saw them on the general's private train," Bonehead furnished.

"You do get around, don't you, Jimmy? Marjie would be so proud of you!"

"Ginger, do me a favor. Stop talking about the . . . Marjie. It's painful."

"Sorry," she said, and then considered what she had said, and went on, "Jimmy, I didn't think. I'm really sorry."

"It's okay, Ginger. Now what was the rumor in the commissary checkout line?"

"Well, she said her friend told her her husband had told her that they were getting General White's train ready for a secret—no, she said, 'unannounced'—for an *unannounced* visit to the Constab units up here. You know, Hersfeld, Wetzlar, Fulda, Kassel, and of course here. And then another lady said, 'He's coming here first. They already flew in the advance party. Just now. Special radios and everything.'"

"Jesus Christ!" Cronley said, shaking his head.

"Jimmy, you're as bad as Bruce. Please don't blaspheme. It's a sin."

"The OLIN is incredible if not always infallible, Jim," Tiny said. "I know. I grew up in it."

"The what?"

"The Officers' Ladies Intelligence Network."

"Well, is he, Jimmy? Is General White coming here?" Ginger asked.

"I have no idea, but having people think we're part of his advance party is even better than having them think we're a soldier show, which is what I told that Air Force officer."

"And even better than having them think we're from the 711th Mobile Kitchen Renovation Company," Tiny said, chuckling. "Ginger, did I hear you say something about something to cut the dust of the trail?"

"Why don't we go in the living room?" Ginger suggested.

There were a number of framed photographs on a side

table in the living room, including one of the Adams-Moriarty wedding party.

"Tiny," Cronley said softly, and when Dunwiddie looked at him, pointed at it.

When Dunwiddie took a closer look, Cronley said, "Second from the left. The late Mrs. James D. Cronley."

"Nice-looking," Tiny said.

"Yeah," Cronley said.

"You never showed me a picture of her."

"I never had one."

Ginger, as she handed them drinks, saw they were looking at the picture.

"Are you married, Captain Tiny?"

"No, ma'am."

"What is it they say, 'Lieutenants should not marry, captains may, and majors must'?"

"My mother told me that," Tiny said. "As a matter of fact, keeps telling me that."

"You're from an Army family?"

"Yes, ma'am."

"Oh, is he from an Army family," Cronley said. "Not only did his grandfather, First Sergeant Dunwiddie of the legendary Tenth U.S. Cavalry Regiment, beat Teddy Roosevelt's Rough Riders up San Juan Hill in the Spanish-American War, but his father, Colonel Dunwiddie, is a 1920 classmate of General White's at Norwich."

"Really?" Ginger asked.

"That's what he was doing on General White's train. Making his manners to his godfather."

"General White is your godfather?" Ginger asked incredulously.

"Yes, ma'am, he is," Tiny said, and glowered at Cronley.

"I would rather have that truth circulating among the ladies at the commissary checkout line than have them wonder what we were doing on the train," Cronley said.

Dunwiddie considered that for a moment, and then, grudgingly, said, "Okay, blabbermouth, point well taken."

"You mean I can tell the girls?"

"Only if the subject comes up, Ginger," Cronley said. "If, and only if, the subject comes up, then and only then, you can say, 'What I heard, girls, is that Captain Dunwiddie is General White's godson.' Okay, Ginger?"

"Got it," she said.

"And now, before we accept Captain Dunwiddie's kind offer to dine with him, at his expense, at the O Club, what else should we talk about?"

Bonehead took the question literally.

"A couple of weeks ago, we had a meeting of Aggies in Kassel. One of them was a classmate of your pal Cletus Frade, before Frade dropped out, I mean. He said he heard he became an ace with the Marines on Guadalcanal early in the war. But that was the last he heard. Did he come through the war all right, Jimmy, do you know?"

"I was about to say," Cronley said, "that it's a small world, isn't it?"

"And I was about to say the trouble with letting one worm out of the can is then the rest want out," Dunwiddie said.

"I don't understand," Ginger said.

"This doesn't get spread among the ladies in the checkout line or anywhere else, okay?"

"Understood."

"Colonel Cletus Frade, Navy Cross, United States Marine Corps . . ."

"He got to be a colonel?" Bonehead asked incredulously.

"A full-bull fire-breathing colonel," Cronley confirmed. "He spent most of the war running the OSS in Argentina. In his spare time, he got married—to a stunning Anglo-Argentine blond named Dorotea—and sired two sons. And one day, when he was visiting Germany . . ." He stopped in midsentence. "The look on Captain Dunwiddie's face tells me he's wondering why I'm telling you all this."

"You're very perceptive," Dunwiddie said.

"I have my reasons," Cronley said. "So let me go off on a tangent for a moment. Bonehead, what kind of a security clearance do you have?"

"Top Secret. As of about a month, six weeks ago."

"I think I know where you're going," Dunwiddie said.

"You're very perceptive. Should I stop?"

"Go on."

"Captain Dunwiddie and I have need, Bonehead, of a white company-grade officer with a Top Secret security clearance to command Company C, 203rd Tank Destroyer Battalion, the enlisted men of which, some of whom you met today, are all of the African persuasion, and most of whom are as large as you are."

"Despite its name and distinguished heritage, Bonehead, Charley Company today has nothing to do with destroying tanks," Dunwiddie said.

"What it does these days is guard two classified installations we run in Bavaria," Cronley said.

"And also supervises Company 'A,' 7002nd Provisional

Security Organization, which is a quasi-military organization whose members are almost entirely Polish displaced persons, which also guards these two classified installations," Dunwiddie furnished. "Would you be interested in assuming that responsibility?"

"You said 'company.' Companies are commanded by captains."

"Not always. In olden times, when I was a second lieutenant, I had the honor of commanding Charley Company," Cronley said.

"If you're not pulling my leg about this, Jimmy, Colonel Fishburn would never let me go. We're short of officers as it is."

"Well, then," Dunwiddie said, "let me rephrase: Presuming Colonel Fishburn would let you go, would you like to command two hundred thirty–odd Black American soldiers and a like number of Polish DPs?" Dunwiddie asked.

"Sir, I just told you, Colonel Fishburn wouldn't let me go."

"You call him 'sir' and refer to me by my nickname? Outrageous!"

"Answer the question, Lieutenant," Dunwiddie said.

Bonehead considered the question a moment, then asked, "Is there a good hospital in Munich?"

"That's a question, not an answer, Bonehead," Cronley said. "Why is a hospital important to— Oh."

"The Ninety-eighth General Hospital in Munich, Lieutenant," Tiny said, "is one of the best in the U.S. Army. Apropos of nothing whatever, its obstetrical services are about the best to be found in Europe."

"No shit?" Bonehead asked.

"Bruce, you're not really thinking of going along with Jimmy, are you?"

"No shit, Bonehead," Cronley said. "It's a great hospital."

"Sweetheart . . ."

"The colonel would be furious if he even thought you're thinking of asking for a transfer."

"Then the both of you better be prepared to act really surprised when his orders come down," Cronley said.

"You're not going to ask Colonel Fishburn?" Ginger asked, but before Cronley could reply, she looked at Dunwiddie and asked, "Can he do that, Captain Tiny?"

"Yes, ma'am," Dunwiddie said. "He can."

"How soon?"

"Well, what we're here for shouldn't take more than three days. A couple of days to finish what we've started here. Say a week."

Presuming, of course, that I'm not strapped to a chair in an NKGB jail cell by then, watching them pull my toenails out with pliers.

Or pushing up daisies in an unmarked Thuringian grave.

Or a blackened corpse sitting in the burned-out fuselage of a crashed or shot-down Storch.

"You seem very confident about this, Jimmy," Ginger said.

"Ginger, that's why my men call me 'Captain Confidence.' Isn't that so, Captain Dunwiddie?"

Dunwiddie shook his head.

"Why don't we go to the O Club?" he suggested. "I saw a sign in the headquarters saying tonight is steak night."

"They import the steak from Norway," Ginger said, then

with great effort and some grunts, she pushed herself out of her chair.

[FIVE]
The Officers' Open Mess
11th Constabulary Regiment
Fritzlar, Hesse
American Zone of Occupation, Germany
1830 19 January 1946

Since all German restaurants and bars were off-limits, the officers of the 11th Constabulary Regiment had three choices for their evening meal: They could eat at home, or have a hamburger or a hot dog at the PX snack bar, or they could go to the officers' open mess. If they wanted a drink, or a beer, they had only their home or the O Club to choose between, as the PX did not serve intoxicants of any kind.

On special occasions, such as "Steak Night," the O Club was usually very crowded. When Cronley, Dunwiddie, and the Moriartys walked in, there was a crowd of people waiting to be seated.

Among them was a young woman who was just about as conspicuously in the family way as Mrs. Moriarty. When she saw Mrs. Moriarty, she went to her, called her by her first name, kissed the air near her cheek, and announced, "Tommy has a theory." She nodded in the direction of her husband. Cronley followed the nod and saw a rather slight lieutenant.

"Tommy says," the woman continued, "the way to get in here quickly is to tell the headwaiter you have a party of eight. Interested?"

Her meaning was clear to Ginger Moriarty. They should

merge parties. But then Ginger did the arithmetic. "But there's only six of us."

"Tell them we're expecting two more. We can't be responsible if they don't show up, can we?"

Cronley went from *Oh, shit, the last thing I need is to sit next to another mother-to-be* to quite the opposite reaction in a split second when he saw on Lieutenant Tommy's chest the silver wings of a liaison aviator.

"Go get the lieutenant, Bonehead," he ordered. "His wife is right. He has a great theory."

He went to the headwaiter and said, "We're a party of eight. Colonel and Mrs. Frade will join us later. When the colonel comes, will you send him and his lady to our table, please?"

"Yes, sir, of course. And which is your table, Captain?"

"I thought you'd tell me," Cronley replied. "Whichever table you've reserved for Colonel Frade. Maybe that empty one over there?"

"If you and your party will follow me, sir?"

"Tom, this is Captain Jim Cronley," Bonehead said, when they were all at the table. "We were at Texas A&M together. And this is Captain . . . I didn't get your first name, sir?"

"My friends call me, for reasons I can't imagine, 'Tiny,'" Dunwiddie said.

". . . Dunwiddie."

"How do you do, sir?" Lieutenant Thomas G. Winters said to Dunwiddie and then to Cronley.

"Why don't you sit across from me, Lieutenant?" Cronley said. "And we'll seat Mrs. Moriarty next to your wife?"

"Yes, sir," Lieutenant Winters said.

"That way she won't get in Captain Dunwiddie's way

when he reaches for the scotch bottle, which he will do again and again and probably again."

"Yes, sir."

"Where is the waiter?" Cronley asked. "Be advised, Lieutenant, that Captain Dunwiddie is picking up the tab tonight, so feel free to order anything."

"You seem to be in a very good mood," Dunwiddie said. "Ginger, how much did you give him to drink at your quarters?"

"Just that one," Ginger said.

The waiter appeared.

"You speak English, I hope?"

From the waiter's reply in English, it was clear he did not speak the language well.

"We'll start off with a bottle of Haig & Haig Pinch," he said in German. "And then bring us the menu."

"Jawohl, Herr Kapitän," the waiter said, and marched off.

"That's very kind of you, sir," Lieutenant Winters said. "But I'm not drinking."

"You don't drink?"

"Not tonight, sir. I'm flying in the morning."

"I thought the rule there was that you had to stop drinking eight hours before you flew."

"Sir, the Army rule is twelve hours before you fly."

Cronley looked at his watch.

"It's 1830," he said. "That means, if you took a drink now, you could take off tomorrow morning at, say, 0630 and still follow the rule. So what do you say?"

"Sir. Thank you, sir, but no thank you."

"You must take your flying very seriously."

"Yes, sir. I do."

"And exactly what kind of flying do you do?"

"Whatever I'm ordered to do, sir."

"Jimmy, what the hell are you up to?" Lieutenant Moriarty asked.

"Put a cork in it, Bonehead," Cronley said.

"Same question," Dunwiddie said. "Lieutenant, Captain Cronley is known for his unusual—some say sick—sense of humor. Don't take him seriously."

"Yes, sir," Winters said, visibly relieved.

"I'm dead serious right now," Cronley said. "Answer the question, Lieutenant. Exactly what kind of flying do you do?"

"Sir, I do whatever is expected of me as an Army aviator."

"Like flying the Hesse/Thuringia border?"

Winter's face tightened, but he did not reply.

"With a photographer in the backseat taking pictures of the picturesque Thuringian countryside?"

Winters stood up.

"The captain will understand that I am not at liberty to discuss the subject he mentions. The lieutenant begs the captain's permission to withdraw."

"Sit down, Lieutenant," Cronley ordered. When Winters remained standing, Cronley said, "That was not a suggestion."

Winters sat down.

"Clever fellow that I am, I suspected it was you the moment I saw the West Point ring. And, of course, the wings."

"Sir?"

"What the hell are you talking about, Jim?" Dunwiddie said, not at all pleasantly.

"You're an intelligence officer . . . and on that subject, show Lieutenant Winters your credentials. And that's not a suggestion, either."

"Jesus!" Tiny said, but handed Winters his credentials folder.

"You may show that to Mrs. Winters, Lieutenant, but you are cautioned not to tell anyone what you saw."

Mrs. Winters's eyes widened when she examined the credentials.

"Now, where were we?" Cronley asked rhetorically. "Oh, yeah. Tell me, Captain Dunwiddie, if you were a West Pointer, and a lieutenant colonel of artillery, and an aviator, and required the services of another aviator to fly a mission . . ."

"Along the border," Dunwiddie picked up. "That you didn't want anybody talking about . . ."

". . . wouldn't you turn first to another graduate of Hudson High who was also an artilleryman?"

Dunwiddie shook his head.

"I thought you were just being a pr— giving him a hard time."

"That thought never entered my mind," Cronley said. "Because if he turned out to be who I thought he was, I wanted to be very nice to him, because first thing tomorrow morning he's going to take me border-flying again. I want to see what he saw and photographed."

"Sir, I couldn't do that without authorization," Winters said.

"Did Colonel Fishburn authorize the flights you already made?"

"No, sir. But—"

"A certain lieutenant colonel, whose name we shall not mention, told you it was all right, right?"

"Yes, sir."

"Did he tell you why we were interested in the fields and back roads of Thuringia?"

"Yes, sir. He said that somebody was going to land a light airplane . . ."

"I'm one of them," Cronley said. "Now, we can go to Colonel Fishburn, which you will note Hot—the unnamed lieutenant colonel . . . did not do . . . and show him our credentials, following which I'm sure he will tell you to take me flying down the border. But if we do that, his sergeant major will hear about it, and so will his wife, and all the girls in what Captain Dunwiddie calls the Officers' Ladies Intelligence Network . . . which would not be a good thing."

Lieutenant Winters looked at Cronley, expressionlessly, for twenty seconds.

Then he said, "Sir, if you'll tell me where you're staying, I'll pick you up at 0530, which will give us time for a cup of coffee and an egg sandwich before we take off at first light."

XII

"What the hell is that?" Lieutenant Thomas Winters, Artillery, inquired of Captain James D. Cronley as they taxied up to the hangar in the L-5.

"I believe it is a C-47, which is the military version of the Douglas DC-3. I'm surprised you don't know that."

There was indeed a C-47 sitting in front of Hangar Two. It had the Constabulary insignia on the nose, which surprised Cronley.

"I mean that funny-looking black airplane they're pushing into the hangar," Winters said, in exasperation.

"I don't see a funny-looking black airplane," Cronley replied. "Possibly because I know that funny-looking black airplanes like that are used only in classified operations I'm not supposed to talk about."

As Winters parked the L-5 and shut it down, a lieutenant wearing Constabulary insignia and aviator's wings walked up to it and saluted.

Cronley got out of the Stinson and returned the salute.

"Colonel Wilson's compliments, gentlemen," the

lieutenant announced. "The colonel would be pleased if you would join him aboard the general's aircraft."

"Lieutenant," Cronley asked, straight faced, "is that the colonel some people call 'Hotshot Billy'?"

"Only full colonels or better can do that, sir," the lieutenant replied. "Anyone of lesser rank who uses that description can expect to die a slow and painful death."

"Lead on, Lieutenant," Cronley said.

A nattily turned-out Constabulary corporal, who looked as if he were several months short of his eighteenth birthday, was standing guard at the steps leading to the rear door of the aircraft. He saluted, then went quickly up the steps and opened the door, which was, Cronley noted, a "civilian" passenger door, rather than the much wider cargo door of C-47 aircraft.

The sergeant came down the steps and Cronley, followed by Winters, went up them.

The interior of the aircraft was not the bare-bones, exposed-ribs interior of a standard Gooney Bird. Nor even the insulation-covered ribs and rows of seats in the interior of a DC-3 in the service of, say, Eastern Airlines. There were eight leather-upholstered armchairs and two tables in the fuselage, making it look not unlike a living room.

General White was not in his aircraft, but Lieutenant Colonel William W. Wilson, Major Harold Wallace, and former Oberst Ludwig Mannberg were, sitting in the armchairs.

"Good morning, gentlemen," Cronley said.

"Where the hell have you been?" Wilson demanded.

Cronley saw on Lieutenant Winters's face that he was now questioning the wisdom of their flight.

"Lieutenant Winters was kind enough to give me a tour

of the Thuringian-Hessian border." He turned to Winters. "I believe you know the colonel, Lieutenant," he said. "And this officer is Major Harold Wallace of the Twenty-third CIC Detachment, and this gentleman is Herr Ludwig Mannberg of the Süd-Deutsche Industrielle Entwicklungsorganisation."

Winters saluted and Wallace and Mannberg offered him their hands.

Wallace ordered Cronley and Winters, who were standing awkwardly on the slanted floor of the airplane, into armchairs with a pointed finger. Wilson waited impatiently until they were seated, and then asked, rather unpleasantly, "Cronley, you're not suggesting that Winters suggested this aerial tour of the border?"

"No, sir, I'm not. But I took one look at him and I could see that Lieutenant Winters is a fine pilot, a credit to the United States Military Academy and Army Aviation generally, and decided on the spot that I would recruit him for service with DCI-Europe. Then I asked him to give me an aerial tour of the area."

"You decided to recruit him for DCI?" Wilson asked incredulously.

"He can do it," Wallace said, smiling. "I think the phrase is 'drunk with newfound authority.'"

"I mention that now because I wanted you to know you can speak freely in his presence about our current enterprise," Cronley said. "He knows all about it. Well, maybe not *all* about it, but a good deal about it."

"And how much did you tell Colonel Fishburn about our current enterprise?" Wallace asked.

"Essentially nothing, sir. When Captain Dunwiddie and

I made our manners to the colonel, he led us to believe that Colonel Wilson had told him that he would explain everything to him when he got here."

"So you didn't tell Colonel Fishburn that you wanted Lieutenant Winters to fly you up and down the border?" Wilson asked.

"When we made our manners to Colonel Fishburn, I hadn't met Lieutenant Winters. We met him at dinner last night."

"In other words, Colonel Fishburn doesn't know that you have been using one of his airplanes and one of his pilots to fly the border?"

"As far as I know, sir, he does not."

"And you didn't think you should tell him?"

"I thought he might object, and I wanted to make that tour."

"I will be damned!" Wilson said.

"Why do you want the lieutenant in DCI?" Wallace asked.

"I thought it would be nice if at least one of the pilots in the aviation section of DCI-Europe was a bona fide U.S. Army aviator."

"I didn't know there was an aviation section of DCI-Europe," Wallace said.

"As of today, there is. Or there will be as soon as I can sign the appropriate documents, which by now Fat Freddy and Brunhilde should have prepared."

"You're going to have an aviation section for the Storchs, is that what you're saying?"

"I'm going to have an aviation section in which I can *hide* the Storchs. There will also be other aircraft, two L-4s or L-5s and, if General Greene can pry one loose from the

Air Force, a C-45. I'm going to tell him just as soon as I can get on the SIGABA, which I think should be up and running by now."

"He's unbelievable! My God, he's only a captain!" Colonel Wilson said. "A very young and junior captain! And he's going to *tell* a general officer what he wants?"

"What's that Jewish word, Billy?" Wallace asked.

Cronley saw on Winters's face that he had picked up on Major Wallace calling Lieutenant Colonel Wilson by the diminutive of his Christian name.

"'Chutzpah'?" Wallace went on, "Meaning audacity? Isn't that what Patton was always saying, *'L'audace, l'audace, toujours l'audace!'*?"

"It also means unmitigated effrontery or impudence," Wilson said.

"I remember when you were a captain, they said the same things about you," Wallace said. "And I remember your defense: 'I did what I believed to be the right thing to do.'"

Cronley now saw on Winters's face his expectation that Major Wallace would now suffer what a major could expect after speaking so disrespectfully to a lieutenant colonel.

"Tom," Cronley said, "now that you're in the intelligence business, you'll have to understand that nothing is ever what it looks like."

Winters looked at him, but did not reply.

"And look at you now, Billy," Wallace went on, "the youngest lieutenant colonel in the Army."

Wilson looked as if he was going to reply, but changed his mind.

"There's more," Cronley said. "Freddy did some research on how the OSS operated administratively, and found out they had people working for them they called 'civilian experts.'"

"So?" Wallace asked.

"So now DCI-Europe has two such civilian experts. They will be paid—I'm quoting what Freddy found out—'the equivalent of the pay of commissioned officers with similar responsibilities, plus a suitable bonus for voluntarily undertaking assignments involving great personal risk, plus a death benefit of ten thousand dollars should they lose their lives in the performance of their duties.'"

"We had a number of such people," Wallace confirmed.

Cronley saw in Winters's expression that he had picked up on the "we."

"And now DCI-Europe has two of them. Maksymilian Ostrowski, former captain, Free Polish Air Force, and Kurt Schröder, former *hauptmann*, Luftwaffe."

"I can't find fault with that," Wallace said. "What about you, Colonel?"

"I hate to admit it, but it makes sense."

"Anything else?"

"A couple of things. When I speak with General Greene, I'm going to ask him to not only transfer to DCI-Europe the six ASA guys he's loaned me, two of whom I brought here with me, but also to get Second Lieutenant Bruce Moriarty of the Eleventh Constabulary Regiment transferred to me. Us."

"Not 'us,' Cronley," Wallace said. "Transferred to *you*, in your role as chief, DCI-Europe. As you know, I have nothing to do with DCI-Europe."

"Sorry."

"But since the subject has come up, what's this all about?

Start with the ASA men," Wallace ordered. "And the last time I looked, Brunhilde is not a guy."

"Freddy had already arranged for Brunhilde to be transferred to DCI. I'm talking about the radio guys. They're smart. Freddy told me that at the Reception Center, when they enlisted or got drafted, they all scored at least 110 on the Army General Classification Test and were given their choice of applying for Officer Candidate School or going into the ASA."

"And these guys didn't want to be officers?"

"They didn't want to serve four years if they could get out of the Army after two," Cronley said. "The point is, they're smart. That has its ups and downs. Because they're smart, they do their jobs well. That's the up. The down is that if somebody else needs them, and Greene transfers them, they'll walk away knowing too much about DCI-Europe, and that makes me uncomfortable."

"Okay. Point taken. But how do you know they want to leave the ASA?"

"Because I offered them an immediate one-stripe promotion if they did, and a second three months after that."

"You can do that?"

"According to Fat Freddy, I can. I promoted him to staff sergeant."

"Okay. What about the lieutenant? Who is he?"

"An A&M classmate of mine. He'll be given command of Company C, 203rd Tank Destroyer Battalion, and the Polish guards."

"That's a lot of responsibility for a second lieutenant," Wallace said.

"He can handle it. And we need somebody to handle it."

"Anything else?"

"I told Brunhilde to look for some clerical help among the WACs in ASA. We're going to need all kinds of help in that department."

"It looks like you're building quite an empire, Cronley," Wilson said. His tone suggested he didn't approve.

Cronley's temper flared and his mouth went on automatic, and as usual, he regretted the words as soon as they came out of his mouth.

"Sir, I'm doing what I believe to be the right thing to do. If my superiors in the DCI decide I'm not doing the right thing, or doing more than I should, they'll relieve me."

Not smart. Not smart. Rubbing what Wallace said to him in his face was not smart.

And that "my superiors" crack sounded as if I'm daring Wallace to relieve me. Not smart.

Stupid.

"I'm sure that would happen," Wallace said.

"We saw one of the black birds as we came in," Cronley said. "Are they both here?"

"The second came in just before you did. They're being serviced. I brought the mechanics I gave you with us."

"I should have thought of that, of servicing the Storchs."

"Yes, you should have," Wallace said, "but nobody's perfect, right?"

"Yes, sir."

"What do we hear from Seven-K?" Cronley asked.

"We have communication scheduled for noon," Mannberg said. It was the first time he'd opened his mouth. "We may get a schedule then."

"Then there's time for Winters to take Schröder on a

tour of the border," Cronley said. "I think that's important. I saw a lot I didn't see in the photos."

"As you may have noticed, Tom," Wilson said, "Captain Cronley has a tendency to volunteer people for things they'd really rather not do. Are you comfortable with what's happening? Are you sure you want to get involved in something like this?"

"Sir, something like this is obviously more important than dropping bags of flour on M-8 armored cars, which is what I've been doing here."

"Tom, you wouldn't be here now if I hadn't asked you to make the first tour of the border, the one with a photographer in the backseat. Then Cronley, who is clever at that sort of thing, and knew about that mission, figured out that it was you who flew it, and then cleverly convinced you that flying the border again with him in the backseat was something I would approve, so you flew it. Correct?"

"Yes, sir."

"That being the case, I feel that I should say this: Intelligence, and especially black operations like this one, are indeed more exciting and important than dropping flour bags on M-8 armored cars. But there's a downside for someone like you. You're a West Pointer, a professional soldier, the son of a general officer. You know there is little love between intelligence types and . . . the Army Establishment. If you go with Cronley, you will almost certainly be kissing your career goodbye. And any chance of pinning stars on your own epaulets one day. And if your father were here, I know he'd agree with me."

"Sir, I got the impression I didn't have any choice in the matter."

"Well, I'm going to give you that choice. Now, and think your answer over carefully before you reply. Let me add there's no need for you to fly the mission Captain Cronley suggests. He can fly Schröder down the border as well as you can. Here's the question: Would you like to just walk out of here and go back to your duties with the Eleventh Constabulary and forget anything like this ever happened? Colonel Fishburn doesn't know you flew this unauthorized mission, and I can see no reason that he should ever learn about it. Think it over carefully."

You sonofabitch! Cronley thought, as his mouth went on automatic.

"I've got something to say," he said.

"No, you don't, Captain Cronley," Wilson snapped. "This is between Lieutenant Winters and myself."

"No, Billy, it isn't," Wallace said. "Cronley's involved. Let's hear what he has to say."

"It's none of Cronley's goddamn business!"

"I disagree," Wallace said. "Go ahead, Jim."

I don't have a goddamn clue what to say, Cronley thought, and then his mouth went on automatic again:

"The first thing I thought when I heard Colonel Wilson just now was that I wished he would keep his nose out of my business," Cronley said. "Then, I thought, well, he's actually a nice guy. Colonel Wallace—"

"Oops!" Wallace interrupted. "Another cow out of the barn. Watch yourself, Jim."

"—has made that clear, and I know it from personal experience."

"Why don't you tell *him* to keep *his* nose out of *my* business?" Wilson asked.

"Pray continue, Captain Cronley," Wallace said.

"And then I remembered another time Colonel Wilson had wisely counseled a junior officer. The day I met him. He knew that I had been promoted to captain from second lieutenant before I had enough time in grade to be a first lieutenant, and he was kind enough . . . as the youngest lieutenant colonel in the army . . . to explain to me what he believed that meant.

"I remember what he said. Word for word. I've thought of it a thousand times since then. And I even quoted it, and the source, when Captain Dunwiddie—another professional soldier like you, Tom—was uncomfortable with the direct commission as a captain I asked the admiral to arrange for him."

"How long do I have to listen to this?" Lieutenant Colonel Wilson protested.

"For however long it takes him to make his point. Put a cork in it, Billy."

"Quote," Cronley said, "'The advantages of getting rank, et cetera, means that you can do things for the good of the service that otherwise you could not do. And that's what we professional soldiers are supposed to do, isn't it? Make contributions to the good of the service?' End quote.

"What I'm suggesting, Tom," Cronley said, "is that you base your decision, as a professional soldier, on where you can make the greater contribution to the good of the service."

After a moment, Wallace said, "Colonel Wilson, in the opinion of the senior officer present, Captain Cronley has just nailed your scrotum to the wall."

"Or I nailed it there myself," Wilson said.

"Your call, Lieutenant Winters," Wallace said.

"Two things, sir," Winters said. "First, Colonel Wilson, sir, I really appreciate your concern. Second, Captain Cronley, sir, is there anything in particular you want me to show the Storch pilot?"

"Welcome to Lunatics Anonymous, Lieutenant," Wallace said.

"What I think we should do now is make our manners to Colonel Fishburn," Wilson said.

"Why don't you do that while I get on the SIGABA and have a chat with the Navy?" Wallace replied.

"I was afraid you'd say that."

"Mitchell has problems with the SIGABA?" Cronley asked.

"No," Wallace said. "According to Dunwiddie, Mitchell has been up and running since about nineteen hundred last night. Why do you ask?"

"I've been wondering why you didn't get on the SIGABA as soon as you got here. And why you're all sitting here in the Gooney Bird. There's a . . . I guess you could call it a 'lounge' in the building. Complete with a coffee machine."

"I was dissuaded from doing just that by Colonel Wilson," Wallace said. "May I tell the captain why, Colonel?"

"Why not? It may add to his professional knowledge."

"Colonel Wilson thought it was entirely likely that Colonel Fishburn would ask him if he'd seen you. And if he replied in the negative, that Colonel Fishburn would wonder why not."

"And if that happened," Wilson said, "and I think it would have, I would have had to tell him you were flying up and down the border in one of his airplanes, which I did not want to do, or profess innocence vis-à-vis knowledge of your whereabouts. Since I am (a) a West Pointer, and (b) not in the intelligence business, I do not knowingly make false statements to senior officers. Now when I make my manners, I can tell him truthfully, repeat, truthfully, that I came to see him immediately after getting off General White's aircraft. I don't expect either you or Major Wallace to understand that, but that's the way it is."

But deceiving him is okay, right?

"I understand, sir," Cronley said.

"And if that question is asked," Wilson said, "and I believe it will be, I can now reply that I had a brief word with you aboard the general's aircraft."

"Yes, sir," Cronley said.

[TWO]
Hangar Two
U.S. Air Force Base, Fritzlar, Hesse
American Zone of Occupation, Germany
1150 20 January 1946

Technical Sergeant Jerry Mitchell and Sergeant Pete Fortin of the ASA started to rise when Cronley, Wallace, Dunwiddie, Mannberg, Ostrowski, and Schröder filed into what looked like it had once been a control tower and now was the radio room.

"Sit," Wallace ordered with a smile.

"How we doing?" Cronley said.

"Waiting, sir," Mitchell said. "They're usually right on time. We've got about nine and a half minutes to wait."

"Which gives us time to run over what's going to happen," Wallace said, "so let's do that."

"Yes, sir. Seven-K initiates the contact. They will transmit, three times, a five-number block. Pete'll type it, and hand it to me. If it matches the number Colonel Mannberg gave us, we will reply with the five-block number he gave us. They'll check that against their list of numbers. Then we'll be open. Protocol is that they send, in the clear, a short phrase, a question to verify that Colonel Mannberg is on this end."

"For example?" Wallace asked.

"Middle name Ludwig," Mannberg said. "My middle name is Christian, so we would send that, for example."

"And then," Mitchell said, "they reply with what they want to send us. We acknowledge, and that's it."

"I hate to sound like a smart-ass," Cronley said.

"Hah!" Wallace said.

"But I think you forgot to turn the SIGABA on."

"It's off, Captain. I was afraid that there might be some interference with the eight slash ten from it."

"With the what?"

Mitchell pointed to three small, battered, black tin boxes. They were connected with cables, and what could be a telegraph key protruded from the side of one of them, and a headset—now on Sergeant Fortin's head—was plugged into one of the boxes.

"That's what we're using," he said. "It's German. The SE 108/10 transceiver."

"Seven-K has one just like it," Mannberg said. "We used them quite successfully from 1942. The slash ten means it's Model 10, based on the original model 108."

"I thought it was something you found in here," Cronley admitted. "And were fooling around with."

"No, sir, that's it. It's a hell of a little radio," Sergeant Fortin said. "Puts out ten watts."

"And that thing with the white button on it sticking out from the side is the telegraph key?" Cronley asked.

"Right," Fortin said.

"Where'd you get it, from Colonel Mannberg?"

"This one, I think, we got from Iron Lung . . . Major McClung. But Colonel Mannberg did give us a couple of them."

Sergeant Fortin, who had been sitting relaxed in his chair before his typewriter, suddenly straightened and began typing. It didn't take long. He ripped the paper from the machine and handed it to Mitchell as he fed a fresh sheet of paper into the typewriter.

Mitchell consulted a sheet of paper in his free hand.

"Send Seven Zero Two Zero Two," he ordered. "I repeat, Seven Zero Two Zero Two."

Fortin put his finger on "the thing with the white button on it" and tapped furiously.

"Seven Zero Two Zero Two sent," he reported.

Thirty seconds later, Fortin's fingers flew over his keyboard for a few seconds. He tore the sheet of paper from the machine, handed it to Mitchell, and then fed a fresh sheet of paper into the typewriter.

"Peanut dog," Mitchell said, and then looked at Colonel Mannberg.

"Franz Josef," Cronley ordered. "Send Franz Josef. I spell."

He then did so, using the Army phonetic alphabet.

Fortin typed what he had said, but did not put his finger on "the thing with the white button on it," instead looking at Sergeant Mitchell for guidance. Mitchell, in turn, looked at Mannberg.

"Send Franz Josef," he ordered.

"Spell again," Fortin ordered.

Cronley did so.

Fortin put his finger on "the thing" and tapped rapidly.

"Franz Josef sent," he reported.

And then, almost immediately, he began to type again. It took him a little longer this time, but less than five seconds had passed before he tore the sheet of paper from the machine and handed it to Mitchell.

"Able Seven," Mitchell read, using the Army phonetic for "A." Then he said, "Dog Tare Tare Fox One Six Oboe Oboe."

"Meaning what?" Wallace demanded impatiently.

"Sir, the protocol is coordinates first. So Able Seven is a place. Dog is D. Tare is T, and Fox is F, so DTTF, which means Date and Time To Follow. Oboe is O, so OO, which means out."

"Acknowledge receipt of the message," Wallace ordered.

"Not necessary. When they sent OO, that meant they were off."

"Rahil is really clever," Mannberg said admiringly. "By asking for the dog's name, she ascertained that Cronley was here—it was very unlikely that anyone else would know the dog's name—and if Cronley was here, it was very likely that I was, too."

"And what if I didn't remember the dog's name?" Cronley asked.

"Then she would have given us one more opportunity to establish our bona fides. She would have posed another question, a difficult one, the answer to which would be known only to me. And if we didn't send the correct response to that, we would have had to start from the beginning."

"What's this Able Seven?" Wallace said. "How far from here is it? Where's the maps and the aerial photos?"

"I've set them up in the room downstairs, sir," Dunwiddie said.

"Why not in here?"

"There's not room for all of them in here, sir," Dunwiddie said.

"Dumb question," Wallace said. "Sorry, Tiny."

[THREE]
Hangar Two
U.S. Air Force Base, Fritzlar, Hesse
American Zone of Occupation, Germany
1225 20 January 1946

"The room downstairs" occupied all of the floor immediately below the radio room/control tower. Dunwiddie had acquired somewhere what looked like a Ping-Pong table, and it was now covered with aerial photographs. Two large maps, one of them topographical, had been taped to the walls.

Wallace first found Able Seven on the topographical map, and then went to the table and started examining the aerial photographs of the site.

Cronley looked at one of the photos and immediately recognized the site. It was a snow-covered field near a thick stand of pine trees. A narrow road ran alongside it.

He then went to the map and, using two fingers as a compass, determined that it was about thirty miles from the Fritzlar Airbase in a straight line, maybe thirty-five miles distant if he flew down the border for most of the way, and then made a ninety-degree turn to the left. Site Able Seven was about a mile, maybe a mile and a half, inside Thuringia.

He sensed that Schröder was looking over his shoulder, and turned and asked, "What do you think?"

"I think I'd like to know what the winds are going to be," Schröder replied. "If they're coming from the North, it means we could make a straight-in approach from our side of the border . . ."

"And if they're from the South, we'll have to fly another couple of miles into Thuringia," Cronley finished for him.

"Precisely."

"If the winds are from East or West, no problem."

"Correct."

"Well, there's no way we could set up a wind sock in that field. Seven-K is going to come down that road two minutes before, or a minute after, we land. She's not going to be able to park on that road and wait for us."

"So we pray for winds from the North," Schröder said, "will be satisfied with either easterly or westerly, and will hope for the best if they're from the South."

"Wait a minute," Cronley said. "Ludwig, could we get a message to Seven-K, asking her to park her car, or whatever she's driving, with the nose, the front, facing into the wind?"

Mannberg considered the question a moment.

"So you'll know the winds on the ground?" he asked. His tone suggested he already knew the answer. "Yes," he went on. "It'll . . . the encryption of the message . . . will take a little doing. But yes, it can be done. And I think it should. I'll get right on it. We don't have much time."

"How much time do you think we do have?" Cronley asked.

"If I had to guess, which I hate to do, I'd say Seven-K would probably want to make the transfer at first light tomorrow, or just before it gets dark tomorrow. Or—she's very cautious—at first light the day after tomorrow. Or just before sunset the day after tomorrow."

"Makes sense. Then, since I have nothing else to do between now and tomorrow morning, I am now going to the O Club and drink the hearty last meal to which condemned men are entitled. Would anyone care to join me?"

"Wrong," Wallace said.

"I don't get a hearty, liquid last meal?"

"You have plenty to do between now and tomorrow morning at the earliest."

"Such as?"

"Such as, presuming you can get Mrs. Likharev and the boys over the border, what are you going to do with them once they are here?"

Cronley actually felt a painful contraction in his stomach, as if he'd been kicked.

"Jesus H. Christ, that never entered my mind. How could I have been so stupid?"

"Because I have been almost that stupid myself, I'm resisting the temptation to say because being stupid comes to you naturally," Wallace said. "I thought about it, but didn't recognize how many problems we have until Hessinger started bringing them to my attention."

"Jesus H. Christ," Cronley repeated.

"You've already said that," Wallace said. "Now, what I

suggest we do is send somebody to the PX snack bar for hamburgers, hot dogs, Coke, and potato chips, which we will consume as we sit at the Ping-Pong table and discuss solutions."

"Yes, sir," Cronley said.

"You are appointed Recorder of this meeting, Captain Cronley, which means you will write everything down on a lined pad as we speak. We can't afford forgetting anything again."

"Yes, sir," Cronley said.

He sat down at the table. Dunwiddie handed him a lined paper tablet and half a dozen pencils.

Wallace, Mannberg, and Dunwiddie sat down. Schröder and Ostrowski looked as if they didn't know what they should do.

"Please be seated, gentlemen," Wallace said. Then he turned to Cronley. "The floor is yours, Captain Cronley."

"Sir, I'd rather you run this. I don't even know where to start."

Wallace looked at him, then opened his mouth, and visibly changed his mind about saying what immediately came to him, and then said, "At the beginning would seem to be a good place.

"Presumption One," he began. "Both planes take off from Thuringia with everybody on board and make it back here.

"Unknowns: Condition of the aircraft and the people on board.

"Worst-case scenario: Airplanes are shot up and there are dead or wounded aboard.

"Medium-case scenario: Airplanes are not shot up and

no wounded. But Mrs. Likharev and either or both boys are sedated.

"Best-case scenario: Airplanes are not shot up. Mrs. Likharev and the boys are wide awake.

"Any other scenario suggestions?"

There were none.

"It seems obvious that there should be two ambulances waiting when the planes land," Wallace said.

"Inside the hangar," Cronley said. "If they are parked outside, people will be curious."

"Point taken," Wallace said. "Recommended solution: We get Colonel Wilson to arrange with Colonel Fishburn for the ambulances and station them inside the hangar. Any objections?"

There were none.

"Comments?"

"Two," Cronley said.

"One at a time, please."

"What do we do if there are wounded in the ambulances?"

"They go first to the regimental aid station here for treatment. If they're in bad shape—where's the nearest field hospital?"

No one knew.

"Tiny," Wallace ordered, "get on the phone."

"And while he's doing that, what if there are dead on the planes?" Cronley asked.

"You, Max, and Kurt wouldn't be a problem."

"That's nice to know," Max said sarcastically.

"I meant, you've got DCI credentials," Wallace said. "They'd get you into the hospital, dead or alive."

"That's comforting," Max said.

"The Likharevs don't have DCI credentials," Cronley said.

"Army hospitals treat indigenous personnel requiring emergency medical attention," Wallace said.

"What's 'indigenous' mean?" Cronley asked.

"Native. German."

"The Likharevs are Russian," Cronley said.

"So we tell the aid station they're German," Wallace said impatiently.

"What if one or more of them are dead?" Cronley asked. "What do we do with the bodies?"

Wallace considered the question.

"More important, what do we tell Colonel Likharev?" Cronley asked.

"Whatever we tell him, he's not going to believe," Wallace said.

"We fly the bodies to Kloster Grünau," Max said. "Where we put them in caskets and bury them with the full rites of the Russian Orthodox Church. The ceremony, and the bodies in the caskets, are photographed. Photographs to be shown to Colonel Likharev."

"The nearest field hospital is the Fifty-seventh, in Giessen," Tiny reported. "There is an airstrip."

"Photographs to be taken to Argentina by Captain Dunwiddie," Wallace said.

"If Mrs. Likharev, or the oldest boy, survives, Dunwiddie takes her, or him, or both and the photographs of the funeral, to Argentina," Cronley said.

"Tiny," Wallace said, "have Colonel Wilson arrange for a Signal Corps photographer to be here from the moment the Storchs take off. When he shows up, put the fear of God in him about running his mouth."

"Yes, sir."

"Our story to Colonel Likharev," Cronley said, straight faced, "would have more credibility if one of us—Max, Kurt, or me—got blown away and Tiny could show the colonel a dozen shots of our bloody, bullet-ridden corpses."

"You're insane, Cronley," Wallace said, but he was smiling.

Ostrowski, shaking his head, but also smiling, gave Cronley the finger.

Kurt Schröder's face showed he neither understood nor appreciated the humor.

"Moving right along," Wallace said. "Best scenario, everybody is standing intact on the hangar floor. Objective, to get them to Argentina. Question: How do we do that?"

"Simple answer. Load them in either the Twin Beech or the Gooney Bird, fly them to Rhine-Main, and load them aboard a South American Airways Constellation bound for Buenos Aires," Cronley said.

"Now let's break that down," Wallace said. "What are the problems there?"

"Well, we don't know when there will be an SAA airplane at Rhine-Main," Cronley said.

"Tiny, maybe—even probably—Hessinger has the SAA schedule. Find out."

"Yes, sir."

"Medium-bad scenario," Wallace went on. "The next SAA flight is not for three days."

"Can we fly them into Eschborn—and we can, in either airplane, I've seen Gooney Birds in there—and stash them at that hotel for the brass—the Schlosshotel Kronberg in Taunus?"

"Yeah," Wallace said.

"Even if one or more of them is 'walking wounded'?" Cronley asked.

"And what if Mrs. Likharev is on the edge of hysteria?" Ostrowski asked.

"And that, the walking wounded, and the possibility of Mother being hysterical, raises the question of how do we care for them while they're en route to either Rhine-Main or Eschborn?" Wallace asked.

"Get a nurse from the aid station here when we get the ambulances," Cronley said. "No. Get a nurse and a doctor."

"Why both?"

"Couple of reasons. The nurse, because the presence of a woman is likely to be comforting to Mrs. Likharev if she is hysterical, or looks like she's about to be, and the doctor to sedate her, or the kids, if that has to be done."

"I don't like the idea of taking a doctor—and that's presuming we can get one—and a nurse to either Rhine-Main or Eschborn," Wallace said.

No one said anything for a long moment.

"What about having Claudette Colbert go to Frankfurt, or Eschborn?" Dunwiddie asked. "Have her in either place when our plane gets there?"

"Permit me a suggestion," Ludwig Mannberg said. "Have both a doctor and a nurse in the hangar when the Storchs return, to take care of every contingency. If any of them are seriously injured, he could determine whether it would be safe to take them to the hospital in Giessen, or even to the Army hospital in Frankfurt . . . what is it?"

"The Ninety-seventh General Hospital," Dunwiddie furnished.

"Ideally, the latter," Mannberg went on. "Instead of the Schlosshotel Kronberg. I suggest that if any of the Likharevs require medical attention, the place to do that would be in Frankfurt, where the good offices of Generals Smith and Greene could be enlisted to discourage the curious.

"If necessary, the doctor or the nurse or both could go on the airplane with the Likharevs. If their services were not required, they wouldn't go. I agree with Cronley that the presence of a woman would be a calming influence on Mrs. Likharev, and suggest that Fraulein Colbert could fill that role."

"I agree with everything he just said," Cronley said.

"How could you not?" Wallace asked sarcastically. "Okay, we're in agreement that Brunhilde can make a contribution, right?"

Wallace looked around the table. Everybody nodded.

"My take on that is, if so, why not get her up here right now? How would we do that?"

"Going down that road," Cronley began, "we get Hot-shot Billy to fly her up here."

[FOUR]
Hangar Two
U.S. Air Force Base, Fritzlar, Hesse
American Zone of Occupation, Germany
1450 20 January 1946

They went down that road, and many others, without interruption—not even to send someone to the PX snack bar for the hot dogs, hamburgers, Cokes, and potato chips Major Wallace had promised—until Sergeant Pete Fortin came into the room.

This stopped their discussion, which was then on how to get photographs of Mrs. Likharev and her sons to former Major Konrad Bischoff in Munich so they could be affixed to the Vatican passports they would need to leave the American Zone of Occupied Germany.

"What is it, Sergeant?" Major Wallace demanded, not very pleasantly.

"Two things, sir. Our next contact is at fifteen hundred . . ."

Wallace looked at his watch and shook his head in what was almost certainly disbelief that it was already that late.

". . . and Sergeant Mitchell says there's something funny going on at the Constab that maybe you want to have a look at it."

"Something funny?" Wallace asked. "Okay. We'll pick this up again just as soon as I finish taking a leak, seeing what's amusing Sergeant Mitchell, and having our chat with Seven-K."

He stood up and went directly to the restroom. There he

stood in front of one of the two urinals. Captain Dunwiddie shouldered Captain Cronley out of the way and assumed a position in front of the adjacent urinal. Former Colonel Mannberg got in line behind Major Wallace, and Kurt Schröder got in line behind him as Max Ostrowski got behind Captain Cronley.

Minutes later, after climbing the stairs, they filed into the radio room in just about that order.

Cronley looked at where Dunwiddie was pointing, out one of the huge plate-glass windows. He saw what looked like three troops of Constabulary troopers lining up on a grassy area half covered with snow in front of the 11th Constabulary Regiment headquarters.

"Okay, I give up," Cronley said. "What's going on?"

"Beats me," Dunwiddie admitted. "It's too early for that to be a retreat formation."

"Jesus, there's even a band," Cronley said.

"Regiments don't have bands," Dunwiddie said.

"This one does," Cronley argued.

"Gentlemen, if you're going to be in the intelligence business, you're really going to have to remember to always look over your shoulder," Major Wallace said, and pointed out the plate-glass window to their immediate rear.

The window gave a panoramic view for miles over the countryside, and in particular of the road down a valley and ending at the air base.

And down it was coming a lengthy parade of vehicles. First came a dozen motorcycles, with police-type flashing lights, ridden side by side. Then a half-dozen M-8 armored cars, in line, and also equipped with flashing police-type lights.

The first thing Cronley thought was, having seen an

almost identical parade up the road from Eschborn to the Schlosshotel Kronberg, that one carrying the supreme commander, Allied Powers Europe, to a golf game, *What the hell is Eisenhower doing in Fritzlar?*

Then he saw the car following the M-8s. Eisenhower had a 1942 Packard Clipper as a staff car. What was in line here was a 1939 Cadillac. Not any '39 Cadillac. A famous one, the one General George S. Patton had been riding in when he had his fatal accident.

"You will recall, I'm sure, Captain Cronley," Major Wallace said, "that Colonel Wilson said that he would speak to General White about some sort of diversion?"

Both of their heads snapped from the open window to the side of the room, where Sergeant Fortin was furiously pounding his typewriter keyboard.

"Seven-K," Wallace said. "Right on time."

Fortin ripped the sheet of paper in the typewriter from it and handed it to Mitchell.

"Jesus Christ!" Mitchell said when he read it.

"Do I acknowledge?" Fortin asked.

"You're sure this is all? You didn't miss anything?"

"That's it."

"What does it say?"

"One Six Zero Zero, Oboe Nan Easy How Oboe Uncle Roger. Repeat One Six Zero Zero, Oboe Nan Easy How."

"Sixteen hundred. One hour." Wallace made the translation.

"Right now?" Cronley asked incredulously. "Today?"

"They sent it twice, Captain," Fortin said.

"And added One Hour, to make sure we understood she meant today," Wallace said.

"Holy shit!" Cronley said.

"Do I acknowledge?" Fortin asked again.

"Jim, can you do it?" Wallace asked. "Can you be at Able Seven in an hour? In fifty-eight minutes?"

Cronley thought it over.

"God willing, and if the creek don't rise," he said.

"Acknowledge receipt, Sergeant Fortin," Wallace ordered.

"Nothing's in place," Cronley said. "No ambulances, no doctor, no nothing."

"Nothing at Able Seven to give us the winds on the ground," Ostrowski said.

"I know," Wallace said.

"Yeah," Cronley said.

"Seven-K wouldn't order this unless she thought she had to," Oberst Mannberg said.

"They just sent Oboe Oboe," Sergeant Fortin said. "They're off."

"Which means we can't ask her to reschedule," Wallace said.

"Kurt," Cronley said, "I guess we better go wind up the rubber bands."

Schröder's face showed he had no idea what Cronley meant.

"Didn't you have model airplanes when you were a kid?" Cronley asked.

Then he mimed winding the rubber bands in a model airplane by turning the propeller.

Schröder smiled, wanly, and then gestured for Cronley to precede him out the door of the radio room.

[FIVE]
Hangar Two
U.S. Air Force Base, Fritzlar, Hesse
American Zone of Occupation, Germany
1510 20 January 1946

"Well?" Wallace asked, when Cronley finished his walk around his Storch.

"I don't think anything important fell off," Cronley said. "Is Tiny in the control tower?"

Wallace nodded.

"Where he has dazzled the Air Force with his DCI credentials," Wallace said. "When you call, they will clear you—both of you—to taxi from the tarmac outside to Taxiway Two, then to the threshold of Runway One Six for immediate takeoff."

"I see the pushers are here," Cronley said, pointing to Tiny's Troopers, who were prepared to push the Storchs from the hangar. "So I guess I better get in, and then you get the doors open."

"I need a couple of minutes in private with you, Schröder, and Ostrowski first," Wallace said.

"What for?"

"Over there," Wallace said, pointing to a door in the rear wall of the hangar. "Now."

Oberst Mannberg was already in the room when Cronley, followed by Ostrowski and Schröder, entered. Wallace closed the door.

"If you're going to deliver some sort of pep talk," Cronley said, "I'd just as soon skip it, thank you just the same."

"Shut up for once, Jim," Wallace said, and then he said,

"Okay, everybody extend your right hand, palm up. I'm going to give you something."

When the three had done so, Wallace dropped what looked like a brown pea into each palm.

"Pay close attention. Cronley, don't open your mouth before I finish. Got it?"

"Yes, sir."

"Those are L-pills," Wallace said. "Inside the protective rubber coating is a glass ampoule. When the ampoule is crushed by the molars of the mouth, sufficient potassium cyanide will be released to cause unconsciousness within three seconds, brain death within sixty seconds, and heart stoppage and death within three minutes. That process is irreversible once begun. Any questions?"

No one had any questions.

"I will not insult anyone's intelligence by asking if you understand the purpose of the L-pills."

"We had something like this in the East," Schröder said.

"Almost identical, Kurt," Mannberg said.

"Is this what Hitler and his mistress used?" Ostrowski asked. "What Magda Goebbels used to kill her children in the Führerbunker?"

Mannberg nodded.

"And what a number of captured agents on both sides chose to use rather than give up what they knew they should not give up," Wallace said. "Or to avoid interrogation by torture."

Cronley, Ostrowski, and Schröder looked at the brown peas in their hands, but made no other move.

"Aside from shirt pockets, the most common place to carry one of these is in one's handkerchief," Wallace said.

"The place of concealment recommended by the OSS, to Jedburghs, was insertion in the anus."

"Really?" Cronley asked, and then began to laugh.

"What the hell can you possibly find amusing about this, Cronley?" Wallace demanded furiously.

"Excuse me, sir," Cronley replied, still laughing, as he moved his hand to his shirt pocket and dropped the L-pill in.

"Sometimes I really question your sanity," Wallace said furiously.

"What I was thinking, sir," Cronley said, stopped to get his laughter under some control, and then continued, "was that the OSS's recommendation for concealment of your pill really gave new meaning to the phrase 'stick it up your ass,' didn't it?"

Then he broke out laughing again.

A moment later, Ostrowski joined in. And then Mannberg. Then Wallace was laughing, and finally Schröder.

"You think 'stick it up your ass' is funny, huh, Kurt?" Cronley asked. "I finally said something that made you laugh!"

"You are out of your mind!" Schröder said, and then, still laughing, went to Cronley and embraced him.

They walked out of the room with their arms around each other and then got in the Storchs.

[SIX]

Hangar Two

U.S. Air Force Base, Fritzlar, Hesse

American Zone of Occupation, Germany

1525 20 January 1946

"Fritzlar clears Army Seven-Oh-Seven a flight of two aircraft as Number One to take off on One Six on a local flight."

Cronley shoved the throttle to takeoff power and then answered, "Fritzlar, Seven-Oh-Seven rolling."

As soon as he was off the ground, Cronley saw that his normal climb-out would take him directly over the three troops of Constabulary soldiers lined up in front of the 11th Constabulary Regiment headquarters.

That would obviously draw the attention of the Constabulary troopers to the two funny-looking black aircraft, which was not a good thing.

On the other hand, it would be a worse thing if he tried to use the amazing flight characteristics of the Storch to make a sharp, low-level turn to the right to avoid flying over the troops and didn't make it.

He pulled his flaps and flew straight.

As he flew over the troops, he saw General White, Colonel Fishburn, and Lieutenant Colonel Wilson looking up at him.

[SEVEN]

Able Seven
(Off Unnamed Unpaved Road Near Eichsfeld,
Thuringia)
Russian Zone of Occupation, Germany
1555 20 January 1946

There was a small truck on the road.

As Cronley flew closer, he saw that it was an old—ancient—Ford stake body truck, and that red stars were painted on the doors.

He remembered seeing on *March of Time* newsreel trucks like that driving over the ice of a lake, or a river, to supply Stalingrad.

A stocky man in what looked like a Russian officer's uniform got out of the cab of the truck . . .

He's wearing a skirt?

That's not a man. That's Seven-K. Rahil.

. . . and went quickly to the back.

A boy jumped out of the truck.

Is that the old one, or the young one?

And then a woman.

Mrs. Likharev.

Mrs. Likharev turned and helped a smaller boy get out of the truck.

Seven-K pointed to the approaching Storchs, and then took the woman's arm and propelled her into the field beside the road.

Cronley signaled to Schröder, who was flying off Cronley's left wing, to land. Schröder nodded and immediately dropped the nose of his Storch.

Cronley slowed the Storch to just above stall speed so that he could watch Schröder land.

Schröder got his Storch safely on the ground, but watching him put Cronley so far down the field that he knew he couldn't—even in the Storch—get in. He would have to go around.

By the time he did so, Mrs. Likharev and the boys were standing alone in the field, making no move to go to Schröder's Storch.

Seven-K was getting into the truck. As soon as she did so, the truck drove off.

Cronley put his Storch on the ground. At the end of his landing roll, he was twenty feet from Schröder's Storch.

Ostrowski was out of Cronley's Storch the instant it stopped, and ran to Mrs. Likharev and the boys. He propelled them toward Schröder's Storch.

Christ, the little one has Franz Josef!

What the hell?

Christ, I've got to turn around.

Why the hell didn't I think about that?

Ostrowski hoisted Mrs. Likharev into Schröder's airplane, and then handed her the smaller boy and the dog.

Schröder's engine roared and he started his takeoff roll.

Ostrowski came to Cronley's Storch, hoisted the larger boy into it, and then got in himself.

Cronley turned the Storch, shoved the throttle to takeoff power, and started to roll.

When he had lifted off, he turned to look at Likharev's elder son, thinking he would reassure him.

He quickly looked away.

He had never before in his life seen absolute terror in anyone's eyes. He saw it now.

[EIGHT]
Hangar Two
U.S. Air Force Base, Fritzlar, Hesse
American Zone of Occupation, Germany
1630 20 January 1946

The hangar doors opened as Cronley taxied up to them. He stopped and killed the engine. Before that process was over, half a dozen of Tiny's Troopers appeared and pushed the Storch into the hangar. Then the doors closed.

Schröder's Storch was already in the hangar, and its passengers had gotten out of the aircraft.

There were two ambulances in the hangar, and what looked like two doctors and twice that many nurses. And someone Cronley really didn't expect to see. The general's wife.

Mrs. White was standing with her arm around Mrs. Likharev. The younger boy was standing beside them with a hot dog in one hand and a Hershey bar in the other. Captain Dunwiddie was holding Franz Josef.

Cronley felt his eyes water and his throat tighten.

"We have a problem with this one," Max Ostrowski said.

"What?"

"He crapped his pants. He pissed his pants and he crapped his pants. I'm soaked with piss from my navel to my knees."

Cronley failed to suppress a giggle. And the laughter that followed.

"Fuck you," Ostrowski said, and then he chuckled, which turned into a giggle.

Cronley put his mouth to the open window and bellowed, "Captain Dunwiddie!"

When Captain Dunwiddie appeared beside the plane, so did Mrs. White and Mrs. Likharev.

"Is there a problem?" Mrs. White inquired.

"Yes, ma'am," Cronley said. "This young man has had an accident, as my mother used to call it."

"Big or little?"

"Both. And Captain Ostrowski has suffered collateral damage."

Mrs. White managed to suppress all but a small giggle.

Then she said, "Captain, I understand you speak Russian?"

"Yes, ma'am, I do."

"Then tell Mrs. Likharev of the problem, and tell her not to worry, Captain Dunwiddie will deal with it."

"Yes, ma'am."

"What am I supposed to do about it?" Dunwiddie asked.

"You're a Cavalry officer, Chauncey, you'll think of something," Mrs. White said.

Captain Dunwiddie stood beside the Storch and told Cronley what he had thought of as a solution to the problem.

"I'll have my guys form a human shield around Max and the boy as they get out of the plane and then march them across the hangar to where we billeted the ASA guys. And while they're having a shower, I'll get them clothing from somewhere."

"Good thinking, Chauncey," Cronley said. "You're a credit to the U.S. Cavalry."

"Fuck you."

Cronley stayed in the plane until Max and the boy, shielded by eight very large, very black soldiers, had been marched across the hangar and into the building at the rear.

Then he climbed out of the Storch.

Mrs. White, Mrs. Likharev, the younger boy, and the dachshund were standing near the ambulances. The boy was feeding Franz Josef a piece of his hot dog.

Cronley exhaled.

Well, it's over. Really, completely over.

Or will be as soon as we get those two some clean clothes.

I feel sorry for the kid. He has to be embarrassed.

For himself.

And for what he did to Max.

And then his mind's eye was filled with the older kid's terror-frozen eyes in the airplane right after they'd taken off.

And then he felt a sudden chill.

And threw up. And then dropped to his knees and threw up again. And then once again.

Jesus H. Christ!

He got awkwardly to his feet.

He felt dizzy and another sudden chill.

Oh, no, not again!

He closed his eyes, put his hands on his hips, leaned his head back, and took a deep breath.

And was not nauseous again.

He opened his eyes and found himself looking at Major Harold Wallace.

"I must have eaten something . . ."

"You all right now, Jim?" Wallace asked.

"I'm fine. A little embarrassed."

"Don't be. It happens to all of us."

"Yes, it does," Lieutenant Colonel William Wilson said. Cronley hadn't been aware of his presence until he spoke. "When I picked the colonel up outside Králický Sněžník, he didn't even wait until we got home. He puked all over the L-4 before we got to two hundred feet."

"Thank you for sharing that, Billy," Wallace said.

"I thought I should. I thought Tex here should hear that."

"And, for once, you're right," Wallace said. "Tex, Schröder made it to the latrine just now before he tossed his cookies. But then he has more experience with this sort of thing than you do."

That's "Tex" twice.

Have I just been christened?

"So what happens now?"

"Odd that you should ask, Tex," Wallace said. "As I was just about to tell you."

[NINE]
Suite 507
Hotel Vier Jahreszeiten
Maximilianstrasse 178
Munich, American Zone of Occupation, Germany
1645 21 January 1946

"I didn't expect to see you until tomorrow, at the earliest," Miss Claudette Colbert said to Captain James D. Cronley Jr. when he walked into the office.

"Nice to see you, too, Miss Colbert."

"Are you going to bring me up to speed, sir?"

"When no one's around, you can call me 'Tex,' Miss Colbert."

"Tex?"

"I have been so dubbed by Major Wallace. Where's Freddy?"

"At the *bahnhof*, meeting General Greene and party."

"Greene is here? What the hell is that all about?"

"There was an unfortunate accident at the *bahnhof* yesterday afternoon."

"What kind of an accident?"

"Major Derwin apparently lost his balance and fell onto the tracks under a freight train as it was passing through. He had just gotten off the Blue Danube from Frankfurt, and was walking down the platform when this happened."

"Is Major Wallace aware of this?"

"'Tell Captain Cronley not to even think assassination option,' end quote."

"Jesus Christ!" Cronley said, and then asked, "And that's why Greene is here?"

"'General Greene is going to meet with the Munich provost marshal to offer the CIC's assistance in the investigation of this unfortunate accident,' end quote."

"What the hell was Derwin doing back here?"

"'He telephoned Lieutenant Colonel Parsons of the War Department's liaison mission to DCI-Europe and told him he had information regarding DCI-Europe that he felt Parsons should have' . . ."

"Jesus!"

". . . continuing the quote, 'which we of course do not know, as that was an ASA telephone intercept.' End quote."

"My God!"

"There was another intercept. General Greene called Colonel Parsons and asked him what he knew about what

Derwin wanted to tell him. Parsons said he had no idea, that he had never even met Derwin."

"Is that another quote?"

"No."

"Then I won't ask where that came from."

"Thank you. Your turn, Tex."

"Okay. You know the Likharevs are in Sonthofen?"

"As guests of General and Mrs. White. And where they will remain until we can get them on the SAA flight to Buenos Aires the day after tomorrow."

"Right," Cronley said. "I didn't know about the day after tomorrow."

"Mrs. Likharev and the colonel have exchanged brief messages over the SIGABA."

"I didn't know that, either. I'm glad."

"Which resulted in this," Claudette said, and handed him a SIGABA printout.

```
PRIORITY

TOP SECRET LINDBERGH

DUPLICATION FORBIDDEN

FROM POLO

VIA VINT HILL TANGO NET

2210 GREENWICH 19 JANUARY 1946
```

```
EYES ONLY ALTARBOY

QUOTE MAY ALL OF GODS MANIFOLD BLESSINGS
FALL ON YOUR SHOULDERS STOP I WILL FOREVER
BE IN YOUR DEBT STOP YOUR LOVING FRIEND
SERGEI ENDQUOTE


POLO


END


TOP SECRET LINDBERGH
```

"Well, you know what they say," Cronley said. "Russians sometimes get carried away."

"You're crying, Tex," Claudette said.

He shrugged.

"I know how to cure that," she said. "But I don't think this is the place to do it. Why don't we go to your room?"

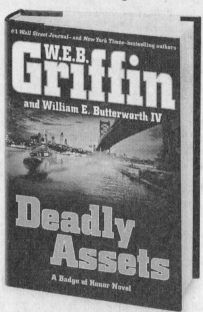